Soleil and the March of Death
Book One

TURN
of the
HOURGLASS

SARAH L NELSON

Swinging Girl Publishing
171 Lakeview
Grosse Pointe Farms, MI 48236
First Printing, 2020
Second Edition, 2022
ISBN: 978-1-7346672-0-2 (Paperback)
ISBN: 978-1-7346672-2-6 (Kindle)
Printed in the United States of America

For the girls of
Yeongyang Girl's School
Especially Hong Ji-Yeon

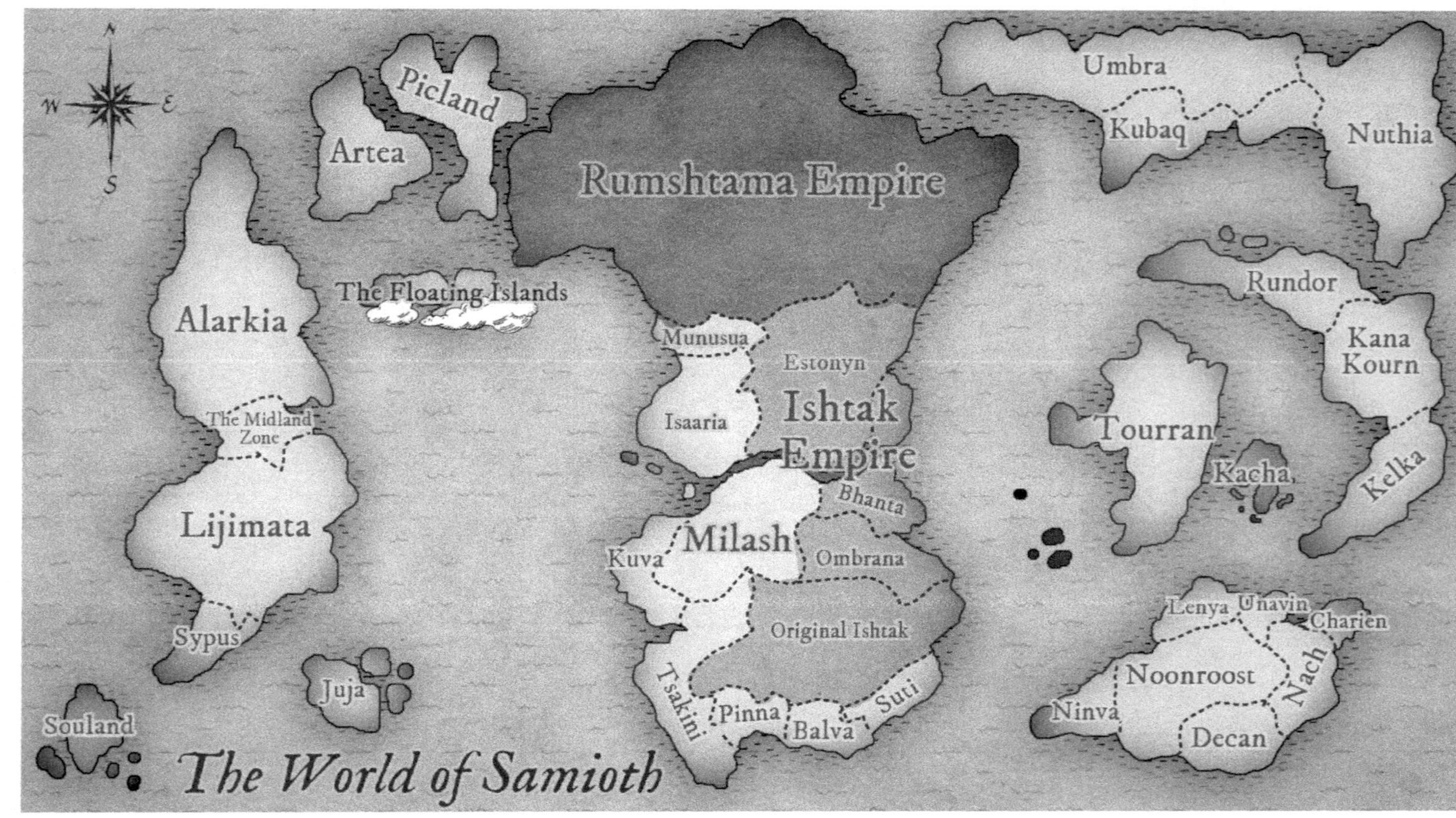
N
W
E
S
Picland
Artea
Rumshtama Empire
Umbra
Kubaq
Nuthia
Alarkia
The Floating Islands
Munusua
Estonyn
Ishtak
Empire
Isaaria
Rundor
Kana
Kourn
Tourran
Kacha
Kelka
The Midland
Zone
Lijimata
Bhanta
Milash
Kuva
Ombrana
Original Ishtak
Sypus
Juja
Tsakini
Pinna
Balva
Suti
Lenya
Unavin
Charien
Noonroost
Nach
Ninva
Decan
Souland
The World of Samioth

One

I OPEN MY EYES AT THE CHIME OF SEVENTH BELL. Six other bells have rung out before, on each hour, but it is the seventh one that wakes me. One would think that a servant girl in the East High Courts University need rise early, before everyone else, to scrub the stone floors and turn back the clocks, brush away snow in the winters and open the awnings in the summers. But while Naomi and the other girls work from fourth bell until twelfth, I begin at sixteenth and go until second, with the older maids. A special allowance, the deal struck by a few clever words from Naomi's father.

The circles under my eyes are permanent at this point, but I cannot help it. No matter how exhausted I am, my eyes snap open at seventh hour, and there I am: awake. This has plagued me all my life, so far as Nusk has told me. There is nothing to be done for it, and my paranoia as a *Khashtani* does not help.

I rise, throwing my blanket off without folding it, and leap down from the loft where Naomi and I sleep when we are too tired to go back to our room in the maid's quarters. I know it annoys Taris to find me or his sister here, but Nusk doesn't mind. He must depend on us for everything his voice can't convince others to give him.

Must be nice, having the fluke of a charmed mouth.

I find my clothes and pull them on: underclothes and base dress, trousers, a thin and long robe that will keep my arms covered and help me carry things in its fluttering tail, headscarf to keep my locks back while working. Gloves to conceal the magical fluke I don't have. Soft servant's boots are strapped to my feet, a pair of knives strapped to my thighs, and a final knife in a sheath that hangs around my neck. I load several dart blades into pressure chambers wrapped around my wrists, and poison needles in a safety container on the inside of my boot.

Not that I'm concerned about this poison; Nusk acclimated me to its effects when I was a child. It was horrendously painful, and left me with dotted scars on my arms, chest, and my shoulders, but it was worth it.

"If that's you, Soleil, you'd better come in quick! There won't be any hot water left!" Korvaan calls to me from the other room.

"Half a minute!" I complain.

I rush to the washroom to splash water on my face and clean my teeth. My hair is a frizzy mess, but no one will notice so long as it stays tucked under my headscarf. I'm checking myself over, making certain I have absolutely everything, when I realize: there is a naked patch on my wrist where usually my fingers find cool metal.

My watch: a necessary component for looking after my principal, and for contacting my *khashak*. And though I have tightened the damn thing until it bites into my skin, it has fallen off and lost itself.

The options for my search are limited, and I know the usual suspects for its location. Of all the things I could misplace, this is one of the least egregious, yet it annoys me to be anything less than a perfect *Khashtani.* I am entrusted with the life of a crown prince. I cannot be afforded mistakes.

My search for the watch takes seconds. It fell off the loft sometime during the night, down onto the wide bed below. I scowl at the damned thing, strap it back to my wrist, and test the buttons to make sure it doesn't require charging in the sun. The noise of irritation I hear from Taris, in the next room, lets me know that my test of the watch's messaging capabilities has caused static feedback for both of us. It's directly in our ears, too, due to the connective hearing pieces pierced there, disguised as earrings. I don't mind the static, but it drives Taris crazy.

Good. Better an irate Taris than a broken watch any day of the week.

I hasten to the adjoining room and am half-assaulted by the aroma of Korvaan's coffee. He's sitting at the table, drowsy and blinking, waiting for his caffeine to finish brewing. With both men here, this tells me Naomi has used one of her time-off stamps, and volunteered to keep a close eye on Rian while the rest of us sort ourselves out. She wouldn't need to, if I were fully operational, but such is the aftermath of my recent knife wound: allowances must be made.

We try not to leave the task of watching Rian solely to Naomi, but on days when Rian's bodyguards have only to escort him around the University, we allow her to step in. Today, I know, I will be doing little around Rian. Taris and Korvaan will look to him, as today is the last day I am meant to hold myself back while my shoulder heals.

Naomi will be displeased when she looks at the wounds, as she always is. She'll say something about me never having enough time to heal properly. She'll lecture about infection and torn stitches and the like, but in the end, she'll do her duty and send me out again. Though not without some sort of complaint about my recklessness. After all, I'd had no idea if the assassin who'd crept onto the grounds a little over a week ago intended to make Rian his target.

But as Comus Day approaches, I grow nervous, and wary. If the coming year's Comus Day passes without incident, and without anyone claiming that Rian is the Lost Heir, I'll have succeeded. Someone else will be crowned king. A false king, perhaps, but this does not concern me much. Proving themselves to the Isaarian people and keeping the throne will be their problem, not mine.

I realized a long time ago that as his *Khashtani,* part of my job is to avoid danger on Rian's behalf whenever possible. I'm not meant to care if he's the Lost Heir. My life's work, my purpose, is to keep him alive whatever the cost, and if he becomes king in this day and age, I'm certain his life will be forfeit. That is what I've been told, that is what I've been taught, that is what I believe.

"What's set you in such a foul mood already?" Korvaan asks me through a yawn as I hunt in the cupboards for a clean mug. If there is leftover hot water from their coffee, I need tea. Naomi will absolutely pitch a fit if I don't drink it.

"I'm not," I say. I think I've found a mug clean enough.

"You've got that scowl on your face that you always get when Rian does something stupid," he says.

"If he's awake, likely he *is* doing something stupid," I mutter.

It is an exaggeration, and a bit unfair, but the man drives me crazy with his antics. One would think he had no idea there could ever be a threat to his life. His father should have told him to be wary until Comus Day passes, but Rian must not think it's possible others might discover who he is. Or what he can do.

"Taris, tell the girl to lighten up," Korvaan complains. "She never observes waking hour properly, that's why she's so bitter. And it'll put off the rest of us."

I roll my eyes. As if I have time to sit an hour in holy meditation in the morning. I know it is a custom many Isaarians observe, but I have other things to see to that don't require me being in my own head.

"Let her be, or you'll make her worse," Taris grunts. He knows better than to demand more cheeriness from me—he'd be one to talk. I've killed assassins with lighter dispositions than his.

Taris stands before the mirror on the sideboard, cropping his beard close to his face and taming his shiny black curls. I'd call him vain, but I know he will not appreciate my teasing the way his siblings might. I can't remember a time when he's chosen to speak with me, outside of when it is necessary; and even then, he is so curt and cold, one might think I'd murdered his lover.

It's almost a shame Korvaan and Naomi both shave their heads clean; I have no one's curls to pluck and tease. My own hair waves in the heat, but is hardly half as voluminous as theirs. When I was still in training, I used to beg Naomi not to cut her hair after she turned eighteen. But, of course, Naomi is unwed, so she keeps to the custom of her father's people.

Not that I had the right to say anything in the first place. My *khashak* are far from home, after all. In Korvaan and Naomi's case, they have never even seen their homeland; and as for Taris, I doubt he remembers it. Milash is as foreign a country to them as it is to me, and though I try to acknowledge this sacrifice to Nusk, he insists time and time again that regardless of present circumstances, he'd always planned to move to Isaaria, for his first wife's sake.

I doubt he knew then that Crown Prince Rian's mother would take interest in Nusk's old job as a *Khashtani,* and commission one to protect her son.

But Nusk has carried his traditions here with him, and passed them on to me and his children. He claims that is enough for him, and he seems to be happy with his simple life here. Naomi always shrugs when I ask whether she would go to Milash if released from my *khashak,* and Korvaan insists he would like to visit, but calls Isaaria his home. They are citizens here as much as anyone else, and have known no other life. They practice the same things they would if Nusk raised them in Milash—only here, they have an odd, pale sister and a smiling, idiot crown prince to protect.

The only one who refuses to follow either Milash or Isaarian traditions is Taris. He has his reasons, I suppose, for accepting neither side of his heritage.

I join Korvaan at the table bench, the tea steeping between my hands. From the back room, I hear a heavy rolling, and soon Nusk joins us in his wheeled chair. Taris has oiled it recently, I note, because it glides smoothly and without jerking, screeches, or squeals.

"Mmm, something burning?" Nusk poses in that croaking voice of his. When I was little, I used to think he sounded like an owl. Or a bullfrog. Wildly different creatures, perhaps, but I've been told I once had an imagination.

"The coffee!" Korvaan cries, and leaps to rescue his pot.

I snort, and sip at my tea. Much better than coffee. I have no taste for the stuff, and must force myself to drink it when necessary, but I sometimes think my *khashak* would rather die than go without it.

Korvaan must have managed to save the bean sludge, because in seconds he has procured cups of it for himself, his father, and Taris. Nusk thanks his second-born son formally, a passive chide for Taris' grunt. We then cradle our warmed drinks in silence. We have long-since become fully grown, but when Nusk's eyes wrinkle that old, pruned brown face, I know he still sees us as children.

With the three of us all sitting on one side of the table, we look like an artist's shading palette: Korvaan so dark, me so light, and Taris in between. I find his skin beautiful, but he hates it. It acts as a reminder that he came from Nusk's first wife. A Native Isaarian, like me.

It's difficult to tell if Taris hates all Native-born Isaarians on principle, or if he simply hates everyone. Were someone to ask, I don't think I could even guess as to his thoughts and feelings about his absent mother, and I have known Taris all my life. It is lucky for him he has Naomi and Korvaan, or else I'm sure he would have absolutely no one in the world who enjoys his company.

I am certainly not partial.

Korvaan has added things to the coffee. Cloves and cinnamon and honey barely conceal the acrid natural scent. Nusk used to say it's my sensitivity to smell that causes my dislike of coffee, but I am more inclined to believe it's a bodily flaw. If only I could inject some form of caffeine directly into my blood; then I could reap the benefits without the musty flavor.

"Soleil, you move better today," Nusk notes. "Naomi has done good work."

"She wants me to meet her," I say. "In the infirmary, so she can take a look at it with the proper materials."

"Taris will take you," Nusk says. "When he goes to watch the prince."

Taris looks like he would rather be bitten by a black adler spider than take me anywhere, but he won't argue with his life-giver any more than I'd dare to.

In fact, he stands and hastily gulps down the last few swallows of coffee before placing the mug in the sink basin, for washing later.

"We'll go now," he says. Eager to get rid of me, I'd wager.

Korvaan flashes their father a look, but Nusk refrains from chiding his eldest. Unbeknownst to them, Taris and I have been locked in an impasse for years, now: he does his job dutifully, though curtly, and I work him ragged. Never more than that, for Rian's sake, but I know there is no point trying to force him into obedience. Taris decided long ago he'd never respect me.

The two of us head out into the heat of a new summer day, Taris in his silver-trimmed guard's uniform, me in my maid's. The paths between buildings on campus are covered, and surrounded by gardens, common spaces, and the like. Plenty of room for everyone, from primary school students to our oldest scholars.

This university has kept us well for years, and I feel what I can only assume is a pang of regret at the realization that these are the last few weeks we'll live here. When Comus Day arrives, Rian will go to the capital, and we will follow him as he presents himself with the rest of the crown princes and princess in contention for the throne. Our country needs its heir now more than ever, and since it has been nearly twenty-five years since the Carsans family delivered their last prophecy, an heir will need to step forward regardless of Fate's original intent.

Rian's parents should have presented him to the Carsans when the Prophecy was first given. After all, I'm told Rian indicated his fluke young, and I know for a fact that he is the true heir to our country. But back then, there were whispers of traitors and assassins, because of what that prophecy ostensibly foretold.

So, Rian's parents kept quiet and ordered Nusk to do so as well, until their son could rule and live safely. Rian does not remember Nusk at all, I should think, nor is he aware of me or my duty to him. But it is for the best. One of the other prospective heirs can take up the position that otherwise would have been his.

There are currently seven crown princes, and one crown princess, hailing from the eight royal families of Isaaria. Any one of them aside from the crown prince of the Carsans family could be the fabled heir, so far as anyone in Isaaria knows. And as far as I know, none of the royals are aware of Rian's identity. He alone is the keeper of his secret, as his parents both died last spring. A tragedy, but an accident.

The rest of the heirs have all but convinced themselves that they still have a chance. Either they plan to cheat, have no care for traditions, or they assume the last prophecy was being highly metaphorical when it said the true heir was born in fire and would have control over air and time. Given their variety of flukes, it's possible some of them truly believe that.

I have never seen Rian use his fluke, but since the Lost Heir has the power to control the passage of time, I suppose it's possible he has used his fluke, and none of us have noticed.

Taris and I make our way to the lecture halls: large, dome-shaped buildings made almost as much of glass as they are of muted sandstone. We Isaarians do so love our natural light and, in the summer at least, it's quite lovely to have so much of it whilst trapped indoors. After all, those with flukes must stand in nature to rejuvenate their abilities. It is only logical to erect our buildings and arrange our cities in a way that accommodates these ancient yet highly relevant practices.

There are many times I have found Naomi standing in the morning sun, bare feet dug into the dirt, her arms outstretched to the sun to feel its warmth. Likewise, I have seen others stand before the moon, and feel themselves connect to the energy that exists within all living things.

For Nusk, the practice requires assistance. Now and again, his sons carry him outside and help him stand in bare feet.

Korvaan, Taris, and I have no flukes, so none of us need participate in such a routine the way many others do. Even so, I occasionally find a rare peace in the feeling of the sun's glow on my face.

There is no such peace to be found this morning with Taris. His usual testiness grates on my own nerves, and we both know better than to engage in casual conversation. Instead, I focus on my surroundings, trying to meditate through observation and gratitude for our world, as Nusk has instructed me. As there is no hope in getting me to observe morning meditation the way he would prefer, Nusk has done his best to adapt the practice, that I might learn to make the decisions necessary for Rian and my *khashak* both.

I count the clicks of Taris' heels on the cobblestone path, to keep my mind busy, but the futile nature of such a task easily frustrates me, and makes me even more vexed with him. It's not as if he can help it: the boots are a part of his uniform. But for some reason, even his footsteps sound condescending to me.

When Taris veers off course to take the path towards the campus housing instead of the lecture halls, it is all I can do to keep my temper in check. I go with him, because I must, but I won't be happy about it.

"I thought you were taking me directly to Naomi," I say.

"We left early. And she enjoys watching Rian's classes with the children. No point in interrupting," Taris says.

I've mastered my face enough to keep from scowling. I'm certain Taris can feel my displeasure, but I have learned there's no point in arguing with him.

He's almost as stubborn as I am.

"Why a detour?" I ask with clenched teeth. I need to stop doing that; I've already ground one of my incisors down so it no longer has a point.

"Prince Mercer sent Rian a belated birthday gift yesterday. I volunteered to deliver it to Rian's rooms, so I'd have a chance to look the package over."

I can't be mad at him for being prudent, but he should have told me Rian's best friend sent him a gift. I need to be aware of all this. Mercer is in the west, now, traveling for "personal enjoyment", and who knows what oddity he might have plucked up as a gift for Rian.

"I'm praying it's completely safe and mundane?" I muse, digging.

It's not that I suspect Mercer of treachery, but last time he sent Rian a foreign gift, it was a miniature sunblood dragon from the Ishtaki Empire. Rian lets the damn thing sleep at the foot of his bed.

"It's a book," Taris says. "Rian's sort. I left it with one of the laundry girls, to rewrap as it was."

"Did she ask any questions?"

"She won't," Taris says, so shortly that I know he either threatened the girl, paid her off, or is already canoodling with her. Typical.

"Where is it now?"

"She left it behind the statue of the Queen of Heaven," Taris claims. "Rian will never know."

"Mmm," I grunt, but I'm pleased.

At this point, I should be able to trust Mercer, as he's done his best to look after our absent-minded Rian. But I don't want to trust any of the crown princes, or the crown princess, even if some of them are Rian's closest friends.

Though I want nothing more than to return to today's scheduled business, I force myself to keep Taris' steady pace as he heads to the servant's washrooms and campus kitchens. The Queen of Heaven and King of Earth statues stand by the entrance to the school gardens, not far from there, and I'm sure his laundry maid had no trouble slipping away for a few minutes to place the parcel there. In fact, this entire gift exchange between Mercer and Rian is so dull, I almost wish there was something mistrustful about it, so that I'd have a reason to keep my mind busy.

It's only as we're making our way to the nobles' quarters with the package that something even mildly exciting occurs. Taris has his cloak folded over his left arm with the package tucked underneath, which is how most guards wear their uniforms while strolling about to keep from getting tangled up. As we head around a staircase, encased by stone on both sides, I recognize the voices of two of the Crown Princes: Crispin Carsans and Magnus Oram.

Taris is to the left of me, in the middle of the staircase. I am near the stone. As the princes approach from the opposite direction, winding towards us, I expect Taris to press himself against the wall, bowing until they pass. But he doesn't.

I curse his stubborn pride and whichever one of his parents gave it to him. I suspect his mother.

Just before the princes come into view, I force my way past Taris, turn, and shove him against the wall before nuzzling up against him, as if we're a pair of lovers caught unawares. He immediately flinches away, but I hold fast.

The princes' conversation quiets as they see us. Crispin Carsans passes by without looking twice, as he cares little for the affairs of those beneath him. But Magnus Oram seems to take it as a personal affront: how dare we allow ourselves to be seen as human, with our own complex lives, instead of simply members of the staff.

"As you were," Magnus says haughtily, looking down on us both with a contemptuous curl of his lip.

He's irritated we do not bow, but I'm worried that Taris will do something brash if I let him go. Magnus waits a beat, then scoffs and continues his conversation with Crispin as they descend the stairs.

We are so far beneath Magnus Oram, in his eyes, that I assume he would react with similar repulsion to see a pair of dogs humping. We could walk past him a hundred times in a day, and remain completely invisible.

The moment they're gone, Taris shoves me away.

"You're impossible," he mutters.

"You're lucky," I snap, straightening my clothes. "Oram could have had you hanged for not showing him the respect he thinks he deserves."

"The University wouldn't let him," Taris mutters gruffly.

"Do you really want to bet your life on that? Or Rian's?"

He does not answer, only continues up the stairs. I follow, but observe him with a degree of shrewdness.

"Do you not approve of Crown Prince Oram?" I ask, wondering why Taris had insisted on doing something so thoughtless in the first place.

"No one should approve of him," he grumbles, but offers me little else.

Magnus Oram may be rude and egocentric, but most of the heirs are, so that on its own should not warrant such a comment from Taris. I make note to delve into Magnus' political career at some point, to see what has bothered Taris so. We may not be the best of friends, but we are both dedicated to Rian; if Magnus Oram possesses any ill will towards our crown prince, I must know.

Luckily for us, we don't run into anyone else for Taris to insult. We deliver Rian's package to his rooms, where his own bodyguards will ensure its safety before allowing him near it. Then we hurry back out of these fanciful quarters, before our presence becomes questionable.

We are careful enough that we have certain liberties with restricted spaces, and in exceptional circumstances, Nusk will use his charmed tongue. But one ought not invite misfortunes by raising suspicions amongst the University security.

Neither Taris nor I mention our run-in with the Crown Princes again, and I know that there is an unspoken agreement between us: we will not mention this to Nusk. Taris will keep to his duties, and me, to mine.

WE MUTELY MAKE OUR WAY to the lecture halls, picking out the building Rian occupies at this early hour. Taris takes off his cloak and hides it in a nearby shrub, and then we stealthily scale the side of the building, our hands and feet having long since memorized the best paths. I'm not sure where Naomi is observing Rian from, but she knows where I prefer to perch amongst the scaffolding in these lecture rooms. Taris waits until I slip in through a window, where decorative carvings on the inside make for excellent vantage points. He take up his post protecting the Crown Prince while Naomi leaves with me.

Normally, I require no escort, but Naomi has been worrying over my shoulder, and I suspect Nusk did not want to risk my scaling the buildings on my own before she clears my full recovery. As our resident medic and member of the *khashak,* still, Naomi has much to see to. I locate her in a position similar to my own as she watches the class below but decide to wait until the end of Rian's lesson to leave. Naomi does find great enjoyment in listening in to Rian teach, and I won't begrudge her a few extra minutes, given how hard she works.

On weekdays, Rian teaches children's classes on behalf of the University. He spent his own years of learning here, in lieu of private tutors, and has a particular bond with the place. Now, he gives lessons on history and literature, not to those pursuing great knowledge and truth, but for children. Given his intellect, his choice surprised many at first, but his reputation has since profited. I'd like to image fewer people will want to kill him knowing of his philanthropy, and surrounding himself with small children only adds to his innocent charm.

It's a history class at this hour, and Rian is closing a lesson on the Isaaria's roots. Or New Isaaria, as some call it.

He stands at the front of the classroom, so filled with energy that I can feel it from my perch.

"Who wants to continue? Or, *a-ha*—I'll call randomly on you instead! Best hope you've studied..." Rian adds mischievously.

Some of the children giggle at the posed threat. It's easy for them to remember what Rian teaches. He phrases everything like a story.

He has drawn a map on the board behind him in chalk: a decent rendering of Isaaria and the surrounding countries, with dotted lines marked across them. Just to the side of the board, at a spare desk, sits a woman with her head rested on a hand. She is watching Rian, but is too far away for me to read what is in her eyes. It hardly matters; I know what I'll find there, and the rest of her appearance gives away her identity regardless of distance. Her dark hair reaches to her elbows, and her eyes are dark as well. Her smooth brown skin has delicate freckles down the backs of her arms, and a smattering of them color her snub nose and cheeks. Her full-lipped smile is a warm, dark pink, and her lashes curl up full and black.

This is Lady Asmer al'Yibna, the half-Bhantian "little flower of Isaaria".

They say she has loved Rian since they were both children, and I know she watches him now with both admiration and dreaming in her eyes.

Rian has called on one of his students, who stands to continue the story of Old Isaaria's fall and New Isaaria's birth, from the refugees who fled invaders and war. These meek but hearty travelers met others along the way, and invited any who shared their faith to create a new country from the ashes of the one lost. Though this was many hundreds of years ago, it partially explains why there is considerable racial diversity in New Isaaria today.

In the student's storytelling, the Old Isaarian refugees have just made a pact with travelers from Tourran and Kacha, who had also left their own lands fleeing religious prosecution, in hopes of finding a more peaceful land to settle.

"And then…Lerri!" Rian calls on another student to continue the tale.

The children stand and sit accordingly, when giving their answers.

"And then they came together and decided to call the new country Isaaria, like the old Isaaria they lost!"

"Exactly. And so, are we all Isaarians, Lerri?" Rian asks.

"Yes, sir," the child answers proudly. "We're all Isaarian, with different heritages depending on where our families came from. But we stand together, and let people live peacefully, with or without flukes."

"Very good," Rian says, and it's a sign for the child to sit. "And what do we call the people who are genetically from Old Isaaria? Mika?"

The child stands. "They are *Native* Isaarians, but only so we can distinguish the difference," she continues knowledgably. "Everyone is equal as New Isaarian citizens. But we may look different, because of our ancestry."

"Naturally so," Rian goes on, motioning for her to sit. He'll speak, now that he's realized the girl's touched upon a much deeper topic. "Not all of us look the same. Even Mika and I look different, and we both have Kachin blood. Mika is Kachin and Native Isaarian, isn't that right?" he clarifies.

The child nods, and Rian grins widely as he continues.

"And does anyone remember the most significant contributors in my family tree?" he asks mischievously. "Where were my foreign ancestors from?"

His students compete heartily to be the ones called to answer.

"Kacha and Tourran!"

"Correct!" Rian says as another child shouts, "Like Lord Aiko's children!"

The mention of the Tourrannese ambassador draws Rian off on a tangent. He cannot help himself. He is a silly little scholar, easily excited by knowledge for its own sake, and greatly enjoys sharing that knowledge with those thirstiest for it. He sits on his desk at the front of the room, clasping his hands together and crossing his ankles. The hour's bell has rung, but was drowned out by the children, and I doubt Rian would have heeded it, regardless.

He's too caught up in the present to comply with the University's schedule, and his students often find themselves in similar situations. But because Rian is this institute's darling, his students are never marked late, even if they have earned themselves that demerit.

"Interesting you mention the Aiko family," Rian says. "True: Lord Aiko married the Kachin princess, and therefore, their children share a similar heritage to my own, genetically speaking. But both Tourran and Kacha are homogeneous countries on the whole. Now, does anyone know what homogeneous means in this context? Ayla?"

Ayla is one of Rian's favorite students. At only eight years of age, she is exceptionally smart, and strives to excel at everything she does. I assume this is because she is one of the orphans the University houses, sponsored by a charitable branch of the Theebin Church of the Holy Three. She looks nothing like Rian, with her long yellow hair and round eyes, but he treats her like his daughter.

"It means that there are not many different types of people, with all different types of looks. The opposite of how things are here," she says.

"Very good. What country would you all say is most *hetero*geneous?" Rian poses, using Ayla's definition and context clues to let the children puzzle out the meaning of the word on their own. "Out of the entire world?"

"Isaaria!" some suggest eagerly with childish patriotism.

Rian chuckles. "We do rank highly in that regard. But consider countries with republics. Yes, Mika?"

"Alarkia?" Mika poses uncertainly.

"The Republic of Alarkia, correct!" Rian praises. "We are the third most diverse independent country in the world. Statistically speaking. Now, next week: we will discuss why you all think that is, and how our different backgrounds have contributed to a culture that is clearly *Isaarian*."

He is trying to dismiss them, but the children have questions for him, too, and refuse to leave.

"Mister Rian," a child says. He's asked them not to call him "crown prince". "Are you going to win Comus Day? And be king?"

"An excellent question," Rian says. "What do you think?" he poses in turn. "Should I be king?"

The students talk over each other, but amidst twenty-five children, the answer is a resounding "yes". Every one of these children are hoping to hear Rian's name announced over the radio when Comus Day comes.

Rian laughs at the children's endearing mirth; they do so love him, as he loves them. "Well, I suppose we'll have to see."

There is something almost suspicious, to me, about how simply he says this. There is no shrewdness, no playfulness. Yet it is a matter of fact that Rian knows he is the Lost Heir. I must be careful to remember that, foolish as he may seem.

As he's about to formally dismiss them, Ayla raises her arm as high as she can stretch it, and Rian curiously acquiesces.

"What if the Carsans' prophecy is wrong?" she asks. "What then?"

"Interesting..." Rian muses. "Well, the Carsans have never been wrong, Ayla. That is why they hold their position. Their family's inherited fluke of prophecy allows us to properly pick the next ruler of the country."

"But if they're not wrong, why has the heir not stepped forward?" she says. "Why do we have to have a Comus Day at all?"

Though I am anxious to meet with Naomi and see to our business, I am intrigued to see how Rian will answer. It is true that a son in every generation of the noble Carsans house inherits the fluke of prophecy, and foretells the next heir of the country. It has been this way since New Isaaria's founding, and has kept our country prosperous and separate from most world conflicts. Sometimes the prophecy simply allows the current ruling family to pass the torch father-to-eldest child, but not this past generation.

By nature of the prophecies, it is usually obvious who the next heir should be. If not obvious, there is always the Currian Council to deliberate and decide. And if, by some chance, the rightful heir does not step forward in the twenty-five years after the prophecy is given: Comus Day, where the current crown princes or princesses will attempt to either prove they fit the prophecy's description or that they are the best suited to rule regardless.

In hundreds of years, we've never once had a Comus Day. The entire country has known for some time now that we will soon host our first.

Rian does not have a proper answer for Ayla. Not that I blame him; he is the heir that was meant to step forward, and never did. He was only four when the prophecy was given, but he could have claimed his birthright at any point afterwards. Even if it meant acting against his parents' wishes.

Still, Rian is not one to leave his class entirely disappointed.

"What makes you think the Carsans' prophecy is wrong?" he asks. "Their reports to the public on the matter have always been vague, never an exact rendition of the prophecies. Perhaps we are meant to have a Comus Day."

Now Lerri has taken up Ayla's torch, determined to find answers.

"But what if the wrong person becomes king?"

All twenty-five children stare at Rian anxiously.

"Well," he starts—and hesitates, I realize, because he doesn't want to admit that he doesn't know. His eyes flick towards Asmer, as if begging for her help.

But Rian is saved as the door swings open to admit one of the most irritating presences on campus. The adopted younger sister of Crown Prince Crispin Carsans: the bubbly, buoyant, and absurdly petty Lady Lune Carsans.

"I am afraid I must steal your teacher," she announces, to the children's disappointed chorus. "You've kept him past the bell, and I have need of him!"

Rian gives Lune a grateful look before turning back to his class.

"All right—you heard the lady. Off you go. I'll be seeing some of you this afternoon, for mythos literature. Otherwise—next week! Enjoy your Fars'day."

He and Asmer both go to meet Lune as the pupils rush off to their next classes.

"Thank the Almighty, Lune," Rian sighs as the last child runs out. "They were bombarding me, and I had no idea what to say. I hate disappointing them. Now, I'll have time to come up with an answer."

"You sound so serious," Asmer notes.

Rian agrees and resorts to his usual dramatics. "I'd better be! My students are my most brilliant companions. I miss them terribly when they are away!"

"A shame we must kidnap you, then, or else your class might have lasted the rest of the day. Come, your majesty," Lune giggles, taking his arm while Asmer slips onto his other. "You've promised us a brunch!"

"Too early for brunch, lively little Lune," Rian corrects, clicking his tongue and chiding her. "Breakfast will do."

"Oh? What time is it?"

"Quarter past eight, dear," Asmer chides. "How late were you up?"

"...Six," Lune admits.

Rian laughs at her and pulls the two women out of the room, sidling through the door so that they can walk arm in arm. I roll my eyes at their childishness, then note that Naomi has left her perch. She has traded off with Taris, then.

So as not to keep Naomi waiting, I scramble from my perch back to the roof and carefully descend from the lecture hall. I am glad I don't have to deal with Rian's entourage today. I do not mind when he spends his time with Crispin and Mercer, or even when he flirts incessantly with Asmer. It's Lune I cannot stand.

It is most difficult, determining what Lune Carsans is. The way she looks at Rian, sometimes, I am certain she is not a friend. There's a slyness hiding behind those round eyes, and the curtains of her caramel hair. She is lovely, yes, but in an otherworldly way. Her hair is not smooth, silky or straight, and get everywhere in its soft waves as it frizzes in the humidity; her lashes are pale without paint; her face is not symmetrical. One of her teeth is crooked, so that her smile is youthful rather than dazzling. It crinkles her nose and eyes.

I suspect she has political machinations like so many others of the court. This may be a danger for Rian, and that playful teasing of hers could mask any ill intent. She keeps too many secrets to be an innocent flower, like Asmer.

Asmer is stunning and sweet and graceful. Quiet. Demure. Smart, but plays at politics predictably. Lune is loud and mysterious and wild. Unpredictable. I believe the two women are something akin to bosom friends, though how two people so different could be so is beyond me.

Once on the ground, I dart across the lawn, looking for Naomi. I catch Rian and his pair of ladies exiting the building as I do so, but I assume they will pay no attention to me, in my maid's clothes.

I am too correct.

Oblivious as she chirps away, Lune skips right into me, and I am forced to let myself fall to the ground instead of adjusting my balance and sliding her off me. Better to play a clumsy maid than perform a feat beyond most folk.

Suddenly, I am struck by the strangest feeling, as if I have lived this moment before. By the time I shake free of it, Rian's boots are practically treading on my fingertips. The buffoon.

"Oh. Sorry about that, dear," he says, and it takes me a moment to realize he's talking to me. "But you really should watch where you're going."

I glance up to find he's smiling.

Rian is rather tall, but not so tall that he towers. Like many, he enjoys maintaining a certain physique, and is willing to adjust to suit the current trends of attractiveness. But he has never done a thing to his eyes. Deep, dark brown eyes, almost black. His stylists always do well to make them shine off his face, for such a color. They are the night sky at its deepest, instead of the murky depths of river silt. His hair is naturally black, but he keeps it white so that the gold ornaments those of his status prefer can catch the light better.

Those ornaments, along with his wondrously stitched clothes and graceful long spine, announce that he is royalty. When I was a girl, it used to intimidate me. I remember, once, thinking that if he were any more perfect, he would be a star in the sky. Now that I'm much older and less childish, I know better.

He is a grinning, laughing lunatic, who does not understand what his destiny means. Many call him the Laughing Prince, and do not perceive him as a viable heir. It is an insult he is too ignorant to notice.

"What a way to start the morning," Lune sighs, standing and brushing herself off as I sheepishly duck my head and lay prone before them, squeaking apologies.

"Forgive her and we can be on our way," Rian says blithely. "She is nothing."

Lune laughs. "Nothing? Only you would think so, Prince Rian. Each person has their place," she says.

Rian shrugs and fiddles with one of the gold earrings dangling towards his shoulders. He should know that, in this position, I could easily crush his testicles, which would ensure he never has an heir to inherit his cursed fluke. I would not dare, as I've sworn an oath to keep Rian from harm, including what *I* might wish him in anger, but he should be warier of strangers.

"Are you quite well?" Lune asks me, trying to get a better look at my face.

I curse her for her interest in me.

"Fine! I'm fine, my lady, my many apologies! Please, forgive me!" I say. With my face hidden, I can roll my eyes, but at least I still sound sincere.

"See? Just a clumsy mishap," Rian says. It sounds as if he's exasperated, and eager to get to breakfast.

They'll have forgotten about me in an hour, and that's a good thing. Even my appearance is easy to overlook, regardless of my uniform.

I do not look the way people expect me to, should they be hunting for a *Khashtani*. I am not short, nor am I enormously tall and broad as Nusk once was, but rest somewhere around the high end of average. I can either hide in a crowd, or put on high-heeled shoes and look above heads. I am not scrawny, nor bulky, but slim and well-muscled; I can pull up my own weight, and carry a medium-sized man, unconscious, across my shoulders, but no one would consider such potential unless I wear revealing or tight clothing, and I have no reason to do so. I am strong, but can make myself look meek, if necessary.

My hair, I prefer to keep a medium length, as it is most versatile that way, and though I have long since lost its original color—dyeing it over and over, for Rian's sake—I recall it once being a light brownish shade.

My eyes are the only thing I refuse to change. I don't know why; perhaps it's some vestige of stubbornness that remains after all Nusk's teaching. I don't believe he's noticed, but Taris has. He snorts and rolls his eyes at my refusal to inject iris pigmentations, see a skin-changer or wear colored lenses imported from Alarkia. Of course, such things would mean nothing to him. He doesn't have to change his appearance, unless he wants to.

But blue eyes are rare. It is, I should think, the one bit of vanity I can allow myself. Everything else, I am perfectly willing to change, but the eyes stay.

It's those same eyes, now, that struggle to avoid Lune. It's Naomi, bless her, who saves me. With my head this close to the ground, I can hear the clack of her heels on the pathway as she runs towards us, and I know her footsteps well.

"There you are!" Naomi cries. "I've been looking all over for you, you clumsy little thing, and—oh! Your majesty," she says, curtseying to Rian, then nodding to both Lune and Asmer. "My ladies. Please forgive my intrusion. This poor girl has an ear infection. Makes her dizzy. Unbalanced. You understand."

Rian laughs. "Think nothing of it, misses. We are just on our way."

Naomi bows again, and stays low until the three have left. Then she straights, sighs, and looks down at me while I rise to my knees.

"Oh, Soleil. Never a dull moment."

"Taris will laugh for weeks," I grunt as Naomi helps me to my feet.

"Your mistake, for crossing paths," she chides. "What were you thinking?"

"That Lune would look where she's going and walk past me instead of in to me," I mutter.

She laughs.

Naomi takes my arm and leads me towards the infirmary. Sometimes we are stared at: by my fellow Native Isaarians who find it strangely intimate that we link arms, and all those who can't help finding Naomi's beauty striking. There are plenty other Milash who have immigrated to Isaaria, as Nusk did, but Naomi is an exceptionally attractive woman, and we have learned this draws attention.

Naomi chatters, and occasionally prompts me to respond, but I'm deep in thought. That unplanned encounter with Rian has left me paranoid, and irritated.

She is nothing.

I am loathe to admit it, but his words do hurt. Not in a sighing way that it might a love-struck girl whose man has dismissed her, but in a bitter, cross way. Like biting into supper and cracking a full clove between your teeth. I have trailed him for nearly twenty years, since I was a girl of eight, protecting him. Learning his habits and his likes and dislikes. Listening to him laugh, complain, sigh, and yawn when he stays up too late poring over his books.

Sometimes I cannot help but think of him as a spoiled brat. *She is nothing.* Ha. Then this "nothing" has been keeping you safe and alive for twenty years.

Still, Nusk would be pleased to know Rian has said this. Part of being a *Khashtani* necessitates one's principal never knows they exist. Granted, I suspect *this* particular rule is one that Nusk made up himself, as he's implied through his stories that he knew his principal well, and they were even friends.

I suppose Nusk hopes I don't grow too attached to Rian in a romantic sense. That could spell catastrophe, so I don't blame him.

The infirmary is empty, save for a cat that Naomi shoos out. We still have another half-hour. This space is only closed for two hours in the morning, before those with talents like Naomi's step in to take their shifts. Somehow, that orange cat has discovered the rotations of this schedule and continually sneaks in when no one is around.

"I don't know how he keeps getting back in," she sighs.

I hop up onto one of the examination tables while she locks the door behind us and starts hunting for the items she'll need.

"He's a curse from Fate, your personal nuisance," I claim, stripping my clothes and weaponry off of my upper half and lying down on my stomach. "Much as Lady Lune is mine."

"Ah, yes. The ever-irksome Lune."

"She *is* irksome. She has no schedule, and when she does, she's never where she's meant to be," I complain.

"Mmm. Perhaps that is intentional. You are destined to be great enemies one day, I should think. Fate has proclaimed it through your naming," Naomi says.

She is quite dramatic, this one. Always has been.

It is not so surprising to me that Lune's name opposes mine. I am the sun; she is the moon. Many Isaarian women have names honoring the sun, moon, or earth. Lune is the only Lune I know, but there are Dianas and Stellas, Selenes and Yues and Mikas.

It is not Lune's name that makes me dislike her, but rather my qualms over a potential seduction of Rian. I could not stand her as his wife. In fact, I rather hope he chooses Asmer. Her cool serenity may temper his impulsive nature some, and she seems as if she could make him happy. After all, as much as I complain and grit my teeth over Rian, I do want him to be happy. I half fell in love with him, once, as one might expect. He has been my entire world since I was very young, it is not surprising to me that I daydreamed about us being the closest of companions as a child and, even worse, lovers when I grew older.

I was a stupid child to want such things with him, but at least now that I know adult Rian well, I understand that.

Naomi sweeps my hair and veil aside, then pokes and prods at the wound on my shoulder. She notes that it is mending well. Between her fluke of stitching and my body's natural ability to heal astoundingly fast, the gash left by an assassin's blade is little more than a subtle reminder for me to watch my back.

"I suppose you're clear to resume your duties with Rian tomorrow morning," Naomi sighs. She's applying salves to my injury all the same, and sticking a bandage on top to keep the skin pulled tight. "But take care, would you? You're lucky this is a scratch and not a stab—you could have died."

"Thanks, N'omi," I say, eager to get off the table.

"Don't 'thanks N'omi' me," she retorts. "I'm not clearing you as a *favor.* I'm doing it because I know that, if I don't, you will find a way to get yourself in trouble again anyways."

I shrug back into my clothes, carefully replacing everything where it belongs. I can feel Naomi watching me, as if waiting for me to flinch as proof that I truly should rest. Eventually, she gives up and starts talking again. Naomi never has been good at handling long silences. Or even short ones.

"Are you ready for Fars'day tomorrow?" she asks.

I sigh. "I suppose so. One of the worst days of the year."

"You say that at nearly every celebration."

"Because they're all a pain in the ass."

I start to help her clean up what mess we've made, obscuring from the other infirmary nurses that she was checking such a significant wound. We have to take care to use the infirmary only during times Naomi is sure no one else will be around, and hide anything that might imply we were here.

"Do you think it would be easier if Rian didn't enjoy parties so much?"

Naomi poses as she closes and locks a cabinet. I wipe down my exam table. "At least he is more of a bookworm than a…well."

"He flirts but never follows through," I agree. I know exactly what she means. "It's curious," I admit, "that he could have any girl he chooses, but rebuffs them whenever they show interest."

"Korvaan and I have a few theories," Naomi smirks. "He's overcompensating. Or he's never done it before. Or he likes men."

I raise an eyebrow at her.

"If he likes men, then he's concealed it well. Remember, Naomi-dear, I had to watch his years of awakening, while he was hardly subtle. His natural interest in scantily dressed women would suggest otherwise."

"He could still be *Inexperienced,"* she insists deviously, unwilling to let go of her pet theories so easily. She wants to imagine Rian as a man with all bark and no bite—someone who knows all the sultry things to whisper in a girl's ear, but would have no idea what to do once he has her in his bed.

"So long as he's alive, he may do as he pleases," I say, and stand to stretch.

It's only partially a lie: emotionally, I don't care in the slightest. But it's less work for me, not having to keep a close eye on women rotating in and out of his bed. It's better for us that he's innocently chaste—it makes work considerably less complicated. But I pity Magnus Oram's and Mercer Ralhan's bodyguards. They must be perpetually terrified that some pretty little assassin is going to flit their way into a successful mission.

"It's a good thing he's such an innocent fool," I grunt. "No one will want him as king, at this rate…And certainly no one will suspect him as the heir."

"If they order a Showing Trial on Comus Day, he'll have to reveal himself," Naomi says.

"Not necessarily," I correct her. "If it comes to that, I'll have Taris meet with him, and teach him how to trick everyone. To play his fluke false."

"What would you have him pretend?"

"Teleportation. They have three days to prepare for a Showing Trial when one is called. I will have him spend that time training himself to travel backwards so minutely that it will appear as if he is teleporting from one place to another. He will have to act simultaneously, slowing time only for himself so he can move to the new spot without anyone seeing it, but if his powers are as great as they are meant to be, he should be able to manage it."

"But what will you have Taris tell him?" Naomi presses. "To explain?"

"I have not decided that," I admit.

There is no good explanation for how Taris would know everything, and why he would want to help Rian, without revealing my position. But Nusk has pounded into my head the second most important rule for a *Khashtani,* after keeping one's principle alive and well, and that is to remain no more than a devastating shadow, killing when necessary to protect the principal, and never revealing oneself except in the direst of circumstances.

The only reason Nusk retired is because the Milash prince he served died of a heart condition—a complete accident, and unavoidable. Most *Khashtani* only retire when death takes us. Nusk is the exception to the rule: most of us will be nothing to the world, forever.

"We could…*let* him become king," Naomi says, trying to be casual about it.

I shoot her a look. "Absolutely not. And you know why."

"Surely it would be best for Isaaria," she presses.

"What would be best for Isaaria is a living ruler," I retort. "You remember the warning Rian's father gave Nusk. If Rian reveals himself on Comus Day, assassins will flock. There are already contracts on each of the crown princes and crown princess. If he is king, it will be even more difficult to protect him."

"That was years ago. He couldn't have known what might happen now."

"I'm not willing to take that chance. There are likely traitors in the courts, as there always are. I will keep Rian out of sight, and out of mind. He will do nothing to impress anyone on Comus Day. He will fade into the background."

Naomi frowns. "But what if, say, Mercer becomes king. As Rian's best friend, surely, he'd keep your prince around at court. Still in danger, then."

"We'll have to hope not," I say. "Now, come along—the servants' kitchens will close soon, and neither of us have eaten."

That pointedly ends our discussion, but this is not the last I'll hear of it from Naomi. All the same, she starts a much more innocent conversation to pass the time, speculating on what Crown Prince Rian and his entourage are having for breakfast as we head back out of the infirmary to see if we can't find some breakfast of our own.

Two

FOR ALL MY GRUMBLING DURING HOLIDAYS, Fars'day truly is a pain. Nothing like large crowds and a thoughtless, hyper-social prince to tease my temperamental nerves. With everyone eager to show off their fluke, it will be difficult to keep track of potential killers, especially considering how generous Rian is with his attention, and how inquisitive he is. Step up to the wrong person, at the wrong time, with the right fluke, and it would take a miracle from me to save his life.

As Naomi and I walk to the kitchens, we can see the preparations for the celebration already in place. Impressive tents are erected on the lawns, a professional stage with lighting and sound equipment powered by flukes or, in some cases, the wonders of electricity have been built underneath the largest of them. Stalls have sprung up, for those who might want to sell their wares after showing off their talents. Tomorrow, the campus will smell of sugar and spices, butter, tender meats, alcohol, sweat, and perfume. Bitter, sweet, sour, pungent, vibrant, violent smells: the sort that make your nose itchy and throat dry.

Tomorrow, if someone pricks Rian with a poison needle and disappears into the crowd, I'll have to choose between catching them and letting him die, or attempting to get him an antidote. I can feel my head buzzing as it calls up multiple ghastly scenarios.

"Do try to quiet your mind, Soleil," Naomi sighs. "I can hear your anxiety."

I huff, but don't argue. It's impossible to be angry with Naomi, and despite starting the day off wrong in every way, her company has brightened my mood, as I suspected it would.

The servants' kitchens are quiet at this time, late as we are, and there are only a few others silently consuming breakfast when Naomi and I enter. We barely make it before the food is cleared away, and sit to hastily consume our spoils.

We eat slices of crisp summer apples and rice porridge that is of decent thickness, if bland. We've arrived too late for there to be much left in the way of seasoning—no sugar or honey or nut-butter to mix in—but that's more due to these additives' popularity than stinginess on the University's part.

I attempt in vain to calm myself as I eat. It's difficult for me to sit still for any length of time unless Rian is in my sights, As my leg bounces up and down under the table, it occasionally brushes up against Naomi's. She puts up with it for a time, but then grows exasperated and tells me to *sit still*: Rian is safe. Taris is perfectly capable of keeping him alive.

Personally, I wouldn't trust Taris to look after Rian for any longer than a day—though I have no proof of it yet, I have the feeling he gets distracted by women too easily—but I don't want to argue with Naomi.

"Consider today your day off," she suggests, and I snort.

"The point of a 'day off' is to relax. If I have a day off, I can't relax. Making this, in a word, point-less."

"Don't sass me, Soleil, or I'll take back clearing you early and make you wait even longer."

"I'd go out after Rian anyway."

"I'd tell Taris to tie you to your bed."

"...Fine," I grumble.

After we clear our plates, Naomi and I part ways. She's off to check the clinic's task board for today, while I head back to the room we share in the servants' quarters. If I'm being forced to take a respite, I might as well review basic training.

I'm paid no attention as I walk down the University paths—the benefit of wearing a maid's uniform. I see Crispin Carsans again, but he's already forgotten, and is likely off to join his sister and Asmer at Rian's table.

Taris will let me know if any of them act suspiciously around Rian. They never have, but I like to take care, anyway.

Inside the servants' dormitories, it's nearly silent. Someone is cleaning their carpets a floor up, but the sound is muted. Naomi and I share one of the rare basement rooms, accessible by small windows close to the ground outside, but I prefer to use the door unless I'm in a hurry. It's more circumspect.

I haven't been back in our tiny apartment for a few days, now—opting at Naomi's insistence to sleep, when necessary, at Nusk's hut. Our room is plain, with few personal belongings. I have weapons and poisons, antidotes, and various mechanical devices all stored beneath the floorboards, in boxes under the bunk beds, and in the back of our closets. Of these weapons, only one is not in my regular rotation, but I continue to practice with it.

I am not inclined to sentimentality, as I am not fond of clutter, but I love my bow. I am fully aware that it is not the most practical weapon; our more modern inventions are better at killing, and some might say that women archers cannot perform as admirably as men due to certain anatomical differences. But my chest has never encumbered me, my arms are good and strong, and my aim is excellent.

That said, I am best with daggers. Specifically: long ones, three-quarters length of my arm, though I can throw well, too. We call them "my knives", and I have a certain fondness for them I refuse to acknowledge even fully to myself.

Excluding the tools of my trade, Naomi and I share a bookcase filled mostly with her medical texts, a washroom that highlights the stark contrast in our nightly care regimens, and our closets. Between my collection of uniforms and civilian garb, I can blend into almost any crowd, depending on the occasion.

I am not a vain woman, but the more variety I have at my disposal, the better chance I have at moving unnoticed. The only person I truly worry about spotting me is Qhan—Rian's lead bodyguard. I did not happen to see him this morning, but that doesn't mean he wasn't around.

Though I am skilled in the art of stealth, Qhan's duty is to notice any and every potential threat to his Crown Prince. And I'm almost positive that Rian's parents never told Qhan anything about a *Khashtani*.

I spend little time in our rooms, staying only to collect some weapons to train with today before heading to the most remote part of campus to strengthen my skills. Though I almost have no time for it regularly, Nusk makes certain I keep to my regular exercises to maintain strength and agility. So long as I'm forced to take a day off, I decide to spend the entire time training. Then, the day will not be a complete waste.

Time always passes more slowly when I'm away from Rian. I pester Taris and Korvaan practically every hour, depending on which of them has eyes on the crown prince. The day passes without any discernable threats, but that does little to calm the nervousness Naomi noted in me.

The morning of Fars'day, I awake feeling no more rested than usual, but I suppose I should have expected as much. My sleep debt is such that, if I don't die young, it will affect my health one day.

Rian, in contrast, sleeps late. I spend hours perched on his balcony, out of view of his window, watching the rest of the campus and occasionally looking in on him. I will not be spotted here, given the angle of my cover and how sensibly I work to make myself invisible. My clothing today is nondescript, plain, and colored similarly to most exterior walls about the campus. This is not perfect camouflage, but it helps.

Until about ten o'clock, all is quiet. When Rian finally rises, he spends an hour dressing, breakfasting, and entertaining both himself and his sunblood dragon. Even I will admit, the little thing has grown on me. Likely because, though it might not be the brightest creature, its loyalty ensures it'll at least try to prevent anyone from doing Rian harm.

By the time Rian digs out a Fars'day-suitable circlet and drapes an embroidered overcoat about his shoulders, another half-hour has passed. The sun has been paying special attention to the back of my neck all morning. A bead of sweat trickles down between my breasts, and pools by my stomach.

Isaarian summers are notoriously humid, and I can already feel my hair crimping out of its braid. Rian, somehow, will spend the entire day acting as if the weather is perfect, regardless of what he's wearing, and I've yet to see so much as a single drop of sweat slide down his face. But I suppose that's the sort of treatment royalty can expect from the world. It probably helps that he nearly always carries a paper fan with him. He essentially has an armada of them, to match whatever he wears—gifts from Asmer, from whenever she travels.

As Rian and his dragon head out the door toward an enclosed spiral staircase, I adjust the picks on my fingers and climb across the building. I stick to where I will not be seen, using the architecture for cover when possible. Rian's pace is easy to match by habit alone, as my body has memorized his walking speeds and can mimic them of its own accord.

Rian calls good morning to everyone he passes, and even if they're in a foul mood, they can't help but brighten at his cheer. He all but skips down the steps, and I catch sight of him now and again through the windows as I scuttle quietly down the building. Between me, the dragon bouncing about behind him, and Qhan waiting at the bottom of the stairs, Rian could hardly be safer.

I am mildly fond of Qhan Khaleem. He's Rian's favorite bodyguard, and mine, too since he is the most vigilant of the lot. Qhan is a fearsome man right at first glance: sharp uniform, a large scimitar at his side, a pistol at his other hip, and ever-watchful eyes. He has a long row of piercings on his left ear: silver loops all the way around. They say each earring is for one of the people he has killed in Rian's defense. I'm sure the only reason there aren't more is because I exist.

I don't know Qhan's genetic heritage, and I suspect he doesn't, either. Milash and Isaarian are likely, but maybe something Ishtak as well, or even

Lijimi. Regardless, he can pack on pounds of muscle easily, and his mind is sharp; that's what matters most, to me.

Rian bids Qhan a friendly good morning as he jumps down the last step. The dragon imitates his master, his little wings flopping as they fill with air, then drop with gravity.

"I think I'll visit the Fars'day market, today, Qhan," Rian claims, as if there was ever any doubt. "Though I feel as if I'm forgetting something..."

"Your gloves, your majesty," Qhan offers, handing them to Rian.

"Ah, I always misplace them, don't I?" Rian says, his good humor unwavering as he tugs the gloves on to protect his hands and fluke.

"Perhaps if his majesty kept to a regular sleep schedule, his memory might improve," Qhan says. There's nothing in his tone to suggest it, but I know that he's teasing Rian. They have that sort of relationship.

"Perhaps it just might," Rian agrees. "So how did you spend your morning free of me, hmm? Give any Fars'day gifts to pretty girls?"

We all know that Qhan spent his morning standing at the base of these stairs, preventing anyone from getting near Rian.

"As I am never free of you, your majesty, I've yet to spot any," Qhan says diplomatically.

"Well, then. We must remedy that. To the fair!" Rian says, and sets off.

Qhan gestures with his fingers, and three other guards form a semi-circle around him and Rian, prepared to step in front of him at a moment's notice.

I stalk Rian and his entourage through the crowds, toeing the sometimes-unnerving line between discretion and proximity. Glittering young noble ladies flit in and out of the crown prince's presence, as do some of his own enamored students, but Rian spends no more than a few minutes with anyone, interested in seeing today's wares.

Nusk has set a stall up for my *khashak,* promoting the crafts they use to calm themselves. I have no such talents, which speaks to my temperament, but Naomi's fluke of stitching makes her excellent at splicing both flesh and fabric. Korvaan's basic carpentry provides glazed wooden furniture many students find to their liking. And Taris, of all people, has a peculiar talent for making the most delicate of figures and jewelry from blown glass.

I've no idea where they find time for these things, but it's a great help during the festival days: a way to keep us all present with a purpose. Even Nusk.

He might not be as strong as he once was, and a charmed mouth won't help much with riflemen aiming for Rian's head, but even so. He's good at helping people with sharp eyes and loud mouths forget they've seen me. Not that I've been noticed since I was sixteen, but no one's perfect.

The only annoying part is seeing Taris' jewelry on all the women around here, including Asmer and Lune. I feel off-put by how close they've come to me and my *khashak*. Lune, in particular, seems to taunt me with how often she indulges herself with Taris' wares. She cannot possibly know how it irritates me, but even so. I'm territorial, and she somehow encroaches on my life in every way I might find offensive.

I will absolutely lose my head if Rian makes her his bride. For now, at least, I'm safe from such worries; he seems to have no desire for a wife, even whilst approaching his thirtieth year. But that won't last. Some day or another, he'll marry either Asmer or Lune. I doubt a new woman will suddenly appear to make a significant impact on his life in that respect. At least, not a new woman I'd trust not to kill him.

Rian somehow manages to chart a course all the way through the fair. He spends time with almost every vendor, and leaves them better off for it even if he does not purchase anything. As for what he does purchase: he taste-tests nearly every filled pastry, grilled meat, and fruit tart he can find. He even stops off for spiced southern coffee at a drinks' stall, managing to hold an entire conversation with the vendor from his seat on the carpet even as the man attends to other customers. Within a few minutes, Rian has finished his drink and is off again.

He examines and-or purchases: silk fans, jewelry, old or rare books, expensive silks, intricate laces, scarves, carved tribal masks from Milash, slippers from Lijimata, Alarkian motorcars and specialty telephones, rare or magical creatures not unlike his own sunblood dragon, typewriters, stationary, pens, perfumes, furniture, gloves, *silverware...*

It can be exhausting to keep up with him. He's too gregarious. Too thoughtless when it comes to his own safety. It's almost difficult to imagine anyone wanting him dead, he's so kind and thoughtful. But Nusk has warned me against trying to make deductions based on Rian's personality. Killing a crown prince is rarely a personal vendetta. And my job is only to keep Rian alive, not to concern myself with his political enemies.

Still: nothing ugly rears its head in the daylight. Rian makes it back to his rooms safely before sunset, and thankfully opts for a simple, private dinner in his chambers. He invites Crispin and Magnus to join him—Crispin because he enjoys the other's company and Magnus, I suspect, to be polite. Asmer and Lune decline their own invitations. Asmer is taking time to beautify herself for tonight, and Lune has sequestered herself in preparation for a performance she's giving.

Lady Lune chooses to keep her fluke a secret officially, but everyone knows it must pertain to music. She pretends to have no talent for instruments besides basic repetition of songs she's heard played. But when she sings, she can treat us to airy, bittersweet lullabies, empowering ballads, or vibrant, soulful music that almost mocks the audience with lyrics none of us fully understand.

She can sing of heartbreak and recovery. She can make grown men cry and jealous ladies stare in amazement.

Tonight, her songs are partially written in a language that I suspect she made up, with trumpets and a fierce beat to accompany her. Tomorrow morning, she will fail to politely receive compliments from Crispin, Rian, and Asmer, opting instead to complain about Crown Prince Mercer's absence. She's used to their praise, after all; Crispin's her brother, Asmer is her best friend, and Rian compliments everyone. Mercer is the one worth impressing

It's easy to hide in the dark while evening falls, and I do not spy anything out of the ordinary at my post outside Rian's rooms. Normally, I would thank the Almighty and think nothing more of it. But this is the Fars'day before Comus Day. One of the last opportunities for an easy kill, if someone wants Rian dead.

It's too good a chance to pass up.

I suffer through Rian's agonizingly tedious dinner with Magnus and Crispin, and occasionally check in with Taris and Korvaan. The former is backup for me, to step in whenever he's needed, and the latter is on standby to help conceal my presence, slip me into places I otherwise couldn't access, and clean up any messes I may or may not leave behind.

The other two crown princes leave for Lune's concert before Rian does. He spends another hour in his room, flicking through his new book, scribbling notes on its contents, and occasionally scratching his dragon behind his short little horns. I'm not unused to this. As Naomi noted yesterday, despite his sociable nature, particularly around the ladies, Rian is more scholar than paramour. He'll flirt with absolutely anyone who shows interest, but all he wants waiting for him in his rooms at night are his books.

I must admit, his antics in this manner can be amusing. He's not a heartbreaker on purpose, but still. It's almost as if he puts on a comedy of errors for my sake whenever I'm growing most bored.

Qhan and his guard have an entourage prepared for Rian by the time he drags himself away from his books to visit the concert tent, and I allow Taris to follow them as I go ahead. I meet Naomi briefly to change into darker clothing, fine enough to pass as party-ware, but not so intricate that it restricts my movements. It's times like these that I wish the Magicsmiths from Rian's old stories were real. They were supposedly the only ones in the world who could imbue things with magic: create magical items. A camouflage fabric, to swap color and texture as needed, would be greatly appreciated.

Still, I've mastered the process well enough that it only takes me a few minutes to become a different person. I send Naomi back to Nusk's cabin on the outskirts of campus, and alert Korvaan that if there's to be danger tonight, it will appear in the next hour or so.

Then I head into the tent.

There are many performances tonight. There are fire-breathers either spitting clouds of alcohol-propelled flame or implementing their flukes to perform the same trick, only with flames that can curl into the shapes of dragons and phoenixes. There are acrobats and jugglers. Sharp-shooters and ribbon dancers.

But everyone knows that they'll want to be in the largest of the tents by nine to catch Lady Lune's performance.

The tent itself is supported by a metal skeleton, with a network of catwalks above that hold spotlights charmed to follow the movements of the performer on stage. It is the most intricate of set ups prepared for those considered the best of tonight's entertainment, which is an Isaarian's way of saying, without verbally expressing, that Lune is more than worth the effort.

As expected, the crowd inside the tent is claustrophobically constricting. Those slipping in late jostle to try and win a better view, and those smart enough to arrive early jostle right back to maintain their positions. It's never physical enough to result in a serious brawl, as Isaarians are, by nature, a bit too prim for that (myself, naturally, excluded).

I send two short questioning blips to Taris over our watches, and he responds with a neutral tone: all is well. Rian has entered the tent, and is officially my responsibility once more.

I find our crown prince quickly despite the crowd, and circle his entourage to take notes. Rian has Lady Asmer on his arm, and whispers something that causes her to cover her mouth with a dainty hand and laugh. Her dress is many-hued pinks, yellows, and purples, like a flower fairy's floating gown. It drapes over her slender shoulders, catches at her waist, and trails out behind her in fluttery waves. Her silk-black hair is piled and coiled and pulled tight into golden hair ornaments, the sort that are in high demand for well-bred ladies like herself, and rests under a gauzy, golden veil. She wears large, dangling bracelets and a complicated gold ear-to-nose chain, set with tiny sparkling jewels.

Rian's own finery does not match hers or any other woman's around, and I think that is telling.

He and Asmer carry Qhan in their wake. His presence soothes my nerves only a little. Qhan is a more than proficient bodyguard, but his fluke is related to sensing the truth in another's words—hardly useful in combat. With Rian in a crowd, Qhan will be focused on keeping him separated from those pinched in around him. In such instances, it is easy to forget to look up.

That's what I'm for.

There are two sets of raised catwalks. One is low, reserved for those with enough wealth to purchase a vantage point above the crowd. Magnus will be up here, as all the crown princes and nobility should be. But Rian prefers to be on the same level as the general public. This makes my job harder, but that's what he likes. Crispin, too, is more of the mingling sort, and Asmer follows their lead, as her only other option is to be trapped in Magnus' company.

He's not the worst of men, but he can be obnoxious. I can't imagine Asmer choosing to spend time alone with him.

The second catwalk stands considerably taller, and holds the spotlights that have replaced the old limelight used for theatrical performances. Our modern age seems to produce new wonders by the year, some incorporating the usage of flukes, some made only from imagination and resolve.

I have set a timer on my watch that buzzes every so often, reminding me to check both the catwalks for threats.

In the meantime, I inspect everyone around Rian, and am pleased to find that Qhan is keeping any considered beneath his station at least an arm's length away from his prince. Asmer holds tight to Rian's arm, and occasionally another noble stops by to try and flatter the two of them, but Rian's bodyguards are earning their pay tonight.

I walk the perimeter of the tent, looking for potential threats. If Qhan is watching anyone close to Rian, that leaves it to me to seek out those hoping to strike from further away.

I head towards the edges of the stage, near the back of the tent, just to be thorough. I can see several of the most anticipated performers waiting back there, including Lune. She stands at the edges of the curtains, wringing her hands and smiling nervously at those who wish her luck.

I can't understand why someone with a song fluke might feel nervous, as I'm certain there's no possible way for her to make a mistake. But if acting unsure of herself is what will garner her more attention, I'm not surprised Lune thinks it proper. Her false humility is grating, but not dangerous.

I watch her for a few more moments before deciding there's nothing about her worth looking at other than her ensemble.

Lady Lune, as always, is a sight to behold. Classy, in her tight-fitting blazer: buttoned, dark blue and sparkling in the light, bangles on the shoulders like a mock general's uniform. Unlike Asmer's sleek, careful coils, her hair is piled up in an artful, soft bird's nest. In the back of her short skirt is a clutch of bunched fabric, forming a ruffled train. She has colored her eyelashes black and the corners of her eyes are adorned with sparkling silver paint.

Her only jewelry is a simple silver band and that disgusting chunky bracelet she almost always wears. It's a box on a chain. A pretty, decorative box, yes, but it's not the sort of piece Crispin Carsans' sister should be wearing. It looks cheap and childish. Even I know that.

There is an announcement being made: Lune's set starts in five minutes. I can feel my heartbeat quickening. Too many people have tried to kill Rian before for me to be given a respite now. Tonight is an unparalleled opportunity. Once Rian is back in the capital, he'll be surrounded by guards, other nobles, and the crown's own standing army. He'll constantly be enclosed on the palace grounds, and once Comus Day ends with him uncrowned, I assume the attempts on his life will stop.

I'm heading back to where Rian is when my watch beeps, reminding me to do what Qhan surely isn't. I look up.

"Fate's Fingers," I hiss.

I do my best to run through the crowd, slipping and ducking around the throngs of drunken people, looking for an easy way up to the upper catwalk.

Lady Lune's music is blaringly loud as she starts her set. High energy. Sensual. Aggressive, and certainly feisty. Women in the crowd suddenly long to be her, and men long to be in her. I hope her magic somehow works on the people I saw creeping around the catwalk and slows them down some. Otherwise, I don't think I'll make it in time. Even if they're after one of the other crown princes, and not Rian, that's a chance I can't afford to take.

So, I do something less than discreet, again hoping that Lune holds the crowd's attention. Jumping up, and glad for my strong legs as I do so, I catch the edge of the lower catwalk, adjust my grip, and pull myself up onto it. I've clearly startled some of those fancier patrons enjoying their overhead view, but many of them are intoxicated. Before anyone can start complaining about an odd woman clambering about where she shouldn't, I start to call for drink requests, stealing a book of money orders from some rich man's pocket and pretending to write them down as I hurry along.

That should be enough to make me invisible again: I am just another one of the staff. No one worth remembering.

I look up again and assess quickly: eight figures, too well-synchronized not to be a team. Too stealthy and surefooted to be a maintenance crew. The parapets above are metal, and solid, but there is still a chance for any blood spilled to get on the crowds below. So: kill all eight, quickly, avoid disrupting Lune's show in any way, and try not to make a mess.

My poison needle blades are best suited for the task. They are coated in one of the deadliest poisons in the world, secreted on the skin of a tachytrarian rainforest frog. In the large doses I prescribe, directly into the blood, it paralyzes before inducing heart failure. It will take a few minutes for the victims to die, of course, and will not instantly incapacitate them, but it will minimize gore and pain.

I run to the end of the lower catwalk until I find the stairs, hidden behind a double flap of the tent wall. Lune's music vibrates through the metal as I race up, almost louder than the clanging of my footsteps as I swing around and around up to the top, jumping over railings when the stairs double back on themselves.

When I reach the top, Lune has begun to sing, and one of the killers is waiting for me, knife in hand. Someone must have warned this bunch about the possibility of a *Khashtani*—or, at least, they'd been warned that most assassins who go after the Crown Prince Rian are never heard from again.

I race forward, automatically dancing the steps Nusk taught me. I've spent years fighting men like Korvaan and Taris, much bigger and stronger than I am.

The man with the knife is skilled, but I am nimbler. Knife fighters are often trained to aim for the chest first, which has many spots where a blade could cause irreparable damage. Then, once their target is off-balance, they'll go for the throat or femoral artery: good spots if you want your victim to bleed out quickly.

So, when he thrusts at my chest, instead of jumping backwards, I slip to the side, grab his arm with both hands, and bring up my leg to kick out the back of his knee. As he falls, I brace a hand on the back of his shoulder and yank back on his wrist, popping his arm from its socket.

If he cries out in pain, no one will hear it.

He's on his knees, the knife lost; I find this a perfectly safe and acceptable position to stick my needle knife between his throat and shoulder. Then I drop him to the catwalk. He'll be dead soon enough, and I have seven others to see to.

Two of them continue forward on their mission. The rest come after me.

Fortunately, the catwalk is relatively narrow, so only two people can come at me at once. Unfortunately, the catwalks are crammed close together, between the platforms and the equipment they hold, and a person with careful hands and feet could easily clamber from one to the other, and come up from behind me.

That's what some of these men try to do.

I focus on the two in front of me first. They're the ones standing between me and the assassins trying to get a clear shot of Rian's head. In the end, the entire scuffle couldn't have lasted more than three minutes, based on the duration of Lune's song. But it always feels longer when I'm working hard to keep Rian safe. Every move feels as if it takes ten seconds instead of half of one.

The first assassin coming at me has a knife not unlike the one I already disposed of, which implies that they want to keep things quiet, too, until they've disposed of the crown prince. This is good news; knives are infinitely easier to avoid than bullets, and only move as fast as the person holding them.

I throw myself to the side against the handrail as he lunges at me, duck under another swipe of his arm to get up close, then jab a needle knife into his belly. He's still got a knife for me to worry about, but he's more easily disarmed with poison working its way through him. I have to trap the knife with my foot when he drops it, to keep it from falling on the audience, and then work my boot under its handle to flick it up in my hand just in time to block the blade of the second man coming at me.

He's faster than his fellow, and this takes more time. I have to work for it.

When our blades meet, he throws an arm up into my face, smashing my nose. The force isn't enough to cause a break, but I'll have bleeding to consider after this, and it is enough of a distraction for him to get a good swipe at me. It results in a scratch my hairline.

Not optimal, but I'll take it over a knife through the skull.

And all the while, Lune continues to sing. The only Isaarian word that I can make out repeatedly is "wait". Her music is a metronome for my movements, and I find it oddly soothing while I fight over a half-dozen men. I don't know what that says about me, and if Rian's life—given his destiny—justifies these deaths, but this is no time for philosophical platitudes.

I finish off the fellow in front of me: three down, five to go. Two behind me, one in front. Two more after Rian.

One of the two behind me traps my arms in a bear hug, presumably in the hope of helping his partner in front dispose of me quickly. But I can make this work.

From here, it's much easier for me to employ the sharpened tip that can slide out from the front of my boot. I swing my leg up to stab one of my assailants in the neck. His hands fly to the gouge in his throat as he drops to his knees. This gives me the opportunity to swing my legs back down and curl forward, with enough surprise force to send the bear-hugger over my head. Granted, he is still holding me, so I'm carried along with him, but I land on top, perfectly positioned to bury an elbow in his gut.

Nusk hates it when I bring fights to the ground, but it sometimes makes my work so much easier.

From here, I stick the poison needle knife in behind his ear, and—

Knife.

Either these fellows are faster than the average killer, or I'm getting slower.

I'm forced to roll backwards, leaving my needle knife in my last opponent. I manage to get my hands under me, and recover by flipping up to my feet. The last of my current quarry holds his knife backhanded, better for swiping than throwing, which is good for me. But he looks confident. Which is less than stellar news when time is of the essence.

I needed my needle knife back, dammit.

When he comes at me, I bring my leg up and kick at his wrist several times. He doesn't drop the knife, but it opens up his chest, with one less arm to defend himself with. From there, it only takes me a few seconds to spin close, into his chest. I grab his wrist with one hand, using my body to keep his arm locked straight, then pop up under it, dislocating his elbow. He still doesn't drop his knife, but he'll have a harder time using it, now.

His free hand scrambles to grab my hair, yanking my head around as he tries to smash my face against the metal railing. It's not my proudest moment, but he's good at keeping his legs away from me when I try to hook back with one of my own and trip him. I do manage to slam back into his body enough to crumple him, pin him against the other side of the railing, and slam his own knife into his head, but it took me longer than I would have liked.

I retrieve my needle knife, wipe the blood from my forehead, and move.

Last two.

They have positioned themselves on another section of the catwalk. When I run straight for them, I must swing myself over a railing and leap, my boots clattering on the metal. It's not elegant, and it alerts them to my presence, but no one below has noticed, yet. We are just scuffling shadows in the dark.

This portion of the catwalk is more dangerous than the other, as it supports most of the lights. They are charmed to match Lune and the others on stage, occasionally getting in my way.

I manage to reach the assassins before the one closest to me is fully standing, and kick him in the face twice before sticking him. The last of them, though, is the one I really have to worry about.

He's not a huge man, but he is significantly bigger than me, and not the slow sort. My first order of business is to wrestle away a gun that I'm sure would have made quick work of Rian's head, had the angle been right. I'm not overly familiar with guns, but I know enough to recognize this one as the sort a sniper would use. It's likely Alarkian, as these assassins may be.

I've no idea why Alarkia would want Rian dead, but it matters little.

I attack as aggressively as I know how, but my blows have little effect. A single hit from him sends me staggering backwards. If feels like a major victory once I finally get the gun from him and send it clattering off far behind us. But he rushes me, slamming into my torso and bouncing us both from one railing to the other. I elbow him to escape, grab the gun, and fling myself back onto the other catwalk.

I decide upon a game of avoidance, for the time being. He can't kill Rian without this gun, but I need a better position to attack from. I work best with trickery and the element of surprise.

The last assassin follows.

On stage, Lady Lune hits a high-note that will make people visibly shiver. The glittering paint near her eyes sparkles under the lights, as do her eyes themselves. She is the triumphant siren, tonight. When she sings, she is queen of the world.

She also, unwittingly, is helping me. Her decision to forgo what is clearly previously planned choreography, and flit about where she pleases, means the lights swing about to keep up with her, making their trajectories unpredictable.

The assassin and I dodge between them. We're both fast, but I have the gun to get in my way, slung across my chest, and he's heavier, with more weight to carry. We occasionally exchange a blow or two when one of us gets too close to the other. But I'm running out of catwalk, and time. So, I dispose of the rounds, but keep hold of the gun itself. When he comes close to me again, I swing it at his face and give him a good crack against the skull.

He bleeds, but doesn't concuss. I use the gun and railings to my advantage, refusing to relent, forcing him onto the defensive. I keep my needle knife at the ready, but if I have to bludgeon the man to death, so be it.

I move to hook behind one of his knees, planning to bring him down and stab him in the eye. But this man's legs are like tree trunks, and while he wavers, he doesn't buckle. Before I know it, he's managed to pin me. *Pin* me. The gun is out of my reach. He's much heavier than me and has pinned my arms over my head with only one of his hands. The other one goes to his hip to pull a knife, and he's wasting no time.

But at the last second, he *hesitates.* I don't know why, and from the confusion in his eyes under his mask, I'm sure he doesn't know, either. Maybe he's finally succumbing to whatever spell Lune has cast on her audience. Maybe he, for whatever reasons, is having second thoughts about killing a woman.

I suppose I'll never know. I take the opportunity to tilt my hips up and tip him forward, breaking free of his grip as he tries to catch himself on his hands. From there, it's a simple swing and flip: getting my legs over his, grabbing one of his wrists and pushing until I have him pinned. I jab my needle knife in under one of his ears and hold him until he stills.

Once his body relaxes, I free myself from our entangled limbs, and stand to survey my surroundings as the audience cheers for Lune. None of the would-be assassins are moving. I sense no other threat present, to either myself or Rian.

I allow the bloodlust buzzing in my ears to fade; it's over. My shoulder aches like I've ripped stitches open, but I know it's healed enough for this pain to be the phantom variety. My left wrist aches from landing on it poorly when I took to the ground, and my nose has started to drip blood, but at least the cut on my forehead isn't gushing, and I've somehow yet to bloody my clothes.

As I catch my breath, I count: one, two, three, four, five, six, seven.

Seven?

Panicking, I scan the tent, checking on Rian, Qhan, Asmer. But no one is moving quickly and quietly through the crowd towards or away from Rian—he's safe. I check in with Taris, seeing if he noticed anyone fleeing the tent, but no. Nothing. No one. I scour my memory instead, trying to recall if I did count eight assailants the first time around, and realize that, the moment I hit the catwalk, I only ever encountered seven. Seven total, not *eight*. Idiot. A simple mistake, perhaps, but one that could have gotten me into trouble. What if there had been eight? I could have gotten myself—or, more importantly, *Rian*–killed.

Maybe Naomi was right; I need more recovery time.

I've spilled more blood than required, but it's no battlefield butchery. As quickly as I can, I use the assassins' clothes to soak up excess blood, lest it drip on the crowd below. By the time it seeps through enough for anyone to notice, Korvaan will have handled the bodies.

Ignoring my injuries, I pile the bodies together near a stack of crates on the furthest end of the catwalk. We'll need to take care of them quickly, but the way I figure, we have at least until tomorrow morning when the tent is taken down, and Korvaan is usually quick. It's routine, now: my *khashak* have a helpful system in place to ensure no evidence is ever found.

Before returning to the ground, I kneel by the bodies. The bottom of one of my boot heels comes off to reveal a hidden chamber that I keep filled with white paint powder, which requires only spit to make a paste. I paint a cross with a circle around it on each assassin's forehead, so that it is recognized in the afterlife that I forgive them for what they attempted to do. No one deserves the Judgement Courts, especially for all eternity. A life taken is a life stolen, always; that's what Nusk taught me. I am a *Khashtani*—I kill when necessary for my principal. But I honor the fallen; at one point, they were someone's newborn son, or daughter. Perhaps someone's spouse, someone's parent.

By the time I get down from the catwalks, I'm woozy, but I've had worse—it's simply the combination of vibrant lighting, minor blood loss, and exercise.

Lady Lune has moved on to her next song, with new choreography. Her legs are going to ache tomorrow morning, I'd say. And her voice should be a hoarse whisper, if she keeps belting like this. At least she's a good distraction.

All eyes are on Lune as I stagger between the partygoers, wiping blood from my nose with my hand. If I stain my clothes, Naomi will turn harpy, and I can't foresee handling that argument well. Korvaan already won't be pleased about the bodies, and I can only handle one of them being irritated with me.

Nusk will be proud that I've once again saved Rian's life, but he won't say anything. Simply nod. His children will also say nothing positive. They expect it of me; success is a foregone conclusion. But Nusk knows all, about everything. He understands that I have no real want for anything beyond keeping Rian safe; he may be a flamboyant, kittenish, oblivious fool, but he's my flamboyant, kittenish, oblivious fool. If he died, I would take my own life in an instant. Not only because it is a *Khashtani*'s vow, but because I would have no reason to live.

I hold down the button on my watch and bring it to my mouth.

"Taris. On you. Alert Korvaan to clean up—seven. Upper catwalk."

The watch cheeps back at me in his response. Taris will keep an eye on Rian while I clean myself up, scowl at Naomi's needle, and pretend as if I was never here in the first place.

As I make my way through the crowd, I steal a lady's large, patterned shawl to cover my torso, another's gaudy necklace, and a third one's hairpiece to throw over my shoulders and neck and pin up my hair in a manner that hopefully obscures the blood in it. Now I'm just another fancied-up lady. Not a perfect disguise, but given the crowd's inebriation, it doesn't need to be.

It should have been easy to slip through the mob and out of the tent, but I hesitate until I can spot Taris. I know it's unnecessary, because I've already killed that pack of assassins and I doubt there's likely to be another set lounging around someplace, but I'm paranoid that way.

Unfortunately, this gives someone the chance to notice me as I waver in place with a hand still pressed to my forehead. As he walks up behind me, it's all I can do not to stab him in the neck. I don't have to glance up to know who it is—he smells like cinnamon, and only one of the princes wears a scent like that.

"Are you well? Miss? You're bleeding," he says.

Damn him. And damn me, for making a novice mistake.

"Fine, fine, I'm fine," I say, forcing my gravelly voice to rise a few octaves. "The crowd is a little rough for me. I think I'll step out—"

"Let me accompany you, and find someone to stitch that cut of yours," he insists, and I curse him another few times by all eighty strings of Fate's loom.

Crispin Carsans is the most courteous of the Crown Princes, which makes him a huge liability. Present him with a bleeding young woman, and he'll help her without considering how opportune such a moment would be for assassination. Not that I think anyone has reason to kill him; as a member of the Carsans family, he can never be king.

Nearly everyone likes him, but still: this tanned, blonde, bulk of a golden boy has little charm to tempt *me* with. I find him nearly as problematic as Lune, but despite her accidental assistance this evening, Crispin's adopted sister still takes first place in terms of which of them aggravates me more.

I let him take my arm, likely feeling proud of himself for helping a lady in need. I damn myself as well as him, for forgetting that, while Crispin drinks, he's more careful about it than others. He's just drunk enough to let some inhibitions down, but not so drunk that he didn't notice my bleeding head.

There's an easy way out of this situation, and I plan to take it, but first—so long as I'm letting Crispin escort me through the crowd—I take my time to look for Taris again. Taris takes his time just long enough to make me anxious, but I finally spot both him and Korvaan on the catwalks.

Success.

Now all that's left is to escape from Crispin's courtesy, and that is done easily enough. I lift my arm out of his so smoothly, he doesn't feel it. I slip back into the crowd, to exit the tent from another side, and disappear into the night. By the time Crispin has made it outside himself, I'll be long gone, and he'll be left wondering if I'd ever been real, or just a ghost brought on by spirits of a different kind.

Three

TARIS AND KORVAAN HANDLE RIAN'S SECURITY, as well as body disposal, while I go to see Naomi in our dormitory. As predicted, she's beside herself that I'm injured again, already, but she only starts her lecture after getting to work. She's done stitching within half an hour, at which point my nose has stopped bleeding and my left wrist no longer aches so badly. Naomi threatens to drag me over to Nusk's cabin to drink some of her sleep-inducing tea, but I manage to haggle her down to a compromise: I will go back out to make sure that Rian makes it to his room safely, sleep, then resume my duties as normal.

This deal weighs heavily in favor of what I'd like to do anyways, and I know my body needs rest, so I don't try to argue for less. Naomi procures a sticky bun, filled with potent coffee-chocolate spread, caramel, and nuts, and demands I consume it before heading back out. The caramel and chocolate hide the coffee flavor well enough, so I agree, knowing I'll need some form of assistance to stay awake as long as I need to.

Then I return to the entertainment tent.

Lune has finished by the time I arrive, and they've moved on to the rest of the night's acts. I find a spot on the upper catwalk and plant myself there to watch Rian, checking our perimeter via Taris and making sure no one attempts to access the upper catwalk whilst a grumbling Korvaan pretends to escort "passed-out drunks" to their rooms. It's a ploy that works startlingly well, but it likely helps that we've only ever implemented it during major events like this, where most folk old enough to still be awake are intoxicated themselves.

Rian has found a spot with an excellent view, which makes the next few hours mercifully easy. He doesn't consume much alcohol over the course of the night, but that doesn't surprise me. The only times I've seen Rian drunk is when he and Mercer are celebrating something he considers significant. I'd claim Mercer's a bad influence, but Qhan usually prevents them from causing trouble, and Mercer is the best friend he can be to Rian, so I can't complain.

By the time the festivities conclude, my muscles are shaking, and I know I should sleep. My *khashak* is more than capable of handling things, now.

After returning to my dormitory, washing, seeing to my teeth and hair, and leaving my soiled clothes to soak in soap and water, I manage a solid four hours of sleep before seventh bell. Naomi is already up and gone, having helpfully hung my clothes up above the bath to dry. She's left me an apple and a note reminding me to drink water—it's a pointless attempt at keeping me healthy, as I find it easier to keep track of Rian without worrying about my own physical needs. I tend to drink water only once I'm in for the night, or when my *khashak* are watching Rian. Otherwise, the interference run by my own bladder is irritating and difficult to plan around.

While I wake at seven and prepare myself for the day, Rian sleeps until a quarter to ten. The only reason he drags himself out of bed at all is because of his plans to meet Crispin, Lune and Asmer to break their fast, and force them all outside. He spends nearly an hour preparing, slow and drowsy as he washes, dresses, and monologues to his dragon about how stupid an idea this was.

By the time he leaves his rooms, I've had to massage a cramp out of my calf three times, and am regretting never acclimating to coffee.

I make it to the gardens before Rian and Qhan do, and am pleased to find excellent cover which will hide me from all, yet provide a good view of the surrounding area.

The gardens are Rian's favorite place on campus, other than the arboretum. The difference is that, while the gardens are often filled with students studying, running about if they're young and nuzzling a lover in a quiet corner if they're older, the arboretum is exclusively for meditation and absorbing power from the earth, moon, and sun. Rian is always casual when he heads there, hands in pockets, distributing smiles and friendly greetings, bare feet all the way.

But it means something, I think, that he always makes certain he has the stores available to use his fluke at any given time. So, however stupid he pretends to be, there's some modicum of caution bouncing around in that head of his.

The gardens are a large maze of Isaaria's natural flora and fauna, speckled by larger clearings with cushioned chairs and covered tables. The University employs those with flukes of nature to keep the garden looked after in every season, and I'll admit, their magic has made the place feel like it belongs out of time. A salon, where life stands still.

Not that Rian and his fellow nobles can be that weary given the luxuries they enjoy, but I know they have their particular struggles, too.

The food has already been served by the time said drowsy nobles have all gathered, each them lackadaisical after the night's events. Asmer has put on a full face of makeup to hide the circles under her eyes. Crispin's golden curls are still damp from a wash. Lune yawns at least once a minute. And Rian ends up eating enough for all four of them combined.

He's brought his miniature sunblood dragon along. *Mango.* It's a ridiculous name for a dragon, and something only Rian could get away with. Though, as a name for any creature, it fits a sunblood best: usually reds, oranges, and yellows, they only ever grow as big as a medium-sized dog. Mango, naturally, is as bright as the fruit whose name he bears. He stomps about imperiously, poking that rounded snout of his everywhere as he searches the breakfast spread.

He hasn't even learned to properly tuck his wings in yet, poor thing, and I've seen them flop about whenever he breaks into a run.

Over the next half hour, the four nobles slowly ameliorate mentally whilst consuming whatever brunch foods suit their fancy. Theirs is quite the banquet: sweet fruit tarts with caramelized topping, creamy egg pies, breakfast custards, hot cakes with sugar powder and jam, fresh fruits of the highest quality, bacon and eggs, juices, coffee, flaky pastry, and thinly sliced fried potatoes with chives. Rian's favorite item—quiche—is missing, but that doesn't deter him.

Their brunch drags on. Lune asks about the end of a book Rian lent her. Crispin has asked a servant to bring him a newspaper. Asmer has been lazily reading one of those cheap romance novels she loves so much, and occasionally takes turns with Rian to feed Mango pieces of fruit.

I take this time, in my limited space, to stretch and rub my sore muscles, half-listening to their conversation.

"Are any of you attending noon High Mass tomorrow?" Lune manages through a yawn, once her literary conversation with Rian comes to a natural end.

"Early at eight per the usual, dear," Rian says.

He's deconstructing a lemon tart, eating it in the most peculiar way he can. It should be noted that this tart is meant to be eaten by twelve people, and Rian is apparently determined to consume the entire thing himself. I'd criticize, only I've done the exact same thing before, albeit with a tart of lesser quality.

"But I don't want to rise early!" Lune complains.

"*You* can still go at noon. I simply prefer the Low Mass time; it forces me to get up in the morning."

"But I wanted to go with you," she pouts.

Crispin flicks a crumb off the table at her.

"Then you'll have to force yourself to go to bed early, moonchild," he teases.

Lune groans and lays her head down on the table, and that appears to be that.

Asmer is the only one of them who does not attend the Church of the Holy Three; she practices Vushan, and their holy day begins at three o'clock on the last day of the week. It means she'll miss whatever activities this lot entertains themselves with later this afternoon, but at least she doesn't have to get up early for worship.

She flips another page in her romance novel, then flushes deeply and skips ahead: not the sort of material to read in public, then. Or perhaps, not the sort of thing she should be reading at all, especially on what she considers a holy day.

"If you must know, I've read that trouble sleeping at night means you aren't out in the sun enough," Asmer says, deciding after a moment to leave her book until another time altogether.

"But I like being up at night," Lune claims. "I prefer it. It's the rest of the world that insists on enforcing a natural circadian rhythm! Or, at least, most of the rest of the world," she adds thoughtfully. "I'm sure there are others like me, just not enough to muster a majority."

"They're called 'the youth', and most of them grow out of insomnia by their twenties," her brother says dryly. "Face it, Lune: you're out of fashion."

"Sleep is a precious commodity," Asmer adds to the teasing.

The lady, predictably, pouts. "You are all impossible."

"There is a point to be made, though," Asmer says. "If you slept more, you could get up earlier and prepare for the day. Organize yourself. Feel ready to take on anything. And…well. You would at least have time to do something about your hair," she adds.

I spend the next minute or so stifling a yawn. This is perhaps the thousandth time Asmer, or Crispin, or one of the other Carsans has mentioned Lune's less than regal appearance. It's a losing battle they insist on fighting. Her hygiene is admittedly fine, and she at least tries to cover her dark circles, and color her face some. But that hair is like my own: unmanageable in the humidity.

"When I was little, I always wished I had silky dark hair like Asmer's; it's so beautiful," Lune sighs. "It would make things so much easier if you and I switched hair—and then you'd see why I never bother with it," she adds.

"You're too pale for dark hair, Lu," Crispin says without looking up at his sister. He flips a page of his newspaper. "You'd constantly look a fright."

Still, Lune pouts. "Then I've missed an opportunity to become a ghost!"

"Here, eat more tart, ghost," Asmer orders, pushing the dish towards Lune. "That should bring some color back into your cheeks."

Lune continues to pout like a child. Rather unoriginal, for a court lady.

"Aw, don't worry, ghostie-girl. You might need more sleep, but you're nearly glowing today! And your hair is beautiful, too," Rian claims, giving her a wry smile. "Let me braid it, little Lady Lune?" he teases. Rian does so enjoy his dalliances with alliteration. "Let me lace your lovely, long locks?"

Lune can't help but smile. I don't know anyone who can withhold a smile from Rian for long, save for myself. And, I'll grant, whoever keeps trying to kill him.

"If you insist," Lune says, swinging around so that her back is to Rian.

"You need to stop babying her sometime. You'll only reinforce her childish behavior," Crispin criticizes. Lune sticks her tongue out at him. "*See?*"

"I'll take my chances," Rian says as he combs Lune's hair with his fingers. "Besides: I like Lune's playfulness—don't ever change; I need you as a reminder there's hope for the rest of us," he adds, and Lune giggles triumphantly.

Crispin snorts and goes back to his newspaper.

Asmer shrugs and flips her own dark locks behind a shoulder.

In the next few minutes, Rian somehow manages to tame Lune humidified tangle into a single, silky braid. Only her still-frazzled bangs remain wild, but I doubt anyone but a professional could find a way to fix that. It almost makes her jealousy of Asmer's straight, thick hair reasonable.

They are, all four of them, undeniably petty. There are so many other things they could concern themselves with, and yet, here they are, chatting away about Lune's hair over a scrumptious brunch, completely unaware of the mortal danger they were in last night.

Mornings like this make me long for Crown Prince Mercer to return. Not only is he easy on the eyes, but he tends to have more scintillating discussions with Rian, and actually gives a damn about what's going on in the world.

He has the potential to make Rian a better heir—and, in fact, better person—than he is right now. Granted, I intend to keep Rian as far away from the crown as possible, but I still hope he becomes a decent Grand Prince after someone else is king. I want him to realize how much power he has, and the opportunities that affords him. I know I shouldn't have wants for him beyond those of his *Khashtani,* but I can't help it. I watched him grow up; I both want him to be nothing to history, and everything.

It's lucky for the world and Rian both, perhaps, that what I want doesn't matter. It's safer, as Nusk has taught me, to keep objective.

There's movement at the table as Asmer stands and stretches gracefully, adjusting the folds of her silk skirt.

"I'll be back shortly," she announces. "Too much juice with breakfast, I'm afraid. Lune, come with me?" she adds prettily.

Lune groans, but doesn't refuse.

"Carry me," she says dramatically, throwing her head back to give her brother an upside-down smile.

"You have legs, Lune."

"But they hurt!"

"And whose fault is that?"

"Rian's," she says. "For demanding a full set when I was already tired."

"My fault?" Rian repeats, playing along. "Why is it always my fault?"

"A better question is when is it not," Lune chimes sweetly.

Asmer allows a small, demure smile.

But in the interest of not forcing Rian to stay in the gardens without company, Lune gets up on her own. The ladies depart for the restroom, leaving myself with Crispin and Rian. And Mango, of course, but the sunblood dragon is busy chasing a dragonfly, so I'm not overly concerned about him.

There are a few seconds of quiet while Rian scrapes his fork across the plate to get every last remnant of lemon tart.

"Lune is in fine spirits today," Crispin finally muses.

"She's been this way for a while, now," Rian agrees. "Something's made her buoyantly blissful, but she won't tell anyone. Says it's a secret, and that she'll let us know soon."

"I hope so. I loathe it when Lune keeps secrets from me…This was a good idea, in any case," Crispin acknowledges. "Good for her, I mean."

He's warming up to admitting to something that may be considered juicy gossip about his own sister; I can tell.

"You're welcome," Rian says wryly. "Thought we should all get together for brunch, or else we'd each sleep 'til noon after a day like yesterday."

"If no one got her up, Lune would probably sleep until evening," Crispin says, and they laugh because it's true.

But then he sobers, and gets to the point he's been trying to ease into.

"Don't tell anyone I said so, but it's nice to see Lune like this again.

She's been so temperamental…up and down in such drastic swings, I've considered having a doctor look at her."

Rian raised an eyebrow. "Why haven't you?"

"Because I brought it up once and she panicked on me. Became erratic and unreasonable. I figure it's best just to keep an eye on her."

That's some interesting information to stow away. I'm not around Lune enough to notice if her behavior has been especially erratic of late, but as we approach Comus Day, there's reason to suspect everyone of treachery, even—or maybe especially—those closest to Rian. I must find time to rotate keeping Rian safe and spying on his compatriots.

Rian has a similar idea, for much different reasons.

"We'll all help keep a watch on her," he suggests.

"Thank you."

Rian shrugs and starts picking through a fruit bowl, looking for something else to feed Mango. "She might be your sister, but Lune's my friend. And I'm sure Asmer and Mercer will agree to help. If we can talk Lune into it, I think Merse will even examine her. See if he can figure out what's wrong without having to take her to hospital."

"Lune will probably be stubborn about that."

"Eh. She's not the only stubborn person I've successfully handled lately."

I roll my eyes. I know exactly what Rian means, and so should Crispin.

A matter of weeks ago, Magnus Oram spent days bothering Rian, insisting he should stop giving classes, stop attending society events "among the people", and had his own guard help double Rian's security.

Which, honestly, is what likely got me injured, as I had twice as many people as usual to evade whilst keeping Rian safe.

Despite Rian's friendly insistences that such concerns were unnecessary, it took a long while to convince Magnus to leave him be.

Sure enough, Crispin remembers, and decides now's the time to divulge to both Rian, and me, what exactly it was he and the other crown prince were talking about yesterday when Taris and I ran into them.

"Speaking of: I had a nice chat with Magnus," Crispin says.

"Oh? And how is the smarmy bastard?" Rian says, tossing a pear to Mango, who snaps it up in a spray of juice. "Still meddling in the affairs of others?"

"Politicking. As one might expect. And don't call him that. He's not… Well. He's not being unreasonable. He says something feels odd. That something big is coming up."

"Are you sure he's not just nervous about Comus Day?" Rian laughs.

"I don't know," Crispin admits. "It's possible, I suppose."

"If he didn't give specifics, don't worry about it now," Rian says with a shrug.

"This is all very odd, though, don't you think?" Crispin points out.

Rian remains comfortably casual. Almost too much so. "What is?"

"The circumstances of Comus Day. Why no heir has come forward. All that. None of us have died, which means someone has to be the Lost Heir. Right?"

I watch Crispin's face as he awaits his answer: this was an unexpected turn for the morning. Almost as if he heard my pleas for information and stimulation both, Crispin has delved into a topic he rarely discusses with anyone, let alone Rian. Either Comus Day's approach is shaking him out of his comfort zone, or something Magnus said has gotten Crispin worried enough to step out of their fantasy world.

Regardless, I'm eager to listen in.

Rian shrugs, not half as excited about these topics as I. "One would think. The other option, of course, is that you Carsans misinterpreted your own prophecy. It doesn't help that you always keep the full thing a secret."

"It's hard to misinterpret the Lost Heir's powers over *time itself,"* Crispin says defensively. "But Rian: indulge me. The Lost Heir, or even the Lost Heir's parents, as we were all so young back then: they never stepped forward, isn't that also strange?"

"So long as I'm indulging you? Sure, I'll admit to that."

"Rian: I'm serious."

"No, you're Crispin," Rian says with a grin.

"Rian," other says sternly. "Please. For once, consider the consequences of all this. By Comus Law–which, please remember, is a *law*—the heir apparent must be presented as soon as it's clear the prophecy relates to them. They will go before the assembled council where, if they truly are the heir, there will be little dispute to their claim, and then that heir will become the ruler of Isaaria until the next prophecy puts someone else in his place—whether it be his or her children, the heir of another royal family, what have you—or allows him to continue his rule for another twenty-five years."

"Not that that's ever happened more than a handful of times in history," Rian claims, rolling his eyes.

"The prophecies are always different, but the outcomes are the same," Crispin lectures. "We've had the crown pass down through one family for up to four generations. We've had kings die before their time is up. We've encountered just about everything and anything before, but never this."

"Precisely my point, and why we shouldn't be concerned," Rian claims.

"What's that supposed to mean?"

"Look, Crispin, when you study as much history as I have, you realize that governments morph over time. Even without, say, revolution or wars, things still change. The fact that the Isaarian government has worked with a single system for so long, and so well, is unprecedented, really. So: no, I don't find it surprising that things are finally turning out differently than expected. It's only strange to you because you're living it, but if you were reading about it fifty years from now, you wouldn't think twice."

Aside from Mango demolishing another fruit, there's silence while Crispin thinks. He's frowning, but Rian's words still make sense.

"I suppose so," he finally allows. "But why wouldn't—"

"Crispin, drop it," Rian interrupts. "You're not the Lost Heir. I'm not the Lost Heir." – (I roll my eyes; filthy little liar.)— "Neither of us is going to be king, someone else will take the spot, life will go on, and one day you'll give the next prophecy and things will either change a little again, or go back to being how they always were. The end."

"Why are you so opposed to talking about this?" Crispin accused. "It concerns us; it's important."

Rian sighs. "Because I want Comus Day done and over with," he says irritably.

"You have no desire at all to be king," Crispin says dubiously.

"Well, no. I do, actually. But I also don't. I'm not entirely sure I'd be good at it, really. It's complicated," Rian decides dismissively. "And what about you—you haven't once considered what it would be like to take the throne?"

"*Ha. Ha*," Crispin says dryly. "No thanks. Even if it wasn't forbidden to a Carsans, I think I'd abdicate the minute a crown touched my head. Ruling a country doesn't sound very appealing; too many rules. Responsibilities. And I've enough of those to memorize already, as a keeper of Comus Law."

"Oh? And those are too much to levy against the benefits of being a king?" Rian counters with a wide grin.

Crispin is defensive. "Rian, Isaaria is already suffering internally, given our eight royal families, the Fae still living in the deep woods, and the Hotisokin demanding full representation at court despite their rejection of the laws set down by the kingdom. And then there's Rumshtama to the north, Kacha and Tourran to the east, Milash and Ishtaki to the south, and on and on…Not to mention, there's been talk of Rumshtama and Ishtaki both suppressing anyone in the Church of the Holy Three, burning down places of worship and rounding Theebins all up in one place. The last thing we need is to be crammed between two holy wars."

Rian grimaces, then looks oddly melancholy as he leans his chair back as far as it will go, tipping it on two legs.

"Why can't everyone just keep the peace?" he sighs to the sky. "No one wants conflict, do they? Why not simply be kind, considerate, and thoughtful?"

"Because you're thinking like a child, and adults are greedy bastards in comparison," Crispin drawls. "You're right, you would be a bad king," he adds. "You're an idealist."

"Too cruel, Crispin—you wound me."

Asmer and Lune are on their way back, now, cutting the rest of what might have been an interesting conversation short. I've always wanted to glean more information about what Rian himself thinks about his destiny, to pick up hints and see what it is he knows and what he doesn't. But he keeps no journal or diary, and rarely writes notes to himself. All I know, I must base on what he says and does. As far as I can tell, Rian has never used or spoken of his fluke, nor has he expressed particular interest or disinterest in being king.

He appears, with rare exceptions, completely neutral on the matter. He'll speak of pros one day, and cons the next. He never indicates that, regardless of personal thoughts, he is the only crown prince with the right to rule, by Comus Law.

It's enough to make me irritated at Lune and Asmer, though they can't help but return to their own brunch.

As expected, they bring the mundane back with them, and the conversation becomes much less entertaining for me.

Eventually, they leave the tables to wander the gardens. The girls entertain themselves by throwing a disk for Mango, who isn't particularly good at even trying to fly, but can manage a wobbly glide if he runs fast enough. They chatter on decidedly unimportant subjects until well into the afternoon. My legs are stiffening from all the crouching I've had to do. I'm sure Qhan, too, is bored to death by all this mindless babble.

Crispin does not bring up Comus Law again, or anything about the Lost Heir. Rian acts as if it was never discussed at all.

Finally, they decide they've other responsibilities or amusements to see to, and Rian courteously notes he'll leave first out of respect to the ladies.

"I'd better head back," he confesses. "I made my Isaarian literature class write their own myths and legends as an assignment, and I'm quite looking forward to reading what the children came up with."

"Meet us for dinner?" Asmer offers.

She fasts on evenings at the end of the week, for religious obligations, but attends dinner anyway for the conversation. Her offer is so hopeful and sweet that it surprises even me when Rian turns her down.

"I think I'll dine alone this evening, if it's all the same," he says. "Last time I brought a book to the table, Lune stole it. And has yet to return it," he adds.

"It's rude when you have perfectly good conversationalists about!" Lune says.

"And in the absence of a good conversationalist?" Asmer poses.

"Well, then, by all means, bring the book. But this is me we're talking about. Of course, the talk will be good."

I'm glad when Rian heads to his rooms.

Back at the nobles' quarters, I wait outside a window at the base of the stairs while Qhan sends someone up to check through Rian's rooms. It's a routine I fully approve of, to make sure no one is lying in wait for the oblivious crown prince. They've never apprehended anyone this way, and find no one there today either, but still—always better to check.

Qhan intends to walk Rian straight up to his door, but Rian begs him off with a smile, claiming something or another about wanting to at least have the experience of walking alone to his rooms. This is pointless, of course, but when it comes to resisting Rian's charm, his bodyguard usually loses that battle.

Crawling carefully along the outside of the building, I keep pace with Rian and Mango, and wait until Rian has unlocked his door and entered his room before finding a place to perch. I head to his north-facing balcony, which he rarely uses, preferring an easterly view. I'm perfectly content to keep an eye on him from there, only when I peer in through his windows, I realize with dread that something isn't right. Rian should have just entered his rooms, and should be at his desk, looking over his students' papers.

But he's not at his desk. Or his bed. Or in either of his chairs: the armchair or the reclining couch. I can see Mango curled up on his pillows, but no Rian.

Now normally, I wouldn't think anything of it. But Rian is a creature of habit, and doesn't often conceal his intentions from his friends. I should be able to see him right now. He should be doing exactly what he said he would be.

My mind races. Could Qhan's man have overlooked something? The food at brunch—had someone checked the food for poison? In the minute I didn't have eyes on Rian, has something happened to him?

I'm jittery from staying in once place all morning on minimal food and sleep. And last night's events aren't helping my nerves.

Before I can force myself to wait, for his sake, I've pried the lock on the window, disabled the trip-alarm I know Qhan has built in, and am standing in Rian's rooms.

There's no point in saying what I could have done, or might have done.

No point in hashing out what I planned to do, or what I would usually do to check on Rian whilst remaining all but invisible to him.

Because the second my toes touch the carpet, Rian walks out of the bathroom, wiping the corner of his mouth on his sleeve. He'd been *cleaning his teeth.* Which is especially peculiar because he only does that in the morning when he wakes and the evening before bed. Never now. As far as I'm concerned, he'd have no reason to do so now at all, unless—

I should have hastily, and stealthily, backed out onto the balcony again and clambered along the side of the building to hide. But I don't, and in a second, he's turned his head, and sees me.

To my surprise, he only looks shocked for a moment. Then he blinks, that moment passes, and Rian's face brightens in a brilliant smile.

While I'm still trying to figure out what to say, he's rushed forward and grabbed me. It's all I can do not to avoid his arms, flip him over onto his back, and put a knife to his neck. So instead, I end up standing frozen while he pulls me into an embrace. Like I'm a close friend he hasn't seen in months.

This feels like a dream. The nightmarish kind.

"By the Almighty, it's about damn time," he sighs, his arms still wrapped around me. "Still—you barely gave me time to brush my teeth, woman. Are you really so impatient you can't wait for proper hygiene to be observed?"

For a second, I'm still stunned by the fact that I nearly just killed my own principal in reactive self-defense. By the time I'm starting to put together some sort of recovery plan for this disgustingly egregious error, Rian has decided that an embrace is not enough. And he kisses me.

I'm not sure how to describe it. I've never been kissed before, after all. I don't have time for romantic inclinations in my line of work. It's…fine, I suppose. Except I have no idea what I'm doing, which leaves him to do the kissing, and me to panic while thinking about how angry Nusk is going to be when he finds out about this. I don't know the protocol for this particular failure in a *Khashtani*, but there will likely be some form of punishment.

By the time Rian stops kissing me, we've backed up against the wall by the balcony doors. He's got one hand behind my neck, and the other arm around my waist. I'm still trying to figure out what the hell I should do.

"That was risky, running right into Lune like that," he chuckles in my ear. "If you wanted my attention, you know how to get it."

I'm not sure what to do other than to push him off me. I've finally managed to find my tongue, but am still lost in terms of what to say, so what finally comes out might be construed as somewhat hostile. Which is unfortunate, but, I think, understandable given the circumstances.

"What are you doing?" I hiss. "I'm not whoever you think I am."

We stare at each other, and I try to read Rian's thoughts through his eyes. I can't tell if he's been drugged, or if he's under the influence of someone's fluke…Nothing.

"I thought," he starts. His face is pale, and his eyes deeply troubled. It is as if I've hurt him far more than I thought he might hurt me. Then Rian's jaw tightens, and I believe I see anger, there. "Of course not," he says bitterly, taking a full step away from me. "Then I've been a fool. Again. And yet I always hope…"

"What?"

"I thought you let me see you," he says. "On purpose."

We stare at one another.

"Soleil," he says hoarsely. "You…"

There's hasty knock at the door, and before Rian gives permission, it swings open., I hastily push him behind me. I draw two throwing knives, and hurl one of them at the intruder, so that it just barely misses his head as he pokes around.

There's a startled cry, and I hold the second knife at the ready.

"Don't move, unless you seek death," I warn, but the man enters anyway, flinging the door closed behind him.

There are two reasons I don't throw the other knife. The first is because I've never seen this man on campus before. He looks western, in a way, but also completely unfamiliar in terms of origin: he is completely albino. The second reason is because he's talking. And he knows my name.

"Hope's *Head,* Soleil!" the albino man snaps. "Why-oh-why must it always, always be 'shoot first' with you? For the love of the Almighty, woman, what happens if you actually hit me?"

All I can do is stare; my long knives tightly gripped in hand. The albino man is muttering to himself, brushing his clothes off and cursing my caginess as if he knows me well.

"It is a damned good thing you warned me about you," I think I hear him say under his breath. "That might have gone through my eye…"

"Who are you?" I demand. "Tell me now, or tell me with a knife to your throat: your choice."

"Oh, don't worry about it, Soleil," Rian says, still speaking as if we're intimate with one another. "We know him." He then peers at the albino man and frowns. "I think. Don't we know you?"

The man sighs. He puts a hand to his forehead and mutters something about the idiocy of trying to keep people sane and how disgustingly overcomplicated "this all is". I'm almost sure I can't have heard him correctly, because that makes the least sense out of anything I've heard today.

He's suddenly pointing an accusing finger at us both. "Taris is an excellent example of someone coming completely unhinged, and apparently no one wants the same for you."

"I won't disagree with you about Taris," I say. "But…how…"

"How do I know Taris? Good question. You are great annoyances to me I hope you know. It would be easier to just let things be…but no. It's too difficult for your silly little heads."

There's a glimmer of something about him that seems familiar, but I can't tell if it's real, or merely his naturally white hair reminding me of Rian's.

"I know you very well," I say. "Don't I?"

"Don't we?" Rian says.

I'm not sure how I feel about being grouped in with Rian that way, as I'm still trying to figure out how he thinks he knows me, but I suppose I can't tell him he doesn't recognize this albino man. So, I let it be.

"We've met many times," the albino says dryly. "But this is not the way. It ends poorly. So: we'll have to fix it."

He takes a step towards us. I'm immediately on guard again, my muscles tense and my knife raised.

"Oh, give it a rest, would you?" the albino says in exasperation.

"Prove you're no threat to the crown prince, then tell me why you're here," I demand in response.

He sighs. Someone else knocks lightly on the door, and then a man's voice says: "Just so you know, Sep: you said five minutes, and you've used up two."

"Give me a second," the albino snaps before turning back to us. "I have to think…I should let you all lose your minds for once and see how *that* goes."

I don't know what to say to that. Rian and I exchange a look, and he gives me an innocent shrug. There's something about this albino man that is familiar to both of us, but neither of us can remember. He doesn't feel dangerous. But I'm not willing to risk Rian's life based on a feeling. I keep a close eye on the man as he hovers a few feet from the door.

"Now here's something we haven't done before…" he mutters. "But I think nothing's lost by trying…Ha. Literally, nothing lost…Except time, but who the hell cares about that?"

"Excuse me," Rian poses, but he's ignored.

"Have to be far enough that no one notices I left…I have Cas, though, so all I need to account for is Jarrod, damn him. Damn them all, actually. Maybe… twelve hours? Twelve hours. Twelve hours is fine…What time is it now?"

I think he's talking to me, and go to check my watch, but the man outside the door replies first with, "Quarter to two!"

The albino man thinks, then shrugs. "That'll do."

Before I can stop him, the albino moves. He's impressively, surprisingly fast, and now stands right before me.

"Do me a favor," he tells me, "and think of the end of Fars'day."

"What?" I say.

"And you," he says, already turning to Rian. Before I can stop him, he presses a finger rather pointedly on Rian's forehead. "Remember, and then forget. And then do what you know you must."

"What?!" I say again.

Next to me, Rian looks as if he's just seen something from another world. He looks as if he realized something mind-blowing. Some sort of cosmic revelation. I hear him whisper a soft, "Oh…" before he turns to me.

"Soleil, you're not going to be happy about this. But it's for the best."

He glances at the albino.

"Do, uh…Do you mind?"

The stranger waves a hand dismissively. "Do what you have to."

I'm confused and suspicious of absolutely everything and everyone now, but I still allow Rian to grab me by the wrist and pull me onto the balcony, closing the doors behind him.

"Am I supposed to have any idea what's going on?" I complain. "Rian—who is he? And what did he do to you—"

"Not right now," the crown prince says. "Look, you need to be more careful. Don't let me see you, even if it's on accident. You give me too much hope, Soleil."

"Would you please stop saying my name?" I say, cringing.

Rian grins. "Don't worry," he says, leading me towards the edge of the balcony and stepping close to me again. "We'll fix this."

I groan, feeling a headache coming on. "I swear, this is a horrible dream," I say. "A nightmare of some sort…"

"Don't worry about that, either," Rian laughs. I don't see anything about this that makes it a laughing matter, but I suppose Rian could laugh while choking on his own blood.

"But what—Oh, *don't do that*," I say as Rian puts an arm around my waist and pulls me closer.

"Never forget me." He breathes the words like they're a prayer he's said so many times, he no longer remembers the meaning.

Then he hastily presses his lips to mine, and before I can say a word, he pushes me off the balcony.

Four

SEVENTH BELL CHIMES; I wake breathless in my own bed. My heart is pounding, there's sweat on my forehead, and my chest feels unbearably tight. If my head ached any more, I'd be forced to find some sort of fluke healer. I force myself to take several long, deep breaths, rubbing at the knot in my chest.

For a moment, I'm too sleep-addled to think straight. But then I remember everything that happened yesterday. Rian kissing me, and pushing me off his balcony. That fall was more than long enough to kill me; I should be dead. I have no idea how I got back into my own bed…

But then I hear noises outside that only lead to further confusion: there's a celebration going on. And it sounds as if it's *Fars'day*. But that's…

Then I know: One of the assassins at the Fars'day Gala. That eighth one that I thought I saw before convincing myself otherwise. He must have gotten to me first, and put me to sleep for Almighty knows how long.

I desperately check my watch. I could have sworn it was seventh bell that woke me, but I am woefully mistaken: the arms point to quarter past three.

It takes me longer than I'd like to get my bearings and head outside. As I run back to the main tent, couples and groups of threes and fours are wandering out of it, laughing, razzing one another, and finishing the last of their drinks. I tell myself that this is a good sign; if anyone had gotten to Rian in the time I was away from him, folks wouldn't be enjoying the end of Fars'day. There'd be screams and panic and all sorts of chaos.

Though I have no way of knowing, I assume Rian is still in the tent and enter.

But Rian isn't there. The lights are off, and night workers are disassembling the stage.

I run to the nobles' quarters. Crispin and Magnus and Asmer are all in their chambers, and Lune is surely somewhere accepting all varieties of praise for her performance, but Rian? Empty rooms. There's only Mango, curled up on his pillow nest and waiting for his master's return.

In seconds, I'm back on solid ground again, running, trying to think.

He's not here, *why is he not here?* What if he wasn't assassinated, but kidnapped, and Qhan is trying to keep it quiet so as not to panic anyone?

What if, what if, what if—

My watch cheeps, startling me. A moment later, I hear Taris' voice:

"Though it's highly entertaining to watch you run around campus like a beheaded chicken, you ought to know your precious prince is perfectly safe."

"Where?" I snap.

"Library. Korvaan is inside with him; I'm on the roof."

I let the tightness in my chest dissipate. If Korvaan is in the library, he'll be watching from the high ceiling, among the arches and columns. I know from experience that it is an excellent vantage point; one can almost see into every corner, so the towering shelves can't possibly hide a lurking menace. And Taris is unlikely to let anyone slip past him to get inside.

"Why the *hell* is that idiot in the library?" I mutter, walking to join my *khashak*.

"Who knows," Taris says.

I can tell from his tone that he'd rather speak in person, if at all. I wait to question him further until I'm perched on the roof of the library, hidden behind the stone carvings. I have Korvaan join us temporarily, as Qhan is inside with Rian, and has guards posted both inside and outside the doors.

Though my hazy dream still makes reality complicated to navigate, I learn from Taris that I did stop the assassins, did tell him and Korvaan to watch Rian and clean up the bodies, and let Naomi patch me up. It's everything afterward that's only fiction.

"When you didn't return, I assumed Naomi forced you to rest, and decided to keep an eye on the crown prince in your place," Taris adds.

"I can't remember," I groan, and shiver as my dried sweat chills me.

"You need a vacation," Korvaan says. "You're wound tighter than a—"

"Korvaan," I warn, and shoot him a look. "Don't. Not now."

"It's only that you look terrible," he says. "Anyone could see it. You're so...pale."

"Korvaan. I'm Isaarian."

"Nah, not, fair-skinned. Pale, as in..."

"Pasty. Ashen. Pallid," Taris rattles.

"Don't hold back," I mutter.

"You should go back to bed, Soleil," Korvaan suggests. He peers at my stitched forehead, as if examining it for bruises. "Guess that bump on your head was worse than you thought."

"Go to your room with N'omi," Taris agrees. "She'll keep an eye on you. Make sure you don't die in your sleep. We'll switch off again in the morning."

I'm loathe to do anything Taris tells me to, but they're right. I need to sleep. Get my head straight.

Exhausted, but relieved Rian is safe, I make my way back to my room. I let Naomi badger me to wash up, and then crawl under my blankets before quickly dropping off to sleep.

When I wake, I swap places with Taris on the balcony and take up a vigilant watch while Rian lazes his morning away. All is well, the assassins from last night will never be found, and Korvaan kept several of their weapons to hand over to Nusk. That mysterious eighth assassin, wherever he or she went, has yet to make an appearance, but I'm sure they're out here somewhere, biding their time.

Rian does not go out to brunch with Crispin, Lune, and Asmer. In fact, he's yet to get out of bed well past the time one might reasonably eat, "brunch".

I use this time to revisit all the events from the past few days that made my dream turn out the way it did: my possible lingering attraction to Rian is mocking me in full, Lune's mention of a brunch that one school-day morning led me to imagine them at such, my observation last night regarding her aching legs, my irritation with Taris and his ridiculous stunt with Crown Prince Magnus, Mercer's latest gift to Rian reminding me of his pet sunblood dragon...

The pieces all fit together too well. It's too contrived a dream.

I try not to think much on it, lest I let myself become distracted, but I cannot help but indulge myself. I'd have to be a fool not to consider the idea that, perhaps, my dream did happen, and Rian pushed back time. Only, from what I understand, Rian does not create new timelines, but simply washes back reality, destroying utterly from Fate's loom whatever events happened, and letting us all play them out again. This means I shouldn't be able to remember anything. Yet, I do.

Curious.

I'll have to discuss the eighth assassin with Nusk and my *khashak* at some point, but for now, I'll simply keep my eyes open, tread with care, and attempt to keep Rian from doing anything too reckless.

Sometime in the afternoon, Rian forces himself out of bed. He takes an hour-long bath, orders nothing but a carafe of coffee for breakfast, and drops down at his desk to study his notes. He's writing a thesis on the history of Magicsmiths and their effect on the world. It's a subject ignored by most of the academic community; if the Families Three did exist, they're certainly extinct at this point. The Smith, Grey, and Wolff families are nothing more than myths, now. And only a few, like Rian, bother studying them with such fervor.

I know little about them myself; only whatever Rian blabbers about to those who'll listen, and the basics, from the stories he likes to tell. Magicsmiths were, supposedly, the only ones in the world whose flukes allowed them to create new things or embed magic into items. There are countless stories of them and their creations: magic mirrors, swords, rope, armor…even ribbons, fruits, and animals. Implications and rumors that a few dragon breeds exist not from evolution, but were born from some Creationist Smith's mind.

I'm a skeptic, but the stuff fascinates Rian, and it's interesting enough to eavesdrop on. I'd rather hear him blather on about the Smiths and the two families meant to balance their power—the Greys and the Wolffs—than suffer through serious talks about Rian's marriage plans.

Fortunately for me, Rian tends to talk to himself (or Mango) when alone, and I'm treated to spurts of information as he works on his thesis. Usually, these little speeches start with a mutter of, "Fascinating…" and then, "You know, Mango…" before he's off describing his latest discovery or conclusion.

A few hours later, his friends come to bother him. Crispin and Asmer have brought with food with them, and clearly have every intention of forcing Rian to take a break. Much like in my dream, Rian is ravenous, and eats an entire noodle dish meant for four people. Crispin is less interested in food, lying sprawled on Rian's bed and lamenting what will likely be a day-long hangover. Asmer nibbles on glazed honey bread, consuming food only out of necessity at this point.

"I think I drank too much last night," Crispin groans.

"It was Fars'day—you get a pass," Rian says.

"Not this time. This is bad. It must have been those Ishtak spirits, but I hallucinated escorting some bleeding girl out of the tent, and when we got outside, she was gone."

"Maybe she was a ghost," Rian suggests. "What did she look like? Maybe she was an innocent maiden killed on campus long ago and now seeks her revenge!"

"I hope not," Crispin mutters. "Who has time for dealings with ghosts?"

"Wear a rope of sage leaves, if you're worried," Asmer says. "That should keep her away."

"Will that keep Lune away, too?" Crispin adds, noticing his pale sister as she's finally dragged herself out of her own rooms and into Rian's. "You look dreadful. Have you considered some herbal medicine? Or needling?"

"What ever happened to, 'Oh, Lune, you sang so wonderfully last night!' 'Oh. Lune. What a marvelous performance!'" she says as she drops down on Rian's bed next to Crispin. Misery comes in pairs today, it seems. "Everything hurts," Lune claims.

"Such is the life of the entertainer," Rian claims as he finishes off his four-person dish, and raises another bowl in offering. "Noodle?"

"No-dle," Lune groans. "Do we have any protein?"

"Yes. Chicken. In with the noodles," Rian claims.

"Then, fine: noodle," Lune agrees, and slides off the bed to sit cross-legged on the ground across from him.

They stay for about an hour, until Asmer leaves to begin preparations for her evening service, and Crispin decides to take Lune into the city for evening coffee. He invites Rian but, thankfully, my crown prince declines.

"I need to grab something I left in the library and then get more work done," Rian says. "Feel free to bring something back for me. I'll be up late again."

"Is your work that important?" Crispin muses.

"Could be," Rian says. "It's possible I've filled in a five-hundred-year ancestry gap for all of the Families Three—Smith, Grey, and Wolff. And I don't even know how to begin to explain the importance of that!"

"You mean you're piecing together a family tree. For an extinct, possibly fictional family line," Crispin says.

"Well, three family lines," Rian corrects. "I was going to write only on the Magicsmiths but it turns out it's impossible to do that without mentioning the Greys and Wolffs, too."

Lune tiredly rolls her eyes. Crispin tries not to laugh.

I follow my crown prince when the trio part ways, leaving the Carsans siblings to attend their own business. Part of me thinks it could be interesting to eavesdrop on what Crispin and Lune talk about when no one else is around, but I know I must see to Rian's needs, always.

As Rian makes his way through the long, covered walkways, I decide to run a test, considering last night's dream. Nothing dangerous; just something to make sure that what happened in his room wasn't real. He recognized me in that dreamscape—knew me, and apparently knew me well. But when I ran into Lune the morning before Fars'day, he showed no indication of recognizing me. He certainly didn't look like he wanted to push me up against a wall and kiss me.

The disparity between the two instances seems to support my dream theory, but I have to be sure.

I get ahead of Rian and, when he rounds a sharp corner, purposefully nearly smack into him. With my uniform and headscarf on, a quick duck of my head and squeaking apologies would usually keep Rian from picking me out of a crowd. But this time, I make sure he sees my face, if only out of the corner of his eye, before bowing my head respectfully.

But Rian barely looks twice at me. In fact, all I've done is irritate him and he waves off my apology with one of his own.

"Excuse me, so sorry," Rian mumbles. "My mistake. But do watch your footing," he adds.

It's all I can do not to sigh in relief.

What a fool I was, to think my dream real. The details of it are already fading, now, to the point where I can barely remember specifics beyond Rian's kiss and the push out a window. Someone must have a fluke over dreamscapes, and is playing a cruel joke on me. Either a joke or, more likely, an attempt to turn me into an obsessed, mad creature that could be used against Rian. I've seen girls hysterical over him before. It's frightening.

If someone in the high courts knows what I know about Rian's untapped power over the bounds of time, they might be trying to exploit it. Or kill him.

Nusk will not be pleased to learn about this.

But perhaps what bothers me most is the implication that somewhere deep down, my little girl self may still want a secret romance with Rian.

I don't. Of course, I don't. It's ridiculous. He doesn't know who I am, nor should he. My dream was a dream, nothing more. It's the absurdity of it all that helps fully convince me that this is not a matter of shifting realities.

When I trade off with Taris later that afternoon, I warn him about the potential eighth assassin, but spare him details. I have much to discuss with his father before making any assumptions.

I decide it's best to try and speak with Nusk straightaway; I have time yet before I'm expected at work, and it only takes me a few seconds to check myself in a mirror to make sure my uniform is in order. I make my way to his hut, certain to pass by the infirmary and take note of Naomi's presence there.

Nusk is in the kitchen when I enter, heating some stew for himself and Korvaan, who slouches at the table, yawning. He'd have helped his father, I'm sure, except Nusk is proud of his near-independence. It insults him when simple tasks are taken from him when he's capable of completing them on his own.

"You seem poorly, Soleil," Nusk says as I enter. "N'omi says you got a bit of a bump on your head."

"*N'omi* did well. Barely three stitches," I claim as I join Korvaan at the table and accept some bread from him. "I'm fine."

"There's worry spelled all over you," Nusk says.

He rolls to the table with three bowls balanced on the folding side-tray of his chair. Nusk has always been able to predict me, this way, and knows that I like to discuss things with him almost every time I save Rian's life.

"What's on your mind, girl?" he asks, smacking Korvaan's arm as his son foregoes a spoon in favor of drinking the thick beef broth out of his bowl.

"I think I've made a mistake," I admit.

"Again?" Korvaan mutters, earning him another, harder, smack on the arm.

"Whatever's been done can always be undone, so long as your principal is still alive," Nusk claims. A favored teaching of his.

I hesitate to admit my mistake to him, but I need his advice.

"It's possible I left one of the assassins from last night alive," I warn. "And now I'm worried for Rian. Especially as the assassin hasn't shown his face again."

Korvaan snorts. "Impossible," he says through a mouthful of stew. I have no idea how he can stand eating food so hot. "I handled all the bodies. Not a chance one of them was alive."

"Not one of those seven," I say. "I first counted eight. But when it was all said and done, there were only seven bodies. I thought I miscounted, but…"

Nusk raises an eyebrow. "But?"

"Then I had a strange dream," I say. "I left Korvaan to clean up, and Taris to watch the crown prince, and went to Naomi. She insisted I get some sleep, but I don't remember that. All I remember is having a strange dream, then waking up not sure if it was real. It felt as if the dream was trying to convince me that Rian and I knew each other. Knew one another… *intimately,"* I add in a mutter, wishing Korvaan wasn't here to hear this.

After a beat, he laughs at me. This earns him a smack on either arm from both his father and me.

"And so, you suspect there's some sort of mischief to handle," Nusk says to me. "You've done well to warn the rest of us. I will inform Taris and Naomi. You wouldn't happen to recall any outstanding features of this fluke dreamer?"

I'm about to answer negatively, defeated. But then a vague memory stirs.

"It's possible he's an albino," I say. "And that he's masquerading as an ally."

"Mm. Well, that will make him easier to find," Nusk croaks.

I drum my fingers against the wood of the table and frown. "Although, if our albino eighth assassin really is still alive and about campus, I have to wonder why he hasn't tried to kill Rian again. Or why he and the others were trying the first time at all. Or who empl—"

"Don't think much of it, Soleil," Nusk interrupts. "It's not a *Khashtani's* duty to get involved in such things, only to shadow your prince, and keep him alive.

I sigh. "I know. I can't help but think about it, sometimes. After all, having assassins come after Rian at least implies that someone out there knows the truth of his inheritance. Right?"

"Let the prince worry about who his enemies are," Nusk says. "Your job is to protect him from them."

"Which would be easier if I knew who they were," I say.

"You would think so, child, because you are still too young to understand," Nusk claims, shaking his head. "But answers to those questions only lead to more questions. If you give yourself too much to carry, you'll drop something, and Rian will pay the price. He is not so incapable as you imagine. Let him discover who wants him dead and strike back as he sees fit. And protect him, in turn, from the consequences. Remember your place."

I want to argue further, but there's no point. Nusk raised and taught all four of us: my *khashak* and me. The way of a *Khashtani* is simple, but dreadfully important, and with so much for me to already keep track of, I know he's right. I should simply let this potential assassin come to me, if he plans to come at all.

Routine and vigilance are more likely to keep Rian alive than sleuthing.

"Eat your stew," Nusk croaks at me, dunking bread into his own. "You need to fuel your mind and body appropriately."

I nod and obey.

"Worst-case, I may need you to speak with the administration," I warn Nusk as I eat. "Convince them that there's some albino murderer about, so the entire campus will be on guard. Not unless we must, of course, but…"

Nusk nods, and I'm pleased to have his approval, despite my earlier mistake.

"Tell me if you want it done, and I will manage the particulars," he says.

It shouldn't be hard for him, given his fluke, to convince the administration that he's a city official come to deliver a grave warning. Such an act will exhaust him, but that is why I ask Nusk to use his fluke sparingly.

"In the meantime, if possible, I would like you to attempt to catch this albino assassin, not kill him," Nusk adds, startling me and Korvaan both.

"But," I start, confused. This goes against almost everything Nusk taught me about eliminating threats.

"I would like to speak with him privately, if such an opportunity presents itself," he adds. "It may not be your place to launch such an investigation, Soleil," he reminds me yet again. "But I think it may be illuminating, were I to do so."

I know better than to ask if he'll share his findings, but I still feel excited about the prospect. So long as Nusk plans any investigation, that means there will be an opportunity, no matter how small, for me to learn more.

The campus bell starts to chime the hour in the distance, but I'm not counting as I should be.

"Aren't you supposed to be working this evening?" Korvaan points out, his mouth half-full. "I didn't think you got today off, too…"

I check my watch, curse, and jolt to my feet.

Maids are supposed to arrive on shift five minutes early, which means I'm already five minutes late.

I drain my soup, sop up what broth remains with my bread, and shove it in my mouth before managing a garbled farewell to Nusk and running out the door. I'm almost sure I can hear him chuckle as I leave.

I'm a decent runner, and manage to make it to the laundry room within three minutes, while the evening matron is giving out orders to the rest of the maids. But my tardiness is, naturally, instantly noticed.

"You—girl! Your name?" she snaps before I have the chance to slip in with the others and start grabbing materials.

I force myself to adopt my humble maid persona. Every few months, I have Nusk make the matrons and staff forget about me, and I make a new one, just in case anyone has noted my sneaking about. But my maid persona is almost exactly the same every time: dull, spacey, and easy to forget.

"Muh-muh-me?" I squeak.

The matron rolls her eyes. Damn if I'm good.

"Yes, you. You're the young one. The special exception, aren't you?"

"Yes'm. Sorry. It's Soli," I say, bobbing into eight or nine hasty bows. The older maids chuckle and shake their heads as they continue on their way.

"You're late," the matron snaps, thrusting a stack of linens into my arms and pointing to a nearby cart piled high with more. "You're on linens. All of Indigo Dormitory needs doing, before the children are finished with recitation and dinner. All eight floors. Then bring the dirty ones to the laundry room, and make sure they're sorted properly. They should have the Lady Lune's linens and towels finished, then; you'll do her room."

Eight floors of Indigo Dormitory, twenty rooms a floor, two to four beds per room, means at least four-hundred beds. There definitely aren't enough bed linens on that cart for so many floors. I'll be making quite a few trips back and forth to the laundry room to get more, sorting and checking off rooms as I go.

The laundry room is a half-mile away from Indigo Dormitory. It's the furthest away on campus.

This ought to keep me busy for a while.

But I've been stuck with Indigo before, and I have a routine. I start at the bottom and move up. Indigo is an all-girls dormitory, hosting middle-class students ages twelve to twenty-two. The younger girls tend to have their classes during a normal day schedule, and both return to their rooms and go to bed earlier. Granted, there aren't any classes as it's end-of-week, and probably half of the students are out with family for Fars'day weekend, but it's a good system. The upper floors are more likely to still be empty later in the day, with the older girls out studying, at the library, or out in the city for a weekend bash.

They're more casual about letting me change their linens while they are in their rooms. The younger girls tend to be scared of me.

I manage to finish up completely by quarter to nine. The sun has nearly set in the warm summer sky, and I take a ten-minute break to find something to eat, rehydrate, and visit the washrooms. Then it's back to the laundry room, where I find Lune's laundry (bedsheets, duvet, silk pillowcases, one of her robes, and slippers) before heading off to her rooms. I'm ahead of schedule, now; if I'm quick, I might be able to stop in and check on Rian before catching a few hours of sleep.

The high court nobles on campus share the same large building; a beautiful, balconied, towered piece that I've crawled up and down time and time again to reach Rian's chambers. He occupies one of the towers, which suits him fine, even if it isolates him. Lune's rooms are approximately down a floor, isolated in their own way, as if she's purposefully backed herself into a corner. I'm guessing her favorite feature is the servants' stairs nearby, easily accessible to her should she wish to slip in and out at odd hours without an escort. Which is a very Lune-Carsans-like thing to do.

This is the staircase I climb to reach her rooms, juggling linens and praying that whoever last saw to her rooms left the proper cleaning materials in the maid's closet on this floor. I'm loathe to go wandering the building in search of missing materials.

This is what I'm thinking about when I forget to knock on her door before using the maid's key I've signed out. Lune is almost never in her rooms at this hour—she typically spends time at the libraries or the night pools before retiring to her room to read—and I walk in on her at an unfortunate moment.

Lune has placed her two identical mirrors so that they face each other, and kneels in between them. Her silken robe has slid off one shoulder to reveal her back, and most of the left side of her chest. Looking at the never-ending reflections of herself, she holds her hair away with one hand and uses the other to press a deadly-sharp scissor tip into her back until blood bubbles up from the puncture. She presses her lips together and twists the blades, and I watch, horrified and mesmerized as she makes sure that the tiny injury leaves a mark. It will match the dozens of other, similar scars across her back.

I plan to slip out and avoided her notice, but Lune must feel someone's eyes on her, because she snaps her head to the side, dropping the scissors and hurrying to cover herself. Attempting to do what I assume anyone else would, I take a hesitant step back, bowing my head.

"I'm so sorry, Lady Lune," I make myself squeak. "I-I-I…"

Faster than I would have expected from her, Lune has flown across the room and grabbed the front of my robe, yanking me closer. With me in my shoes and her bare-footed, I'm a good half-hand taller than her, and yet, she manages to be somewhat intimidating. It's the angry flash in her eyes, instead of embarrassment, and the snarl on her upper lip.

"Whatever you saw, you're too stupid to understand," she snaps.

Harsh: first, because I never thought her particularly bright and second, because I did not expect such a thing from her.

"I'll come back later," I mumble, but her grip does not loosen.

"No," she orders. "Do what you would with the room. Put the mirrors back."

I nod, figuring why not inquire and see if she'll tell me what exactly the marks on her back are now that I'm in on her secret.

"What…That is, why—"

"It's none of your business," she interrupts, and then lets me go, shoving me backwards for good measure. "I'm going out. Tell no one of this," she demands, and though I want to scoff at her pitiful threat—I significantly outweigh her—I know I must play my part.

I maintain my low bow, mumbling mouse apologies as she stalks past me out of the room, yanking her robe back over her shoulder. I'm not sure where she thinks she's going in her skimpy nightclothes, but as it's Lune, I'm also certain that no one will think twice about it.

The moment she's gone, I juggle the linens in my arms and raise my watch to my mouth, using the fingernail on my opposite thumb to press the button.

"Taris. Wake Korvaan to swap with you. I need you to tail Lune. I need to know where she goes tonight, who she talks to, what she does. Understand?"

There are a few moments of silence, then a blip in response: affirmative. Taris will follow Lune and report to me in the morning.

I add a few more orders for good measure: "Once I'm done, I'll join Korvaan. You, go sleep for a few hours after Lune returns to her rooms. That way, tomorrow, we can swap and I'll sleep for a few hours while you watch the crown prince. Yes?"

Another blip, quicker this time.

"Warn me if Lune's coming back," I add.

Then I get to work.

I'll have to make up the room as I go, naturally, but that's no trouble. Worst case, if Lune returns shortly, I'll pretend as if there was a problem with the linens or the towels weren't fresh enough, and claim I had to go to the laundry room for more. But while I work, I'll be looking for clues. Secrets Lune might have squirreled away someplace in her chambers.

Stupid girl: I might look like nothing more than a maid, but this is a very easy way for someone with ill intent to access Lune's rooms. Granted, I'm only allowed in here because the guard's downstairs recognize me. But a maid can be bought off. A maid can be a spy.

Lune should have someone she trusts up here with me at all times. One of her ladies' maids, or Asmer, or a supervisor. But she never does.

I quickly head back out to grab the cleaning cart from the maid's closet, and then decide to investigate first where I expect least to find anything, in case Lune comes back for a coat or shoes. Only once she's been gone for a quarter of an hour will I consider it safe enough to do any real meddling.

Her bathroom smells like she's been sick recently and sprayed perfume over the top, but is otherwise clean, unlike some of the other nobles'.

I wash her aqua-tiled modern shower, luxury bathtub, toilet, sink, and floor. While cleaning the mirror and vanity, I poke about in search of something interesting, but come up only with hair pieces, ribbons, combs, jewelry, tooth cleaners and bleachers, depilatories and wax, and minor medical supplies like gauze, small adhesive bandages, and creams.

In the end, there's little of note. Though I do discover, while emptying her trash, a pair of undergarments spotted with blood.

At least that explains her mood.

Enough time has passed now that I feel comfortable rooting through

Lune's study and bedroom. The first thing I do is move the mirrors back to their places, as Lune requested, and change the bedclothes. I check whilst plumping her eighteen pillows that she hasn't hidden anything inside, but no: nothing.

That's almost suspicious. I'm not exactly an expert on how court ladies think, but I know for a fact that even sweet little Asmer keeps a knife under her pillow, just in case. So, either Lune really is an idiot and trusts folk more than she should, or she's cleverer than I've given her credit for.

The rest of her room yields equally disappointing results. There's nothing in her wardrobe, drawers, or cabinets but clothes, clothes, more clothes, and notes for some lyrics she's writing. Of the books on her shelves, there's nothing stuffed between the pages or hidden in a hollowed-out tome. I note a disproportionate amount of Magicsmith fairy tale collections and world history books compared to the romance novels and musical theory works I expected, but if I had to guess, I'd say this is because she's trying to read what she suspects Rian does so they'll appear more alike. Since Rian is passionate about this Magicsmith project of his, that's actually a decent ploy.

I search through all the papers on her desk, looking for hints of treachery or sedition. But the most personal thing I find are a series of short correspondences between herself and Crown Prince Magnus; it appears he was secretly courting her for a period of time.

Attempting to court her, is more like. Lune is a bit of a tart, true, but from what I can gather from a one-sided conversation, she must have been more resistant to Magnus's advances than he's used to.

Considering all the suitors she's turned away, there are plenty of rumors that she favors her own sex, but I know the truth. She's aiming high, whether she knows it or not. She wants Rian. At best, it's because he's attractive, as gregarious as his pet dragon, and she likes him.

At worst, it's because she knows who he is, and she wants to be queen.

There's nothing else to find in her rooms—or, if there is something, I don't have time to search for it. I'd stay but, in addition to the ticking clock of Lune's inevitable return, I'm exhausted, and have no idea where to start were I to continue poking around.

Disappointed, but not surprised, I finish cleaning Lune's quarters, return my maid's cart, and leave the tower by first bell's chime. I'll check in with Taris sometime in the morning to see what Lune was up to tonight. And, naturally, I'll stay extra wary of her. But, otherwise, I see no point in tempting Fate to weave something especially troublesome for me in his tapestry.

THE FIRST DAY OF the week for Rian starts with Mass in the campus' Theebin chapel, and since he goes, I go. I can't say I believe in anything specific, but my speech patterns, at least, have been affected enough that it sounds as if I do. Perhaps that's the real test: curse against a god, and you must believe in one.

Mass is at eight, which, for Rian, Crispin and Lune, is dreadfully early. Rian manages to drag himself out of bed by half-past seven, feed Mango, dress, and get out the door within fifteen minutes, but he's barely awake. No food before Mass, after all, and that includes coffee.

The chapel is brilliantly old-fashioned, with its pillars and arches, stained-glass windows, and high ceiling, which gives me ample space to lounge about from on-high. Naturally, there are guards posted all over the chapel's entrances, and Qhan is around to keep an eye on Rian, but I'm too on edge about that eighth assassin to allow Rian out of my sight when I can afford to watch.

Cautious as I am, nothing happens for all of Mass.

Rian manages to stay awake the entire time, but rubs his eyes every few minutes and has yet to realize that his jacket is buttoned wrong. Lune stares at her missal with intense concentration, re-reading over and over in an attempt not to fall asleep, and likely ignoring the exact same passages as they're read slowly out loud. Her Mass veil is slipping off the back of her head and Crispin keeps fixing it for her without her noticing. I have no idea what she did last night after I caught her pricking herself in the back, but she clearly did not sleep well, if at all.

I've yet to hear back from Taris about where she went last night, which is irksome, but hardly an urgent matter.

Mass ends, and Crispin manages to drag an exhausted Lune and Rian to breakfast, where they meet up with Asmer. The four lounge the hours away on a lazy start-of-week day. It's almost an agreeable day, even for me.

Until about noon, when I'm reminded that fighting assassins on catwalks isn't the only time I need to worry about bleeding.

We have a protocol for this and, compared to some, I have it easy. I don't suffer from horrendous cramps or body aches; the damned thing is just wildly unpredictable, when it bothers to show up. I only have to call Taris in to replace me for about an hour or two, and then I can get back to work as usual. So, it's not a major complication.

That said, when we all decided to give me an hour or two in these cases to put myself together, *I expect to get the full hour. At least.*

So imagine my irritation when, after barely managing to clean up, Taris beeps my watch in summons. This is no emergency acknowledgement, but still. Without further information, it's best I find him and see what he wants.

I know where Rian will be at this time. It's practically a weekly tradition that ensures a crowd has gathered around the performance space in the campus' main square, backed up against one of its most impressive sandy-stoned buildings. The front row of the crowd is mostly children. They sit on a stretch of grass with a sun-sleepy Mango, as close as they can get to where Rian is sitting above them on the dais. Behind the youngest children are older students pretending as if they didn't purposefully stop by. I catch sight of Asmer, close to the children, as she'd never once miss hearing Rian speak. Crispin and Lune are nowhere to be found, but this is almost a relief; fewer nobles for me to worry about.

Everyone else is too distracted to notice me slipping between them, lost in their own imaginations: Rian is giving a reading for the children. His voice carries them far, far away, into today's chosen myth, where monsters and spirits of all sorts fly through the night, birds sing warnings for wary warriors braving dreaded forests, and tall grasses whisper secrets in virgins' ears. His voice for stories is the same as his speaking voice, and yet completely different. I have listened to him for years and still I cannot quite describe the way he speaks when telling stories.

It is somehow theatrical, but not melodramatic. Charming, teasing its listeners one second, then dark, lamenting the next.

I find Taris standing near the back of the crowd. He's tall enough to see above everyone else's head, and is watching Rian like he's in a trance. That's practically everyone's reaction to listening to Rian's stories, captivating as his voice can be, but I expect more from Taris.

Sidling up next to him, I pretend as if I, too, am merely here for the story, but then jab Taris sharply in the side with my hand and try to give him *a look*.

"Did you call me here to listen to children's stories?" I hiss at him.

Taris doesn't glance my way. "Shh," he says instead. "We're just coming to the best part, now."

"Where did Lune go last night? And what's so important?"

"Later."

I huff, but settle in to wait. I can't exactly force him to talk.

It takes a sentence or two, but I recognize the story Rian is telling: "Of Crow and the Death". It's a short tale, with just enough of it to tell for this sort of crowd. Taris isn't wrong: Rian is coming to the close of the tale, after the Crow's friend, the Blue Jay, has died, and the Death already came to claim him. This end portion is the moral or lesson. That is, arguably, the best part. If not for the story itself, then for the way that Rian tells it.

"...And with the Death still before him, the Crow began to cry, no longer caring to present a brave face. The Death had seen as much before, and was moved not one bit, but what was said next gave him pause, as an idea took hold to present an old test. One that no one else he'd presented it to before had passed.

'If only there were some way to bring my friend the Blue back!' the Crow lamented.

'Ah, alas, but there is not,' the Death said. 'Not without a sacrifice worthy, in return.'

It did not take the Crow but a moment to offer such a sacrifice, pledging, 'Take me, reaper of souls, and spare the Blue instead! I love too deeply to live knowing I could have saved him and did not.'

The Death did not, at first accept, questioning the Crow again. 'And for what reason would you do this? Why offer yourself in his place when you have no way of knowing that I will keep my word? Do you not know Death is eternal?'

'Is it? ...Perhaps it may be so, but the Blue is my friend. And I am willing to take that chance, and die for him, as I know that he would do the same for me. Death may be eternal, but so is love.'

'Love is fleeting and fickle,' the Death said, as he believed he'd seen as much in his own interactions with Love. 'Common and bland. Lament now, if you wish, and in time, you will love again. Why waste yourself, now, for one iteration of it? I promise, you will regret it later.'

But though Love might have seemed the fickle sort, the Crow, for certain, was not. 'Perhaps many love, in what seems like the same way, over and over. But I do not find it so. Maybe I will find another to love, but I will never find someone to love as I did my friend and brother the Blue. For he is the only him in the entire world, and I would know.'

'There is no nobler thing, than to give up one's life for their friend,' the Death mused, and then posed his bargain. 'Give up your life, as your friend the Blue gave his for you, and I will restore him.'

The Crow took barely a second to reply, having made up his mind. 'Then I'll do so for him, as I know for fact he would have, and has done, for me.'

'Are you certain?' the Death said. 'Perhaps you have not thought it through.'

'I've thought on it as much as I can bear,' the Crow said. 'I was the one meant to die, not my friend. It would not be right for me to hesitate, now, when given the chance to return the favor.'

Still, it was the Death who hesitated. He looked into the Crow's heart, searching for a seed of selfishness, a weak will, a way to prove that the Crow's words were words alone. But he found nothing but true courage, love, and honesty. An utterly unselfish act, made for utterly unselfish reasons.

And so, with a sweep of his white cloak, the Death restored the Blue, and fulfilled what the Almighty said he would do, exactly as he was told to do it. The Crow was surprised to find that the Death did not take his life in turn, but instead seemed chastised. His own lesson had been learnt just as well as the one he meant to teach.

'It is not that you sacrificed, but your willingness, without question, that has saved you,' the Death claimed. 'Go. Live your time allotted. I will be back for you one day, but not this day. Know, now, the cost of a life well-lived.'

And the two bid a polite farewell and flew off from him, intent on doing as they were told. In his lingering suspicions on the nature of Love, the Death occasionally looked in upon the two, but their friendship never once broke. It frayed, from time to time, but never in a way that could not be fixed, and never once did either of them forget their sacrifices.

The Death thought on this for many years, and was forced, in the end, to conclude, that there had to be something more than what he saw to Love's nature, even if he did not understand it. Because love is more than a word, or a look. Love is more than fleeting pleasures or constant joy. Love is a mystery. Love is divine. Love is more."

For a while, after the last of Rian's words linger in the air, there is nothing but awed silence.

Rian brings so much meaning and passion to the simplest stories like this one that it's as if there's resounding truth to the tale. But Rian is a romantic. And, much like Lune can capture a crowd with her singing, he has discovered a way to convey just how much he believes in what he's reading that, for a few seconds, everyone listening believes in it, too.

The illusion fades in a matter of seconds. People still appreciate the reading, but return to their own philosophies and the modern belief that love is fleeting, or superficial. For some, maybe it's pointless. For others, unreachable or cruel. Nothing divine, mysterious, or sweet. But not Rian. And, I notice, not Asmer: he's moved her to tears. I wonder if he told this story about love for her sake. I wonder if this is his way of making a promise to her.

Personally, I find the tale overdramatic and childish, but maybe I'd change my mind if I'd heard Rian tell the whole thing through. It's the setup that makes the payoff at the end mean something, after all.

Moments later, Rian's accepting the applause and thanks and compliments, and I take the opportunity to force some answers out of Taris.

"Where was Lune last night?" I mutter.

"Doctor's," he claims, and I frown, shooting him a quick look.

We have nursing staff available on campus at all times, but no consistently accessible doctors.

"She went to the city to see a doctor? She was only wearing her robe."

He sighs, exasperated with me, but that's nothing new. "She hailed a coach, drove all the way into the city, downtown, and went to some doctor. Why? I don't know. I couldn't get close enough to listen in. Obviously, no procedure was performed. I looked up the doctor, after: his practice is legitimate, but I suppose that Lune wanted to meet with him some place private. For private reasons."

"Did she have him look at her back?" I ask.

Now it's Taris' turn to give me an odd look. "No. Why?"

I think back to last night. I suppose there's a simple enough answer, considering how she'd been sick up and had those blood-spotted drawers in her trash. Lune was having some complications with her monthly courses and was too embarrassed to go to the clinic on campus to seek assistance. It doesn't explain why she was stabbing herself in the back with scissors, but if her cramping is bad enough to cause nausea, I can understand why she might want to see a doctor.

"Never mind. Did she go anywhere else?"

"A bar," he admits. "Didn't drink anything, but sang for a while. Patrons loved it. Pianist looked like he, uh, was interested. She sang a little with him. Patrons loved that even more. Returned to her rooms. Fell asleep."

"No, ah…nighttime visitors?"

"Not unless they went to watch her sleep after I left."

"Point made. Good work," I admit grudgingly. "Remind me to look into this doctor later and see if I can figure out what she saw him for."

"I'll do it," he offers.

Even better.

"Good. Now: why am I here?" I demand, sure to turn my full ire on him.

"I wanted to test something."

"And this test was fruitful?" I ask.

Don't grit your teeth, Soleil, don't do it.

"Immensely," Taris claims, and hands me something so small it can fit on my fingertip.

"What's this?"

"A bug. New from Alarkia. Much smaller and clearer than others. I stuck one on the crown prince, then put myself all the way back here to hear him speak: clear as day, as if I were right up front with the children. Now we can listen in to whatever is being said to the crown prince at a safer distance. Besides—I thought you'd like to be here yourself, today," he adds.

"Why…?"

With a nod and gesture, Taris points out a man I recognize instantly: taller than Rian, and much more muscular, with fair Native Isaarian skin, barely tamable dark hair, a strong bone structure, and a mouth that more often than not is quirked either mischievously or flirtatiously. A well-worn travel satchel is slung across his shoulders, though I'm sure maids have fallen over themselves offering to take the rest of his luggage back to his rooms.

Crown Prince Mercer Ralhan is weaving through the crowd, holding a finger to his lips and playfully shushing people while he sneaks up on a distracted Rian. So, Mercer's back from whatever thrilling adventure awaited him abroad. Rian will be overjoyed, and I can't help but be relieved as well. Part of me is worried that, when abroad, Mercer will get himself held ransom by the powers of a foreign country, or meet his demise at the hands of some fearsome beast.

His return is good news both for me and Rian. And, yes: Taris is right in assuming I'd want to watch the pair's reunion.

I don't want to be pleased with Taris, because I'm annoyed at him for forcing me to listen to Rian's sentimental story, but I have to admit: this is good work.

"You're not entirely wrong," I say, but I don't dare congratulate him.

I can't afford for his head to get any bigger than it already is.

"You have one of the corresponding transmitters for me, I assume?" I prompt him, and let him stick said transmitter in the curve of my ear, under the guise of tucking back a strand of my hair.

"I have an entire box of bugs," Taris goes on to claim.

"Good. We're likely to go through them fast, with Rian's laundry the way it is, unless I can start sticking them to his shoes," I note.

"I got it on his diamond earring," Taris admits.

I have to jerk my head up at him to that.

Taris shrugs. "I pretended there was a bee in his hair and fished it out for him."

Bees are attracted to the gold ornaments in Rian's hair; Qhan, the campus guards, and even Crispin are almost constantly plucking them out of Rian's hair. I doubt he thought twice about Taris offering to do so. I'm only jealous because I think Rian would have noticed if I ever tried to do the same.

The guards have a different level of familiarity with the nobles than us maids. And Taris knows it.

"As he rarely takes that thing out even when he should, I think we're fine, for now," he continues. "The only thing we have to worry about is him accidentally brushing it off when he takes out the dangling ones, and even that's unlikely."

"Good work," I'm forced to admit, and try to ignore Taris' smirk.

"I've also already set them up with our transmitters. So...Did you want to take over for the rest of the day, then, until your maid's duties require your attention, or—" he starts, clearly mocking me.

I press a button on my watch until our proximity causes a startling amount of feedback.

Taris glares at me, then heads off his own way.

I'm back with Rian for the rest of the afternoon.

Five

I MUST ADMIT, AS the day wears on, that Taris' new Alarkian bugs work even better than expected. I suppose he noticed someone with them during Fars'day and purchased a box. They'll make my life easier, at least: I no longer have to stay close enough to hear what Rian's saying, and can instead keep to shadows. Better positioned to see all around.

I'll never thank Taris for this again, but at least he does a decent job trying to keep Rian alive. Some part of him cares.

I find a hiding spot by a nearby walkway pillar, behind where Mercer is about to surprise my crown prince. When they move, I'll be able to scramble up to the top of the covered walkways, and use the lip there to stay hidden while following them. I'm certain they'll be off, soon, to find some privacy and catch up with one another. They've been best friends since childhood.

"An excellent performance, my friend!" Mercer congratulates, throwing an arm around Rian's slimmer shoulders. "You never fail to impress."

"Mercer!" Rian laughs. "I didn't know you were back today! You missed Fars'day by just a few nights."

"Ah, I know," Crown Prince Mercer groans. "I heard Lune put on quite the show. I'm sorry I missed it."

"She'll forgive you if you've brought her a present," Rian teases.

"Ah, but of course. I've a little something for everyone. Even you—in addition to your birthday gift, of course."

"Mercer…You shouldn't have," Rian says.

"I know. I can't help myself. Besides, it's not as if I bought you a *Pterano*."

"I don't think the University would let us keep one if you did."

There's no doubt about that. Crown Prince or no, there are limits to what Mercer can get away with, particularly in the field of exotic gifts. A sunblood dragon is one thing, but Mango is docile and miniature. Pteranos have giant wingspans, sharp beaks, extreme intelligence, and speed unmatched by almost any other bird of prey in the air. There might be tales of folks riding Pterano birds in the north, but I wouldn't bet Rian's life on one not suddenly deciding it's hungry for a little laughing snack.

The only way Rian's riding a Pterano bird is if I'm dead and buried.

"Come on," Mercer adds, steering Rian towards the gardens. "You owe me a story about what made this Fars'day so special…and in return, I'll tell you all about my travels in the west."

"An excellent deal, if I've ever heard one," Rian claims.

"Oh, I'd like to think so."

After they're a few feet down the path, Rian whistles and calls, "Mango!"

The dragon perks up and flops his way free of the gaggle of children around him. He dutifully follows behind his master, thinking himself more fearsome a protector than he really is. He tromps about making little hissing noises if anyone comes too close to Rian.

"The necklace is new," Rian notes. "And it's in good taste, well done, you."

Mercer is surprised by the backhanded compliment. He glances down to pick up the chain dangling from his neck, as if he'd forgotten he had it on.

"Oh, this? I picked it up somewhere in Alarkia, I think. Don't remember where. But it's nice, isn't it? And it goes with most everything I like to wear, so as long as I remember to keep slinging it around my neck, no one can complain about me not looking princely enough."

"Eh. It would likely help if you didn't, ah, *dabble under the duvets of dozens of different dames,*" Rian says, somehow managing to both be tactful and tacky.

Him and his damn alliteration.

"You seem to have enough decorum for the both of us," Mercer teases.

Rian rolls his eyes. "That's because while you flounce around the world, kissing pretty girls, I've been preparing for the new king's crowning. We should be making ourselves proper Grand Princes, by procuring *wives*."

"Oh, I'll get around to it," Mercer claims, blasé. "Besides, what are you worried about? You've had women all over you since we were youths."

"Yes, but wives care less about looks and more about quality."

This is puzzling coming from Rian, as I've seen little effort on his part to start preparing for a wedding. Nor have I seen him actively pursue anyone. This concerns me.

"What about Asmer?" Mercer says, too casually.

"What about Asmer?"

Mercer almost stops walking to emphasize his apparent shock.

"You're mocking me; you must be. You can't have not noticed. She's smitten with you. Practically hangs on your every word."

The look on Rian's face is a grimace. "But she's like my little sister."

Now, I'm panicking. Because the only other woman hanging about Rian has been Lune. But Rian can't marry her. I absolutely won't allow it.

The crown princes lose themselves in the gardens while I tag along, staying concealed and discreet. Rian and Mercer's bodyguards might be hanging back to give them privacy, but I will not. Nothing in Rian's life is private from me, nor can it be, for his sake.

The two settle in their favorite spot: a little corner under a pair of large apple trees that faces an open field. The seating offers an excellent view of the clear, blue sky and waves of bright green grass.

Mango immediately picks up a fallen apple and prances around by Rian's feet. Chuckling, Rian plucks the fruit out of his dragon's mouth to oblige him.

"Mango – fetch!"

The dragon darts away, pleased his master is engaging him in a game.

Mercer and Rian take their seats on the cushions of swirled white-iron chairs, where they'll soon be served whatever drinks and sweets they fancy. Rian has already plucked a peach from the top of their table's centerpiece and takes a large bite, somehow managing not to get juice all over his fingers.

"How were things? Across the sea?" he poses.

His fellow crown prince sighs and shakes his head.

"Not well, Rian. Not well at all. The war between Alarkia and Lijimata is devastating the west, draining it of all that once made it so prosperous."

Rian frowns, concerned. It's a side of him I'm not used to seeing. Though my observation of his brunch conversation with Crispin was merely a dream, it was accurate: at times like this, Rian usually launches into what seems like a prepared speech on silver linings, sometimes overshadowing the problem. But not this time.

"I thought they were negotiating," he says. "It's been, what, seven years?"

"I did, too. But it was too good to be true."

"This is a mess," Rian claims. "Alarkia had no reason to go to war with Lijimata, and no reason to kill its king and queen in the first place!"

Mercer sighs. "It's too late, I'm afraid. Someone killed the king and queen of Lijimata, their magic-blind daughter Emmelina retaliated by killing the Alarkian ambassador and his daughter…and just when things seemed to be winding to a close, with these peace treaties, someone went and assassinated Emmelina's cousin. And this happened only a few months ago, Rian. Months. The west is an abomination. There's almost no point in trying to lend either side aid. It's almost as if they want to remain at war. Pick up right where they left off eighty years ago and finish what they started."

Rian's expression twists. "Don't they realize all they're losing? Their people, their whole culture: dead, lost, and ignored amidst their stubbornness for war?"

Mercer only shrugs.

"What about the Lijimi prince? Doesn't Emmelina have a younger brother?"

"Crown Prince Castel? He's been missing since the beginning of the war. I doubt he's still alive, and if he is, he'd be smart to stay away. Lijimi royalty's being killed like they're in season."

Mango has returned with his bite-covered apple, and is weaving between the delicate legs of the princes' table, occasionally nudging Rian's shoe to try and get his attention. Barely looking, Rian takes the apple and throws it again. His own piece of fruit has been forgotten entirely.

"But the trip... There must have been something nice about it?" Rian poses, distressed by the idea that his friend might have spent the last few months on the other side of the world absolutely miserable.

Mercer considers this. "Well, yes. There are pockets of peace, still. And I'll admit, I'm making it sound all doom and gloom, but that's truly how it felt. And I did purposefully seek out places where I might find injured citizens, regardless of what country I was in. I figured, so long as I was there, I might as well do what I could for the people. Medically speaking."

There's a beat of morose silence. The sun seems to disappear from the sky.

"Sometimes all I could do was leave behind enough painkillers to keep them doped up until they died," Mercer admits quietly. "There was this little Alarkian girl, Rian, maybe only four years old—"

"Mercer—I really can't. Not with kids. Please," Rian interrupts. I'm sure he's thinking of his own students. Of Ayla, whom he's grown particularly close to.

Mercer sighs, but nods. "I only want you to understand. We can't keep living in a world like this, Rian. There has to be a way to stop this sort of thing from ever happening again."

"War?"

"Tragedy. In general. Suffering."

"Well, you'll be hard-pressed to stop that completely," Rian chides.

"Maybe," Mercer mutters. But he notes Rian's attempts to bring their conversation to a lighter topic and leaves things there.

I'm grateful to him for that. Mercer has no desire for children of his own, but he understands and respects Rian's view. And Rian has always wanted to raise children. He adores them, and can't bear to hear stories of any child's anguish, regardless of loyalties or heritage.

It's things like that which remind me of how soft-hearted he is.

"Ah!" Mercer exclaims, smiling and reaching down to dig in his bag. "Your present! I nearly forgot."

Rian's smiling, too, bloodshed and dead children momentarily forgotten. "Mercer…"

Mango has returned and leapt up on his lap, now munching on that apple.

"No, no, no," Mercer insists. "You can't protest. That was the deal. Besides—I always bring gifts back when I travel, regardless of birthdays, so it wouldn't make sense not to bring you back two."

Rian rolls his eyes, but can't argue with that.

Mercer's hand suddenly stops digging around; he's found what he's looking for, and I'm almost as anxious to see it as Rian.

"The book I sent you—you like it?" the Mercer prompts, raising an eyebrow.

"Well, of course! You knew I would, Merse; it's gorgeous," Rian says. "The illustrated lettering is the finest I've seen this side of the century, and that's saying something! You know—"

"Yes, yes, I'm sure you could lecture me on the art's entire history," Mercer deflects, rolling his eyes. "But I got to meet the girl who worked on them, Rian. And hear this: she's fourteen."

Even I'm startled to hear this. I've seen the book open on Rian's desk over the past few days, and though I'm hardly an expert, I can appreciate pretty artwork when I see it. I'm impressed that a mere girl could create such delicate beauty.

"The world isn't fair, Mercer," Rian says. "Not fair at all. Fourteen?"

He tilts his head back to look up at the sky.

"Why the hell would you give that sort of talent to a child?" he demands, presumably of the Almighty.

Mercer laughs. "Well, if you're impressed by that, just wait. So, I got to talk to her, yes? I purchased the book for you, and it came up in conversation that you are part Kachin, and interested in history. And she says she has something else to give you—one of *Isaaria's crown princes*—and pulls out this."

He takes out something from his bag that it takes me a moment to identify. Even once I do, I don't understand why it's important.

It's a Kachin royal hairpiece; maybe a queen's, by the look of it. It's golden, anyway, with a bejeweled animal—a southeast Kourn feather-dragon—wrapped around the top amidst a cluster of tiny, gold-and-jewel leaves and flowers.

"Hope's Head, Mercer," Rian rasps in awe. "This…This is…"

"And, take a look at this," Mercer says, pulling the hairpin apart to reveal it's made of two pieces: a sheath, and the actual pin, which is sharpened into a dirk. "Handy for a lady trying to look after herself."

He sheathes the dirk into its base and hands it over to Rian, who handles the hairpin with such care, one would think it was made of glass. He examines it, pushing Mango's snout away when the sunblood tries to lick the gold—greedy little mite.

"She said this one allegedly belonged to Queen Kim Mi-Sun; I believe the current Kachin princess is named after her, isn't she?" Mercer says.

"Mm? Oh, yes. Princess Park Mi-Sun. Second in line to the throne, after their crown prince. But I thought—"

Rian cuts himself off.

Mercer grins widely.

I wish I knew what was going on.

"Mercer, you didn't. This isn't."

"I did. And it's a possibility."

Rian stares. "Did that girl understand the value of this thing? She can't have. She wouldn't have given it to you if you did."

"Oh, she knew," Mercer claims. "She told me it's possible this hairpin is the very one the Magicsmiths gifted Queen Mi-Sun over seven-hundred years ago. I believe that's why she wanted you to have it."

Rian stares at his friend, then back down at the pin, and I finally understand.

If this hairpin somehow proves magical, it's a valuable addition to Rian's thesis about the Magicsmiths. This hairpin might be able to demonstrate the nature of the Magicsmiths' powers: the power to create entirely new things, while everyone else with a fluke can merely manipulate or alter. That's a significant discovery for the historical and mythical literature communities.

If the hairpin is magical in nature, it could be worth more than the entire University.

"This is incredible," Rian says. "Mercer, this is beyond words. Thank you."

He's overcome with wonder and admiration for his friend. If he weren't already sitting down, I'd be afraid of him passing out.

"But that's not all," Mercer says. "Well, it's all in terms of physical gifts, but I've got more to tell you. Rian: this girl also had a magic mirror."

Rian's eyes are so wide, I can see his pupils have dilated. *"No."*

"*Yes!*"

"Did you get the chance to speak with it?" Rian demands, now so excited that he's half-stood up from the table, leaning across it.

"Oh, yes," Mercer crows. "Its name is Reginald. He has several mirror interfaces, including this girl's compact mirror; and he was *opinionated.* He said my hair was good, but my nose could use some work."

Rian throws himself back in his chair and bursts out laughing.

Magic mirrors are also rumored to have been created by Magicsmiths, but that's a difficult thing to prove. The hairpin, though only a few hundred years old, could be identified via paintings or historical documentation. But the magic mirror theory is based on a fable. It's not the same quality of evidence as the hairpin, but still: they are rare and important artifacts. The fact that this Alarkian girl had both is astounding. Almost inconceivable.

The fact that Mercer managed to run in to her at all is almost too fortuitous.

"Almighty bless, Mercer!" Rian cries. "I have so many questions for her! How did she get them? Family artifacts? But how would an Alarkian family get a Kachin royal's hairpiece?! And a magic mirror, what the hell, Merse! Why didn't you just steal her away!?"

Mango can sense his master's excitement, and he pouts, jealous. Rian notices and scratches between Mango's ears and little horns.

"Oh, I would have if I could," Mercer claims. "But she said her *fiancé* wouldn't be too happy about that."

Rian's mirth falters. He looks at his friend with suspicion, and a frown.

"Fiancé? Mercer, I thought you said she was fourteen?"

Mercer shrugs. "Well, *betrothed,* I suppose, but that's the same as having a fiancé, isn't it?"

I can tell Rian is uncomfortable with this. He teaches a class of thirteen and fourteen-year-olds; he's aware of how young that really is, and how a girl that age is in no position to be married. Even hundreds and hundreds of years ago, when life expectancy was much shorter, no one married that young. It was too dangerous to expect a girl to bear children, especially at a time when childbirth was more likely to result in death for the mother.

Though occasionally nobles married their children off young, the so-called happy couple usually didn't see each other again post-marriage for five or six years, during which time they learned how to govern their lands. It annoys Rian when those on the fringes of the historical community try to claim otherwise; he's convinced most of them have a sexual perversion they're trying to hide.

His favorite retort in such debates tends to be along the lines of, "Are you sure you're not part Fae?", and that usually disgusts the other party enough that they don't try to fight him on historical accuracy anymore.

"They still do that over there?" Rian asks, and I can tell he's thinking about how that girl's life might have changed if Mercer had brought her back with him. "I thought Alarkia was rather progressive."

"I suppose...well. The war and all. I doubt she's marrying anytime soon, but folks with power in Alarkia are snatching up anyone with promising talent for arranged marriages."

Rian's frown remains. "As in political power?" he asks, hesitant.

If Mercer had been seen purchasing rare and expensive things from the fiancée of some Alarkian politician's son, some folks might assume that Isaaria was taking a side in the war.

"Eh, I doubt it," Mercer says. "More upper class. Wealthy."

"Be careful, Merse," Rian sighs. "I know you enjoy your travel, but it's getting to be a dangerous world. Especially after Comus Day...Things will be different."

"I thought this new king will usher in a time of peace?" Mercer points out. "The Carsans can't have been wrong about that. As bad as things may seem, they can only get better, can't they?"

"I suppose so," Rian says thoughtfully.

There's an awkward beat between them, then Rian smiles and lets Mango off his lap again. He plucks up another piece of fruit and throws it into the field.

"Well, come on," he says, scooting closer to Mercer. "Show me what you got everyone else. By my reckoning, you've got gifts for Lune, Asmer, Crispin, and little Soren, too, didn't you?"

The tension between them dissipates. There will be no more talk of the war between Lijimata and Alarkia. Mercer only ever mentions the countries again in the context of where and how he acquired the other gifts he intends to bestow.

He and Rian are so different, and yet so similar. I can't imagine Mercer will try very hard to win the mantle of king, what with that wanderlust of his, but I almost wish he would. He's seen so much of the world; if anyone can determine a way to restore peace between all the countries, I'm sure it's him.

The two take a late lunch as the afternoon wears on. Mercer tells frivolous stories of travel mishaps, and Rian regales his best friend with a detailed account of Fars'day, as well as the little run-ins he had with a number of students of his earlier in the day. He admits, more seriously, that he's considering adopting one of his students after Comus Day (I'm sure it's Ayla), and Mercer jokes again about Rian trying too hard to settle down.

It's quarter to four when Taris shows to take my place. Mercer and Rian are further out in the field with Mango, but close enough that I could reach them if need be. Qhan is not far from them, either, and he's keeping a sharp eye.

I'm watching them when a whine of feedback startles me, blaring right in my ear. I manage to keep from jumping and upsetting my position, but still.

I clamp my hands over my ears to let Taris know he's made his point, and whirl in time to see him release the button on his watch.

"What the *hell,* Taris?" I snap, glaring up at him.

The feedback's annoying, but I'm irritated further by the fact that he's bigger and stronger than me and he can still manage to sneak up on me. It isn't fair.

He shrugs. "Payback."

"You're so immature," I mutter under my breath.

"And you're an idiot, but at least you enjoy flaunting your faults."

I swear to the Almighty, if I didn't need Taris, I'd have killed him already.

"Why do you hate me so?" I demand, exasperated with his childishness.

"It's not hate," Taris claims, looking at me with disgust. "I just expect more."

"What more do you want from me?" I ask, incredulous.

"I want you to start thinking for yourself," he says bitterly, "instead of just doing whatever my father tells you to."

He slips past me to take up his position watching Rian before I can answer, leaving me to wonder what he meant by that. I can't begin to think why Taris would hold so much animosity towards his father, who has done nothing but care for and love us all for our entire lives.

THAT EVENING, FATE treats me to a little show. I've been assigned to pick up and return library books from the stacks outside the dormitories, so the librarians' assistants can sort them back into their proper places, and then mop the covered walkways around campus. The hour is late when I find a handful of books that belong in the southern lecture halls, not the library.

I'm irritated, mainly because this means a walk for me, so I leave those books for last. It's a quarter past midnight by the time I've found the room where they belong. I've just finished replacing them when I hear a door bang open to admit someone to the building. Curious, I peek through my room's tiny window to see who's wandering about at this hour. I'm expecting an exhausted student with a thesis due, but it's Magnus Oram of all people.

He loiters in place for a full two minutes, long enough for me to know he's waiting for someone. A second later, the door at the opposite end of the hall opens, and who should stride in but Crispin Carsans.

"I didn't think you'd come," Magnus admits. "Where's your sister?"

"Running late, likely," Crispin says. "What's all this about?"

"I'd rather say it once. Did you not stop by her room to pick her up on your way here?" Magnus says, and his insistence on Lune's presence implies that this conversation is about her.

"I wasn't headed that way," Crispin says. "She will be here."

"Mmm. Aren't you worried about leaving her alone?" Magnus says, starting to dig his own burial site. "Lune is a bit of a tart—you know that. And she does so enjoy the company of our fellow crown princes."

Crispin snorts. "Rian's a good man. He'd never do anything improper to Lune."

"What about Mercer? Or Yuugo and Detrus? And perhaps most importantly, *Vásan?* Lune might be dancing close to Rian, but I've noticed your little sister sidling up to crown princes at every opportunity. As if she expects something from them. Aren't you worried one of them might give it?"

My view of the two isn't stellar from my current position, but I see Crispin stiffen. His face is concealed by shadows, but his stern tone of voice is more than adequate to convey how he feels about that last part.

"I respect what you've done to look out for us all, Magnus, but don't cross that line," he warns.

"And why not?" Magnus challenges. "Why is 'Lune Carsans' the exception to the rule? In fact, why do any of you Carsans get to be the exceptions? No one can ever say a bad word about you or Lune, or your crippled brother—"

When Crispin steps toward him, I think there are about to be blows exchanged. Magnus clearly thinks so too, because he jumps back and cuts himself off. Magnus isn't a small man, but Mercer and Crispin are definitely the most physically intimidating of the princes, and Crispin is the tallest.

I'm certain the only reason Crispin's holding back is because he respects Magnus's position. Nothing more.

"Leave Lune be," he hisses. "And don't you dare say anything about Soren ever again."

"But she isn't quite your sister, is she? Lune?" Magnus mocks. "Greedy little songbird, sneaking about, trying to get more than she deserves…"

Crispin does not rise to that bait. "I don't care what you're playing at, and I don't care about what you want anymore, Oram: stay away from Lune, or I will make you regret it."

"She knows more than she claims," Magnus spits back, grabbing Crispin's arm. "She's a clever liar, your 'sister'. Flouncing about, teasing folk, then pushing them away…"

I may be wary of Lune's intentions, but Magnus's painted picture of her as this sultry seductress is highly inaccurate.

"She's taunting us with what she knows. I've no doubt, whatever's really about to happen this Comus Day, Lune knows about it."

I realize that there is more to Magnus than I first thought. Maybe some part of him only wants a night in Lune's bed, to make her another one of his conquests, but he has other goals. He haunts Lune's footsteps not because of her enticement, but because he's likely gotten information out of women in his bed before, and he's hoping to repeat the process with her.

That means Lune knows something worthwhile. That means Lune has a secret Magnus is willing to risk Crispin Carsans' wrath for. Magnus might be a worm, but he still knows where to go digging, and I make a note to follow his example. Perhaps I have been too forgiving of Lune lately, after her performance unintentionally helped me protect Rian. Perhaps my original instincts to be wary of her were right after all.

"Is that what you want?" Crispin says in confusion and disgust. "What, you—you think Lune *'knows something'* and you…You what? You want her to share that information?"

Crispin's not brilliant, but in this case, I find his confusion understandable. I'm not sure why Magnus approached this conversation the way he did, or why he's leading into it after making it clear he wanted Lune here first, but now that he's telling all, I will sit back and observe.

Crispin's talking again before Magnus can answer.

"I don't know what you think Lune knows, but you're wrong. She hasn't done anything wrong—"

"Forgive me if I expect more proof beyond your word."

Crispin stares at him for a second, then stalks past him. "I don't have to stand here and listen to this. In fact, I'm glad Lune's not here."

"And what's wrong with wanting insurance?" the other challenges, but Crispin's already gone.

And I'm stuck on the other side of the door while Magnus stands out in that dark hallway.

On the one hand, Magnus isn't wrong; he shouldn't trust someone based on word alone. But he went about this play so oddly—his execution so poorly planned—that I'm forced to wonder if he put together his plan to confront the Carsans siblings only recently. Which implies that Lune has done something to warrant this wariness. I'm curious about this most of all, because I want to know what suspicious thing Lune's done that I've missed.

I'm waiting for Magnus to walk off so that I can slip out, but the door in the hall suddenly bangs open and there's a loud clack of heels against the marble.

"Sorry I'm late," Lune sings, waltzing in as dramatically as she can. "I forgot about this entirely, took all my makeup off, and then had to put it on again!"

She's acting like a ditz, but she's wearing heels high enough to make her eye-level with Magnus, and a skirt short enough to imply that she's got something hidden up there to protect herself with. She's still smaller than he is, but she's come here with the intent to intimidate him just as much as she's sure he plans to intimidate her.

Coupled with her recent threat to me, Lune has more teeth than I've given her credit for. Perhaps all the Carsans do.

"You're more than late," Magnus snaps. "You've missed it. Your brother's left, and I'd meant to speak to you together."

Lune gives him a pout. "Not my fault the two of you couldn't find something to talk about while you were waiting. Well, ta-ta for now, Magnus. Might want to pick a better time to meet. I'm excellent at making it to brunch—"

She's turned to leave, but Magnus leaps forward and grabs her arm, yanking her back. Crispin might have restrained himself from becoming physical with the other prince, but Magnus is offering no such courtesy to Lune.

Lune is startled, but after an awkward moment, she looks at Magnus, then down at his hand on her arm, then back up again.

"Do you mind? That's going to bruise."

"I'll let you go once you tell me whatever it is that you and Crispin know about the Lost Heir. Why we're about to have the first Comus Day in history," Magnus demands. "And don't lie. I know you both know something; I'm just not sure of who knows what. You, I suspect, have all sorts of secrets locked in that fuzzy little head of yours, don't you?"

"Well, which is it: are Crispin and I keeping secrets together, or are you unsure of which of us knows what?" Lune challenges.

It forces him to think for a second.

"Both," Magnus snaps. "They're not mutually exclusive. I've been watching you long enough to know that you're both…aware of…*something.*"

Lune sighs and reaches down to unpeel his fingers from her arm. "Well, sorry to disappoint, but you know I'm not fond of politics. And all Crispin has to do is keep Comus law. He doesn't know what's going on any more than anyone else."

Magnus renews his tight grip. "But you do."

"Did I say that?"

"I know you do, Lune. Don't bother trying to hide it."

Lune raises an eyebrow. "Last I checked, our justice system still worked in favor of laying the burden of proof on those who claim, 'guilty'."

"Why mention innocence and guilt at all?" the crown prince challenges. "All I said is that you had information. Feeling guilty about something, then?"

Lune laughs, but she sounds uneasy. "Not at all. You—"

"Tell me who the Lost Heir is, Lune," Magnus interrupts, and Lune stops so quickly she has to catch her breath. He's startled her.

For a moment my heart stops—I had suspected that Lune knew who Rian was. It would explain her potential motives for getting close to him, at least. And if she tells Magnus, then my world is about to become hell.

But she says nothing, and Magnus goes on:

"All I know is it's not me, and it's not Crispin," he says. "That still leaves five crown princes and one crown princess. I thought, then, that it must be Rian or Mercer, as you're always so close to them, but I've spent time around all the potential heirs, and they're playing this all very close to their chests."

"As they should; they're being cautious. Let go of me."

Magnus ignores her. "At first, I thought I'd be forced to wait until Comus Day with everyone else. But then I got to thinking—"

"Must be new for you," Lune snaps, and finally manages to yank her arm free. "Now: let me leave, or you'll regret it. I promise you, Magnus, you're probably right that there must be something exceptional about to happen, but I know nothing about that. I swear. I'm as clueless as anyone else."

"Then explain who the man is you keep meeting. The one you whisper to in bars, in the dark, in your own room. Why keep it a secret, Lune? Why not let our securities be aware of him…unless you're up to something?"

For a moment, no one speaks. Lune is shocked. I'm shocked. Magnus looks somewhat triumphant.

I'm most startled because I remember asking Taris if someone visited Lune's rooms. I didn't think much of the question at the time, nor was I sure why I asked it, but my instincts are proving correct once again. But Taris would have no reason to lie about whether Lune had invited a man to her rooms—for all his faults, he does care enough about Rian to do his best to neutralize threats. This leaves me to conclude that Magnus saw Lune and her mystery man sometime before that…

And I realize the perfect night for it: right after her concert on Fars'day evening.

The same night of the assassination attempt. And the missing albino.

"Your family is conspiring something, Lune, admit it," Magnus pressures. "For good or ill, I don't yet know, but this will go easier for you if you confess to me, now."

She snorts and rolls her eyes.

"If I'm to be a grand prince to a missing heir, I should at least know who I'm meant to advise and protect," he adds.

"Oh, don't pretend to be so noble—"

"Tell me who it is!" Magnus demands. "I know you know, you little *snake*. Tell me who the Lost Heir is and what your intent is for them…And maybe I'll see to it that you become a proper princess."

Lune looks Magnus up and down and laughs in his face. "Oh, Almighty help me, I hope not!"

She moves to slip past him. I don't know if Magnus ever intended to hurt her, but he reacts out of desperation to keep her from leaving. He snags Lune and throws her against the wall, pressing into her shoulders to pin her. I can't see her face from this angle, but she must be scared, because she says nothing.

"What are you up to?" Magnus demands, his voice low now. "Why haven't the Carsans presented the very heir meant to bring *peace* to the world, in times when women are children are being slaughtered in the west? *Why has your family done nothing but sit back until the law forces you to act?*

"I can't have been the only one to notice," Magnus goes on. "I'm not the only person wondering where our country's king is. What your family has to do with this all. *If the Carsans lied about the prophecy.*"

"…I'm not really a Carsans," she says.

"Oh, I'm aware. But you have a powerful fluke if used correctly, Lune. I wonder, what exactly have you been singing to us, all these years? *What is your host family up to?* Answer me!"

He shakes her so she knocks against the wall again. I almost step in to help her. But before I can act, Lune has reached under her skirt and flipped out a butterfly knife. With Magnus already so close, it's easy for her to press the knife against his neck; though he holds her by her shoulders, she has all the power. He stiffens. She could easily slit his throat. Purposefully or not.

He makes a show of slowly releasing her, and holding up his hands.

"Lune, don't. I—"

"I heard what you said to my brother," Lune warns. "You're lucky

Crispin didn't flatten you. So, know this, crown prince. You might have all the power in the world, but you must share it with seven others, and my brother is one of them. Test us again, and you'll suffer more than a little scratch."

She pushes Magnus away, but not before ensuring her knife has cut the side of his neck. It is by no means a lethal injury, but it is a significant warning.

I've clearly been right to suspect Lune of something all these years.

"Tell me what you know!" Magnus all but screeches at her, holding a hand to his bleeding neck. "Our entire world might depend on it!"

Lune whirls on him again, brandishing her knife.

"Continue down this path, and I will be forced to end you. There is more happening than you could possibly understand, so stop trying," Lune warns. She sounds so cold, so different; it's hard to say if she is being possessed by another party, or if this is a side of herself that she's hidden all these years.

"Forced by who?" Magnus demands, though he sounds a little hoarse, now.

Lune gives a nervous laugh, then sheaths her knife and turns to leave.

"Forced by who, Lune?! Grand Prince Carsans and his wife? *Crispin*? Who?!"

"Stay away from me, Magnus," Lune sings sweetly, and I watch his muscles stiffen. He can't refuse her caroled word, her siren's tongue. It makes both him and I wonder why she didn't use her fluke before. "Touch or threaten me again, and I'll make you cut out your own tongue!"

Magnus opens and closes his mouth twice before wisely deciding to keep silent. In a few more seconds, Lune's slipped out the door, letting it bang shut. The second she's gone, someone else enters the hall from the room just next to mine, making me wonder how close we came to crossing paths.

He's little more than a shadowy bulk, in this light and from this angle. But context helps me place a name and face, as does his voice. Griffith Reach is Magnus' most loyal bodyguard, much as Qhan is Rian's. I've never run into the man, or observed enough of him to form an opinion, but he's never far from Magnus' side.

I'm curious to see how this next scene plays out, and what I might learn.

It's not every day the king of Isaaria's own son bids his bodyguard hang back while a court lady threatens him with a knife.

"I'm sorry, sir," Griffith's insisting, already examining Magnus's neck. "She moved so quickly—"

"It's not your fault," Magnus interrupts. "I told you not to interfere."

"Even so. This is unacceptable. The Carsans have taken things too far—if your father knew of this, it would be considered treason. I'll alert the guard to detain them both, and find you a doctor," Griffith promises, and is halfway to the door before Magnus stops him.

"No!" the crown prince snaps, and Griffith freezes. "No," he repeats, and pulls his hand away from his neck for a moment before pressing it back again. "Leave her be. Keep this quiet. If the Carsans really are a threat to the true heir, we need to know. Someone needs to know. And I've no doubt Lune will keep her lips tightly shut if tonight's events come to light. She'll let her proprietor know. Pull back. Change plans…"

I can hear the frustration in Magnus' voice: even he knows tonight was a mistake, but I suspect he acted in desperation. Time until Comus Day is quickly ticking down, after all. And what he said about violence in the west and the Lost Heir is right: in times like this, the Carsans family potentially does have the most to gain, depending on what tricks they have up their sleeves.

"No," Magnus repeats. "We must wait, and hope that I have not ruined our chances of putting the rightful heir on the throne."

"But sir, your neck—!"

"There are more important things to concern ourselves with," Magnus claims, narrowing his eyes. "Including what we may be forced to do if it is true one of the eight families has treacherous intent."

I can tell Griffith is displeased with this arrangement, and I understand why. He is close to Magnus, and to allow such an injury on his watch is an egregious failure. If Lune had intended Magnus true harm, there would have been nothing Griffith could do to stop it.

"Sir, you have a recording of them," Griffith presses. "Those are their voices, and Lady Lune using her fluke on you. That's ample evidence!"

"Evidence of a response to an invasion of their privacy," Magnus retorts. "And for anyone else, that might be enough. But my father is king, and would remain so if no heir ever stepped forward, if not for Comus Law. Of all the families this business of missing heirs looks worst for, it's the Orams, and I'm all-too aware of that. No one would believe I mean well, without solid proof. No one."

I should have known better than to assume Magnus stupid enough to meet with Crispin or Lune alone, or without something to make a meeting valuable. Now, at least, he has both of their threats on record, with both a tape and a witness. If this somehow comes to a trial of sorts, Magnus is making certain he has enough evidence to make a compelling argument.

I leave before Magnus and Griffith do, exiting the building through a window. I'd have liked to listen a little more, but I'm not about to test my luck.

I'm now finding it unfortunate that Rian does not hang about Magnus much, because it gives me limited opportunities to see what the most mistrustful of the crown princes is up to. And what he might have uncovered in our inadvertently joint investigation. But at least there's Crispin and Lune to watch, and I'll have plenty of opportunities to do so.

This, I've decided, is less a question of who is up to something (as I'm certain Magnus is right about Crispin and Lune, given their antics tonight), and rather a triple question of what they're up to, if they're a threat to Rian, and what I can do about it this early in the conspiracy. If anything.

Well, I'll amend that. Four questions remain, the last being the most obvious and most important: how many players are in this game? I haven't ruled out the existence of other parties, larger and smaller. I doubt the elder Carsans siblings are criminal masterminds, but they're perfect puppets.

I know to be watchful of them as I'm forced back to the daily business of minding Rian: Rian teaches his morning classes, Rian goes for a swim, Rian takes Mango out to try and help him fly, Rian has lunch with Mercer and Asmer, Rian returns for afternoon classes. And so on and so on.

Nearly a week of routine passes. My prince and his crew go about their normal business, as if Comus Day isn't sneaking up week by week, and are so predictably dull that if I almost wish for some action. Sparse amusements crops up here and there—Asmer is adorably awed her father has asked her to represent their family on his behalf at Comus Day, Mercer gets himself into a bit of trouble with a pair of blondes he didn't realize were twins—but these are minor distractions.

There's been no sign of that albino assassin. I try to keep from thinking about what might have happened to him, and if he had a different mission than the other seven. Nusk would be disappointed if he knew I was letting my mind wander, but I cannot help myself.

Some things are simply too strange, too suspicious, to brush off.

And then, one morning, after Rian's Isaarian history and relations class, Lune doesn't appear to escort him to breakfast. He, Mercer, and Asmer wait for her, but Lune doesn't show. Eventually, the trio is forced to head to breakfast one person short, reassuring one another that Lune will meet them there, but she doesn't. In fact, Crispin doesn't join them until long after they've finished and are strolling about the grounds.

Crispin acts casually when he finally makes his appearance, but he's careful about his timing. Mercer and one of the aforementioned blondes have bumped into one another, and Rian and Asmer are hanging back to privately mock their friend while he tries to sort things out.

"I see it hasn't taken Mercer long to get himself back into trouble," Crispin notes as he joins them.

"Not that it should surprise any of us. Where's Lune this morning?" Rian asks. He's trying to be casual, but I can tell he's concerned. "I'm sure she'd love this."

Crispin sighs. "Sick. Apparently. Or at least, too anemic to get up when I went to see her. She has no cough or fever, but she's woozy, and so pale she truly does look like a ghost."

Rian and Asmer exchange a look.

"Perhaps we should stop in and see her," Asmer suggests. "To let her know we're thinking of her, if nothing else."

"She's in a terrible temper," Crispin warns, but this doesn't dissuade the pair.

"We'll be quick," my crown prince promises.

"You stay with Mercer," Asmer adds, trying to sound reassuring. "Try to keep him from being thrown out of the University, if you can."

Crispin is less than enthused with their plan, but agrees there's likely no harm in the pair stopping in to see Lune. Still, his initial resistance makes me curious. There are many possibilities of why, none of them good. Though the fact that Crispin is saying Lune is merely ill implies that he either is unaware of the truth, or he's better at lying than I've ever given him credit for.

I want to know what the Carsans are planning that they'd think it prudent for Lune to stay in her rooms today. After all, she looked perfectly fine yesterday. The odds of her suddenly being too weak and sick to stand are slim. So, while I follow Asmer and Rian for my prince's protection, I also do it to spy on Lune.

While Rian and Asmer take the staircase, leaving Qhan to stand guard at the bottom, I scale the wall. Lune doesn't have a large balcony like Rian's, but there's still a ledge on one of her windows for flowers. She doesn't bother with plants, and covers her window with curtains, but there's enough of a crack to allow me some visibility, if I close one eye and peer in. Rian has that bug on him, still, but I carefully crack the unlocked window anyway.

Even with the window opened only slightly, I'm instantly assaulted by an overwhelming aroma of incense and perfume. As if there's another smell underneath that Lune wants covered up. Lune herself is a lump on her mattress, curled up with the duvet pulled up over her head. I only have a few seconds to get my bearings, and try to ignore that dizzying scent combination, when there's a light rap on her door.

"Lune?"

It's Rian's muffled voice.

I ensure I'm concealed behind the curtains, glad they're thick enough to hide me on the other side of the window, then watch as Rian creaks the door open. He and Asmer enter and make their way to Lune's side.

"Lune?" Rian asks again, and perches on the side of the bed.

"You all right, sweetheart?" Asmer adds, her genuine sympathy nettling me for reasons I can't explain.

Beneath the sheets, a sniffling noise confirms that Lune is awake.

After several long seconds, there's a very quiet: "No."

"Crispin said you're feeling poorly," Rian goes on, hesitant. "Is there anything we can do, or—"

"Please go away," Lune whispers. *"Please. Leave me alone."*

It sounds as if she's been crying.

Rian is concerned. He glances up at Asmer but she is equally helpless and her expression says as much.

"Very well," Asmer says slowly. "If you're sure. Have one of your maids call my rooms if you need anything, and I'll get it myself, yes?"

Lune doesn't respond.

"Lu?" Asmer says, quieter.

"Mmm."

Asmer tries to meet Rian's eyes, but he's still peering at Lune with a serious frown. Asmer's of the mind that they should leave Lune be, as she's requested, but I can tell that my crown prince isn't the sort to leave well enough alone. Lune might want solitude, but Rian doesn't want to grant it.

"Rian," Asmer whispers—I can hear her only because of the bug on his earring, but I'm sure Lune can't. "We should go."

Asmer heads slowly for the door, waiting for him, but Rian makes it only halfway before changing his mind.

"I'll be there in a moment. You don't have to wait; I'm going to my rooms after this for a spell. Let Qhan know, if you wouldn't mind?" Rian requests.

He waits for a perplexed affirmative from Asmer, then returns to Lune. He sits once more on the side of her bed, as close to her as he can get without invading her personal space.

"Lune?" he poses again.

"I said go away," she retorts, her voice cracking, but Rian gently puts a hand on her shoulder. She doesn't flinch away.

"Lu, did someone hurt you?" he murmurs, almost as if he expected something like this. I don't think he has any idea of who might have hurt her, or why, but his instincts tells him it's possible.

She doesn't respond, but sniffles.

"Lu, what's wrong?" Rian presses. "You're not just sick. Please, tell me?"

I can hear a rustling noise from the bug, and when I adjust my position, I see Lune finishing a few shakes of her head against her pillow.

"You can talk to me, you know," Rian promises. "Even if you don't want to tell Crispin or Asmer—you can at least tell me. I won't spread it around, you know that. You can trust me."

She hesitates. I'm forced to wonder, again, if Lune knows who Rian really is, or if whatever she's up to does not require that specific information. Is it by design or chance that she's almost constantly around the Lost Heir of Isaaria?

Too many questions. Not enough information.

"I know," Lune finally admits.

"So, tell me what's wrong?" Rian prompts, a ghost of playfulness in his tone.

"I…can't," she insists.

Rian knows not to press further. He gently places a hand on Lune's head and strokes her hair while she cries.

It's moments like this that I'm not at all worried about Rian's potential interest in Lune: he is three and a half years older than her, and right now, he is treating Lune as he claims he sees Asmer: a little sister. Nothing more.

"It's all right, Lune," he says. "If you need a few days' break from everything and everyone, then take it. But you decide you want to talk to someone, you will always have me."

"Thank you," she sniffs.

"Is there anything I can do, before I leave?" he offers.

"Could you…Could you please call one of my maids in?" she asks weakly. "I want to bathe."

"All right," he agrees, and after a moment, leans back down to plant a kiss on her head. "I love you, little Lune. So do Merse and Asmer. Take care of yourself."

Platonic love, I try to calm myself. *He means platonic love. That's why he mentioned Asmer and Mercer as well.*

But I can't entirely ignore how uncomfortable I am to hear Rian tell Lune he loves her at all.

Rian departs, but I remain. He is only going back to his rooms, after all, and there's little threat to him there with his own bodyguards about. Besides, I'm curious to see if I might glean anything else now that I have Lune alone. At first, I'm disappointed, as she does nothing but scrunch up tightly on the bed and sniffle. But then that maid she asked for appears.

"My lady?" the maid asks gently. "Are you still feeling unwell? Do you want me to send for a doctor—"

"No doctors," Lune interrupts. "Fill the bath for me, please? And then…you can leave. Have someone come clean the bed while I'm away. Please. But *only the bed.* Don't touch anything else."

The maid is a little taken aback by this request, but recovers. "Of course, my lady," she soothes. "Whatever you need."

She heads dutifully to the bathroom, and I can hear her jostle several glass bottles after turning on the water, adding soaps and perfumes that are likely meant to help Lune relax. It takes several minutes for the tub to fill, after which the maid returns to find that Lune has not moved an inch.

"My lady? Your bath is ready," the woman says.

"Thank you," Lune mumbles. "You may leave."

She's not cold, but certainly curt. Dismissive.

"Do not hesitate to call for me if you require anything else," Lune's maid adds, and I can tell she's worried about her mistress, but not enough to disobey one of Lune's requests outright.

With a few quiet strides and the gentle click of the door, the maid leaves, and Lune and I are alone again. She's slow to move, but after a rustling of bedcovers and a thump as one of her pillows falls to the ground, Lune's feet slide over the edge of the bed. I rearrange my position to watch her. She does not storm to her bath in a rage, but instead staggers, hunched over as if truly ill. She's dressed in a dirty shift, not even her nightgown, as if she couldn't be bothered to put on something else before dragging herself into bed last night.

I note that her feet are caked with dried mud and dirt, and there's some on her hands as well, up to her wrists. Her eyes are red, her makeup smeared and trailing down her face in obvious tear tracks. Interesting, but not enough.

Lune shuts the washroom door, and I can hear her settle into the water. I make an impulsive, perhaps irrational decision. One thorough search of Lune's room revealed nothing, but if she has secrets, now is the time to find them.

Stealthy as I am, I manage slip in through the window and land on the floor in a careful crouch. I have perhaps minutes before a maid appears to clean Lune's bed, and I *cannot* be seen in here. The first time around, I didn't know where to start looking. But I'm rather sensitive to smell, and now that I'm in her room, Lune's attempts to cover up a pungent scent are not entirely successful.

There is something else. Something beneath the perfumes that, I'm sure, no one else noticed. Likely they assumed Lune only meant to cover up the smell of sick, but last time she was ill, she sprayed only in her washroom. Now, the whole chamber is full of it.

It does not take me long to instinctively check beneath her bed—as she was so insistent on its cleanliness—and I find exactly what I'm looking for.

At first, when I pull the puffy fabric free, I'm disappointed. It's only one of Lune's dresses, as if she's kicked it under the bed after a hard night out drinking and singing. But as I shake it open, something thumps to the floor in the skirt. As I spread the dress wide, I find a large stain covering it from the waist down. The source of the smell. Lune's dark secret.

Blood. Blood spilled all down her skirt like a butcher's apron, coating it. It's dried, now, and has stiffened the fabric so that it cracks when I move it. And, wrapped carefully in the folds of the skirt so that I almost miss it: an equally blood-stained knife. Not Lune's butterfly knife; this one is heftier.

I stare at the two hidden objects, my mind racing to recall who I might not have seen in the past few days. Who Lune might have reason to do away with. But I come up with nothing. I'm left to wonder, even as I escape her room, leaving her bloody belongings in their places: Who did she kill?

Six

I CANNOT STOP THINKING about Lune and the bloody dress. I am obsessed with the idea that she harbors some ill will toward Rian, but all I know for certain is that she has killed someone. It's clear she attempted to hide it by pretending she's ill, but that charade was set to work only if her friends avoided her, which they did not. Lune is no great actress, and from what I can piece together, not much of a murderess either. Regardless of what schemes she might have in motion, or regardless of whoever she's working for, she has no stomach for killing, and greatly regrets having to do it.

That matches with what I believe she is: an informant. I've seen enough assassins after Rian to know she can't fill that role. What I don't know, and what is now driving me to the brink of insanity, is who she's working for or with, if she plans on betraying that person, what her intentions are for Rian, and who she might have killed and why.

At first, I thought, naturally: Magnus. He must have found out something he shouldn't, or maybe he was digging too close to the truth, and Lune was told to kill him and cover things up. But I've seen Magnus around and about since discovering Lune's bloody secrets; aside from the scratch Lune gave him, he's perfectly fine.

Regardless, this proves that Magnus was right. Lune knows something, and whoever else might have shared that knowledge could be dead. If Magnus's further predictions prove correct, then the Carsans may be a great danger to the heirs. As Magnus has seen more sides of the Carsans than I have, simply because they're always so innocent around Rian, I can't disregard his opinion.

The only problem is motive, because Lune wanting to harm Rian contradicts my other worry regarding her intention to make herself his bride.

I think back to the night I walked in on Lune with the scissors, which now makes more sense. Lune must have been told her assignment then: she was to murder someone her puppeteer wanted out of the way. The prospect made her queasy and she could not keep her dinner down, making her sick up in her bathroom. The stress of it caused her menstrual cycle to start earlier than she was prepared for, explaining those ruined drawers. The marks on her back—some form of self-harm out of loathing. Her visit to the doctor in the alley: to know what parts of a man or woman to cut to ensure they die quickly.

She must have severed an artery, hence the blood. And the knife.

Rian does little of interest for the rest of the day, so I'm trapped running these things over and over in my head, trying to make sense of them. Though I already suspect what Nusk will say, I decide I need to tell him about this, and see what he thinks I should do. The Carsans' threat is too great to go ignored.

For once, Taris shows up early enough that I have about an hour to head to Nusk's cabin for a short chat. He's reading in the kitchen while Naomi cuts a slice of bread and slathers it in jam and butter.

"Taris relieved me early. We need to talk," I announce before Nusk can ask about my sudden appearance.

Naomi glances at her father, and starts to leave the room.

"N'omi can stay," I add shortly, taking a seat at the table across from Nusk.

He nods to his daughter as he sets down his book, marking his spot. Naomi perches delicately on the edge of a chair, as if ready to rush out if she decides she doesn't want to hear what I have to say. She and Nusk keep from questioning me while I fill them in on Magnus's suspicions, his arguments with the Carsans siblings, Lune pulling a knife on him, and the bloody dress beneath her bed.

When I finish, I wait expectantly for Nusk's advice on handling the situation. How to spy on the Carsans and discover their plans, or otherwise ensure Rian's safety. But he merely taps his fingers thoughtfully against the tabletop, then runs his hand over the grooves and swipes some of Naomi's crumbs into his hand.

"And so?" he poses, and for a few seconds, I'm stunned.

"So, I think Lune Carsans is a traitor," I say. "I think she murdered someone."

Nusk's face remains distressingly impassive.

"Does this in any way affect the crown prince?" he points out, and I have to think about that one. "Directly?"

"Well, no," I admit. "Not that I can tell."

"Then leave it be."

Nusk wheels over to the sink basin to dispose of Naomi's crumbs. Naomi herself shifts uncomfortably, watching us like we're lions prepared to pounce at one another. I turn in my seat on the bench as well, so I can still face Nusk.

"But it could!" I press. "Magnus Oram said—"

He whirls his chair back on me suddenly, and I feel like a little girl again. Not that Nusk has ever threatened me seriously, or raised a hand to me other than a light smack to get me moving in training, but even so. I can tell he is disappointed in me, and his next words reveal why.

"When was Crown Prince Oram near Rian recently?" he demands.

I say nothing. Because we both know what this means.

"Then you mean to say that you are stalking and spying on another of the crown princes, endangering your principal by giving Oram an opportunity to catch you, a lowly little maid, eavesdropping."

Nusk expects my chagrined silence, but I feel I have a valid point. Taking risks is part of my assignment. As I've been taking said risks on Rian's behalf—and discovering pertinent information whilst doing so–I'm forced to conclude that my instincts aren't as terrible as proposed. My spying, if that's what we want to call it, has been done in a manner that I do not find unbefitting a *Khashtani.*

"But he didn't catch me," I argue. "And neither did Griffith Reach—and he should have been on the lookout for someone like me, and…My point stands, Nusk," I sigh. "There is a threat to Rian amongst these backstabbing politicians, and I can't even know if it's because they understand who he is, or because some of them have their own bid for the throne and think he'll be in the way—"

"Soleil, quiet," Nusk suddenly snaps, and it takes me a moment to realize he's used his fluke on me, to make me silent.

I can hear Naomi's anxiety with each deep breath. Her eyes flick between the two of us, and I realize I should not have said she could stay for this. We are both stuck there, saying nothing, while Nusk runs a hand over his face and sighs. He takes a moment to think before looking up at me again, and I should note the exhaustion in his eyes, but all I can feel is building frustration.

"Soleil: don't obsess," Nusk chides, his tone softer than before. "It is not your responsibility to know who or why, only to stop them. Go down this path, and you will become sloppy. Keep to your routine, and keep the crown prince safe. So long as you keep him alive, it matters little who might want him dead."

I cross my arms. I manage to keep from glaring, I think, but my body language still makes my opinions clear, even if my tongue can't.

This is the most dangerous time in Rian's life, and I cannot make a single mistake. Even during his own time as a *Khashtani,* Nusk never faced anything quite like this. In general, I trust his opinion and his wisdom, but that wisdom is not infinite. That experience, not infallible.

My mentor will not sway me so easily, now, and he knows it.

"Naomi, leave," Nusk says shortly, and she all but flees the room.

Tension seethes between Nusk and me. Most times, I'd have relented by now. Allowed my shoulders to drop, submitted with an apology. But for some reason, despite all the obedience Nusk has drilled into me, I don't. Our little family has functioned on the premise that the Qurvo children and I obey Nusk without question, and when I was young, this made sense: Rian's life depended on such things, and Nusk seemed to know everything.

But I am not a child any longer. Nusk has no right to make me obey without question, whilst still reprimanding me for not being the perfect *Khashtani.*

Nusk relents first, and I can't help but feel mild triumph. He is the only father I've ever known, and I know I should still respect him as such, but he needs to learn, too, that I am a different person. The *Khashtani* tradition is not even mine–I am the only Isaarian Living Shield in existence.

By that fact alone, my experience and Nusk's will never be the same.

"Oh, Soleil," he finally croaks. "There is still so much you don't understand."

"If that's true, we might as well say that there's much no one will ever understand," I retort.

I'm prepared for him to volley back with something about his own superior experience, but he doesn't.

"You are still thinking like a child," he says instead.

That takes me by surprise.

Not only because it's an insult, but because it feels like something I've heard before. Not from Nusk, and not said to me, but the sentiment is familiar.

Perhaps it is this reminder of Nusk's view of me—one of his children—that makes me soften towards him. It's hard to stay angry at a man who has dedicated both his life and the lives of all three of his children to protect Rian. Granted, my life was chosen for me, too, but I was an abandoned child plucked from the middle of nowhere, given a purpose. Nusk chose to want me.

"I'm not a child any longer," I remind him unnecessarily.

"Yet," Nusk says. "You still think yourself invincible. You stretch yourself too thin. You cannot be with Rian constantly, let alone everywhere at once, and yet, you try. You're worse than that, in fact, because you try to delve into more than you're meant to. You think your purpose isn't enough."

This is a criticism not of how I see myself, but one of hubris.

"Well, perhaps I could speak with Rian and tell him everything," I retort flippantly. "I wouldn't be spreading myself too thin, then, would I?"

"Soleil," he says, and gives me a stern look.

We're silent again for a few seconds.

"I'd like this to be the last argument we have," Nusk says. "I'm too old for it, Soleil. I won't live for much longer, and I can't be at peace knowing that you might not be the best *Khashtani* I could have created for the crown prince."

"But are you certain we're doing the right thing? Suppressing the Carsans' prophecy like this?" I challenge.

Nusk gives me a stern look. "We've spoken on this before, Soleil."

"You've dismissed the question before," I challenge. "But what if we did allow Rian to be king? Would that truly be so bad? I've always convinced myself otherwise, but…He would have more bodyguards, as king. He would—"

"What is the purpose of torturing yourself with these hypotheticals?" Nusk interrupts. For some reason, he sounds angry. "Soleil—you may think yourself this great, mysterious force, changing the fate of the world by keeping one man alive, but you are not meant to consider these things. Consider the crown prince, yes; consider his life, your duty to it. But your duty is to keep him alive at all costs. That is why the crown prince's parents had me make you into what you are. And for no other reason."

"But they were people, just like we're people," I retort. "Maybe they made the wrong decision. Maybe they made one in fear, and maybe… someone should change that decision."

"They did not want their son endangered by becoming king, and you should respect their wishes as Rian has," Nusk warns me.

"What about what Rian wants?" I challenge.

Nusk is exasperated with me, but manages not to lose his temper again.

"If the crown prince wanted to become king, we would have to find a way to stop him. But he has made no indication that he desires such a thing, and I believe this is for the best. He might be the crown prince Fate chose, but he is not the only option. He is not the only good man in the world, Soleil. There will be another. One who has been preparing all these years while your little scholar frivols his time away on Magicsmiths and children's classes."

I can't fully disagree with him on this, and must look down at the table to avoid letting him see that. Rian hasn't done much in the way of preparing to be king, were he called to it. And beyond the truth that I know, based on a vague prophecy that I've never heard, I have no idea if he'd be a good king. Just the chosen one.

Nusk has a point, and I know it's better than mine. But it's frustrating to hear so many restrictions. To know my information on the Carsans and Magnus should be treated as nothing. To worry that it could become important in the future, and I'll still be expected to ignore it unless it threatens Rian.

"Your place is to stop assassins, not to dabble in politics. It is a world in which you don't belong, and its complications could easily undo everything we've worked to maintain," Nusk says. "You can no more keep Rian from the court he lives in than I could my principal from the disease that killed him. You must understand this, Soleil. There are limits to what you can do. Limits to what you should do. Your actions, the lives you take—it all means something."

"I know that," I snap, bristling.

I hate it when Nusk implies I have less compassion than anyone else. Maybe I do. Maybe I don't care as much about life as I should, but I want to. Isn't that enough?

"Do not mistake me, Soleil," Nusk continues, "your intentions are admirable, and ambitious. But too ambitious for a *Khashtani.* I would like you to meditate on this, this afternoon," he goes on, beginning a dismissal, and I grumble as I get to my feet, realizing we'd done nothing but waste time talking in circles.

"No promises," I mutter. "But I'll stay away from Oram and the Carsans. If *that's what you wish."*

"It is."

"Fine."

I stalk to the door.

"Soleil," Nusk says again. "Do meditate on it. You must know your place."

I nod, but know that I won't. Oh, I'll bear in mind what Nusk has told me, and I'll stay away from one of the most interesting and dangerous intrigues that I've ever come across, because he's told me so. But I refuse to be at peace with that decision because I don't like it.

Naomi is waiting for me outside the door. She falls hesitantly into step behind me as I leave the path, tromping across the grass to take a shortcut to our dormitory. I have time before I must report to work: I might as well return there.

We walk for only a few short seconds before Naomi tries to relieve me of my irritation. I wish she wouldn't.

"He means it in the best way," she says. "It's not that he thinks that you're incapable of helping Rian further. But there's a reason a *Khashtani* is only meant to serve and protect. You're one person. You can't do everything."

"I'm not trying to do everything. Just everything encompassed in my job," I mutter. I try not to sound too irritable, so Naomi won't think I'm mad at her.

"But you have to admit, Soleil, the more you divide your attention, the greater the odds are of something bad happening. To the crown prince," Naomi warns me. It bothers me that she sounds tentative.

"Not to mention, I know you'd be terribly upset if anything happened to any of us," she adds quietly. "You don't have to say anything," she says when I miss the beat she left for a response. "But I know it's not just Rian you're trying to protect. That's already more for you to do, in addition to keeping him safe and away from the crown."

I wish she'd stop talking, but Naomi is intent on reassuring herself that Nusk and I are no longer at odds. She wants me to concede, and admit that I'm wrong.

But I'm not going to, because I'm not.

"Get to your point, N'omi," I sigh.

"I agree with my father, Soleil: let Rian manage the politics. I've watched him, too, you know. He's smarter than he lets on. You have to trust him."

"You're probably right," I force myself to say, but I'm irritated by the fact that this means I can't fully count on Naomi or Korvaan, now.

Korvaan tells his father absolutely everything, and Naomi is siding with Nusk on this one. If I want to uncover whatever secret plots might do Rian harm, I'm completely on my own. That is, unless I decide to trust Taris enough to bring him in, but I can't make that decision quickly. Taris likes to be contrary. He might side with me, out of that odd spite he has for his father, but we're hardly bosom pals.

I do not know what will happen if Nusk discovers I'm planning to defy his wishes, and I don't have any desire to find out. So, I'll play along, for now. And keep my eyes on the Carsans siblings every spare second.

My act—thus far, at least—seems to fool Naomi. With my submission, she's already cheerier than before. Relieved.

"Besides, you're a *Khashtani*, not a nanny," she says wryly, trying to tease me. "All Rian needs is for you to keep him safe from daggers in the dark, not hold his hand every step he takes."

"You're also the one who brought up letting him become king," I challenge her. "And got me thinking such things in the first place."

"It's only an idea, though, Soleil," Naomi claims. "It's a way for me to see your thoughts. Make sure you know you're doing all this for the right reasons. But though we might be friends, I am still a member of your *khashak*. You are right to chide me when I present such silly ideas."

The way she says this tells me Nusk likely already knew about Korvaan and N'omi discussing Rian—his sexual preferences, the possibility of crowning him, his personal life—and has not approved. He's reminded them of their places, as he so does endeavor to remind me of mine. It's not the stubbornness in my blood that wants to argue with Nusk and reject the fundamental tenets of his lessons; I genuinely can't understand why it would be bad for me to catch the Carsans before they try to harm Rian.

But that's not all I have to consider, now; Naomi's right when she says she's merely a member of my *khashak*. That's how she's meant to see herself. Not as my sister, not as my friend.

It's enough to completely sour my mood, and my thoughts are tumbling over and over in my head as we return to our room. Naomi immediately crosses to throw herself on the bed. She's complaining about the heat of the day, and sweat glistens on her forehead to validate her grievance.

"Soleil?" Naomi says, and I realize that I've done nothing but stand by the door for the past minute.

"Mmm."

"Don't you think?"

"Don't I think what?"

Naomi stares at me, then sighs. "I swear, you never listen to me."

This irritates me further.

"That's not true," I insist, and cross the room. Still, before sitting next to her, I check my watch for the time, and Naomi notices. "I bet I could tell you what you'd do if you weren't in my *khashak,"* I add, in an attempt to distract her.

"Really," she says, unimpressed.

I almost smirk, because, for once, I do have the answer to this.

"Well, assuming the name Valor Ondra means anything to you," I drawl, and Naomi's flushes so deeply I can see the red. "If I released you from your *khashak* bonds, would you grow your hair out for him?" I add.

"He...has come to the infirmary a few times," she admits sheepishly. "Always when I'm there. And waits until I'm free. But it's not...He...We haven't..."

I can tell there's more that she wants to say, but she isn't sure if she should say so around me: But we can't do anything further, anyways.

"If you ran away with him tomorrow, I would never say anything," I sing, and Naomi covers her face.

"So-leil," she groans, embarrassed. "I barely know him. Besides, he's one of Rian's guards. It would mean depriving the crown prince of someone to keep him safe. I could never do that."

I know she cannot, but I shrug anyway, as if acknowledging there's true merit to the idea. And as far as I know—why not let Naomi have her little daydreams? Nusk must have some idea of what will happen to all of us after Comus Day, if all goes according to plan. Or, Nusk's plan, I now must note. Perhaps I will release my *khashak,* then. Perhaps it will be better to be without them, now that I'm starting to think they're holding me back.

"Well, what about you?" Naomi challenges, turning my question against me. "What would you do if you were released from being a *Khashtani* right now? What do you want, Soleil?"

I roll my eyes and open my mouth to say one thing: the expected answer, the lecture about how, if I were not a *Khashtani,* Rian would have to be dead.

That isn't what comes out.

"I want children," I answer automatically, and then frown.

I have no idea where that came from.

"I don't know why I said that," I insist. Naomi's mouth is partially agape. "I don't want children. *Rian* wants children. I think I was only channeling…I don't know what I would want."

"I thought you were going to say…" Naomi starts, and then stops again, and her blush returns.

"Say what? *N'omi?"*

"It's nothing," she mutters.

She refuses to meet my eyes. So here we are, then. Forever separated from what we used to have and what we might want.

I glance at my watch again. Time is up. It shames me, but I'm relieved.

"Work is soon," I say in self-dismissal, standing. "I'd best be going."

"I'll stay up for you, if you like?" Naomi offers.

"Don't bother," I insist. "You rise early, I stay late. We'll return to the schedule and…let all these nobles' nonsense go on as usual."

Naomi nods and bids me farewell. I leave for my own duties, making note that this is yet another thing I must mend. But no matter how much I value my relationship with N'omi, I cannot abandon the very thing that's caused the rift between myself and Nusk. He might refuse to see the dangers circling about Rian until the last few seconds, but I tire of sitting in wait.

The next time someone seeks to do Rian harm, I will strike them down before they get within a hundred yards of him. Regardless of whether that person is noble-born or not.

SEVERAL MORE DAYS PASS, and I hear little official news on Lune Carsans. The servants and the students and scholars whisper, wondering if she's gotten herself with child or was spurned by a secret lover. But among the more prominent nobles on campus, not much is said. Asmer offers helpless shrugs when Lune fails to appear for breakfast, or brunch, or dinner. Crispin answers with short, sighing responses when Rian asks. Magnus has all but sequestered himself after the night Lune nearly slit his throat, and Mercer seems determined to keep everyone else from worrying by perpetually changing the topic.

There are no attempts on Rian's life, nothing unusual, no albino assassin or informant or whoever the hell such a person was—I can't even be sure if they exist at this point.

I am dreadfully anxious.

It's the start of a new week before something finally happens. Lune skips Mass this morning—highly unusual for her—leaving only Rian and Crispin to attend. They don't talk much afterward, and Rian returns to his rooms to fetch Mango before taking the dragon out to the fields and trying (once again) to get him to fly.

Mango's loyal, but not bright, and doesn't seem to understand the function of his own wings. Rian likes to run with him, holding Mango up in the air like a disagreeable kite as he tries to get him to glide. He hasn't made much progress, yet. It's entertaining, though: watching the dragon's surprise to feel air beneath those flappy appendages, and his panic whenever Rian tries to let go of him.

At one point, some of the University students join them. Rian lets them chase Mango, and himself, playing like an older brother or fond uncle. I'd enjoy seeing him this happy if I weren't so suspicious of what Lune and Crispin Carsans are up to in the meantime.

Keeping an eye on them whilst avoiding Nusk and my own *khashak* and maintaining my duties as a maid is going to be complicated.

That's not to say I plan to let this obsession get in the way of doing what's best for Rian, as Nusk worries; quite the contrary. I'm suspicious of Crispin and Lune because all current evidence points to them, but I'm not so foolish as to ignore Nusk's advice entirely. I must keep my focus broad, to see the whole picture. Mercer, for example, is Rian's best friend, and would be the perfect person to dramatically betray him. He has even less motive than the Carsans, granted, but even so. The only one I'm least suspicious of is Magnus, and that's only because I've heard him say himself why he's looking for answers.

Then there are the rest of the crown princes and the Crown Princess Nissa. Any one of them might wish Rian ill, for obvious reasons.

I have seven prime suspects, all equally likely and unlikely in their own ways. But they're the only ones, that I can see, who'd want the Lost Heir dead. Likely one of them believes that they deserve the throne, "Lost Heir" or no, and are more than capable of ushering in a time of great peace themselves.

Nusk often warns me against hubris, but something tells me no one has done the Isaarian heirs such a favor.

The rest of Rian's afternoon consists of lessons that bring me no closer to the Carsans. They are not his usual kind of lesson, either; today, he is a student. He has Qhan teach him swordplay in a private room, to keep folks from watching and making commentary. Rian does have some aptitude for swordsmanship, but I doubt he'll ever be in a situation where he needs to fight for his life in such a way. Almost all the princes carry ceremonial swords, but none of them have seen real battle except for Mercer, and even he has never participated.

Mercer himself decides to seek out Rian while the poor man's hair is still wet, in the hopes of dragging him into a social life.

"Do you have plans?" he asks Rian while I'm perched outside the window.

Mercer scratches behind Mango's ears, making him purr with delight.

"Plans? Not really," Rian says, trying to towel off his hair.

"Then we need to go out," Mercer announces dramatically. "To the city for a few hours, and enjoy ourselves. No-no: don't argue," he adds, cutting off Rian. "You have plenty of time to sit in your rooms and pore over books. But you and I both know you need this."

I can tell Rian doesn't really want to go out, but he won't argue with Mercer, even over something so simple.

"Well…I could always use the time to—"

"Oh, do it tomorrow!" Mercer insists. He's grabbed Rian about the shoulders and is steering him towards the door.

"What can I say? You win, you merciless man. If we must go out in celebration, I suppose…we must," Rian says, unable to keep from smiling.

"Goodnight, Mango, I'll bring your master back by sunrise!" Mercer says before they close the door and leave the sunblood to amuse himself.

"*Sunrise!*" I hear Rian say as they head down the stairs. "Merse, really. I *do* have to get up at a reasonable hour tomorrow. The students depend on me."

"Call in sick! No one would mind."

"From the administration. My students will be terribly disappointed…"

I'm about to follow them down the tower, planning how to tail them into the city without getting left behind or spotted, when someone grabs me by the back of my clothes like a disobedient puppy and hauls me onto the balcony. I've a knife drawn up against my palm, ready to strike it through an eyeball, but scowl when I see who it is.

"Taris! You—!" I start, sheathing the knife when I realize he and Korvaan have invaded my space, one looking significantly more chagrined than the other.

"There's a visiting dignitary tomorrow," Taris interrupts. "No one will say who, yet, but all the maids have been recruited to clean and prepare until the moment they step foot on the ground. Guess who that includes?"

I scowl. "I need to be with Rian tonight. They're going into the city."

Taris raises an eyebrow.

"You've been watching him all morning and afternoon," Korvaan says. "It'll upset the schedule."

"I can do two shifts," I insist. "I'll tail Rian tonight, swap with you tomorrow morning, and we'll work out putting the schedule back again afterwards. It's fine."

"And how are you supposed to get yourself out of work?" Korvaan says. "They do expect you to continue making an appearance."

"We'll sort something out," I claim, trying not to be nasty.

Korvaan chuckles. "Oh, no. I'm not going to be a part of that," he insists. "Those matrons are *cold-hearted snakes*. If someone's going to them making excuses for you, it's not going to be me."

I'm not pleased with the situation, but I've been too lax with my maid cover lately. If I try and slip out of work tonight, it will draw suspicion. We could always ask Nusk to intercede, but though flukes are magical in nature, they are no cure-all. Naomi, with her ability to stitch fabric or flesh, could not save a patient if they bleed out during a procedure. Those with healing capabilities can't mend afflictions a person was born with, or old injuries. And though Nusk can issue commands with his charmed tongue, they could still re-discover something that he's told them to forget. He has no mastery over a person's memories, and cannot create new ones or false ones. Only a Smith could do such things; so, in effect, it happens only in stories.

"Fine," I relent. "Taris, you watch Rian. Korvaan, I don't know. You two sort it out. And do it fast."

They're both surprised that I've left the decision to them, but I'm not at all in the mood for Taris' snarky commentary. After climbing down the tower, I head for the maid's posting board, where I assume Taris spotted the summons.

He was right: details are minimal, but someone's coming from the capital to visit tomorrow, and all maids are to work past their usual hours on an amended schedule: twelve-hour shifts. On one hand, this gives me a few extra hours before I'm expected to start work. But Taris wasn't wrong: it would give me no chance at all to tail Rian and Mercer into the city, as I'm certain they plan on spending the entire evening and perhaps even part of the early morning there.

I decide to use the next two hours as I please, after ensuring that my *khashak* are aware of this change in plans. If I'm going to be forced into constant work, I may as well indulge in some leisure time.

I find a sequestered, lonely spot, dig out my bow, and practice shooting. Bows are almost obsolete, now, with the introduction of firearms and their continual advancement, but I'm not fond of guns. Too noisy. Besides this is the only hobby I can have, as it still sharpens my skills while, strangely, allowing me some level of peace. I make a note to myself to speak with Nusk, later, and see if having a quiet mind while shooting counts as meditating.

Suppertime approaches, and I take a break to eat some cold tomato-pepper soup and cheese bread before heading to work. I try to duplicate the same mindfulness I managed while shooting, to help the menial labor go quicker, but it's difficult, knowing Rian is in the city without me.

The clock has struck nine and I'm carrying my bucket and mop back to the supply closet when I see a swarm of maids. Curious, I lean my tools up against a wall, sure someone else will return them for me, and inquire.

These girls are all young—day maids. The fact that they're crowded about long after their grueling workday is peculiar, but as I make my way through the throng, I see why: standing at the head of the pack is Crispin Carsans. The girls must have heard that he needed help with something and are now attempting to catch his eye in hopes of some fairy-tale romance.

They all read too much fiction. Besides, they should know they'd have better luck with Mercer; all they'd have to do is breathe to get his attention.

It doesn't take long with these gossiping busy-bodies to learn what Crispin wants. Lune, apparently, has disappeared off-campus, and her brother is here to recruit some assistance.

Immediately, I see my way out of here.

"Maybe she went to the city. That's where Crown Princes Mercer and Rian went," I murmur to a maid, starting the rumor so it's passed up to Crispin.

"Who said that?" he demands, looking over us, and I allow the other girls to push me forward.

Crispin does not bother to ask my name. "Do you have any idea where they went? The other crown princes?"

No, but I know their usual haunts.

"Yes, sir. I do not know for certain if the lady joined them, but it wouldn't be unlike her," I add.

Crispin thinks for a second.

"You and…you, you, you, and you," he says, pointing to several of us, "come with me."

He leads us toward the west end of campus, where coaches park for the usage of students and faculty. We have a dozen coaches and drivers on staff here, to bring folk to and from the city or the train station. Rumor has it we'll be getting Alarkian motorcars as well, soon, which further proves a point Nusk has been making for years: even in the middle of a war, industry never dies. If money can be made, it will be.

Crispin marches up to a trio of coachmen hanging about with smokes, and one of them reluctantly steps forward to take his orders.

"All you on to the city, then?" the coachman asks, nodding to us as he fixes his cap and rebuttons the top of his jacket.

"Only the maids," Crispin corrects. "If they find my sister, bring her home; otherwise, bring these girls back before midnight. I don't want them alone late," he insists, pressing money into the coachman's hand.

He turns and finds me again. I would be concerned, but I suspect Crispin will forget my face the moment Lune's found.

"You, sit up front," he says. "Instruct him once you're in the city limits."

"Yes, sir," I acknowledge.

It takes us about an hour to make it to the city, and another fifteen minutes to reach the quarters with the busiest bars and restaurants. I thank the coachman and leap off the bench, already plotting how to lose the other girls. They clamber out of the coach, some of them excited, the others pressing close nervously.

"Should we split up?" one of them poses.

"I don't think Crown Prince Crispin would want us to," a more anxious one demurs. "We are all alone out here, like he said…"

"You do whatever you want. I'm headed in there," I say, gesturing to the most likely place I'll find Rian. "We can all meet back here at half-past eleven."

I'm just heading off when two different girls grab at my arms, and nearly all of them begin to plead with me not to leave them.

I sigh and brush them off. "If the Lady Lune is in the city, she's likely looking for her friends. Lady Asmer is her closest. Asmer's with two of the crown princes, and *that pub* looks the most like a security nightmare. Safe to say, that's where Crown Prince Mercer is."

I'm not trying to be funny, but two of the girls look at each other and giggle behind their hands.

"You can come with me if you want," I say, "but we'll have to split up once we're inside to search. Otherwise, we're not using our time efficiently."

And hopefully, if Mercer and Rian aren't there, I can slip away in the crowd. Based on what I can see and hear, the establishment looks plenty busy.

The maids tentatively agree to my plan and follow me into the bar. I assume none of them have been to a place like this in their lives, and are too busy thinking about what an experience this is to fully understand the potential consequences of our mission. If we don't find Lune, either the entire campus and half the country will be alerted by tomorrow morning, or Crispin will swear us to secrecy for the rest of our lives.

The lighting inside the bar is uncomfortably yellow-tinged, and dull. The establishment is of medium size, but packed wall to wall so that we have to squirm between patrons. The maids do their best to stay with me, but I quickly lose them.

Within ten seconds, I can hear Mercer's bellowing laugh from a corner. After standing on a chair, I spot Rian not but two feet away from his best friend, grinning and laughing.

I've hopped off the chair and am just about to make my way over to Rian when someone grabs my arm and whirls me around. The only reason I don't stab him in the neck is because this is a highly populated environment and because I can smell a certain cologne that I'm unfortunately far too familiar with.

"*Soleil," Taris* hisses.

"Hel-lo Taris," I say. "Any particular reason you've decided to accost me?"

"What are you doing here?" he demands.

I briefly consider lying to him, but there's no point.

"Crispin has some maids out looking for his sister. He might have reason to want to keep her close. Rian's not on the verge of passing out drunk, I'm assuming?" I add, and Taris grunts.

"They're testing which of them can consume more: Mercer drinking, or Rian eating."

"Idiots," I mutter.

"I agree. And yet, Qhan will keep them from too much trouble. Currently, I believe, they're talking about women."

I snort so hard snot almost comes out. "Well, that's…simply…"

I don't know why I find that idea so laughable. And uncomfortable.

"Hilarious," Taris offers.

"Right, right," I say.

"Why is it hilarious?"

"You're the one who said that. Suggested it," I insist awkwardly.

Taris shrugs. I hate him.

"Oh, and look at that," Taris says. "Your quarry has shown herself."

I turn to see a barefoot Lune wobbling on top of the bar, stumbling down it rather tipsily while several of the closest men cheer her on. Some try to look up her skirt. They want her to sing, given their slurred calls. And she—half-giggling as she starts up—is willing to oblige.

"Wonderful," I groan, prepared to barge through the crowd.

"You want to drag her down? Here?" Taris points out.

I cross my arms and scowl, but am willing to let Lune perform for now, if she must. After, I'll gather up the rest of our maid brigade and get her home, where I'll try and eavesdrop on whatever it is Crispin chides her over.

At first, Lune's singing is what I'd expect: a jaunty tune to send everyone into a celebratory roar. The sound of her voice is enough to quiet the room down, in anticipation, but once she has silence on her side, Lune uses it to transform her song into something lonely, and depressed. Almost a dirge.

And yet, no one heckles her down off the bar. No one insists she sing something different. Everyone listening: those who'd been eyeing her up, Mercer and Rian, Asmer with her friends, the maids, Taris: they're all captivated.

"She's upset about something highly…personal," Taris murmurs, and I glance over at him to see him grimacing.

Every time Lune's voice swells, he looks as if he's in physical pain, and I see he's not the only one reacting this way.

"Why don't I feel it?" I demand.

"You're not a man," Taris grunts, and flinches again when Lune strikes back into her chorus.

"Does it hurt?" I ask Taris, fully prepared to send him away in case Lune means to incapacitate all the men in the room, but Taris shakes his head.

"Not in a way you would understand."

I frown. "You mean it's like getting kicked in the balls?"

"No, it's as if…someone you care for is hurting deeply, so you hurt for them."

That surprises me. I can't think of anything Lune might be hurting over.

Looking to Taris, I wonder if he's the one misinterpreting things. But how could that be, if Lune's using her fluke? Wouldn't he then feel whatever it is she intends for men to feel, when they listen to this song? I don't know the language she's singing in, so the lyrics, at least, are of no help to me.

I glance at Lune, singing her heartbreaking tune with her eyes closed. Then, I flick my eyes back to Taris, and watch him close his watery eyes and shiver; he is not the only man in the crowd to do so. I must be particularly careful to watch him and Korvaan—if Lune notices they are about and puts the pieces of my *khashak* together, I know now she could enchant Taris easily. And he is the stronger-willed of the brothers.

Her fluke is a dangerous one. If not for the catch that she must sing to activate it, and that it does not last long, I'm sure she'd have the entire University under her sway by now.

It's painful to listen for the three minutes or so that she spends singing—or, at least I assume it's only about three minutes, but it feels much longer. Once she's finished, leaving her audience staring off emptily, Lune plucks a drink out of someone's hand for her own consumption. Something in the back of my head tells me I should go up to the bar and pull Lune down despite what Taris and I already agreed, but I'm immobilized, too. I'm not sure if it's melancholy that disables me, but something curious is happening in my head. As if I'm lamenting things I've never seen and mourning deaths that have never happened.

It's Mercer who finally makes it up to the bar and grabs Lune, letting her spill her drink all over him as he throws her over a shoulder to carry her toward the door. Once Lune starts complaining, calling Mercer some rather unkind names, the room suddenly breathes again.

"What in Fate's Fingers was that?" I hiss to Taris.

He's blinking, like he's just come out of a waking dream. There are tear tracks on his cheeks, and he's only one of many.

"I…She…Soleil, I…I'm…" he starts, looking dazed.

"Ugh. Forget it. Watch Rian—" I start, and groan once I catch sight of my crown prince.

Rian, of course, has followed Mercer to the door and is hanging about with Qhan and Asmer while Mercer talks with one of the maids. I wouldn't care, except where Lune goes, now, I also must go. I might have been able to slip away earlier if I managed to prolong the hunt for Lune while I checked on Rian. But I can see the maid near Mercer looking around for the rest of our party, ready to gather us up and leave.

Damn. Damn, damn, damn. And damn Lune, specifically, while I'm at it.

I whirl back to Taris.

"Are you going to be fine, here?" I demand. "Because I've better things to do than babysit the Loon, but it looks like I'm not going to have a choice."

He scoffs. Back to normal Taris again.

"I'm perfectly capable of looking after the little prince," he sneers. "And Korvaan's close. Keeping a watch on the perimeter. No one's getting near him."

"They'd better not," I growl.

By the time I rejoin the rest of the maids, and glance back towards Taris, I find he's gone without a trace. So at least he can get that right. I've no doubt he's making his way out a window, and will tail Rian for the rest of the night. He won't tell Nusk about my being here which, at this point, is for the best. And I doubt Korvaan will be able to pick me out amongst the other maids from above, so long as I keep my hair covered and head down.

I pretend to be listening to the whispered gossip of the other girls as they trade concerned looks. Mercer pays them no heed and is fussing over Lune. He's put her back on her feet and is holding both of her wrists, checking her pulses, but it doesn't look like she'll be able to stay standing for long.

"How much have you had?" Mercer demands once he lets go of her.

Lune sways on her feet and giggles, but it is by no means a joyous sound. "No-o-o," she says, and falls into him. "None," she corrects herself, then amends again when Mercer gives her a serious look. "Not…much."

I catch the sharp look Asmer gives Rian, but I don't know if anyone else does, besides maybe Qhan. Mercer grumbles something to himself that sounds like several curses, and then hefts Lune over a shoulder again heedless of her protests.

"Let's go, then," he says, all but stomping out as the rest of us follow behind in a clustered train. "Rian?"

"Right behind you," he answers, and there is no trace of the Laughing Prince.

Our party slips into the street, the maids clumped together in the middle. I do my best to blend in with them, though I'm curious to hear what Rian and Asmer are muttering about as they trail behind. I won't risk getting any closer to them, but I can turn on my earpiece and eavesdrop that way. It's not hard to catch up to their conversation, given recent events.

"It was pretty, but sad. So *very* sad," Asmer says, her brow crumpled in distress.

Asmer couldn't have felt what Taris did, but she and I still aren't deaf. There's a melancholy over everyone who heard Lune sing, and it was clearly done on purpose. The general levels of mirth in the bar have plummeted as we leave it behind. Conversations have dropped off or lowered into mutters.

"Sad? Depressive, more like," Rian says.

"I'm worried about her," Asmer whispers. "What if she…What if she plans on hurting herself?"

"Lune wouldn't do that," Rian reassures her.

"But how do you know?"

"I'm hoping she wouldn't do that," he's forced to admit.

"I'm going to pray for guidance. And then act," Asmer decides. "She needs some kind of help. I simply don't know what kind, yet."

"You are the sweetest thing, Asmer," Rian sighs. "And a good friend. Look after her well. I appreciate it. I'm sure Crispin does, too."

I appreciate it.

Why would Rian appreciate Asmer looking after Lune any more than anyone else? I try not to let such an innocent comment rankle me, but it's concerning. All I can think of is that *it's Lune: Lune* is the woman that Rian might marry. And regardless of what I've seen to make me pity her, she is a murderer.

The coachman has parked in a designated area to wait for us, and is smoking with several of his fellows. He looks surprised to see us back so soon, and with two of the crown princes in tow, but immediately hurries to accommodate us. He pulls the coach forward and opens the door for Mercer. Lune has long-since stopped giggling, and is on the verge of tears, likely missing her audience. But Mercer doesn't deviate, heading directly up to the carriage step to stuff her inside.

Asmer leans closer to Rian and stands on her tiptoes to whisper to him, but I turn off my earpiece. I'm standing too close to everyone else, now, to risk someone noticing their voice has an echo.

Mercer steps back out of the coach, dusting his hands off, and returns to Rian, already muttering loud enough for me to hear.

"That girl's head is…" He whistles and gestures upwards. "I'd guess at the medications, Rian, but I honestly have no idea."

Rian's eyes widen. *"Medications?"*

Asmer looks horrified.

"Not the sort any doctor I know would prescribe her. I'd have someone tell Crispin," Mercer continues. "Maybe ask someone to search her room."

Asmer presses her lips together tightly. "I'll go with," she offers. "Should I get a doctor in to see her?"

"Not necessary," Mercer says. "But make sure she gets to bed and doesn't take anything else."

He's not as concerned about this as Asmer, who has gone back to biting her fingernails—a bad habit that I'm sure everyone hoped she'd broken years ago; it's not suitable for a lady of her station to show distress in that childish way.

Mercer gets the maids piled into the coach, an event that leaves most of them flushing and tittering, and I can't blame them. Everyone knows Mercer is a tremendous flirt, and it must be special for these girls to get such attention from a prince. It will be something they tell their children one day, reminiscing about the times they were toe-to-toe with royalty.

This time, I'm sent to the back instead of sitting with the driver, which would concern me except Lune is so incapacitated that I highly doubt she'll recognize me. It's cramped in the carriage, but none of the girls are particularly big, and if I sit with my legs crossed, I have just enough personal space. The maids are giggly for a while, watching Rian, Asmer and Mercer talk outside, but once Asmer clambers inside and the driver has set off, they quiet.

I pretend to keep watching out the window, but there's little to see after we leave the city and the lights fade into pinpricks behind us. Two of the maids start whispering about Mercer's ass and think I can't hear them. Asmer picks at the lace overlay of her skirt and keeps glancing at Lune. I can tell she doesn't want to discuss things with Lune in front of us maids, but she can't imagine waiting and running the risk of never getting the chance to talk about it again. After all, who can say tomorrow won't start with Lune curled back up on her bed, sobbing over the person she murdered.

"The song you sang is different than what you usually perform," Asmer finally says, attempting to sound innocently curious while keeping her voice relatively low. As if all us maids aren't listening in for all we're worth. "I can't decide if I liked it or not yet. What's it called?"

"Haven't named it," Lune mumbles, and closes her eyes. "Never will, now."

I watch Asmer's brow furrow. Usually, she's careful not to do that, as she's been concerned about wrinkles after one appeared at the corner of her mouth from smiling too often.

"Why not? Lune? Won't you ever sing it again?"

"No."

"Oh. Is there a reason?" She waits a beat, then continues when Lune says nothing. "Is something the matter? You act as if something is bothering you."

Lune snorts.

"You skipped Mass this morning," Asmer whispers, gently prying. "You never miss Mass. Maybe tomorrow you should go and see if you can talk with—"

"I'm not going again," Lune interrupts, her voice suddenly darker. Huskier. "They can't do anything for me there, anymore."

Asmer quiets. Several maids shoot looks at each other, and I can tell they're trying to decide if this is gossip that they can safely share once they're back in their dormitories, or if they could get dismissed for spreading such things around.

As awkward as it was to listen to Asmer's tactless interrogation, I can't help but wish someone would attempt a proper conversation as we bump through the night back to campus. There are quiet whispers, but nothing to draw Lune out and force her to talk. Considering she's mentally incapacitated if Mercer's assessment of her is correct, this is my best chance to hear her slip.

But drunk Lune is, unfortunately, silent as can be.

Or at least, she's silent for a while. And then, very quietly, she starts humming under her breath. At first, I don't think anything of it and neither does anyone else. But then Lune's humming triggers something in my memories. Something that feels intimately familiar to me, and almost intrusive.

My head jerks away from the window. Lune doesn't notice my gaze, just continues to hum, lost in thought. I attempt to recall where I might know such a tune from, but when I try to delve into my memories, all I find is a pressing headache. It sounds like a lullaby, but I can't identify the song. All I know is that it's painful to hear her hum it, and I want her to stop.

"What is that you are humming?" I demand hoarsely.

Everyone in the coach stares except for Lune, who stops humming, but continues to look out the window while fiddling with that ugly bracelet of hers. She takes her time before finally turning her head to look at me, and when our eyes meet, hers are dull and disinterested. As if it means nothing to her, to have a maid ask such a question of her. And so rudely.

"That song," I repeat. "What is that song—?!"

The coach suddenly jerks to a stop, nearly tossing one of the maids into Lune's lap, and another lurches toward Asmer. I automatically throw my arms out to either side, bracing them against the walls to keep anyone else from being jumbled about. There's no time for apologies as the horses continue to complain, refusing to go any further and reacting poorly when the coachmen attempts to press on.

"Not to worry, ladies!" the coachman calls to us. "The horses are fussy. I'll get them straightened out and we'll be on our way presently!"

But I can tell from his tone that this is a pacifying statement. The coachman has no idea what is wrong with the horses any more than I might. We can hear him trying to soothe them, growing frustrated as the horses refuse to go forward.

"What's wrong with them?" one of the girls asks, terrified.

I force myself through the full carriage, grateful to be close to one of the exits. The door jams slightly when I try to open it, but by putting my shoulder into it, I manage to swing it open and jump down.

"Driver!" I call, squinting to try and let my eyes adjust to the dark, which is difficult with the two lanterns at the head of the coach. "What's wrong? Why are they acting up? It's bothering their ladyships."

"Terribly sorry, miss," the coachman says. "They're usually very good horses. Swear by Hope's Head. Never act up."

"Can't say that anymore," I mutter, and jump out of the way to avoid getting my toes squished. "You've no idea what's causing this?"

"None at all! Not unless by some chance there's something ahead, but there are no dangerous animals on this road."

I frown into the dark. Curious. The coachman clearly has no idea what to do, but his talk of wild animals has got me thinking. Perhaps there's something the horses can smell up ahead that we can't. Something that makes them nervous.

"What is it?" one of the maids asks, poking her head out of the window.

"Should we be concerned?" Asmer asks.

I realize neither Lune nor Asmer have proper security with them. Lune, obviously, slipped out on her own, but I have to wonder about Asmer. She's not exactly royalty, but her father is lord and warden of the southern border. The al'Yibna family holds significant importance to the country, and the lady would make an excellent hostage. Or worse.

Protecting Asmer and Lune is hardly my responsibility, but if something happens to either of them it will complicate my work. Regardless of what I think of them, Rian cares for them both. And I'm not heartless. I wouldn't wish to see either of them harmed.

"Stay with the coach," I say, throwing the door closed.

Before anyone can argue, I flick a knife down into my hand and head out to see what waits ahead.

The further I get from the coach, the darker the night becomes, until the sounds of the horses fade and the lights disappear from sight. Despite my care to keep quiet, the night is so still that I can faintly hear my own footsteps. Perhaps I'm only noticing because I'm listening for it, but it makes me feel obtuse, and painfully conspicuous.

A drop of water drips slowly onto a stone somewhere, which I let annoy me because my only other option is to let fear creep in. I hate to admit how eerie my surroundings feel, and how I'm starting to wish I had Korvaan or Taris with me. I'm perfectly capable of looking after myself, but it might be nice to have one of them watching my back. Or perhaps I could have left them with the coach, to keep an eye on things.

After a few minutes of walking, and trying not to let the darkness spark the more gruesome side of my imagination, I start to feel silly. I don't see anything that might frighten the horses. In fact, perhaps they've calmed while I've been away, and my party is waiting for me to return so we can be off again.

But then I hear it: a strange, moist snick-snacking noise. And then a low sort of grunt, or a snarl.

It takes me a while to recognize the sound of *gnawing.*

I freeze. I don't dare turn back or advance, but try to focus my eyes on the road ahead, to see the thing ahead of me. It's only then that I realize why it's so difficult for me to see: there's no moon tonight. All I can do is stand there in horror and listen to the grotesque, moist slurping sounds of something feeding in the night. Occasionally, there's a series of crunches: *bones.*

Against my better judgment, I begin to creep forward, towards it. I don't get a good look, but I do identify that this creature is no wild animal that I'm familiar with—magical or otherwise. It appears to have wings, and claws, and long, sharp teeth. Most importantly, it is much, much bigger than me.

"Fate's Fingers," I whisper, taking a few stumbling steps backwards.

At the sudden sound, the creature stops devouring its prey. Its head jerks up, and I can hear it sniffing about. There's a series of clicking noises.

I force myself to stay calm. I don't dare move, and barely breathe, praying that it does not notice me. Never in my life have I felt such fear, and I'm unaccustomed with how it takes over my body. It makes me feel weak, my mind muddled and useless.

It's such a relief when I hear the thing go back to its meal that all I can do is turn and run. My footsteps are quick and quiet, from practice, but I'm certain if I were anyone else, the thing would have taken notice of me and given chase.

The pressure in my chest eases when I see the lights from the carriage.

"There's another path we can take, but we'll have to go back some ways and it will be a longer journey—" the coachman starts as I approach.

"Take it. Now," I demand, tucking my knife back in place and throwing open the door to the carriage.

I've startled the girls inside, but I don't care. I can't risk the driver forcing the horses to carry this gift basket of desserts into the claws of that monster.

Some of the girls ask what I saw, if anything, while the coachman turns the horses about. Lune has gone back to staring out the window. Asmer is pale and practically shaking, her breathing irregular. I wonder absently what time it is, and when she last took her medicine, but it is less of my concern than the present dangers to our party.

"Nothing," I force myself to say, attempting to brighten my tone. "There's nothing. But if the horses are spooked, best to go the long way. We can't stay out on the road all night."

That suits most of them, enough that they tease the others about worrying so much. Even Asmer is nodding to herself, though I can see a small statue of the Vushan goddess of good fortune gripped in her tiny hands. She carries her patron goddess in her pocket, as all who follow Vushan do, but almost never brings it out publicly. Clearly this occasion merits fervent prayer.

Eventually, she returns it to her skirt pocket, likely telling herself that these things happen, and it hardly matters what startled the horses so long as we return to the campus safely.

But Lune is glancing at me out of the corner of her eyes. She doesn't change her expression, or even blink. Nor does she avert her gaze when she notices I've seen her. She simply stares at me, almost in accusation. As if she might have forgotten about the incident with her humming, but she still wants me to know for a fact that *she knows what I saw.*

Seven

IT'S BEEN SEVERAL dull days since Lune's impromptu concert, and though I had hoped to discover something interesting in the days since, I've gathered precious little. The so-called important dignitary arrived: a representative from the Currian Council who spoke to each prince here to make them aware of the preparations involved for Comus Day. I found his presence irritating, as the matrons had every maid working overtime to keep the University spotless. I suppose they feared the king might not continue to fund this place so generously if he thought Magnus's living conditions unsuited to his station.

It's the thirty-ninth day of summer. Comus Day is a little over a month away, which feels both too close and too far. I'm itching for some excitement, even if it's just Rian bringing in some sort of magical creature for his classes to stare at. I'm sure there are several types of fairies who'd happily volunteer—they love the attention—but I don't think the University would allow it. They do have some rules Rian must follow.

It's a sweltering, humid day, and the approach of evening hasn't done much to help. Most formal clothing save for gloves have been abandoned. Classes have been canceled, and everyone aside from the guards has been given the day off. It is unbearably hot out. Almost everyone has found some body of water to lounge in, or sought out someone with a useful fluke for cooling off. Rian has filled his bathtub with cold water and ice for Mango to splash around in all day, only coming out when necessary. Even Asmer, who is as demure and modest as can be, has donned a dress made out of light material that swishes around her legs when she leans from side to side.

I've had to abandon my maid's costume in favor of something more casual: cropped, loose trousers and a sleeveless, shortened top piece that helps keep me from sweating through my clothes completely.

As a hot, sleepless night approaches, campus fails to wind down. Students who live in the city or with parents haven't bothered to come in today, but there are still plenty of students of all ages trying to entertain themselves while staying cool. It's almost too hot to eat, but there are ice drinks and cold cream sweets thanks to the University. Some children are running around with giant, dragon-wing kites flying behind them, creating a manufactured breeze.

Rian is dozing off under a tree with Mercer and a bottle of fruity chilled wine.

Naomi has volunteered, along with a handful of others, to make sure no one overheats and collapses. Taris is trading shifts with me so I can take an hour's nap to combat the drowsiness of the heat, and Korvaan is on shift with his regular guard's duties.

I'm heading to Nusk's cabin to check on him when I notice a gaggle of folk heading in the same direction, as if surging to take a look at an exhibit. At first, I don't think anything of it, until I realize they're moving towards the infirmary.

I reassure myself it's impossible for Rian to be the one injured. I saw him only minutes ago, at the orchard with Mercer.

And yet, I worry.

I follow the crowd as quickly as I can without warranting suspicion. I try to catch snatches of conversation as I go, but the blood is pounding too loudly in my ears. I'm not sure why I'm so nervous—or why I don't go check under the tree again if I'm so concerned about Rian's well-being. But perhaps there is something else driving me towards the infirmary. Something more instinctive.

I'm about to dive into the crowd when someone grabs my elbow and yanks me backward. N'omi. I'd lecture her about startling me like that, but at this point I think it's just something all my *khashak* are going to torture me with.

"What are you doing here? You should be trying to rest!" Naomi's insisting. Her words sound like she's shouting them to me underwater.

I gesture to the crowd. "What…Why?"

"Oh, you hadn't heard?" Naomi says.

"Heard what?"

"Lady Lune is hurt," Naomi reports. "Some say she fell down the stairs. Others say she was pushed…"

I think of the last angry letter Crown Prince Magnus Oram sent her.

I think of the last time I saw the two together. How he'd grabbed her, and threatened her, and she'd cut him.

I think about the fact that she's killed someone.

"I would not find that surprising," I say.

I raise my watch to my mouth. By now, Rian and Mercer may have heard the rumors and moved from their idyllic spot under the tree. I need to make sure Qhan escorts them back to their rooms. I'm sure he would, and ignore their protests, so long as he's aware of what's going on. But if he doesn't, I'm going to need Taris to intervene.

Regardless of whether it was Magnus or not, if someone's killing off nobles, I need to make sure they aren't planning to go after Rian next.

"Taris, eyes on Rian?" I ask.

Strangely, there's no answer. Taris wouldn't ignore me. Not over something this important.

"Taris, can you see Rian?" I repeat, and then wait.

Nothing.

"Is something wrong?" N'omi asks. "Is the watch not working?"

"It's working fine. Taris—"

"Is he all right?" Naomi interrupts.

"I don't know," I admit, still pressing buttons on my watch. "Wherever he is right now, I don't think he's with Rian."

But I saw him change shifts with me. Which means that in the few minutes it took me to get from Rian to Naomi, something happened. To Taris, to Rian; who knows. It's my job to find out, and attempt damage control.

Naomi bites her lip, moving from concern to fear. "Soleil, you don't think—"

"Not now," I say. "Go get Korvaan to join me; we need to find Rian and make sure he's safe. Then we'll worry about your brother."

Before dashing off again, it occurs to me that I can't have Naomi panicking on me. Not now.

"N'omi," I start, taking hold of her arm in a way that I hope is somewhat reassuring. Or at least something a sibling would do. "Don't worry. Taris can more than look after himself. I'm sure he's fine."

In fact, I suspect the reason he hasn't responded to me is because he's gotten distracted and made the horrible assumption that he wouldn't be missed at his post for an hour on a day like today. When I do find him, I'm going to wring his neck. And maybe go to Nusk to see what I can do about banning Taris from women. At least for a few months.

Naomi thinks too highly of her older brother to consider such things. She hesitates, then forces a nod. If I were better with words, I might have stayed longer and attempted to calm her down. But I never know what to say in times like these, and I don't have the time to spare. So, yet again, Naomi suffers for it. Not fair of me, I know. But there will be time for apologies later. I hope.

The crowd in front of the infirmary has grown significantly. They're currently banned from entering, but that doesn't stop them from whispering nervously, spreading the rumor: Lady Lune is dead. Her injury turned out to be far worse than suspected. She really was pushed down the stairs. Someone has killed her. Perhaps on accident, but even so.

I hate to sound callous, in case Lune really is dead, but I have no time for idle gossip. The obvious answer is that Lune was working for someone, and either Magnus killed her out of anger or her employer recently found her redundant. Regardless, I need to reach Rian, and fast.

Damn you, Taris. If you wanted me to fail so badly, why not just push me down some stairs? But for the love of the Almighty, do your job and duty to Rian, you coward.

I rush straight back to the tree, but Mercer and Rian are gone. The news about Lune may have made them move, or they happened to get up in the past ten minutes to lounge elsewhere, or something has gotten to them. I try my watch again, but there is no response. I suspect that Taris has taken it off. It would take a miracle, at this point, to locate him. I focus instead on Rian, and scroll through his usual haunts.

But I can't find him.

I have lost the true heir, rightful heir—whatever you want to call him, he is the most important person in the world, and I've lost him.

Nusk is going to kill me. I'm going to kill Taris.

I'm hurrying down a covered hallway, abandoned at this point in the day, when someone whistles. There's no one else around, so the sound is directed at me, as if to try and get my attention.

I whirl to see someone stepping out from behind one of the pillars, a good distance behind me, as if wary of me. Someone with a grain of sense, then.

I'm startled when I recognize him.

The albino man.

I knew I hadn't imagined him. And I knew I couldn't trust him.

I look him over as carefully as I can, to commit his appearance to memory, but for some reason, I struggle. I can only recall his most obvious features: his albinism, a slight figure, his height only about equal to my own. Physically, he's less a threat than Rian, and certainly much less so compared to, say, Taris. He's also startlingly young—perhaps only twenty.

Yet, something tells me to be wary. Something tells me he is dangerous.

He sighs. "You're going to have to try and do better than this, Soleil," he says. Disappointed.

I flick one of my knives out. "Who are you? What do you want?"

"There's no point in telling you," he claims. "Honestly. You'll only be angry, and no one wants to upset you, Soleil. Least of all, me."

I tighten my grip. "Allow me to clarify: answer my questions or bleed."

"You won't hurt me," he says.

"Want to bet your life on that?" I snap.

"I have before," he says, which tells me something at least. And then he grins, a tortured, mocking thing. "Besides, you can't kill anyone you know more than a few minutes, not even to save your own life. Only strangers you tell yourself don't matter."

"I'll bleed anyone I consider a threat to my principal," I hiss.

"Oh? Let's test that…Goodbye, Soleil. We'll see each other again, soon."

He's about to step behind the pillar again, and vanish. I don't plan on letting him. But plans so often go awry.

"Soleil," a deep voice says from behind me.

The hair on my arms stands up for a moment, but I recognize the voice, and his ability to sneak up on me, and make myself relax.

"Taris. *What* in the hell have you—" I start as I turn, but cut myself off.

It is Taris standing just a few feet from me, but something is undeniably wrong with this picture. There's a dagger in his hands. A redness around his dead eyes. He looks strangely whitish—no, grey. His muscles shake, but when he speaks, his voice doesn't. It's hatred that I sense and hear from him, and though little frightens me, this does.

"What are you doing? Taris…?"

I take a small, hesitant step away, putting my weight on my back foot.

"I'd say I'm sorry for this," he says callously. "But I'm not."

I don't know why I don't attack first. I should. I have every reason to believe that Taris is going to hurt me, and yet I have trouble forcing myself to try and kill him first. Even when he lunges, my first instinct is to run, not use the knife in my fist. I'm stumbling backwards, confused.

It takes until Taris cuts open my cheek for me to realize that he's not going to stop. He's *going to kill me.* He might have also already hurt Rian.

When Taris comes at me again, I fight back.

Unfortunately, since his knife is already out, I'm starting at a disadvantage. Disarming techniques are much easier to perform when an opponent is pulling a weapon or trying to conceal one. If I want that knife out of his hands, I have to get in close.

When he goes to stab me, I surprise him by dropping my own knife, slipping to the side, and grabbing his wrist. I use his own momentum. Spin, pull him forward, drive my knee into his face. Drop him to the ground on his knees.

Part of me hesitates after that, hoping that a knee to the face and a bloody nose will free Taris from whatever spell he's under. I don't want to take things further than this, and I'd rather have him by my side. I have his knife in my hand, and could easily stab him, but I wait a second, and then it's too late.

Taris is back on his feet, lurching forward to tackle me. Again, I let momentum control the fight, and roll backward over my head the second my shoulders hit the ground. I get up to a crouch before him and whirl, his own knife held tightly in my fist. I go on the offensive and slash at him, backing him up to control the distance between us.

I try to think up a good place to stick him that won't end lethally, but it's like trying to fight against my own instincts.

I forgo the knife and fling it away; better for neither of us to have it. And I have extra, if I need them. Instead, I use the pressure chambers at my wrist to try and hit him with the poisoned darts. He's accustomed to this type of poison, but it should still cause nasty complications. If I hit Taris in the right spot, it won't kill him, but it'll make him sick, and hopefully take him out of the fight.

Taris notices what I'm about to do and rolls behind one of the pillars so that my darts ping off the marble. I'm sure I've got him, now, until I remember that Taris has projectile weapons as well, and his are a little more lethal.

Standard issue weapons for the university guards: *guns.*

I find cover of my own behind one of the pillars just in time and reload my pressure chambers while Taris wastes his rounds. If he wants to engage in this game, I can play. I catch sight of the albino still hovering behind a pillar of his own, on the same side of the walkway as me, and shoot a few darts at him, too. I don't hit him, but at least he's trapped behind one of the pillars. And so long as he's still around, he can't be hurting Rian.

When there's a pause in the shooting, and I break from cover to try and dash across and take Taris by surprise, I find that he had the same idea. And he's right in front of me.

Taris grabs my wrist, squeezing at the pressure chamber until we both hear a crunch. I in turn grip the front of his uniform and slam him backwards against a pillar. In an ideal world, this would have been enough to force him to release me and I'd be able to slip away and reassess.

Instead, he grabs the front of my top at my shoulders and pushes back, so I'm slammed against the pillar behind me and get the breath knocked out of me.

I kick at the button on one of my heels and out comes my boot knife. Taris releases me, and I scramble to get some distance between us again. But then I'm moving in the wrong direction. I've been flung backward onto the walkway again, and I realize that Taris managed to grab my hair.

The next thing I know, Taris has me pinned on my back and my arms against my sides. I'd buck my hips to throw him off, but he knows this move. He has his ankles locked together under my legs, so he's more stable. I can't flip him.

He also knows I'm weak when pinned on my back. It's the hardest position for me to escape from, especially when my opponent is heavier than I am.

We're both panting. I glare at him. He has me pinned, but he's hesitating.

"Taris," I hiss. "You bastard. I swear, if you don't let me go, I'll—"

The hesitation's gone. He wraps his hands around my throat and presses. I immediately forget how I'm supposed to react to being strangled and start to panic. Because in all our training, it was always someone unknown trying to choke me out. An enemy. Someone I wouldn't mind gutting. Stabbing in the throat. Slicing open their face.

Unfortunately, the albino man was right: it's not the same, when it's Taris.

I struggle, and finally remember to tilt my head back, to try and suck in air. I manage to wriggle a hand free and scramble for my knife—I'm sure it's fallen around here someplace. But I can't find it.

I can hear my own urgent attempts at breathing, my involuntary noises of panic. I can't force my voice to work. It feels as if my mind has been split in half; part of me is trying to decide what to do next, how to free myself, and how to keep Rian safe. The other half can do nothing but scream *WHY, WHY, WHY, WHY, NO, NO, NO, NO.*

And then, through it all, comes a cold, dreaded realization: Taris is stronger than me. He is faster than me. He has me solidly pinned. I am going to die.

That albino man is going to stand there and watch, and Taris is going to kill me. My vision becomes spotty. My chest feels tensed to explode and there's a headache pulsing at my temples as if all the blood in my body is pooling there. I realize my arm has fallen dead against the ground and is no longer helping me fight. As if it's gone to sleep already. Admitted defeat.

I'm not ready to give up.

But my body is.

I AWAKE WITH A START, my forehead damp with sweat, the night still dark around me. This is the second time I've woken, but after the first, I was so exhausted, and so relieved to be back in my own bed, that I drifted back to sleep instantly. I can't know for sure how long I've been out, but it's memories of prior terror that force me awake once more. My heart beats so fast it's painful. In an instant, my watch is to my mouth, my finger on the button.

"Taris," I rasp.

"Your crown prince is fine," Taris replies dryly. I flinch to hear his voice, but at least he sounds normal again. Not that monster from my dream. "He's flirting with Asmer and Lune at the night pool. His bodyguards are close. Mercer and Crispin are with them."

I frown and check my watch face.

"This late?"

"No one ever said any of them had common sense."

"Wait, Lune is there?" I say, allowing my brow to crease. Because the last I'd heard, she was hurt and possibly dead.

"Unless she's got a sister I don't know about."

"How long has she been there?"

"A few minutes. Why does it matter?"

I've managed to slow my breathing properly. I need time to think, to consider what all this means. What's happened.

"Stay alert," is all I say to Taris, and then let the line go dead.

For a few moments, I allow myself to do nothing but breathe. There's still a pounding in the front of my scalp, and a tightness in my chest.

I look around: I'm in my dormitory room, with Naomi. It's a little past two in the morning, and I've barely slept. The fake-day I experienced in my dream, with Lune's death and Taris' attack, has exhausted me, and I want nothing more than a solid twelve hours of sleep.

There will be time for that later.

I jump down from my bed. It's not the sound that wakes Naomi, because I'm quiet as a cat. But she must have sensed there's something wrong. By the time I start to dress, I hear a quiet and tentative, "Soleil?".

"Not now, N'omi," I say shortly. "Go back to sleep."

"Why are you up?" she asks drowsily.

"What day is it?" I demand. If she's going to insist on being up, the least Naomi can do is be a little helpful.

"The…thirty-seventh day of summer?" Naomi offers, partially confirming my original suspicions.

In my dream, it had been the thirty-ninth.

"Is Lady Lune dead?" I go on.

Naomi raises an eyebrow. "What are you talking about? Are you feeling well?"

I let out a slow breath. So, Lune's death wasn't real. That was something I dreamed of, possibly because of my distaste for her; I'm not ashamed to admit it.

"Did she perform, though?" I press. "Sing some dreary song a few nights ago that had Taris and Rian and practically every other man there teary-eyed?"

Naomi frowns. "Yes? Taris said it was painful to listen to."

"And a representative from the king has been here?"

"Yes. For the past few days. What's going on? Soleil?"

So, then. That, at least, had been real.

I blow out a slow breath and scrunch my hair up in my hands. I need to sort this out. I need to think.

This is the second dream sequence when something strange has happened: the first, the third-worst case for a *Khashtani*. Rian had "discovered" me and was in "love" with me. Second worst scenario*:* Taris, my *khashak,* betraying me.

I'm worried that, in a last scenario, Rian will die, and I won't be able to tell if it's real or not.

"Soleil?" N'omi says again, nervously, as if she thinks I've lost my mind.

Then again, I'm making an assumption. I don't know that the albino man's goal is to kill Rian. I'm just not sure why he'd be hanging about the University if it wasn't. He might want to kidnap Rian. Or force him to become king, and then manipulate him, using him like a pawn. A husk.

I suppose it's all the same in the end: he's still a threat to Rian. He needs to be stopped. And he did appear at the same time as those other assassins, which means my safest bet is to assume for now that he does mean Rian physical harm.

Whether I like it or not, there is one member of my *khashak* most prepared to help prevent physical attacks on Rian. One member who I, ironically, think I can trust, because as his brother once said, it's almost like the two of us compete to see who can protect Rian best.

Time to don a little humility.

"Soleil, is something wrong?" Naomi asks, as if afraid of my answer.

"I don't know, yet," I say.

I throw on the rest of my clothes and tie back my maid's veil, wrapping up my hair.

"I need to talk with Taris," I tell her sharply. *"Alone."*

Naomi's startled, but nods. "I'll wake Korvaan. And see what we can do. Should I tell Nusk?"

"Don't worry him. It's personal," I lie quickly.

She frowns. "But nothing's personal for—"

"I need Taris to needle me. I'm having some health issues. Now, go get him."

"Oh. Yes, I'll…I'll go now."

She runs off, and I instantly regret being so curt. But given my last exchange with her and her father, I can't trust Naomi not to go straight to Nusk with whatever I say about the albino man. I don't know why this man is manipulating me, but his motives are clearly different than any previous assassin's. If I do as Nusk asks and simply catch and deliver him, I might never get the chance to speak with him myself. And Nusk will never tell me what he uncovers.

That means this is something I must do without most of my *khashak*. And, unfortunately, the only one of them I can truly trust right now is Taris.

With Korvaan taking over for his brother, and Naomi giving him my hasty excuse about illness, I'll have about an hour with Taris before suspicions fester amongst my own *khashak*. We can't break into the infirmary at this hour, and I don't dare head to Nusk's cabin in case he overhears something he shouldn't. So, I have Taris meet me in one of the empty classrooms, where we can speak privately with no prying eyes or pricked ears.

Taris is hard to read when he joins me. He's brought his kit, with a variety of materials he usually uses for needling, and is so quick that he's half unpacked before I can open my mouth. I'd appreciate his efficiency if not for the fact that it's of no current use.

"Don't bother. I don't need the needles," I claim, and Taris looks exasperated, but curiosity can't quite beat out his desire to say something snarky.

"Then what is this about? And what was that check-up of yours earlier? Do you really not trust me to look after the prince—?"

"I had a nightmare that you tried to kill me," I interrupt.

Taris blinks. "Well. Then. Nice to know what you think of me, Soleil."

I bristle. Leave it to Taris to take this so personally.

"I'm not trying to pick a fight," I finally make myself say.

"Why else tell me?"

I force myself not to snap. I take a deep breath in and let it out, reminding myself over and over: I need Taris. I might not like it, but I do. I have to tell him this, and try to uphold our partnership. For Rian's sake.

"Because I've been thinking about Fars'day," I say. "About the assassins. I think one of them has a fluke related to dreams, and I think I somehow let him get away. A Dream Walker. Or Nightmare Feeder, I'm not sure. But ever since, my nightmares, my dreams, they are so much like reality, I can hardly tell them apart."

Taris raises an eyebrow at me. "And you're sure this isn't Rian using his fluke?" he asks, which is something I've considered.

I shake my head. "If he did, he'd be rewriting time. I wouldn't remember it," I point out. "And besides: he'd have no reason to do it when you 'attacked' me. He wouldn't even know it was happening. Or have any sort of motive to rewrite all of history to help me: all he'd see was a guard murdering a maid. Tragic, maybe, but not worth changing the past over."

Taris looks at me, then begins to slowly repack his things.

"I see," he says after a long while.

"What?" I demand, sure he's mocking me.

Taris snaps his bag shut.

"Nothing. I'm only surprised you're trusting me with this. Pleased," he admits. "But…surprised."

I narrow my eyes at him. "Why would you be surprised?"

But Taris sighs. "And that: that's exactly my point," he says, gesturing to me. "You're suspicious of everyone, Soleil. Even us. You barely tell me more than you think I need to know. It's annoying."

"Annoying?" I repeat. "Oh, so sorry I'm irritating you in doing my job–"

"Our job," Taris corrects sharply.

It's the anger in his tone that keeps me from continuing.

"You might be the *Khashtani* for the prince," he snaps, "but don't make the mistake of thinking that makes you the one and only person trying their damnedest to keep him alive."

I try to keep glaring at him until he says something else, but I can't manage it.

"Why should you care about Rian?"

"Why do you?" he challenges, and that startles me. "Why do you allow yourself emotional attachment to him, and use your twenty-years' sentry as an excuse, but refuse to recognize the rest of us may feel the same?"

Deep down in the depths of my wit, I might have a good answer, but I can't think of it straightaway. And then Taris is talking again—well, ranting, really—and my opportunity is lost.

"Think about me, Soleil, and ask yourself: do you really think I do any of this out of loyalty to you?"

I give him a look. "I know you don't."

Rather than rise to my bait, Taris soldiers on with a rare sort of passion in his tone. "Rian is a good man. A good prince. One of the few people who can be given power and not be corrupted by it."

I'm wary of what he's hinting at. "Rian cannot be king. Your father's said as much, and is most insistent we agree."

Taris hesitates for far too long, and then looks away from me and shrugs.

"You think otherwise?" I challenge.

"I think we should consider all our options with care."

We both wait a beat.

"Well?" Taris prompts.

"Well, what?"

"Do you agree. It's not necessarily the end of the world if Rian happens to become king. In fact, it might be easier if he were."

His suggestion makes me uncomfortable, because it goes against something I thought was known. No matter how many mysteries sprang up and how overly complicated my job became, at least I knew one sure goal was to keep Rian from the throne. Even if I wavered back and forth on it from time to time, since Rian seems to have no desire to be king, it was an easy goal to maintain.

It's one thing to question the possibility—to argue with Nusk about allowing Rian to do what he wants, if he wants it. It's another to do what Taris is suggesting, which is to actively ensure Rian is crowned.

"Never mind," Taris sighs before I can open my mouth. "We'll deal with that later. I suppose this new threat to Rian is of more importance?"

"Oh. Yes. Definitely," I agree, feeling strangely relieved.

"This 'assassin with a fluke over dreams'," Taris muses. "At least, that's what you've assumed?"

"That's what I've concluded considering the circumstances and the evidence."

"And you're positive that these are merely dreams?" he asks again.

"Don't laugh," I warn him, thought I already know he will. "But in the first one, before he threw me out the window, Rian knew who I was—and he pushed me up against a wall and kissed me."

Taris hesitates for what feels like a long time. Then he laughs. The bastard.

"Shut up. I don't want to hear about this again, understand?"

"Yes, your highness," he snickers.

I give him a glowering look, and he sobers.

"Look, I wouldn't have said anything if it wasn't relevant," I insist. "The fact that these two 'dream sequences' have been related to the worst things that could happen to a *Khashtani* implies something even worse down the road."

Taris is smart enough to guess. "This assassin of yours wants to kill his target without risking his own life by getting close to you. If he can disorient you enough with these…false worst-case scenarios, you're going to make a real mistake. Allow an opening to Rian. And that's all a cowardly assassin need."

"I can't stand these fluke dreams, and this has only been the second time," I hiss in irritation. I'm half-tempted to threaten not to draw the penance cross on his forehead when I end his life, but I know that will irritate Taris.

If only Rian knew about me. If only I were allowed to speak with him, we could avoid assassins forever and a day, traveling through time. But I know I cannot. Beyond what the rules of the *Khashtani* state, it is taboo to reveal a hidden fluke to someone who has not yet discovered their power. And I have no way of knowing if Rian is aware of who he is or what he is capable of. Oh, he surely has some idea, given what his parents must have told him, but…From what I've seen of him, I don't think he truly understands his destiny.

"So?" Taris prompts, making me realize I've suddenly fallen silent. "What do you want to do?"

I'm almost certain this is the first time Taris has ever sincerely asked for my advice. The first time he's admitted that, in a way, I am his superior. I'm surprised to find that it doesn't make me feel particularly good about myself. Only relieved that I can at least trust Taris to do what's right, even if he hates me.

"We'll need to find a way to help me determine what is real and what's not," I say. "And it will have to work for the both of us, in case this fluke dreamer assassin he targets you, too."

"I'm not too worried about a star-crossed lovers' fantasy with the crown prince tripping me up," Taris says wryly.

"Well, he won't use that, then, will he?" I snap. "We need to be careful, now, Taris. Whoever is doing this must know about Rian's powers. They must know enough to want me to think that Rian's rewriting time, to confuse me. Make me forget to look for him, like you said—"

"You know it's a man?" Taris interrupts.

"An albino man. I think," I admit. "I told your father as much, but—"

I stop myself and frown, remembering how Nusk had promised me he would fill in Naomi and Taris himself.

"But he didn't tell you," I mutter half to myself, suddenly suspicious.

These suspicions, however, are not directed at Taris. Much as it pains me to admit, even to myself, it's his father I'm worried I can't trust. As much of a bastard as Taris can be, at least he's never lied to me. That brutal honesty isn't always appreciated, but he's not a liar.

Nusk told me he'd warn Naomi and Taris about the albino man.

He hasn't.

Only he, me, and Korvaan know, and Korvaan wouldn't dare breathe a word of it if his father told him not to. He's too loyal. Too obedient. Too well-trained as a *khashak*.

"What's your point, Soleil?" Taris sighs.

"I think your father's hiding something," I blurt.

I immediately regret it, assuming that this will insult Taris, in a way—this is his father I'm accusing, after all. Instead, he rolls his eyes.

"Excellent, Soleil. Your epiphany is the exact thing that I've known forever."

I scowl. "Well, it isn't as if you've bothered to tell me. Or warn me."

"How could I know you wouldn't immediately report to Nusk?" Taris points out. "How could I assume you'd pick an allegiance with me over him?"

It's annoying when he makes good points like this.

"Fine," I say. "Let's start over, here: now you can trust me, and I can trust you. Everyone else is on a separate tier, at least for now, agreed?"

Taris grunts and nods. I'll take that as a yes.

"As far as I'm concerned, Nusk and his secrets are a secondary concern so long as they pose no immediate threat to Rian, and I don't think they do. Would you agree with that assessment?" I ask.

"I would."

"Then we'll keep an eye out for anything we find suspicious from him, and I'll casually attempt to probe him for answers when I can," I suggest. "He'll suspect me less than you."

"He thinks you're naïve," Taris agrees.

I'm not too surprised to hear that, but it still hurts.

"So, we're looking for an albino man with a fluke relating to dream manipulation," Taris says. "And a powerful fluke, at that."

"And a fluke that works well over distance, without having to touch the victim," I add. "It's not a lot to go off of, I know, but…"

"But how many albino men are in Isaaria," he finishes for me.

"Exactly."

"I'll be on the lookout," he grunts.

"Don't tell your father I've told you about the albino," I warn. "Really, Taris. Don't. It will exasperate him."

In the seconds he makes me wait for him to respond, I'm worried that I've made a mistake with that. But his facial muscles don't even twitch.

"I wouldn't worry," he says. "This wouldn't be the first secret I've kept from Nusk…Now what?"

"Now, you watch for an albino, and keep a special eye on those Rian hangs around. I'm certain if he's going to be betrayed, it will be by someone close to him. Once we're nearer to Comus Day, we'll be able to investigate the other crown princes, and the princess, but for now, we'll focus on the Carsans, Mercer, Magnus, and Asmer."

"The Carsans?" Taris repeats. "Wouldn't they have the least motive of all? Crispin can't be king—"

"That's assuming the crown is what Rian's enemies are after," I say. "And while they could be, we don't know that yet. So, report to me on everything you see that looks suspicious. From any of them."

Taris hesitates, but nods. "We'll take it a day at a time, then," he agrees. "And Soleil: I do appreciate you trusting me," he adds.

He sounds remarkably sincere.

"You're welcome," I say, then clear my throat and check my watch. "Well, then. I think we have another half-hour to waste here for the sake of convincing Korvaan and N'omi that you're needling me."

"Maybe I should," Taris offers. "To pass the time."

But he's already packed everything up, and as he hasn't offered any medical assessment of why he should needle me, I decline. I hop up onto one of the students' worktables instead, my legs dangling down as I prepare to settle in and wait. Taris leans against the wall near the door and crosses his arms.

I try to think up a conversation topic I could entertain with Taris, the same way I might his brother, but nothing comes to mind. The sorts of things Korvaan and I speak about in jest, I feel as if Taris wouldn't understand. He'd take things too seriously, or find the entire conversation trivial. I know Korvaan said Taris likes Rian's stories, but after several minutes of trying to think up an introduction for such a topic, I decide I'd feel awkward discussing fiction with Taris.

There's something too real about him. Something too physical. Taris, to me, has not a speck of fantasy in his head. He's not a dreamer, or an optimist, or the sort of person drawn to any distractions that aren't, again, physical.

So instead of asking him why his favorite tale is "Of Crow and the Death", or what he thinks of Magicsmiths and the Families Three, or if he's ever felt tempted by the wandering quests heroes always seem to venture on, I say nothing. So, Taris says nothing. And we languish in silence.

Fate's Fingers, but we must be damned depressing to be around.

After another twenty minutes, we decide enough is enough and head out of the classroom again. Naturally, that's around the time that I think of something I want to know about Taris. Something that I think I could ask him without upsetting him, that I already have an answer from Naomi for.

"Taris, what do you want in this world?" I ask as I hover in the doorway.

Taris hesitates. I suppose this is a more complex question than I'd thought, because it takes him quite some time to answer. When he does speak, he sounds aggressive. I thought we'd managed to get past that, but perhaps not yet.

"I want the people I love to be safe. And I'll do anything to achieve that. It's all I care about," he says sharply, and this surprises me.

I would have thought, for sure, he would say something along the lines of leaving his family and me far behind and never thinking of us ever again. After all, though he might soften around his siblings, from what I can tell, there is little love lost between me and Taris, or Taris and Nusk.

Eight

"YOU NEED TO take better care of yourself, little cub," Nusk's gruff voice wakes me. I groan and rub my eyes while checking my watch: quarter to six. Damn. I must have stumbled back to Nusk's cabin and fallen asleep after my late-night conversation with Taris. Poor N'omi: she must be wondering where in the world I went.

"But, even more important: you must keep sharp," I hear Nusk add.

The next thing I know, he's hooked a cane around one of my ankles and yanked. Nusk might be chair-bound, but he's kept his arms mightily strong, and the force is more than enough to pull me straight out of the loft.

I manage to land in a crouch, but it's not my favorite way to wake up in the morning. Nusk used to do it to me all the time, back when I was training: sporadically, and without warning.

"N'omi told you I had trouble sleeping last night," I guess as I rise and stretch.

"Mmm. It is not only last night. She's told me you have not been the same for quite some time, now. Since around the time Mercer Ralhan returned. You're not as sloppy as I feared, but still: you are distracted," Nusk lectures.

"I'm fine," I insist, pulling my hair back. "Only—"

"If you are about to make an excuse, then you are not 'fine'," Nusk lectures. "There is no such thing as a mistake for us. We cannot be sloppy. Cannot be drowsy. Cannot fall into the routines that our principals do. To allow such a thing is to invite disaster, and I know that is not your intent."

He's probing to see if I've done as he asked the last time we talked, and resumed my *Khashtani* duties without attempting anything *"beyond myself"*.

I groan.

"You know I am right, Soleil," Nusk says. He starts to roll himself to the kitchen. "Now get yourself in order and join me for breakfast. You'll have time."

And then he's gone, to give me some privacy.

Given the fact that he's woken me so early, he's not wrong. I rearrange the day's schedule in my head and figure this won't make too much trouble for me. I'm going to be tired, but I've had worse days. I'll be fine so long as I keep myself stimulated.

Since I have the time, I give myself an extra three minutes while washing to clean my hair. It'll frizz the moment I step outside, but at least it'll smell nice. Afterward, I stand under the water for a few minutes for no particular reason, enjoying the stream of water. Imagining it taking the tightness in my head and draining it down, out, away, and swirling into the drain. Maybe it's wishful thinking, but I feel as if it helps.

I keep my watch nearby, in case I'm called in to help Rian, but I trust Taris to look after him.

In the kitchen, I can smell Nusk cooking eggs, and there are flaky rolls stacked up on a plate at the table. He might have woken me with a chiding, but I suppose Naomi must have truly sounded worried about me, because she inadvertently convinced him that I need a break.

"Sit," Nusk tells me. "We'll eat in just a moment."

I take a spot on the bench in front of one of the mugs at the table, pleased to smell warmed chocolate inside. It makes me smile, remembering how rarely Nusk would allow us to drink hot chocolate when we were young.

"I heard Mercer tell Rian once that they drink chocolate in the west, too," I say, taking a long sip. "In Lijimata, they cook it so thick, it's more like a paste. You need to eat it with a *spoon–*"

"And sometimes even spread on toast," Nusk finishes as he brings his pan of eggs to the table, for the two of us to split without bothering with extra dishes. "Yes, Taris told me."

He joins me to eat, on his side of the table, and grabs one of the rolls.

"I think Taris always beats me to telling you the interesting things Mercer shares," I admit, rolling my eyes.

"Taris is highly competitive," Nusk agrees. "You're slightly less so. That's why you're such a good *Khashtani*. You have enough drive to keep the crown prince safe, but not so much that you might endanger him whilst trying to prove someone wrong. It's further proof I chose well."

I take one of the rolls, but hold it in my hands for a few seconds, mulling over his words.

"Why did you pick me?" I ask. "To be a *Khashtani?* How could you have seen me as a child and known that I would be any good at this?"

Nusk shrugs. A smile plays at his mouth. "I didn't," he says. "In fact, Taris was meant to be the crown prince's *Khashtani*. You were meant to fulfill a role as the last member of his *khashak*, with Naomi and Korvaan. But when the time came, I made a different choice."

I stare at him. For so long, Nusk kept this from me. From all of us.

"Taris was, and is, too reckless," Nusk continues. "Too emotionally driven. You, at least, can turn off those emotions, as you know is necessary. You may be brash sometimes, Soleil, but you are not as foolish as your brother. Taris could never fulfill the duties of a *Khashtani*. Not completely. He refuses to sacrifice what he should. And must."

That was not at all what I was expecting him to say.

Nor did I expect him to refer to Taris as my brother. Of course, I'd always seen my *khashak* in that way, but it was different, hearing Nusk say it. Hearing him imply he sees me like a second daughter.

"And what's that?" I ask. "What is he supposed to sacrifice that he won't?"

Nusk looks startled, as if he never expected I'd inquire, but then his features soften, and he chuckles. "That is his own business, Soleil. It is between him and me, and will remain so unless it becomes a danger to the crown prince."

I don't bother to mask my disappointment.

"All you need to know, Soleil, is that Taris has an unreasonably selfish side of himself," Nusk humors me. "Like all of us do. My only concern is that he may feel he deserves to indulge it, when he does not."

I frown. "What do you mean?"

I'm nervous about this sudden scrutiny of Taris. As if Nusk somehow knows we talked last night, and about our tentative, secret alliance inside our already small circle of five.

Nusk tries to brush it aside. "It's nothing you need to concern yourself with, Soleil. It's…a matter that Taris and I have disagreed on for many years."

He's back to eating his eggs, as if that's meant to be the final word. I might have pressed him for more if not for Naomi, who chooses now to sweep into the house with a basket of fresh berries and a cheery expression.

"Good morning," she sings. "I've brought a gift. Someone dropped it off for me at the infirmary. In thanks."

I check my watch. "Shouldn't you be at the infirmary now?"

Naomi ignores me and sets the basket on the counter, preparing to rinse the berries and settle the freshest ones in a bowl for our consumption. She's absently humming to herself.

Nusk and I look at each other, and he raises an eyebrow.

Considering how much Nusk seems to know about everything, I've no doubt that he's aware of the tentative and unofficial courtship Naomi has accidentally started with Valor Ondra.

I consider this. Nusk, for some reason, has not chided Naomi's frivolity, nor has he done anything to make it look as if he endorses such a relationship. So, does he think I should release Naomi from the *khashak?* Should I let all of my *khashak* see to their own lives instead of obsessing over Rian's, the way I do?

Of course, the other option is Nusk suspects that after Comus Day, there won't be a need for any of us any longer. I'm tempted to ask why he might think so, but he's been lecturing me so much about overthinking, and living in the future instead of the present. I don't want to irritate him or make him suspicious when things are going so well this morning…

"Soleil!" Naomi says.

I jerk my head up to realize that this is the third time she's said my name. She and Nusk are both looking at me with some concern.

"Are you feeling all right?" Naomi adds.

"I'm exhausted. But I'll be fine," I add quickly. "I've had worse days."

I half-expect Nusk to launch into another lecture about how I should be more careful to look after myself and try to settle my mind through meditation. I suppose I must have accidentally given him an exceptional reason to worry, because he doesn't say a word. But he does look to Naomi, as if confirming something to her that they've discussed previously.

"What?" I say.

"Soleil, I want you needled again," Naomi warns. "Whatever Taris did last night, I'm not positive it worked."

"I don't want needling. I don't need it," I argue. "I don't have the time—"

She raises an eyebrow. "Don't you? Soleil, your body is going to start shutting down on you."

"But what about Rian?" I point out. "If I can keep up my work, I should. Someone needs to be with him. And if Taris is with me, and we spend the next hour in a session—" I pointedly check my watch. "There's not enough time."

"I'll stay with Rian," Naomi interrupts.

"That won't work."

"Yes, it will. Things have been quiet for a while," Naomi continues.

If only she knew.

"Allow me to watch Rian this morning, and relax. We can trade off this afternoon, just before his mythology class. That should be plenty of time, don't you think? And Korvaan can help. I think that's more than reasonable."

"You'd have to use another one of your time off stamps. And that's not—"

"Fair?" Naomi says. She laughs genuinely. "Soleil, I know in the back of your head you have this fantasy where we only take time off for ourselves when we deserve it, but let's be realistic. When, in the many years that I've worked in the infirmary, have I ever taken a day off for myself?"

I can't argue with her there, because I know I'm not being reasonable.

"Fine," I relent. "Let Taris know we'll do it here. But let's make it quick."

I have to wonder if the reason Naomi isn't currently at work is because she and Nusk already planned this, and she only went to the infirmary in the first place to let them know she needed a day off.

I return to the boys' room with the loft for the time being, while Naomi triumphantly contacts Taris to let him know about the change in plans.

As gruff as he is, Taris is the only one of us trained in needling, and he's good at it. His hands are rough and strong, but his fingers are nimble. He knows the points for both pressure and needles, and can stick them in so well I barely feel it, unless he's dry needling. Then again, dry needling is known to make even the most stoic soldiers scream, and I can get through it by only gritting my teeth, so perhaps Taris is terrible at needling and I have a high pain tolerance.

It's not that I mind the needling sessions; if I'm entirely honest, I enjoy them. But it occasionally feels unnecessary. Acupuncture is something that should be reserved for people with more time. And more physical maladies.

When Taris arrives, it's long past the time I'm supposed to have swapped with him to look after Rian. Naomi's gone in my stead, to watch Rian teach his first class of children about how their own country came to be. At least Qhan will be there. I need to stop worrying.

"So. More needling?" Taris says as he enters with his bag.

I appreciate that he's bothering to make it seem as if this is only hours after our last session, even though we should have privacy.

"N'omi and Nusk think whatever you did last time didn't work," I say as he pulls out his cushioned work table from under the bed and unfolds it. I take the other end, to set up.

"Guess we'll have to try something more aggressive, then. And I'd like to do some dry needling around your shoulder injury first," Taris admits. "I don't think you've noticed, but you've been overcompensating for it."

"Do whatever you want," I mutter.

He gives me a look. "Are you annoyed with me?"

"No," I snap, and start stripping off my clothes. "Turn around. I'm annoyed with everyone," I add after Taris turns his back and allows me to bare most of my skin before laying down flat on the table.

"Am I not included in 'everyone'?"

"Usually, you would be. But you're about to stick a bunch of needles in me, so I'm going to say 'no' for now."

"Probably a good idea," Taris says.

"I thought so."

The dry needling is painful. Taris is using a needle to separate layers of tightened and twisted muscle, after all. But afterwards my shoulder feels as if it's received a good stretch. He has me flip over on my back and puts a towel over my chest so he can switch to thinner, less intrusive needles for acupuncture.

All I can think of, the entire time, is a story Rian told once about the origins of acupuncture and its relation to flukes. Something metaphorical, I think. I'm struggling to remember the details, but I did enjoy it. There's a lot behind the tale in connection with flukes, in fact. After all, the use of flukes is merely a redirection of energy. All the needles do is straighten crooked or blocked inner channels so that energy can flow freely for proper harnessing.

I can't remember who thought Taris should learn the skill—if it was his own idea, or something Nusk made him do—but he's good at it. He occasionally checks my pulses to see what I need done, presses at certain pressure points to see if they're tender, and adjusts course dependent on how I feel.

It's relaxing enough that I allow myself to close my eyes and drift a little.

"I must admit, that feels good," I mumble.

I can picture Taris' smirk. It makes me want to smack him in his smug face. But that's not particularly practical now that I'm depending on him to help me unravel the secrets of the Isaarian courts. Especially since I'd have to get up to do so, and I'm not keen on letting Taris see my breasts.

"You're blocked all over, so, yes, I suspect remedying that might feel good," Taris says. "Have you tried standing out in the sun and connecting with the world?" he adds, and I groan.

I have, on occasion. But after a few seconds, I feel silly, and as if someone's watching me, laughing. So, I don't make it a habit.

"No point. I don't have a fluke."

"It's still good for you," he presses. "I do it, on occasion. So does Korvaan."

"I hadn't noticed."

"Yes, you have. Don't be stubborn. I guarantee, it'll make you feel better. Headache gone?"

"Mm? Oh. Yes. It's drained."

"Good. I'm going to do some in your feet and head, and then we'll be done."

"Mmhmm."

The feet needles are ones I hate the most, but at least Taris doesn't leave them in. It's just a quick poke, in and out. He must know the more time he takes, the more anxious I'll be to get back to Rian. If he's going to insist that I take up even more time, standing out in the sun with him with my shoes off, he won't make me lie on the table with needles in me for half an hour.

When the two of us emerge from the back bedroom and Taris explains his plan to his father, I can tell Nusk is pleased. Despite what he claims Taris lacks, or how he's more emotionally driven than I am, at least Taris can meditate. Our mentor clearly hopes the habit will rub off on me.

The sun is bright in a cloudless sky when Taris and I step out the back door, behind the cabin. He leans against the wall and I sit on the doorstep to take off our shoes, and he rolls up his sleeves and trouser legs as well. Without most of his guard's uniform, he looks casual. Somehow more natural.

"Out you get," he says once he's standing with his toes digging into the grass. I'm still stuck back on the doorstep. "And close the door behind you," he adds.

I reluctantly join him. At least there's a mild breeze to cut the heat.

It's strange to see Taris so peaceful. He can stand here, half-undressed, with his eyes closed, head up towards the sun and his feet in the dirt, and look happy. If he can manage it, why can't I? It's almost unfair.

"Close your eyes, Soleil," Taris drawls, as if he can tell I'm looking at him.

I shouldn't scowl—that doesn't seem very relaxing—but close my eyes.

It feels as if hours pass. I can practically hear a clock ticking in my ears, as if to remind me what a waste of time this is. And I can hear Taris breathing. That doesn't help. How can he calm himself so easily? It frustrates me that this isn't difficult for him.

"I'd relax more easily if you weren't here, you know," I finally mutter.

"I didn't say anything," Taris points out.

"But you're here."

"Fine. I'll get Korvaan, and take over from him," Taris says simply. "Work on emptying your mind in the meantime. I'd tell you to fill it with prayer, but I know you won't do that. We'll talk later."

Before I can think of something snarky to say, he's dropped his arms and walked back to the hut, gathering his things up as he goes.

It surprises me when I realized I'm disappointed to know that Korvaan will be taking his place. Not because I don't like Korvaan—I'm fonder of his company than his brother's, and always have been. But I suppose I've never realized before that there is some part of Taris' presence that I do enjoy.

I throw myself down to sit cross-legged and begin picking at the grass. My fingers move, to braid the strands together, making a chain. It's strange that I know how to do this, as I have no memory of making daisy chains with N'omi, and I can't imagine Nusk giving us time to do so when we were young.

As pointless as this exercise is, it passes the time while I wait for Korvaan. And as I reflect, I realize it was only how well Taris was meditating, compared to me, that bothered me. But since it's too late to stop Taris from switching with his brother, I decide not to worry about it, and continue with my craft, sitting out in the sun.

When Korvaan sits down next to me, I've made three different flower crowns with wildflowers and daisies.

"Feel relaxed?" Korvaan asks, teasing but interested in my response.

"Strangely, yes," I admit. "And my headache is gone. Though, to be fair, that's all thanks to Taris."

"He is good at what he does," Korvaan agrees. "Whether it's needling you, or *needling you.*"

I almost laugh at that. I feel startlingly good.

"Yes, well. I think even if he were here right now, Taris would bother me less," I say. "I guess I didn't realize how calming doing nothing can be."

"You're not doing nothing—you're making crowns!" Korvaan claims, taking one of my flower chains and dropping it on his head.

"Regardless," I say. "I don't mind meditation so much when it's done this way. I'm not much one for prayer in the Theebin way, I suppose."

"Plan on making it a habit?" Korvaan suggests, giving me a hopeful look.

I have to wonder how long they've all watched me drive myself mad with stress, hoping I'd figure out some form of outlet.

"I haven't decided," I say. "It depends on timing. And who is watching Rian."

"It doesn't take long," he insists, "fifteen minutes or so is all you need. And I'm sure Taris wouldn't mind watching the prince for an extra quarter hour."

"Mmm," I say, and watch the wind bend the grass down for a few seconds. "Do you find it helpful? Taris says both of you bother to take the time out of your own days, even though neither of you have flukes."

Korvaan shrugs. "I suppose. I can't imagine not doing it, in any case. We've done it for as long as I can remember. I think N'omi started when she was little, because she showed her fluke early. And when Nusk had her start, Taris and I didn't see any reason why we shouldn't do it, too."

I frown. "Was I around, when N'omi showed her fluke? I don't remember."

"Oh, who's to know. We were all young. Probably my father could tell you, if you asked him."

"I'm sure he would," I lie in agreement. "But Korvaan: do you remember what things were like? Before Nusk…found me?"

"Not much," he admits, and then grins at me. "But that was a long time ago. Now it feels like we've known each other for hundreds of years!"

"Surely not that long."

"I only said what it felt like. And Soleil, you know our lives would be much different if you weren't here."

"Yes, of course. You wouldn't be trapped in a *khashak,* spending your lives helping me protect the crown prince," I say bitterly.

He gives me a confused look. "Soleil, we would still be a *khashak.* Our father agreed to that for us. A deal he made, with the Yakaramis. We would just have a different *Khashtani.*"

You would have Taris, I think, but I don't say so. I don't know what Korvaan has been told about Nusk's original agreement with the Yakaramis, and I don't know if he's aware that his brother was meant to be Rian's *Khashtani.* I don't even know if Taris himself knows. After all, Nusk revealed it to me this morning. Perhaps he had a reason for keeping it a secret from us this long. Maybe he hopes that telling me will somehow make me feel like I'm doing a good job, and continue to keep my nose down. Forget about my investigations.

After another ten minutes, I head back inside with Korvaan and find N'omi arranging a vase of flowers. I have to wonder if those are yet another gift from her suitor, or if she picked them herself.

"Taris came to watch Rian and told me he could handle it on his own," she says, giving me a look. She wants to know why I decided to alter her plan.

"Ah," I say, and go about fixing my feet back into my shoes.

So much commotion happening this morning, all for my sake. I'm surprised that I manage not to feel guilty about it, but Korvaan was right: it's a simple matter of allowing myself time to at least try and do nothing. Perhaps I can't meditate, but when I was braiding flower crowns, positive that Rian was safe in the care of my *khashak,* I was not worrying over him.

I can tell Naomi wants to say something more to me, because she's hovering, poking her flowers into a particular arrangement. Moving them practically petal by petal. Korvaan's left to see to other things, and I plan to follow him shortly. I'm just about to swing out the door calling my farewells to Naomi and Nusk, wherever he is, when Naomi stops me to say her extra piece.

"Soleil: did you really have Taris and Korvaan swap with so you could try and stand out in the sun for a few minutes?" she accuses.

"I might have," I allow, hand still on the doorknob. "Why?"

She rolls her eyes. "Oh, never mind," she says unconvincingly.

"What?"

"Nothing. Only I wish you and Taris would get along better," Naomi sighs. "It would make things simpler, for the rest of us. The crown prince included."

With anyone else, I would snap something about it being all Taris' fault. But I can't do that to Naomi. I've been too harsh with her lately, and I never should have done so to begin with. Besides: she's not wrong. And as much of an ass as he can be, Taris has always been a good older brother to Korvaan and N'omi. And now that I've shared with him all my secret plans regarding the albino assassin and the Carsans siblings, I need him. More than that, I trust him.

"I'll do better," I promise her. And for once, I mean it.

RIAN'S REACHING THE end of one of his afternoon classes, the one on Isaaria myths and legends. Asmer's there, too, smiling from her seat in the corner. Today, they're discussing the Fae that still live on our lands—the last real haven for the Sacred Trees that grant their long lives. The children are excited to be speaking of the mysterious and beautiful Fae, but this is due to ignorance. Rian and the rest of the heirs have met the Fae, and Rian is not fond of them. From what I've gathered from his complaints to Mercer, the simplest way to put it is this: they're assholes.

Still, it's difficult for people to understand, especially children. To them, hearing about Fae is even more captivating than dragons or griffins, gildhorns or undine, because those creatures are still relatively lively in Samioth. You might see them now and again, out in nature, or even tamed as pets. But there is only one place remaining in the world for the Fae, and it is right in the backyard of Pyrian City.

Rian fields his class's questions dutifully, but can't hide his irritation when it comes to the Fae. I'm not sure what they've done to annoy him, but it must have been bad to merit this sort of grudge from the Laughing Prince.

I wouldn't know: by chance alone, Taris is the only one who has been on duty with Rian whenever he met with the Fae.

Ayla is in this class, too, and I wonder if she begged the administration to put her in as many of Rian's classes as possible. The two are endearingly close, and have been for about a year now, after Ayla shyly sought Rian out after one of his readings to ask him some questions. She's a bright girl. All of Rian's students are smart children, but Ayla especially so. It's because, I think, her passion drives her to excel beyond even Rian's expectations.

It probably helps that he doesn't talk down to his students, or try to limit them. They might be children, but they have a natural love for learning and questioning that Rian tries to cultivate.

Currently, the students are trying to puzzle out why the Fae are slowly going extinct, and how to prevent such a thing. They're far too pure of heart: the Fae's lack of progeny in this world is their own fault, not because of anything humankind has done directly. There's little we can do to help them, either. Assuming they'd ever accept our help. They're fickle, disdainful things.

"Well, as I'm sure you've noticed, people in general don't have as many children as they once did," Rian is saying. "For good or bad—that's irrelevant, really, and I don't think it would be appropriate to tell you my opinion—but Fae are highly influenced by our world. And so, as birth rates decline for humans by choice, Fae have slowly forgotten how to reproduce. Well, the, ah, *act itself* isn't something they've forgotten. But the joy of having children about: all those memories are lost. So, they can't remember why or how they should."

"That's so sad," Ayla laments.

"It can be, depending on how you think about it," Rian admits. "But the Fae are resilient folk. They've lasted this long, and just like blaming humanity for their losses. We've practically got a sanctuary for them. If they go extinct at this point, it's their own damned fault."

Asmer perks up in the corner, and clears her throat gently, as if to remind Rian he shouldn't be cursing in front of children.

"But you've met the Fae before, haven't you, Mister Rian?" one of the children asks excitedly.

"Well, yes. All the heirs have," Rian says, leaning back against his desk. "It was more a meeting with their leaders." He adds in a mutter under his breath, "And *one leader* in particular…"

If he weren't in class, he'd be snarling. I know precisely which Fae he's talking about, and it's because he rants about the fellow every time they're brought up: Clanaugh, the closest thing the Fae have to a king. He's one of the few creatures in Samioth who can make Rian truly angry.

"What do the Fae look like?" a child prompts. "Are they really beautiful?"

"Are they delicate and made out of paper-like? Same as dryads?"

"Do they look like people, or like plants and animals and such?"

"Did you ever see a Fae *child?"*

Rian fields the questions smoothly, used to the children's energetic requests.

"Well, when they appear to *us,* they usually take a more human shape," he explains. "They'll look like the most beautiful people you'd ever seen, but…you won't want to look."

It's clear that the children are too young to understand what he's talking about. They can't imagine not wanting to meet a Fae; such creatures are mystical and mysterious to them. Rian sees this, and tries to clarify.

"Ah, Lady al'Yibna, if you wouldn't mind assisting me for a moment?" he says, and gestures for Asmer to come up and join him.

He presents her to the class.

"Now, we can all say Lady Asmer's lovely, can't we?" he begins, and Asmer flushes slightly as the children agree. "And she's very nice to look at. The Fae, then, would look even more beautiful—if you can believe it—but you won't like looking. You'll want to look away."

"Like the sun!" Ayla says. "Pretty, but if you look directly at it, it hurts!"

"Exactly," Rian says, then pats Asmer on the shoulder. "Thank you, Asmer, I think they've got it now."

She retakes her seat, still red with the innocent compliments of the children, and from Rian.

"But what about the child Fae?" that one student prompts again. "Did you ever get to see one? Since they're so rare?"

"Once," Rian admits. "One of Clanaugh's sons, the first time I met him."

The classroom rumbles with the children's whispers.

"Clanaugh?" one of them repeats. "The king of the Fae?"

"Well, not quite," Rian corrects. "But he's definitely powerful. And he's made certain that every Isaarian king is aware of that. We have a pact with Clanaugh, you see. In exchange for letting the Fae continue to live on our lands."

"I thought they were here first," Ayla points out.

"Not in Isaaria," Rian corrects. "They fled here. Much as our ancestors did, when New Isaaria was formed. And since Clanaugh likes to steal travelers as household pets, dressing them up to show off at whatever passes for a Fae party, it became necessary to make a pact with him. To protect Isaarian citizens from such a thing."

The children are too busy chatting amongst themselves to absorb this. They're listening to Rian, but they don't agree with his sentiment. To most of them, being kidnapped by Fae sounds enchanting. Something out of a romance. They don't understand that the Fae's pets live barely-lucid lives, kept alive by Clanaugh's magic for as long as they manage to entertain him.

Such an idea partially terrifies Rian; I don't think he'd like living forever in the Fae's bubble while the rest of the world turns around him. But Fae prefer those with high levels of magic in their blood. Powerful or rare flukes and such. Given how powerful a fluke Rian has, I'm sure Clanaugh is tempted to break the "right of the Isaarian heir" and kidnap my crown prince. A creature like him would be thrilled to hold the power of time in the palm of his hand.

Rian rolls his eyes. "Clanaugh's not all that wonderful, boys and girls. Will I respect the fact that he's one of the oldest and most powerful Fae today? Yes. But he's a right bas—"

Asmer feigns a noisy coughing fit to censor him. Rian does not notice she's done so on purpose and looks to her with both confusion and concern.

"Are you quite all right over there, dear?"

"Perfectly fine," Asmer says hoarsely.

The bell rings right on cue: end of class. Rian is quick to dismiss his students, ushering them out before they can think up more questions to ask.

The children leave, still chattering about the Fae, while Rian reminds them of supplemental reading they might explore if they're interested. Next time, he wants to start next class with an examination of how certain mythical creatures are portrayed in Isaarian stories compared to other countries.

I know he can't wait to get to one of his favorite mythical figures: Kang, the man cursed with dragon's blood. There are so many stories with Kang in them, including modern series in which he is mentioned or even a prominent character. Rian owns many of these books. His favorite portrayal of Kang is a series whose manuscripts have mysterious origins: each volume is left on the doorstep of an Alarkian publishing company, with instructions on how to deliver royalties, and an obvious pseudonym for the author, K.A. Manna.

Rian does so love his mysteries. If he weren't such a scholar, I sometimes think he and Mercer would make an excellent team: going out around the world and discovering things supposedly lost to time. But Mercer is a man of medicine and science; he claims to have no time for theories on the fantastical. And Rian hates travel. He loves his creature comforts of home.

Asmer sweeps out with the children as they leave the classroom. She claims her brother Raj has promised to telephone her this afternoon, and she does not want to miss him. Eventually, only one student remains while Rian packs up his things and Qhan lingers by the doorway. Ayla.

"More questions for me, Ayla?" Rian teases her.

The administration, sadly, doesn't allow Rian to tutor any students, and prefers he only interact with them during class to avoid favoritism. But he and Ayla occasionally find ways to bend the rules.

"I want to know more about the Fae," she presses. "And what they're like."

"They are not as charming as you probably hope," he laughs, trying to let her down easily.

"I don't care if they're charming or not," Ayla says as they leave the room, and I continue to listen in as I clamber across the roof, planning a path that will allow me to follow them when they leave the building.

"Don't you?" Rian says.

"You said Clanaugh's not nice, and I believe you," Ayla says. "But if I knew more about them, then I'd be able to help you with your Magicsmith research."

"Oh, really?"

"Mmhmm," Ayla says. "Because you told us that Fae tend to kidnap people with powerful flukes. Magicsmiths have powerful flukes, right? So, what if Clanaugh had one?"

"Not bad thinking, Ayla," Rian admits, though he's already traveled down such an avenue. He doesn't want to disappoint her, since she's given this quite a bit of thought, but if Clanaugh had a pet Magicsmith he'd been keeping alive for centuries, Rian would be one of the first to know.

"Tell you what," he says. "One of these times, I'll give a story-telling and focus on something or another about Clanaugh and the Fae, how about that?"

"Will you be telling another story this afternoon?" Ayla prompts innocently, bouncing at Rian's elbow so that her sunny hair flounces up and down.

Rian can't help but laugh, and puts a hand on her head as if to still her. "I might, rabbit. Why—do you not have enough work from your teachers to keep you busy?"

"I like hearing them," she insists. "It doesn't even have to be one about the Fae, this time. I like all your stories. No one ever told stories at the orphanage. And I like having you as our teacher."

Rian laughs heartily. "Ah, well. I'm glad you think so, Ayla. I quite enjoy your company, too," he says, rubbing her hair so she has to straighten it out again through her giggles.

"In fact, you don't need to give me an answer now, Ayla," he warns her.

"But I've been meaning to ask you for some time: once Comus Day is over and everything settles…what would you say about coming to live with me? That is, I'm saying…Would you be all right with my adopting you?"

Ayla stares up at him for several seconds. When she speaks, she's breathless, as if she doesn't dare hope, but still: "You're adopting me?" she repeats. "I'd be like your daughter?"

Rian is bashful; her questions are proof that this hasn't gone quite as he intended. "Ah, well. Yes, I would like to adopt you. If you approve. You'd be my daughter, so—"

Ayla flings herself at him, wrapping her arms around him and crying with delight as she repeatedly accepts his offer. For a moment, Rian is startled. Then he laughs and hugs her back. It occurs to me that I'm experiencing a strange, buoyant happiness to see Rian so joyful; I approve of his idea of adopting Ayla, and I think he'd do a wonderful job raising her.

But it does seem to imply that he has someone in mind to wife. As good a job Rian might do on his own, there are some things it will be easier for Ayla to experience with a mother than with him.

"Yes!" Ayla cries. "I'd say 'yes', I want to! It's the best idea in the world!"

Her smile and glassy eyes are absolutely endearing. I can almost imagine what Rian is feeling to see her this happy. It's refreshing.

"Does this mean I get to come and live with you forever?" she asks.

"More or less," Rian admits. "Where that ends up being is still undetermined, honestly, but Ayla: we'll get to be together. I promise."

"Will I be a princess, then, or do I still get to be a normal person?"

"What would you prefer?"

Ayla considers this. "I don't know, yet. I didn't know I got to pick."

"Well, little Ayla, by definition, you will be a lady of the court so long as I'm a crown prince. We'll see about the title of 'princess' when the time comes. And regardless, we'll still have each other."

"But aren't you going to try your very hardest to be king?" Ayla asks.

"Eh, I'll do what I can, but I doubt it will be me," Rian says. "Whoever is meant to be king will be king, Ayla. That's how it works."

Ayla doesn't entirely understand. "Oh," she says, frowning. "Well, who do you think is going to be king, then? If it's not going to be you?"

"Probably Vásan," Rian admits with a shrug, and I'm startled to hear this.

I haven't thought about Crown Prince Vásan Pike in weeks. I haven't thought about the other four heirs in such a long time, they've all but faded from my mind entirely. With Comus Day approaching, I need to be better in researching them. Seeing what they've spent their lives doing. What people think of them. What they think of being the next ruler of our country.

I know the basics, of course: what's said around campus, gossip, news, truth. Everything in between. But information must be precise in my line of work.

If Rian thinks Vásan will be the next king, I need to know why he thinks so, what kind of ruler Vásan would be, and what it means for me that Rian appears to have no interest in contesting the other's claim. Two months ago, I'd simply be relieved. Now, for some reason, I feel as if Rian will be wasting his potential as a mere grand prince. As if misguided pride is keeping the rightful king from the throne.

"Oh," Ayla says, thinking. "Do you like Crown Prince Vásan?"

"Well enough," Rian says. "I don't know him that well, but he has more than proven his leadership skills in the past few years. He's been acting Grand-Prince in his father's stead since Aloysius died four years ago, and the people seem to approve of him. That's good, for a crown prince. Even better, for a would-be-king. I think, as heir with the most experience, even more than Magnus, Vásan is the one the Currian Council will choose."

"Huh," Ayla says.

She was expecting a simpler answer, but she's smart enough to understand what Rian is saying.

"He's responsible, dear," Rian continues with a smile. "And while he won't be the most charming or kindly king, perhaps that's not what's needed right now."

"What do you mean?"

"Never mind it, Ayla. I'll explain it when you're older. You're too young to be worrying about these things."

"But not too old for your stories," Ayla contributes pointedly, hinting at what she really wants.

Rian checks the clock tower for the time before making a decision.

"Oh, go gather your classmates. I'm sure they'll whip up a crowd," he says, unable to resist her. "I've got a few minutes; we'll do a story right here and now."

Grinning with excitement, Ayla dashes off, holding up the split skirts of her uniform's kirtle to show off her tall socks and skinny legs. I watch her go, shoes click-clacking on the stones as she calls her fellow students. Announcing Crown Prince Rian's intentions of telling another story this afternoon.

Rian chuckles, smiling after her.

"I think she took that well," Qhan says, coming up to stand with Rian instead of lurking in his shadow.

"She is an absolute ray of sunshine," Rian agrees, almost proudly.

I find I'm smiling, too, for some reason.

Rian finds a Qhan-approved spot to get comfortable: the base of a tree atop a slope. It doesn't take Ayla long to return, trailing students behind her. They arrange themselves on the grass around Rian. When he finally begins, deciding enough folk have arrived to give him a proper audience, I find myself fighting not to fall under the spell of his story-telling once more.

Rian has chosen to tell the beginning of the Families Three—the so-called oldest and most powerful magic families in all of Samioth, meant to keep the peace. Naturally, it's only a story: the unrest and violence in the west is proof of that, if there was ever doubt. It is a fairy tale; something to give that extra dash of wonder to children whose world is already filled with magic. It's not even as popular a story as it once was. It is dark, and long, and filled with blood and gruesome sacrifice. But the beginning, at least, is instructive, and I'm certain there's some sort of lesson Rian wishes the children to take away from this.

"Many, many, many years ago," he starts, "when even Old Isaaria was in its infancy, there came to be three families in Samioth with whom magic was first instilled: The Greys, the Von Wolffs, and the Smiths. The Greys were named such for the coloring of their patriarch, whose hair was solid grey with age, but whose face appeared youthful, for their lives were long and their flukes strong. They ruled prosperously over the ancient kingdom of Lusch, having made themselves royalty from nothing.

"The Von Wolffs' leaders were a Valeian prince raised in the wild by animals, who grew into a fair king, and a forest woman of raven hair and fairest skin, said to be a dryad herself, whom he married. In them, many blue-blood lines mixed, from noble northern houses. Finally, the Smiths were named such because, of all the people in the land, they were the only ones who could take magic and make things entirely new, enchanted, and unspeakably wonderful. As a blacksmith makes swords and a coinsmith marks currencies, they made things of magic, and thus were called *Magicsmiths.*

"It is rumored that the Smiths hold in their family line the blood of the Fair Folk, whose own magic has passed through their line, strengthening it into something unique, and powerful."

Rian hesitates, and I can tell that part of him wants to pause the story, escape from the spell he's put everyone under and explain in excruciating detail why it's important to differentiate the Fair Folk from the Fae. But he thankfully decides against it, and moves on.

"At this point in history, the world was full of danger, not only from magical creatures, but also from man. As more and more family lines absorbed magic, flukes began to surface, and some of their bearers carried bloodthirstiness in their veins. A greed for power or glory or riches grew within them, and they intended to use this magic in the worst of ways. So, one of the seven angels came down to each of the original Families Three: Fate, to the Greys, Hope, to the Smiths. And to the Wolffs came the Death. They were instructed to use their own given-flukes to help the world: not by joining wars on any particular side, or taking from those with over-full vaults, but to end the very things tempting humankind into using their flukes for wrong: demons.

"The Greys were to be hunters of monsters born from demons. To kill them, and prevent them from preying on folk either in mind or body. They learned to track demons, how to spear personal ones and scare off those hungry for human flesh, how to make certain one's thread—as woven by Fate himself—wasn't tangled, or cut early, by demonic intervention.

"The Smiths were called by Hope to create a new world for those eager to fight the monsters by living their lives justly and peacefully. The Magicsmiths began to create, as they were meant to: household utilities, advice-giving mirrors, staffs and jewels for rulers, and demon-killing weapons for the Greys. They were the champions of hope. The ones meant to lead the world into new eras while the Greys hunted monsters in the shadows.

"And to the Wolffs, the Death gave a most perilous calling: to protect the veil between our world and the Otherworld. The Otherworld, from whose bottom tiers the demons sprang, and whose heavens the angels had come. When the Death came to collect the souls of those perished, the Wolffs were to help keep the world in balance: to make certain that as many souls as possible were taken by the Death, and not by *the Other One*. The Fallen One. *The Dark.*"

The way he mentions the Dark makes some of the children shiver, or shove at each other, whispering. I'll admit, Rian's voice even sends a shiver down my spine, though I'll be the first to insist I don't believe in the most popular haunt of children's nightmares and scary stories.

Yet, Rian's telling makes one want to call down all seven of the Theebins' sacred angels for protection: Fate sometimes called Justice, Faith, Peace, Hope, Love, Courage, and even the Death.

I tell myself it's all nonsense. But when Rian speaks of the Dark and all its evil machinations, it makes a person desperate for some form of sure protection. Something to help them sleep at night.

"These charges to protect mankind's bodies, minds, and souls were dangerous," Rian continues, "and often shed blood amongst the Families Three. Thus, their abilities and lines rarely spread far. Most of the families' members met gruesome ends as the prey of bloodthirsiness. Otherwise, they often ended up sacrificing themselves for the sake of others, becoming martyrs of religious prosecution or dedicating themselves to their faith and procuring no heirs.

"During particularly dark times, the Grey family came up with a system of choosing heirs and match-making their children with strong spouses, to ensure that at least one or two sons survived to carry the line. As this system placed preferential treatment on sons instead of daughters, the Smiths and Wolffs opposed, instead adopting separate practices with significant adjustments.

"For some time, the Families Three survived, and occasionally even thrived, whilst discharging their duties to humanity, keeping us safe from the monsters only the Dark could think up. Until an heir of the Grey family—a young man by the name of Kryto—made a discovery he thought brilliant. A way to fight the Dark's forces in even greater numbers. A way to, perhaps, kill the Dark itself.

"The practice, called witchcraft by some and pure evil by others, came to be known as *Dadj'zcha:* the magic of sacrificing blood and flesh to procure powerful results. Kryto Grey thought himself a savior of man. He did not realize that the whispers urging him on were from the Dark himself, who had finally discovered the greatest sin of the Grey family; the way to twist and corrupt them until his greatest adversaries became his most useful tools: their pride.

"When the Smiths and Wolffs discovered the spread of this shadowy practice, they spoke against it. But it soon became clear that the Greys were corrupted from within, and no longer honored Fate's design. Bloody fights sprang up amongst the families, two fighting against one. At the end, the Wolff family was all but extinct, and the fighting looked as if it would never cease. Until they and the rest of mankind grew so weak and broken that Love's angel begged her God to allow her intercession. She was granted such, and from there, no one quite knows what happened to the remains of the Families Three. Only that the rest of the world went on, and it cannot be said for sure whether the Families' promises were renewed and they continued their work in secret, or they were allowed to die out completely.

"Now, there came to be in Old Isaaria a most noble family of magical breeding, whose line carried the fluke of prophecy. The Carsans."

The melancholy that's fallen over the crowd lifts at mention of the Carsans. Rian is coming to the end of his abridged tale. And I'm certain that regardless of what is known or not, he plans on leaving everyone with something to hope for. Something to make this story's end a "good" one.

"The Carsans family gave many prophecies about the fate of Isaaria, and were instrumental in guiding our people to a new home. But they also were given a prophecy by Fate: a way to ensure that those tempted by the

Dark did not endanger the world ever again. This prophecy was lost to time, but I am certain there are still those who remember it. And, when the world is most in need of guidance, these individuals might step forward to call upon heroes to do as the Families Three once did, to keep mankind safe."

I can tell that Rian is not as satisfied with his story-telling as his audience is. In fact, I notice that this is the largest group of people ever gathered to listen. So, while they might all tease about how pointless Rian's research into Magicsmiths and other fictions are, they, too, are all intrigued by it. They, too, want to know about what might or what could have been, a long time ago. Back in a time history has forgotten.

I catch Crispin Carsans slipping away from the back of the crowd without a word. Strange. And curious. I'm tempted to call in and ask Taris to ghost him, but I don't think now's the time to spy on the Carsans, and I need Taris to be well-rested for future inquiries.

I hang about, watching people ask Rian questions or compliment him. The crowd is slow to dissipate as students turn to one another, theorizing. Asking questions about bits some of them missed, having arrived late. Wondering about where they could find the rest of the story, or if Rian has all the Magicsmith books from the library up in his room.

When the bell chimes an afternoon hour, the students are forced to start dispersing; many of them have classes, and are already late. But Ayla lingers near Rian, eager to capture him for a few moments more.

"That was wonderful," she says. Her tone is hushed. Awed. I have no doubt that she sees Rian as her personal hero, and all merely for telling a good story.

"I don't know how you do it," Ayla continues. "But when you tell stories, it…it's like having the story happen right here, in front of us. Your fluke doesn't have to do with story-telling at all, does it?" she adds.

"Not even remotely," Rian promises. "Besides, I left out a lot. Specific events, and characters. Theories, connections to history and the Theebin religion and such. I didn't mention the Seven Eyes of Death at all, or the Curse of the Dragon's Tooth, and…well. Perhaps it wasn't the best choice of story, this time. There is simply too much involved to do it justice all in one take."

"Well, I liked it," Ayla insists. "I should go to mathematics, now. But will you ever tell me all of it?"

"Maybe. Sometime," Rian says. "Once I have the whole story to tell."

This is enough to satisfy Ayla. Once she thinks no one is watching, she lunges forward to give Rian a brief, heart-felt embrace, then grabs her bag and runs off, her gold hair flying out behind her.

Soon, the only ones left are Rian, Qhan, the usual bodyguards and Mercer, of all people.

He, like Crispin, must have snuck into the crowd, but I hadn't noticed him up until now. Sloppy of me, but I was too preoccupied with Rian and Ayla. I'll have to take care that their budding father-daughter love story doesn't distract me in the future.

"Again, I bow to your superior skill at commanding a crowd," Mercer says, his tone and body language full of good-natured pomp at Rian's expense.

"Oh, don't do that," Rian insists. "It's the stories they want. All that makes me is a good entertainer, and perhaps historian. Not a politician."

"Historian? You still think so?" Mercer asks, playfully critical. "I mean, that hairpin of yours came from somewhere, and it's possible that it was a gift from an alleged Magicsmith, but it's one thing to acknowledge a possibility and quite another to blindly believe something that's never been proven."

Rian shrugs and grins. "And why not? I believe what's written in the oldest of texts from the Theebin church, and stories of the Families Three have as much historical accuracy to them to hint at their truthfulness. Perhaps they are not entirely reliable, but even so. Those families, or at least iterations of them, did exist. Who's to say the stories told of them aren't true?"

Mercer raises an eyebrow. "If they are, it means there could be Magicsmiths out in the world, refusing to help while countries turn on each other, and the Grey family out still trying to do…oh, whatever it is they intended to do when they turned on the other two. You weren't clear on that point, actually. There! Some criticism for you."

"You saw that magic mirror yourself, Merse," Rian chides, ignoring Mercer's last point. "And you were just as excited about that hairpin as I was."

"I was excited because I knew how much it meant to you."

"So you say," Rian teases him. "But you want to believe just as much as the children do. You've just turned a skeptic, now, because you believe being an adult should dictate such. Besides: magic mirror…"

"There is an astoundingly more likely theory that the magic mirrors were gifts from the Fae," Mercer says dryly. "And having met Clanaugh as many times as you have, I wouldn't put it past someone like him to 'gift' magic mirrors to humanity. He'd likely think it hysterical, and I suspect his kingly Fae brethren are just the same. Ah, were the same, I suppose."

"Or," Rian drags the word out, "Horacio Smith made the magic mirrors after a nobleman said his talent was worthless and his claim as a Magicsmith, false Ironic, given how little credit he's received for their creation."

"Which seems to indicate that they were made by Fae."

"Did you ask Reginald the Mirror when you happened to have him before you?" Rian challenges.

It takes Mercer a beat. "I'm amazed you remember its name."

"His name," Rian corrects.

"Yes, well, *Reginald* wasn't inclined to be very helpful in the field of historical accuracy," Mercer claims. "I did ask him about your Horacio Smith, and he answered only, 'a magic what?', which implies I'm right."

"Or, I, the expert on the subject, am, in fact, correct," Rian says. "Besides, magic mirrors are known for lying."

"Given how few of them have graced the world stage with their presence, I doubt they can really be 'known' for anything outside of your stories," Mercer drawls. "Wasn't your Magicsmith supposed to have made hundreds of them?"

"Ah, yes. By the end of his life, Horacio Smith had managed to create five-thousand and seventy-two magic mirrors, who in turn, created their own societal rules and hierarchy in a system they refer to as the 'Gilded Guild'. And honestly, my good friend, history does not get much better than that."

"You only like it because 'Gilded Guild' is both alliterative and a pun," Mercer accuses.

"Possibly. But I also admire the tenacity of Horacio Smith for dedicating his entire life to petty revenge for the off-handed comment of one person."

"Admit it: I'm right. I've been all over the world, Rian, and I haven't seen a single thing aside from a few debatable trinkets to prove there are Magicsmiths around, or that there ever were."

"Just because you've traveled the world doesn't mean you've seen all of it," Rian chides. "You haven't even seen every corner of Isaaria! Who knows what's still out there? Who knows what we'd find, if we went looking?"

"Then let's look," Mercer suggests. "Let's make a pact right now: once Comus Day has passed, king crowned and country settled, let's go poking around for Magicsmiths."

"Oh, you know I couldn't. Besides. I, ah…may or may not have… parental obligations."

Mercer stares at him. He hasn't decided if he's more displeased or shocked, but from what I can see, he's closer to the latter.

"Hope's Head, Rian; what did you do, who did you do it to, and do I need to start preparing a best man's speech for the world's hastiest marriage?"

Rian can't help but laugh, though there's a nervousness to it that I'm sure puts Mercer on edge. My crown prince is quick to remedy the situation, but for a few seconds, Mercer looks certain he'd accidentally guessed correctly.

"Nothing like that," Rian reassures his friend. "It's Ayla. I'm adopting her."

Mercer's shoulders visibly relax.

"The little blond child who's enamored with you? Well, then. When do I get to meet her, Rian? You kept telling me all about her, and yet you've never once bothered with a proper introduction! Is this how I'm going to end up meeting your future wife, too? You'll pull some girl out behind a curtain and give her your name without even letting me approve of her first?!"

"Oh, don't be like that, Merse," Rian insists. "It's not like I've told anyone else about Ayla. Well, except for Qhan, of course."

"Qhan!" Mercer repeats, and whirls on the bodyguard. "You traitor! How could you not tell me?"

Qhan shrugs. "Sorry, sir. I was sworn to secrecy," he adds. "And I needed to know—for the crown prince's security."

Mercer groans dramatically.

"Besides," Rian continues, "I think you'll agree it's much more important for you to approve of my future wife than a little girl I want to adopt."

"Yes, yes, all right. An unfair comparison," Mercer relents. "It's only…I didn't think we kept secrets from each other, Rian. Everyone else does in the courts, that's undeniable, but…not…*us.*"

"It was hardly a secret," Rian demurs. "You've been busy, out and about all around the world. I only started seriously considering it after you went west, anyways. Trust me—you haven't missed any big milestones."

Mercer harrumphs, a sound only Rian can get him to make. Regardless of his friend's reassurances, I'm certain he's just as suspicious as I am that Rian has been hiding a secret bride somewhere.

"Well, so long as you promise to keep me updated. At least let me take you out to celebrate!" he insists. "You can introduce me to Ayla later. Tomorrow, if we're not too hungover. It's not every day you decide to raise a child!"

"Ah, I appreciate it. Really. But not today," Rian excuses himself after another check of the clock tower. "Sorry, Merse. I have *business* to see to this afternoon."

"…*Oh.* I see. Want accompaniment?" Mercer suggests.

But I know where it is Rian is going, and know, before he opens his mouth, that he'll decline. And since Mercer already knows about it and casually offered his company out of support, not curiosity, he's not offended.

This is a private matter.

Nine

RIAN COULD HAVE used his princely title to have a coach ready for him immediately, but instead opts to wait in the queue for half-an-hour, standing silently with Qhan and rocking back and forth on his heels. Hands stuffed in pockets. It's not that this isn't important enough for him to proceed with haste, but Rian does not like having a paper trail of where he goes. Using his power as a crown prince ensures one, as the coachmen must document his jumping to the front of the line for legal purposes in case someone complains about how long it took for them to get a ride. Waiting like anyone else for the next available driver does not.

I'll follow Rian and his guards in a coach of my own and keep my distance once we've reached the city. I know where Rian is going. He takes the same path every time, as if he's never considered someone might follow him. It's a good thing he has Qhan close by.

Rian is visiting the apothecary known as Mallin Cruz. Or at least, everyone *claims* he's an apothecary. It's a dying business: most would rather see their own doctor or visit a clinic to receive a prescription to be filled at a local pharmacy. Apothecaries still in thriving business are considered less-than-trustworthy, as it's likely they've supplemented their wares with illegal materials. But regardless, Rian trusts Mallin.

I think the greatest appeal is that of discretion. Since I know what Rian intends to purchase, I understand why he covets such a thing.

I was not so calm the first time Rian ventured into the seedy part of city that houses Mallin Cruz's shop. It was ten years ago, now, and I'd been a jumpy teenager, prone to overreacting whenever Rian "deviated from the schedule". Nusk used to laugh at me over that, claiming I worried too much.

He sent Taris with me until I became accustomed to Rian's apothecary outings.

Now, all I have to do is tell a driver to follow the coach that's just left and turn on my earpiece so I can listen in on Rian during the ride. Nothing's ever happened to Rian on his way to the city—strangely enough, or perhaps because of my precautions, no one's even tried to attack him in-transit—but it's nice to sit and listen to him jabber, sometimes.

Today is not as blistering hot as the past few days have been, with a gentle, cool breeze blowing through both the city and University campus. I keep the windows of my coach open, and the curtains pulled back, and gnaw on mint leaves to keep from grinding my teeth.

"Times are about to change, Qhan," Rian announces once we are well on our way. "In many, many ways…"

"I can only imagine, sir," Qhan says.

"In a few years, I'm sure the University will replace most of the coaches with some of those Alarkian contraptions," Rian continues, pretending this is what he was talking about all along. "I wonder if I should petition to have the coachmen receive free teaching if they desire, so they can learn how to drive those beasts. I'd hate for them to lose their jobs."

"If they're motivated to keep their jobs, they'll find a way," Qhan claims. "If not, they'll learn to adapt. You're too kind, crown prince," he adds, and I can tell that Rian's disappointed.

"Yes, but I like our coachmen," Rian complains. "And they work for the University. So, if the University is going to change from horses to machinery, shouldn't the coachmen have some sort of…job security?"

"I wouldn't know, sir. I'd say it's a matter between them and the University."

"I suppose I am making a bit of an assumption," Rian admits. "But if I were a coachman who had loyally served for years, I should think I'd like a little reassurance that my hard work had been noted. No one likes being thought of as expendable, you know. And according to Fate, none of us are, so why should we humans say otherwise?"

"As always, your majesty, I have no answer you'd find satisfying," Qhan says.

They go on: Rian trying to force opinions out of Qhan, who is not the sort of man who enjoys letting his thoughts run wild in the hypothetical. He pretends to be impassive, though I am certain he enjoys listening to Rian's blather just as much as I, or Mercer, or Ayla, or anyone else on campus seems to.

When we arrive in the city's center, Rian has the coachman stop so he and his guards can walk the rest of the way. He enjoys the exercise, and doesn't want to encourage speculation back at campus about where he might be going.

Sumouel City is arguably the safest city in Isaaria, even at night. There's not even much mugging to worry about; drunken disorderly is the most common fine issued by the peacekeepers. Even the dirtiest and darkest part of the city is simply underpopulated and lacking janitorial upkeep, but I hardly consider it dangerous. I would prefer Rian not venture out at all, of course, but he has me and his guards and Qhan. We'll keep him safe.

I walk behind them at a distance, keeping to the shadows. There are a few less than reputable folk walking down the street as well, but they ignore me, some of them to the point of nearly walking into me.

We are close to the apothecary when I spy a ragged figure propped against the wall of a broken-down building. He has a tin cup next to him, but he's not actively pandering. In fact, he makes no sound at all, nor does he move.

It's only when I'm right in front of him that I realize what I'm looking at.

A magic-sick. I flick my eyes away from him; poor fellow. He's so thin, and covered in the characteristic small, dotted sores on his face, neck, and shoulders. His eyes are glazed and mouth slightly open, so I can tell that he is in the last stages of the sickness, where victims of corrupted magic are often no longer themselves. They are allegedly stripped of personality, yet they cling to life until the very end. There's no way to know for sure what happens in a magic-sick's head, but mind-readers have hedged there may be something there that they simply cannot reach. Magic-sick could be prisoners of their own bodies, unable to beg for help.

It's saddening in every way, and multiple law-makers have attempted to pass an edict to euthanize those who come into contact with such corrupt magic. The intent is one of pity and mercy, but doomed as they may be, magic-sick can still live for a long time in the final stages, so long as there is someone who does not mind caring for them. I've heard Rian say that in the end it becomes less a matter of mercy, and more one of convenience. And he believes the value of human life should not depend on convenience.

He and Mercer both give anonymous yearly donations to help researchers find a cure for magic-sickness. I know, because I remember them staying up all night seven years ago, discussing the ethics of it all. But no one else has any idea about their secret charity, and I think there's something noble in that.

Glancing around first to make sure Rian isn't too far ahead, I dig in my coin purse, tied under my skirt. I take care to place my contribution directly into the magic-sick's tin cup. I try to look at him straight on, searching for anything in his eyes to indicate he might know how to use currency, but I can't tell.

I don't dare linger longer, and hurry on after Rian and Qhan. There's nothing more I can do for this fellow, anyway.

Pushing the magic-sick from my mind, I find a nearby building to climb, taking to the roof. I need to be up high anyway.

Like many old Isaarian public buildings, the apothecary has a skylight that can be covered easily in the winter and opened up in the summer to allow airflow, and combat the humidity. It's perfect for me to peek in from above and keep an eye on Rian while he does his business. No one can sneak in or out of the shop without me noticing, and I have an easy way in if Rian needs help.

I take my position up top while Qhan stands guard at the doorway. He won't block others from entering, but his presence alone will dissuade other customers from stopping by until Rian has left.

Qhan sends another of Rian's bodyguards to check the inside of the building, and he eventually emerges with a nod: it's safe to enter. Rian does so, brushing past the curtained doorway filled with bell, chimes, and all sorts of dangling, superstitious charms meant to ward off malicious spirits. Normally, I'd scoff at such a thing. But the creature I saw on the road back from the city that night has unnerved me enough not to outright laugh at such precautions anymore.

Considering my recent kill count and how many bad dreams I've had lately, maybe I should stop into Mallin's shop myself. And invest.

I lay on my stomach to watch Rian through the skylight. I have a good view of almost the entire shop without having to move around, and can see Rian's full transaction with the apothecary from beginning to end.

Mallin Cruz is Lijimi, though he's lived in Isaaria almost as long as Rian has been at the University, and is not a refugee from the ongoing war. From what I've seen of him, Mallin appears to have few patriotic inclinations when it comes to his birthplace, and has never once mentioned politics to Rian.

Compared to Rian, Mallin is a short man, perhaps my own height or a little smaller, and his skin is a much tanner color. When he smiles, which he often does when he sees Rian enter his shop, he reveals teeth stained with tobacco and Umbra leaves, as well as three gold teeth and one silver one.

"Ah, Crown Prince Rian!" Mallin announces, and thankfully there is no one else in the shop to hear.

"Mister Cruz," Rian says respectfully. Well, perhaps it's not quite respectful, given how many times Mallin has insisted on being referred to by his first name only. "Always a pleasure."

"Your usual, Crown Prince?" Mallin says gleefully.

He takes a perverse joy in the fact that someone of Rian's station frequents his shop, as if something is forcing Rian to do so, though we all know it's simply a personal preference.

"That would be appreciated. Thank you," Rian says.

He doesn't grow exasperated with Mallin for not having his order ready, though this was clearly done on purpose in an attempt to get a rise out of him.

"I'll need only a few minutes, and then you can be on your way," Mallin claims, and holds out a hand.

He always makes Rian pay him first, as if he suspects the crown prince might try to haggle or cheat him out of fair payment. I don't know what sorts of nobles Mallin has dealt with in the past, but it's clear he doesn't trust them. Not that I blame him, and I suspect Rian doesn't either. He hands over the coins promptly. Mallin disappears into his back room, leaving Rian alone in the shop.

It is beneficial in a superficial way that Mallin moves wares quickly; every time Rian visits, there's something new to examine while he waits. This may be an apothecary, but Mallin also sells all sorts of charms, crystals, and gems. Even eastern herbs and blood-mapping kits. Sage ropes to ward off angry ghosts and small animal skeletons to frighten malicious spirits hang right along displays of tinctures meant to cure headache, literal heartache, cramps, and so on. He even sells burlap bags stuffed with herbs and spices for cooking, which Rian always seems to take an interest in, even if he never purchases any. At the very least, it keeps the place from smelling like squirrel corpses.

The shop itself isn't large—most of the products Mallin puts on display either line the walls, or sit in three glass display cases in the middle of the shop. Everything else he keeps in "the back", in a room behind the desk and the storage chamber beneath the shop, accessible by ladder. Normal patrons likely aren't meant to know about said basement room, but something tells me Mallin Cruz isn't worried about Rian bringing the peacekeepers to his door.

Rian is leaning near the wall, his hands clasped behind his back as he peers at some sort of fanciful bong, when Mallin returns with a draw-string bag.

"Will that be all, princeling?" he inquires, grinning so his fake teeth glint.

Rian approaches the front desk to take the bag, opening it to make sure Mallin gave him what he paid for: two vials, two medicines.

"Actually, I'm curious if you might have that certain something I asked after a few months ago," Rian prompts. Not the usual script. "In fact, at this point, I may as well tell you that if you haven't procured it yet, you needn't bother. Today's the last day I'd be interested in buying."

This caveat instantly forestalls any attempts at trickery or bartering. Usually Mallin would tease Rian, forcing him to pay much more than necessary. But if it's now or never, he will sell without complications.

"I will check the back again. I'm certain it arrived yesterday," Mallin claims. A lie, likely, but it hardly matters so long as he gives Rian what he wants.

But what Mallin says next surprises both me and Rian, because as I said, most times the crown prince has the apothecary to himself.

"Just allow me to see what this customer needs first, in case it takes me a moment to dig out your order," he says, and gestures just behind Rian.

Rian turns to the figure behind him, and I'm shocked as well. I hadn't noticed someone enter. And a quick glance at Qhan tells me that he, too, is unaware of another person in the apothecary. They must have snuck in, perhaps using a fluke. They are wearing a hooded cloak, so clearly anonymity is in order. That's not unusual. And since the newcomer doesn't turn their head to watch Rian as he graciously steps aside from the counter, I decide they are not a threat to him. At least, not yet.

"And how might I help you?" Mallin says cheerfully.

If the hooded figure is a regular customer, he's giving no indication. Rian begins to make another round about the shop, feigning disinterest.

"I need some rare materials," the hooded person says, and I realize that it's a woman. A tall woman—she's nearly Rian's height and, like him, practically towers over the apothecary.

"Of course," Mallin agrees. "It's my specialty. What's your practice?"

"*Dadj'zcha*."

The air suddenly feels a mite chillier.

It is strange, and startling, to hear the word so soon after Rian's mention of it. Only this is no ancient tale of old heroes: when spoken aloud, now, there is no doubt that the woman is referring to the modern practice of *Dadj'zcha*. There may be disputes as to whether the Families Three ever existed, but no one can deny the fact that the practice of *Dadj'zcha* is very real, and very dangerous.

I swear, I can see the hairs stand up on the back of Rian's neck, though he pretends to continue to browse and mind his own business. I am glad to be so close to him, now; anyone involved in *Dadj'zcha* is not good news. Whoever this woman is, she cannot have pure intentions.

"Give me a few moments and we'll talk specifics," Mallin says without skipping a beat. As if this is a request that he hears every day.

It can't be.

Dadj'zcha is a dangerous practice, and though it isn't technically illegal in Isaaria, it's considered taboo. Wrong. Twisted. Cavorting with the Dark.

I admittedly know little of its workings, but I understand the basics as well as any child: flukes are magic. Gifts given at birth. A part of a person. They draw upon energy granted to them through the sun, moon, and earth, and channel it. The gifts must be maintained through practice and hard work, and often have built-in boundaries, too, based on how much a person can do without exhausting or injuring themselves. There are limits.

With *Dadj'zcha*, there are presumably no limits. But only a fool would believe that comes without cost.

I'm sure Rian is nervous to be around this woman. The likelihood of her ever doing something to hurt him is slim, but I can understand his apprehension. Those who practice *Dadj'zcha* tend to be unpredictable and violent. And they generally hate anyone who represents authority in any form.

Rian is a crown prince.

I move into a crouch and ready myself for action.

Mallin returns to the back again, leaving the *Dadj'zcha* woman and Rian alone to browse his wares while doing their best to spy on one another. Neither of them turns around fully as they slowly dance from one corner of the room to the other. Rian passes in front of the old Tourrannese ceremonial masks and looks them up and down, like he's considering purchasing one. The woman is in front of the dried lizards and bugs, in their glass cases. Next to them are the flowers—also in glass. Some of them are toxic.

I sit there and tell myself I am more concerned about toxic flowers than the woman looking at exsanguinated mammals as if she's genuinely interested in purchasing some.

Hunched over the skylight, knife in hand, one wrist poised to shoot a poison dart into that bitch's neck if necessary, I count my drops of sweat and wait. She doesn't make a move towards Rian. She doesn't speak to him. But she starts humming an eerie tune that makes me want to end her, if only to make it stop.

I notice for the first time, as she reaches out to stroke a leaf of Devil's Ivy, something that makes me tighten my grip on my knife. Something that it took me a long time to realize, I'm so unused to seeing Isaarians' bare hands: *she's not wearing gloves.*

"Ah, and here it is, sir!" Mallin announces, appearing behind his counter once again. I'm sure it is not lost on Rian that, for once, the apothecary is not using his title. "You're right. I had it in the back all this time."

He hands Rian a cheap white box, the sort one might use to transport a custom cake in. There's something unnaturally cheerful about the thing, as if one's supposed to naturally assume whoever carries it is off to celebrate something. Rian pours more coins into Mallin's hand in exchange, and carefully balances the box as if there's something delicate inside.

He thanks the apothecary, dips his head politely to the cloaked woman, and heads out of the shop as if he's in no hurry.

As intrigued as I am to observe Mallin's sale with the woman, I follow Rian and adjust my position. Once he's a few steps out the door, the chimes still swinging after brushing over his shoulders, he looks back and shudders. Qhan is at his side in a moment, already apologizing, claiming he has no idea how that woman got in. He never saw her.

Rian refuses to accept his apologies. If Qhan didn't notice that woman, no one else was going to.

The two continue on their walk. The magic-sick is gone, now, which I assume means someone must have come by and removed him.

I follow on the rooftops, maintaining an angle that allows me to watch Rian and reach him quickly if need be. Vigilant as I am, I spot Crown Prince Magnus and Griffith Reach before Rian or Qhan. As Magnus poses no current physical threat to Rian, I do not intervene.

It's almost comical, watching the two crown princes and their sets of guards bump into one another. Qhan and Griffith are the ones closest to their princes, yes, but there's a decent perimeter set up around the nearest block. While still in this abandoned area, there will be no one around to interrupt.

"What are you doing here?" Rian blurts.

"Following you—what are you doing here?" Magnus retorts. Somehow, when he says it, it sounds much more accusatory. "This is not the most reputable place, Yakarami," he adds, giving Rian's box and bag a deserved suspicious look.

"Oh, I'm aware. I wasn't aware our movements were being restricted. It's not as if I've done anything illegal," he adds, and it's clear given his smile and tone of voice that this was said in jest. In an attempt to alleviate tension.

With Magnus, it doesn't work.

Crown Prince Magnus holds up something that I recognize as a tracking receiver. I realize he must have planted a bug of his own on Rian, and I can only hope that he didn't happen to pick up the frequency of the one Taris stuck to Rian's earring.

"You must be more careful, Yakarami," Magnus warns, while Rian is too busy being aghast to speak. "I could have been just anyone, planting a tracker on you. I could have been an assassin, following you to this secluded part of the city to do you in."

Rian is speechless. Qhan, however, isn't.

"I would never allow such a thing. Your majesty," he says.

His tone is polite enough, but I can tell from the fact that his hand is still on the hilt of his scimitar that he's irritated with Magnus for pulling such a stunt. Now that he knows to look for something, Qhan leans over and plucks a clip from the strap of Rian's satchel. Who knows when Magnus planted it there? Qhan tosses the tracker at Magnus, but Griffith is the one who snatches it from the air. Magnus doesn't even flinch.

By then, Rian has recovered from his shock enough to speak.

"I, ah, is there a reason you decided to follow me out here today, Magnus? Not that I don't appreciate the company, but if I'd known you were interested in what I was up to, I would have invited you along."

That's a blatant lie, but I appreciate that Rian's trying to cover his tracks.

"Comus Day is approaching," Magnus says.

Rian nods. "I had noticed that, yes."

"And I think we should form an alliance in preparation."

Rian continues to nod. "I think that's a terrible idea," he says, in the same tone of voice, so that it takes Magnus a few seconds to process what he's said.

"Good, because, I—" Magnus starts, and then has to force himself to stop. "Wait. Did you just—"

"Say no to you?" Rian finishes. "Why, yes. That does happen sometimes, Magnus. I suggest you prepare yourself for potential proximate pain by prioritizing this moment in your memory."

He flashes what I know is his genuine smile, which makes this situation even worse for someone like Magnus.

"Excuse me, *what?*" he splutters. "I always thought it was a necessary fiction: you acting the fool."

It seems as if he can't quite comprehend another reason why Rian wouldn't want to form an official alliance in the coming days.

"I'm trying to recruit you for a good cause, Yakarami," Magnus presses. "Isaaria needs its future heir. If the Carsans aren't going to do their job and track down who it's meant to be, then someone must."

I suspect he intends to use this moment to hook Rian in, then reveal what other things he suspects the Carsans of, but my crown prince isn't having any of it. He has plans for today, and given how personal they are in nature, they take precedence over Magnus' paranoia.

"Look, Magnus," Rian sighs. "I know you like to look around at the rest of us, trying to figure out who dodged out of being crowned king as a child—"

"Or queen," Magnus interrupts.

"Right, right. Or queen. But my point is: no one else seems to care. Not at the moment. It doesn't matter who should have been the next king, only who's going to be. And whatever trials await us at Comus Day will determine that. Fifty years from now, no one will even care that there was a missing 'True Heir'. Because it simply won't matter anymore."

Magnus narrows his eyes at him.

"Now, if you don't mind, I'll be off," Rian says. "Lovely surprise to see you, Magnus. Enjoy your day."

"Where are you going?"

"I have an appointment."

Magnus frowns. "Now is not the time to start keeping secrets, Yakarami."

"It's not a secret," Rian sighs. "It's a matter of privacy. Trust me, if anything changes and I'm suddenly perfectly fine with everyone in the world knowing my business, you'll be the first person I gab to. Fair enough?"

He flashes that perfect smile of his again, pats Magnus on the shoulder, and strides confidently past to go on his merry way. I'm about to hop to a nearby rooftop when I'm stopped by further words spoken. This is far from over.

"For the record, Yakarami, I'd be very careful about the stories you tell on campus," Magnus says, raising his voice slightly at the end to get Rian's attention.

Of course, Rian turns, a look of confusion on his face.

"What's that supposed to mean?" he asks hesitantly.

"Only that you know the basic stories as well as anyone else," Magnus says. "And the Families Three are meant to be three. Together. They're heroes. For some, they're gods. They're supposed to be untouchable. It's not exactly helpful for you to lounge on your grassy knoll spouting tales about how they all betrayed and killed one another."

"That's history," Rian says.

"Yes," Magnus agrees. "History. No one wants the details anymore. Not the grimy bits, anyway. No one tells stories about the end of the Families Three. Did you ever consider that there's probably a reason why what you study is buried so deep that your subject is considered ancient and irrelevant?"

Rian shifts uncomfortably. "Well, I wouldn't say irrelevant," he mutters.

Magnus takes a few ambling steps closer to him, and Qhan pointedly rests his hand back on the hilt of his scimitar. I'm not that concerned, but I'm glad Qhan is doing his job.

"There's a reason the only stories people tell are the good ones, Yakarami. They always have good endings. Because the heroes of the old stories are supposed to stay that way."

The two of them stare at one another.

"Are you…threatening me?" Rian asks with an awkward laugh, as if he can't quite believe it.

"I'd never do that, Yakarami," Magnus says. "Really, I wouldn't. But think about it. Our country is about to go through a tremendous change. All of us heirs are being scrutinized now more than ever. Every single child at that University looks at you with stars in their eyes. And there you are, telling them that the bedtime stories their parents told them at night are all lies. Do you understand what kind of power we have? That every little thing you say influences our country, and our people?"

Rian gives another nervous laugh. "I'm telling stories, Magnus. There's nothing sinister about it. Unless this is some sort of metaphor for spilling royal secrets, in which case, I should think it's obvious you don't need to worry about that," he blathers. "I'm no gossip."

"Just remember who you're talking to, Yakarami," Magnus sighs, shaking his head. "You had the luxury of growing up ignored. The least likely of any of the heirs to be worth anything. I had to be 'the son of the king'."

He brushes past Rian, choosing to leave first. I doubt he's even planning on going in the direction he's currently walking for more than a block; he merely wants to be the one to end the conversation.

Griffith makes a point of nodding to Qhan, almost in what I assume is respect or deference. Magnus has potentially had just as many attempts on his life as Rian, only for completely different reasons.

Qhan returns the nod. The two have some sort of understanding with one another, as professions that care genuinely about their principals.

Rian stands still for a moment, watching Magnus leave, then rolls his eyes and continues on his own way. Usually, my crown prince is a likeable, light-hearted fellow, and he does his best now to reoccupy that persona. But I can tell that what Magnus said has bothered him. He doesn't like confrontation. And much of what the king's son said hints at trouble to come amongst the eight royal families.

Sides may be chosen once a new king is crowned.

Rian will not do well with that.

"I apologize for the apparent rivalry I've started," he sighs. "If Magnus and I got along better, I think you and Griffith might make good friends."

"I'd prefer to have drinks with Marques," Qhan admits, straight-faced.

That draws a good laugh from Rian, and he's grinning again.

Talan Marques is Mercer's bodyguard. Sometimes even I have to wonder if the man exists, because while Mercer's life is obviously well-preserved despite all his traveling, I almost never see Marques. Personally,

I'd prefer Griffith any day of the week, because at least I can watch him. Marques could be anywhere, at any given point in time, and I might never know. The last time I saw him was almost a year ago, during a University party Mercer attended.

"That was a little confusing," Rian admits, glancing back to where they'd left Magnus and Griffith behind. "Do you have any idea what he was jabbering on about at the end, there, about my storytelling? It is simply telling stories, you know. I don't have ulterior motives."

I follow along on the roofs, listening over my earpiece while they talk. There's a brief moment of silence, making it clear that Qhan does not entirely agree with his principal. When he speaks, I find I'm relieved; Rian needs someone willing to give him good advice, and sometimes folk are too scared to speak up against a royal. Even one like Rian.

"He does have a point, sir," Qhan says. "I should think your run-in with that *Dadj'zcha* practitioner should be enough proof for you: that woman is nothing to us. You'll likely never see her again. But she's a practitioner of *Dadj'zcha*, the dark art the Greys started, and you're telling stories making them out to be villains. As I'm certain Mercer's tried to inform you, what remains of peace in the world is tenuously balanced between Isaaria and our allies. It would be unfortunate if you somehow managed to anger some outside group. Our country has enough troubles."

"Huh."

"And Crown Prince Magnus has always tried to look after the rest of the heirs," Qhan goes on. "I suspect he's not pleased to learn you're spreading around potentially controversial material. Not with Comus Day so close."

Rian thinks for a few moments. He hadn't considered this.

"I suppose," he says. "But it's not as if I'm changing the story for my own purposes. History shows that the Greys did begin practicing a dangerous and corrupt art instead of depending on their gifted flukes. They did turn on the other two families—all but destroying the Wolffs. And actually, you know, I didn't think it appropriate to mention it in front of children, but they started capturing Magicsmiths to keep under their thumbs, like pets. Killing off all but a few children in each family, to ensure they always had control of the 'first-born Magicsmiths' of each generation. Now, I haven't discovered why, yet, exactly, but you know—"

And on he goes. If Mango were here, he would likely be even more animated as he blathers on about the Magicsmiths and the many lost stories about them.

But I'm too busy thinking to listen. Because, as clarified by Qhan, Magnus has a point. Perhaps at least some of the killers haunting Rian's steps aren't after him because of his position as one of eight heirs of Isaaria.

And perhaps they aren't after him because of his fluke, or the Carsans prophecy, or politics.

Perhaps Rian-the-Scholar has dug up something he wasn't supposed to. And someone wants that information to stay hidden.

RIAN'S STRIDE IS ALMOST aggressively brisk for the entirety of his trek to the opposite end of the city. This is part of his routine, after every visit he makes to Mallin's. His destination is a private care facility: high-end, regulated strictly, with some of the best on-staff physicians one could hope for. They cater exclusively to family needs, allowing those with life-threatening illnesses to live as freely as possible while staying close by the assistance necessary to keep them safe. Qhan has the guards clear the place of potential threats, then stations them around the building while Rian enters alone to conduct his business.

I know this is a building old enough to still house its original ventilation system, a system large enough for me to use. Granted, a potential assassin might use the same vents to go after Rian, but given how few people know he comes here, it's unlikely.

I wrap rubber soles around my shoes to keep them quiet in the vents, then steal inside the building before Rian's guards start their rotation.

As Rian is only a little late compared to the time he alerted the staff to expect him, there is a nurse still standing by to wait for him. They never require him to sign in as they do other guests, and Rian surely knows the way to go at this point, but the nurses take care to greet him and give him any necessary updates each time he visits. Even the feel of the facility, and the way it is decorated, is comfortable and personable. Nothing cold and clinical about it at all, except the staff's stiff white and blue uniforms.

The nurse smiles when she sees Rian, but there's sadness in her eyes that even I notice, at a distance.

"Crown Prince," she says, as she rises from her curtsey and straightens out her apron. "How was your trip into the city today?"

"Not at all strenuous," Rian says, handing the nurse the drawstring bag from Mallin's. "There's her medicine in there, as well as Asmer's."

The nurse nods. Since Asmer al'Yibna's medical condition is meant to be a secret, her father and the rest of the royals go to great pains to pretend as if it doesn't exist. Mercer primarily acts as her doctor, and since it could endanger his reputation to steal medicine for her, Rian purchases it discreetly through Mallin Cruz and has it passed on by people he trusts.

He'll be visiting the apothecary anyway, after all, and Mercer's aware of this, even if others are not.

It occurs to me that Rian could have simply told Magnus he was helping Asmer, and Magnus would not have asked anything more about it. Since Asmer is endeared to practically everyone, it would have been an excellent excuse. But I suppose protecting her privacy, and Mercer's career, are more important to him than deflecting Magnus' suspicion.

I may have judged my crown prince too harshly; he might not like conflict, but he'll suffer it for those he cares about.

"How is she today?" Rian asks.

The nurse hesitates, but gives him the truth. "She is happy, but her health has continued to decline. To be honest, most of us thought she would pass before your next visit. It's a miracle the Almighty has allowed her to stay this long."

"Then we shall have to pray in thanksgiving, won't we?" Rian suggests, his tone still light, but forced. "I'll stop in to see her—it has been some time."

The nurse nods, still holding the medicine bag. I wonder if she's aware of where Rian gets that medicine from, or if she simply doesn't care.

It certainly cuts down on expenses for the facility, letting him bring it through such obscure channels.

I clamber through the vents ahead of Rian as he heads down the hall, and manage to position myself comfortably behind a grate to watch as he opens the door to the room housing the only living family he has left. His grandmother has been here for the better part of fifteen years, now, and most other royals have assumed her dead. When Rian's parents passed, it certainly drew any remaining attention away from Sakia Yakarami, former Grand Princess of Isaaria.

Rian used to see her every other week; sometimes more, if he could. But as sick as she is, his grandmother can barely muster the energy for those relatively sparse visits from him. Her doctor explained to Rian long ago that though his visits bring her joy, they are taxing on her health, and Rian is too selfless to try and see her more often for his own sake.

She looks especially sick and small now, asleep in her bed, blue blankets pulled up under her arms, her thinned silver hair braided loosely behind her head on the pillow. I've seen a few official photographs from her mid-life, and royal portraits of the Yakaramis from when she was younger. Sakia Yakarami was a beautiful woman, and I know from historical texts that she was quickly widowed after giving birth to Rian's father. She raised him on her own, and helped look after Rian, too.

She has lived an interesting life, and I know Rian enjoys visiting her.

"Amami. It's me," Rian says, reaching across the bed to take her hand.

He's still smiling that bright, young smile without a hint of sadness to it. "Amami?"

"O-ah. Ree-on," she says drowsily, as she wakes. "Baby boy. So good of you to come see me again. You are too-good-to-me," she says, patting his hand four times of those last four words, to emphasize her point.

"I'm sorry I haven't been in much lately," he apologizes. "Things have been…hectic, but I should have tried harder."

"No, no, no," his grandmother insists. "You have your own life to live. You don't need to keep spending so much time with me."

"Nonsense," Rian claims, and helps prop her up on her pillows.

Sakia Yakarami no longer has the strength to sit up for long, but with enough pillows behind her she can at least lie at an angle.

"I brought something for you," Rian says.

He pulls a chair closer to her bed, settles himself down, and then transfers his box from the floor to his lap.

"I know I'm not supposed to be here often, bringing in outside germs. But it's Sakamoura today—Kachin holiday for honoring grandparents," he tells her. "So, instead of just bringing your medicine, I asked Mallin to find me a Roustia."

I can't imagine how much Mallin charged for that flower; Roustias never die. They can be dangerous to acquire, and are not native to anywhere in Isaaria except in the parts of the forest occupied by the Fae.

Rian unfolds the white box to reveal a large, beautiful blossom. It glows in the dim room, it's so golden, and I know that, were we in complete darkness, it would emit a soft, romantic light to attract fairies, pixies, and even nymphs. If Rian leaves the flower in his grandmother's window, she might get to see a few fluttering folk hovering outside to bask in the Roustia's light.

"Oh, Rian. So beautiful," his grandmother croaks as he places the flower and its delicate, folding petals gently atop her hands.

"And it will live forever, so you'll always have something from outside here," he promises before she can thank him. "Something magic."

She smiles at the flower and strokes one of its petals. I practically expect to see a sleepy fairy rouse from the center, yawning.

"Amami," Rian goes on. "After Comus Day, everything will be different. All this madness will be over, and I'll have you come live with me. I can take you out in a wheeled chair, like little Soren Carsans, do you remember him? We can go out near the forest every day. And see all sorts of magic. Would you like that?"

"I would hate to be a burden to you. You are still so young! You have your own life to see to," she protests weakly.

Rian doesn't like that one bit.

"Amami, you are not a burden," he insists. "I'd have you come live with me now, if I could. Let's think about it," he suggests, trying to lighten the mood more. "When we're finished with all this 'Lost Heir' nonsense, and I can give you whatever you want, what would you like?"

Sakia Yakarami makes a great show of thinking about this.

"Great-grandchildren!" she cheers, and Rian laughs.

"Well," he says. "We'll see."

He does not mention his plans to adopt Ayla, but I understand why: his grandmother is going to die, soon. There will be no moving in with him, no seeing great-grandchildren. He does not want Sakia to pass knowing she had a great-granddaughter whom she never got the chance to meet.

"What else?" he presses.

His grandmother's answers are halting, and often slightly slurred, but I can hear her well enough.

"Mmm…I would like to go out in the forests again, under the moonlight in bare feet. I did that as a girl, did I ever tell you?"

"Yes. All the time, you said. You said Great-Grandfather always pretended it infuriated him, but he loved you too much to stop you."

She continues, remembering. "I'd like to see the night fairies again," she claims. "Some of them glow in the dark. And they sing such beautiful songs…I always wondered what they were about…And the naiads and the dryads…And the little reptilian dragons scampering about the forest floor, or the ones with feathers, perched on tree-branches, trying to spring after birds!... I wonder if they miss me. Or if I was always just another human to them."

"I'm sure they'd remember you," Rian promises her. "I don't think I've gotten the chance to introduce you to Mango, yet. But do you remember, I told you about him? My little sunblood dragon?"

"Oh, yes!" Sakia Yakarami chirps happily to be reminded. "Has he figured out he's meant to fly, yet?"

Rian laughs. "Not yet. Poor thing. When I first got him, I learned he was separated from the rest of his litter when he was a baby. He thinks he's a cat, not a dragon. In all other ways he acts like one, though. I'll have to bring him by for you to see. Would you like that? More visitors?"

Rian must know there's no chance his grandmother could handle seeing any more people right now, let alone a dragon. No matter how miniature Mango is. There's stress and germs and excitement involved. I can't decide if it's cruel or not, for him to offer such a thing when he knows he can never deliver.

"Oh, yes. Bring more folks in! Soon as I get stronger, I'll be back and out in society again, fit as ever! Where's that handsome friend of yours? Mer-cer!" she croaks, remembering his name. "Always a charming lad. Bit of a wandering in his bones, though. Bring him by, if you can pin him down."

Rian smiles. "Oh, he's still around for now. But you're right—he does like to go out and about in the world. Wants to see everything…"

They continue to talk. Or, Rian does. He tells his grandmother entertaining things about his life. He does not mention Comus Day, only the fact that Mercer is back and has brought wondrous gifts for everyone. He does not say anything about Lune's peculiar moods, but describes her concert. He says nothing about his recent run-in with Magnus, or the political monster he will face in the coming weeks, but instead regales her with the stories he's telling his students, and his Magicsmith research.

Sakia Yakarami nods now and again, or smiles. She tires and says she's going to close her eyes to rest a bit.

Rian suggests he tell her a story to see her off to sleep, and repeats his own tale from earlier today. The one he graced Ayla and her friends with, about the Families Three. This time, he utilizes more detail, according to the Church of the Holy Three and the Theebin religion, as he has no one to offend. And he makes it more dramatic. It's still not as detailed as I'm sure he would like, given the centuries its arc spans, but he mentions more names. He is working on those family trees, after all.

When he's finally done, he looks over at his grandmother and the Roustia flower resting on her hands. He looks for a painfully long time, and then reaches out to feel for a beating at her wrist. I don't need to be taking her pulse to know: she stopped breathing several minutes ago.

Rian puts his head down in his hands and stays like that for a long while. I almost wish I could crawl out from the vent and wrap my arms around him. Today has been so hard on him, and though I know I should be ignoring these feelings and impulses, I can't help but want to comfort him.

He does mean so much to me.

Eventually, he wearily raises his head, reaches into his bag, and pulls out a plain envelope to lean against the Roustia. Then he stands and quietly exits the room. As if his grandmother is only asleep, and he does not wish to wake her. He makes his way back up to the lobby, to track down the nurse from before. I'm certain the staff won't be surprised to learn of Sakia's death. After all, they were shocked she lasted this long.

But there is still pity, and sadness, when Rian tells the nurse the news. She frowns, and her brow furrows. I think she's examining him for signs of grief, and the fact that she can tell he's attempting to put up a mask only makes her feel more for him. He is trying to be practical about it, but that's not Rian.

"I've left full details, of how she said she'd like to be buried, in an envelope on the bed," he says, and I realize that he brought that fully expectant of today's events. "There is a flower in her room, now, to be planted on the site. Could you contact the right people, and have it seen to? I'll pay for all of it."

"Yes, we will take care of that," the nurse says gently.

"I…I'd like to have a full service for her. But I…Can't. Right now. Things are…I'd like to come back, with my family, and have something of a ceremony, after the new king is crowned. Would that be possible?"

"Of course, crown prince," the nurse says, bowing her head. She doesn't ask what he means by "family", though she's aware that Rian's grandmother was officially his last living relative. "We are all greatly troubled by your loss," she adds.

Rian hesitates. "She…lived for a very long time," he finally says. "I'm lucky to have had her this long, and should be happy she'll have a chance to traverse the Otherworld, now. She lived a good life. I'm sure her travels will take her on a heavenly course."

"Yes, crown prince. We are all sure of that," the nurse agrees.

Rian clears his throat and becomes awkwardly over-aware of his hands.

"Well. Then," he manages. "I expect I will not be back here again for some time. Thank you. For all your help."

The nurse nods.

I disengage from the scene and make my way up the vent to a grating on the roof to exit the building. It's strange to know as I leave that this is likely the last time in my life I'll follow Rian here. It became so routine. Though it sounds foolish, and stupid, some part of my brain assumed that this would go on forever. It became a limbo, like the days at the University.

I find Rian outside, in front of the doors. I can see him from an angle, but from the top-down he'd be hidden by the building's overhang. He stands on the steps, not moving. I can't imagine what he's doing until I hear Qhan call for him and he reaches up to wipe at his face. Crying, then.

Qhan regards Rian with great concern.

"Are you well, little prince?" he asks quietly. From him, it's an endearment.

Rian takes a few seconds to compose himself before answering. I understand he doesn't want to look weak, but there must be someone who's permitted to see our Laughing Prince emotional. He must find someone he trusts with all these things. Otherwise, it'll only be a matter of time before he breaks.

"I'm fine," he says, his voice thick. "It's something I expected. And yet...I'm glad I have you, Qhan. And Mercer, the Carsans, Asmer…"

"And Miss Ayla, soon enough," Qhan prompts.

"Yes," Rian agrees with a watery smile. "I will have Ayla, too."

He lets Qhan lead him away, to call a coach and return to the University and pretend as if this tragedy never happened. Rian is good at covering such things up, though he and Qhan and I will always know who he's lost. But as Qhan said, Rian will always have his bodyguard, and his friends, and Ayla.

And me, I can't help but think as I trail at a distance, not daring to even step close to Rian's shadow.

You will never be alone, my sad little prince. Because I'll be one step behind you, keeping you safe.

Ten

IT'S NOT ENTIRELY FAIR to say that Taris is cantankerous and self-absorbed all the time. There is, in fact, a mildly good-humored side to him that appears now and again around his siblings, particularly when playing games, but it tends to dissipate instantly when I enter the room. This afternoon's events proved to be a rare exception.

It has been about three weeks since the death of Rian's grandmother. Comus Day is only ten days away, and tomorrow morning, the royals of the University will depart for the capital in preparation.

Magnus is practically panicking. It would be funny to watch if I, too, weren't growing nervous.

I have been watching all the royals closely, but whatever machinations are in place behind the scenes, there have been few hints of them. It's a quiet warning before the storm breaks, and I feel woefully unprepared for rain.

I've left Naomi alone with Rian for a few minutes, expecting Korvaan to take my place as previously decided, but return to Nusk's cabin to find that he and Taris are engaged in a serious game of yi-cheon. I'd be irritated with him, except it looks as if their game is drawing to a close.

Today's schedule is bound to be unusual, anyway: there's an official send-off for the royals this evening, and it's sure to be quite an event. I plan to spend most of my time there watching Rian while my *khashak* finish our preparations to leave: wiping clean the rest of our lives here, and making the final arrangements to ferry us all to the capital without raising suspicions.

When I enter the cabin, it's stripped almost completely bare. Nusk hasn't fully divulged his plan to me, but I trust he has made most of the arrangements on his own. Whatever lies he's told and orders he's given with his fluke, I've noticed he's needed to be brought out in the sun more frequently over the past week. For Korvaan and Taris, it's exhausting.

So, I don't begrudge them a friendly game, mainly because I'm tired of barking orders at them. I truly have been trying to keep my promise to Naomi about getting along with Taris now that we need each other. Not that our partnership has borne much fruit, unfortunately.

"Are you holding three and eight?" Korvaan accuses his brother.

Taris says nothing, but gives a wry smirk.

Korvaan tisks and scowls down at his own tiles, certain that he's lost. If Taris truly is holding a three and eight, Korvaan's right—that's the best pair in the game. He has no chance.

Korvaan sighs. "I swear, he's impossible to beat," he complains to me. "Fate most definitely has favorites, and Taris is one of them."

"That's luck's hand, not Fate's," I point out as I circle to the cabinet for a mug before realizing they've all been packed up. "And aren't you supposed to be watching our crown prince?"

"Give me a minute, Soleil," Korvaan says, staring at his tiles. One might think this was a matter of life and death. "If he does have three and eight, the game's over, I'm dead. But, if he doesn't—"

I lean over so I can peer over Taris' hands at his tiles.

"He does."

Korvaan's reaction is dramatic enough that Taris and I share smiles before we can remember we're meant to tolerate each other for business purposes only.

"What the hell, Taris?" Korvaan complains, throwing his tiles down on the table. "How the…Are you cheating?"

Taris shrugs, places his own tiles carefully down with the rest, and stands from the table. "If I were, I wouldn't tell you," he says. "But I'm not."

Korvaan clicks his tongue in irritation. "Bastard," he mutters.

"Only compared to you," Taris retorts.

For a moment we stare at each other, and then cannot help but laugh. I never thought Taris would make a joke about the circumstances of his birth, but here we are.

"What is this, camaraderie?" I say.

I swear to the Almighty, if this is another one of that albino's damned dreams, the first thing I'm going to do when I find him is stab him through the eye. I don't care if I don't get the answers we need.

"It's almost as if we like each other," Korvaan says.

"Don't tell N'omi; she'll be jealous," Taris mutters. "This isn't likely to happen again, and she's missed it."

"Oh—speaking of N'omi, once I relieve her, she'll want to see you in your dormitory," Korvaan tells me, with a sort of grin that says he knows why. Some surprise, I suppose.

Fine. We're steeped in enough counterfeit mirth already for me to play along. I mean, Taris is right: it won't last. But it is nice to pretend.

"I'll see her shortly, then," I say. "The crown prince is in his room, preparing for the evening's festivities with Mango and Qhan. I believe he's requesting the opinions of both."

Korvaan rolls his eyes, but grins as he pulls his uniform coat on. He buttons it on his way out the door, leaving Taris and me to clean up the yi-cheon tiles.

"What time does the show start?" Taris asks while sweeping a handful of tiles back into their drawstring bag.

"For me? The moment Rian leaves for the party. Which won't be before seven, I should think," I say. "I'll be with him until he's returned to his rooms. You'll stay, then, while the rest of us prepare for the move tomorrow. You can sleep on the train."

"Fair enough."

"You'll be especially careful tonight, won't you? I'd hate to have to kill you if anything were to happen to Rian on his last night here."

Taris gives me a supercilious look. "Please," he drawls. "As if I've ever let anyone close to the crown prince."

"Don't ruin this for me, Qurvo. I don't feel like digging a grave tonight."

"In your dreams, Marson. If anyone's going to ruin things, I think we both know it'll be you."

We smirk at each other.

I think I like being on good terms with Taris. We can still mock each other constantly without me having to be angry about it. Instead, it's almost enjoyable. And this is not a relationship I could maintain with N'omi or Korvaan, as I think Naomi's feelings would genuinely be hurt, and Korvaan isn't the quickest when it comes to banter.

"Best get a move on," Taris says. "N'omi's been preparing something for you over the past year. I'm sure she's all but sprinting back to your dormitory."

I raise an eyebrow. "Has she, now?"

"Don't disappoint my sister, Soleil," he warns.

I roll my eyes and make my exit. Regardless of what N'omi has made for me, the two of us still need to move all our things out of our dorm. Whatever we're bringing with has been packed up and must be brought to the back of Nusk's cabin, while anything else is being donated. We're not the only ones doing this, as the nobles' entourages are all preparing for the move back to the capital. I don't think my team has all secured proper positions, yet, but there's time. Nobles are notorious for allowing things to be done last minute.

Campus isn't half as festive as it was for Fars'day, but to be fair, Fars'day is a major event all of Isaaria celebrates. Tonight's celebration is to be held in the campus' large ballroom, and does not require tents and stalls. It's supposed to be, I'm told, a much classier affair.

As predicted, Naomi is in our room waiting for me. If I had to guess, she could only have beaten me by a minute or two, but she's already gone to work emptying our room out. All we're really keeping are my tools, and a few pairs of clothing each. Everything else, for me at least, is unnecessary.

"Oh—Soleil, good," Naomi says when she sees me. "Sit down, sit down! I have something for you."

She certainly looks excited. Her smile practically glows. I'm tempted to ask if part of her good mood is because Valor Ondra will also be going back to the capital with Rian, but I don't.

I perch on the edge of the bed as bidden, feeling a strange, sudden surge of excitement. I can't remember anyone giving me a present before. Not something for the sake of my expected enjoyment, anyway; usually anything from Nusk is meant for work. And the one wooden table Korvaan made for Naomi and I was for the sake of adding necessary furniture to our room.

Naomi is digging around her side of the closet, and I can tell from how long it's taking her that she did her best to hide my gift somewhere I would never think to look for it. When she returns to me, it's with a beaming smile on her face, and something made of dark fabric draped over an arm. Before I can ask, she's lifted the fabric up to display it to me.

It's a long, lightweight coat with fluttered decorations on the shoulders, bottoms of the sleeves, and trim. Around the middle, there are ties hanging off of the waistband so I can roll and secure the bottom of the coat to keep it from being a nuisance if I need to climb.

Naomi smiles, pleased with my reaction. "I knew you'd like it," she claims, deservedly smug. "I've been working on it for months, just a few minutes here and there. It's not anything a *Magicsmith* could conjure up, of course, but—"

"But you could have fooled me," I interrupt, finally finding my tongue.

I stand to accept the coat and Naomi surprises me further with a pair of matching gloves, a sly little grin on her face. She's clearly pleased with herself, and I'd say she has a right to be.

"Can't forget these," she claims. "You must match."

"They're beautiful, N'omi. And perfect. Thank you."

I take off one of my own gloves and slip on the black silk instead. They fit me exactly: no extra space at the fingertips, no bunched fabric across my palms. The tips of the fingers have small holes to allow my climbing hooks through.

"I thought you could wear it tonight," Naomi says. "So that you can blend in with all the fancy-wear of the party, but still move however you want."

"That's because you're brilliant," I say.

She beams.

I don't deserve Naomi, but I am glad to have her. Even if she is more loyal to her father than me. Even if I cannot speak to her about everything I would like, Naomi is the greatest gift the world has allowed me, as a *Khashtani.*

She does things out of the sheer kindness of her heart. She sees what's needed, and does it. She is selfless by nature. And that is the one thing I know I can never learn to be.

"You can wear it on Comus Day, too, like how the royals do." Naomi is still talking on and on.

"Yes…Yes, I think that's a perfect idea," I murmur, trying to think of how best to tell Naomi the idea I've been rolling around in my head for the past few days.

Her gift has inspired me to tell her now instead of waiting as I planned. I want to be able to pay her back somehow for doing this for me.

She can tell I'm thinking hard about something and frowns. I take a deep breath and decide that if I don't tell her now, she'll think she's done something wrong.

"N'omi, when Comus Day is over, I'm releasing you and your brothers from my *khashak," I* say, and I watch the shock settle in.

"You deserve a better life than this," I add.

"But you need us!" she insists.

"I do," I agree. "But the threats to Rian's life will lessen in ten days, if not disappear. I'll have Qhan, and the rest of the guard, and I've no doubt Taris will stay, because he'll have nothing else to do. But don't deny that you and Korvaan both desire more from your lives. I won't be the thing standing in the way of that. Not after everything you've done—not only for Rian, but for me."

Am I releasing them from their *khashak* bonds out of selfishness? Making myself feel better about a debt I can never repay? Almost certainly. But Nusk's children have always been more like siblings to me than a *khashak,* anyway. I am, admittedly, emotionally attached to them. So, while the decision is not entirely altruistic, I'll allow that there is some sacrifice on my part. Perhaps not enough to redeem me, or make me a decent person, but still.

Naomi shifts from one foot to the other, not sure how to react. I can tell that this is news she's excited and even happy to hear, and is now struggling with that reaction. It makes her feel disloyal to me and Rian, but it shouldn't. There's so much time for her to do other things with her life; she could head off with Valor Ondra, she could start her own business—or two businesses—using the gifts her fluke has lent her.

Naomi bites her lip.

"What did Taris do?" she finally asks. "What did he do to make you this upset with all of us? To want to get rid of us?"

"N'omi, no," I sigh. "It's not that. It's because I think it's selfish to ask you to look after Rian with me for the rest of your lives. You didn't ask for this. None of you agreed to do this. You were assigned these positions because of your father. And I'm not saying that what Nusk did was wrong. All I'm saying is that I think letting you go on with your own lives is the right thing to do."

"And what if we stay with you anyways?" she challenges me.

I shrug. "If you want to keep being my *khashak,* I can't stop you. But it should be a choice. And Nusk never gave that to any of you."

"Any of *us,*" Naomi says, a bit aggressively. "You didn't get a choice, either."

I'm about to argue that doesn't matter, but I can't come up with a way to say so that doesn't make me sound like a hypocrite. Which is likely Naomi's point.

I try to check my watch discreetly, and Naomi laughs at me.

"Nice try, Soleil. I think we both know you have time before you're expected to take over from Korvaan."

"Aa-and we'll be spending that time moving out," I decide.

"While talking about this. We can multitask," she says wryly.

"Impossible."

I don't want to talk about this because I don't generally dwell on my feelings about my life. Yes, I have my opinions on Rian, but I haven't ever considered a life without him. I don't want to tell N'omi because it feels ridiculous and sentimental, but I feel as if I'm meant to be here. Like I'm meant to be Rian's *Khashtani.* When Nusk found me, I was just some orphan no one wanted.

But Rian is the most important person in the world. Constantly saving his life may or may not make me feel important, too.

Naomi, to her credit, teases me with questions while we spend the next few hours moving out of our room. But I am stubborn and resilient: I am not going to let her break me and say something ridiculous. I'm overly cautious ever since that unprecedented outburst about my wanting children.

The fact that she's somewhat smug when I leave tells me that Naomi knows she can always corner me later and force me into continuing the conversation. She heads off to Nusk's cabin with the belongings we hope to take with us while I turn to the campus' ballroom for the farewell party. I'll be watching Rian, Taris will be watching the perimeter, and Korvaan will wait with N'omi and Nusk in case he's needed.

The university's ballroom, reserved for only the grandest events, is perfect in that the slanted, triangular rooftop is made almost entirely of paneled glass to show off the night sky. During the summer, the sun won't start to set until seven o'clock, which means it will take some time before those celebrating are exposed to the moon and stars, but I don't think any of them will complain about being treated to such a spectacular sunset first.

Naturally, the glass itself is more interesting to me than the view: I've been practicing these past few days, and it turns out that it's easy to climb up onto the edge of the roof, crack open a panel, and slip inside. There's an upper floor to the ballroom that circles around the outside to create a hexagonal balcony for a person to walk the perimeter and watch the celebration below.

No one notices me slip inside onto the balcony. It helps that, this early in the evening, most people are down on the ballroom floor itself, leaving me in the darker eaves of the upper level.

I plan to mainly stay up here, if I can. It minimizes my chances of accidentally running into someone who might recognize me. Usually I wouldn't worry—I'm forgettable, after all. But given how close I've been sniffing around the Carsans lately, Crispin might finally realize I'm the woman who gave him the slip on Fars'day as well as the maid he sent after Lune.

I wander around, pretending to enjoy the view of the open floor below while searching for a good angle on Rian. Since all adult students have been invited tonight to see all the royals and their folk off, the room is crowded. There are guards along the outside of the ballroom, checking the identities of all who enter by way of the doors. I'd be concerned about this security breach, except I'm meant to be a security breach.

The first person I see is Crispin Carsans. It's difficult not to: he's huge, and dressed in fine black silk with intricate embroidery. It's an old-fashioned piece, modernized for the occasion, but it suits him.

The second and third people I see are Lune and Rian.

Rian looks perfect, as always. I know he's been looking forward to donning these clothes for months, ever since they were made for him. His long sleeveless overcoat is white trimmed with gold to match his hair, and he lazily waves at himself with a paper fan decorated with similar motifs, to combat the evening heat. Beneath: his double-layered, finely folded black silk suit, with white ribbons tied up from his shoes, around his ankles. He always looks so refined, it's almost enough to convince me he's not entirely human.

Beside him, Lune wears a gown patterned like a distant galaxy, sparkling silver amongst blue-gray space with shimmers of purple and pink and white. A silver circlet of stars rests at her brow; something she should not be wearing as, despite her connections to the Carsans, she is not royalty. With her high heels on, she seems long and elegant, and stands close by to Rian.

She could turn her head, tilt it up and kiss him. In which case I'd probably decapitate her, I decide.

But—mercifully—Asmer is there, too. She wears a lovely gown in various shades of faded pink. It's relatively conservative in the front, held up by a collar of clear, sparkling jewels and a belt in the same fashion, but the back is open to her waist, revealing her perfect, smooth skin. She steps up to Rian's other side, exchanges a smile with him, and I feel slightly relieved.

All of them bear a traditional Isaarian sash hosting the creature and flora associated with their house. Asmer's is, naturally, the simplest, but that hardly detracts from her costuming. I personally approve of the dragon and climbing jasmine of the Yakaramis, in how majestic it makes Rian look, though I find Lune's golden peonies missing the Carsans' griffon clashes with her gown. She somehow manages to lose it not long into the evening.

This is what they will wear when the new king is announced. But they are presenting the costumes tonight to the University, as a special treat. Most will only be able to hear through radio of what the royals wear on Comus Day, and later see pictures circulated through the news, but it's different, getting to see all of their colorful splendor in person.

Even Qhan's uniform entertains some additional frippery for the occasion. I suspect it was all Rian's idea, but Qhan is indulging him, which is exactly what I would expect from him.

I'm especially grateful for Taris' bugs, tonight. I'll be able to hear much of what's happening while staying far above it all.

I search the crowd again, looking for the rest of the usual suspects. I find the king's son easily enough. Quite the crowd has gathered around him: folks hoping to get one last audience before he returns to the capital. After all, until Comus Day, the king is still the king, and Magnus is still his son.

Magnus' neck has healed well, but even if it scarred, the collar of his carefully embroidered dark blue tunic covers it well while complimenting his dark skin and fit build. There's gold jewelry in his hair, like all the other princes tonight, as well as a simple crown, a subtle reminder of his parents' status. He looks, I'll admit, more attractive than usual, apart from the scowl that's making one side of his mouth twitch. His date is a minor noblewoman that ranks lower than Asmer, and I can tell she's upset that Magnus' attention is not solely on her.

He's too busy glaring at Lune.

I don't blame him. She hasn't done anything particularly suspicious in the past few weeks, but I still don't trust her, or her brother. And she did scar his neck.

Lune, thankfully, has left Rian's side and is flitting through the crowd, enjoying all the compliments for her galaxy dress. I suspect she's trying her best to enjoy the attention while she can. The moment they return to the capital, she loses it all.

There's a movement in the crowd that draws my eye: Mercer, looking rather dashing in red silk as he sidles closer to Rian, is waving to get my crown prince's attention over all this noise.

I turn on my earpiece and continue to circle the upper level, checking for threats. Anyone moving quickly towards Rian. Anyone who doesn't belong. And in between these routine checks, I always glance back at Rian himself.

Mercer's tucked close to Rian, leaning in. It's so loud in here with all the guests and music that anyone who wants to talk to another has to shout in their ears.

"Enjoying yourself?" Mercer asks.

"I can barely hear myself think!" Rian replies. "What do you want, Merse? I think we both know you're looking for a girl to roll before tomorrow morning. Why would you ever be interested in talking to me on a night like this?"

He's teasing, but it's not entirely unfair of him to say.

"Ha. Ha," Mercer says, his dryness undercut by the volume at which he's forced to say it. "The night is still young, my friend. No, it's...something else..."

"What?" Rian asks. "You need a recommendation?"

"It's not that," Mercer says, and for once, he sounds serious. He even sighs and takes a minute, as if he's reconsidering what he's going to say. "Has Lune been acting strange?"

I have to press my earpiece in even closer to hear them, and with my arm blocking my vision for a second, I nearly bump into innocent partygoers. It's a dance of mouthed apologies and head bows while I move on. I look down and find Rian and Mercer have moved to a slightly quieter place to talk. I keep my eyes on my crown prince for the next few minutes while I pretend to nurse a tall champagne flute I grab off a waiter's tray.

Rian is frowning. "A bit," he admits. "Why?"

Mercer hesitates again, but forges on. "I was talking with Magnus. And he doesn't want to point fingers without evidence, but he says Lune and Crispin have been acting peculiar."

"And so? They are a little peculiar," Rian tries to laugh it off. "We all are. And I'd say Lune has been a bit off, sure, but Crispin's been the same as always."

"I know, and I don't want to go off of Magnus' word alone, but… Even so. Watch your back tonight," Mercer warns. "And all nights moving forward. And be careful what you tell them. Magnus' methods might be questionable, but he's always looked out for us heirs, as the oldest. I want to be sure you don't get hurt."

Rian mulls this over, considering the implications. So do I: if even Mercer is starting to suspect the Carsans, then I was on to something.

"There's no reason why Crispin or Lune would ever betray us," Rian insists, bothered by this idea. "Crispin could never be king, by Comus Law. And Lune doesn't want for anything she doesn't already have."

Mercer sighs. "Rian, I'm not saying to stop being friends, I just want you to be careful. We all need to be, the closer we get to Comus Day. No one knows why the heir hasn't stepped forward, but I've suspected for a long time that something sinister is going on. So, stay safe."

Rian gives a seemingly genuine laugh. "Why would anyone come after me?" he claims. "Even as a crown prince, I'm practically a nobody."

Mercer rolls his eyes. "Right, right. But even a nobody has the potential to be someone's loose end. Promise me you'll be extra careful until Comus Day has passed?" he adds with a barely audible sigh.

"If it lets you sleep at night: certainly," Rian grins.

"And don't trust anybody."

"I'll try, but no guarantees."

Mercer gives him a good, long look. I can tell he's concerned about Rian, but he won't try and convince his friend any further.

"Take good care of him, Qhan," he says instead, clapping Rian's bodyguard on the shoulder. "He's an idiot."

"Duly noted, your majesty," Qhan says.

Mercer's back to his old self when he heads off, and Rian quickly shakes off the warning to return to the celebrations. Mercer's off to find a girl like Rian suggested. Asmer is now returning with a drink in each hand. Lune's dancing with a very excited young man who probably got dragged here by his friends and now has something to write home about. I've no idea where Crispin wandered off to, but I hope he stays there.

A quick check-in with Taris: all is quiet outside.

I keep my eyes and mind busy as the minutes pass and the revelry continues into the night. I can't tell from his body language if Mercer's warning put Rian out, but I, at least, am still thinking.

Mercer came to Rian on his own. Granted, Magnus told Mercer to watch out for the Carsans in the first place, but Mercer must also think them a viable threat to bother warning his best friend. Otherwise, knowing him, he'd brush it off. I know for a fact that he likes both Crispin and Lune; he wouldn't count their friendship for nothing.

And then there's the fact that Magnus told Mercer in the first place. While I wouldn't put it past Magnus to spread angry rumors about Lune after their run-in, I can't imagine him accusing her of treason, which is what his talking to Mercer was, in a veiled, hushed sort of way. But there's still room for discretion. For mistakes. One would think, if he truly wanted revenge, he'd be shouting her treachery from the rooftops. Instead, all he has done is warn Mercer, and by proxy Rian, to be careful around her and Crispin.

I file this new information away, and tell myself to keep an eye on Lune and Crispin tonight: they're most definitely a threat.

It's a quarter past midnight when I finally spot something worth my full attention. Up until now, it's been non-stop dancing and drinking and eating. I noticed Mercer disappear three minutes ago dragging a giggly young woman behind him, and I'm sure they're going to his room. Or a nearby lecture hall. And with him gone, Crispin is making his way towards where Rian is, pretending he's too drunk to listen to Magnus' blabbing. Nothing serious, for once: just an awkward apology for their encounter in the city.

Apparently, Mercer explained things. Not about Sakia, but the procurement of Asmer's medicine. Even Magnus, like everyone else, has a soft spot for the Little Flower of Isaaria. Rian has accepted the apology, aloud at least, but I can tell he feels as if he should still be wary of Magnus. His concern is overblown—I don't think Magnus' threat was meant to be taken seriously, or at least not as seriously as I'm taking the potential threat of the Carsans. I think it was a case of the king's son letting his emotions get the best of him while seeking an ally among his peers.

Likely it's finally occurred to Magnus, so close to Comus Day, that people don't like him very much. I think it bothers him.

Crispin is shouting something to the other two crown princes that they can't hear. Rian squints, his brow furrowing, and leans closer, putting a hand to his ear while very clearly asking, "What?"

Qhan helps Crispin muscle his way through the crowd to get closer, and Magnus' body language is doing absolutely everything to ensure that Crispin knows his company is not appreciated.

"Lune," Crispin repeats over the din. "Have you seen Lune? I can't find her."

"Good riddance," Magnus mutters, tossing his drink back.

Crispin narrows his eyes.

"I swear to the Almighty, Magnus, crown prince or no, if you've been harassing my sister—"

"Harassing?" Magnus says incredulously. "Fate's Favored Lune?" he sneers. "Oh, who would dare?"

"You were saying unflattering things about her last I heard," Crispin says.

Poor Rian has no idea what to do and looks to Qhan for help. But they're backed into an alcove, surrounded by tables that have been pushed aside from the main floor, and there's nowhere Rian can escape to.

"Oh, she deserved it," Magnus chuckles bitterly to himself.

He is about to take a swig of a drink he's picked up from a nearby table when Crispin reaches to grab him. Both of them are at least tipsy, and I'm glad that Griffith is suddenly there to push them off one another; otherwise, they could have started a brawl. Idiots.

Rian blinks and glances at the drink in his hand; things happened so fast, he's not sure if he saw it all correctly.

"I saw those bruises on her arm," Crispin snaps. "She said not to do anything about it, but I know they're from you."

Griffith is barely holding him back, and is radioing for someone to escort Crown Prince Carsans back to his rooms.

Magnus retaliates by reaching up and grabbing at his own collar, ripping it in his haste to reveal the mark on his neck.

"You see this?" Magnus hisses. "This is from your little sister."

Crispin is now uneasy. "You must have hurt her," he decides. "Lune wouldn't do that for no reason."

But Magnus and I both know that if Crispin really thought Magnus had hurt Lune, he would be beating his face in.

"You'd best stop defending her, Crispin," Magnus warns with a sneer. "You come from a good family, but let's face it: she's not really your sister, is she?"

I've seen little to sway me one way or the other, but it's clear that Magnus' suspicions of the Carsans family have shifted specifically onto Lune. Either that, or he's trying to trick Crispin into revealing something.

I cast my gaze about the room again. Crispin's right: Lune's gone.

Crispin is being escorted out as requested, but I'm no longer paying attention. I need to make a decision. Either I stay here with Rian—as I'm meant to—or I leave to see if I can find Lune. I know I only have seconds, but it's a difficult choice: if I play the odds, even if there is a threat against Rian tonight, Taris and Qhan together can easily thwart it. It may go against all my natural instincts, but leaving Rian might give me my one and only chance to uncover the threat to him.

I know, as I'm slipping out of the dimly lit ballroom to begin my search for Lune, that I should alert Taris. He's my partner, now, even more than he was meant to be before, and he could help with this.

But I know that Taris will continue to do his job if I don't say anything to him. If I do tell him, he might become distracted. He might insist on being the one to follow Lune, when this is something I want to do myself. I trust him, but I'm the one who started this. I need to be the one to see it through.

Given what I assume Lune's doing, she'll have sought out someplace obscure and dark. A place no one would go at this hour. Even Mercer heading off to an empty lecture hall is risky—there could be other pairs looking for a place alone, and Lune should know that. There are only a few places absolutely no one would dare go, and I am familiar with all of them.

The University doesn't have many rules when it comes to curfew, but there are a number of locations that they request no one frequent after hours. One of them is the professors' offices, but Lune wouldn't attempt that. Another is the stables, and the loading bay for the carriages. And lastly: shipping and receiving for anything being sent to or from the University.

This last spot is furthest from the ballroom, so that's where I head first, but there is no sign of Lune when I arrive.

While leaving, I spot a group of large storage crates at the delivery bay and cannot help but wonder what's inside. One might excuse such a set leaving the University given the circumstances, filled with the many belongings of Mercer or Magnus. But why would they be arriving?

I walk on, trying not to overthink it. I check the carriage storage next. There's a dark, narrow alleyway I'm aware of down there, which I can imagine is a perfect meeting spot for those up to no good.

It's all I can do not to laugh when I'm proven correct; as I draw near to the alley, I can hear hushed voices, and one of them sounds like Lune. Admittedly, I haven't approached the alley in a way conducive to espionage, but even if I cannot see them, I can hear them. I press myself close to the wall, near the corner, and listen intently. I even turn off my earpiece; it's unnerving, not being able to hear Rian anymore.

"—as Sep said last time?" I hear Lune whisper.

I find I am frozen, because I have no idea why Lune Carsans would be saying that. I might not be brilliant, but from time to time my memory picks one or two obscure things to hold on to during times of stress, and I know that name. I know it because the first time I encountered the albino man, in Rian's rooms, in that dream, that's what the albino's companion called him.

"Hard to say," a low voice answers her. A man. His accent is Lijimi.

Her employer? Contact? It's hard to say, but he is speaking too low for me to tell if I recognize his voice, as if he is purposefully altering it.

Lune huffs. "I'd rather I knew for certain," she says. "I hate all this dancing around in the dark, following orders blindly from a man I don't fully trust."

Her companion chuckles almost bitterly. "Oh, Lune. I know. How do you think all of this has been for me?"

Lune is less than empathetic. "Hmph. Well. Tell that little fool when you see him that he'd best have an answer for me next time. I'm tired of killing myself over and over again for him."

"He's in a very taxing position, you must know that."

"Are we not?"

"There are many cogs turning. So much to consider…"

There's a pregnant pause, and I try to sneak forward. If possible, I want to get a good angle on them and see the Lijimi man.

"I heard about what happened," he says, even quieter. I can barely hear him. "I'm sorry you had to go through that. And to bury the body alone—"

"I'd rather not talk about it," Lune snaps.

I can't imagine she wants to remember having to dispose of someone. I still cannot determine who it is she's killed, but I now know for certain that Lune does not enjoy taking lives. She'll do it, but it affects her poorly. And her conspirators, if they can be believed, never meant to put her in that position.

"Of course. I pray you do not experience it again," the man says.

"So do I," Lune sighs. "But it's not as if I have any control over it… There's been an influx, lately," she adds quickly, changing the subject. "I thought you should know. Any chance you could get our oh-so-brilliant leader to tell me why that might be happening?"

"Isn't it early for that?"

"Precisely my point. Teresa's only fourteen, and all the others are dead and gone, so that's out. And as far as I know, out of the Seven, the only ones we've lost are the twin and Erikson's daughter. But only *He* has any idea what exactly is going on and why and how, so—"

There's a sudden sound from above. Like pebbles falling, or something shifting against the building. Lune takes in a sharp breath and falls silent. When she speaks again, her voice is exceptionally low. I must strain my ears to hear her, and even then, I'm partially guessing at her words.

"Were you followed, here?" she whispers, fear coloring her tone deeply.

"I'm not sure," he says, hesitant. "I'm not sure how I could have been, but—"

"It doesn't matter how. There's almost nothing they can't do. *Get out of here.* We can't lose you like this."

"Yes," he says, breathless. "You're right. But first: allow me."

There's a strange sound I can't identify. It's brief; a whooshing or whirling and then a quiet pop. When I round the corner, Lune and her companion have vanished. His fluke. It must be. I have some idea of what Lune's is, after all, and I do not believe she has used it lately.

I should have moved earlier. Possibly, I should have attempted to confront Lune, but it's too late, now.

I curse and rush out of the alley. If something is following Lune, I don't want its attention in her absence. I cannot know where Lune and her contact have vanished to, but I'm not sure it matters. I doubt I'll get any more answers from them, tonight. But there's someone else whom I suspect might tell me something.

Nusk. Nusk must know something about this. He's the one who told me he wanted to speak to the albino man if I managed to catch him. He's the one who was not surprised to learn of an albino assassin. Taris and I previously decided to keep our investigation from Nusk, but I'm beginning to believe I must interrogate my own surrogate father, and learn whatever it is I can about this albino man. He is too much a part of all this.

I must know who he is and how both Nusk and Lune know him.

Turning my earpiece on and then off again, I quickly determine that Rian is retiring for the evening. Escorted by Qhan, and with Taris watching over him, I'm not worried.

I run all the way to Nusk's cabin. Sleep will be a distant luxury, tonight.

When I burst through the front door, I find Nusk, Naomi and Korvaan in the kitchen. Korvaan's leaning up against the wall, yawning, while Naomi makes tea, and Nusk sits in his chair on his side of the table. They all stare at me when I enter. Naomi and Korvaan are surprised, but when Nusk sees the expression on my face, he knows.

"I need to speak with you," I say.

"I'm afraid I can't do that, Soleil," Nusk says calmly. "And who is with the crown prince? If you're here?"

"Taris," I say shortly.

"Not your wisest choice," Nusk murmurs. "I told you, Soleil: my son is too emotional. You can't trust him to make the logical choice. And by that same token, you cannot trust me, either."

I turn defensive. "And what am I supposed to make of that?"

But Nusk is shaking his head. "You never really learn, Soleil."

I'm done playing this game. Enough of the secrets and the lies.

"Tell me of the albino man," I demand. "Tell me what threat he is to Rian, and tell me what he's doing. Why is he here?"

Nusk looks sadly at the tabletop.

"Naomi, be a dear and continue with the tea," he says, as both of his children have done nothing but stare at us for the past few seconds.

She hesitates, but nods and starts to turn towards me so she can get back to the stovetop.

Korvaan sighs. "What in the *world* is all this about—?" he starts.

Naomi suddenly screams. She drops the teapot on the ground.

"There you are, little sunchild," a terrifyingly deep voice growls behind me.

An arm wraps around my throat and pulls me directly off the ground.

I pull a knife, but my attacker's other hand catches my wrist. He keeps me from stabbing him through the head, and no matter how hard I push, it's difficult to attack from this angle, swinging backwards. He peels my fingers away from the knife, his other arm still securely around my throat.

There are many tricks for getting out of this hold, but the first two I try immediately fail, and that panics me. This man is massive; bigger than Taris, bigger than Nusk once was when he could use his legs. He's tall enough that I'm sure he had to duck down to get in through the doorway.

I'm dangling before him, my legs kicking at the air. Though I manage to make contact with his shins, he doesn't react. Even my boot-knife is of no help. My vision is clouding, but I manage to process that we are being invaded. I cannot count how many, but while Korvaan has his pistol out, he's hesitating. I don't think he wants to risk injuring me. Or else, he doesn't know where to shoot first.

I can hear myself squeaking. The air catching in my throat.

I can't breathe.

No one's moving. I don't know what it is about being choked that terrifies me so much, but I'm doing my best to escape and failing.

"I don't want to kill her," my assailant mocks. "You must know that, *Khas Qurvo.* But I will if I must. And if you open your mouth to say anything other than what I want, I'll find someone to decorate your pretty daughter's head."

I think I can hear Naomi crying.

"It's been a long time, general," Nusk says slowly. "Or aren't you a general, yet? You're younger than I remember. Do you remember? Or does your father still find you lacking?"

"That's irrelevant," the man snaps. "Either you answer my questions, or you don't speak at all. For the sake of your daughter and Miss Marson, here."

This rankles me. I refuse to be used as a hostage. I'm Soleil Marson. You might have gotten the best of me, taking me by surprise like this, but I still have options. I still have...I still have...

Climbing hooks.

"We already know where the little prince is," the man continues, smug bastard. "He's not my interest tonight. Now, where's the other—"

I flick my climbing hooks through Naomi's gloves and scratch him across the face. I do not manage to dig into his eye, but the injury is enough to force him to drop me, bellowing. The moment I hit the floor, I swing my legs out to kick the backs of his knees and while he doesn't hit the ground, he at least falls back into the wall.

Korvaan and N'omi are moving, too. Korvaan had two men by him, likely about to restrain him in some way, but he takes out one of them instantly.

Naomi pulls a throwing knife from her sleeve and hurls it into the eye of her brother's second attacker. She's quick to duck behind the door frame afterward, as I know Naomi rarely carries more than two knives on her at a time. I sincerely hope she's about to run out the back door and out to safety, so she can't be used against us.

Despite the scratching in my throat while I gasp for air, I scramble to my feet and recover my knife from where it's stuck in the wood floor. Korvaan empties his pistol into two more enemies, and I count five left. Including the general whose face I've scratched open.

I think Korvaan and I can manage them.

Korvaan vaults over the table, pushing Nusk's chair away as he goes. I whirl with my knife just in time to sink it into the head of the man who's decided to grab my hair and yank. One down already, though he's taken my knife with him.

"Soleil!"

Korvaan throws me my bow, and even without arrows, I can use it. I can feel someone close behind me, so the moment the bow hits my hand, I swing and use my momentum to smack them across the face.

My newest attacker grabs onto the bow, trying to wrest it from me. There's a red welt across his face where I struck him, but it hasn't slowed him. I manage to free the bow whilst trying to knock his knees out from under him, but my victory is fleeting. He manages to get in two good hits, one in my solar plexus and one directly across my face.

I let the motion carry me—my face should bruise less if I don't resist—but don't fall to the floor. I let my body bend enough so I can snatch up the metal teapot with my free hand, then turn back and swing. My intent was to bash the man in the head, but he avoids me, and I swing wildly at him like a drunkard.

These are cramped quarters. There's little room to move, let alone make mistakes. I can see Korvaan struggling with three men at once while I'm left with the fourth. That big one is going to be a problem; I need to finish this and help Korvaan. What I can do for him, now, is to use up the poison darts in my bolt-shooter, spreading my aim amongst all three of the attackers, and hope one of those lucky spines hits flesh.

My own quarry seems to think it's a good idea to bear-hug me from behind. Not his best decision. He's not as big as his general, and I am strong for a woman. I swing my legs down, plant both feet firmly on the ground, and fling him over my head. He does not let go, so I flip over with him, freeing myself as he lands on his back. I've got the bow and the teapot, still, not to mention my own elbows. A combination of all three can cause what I hope will be irreversible brain hemorrhaging.

I'm startled by N'omi's sudden scream. My head whips around to see her flung back into the kitchen from the hall. I thought she'd escaped out the back door, but given the man that follows her in, I suspect she's been trying to evade him.

I had not considered someone guarding the back door. I miscounted. That seems to be a failing of mine, lately.

I'm fully prepared to leap over the table and go to Naomi's rescue. But at the last second, someone grabs my ankle and I nearly hit my face on the side of the table. The fellow I smacked across the head with the teapot is resilient. I should have known better than to think he was down.

I flip over and brace myself against the edge of the table while he struggles to keep my ankles restrained. I likely would have made quick enough work of him once I got my balance. But I suppose the invaders and their general decided only two of them needed to attack Korvaan, as one comes up from behind me and lifts me off the table with a headlock.

I've much less leverage whilst almost horizontal.

"Someone doesn't like having their neck touched, do they?" he mocks.

This is a correct observation.

The good news is that I don't believe this fellow was paying attention when I freed myself from his general's grasp, because otherwise he would have remembered I keep hooks on my fingers.

Regardless, I'm taking too long. It's not as if Naomi's attacker is waiting with baited breath to see what happens to me when he has her right in front of him. He hits Naomi, and the force of it is enough to spin her and send her sprawling across the table. While I'm doing my best to finish off the two irritants keeping me from reaching her, Naomi's gotten herself pinned, and I know she's too weak to free herself from a man so much stronger than her.

I realize I'm about to watch Naomi's throat being slit when a dagger appears in the forehead of the man trying to kill her. His body staggers, loosens, and collapses onto the floor.

There are six, sudden, loud bursts. I know what a pistol sounds like, but it takes me a moment to identify it. Next thing I know, I'm flat on my back, gasping for air, ears ringing.

I try my best to process what has happened as the room spins and warps around me. Six shots, three men down, plus one felled by a throwing knife I recognize. I've almost forgotten how good Taris is at killing. In fact, I'll be the first to admit he's much better at it than even I am.

It's frightening.

Only the general is left, now, and he no longer has any interest in Korvaan, Naomi, or me. Taris recoils and, for a moment, I think he's about to duck out the door again to protect himself. But while anyone in their right mind would simply shoot Taris, the general grins and snaps his pistol back into its holster. He gives a devilish grin and gestures for Taris to attack. If I didn't know better, I'd say this was a long-awaited rematch.

I'm only vaguely aware of them. My head is pounding, my back aches fiercely, and my ears are ringing from the gunshots and lack of air both. My throat feels as if part of it has cracked and pushed inward on itself. As my hearing trickles back, I flinch at the commotion created by Taris and his opponent, but while I'm highly invested in the outcome of their fight, I cannot force myself to watch.

After another fifteen seconds, I manage to flip myself over and crawl a little. I can still hear the general and Taris, but I can't tell which of them is doing better, only that neither is dead yet. I see Korvaan dragging himself toward Naomi, and am trying my best to assess them for injuries. There's blood on Naomi's left arm, but she's moving it well enough, and while Korvaan is moving weakly, it's from exhaustion. I conclude they are dazed and panicked, but not vitally injured.

I do not have long to feel relief. There is a loud thudding noise and when I glance over, I see Taris is not doing so well against the general as I'd hoped. He's not fully pinned, but the general has unclipped his pistol again. I suppose he's had his fun, though their fight couldn't have lasted more than a minute, and Taris is doing his best to keep the gun pointed away from his head. I don't know exactly what this man intends, but he does not want the Qurvos alive.

"Such a pitiful death, for a man like you," the general mocks. He's not sounding his best, but he's still smug over besting Taris. "The son of Khas Qurvo," he says dramatically. "Put down like a lame horse…"

Panting, and pushing my sweaty stray strands of hair back, I force myself to my feet again. I don't purposefully take my time, but I'm exhausted, and my body aches. I pluck my knife up from the ground, walk up behind the general, and quickly, professionally, slit his throat.

When his body collapses backwards off Taris, I fall to my knees, too. I'm tired. So tired. There's a fuzziness to my vision, and I have to force myself not to faint. I am struck by the sudden urge to scream. I have killed men before, to protect Rian, but this time, it bothers me more than it should.

There is silence but for our breathing when my vision has cleared and I've managed to pull myself to my hands and knees. I glance to where Taris is lying, shocked, and he looks back at me. From under the table, Naomi and Korvaan are starring, too.

I realize who I've forgotten to account for all this time.

I can see Nusk lying on the ground, his head turned away from me. I don't know what happened, and I probably never will. There's so much blood on the floor and spattered about the room that I cannot tell if any is Nusk's, but while I can see his chest moving, he's making no attempts to sit.

"Nusk," I croak, starting to crawl over to him. *"Nusk."*

I start to cough as I move. There's a throbbing in my scalp, and my throat aches. When I reach Nusk, there is blood soaked through his clothes, but I can't tell where it's coming from. I don't know who did it. We all saw Korvaan push Nusk away, so in all of our minds, he was free of the fight. A component we did not have to consider until afterwards.

Nusk's still breathing when I sit and pull him onto my lap, but he's pale.

"Where? There's blood. It's coming. From someplace," I'm babbling.

"Nusk?" I manage to say again.

Taris has gone to his siblings. I'm too concerned with Nusk to be angry at him for leaving Rian. He says something in Milash that only his father could understand, but Nusk does not answer. Even when Taris speaks again, more vehemently, Nusk is only looking at me.

"Forgive me, child," he says, stroking at my arm with a feebleness I would have never ascribed to him. He wants to be stroking my hair, but is too weak to raise his arm that high.

"Hush," I say. "We will get a healer. They will help you; save your strength."

I turn to my shocked *khashak* and snap, "N'omi: get needle and thread. Get cloths. To stop the blood. Korvaan: find someone. Find a fluke healer. *Now!"*

But they don't move. They're all but frozen.

"Soleil," Naomi finally whispers. Her eyes are large, her voice choked, and her forehead crumpled as she tries not to let her emotions overcome her.

Her brothers say nothing, and that's enough.

It takes me too long to do it—I don't want to. I know what I'm going to find, and I don't want to see it. Because once I do, it's real. But I force myself to look back to Nusk. The only father I have ever known.

He is already dead.

Eleven

FOR SEVERAL LONG MOMENTS, it's silent. I still feel dizzy, my head cottony enough to make me swoon whilst kneeling. It takes me a long time before I move to draw Nusk's eyes closed. It's more habit than duty. Finally, I slide Nusk off of my lap and arrange his body on the floor as best I can. Naomi begins crying in earnest. I can feel the tension rising, from myself, Korvaan and Taris.

I glance at the bodies on the ground. Not one of them has moved since they were felled, and though I watch for covert breaths, I find none. We've killed them all, and the skeleton of what was once Nusk's cabin is littered with corpses. Naomi and Taris are both covered in blood that's not theirs.

I feel no pride in this massacre. In fact, the more I try, the more I feel nothing.

Without Nusk to order us to action, none of us know what to do.

"I don't understand," I say hoarsely. "Why would they go after us?"

"They didn't go after us, they went after you," Taris snaps. "I suppose whoever wants the crown prince dead finally decided it's too much work, trying to get around you. Best to end you first."

My anger sparks, and instead of trying to contain it, I let myself and Taris both fuel each other's flames. It's a better alternative to acting as Naomi is, anyways.

"Don't you dare blame me for this," I hiss.

"If you hadn't gone running out across the campus to spy on Lune Carsans, they never would have seen you," he accuses. "If you'd done your job, and stayed close to Rian, they never would have seen you. They would not have followed you here, and they would not have killed Nusk."

I splutter. "What about you! You abandoned your post as well!"

"And if I hadn't, you'd all be dead," Taris snaps. "You made your choice and I made mine, but only one of us was doing damage control."

We glare at one another. Korvaan is attempting to comfort his sister, but his words are stilted. He is in shock, and does not know how to react. Between the different ways we're coping with what has happened, I'm not sure whose is best.

"What are we going to do now?" Korvaan finally forces himself to say.

Naomi is trying her best to be quiet. She's covering her mouth in shame, her face turned away from us all as her body shakes.

Taris scoffs. "Now we do our best to salvage this. We go to Pyrian City with Rian, and do whatever it takes to keep him alive. To make sure he becomes king, as he's meant to."

Korvaan and I both stare at him, for different reasons.

"Soleil will approach the crown prince and explain everything to him," Taris continues, ignoring us both. "We'll pull him into our circle and make certain he understands what he has to do. For Isaaria."

"The law of the *Khashtani*–" Korvaan starts.

"To hell with that!" Taris snaps. "What do the rules matter, if they keep us from our life's work? We must protect the heir, no matter what. Nusk is dead, now. We're at a disadvantage. The only thing we can do now to ensure Rian stays alive is to get Soleil as close as possible to him. If that means breaking the laws of the *Khashtani*, then so be it."

"They are all we have left of our father," Korvaan claims.

"The foremost principle of which has always been to look after the living, not the dead," Taris snaps.

We listen to his heavy breaths for a few moments before I exchange a look with Naomi. She's tear-stricken, but nods; whatever I decide, she'll follow me, regardless of what her brothers believe.

"We stay with Rian," I decide. "We protect him from all harm, at any cost. If that means revealing myself to him, and breaking every *Khashtani* law that Nusk ever gave us, then so be it. But I will not do so intentionally. And I will not force him to become king."

I know Korvaan is angered by this, and Naomi frowns, despite agreeing to follow my lead. But they know not to disobey me. With Nusk gone, my *khashak* must follow my every order. For our principal's sake.

Taris gives me a long, hard stare, then nods. He might push me again, later, but not now. Even Korvaan, who glares at the floor, holds too much respect for his position to disagree with his *Khashtani,* especially given his position on the laws of such.

I'm greatly relieved by this. There is too much to do tonight for us to be squabbling.

In my head, I struggle to make up a list of all our responsibilities.

"We need to clean this up. Pack what we can, what we might still need, and burn everything else, or bury it. Make certain of our new positions," I say, and once I start, I can't stop. "We need to be close to the royals, so we'll have an excuse to accompany them. Nusk would have done so for us, but—"

I cut myself off. We spend several seconds trying not to look at one another.

"I will see to the arrangements," Naomi murmurs. "We'll accompany the crown prince to Pyrian."

She wipes the tears from her face and heads to the washroom first.

"If you can't get us all assigned to him, you've still Crispin, Mercer, Asmer and Lune," Taris reminds her. "We can travel with any one of them and remain unnoticed. Don't press your luck."

Naomi nods, but there's a dullness to her eyes.

"We clean this place, scrupulously," I demand once she's gone. "We strip it of anything that suggests we were ever here, and at dawn, we will complete burial rites for Nusk. Then we leave."

"And by 'we', you mean me and Taris," Korvaan sighs. I know that what I say next will displease him.

"No, I mean you and Naomi when she returns," I say. "Taris—with me. We have a job to do."

Korvaan's mouth opens, but Taris shoots his brother a look, and neither of them protest. At least, not to me. When Taris goes to move past him and join me, Korvaan grabs his arm tightly and yanks him back.

"Does our own father's death mean nothing to you?" I hear Korvaan hiss.

Taris yanks his arm free. "Very little means anything to me anymore."

Korvaan scowls at us both, angrier than I've ever seen him before, angrier than I could have imagined. Then he stalks off to the back. He has bodies to bury, and tools to unpack to do so.

Then it's Taris and me, in a room full of bodies. He says nothing to me, simply heads to the front door. He even passes me by when I can't help but stop before walking around the body of the man Nusk called a general.

Despite what little time we have to waste, I hesitate. As I noted before, the general is a large, strong man—much bigger than me, with a naturally muscular build. Bloodied dark hair has stiffened into a plaster against his forehead, and his dull, still-open eyes are also dark in color. There is something frighteningly, hauntingly familiar about him. He cannot be older than twenty-five, which means it's unlikely I encountered him years ago, only to forget.

I frown and at him long enough for Taris to notice. He pauses, waiting for me, a question hanging in the air.

"It's strange," I admit, "but I feel as if…"

As if I've killed this man before.

There is a silver-carved insignia on the left side of the dead man's chest, partially hidden beneath a folded-over portion of his jacket. Curious, I kneel and push his jacket to aside. The pin is mostly round, with longer and shorter jagged portions springing out from a smaller circle inside, like an odd sun, or starbursts. Etched into the inner portion is a simplistic outline of a firebird. Around the ring of the center circle are several words in a language I don't know.

I have seen this symbol before. I cannot recall where, or how, but I'm certain I have. It does not belong to the eight Isaarian royal families. I'd have recognized it. No one has a firebird. So how do I know this sign?

I rip the pin off his jacket and slip it into my pocket.

Taris snorts. "Memento?"

I hastily stand again.

"Follow me," I snap, and head out into the dark without another word.

The night is still relatively young, and there is enough excitement about to ensure that few people will notice Taris or me, and no one at all heard the commotion in the cabin. It's astounding what most people don't notice. They're so laughably self-absorbed, I could probably follow a pair of maids, listening in on their entire conversation, and they'd never notice me there so long as we were moving along a traffic-heavy path.

Taris and I are nobodies tonight. For a long while, there is silence between us, and he does not question where we are going, though it's obvious we aren't off to attend Rian. No, Taris made the right decision, coming to look for me as soon as he realized I'd abandoned my post. He saved all of our lives, as he said, and I cannot bring myself to thank him for it.

We are well on our way to the campus' garden supply shed when I can't stand the silence any longer.

"I don't like the circumstances of this," I admit. "You weren't there, at the beginning, but those men knew Nusk. You didn't recognize them, did you?"

"No," Taris says plainly.

"But they know us."

"Apparently."

"And there's no asking Nusk. Now that he's…"

I can't bring myself to finish, because I know my voice will crack if I do, and I cannot let Taris see me fall apart.

"Your face does not speak of mourning," he accuses me anyway.

"Yours doesn't, either."

Taris shrugs. "My father taught us to keep our faces masked and our hearts sealed. I suppose neither of us should look as if we mourn."

"Perhaps we shouldn't," I say, but I can still feel him judging me. Assessing my actions. Reminding himself over and over of his conclusion that, if not for my arrogance, his father would still be alive.

I crouch to pick the garden shed's lock while Taris keeps watch. He still has not asked what we are doing, though he must be wondering. Either that, or the events of tonight have affected him more negatively than I thought.

It occurs to me that there is likely no small amount of blood on us, and that we should take some workman's jackets from the shed as well, to cover ourselves up until we can wash. I realize I have ruined Naomi's gift. Only the gloves are salvageable, and sturdy. I decide to wear them as much as possible, by means of apology.

Frustratingly, it takes me a full two minutes to pick the lock. My usually nimble fingers, the same ones so talented at untangling knots, are shaking. Perhaps, after washing up, I might need to get some sustenance in me. It must be those sips of alcohol I'd had while at the party. Another stupid mistake.

"Come on," I tell Taris once I've entered the shed. "Regardless of your father's death, and perhaps even in light of it, there's work for us to do."

Taris takes his time before joining me, and this makes me uncomfortable.

"...It is a shock to be sure, but Nusk would have wanted us to continue our work without allowing this to ruin us," I say.

Taris raises an eyebrow, and I can tell that he's mocking me. I don't know how he's kept his calm through all this. I don't know how he's managing to stay so impassive while I'm struggling to do the same.

"A shock? This shouldn't have come as a surprise," he claims. "The mentor figure always dies, in stories."

It's all I can do not to slam him against the wall when I grab him by his shirtfront and yank him closer to my level.

"This is not one of Rian's damned stories," I hiss. "Your father is dead, you cold-hearted machine."

He puts his hand over mine and squeezes it until my bones ache.

"Yes," he retorts. "And whose fault is that?"

I release him. My emotions are running erratically, and I force myself to take several deep breaths.

"I...didn't intend that," I force myself to growl.

"There's a dark side to everything," Taris warns me, not at all sympathetic. "You should know that. Your intentions don't matter. All that matters is what happened."

He waits with his arms crossed while I breathe. I appreciate that he doesn't say much more.

"Grab a shovel," I finally say. "You remember where Korvaan buried the assassins from Fars'day?"

"You want me…to help you dig up bodies," Taris clarifies in distaste.

"Yes," I say. "I need to see if any of the killers we've buried before are similar to our attackers tonight. Nusk called that one man a general—I want to see if the uniforms match. And check if any of them are wearing this," I add, showing Taris the pin I snatched.

He takes it and stares at it for a very long time, blinking impassively.

"I took it off the man Nusk called a general—"

"Yes, I noticed," Taris snaps, handing it back to me. "Why does it matter?"

"I think, possibly, the albino had the same pin."

"I thought you didn't remember much about him?" he says suspiciously.

"I don't," I admit. "But this pin…This symbol. There's more to it. And there's something else. Whoever the albino man is, Lune knows him. And he has other agents around here."

Taris looks thoughtful. He does not meet my eyes.

"I'm starting to think we have at least two sets of unknowns, here," I say. "Lune and whoever she's working for, and the people who wear this pin. I think the man Lune's working for is the albino. I think he was one of them, and he's changed his mind about a method of theirs. Regardless: I think both of them want the Lost Heir of Isaaria dead. For various reasons. At the very least, they don't want him to become king."

"That's quite the theory," Taris says.

"We don't know anything for certain yet," I admit. "But it's better to assume the worst and be surprised for the better than the other way around."

Despite his anger, Taris agrees agree with me on that.

He takes a few moments to think, looking almost pained. I wonder why he doesn't tell me what's running through his head, but I suppose he never was one to share.

"I'll dig up the bodies," he agrees with a heavy sigh. "Hopefully you'll learn something from it. But Fate's Fingers, Soleil, if you ever ask me to do anything like this again—"

"I won't," I promise him.

He grabs the shovels, and I scrounge up a pair of workmen's covers for us. It's incredible how few people ask questions so long as you look the part.

I allow Taris to lead the way to the unofficial gravesites. I already know the smell is going to be dreadful, and I'm almost glad that we didn't try to clean up beforehand.

It takes us a full hour to unearth the bodies, and though Taris does not say anything about it, I'm not sure if our hard work was worth it or not. While I check the top-most cadavers, he leaves me to begin digging a fresh grave. I don't have to ask; I know he intends to bury his father here. I question his choice to do so next to where we generally hide the bodies of our enemies, but I suppose it doesn't matter where we put the bodies in the end.

The Fars'day assassins aren't wearing uniforms, and they do not in any way resemble our attackers tonight. Nor do I find any symbol that bears resemblance to the pin. But each of the bodies *do* have something strange about them that I wouldn't have noticed except by chance and a diligent second-check.

All of them have a small cut on their right arm that has now festered with decay. I would have thought it mere coincidence, but each body is also missing a patch of hair in the same spot on their heads. Again, it could have simply been due to decay, but two signs? Done to all of them, all in the same location?

"Taris, for what reasons would someone need hair and blood?" I ask.

He shrugs. "*Dadj'zcha*?"

"I'm being serious."

"So am I."

"Fate's Fingers," I curse.

Every time I think I've uncovered some clue; it only adds another confusing angle to the equation.

By the time Taris and I have reburied the bodies, it's nearly four in the morning. We have a limited amount of time to finish, here, and make certain we're presentable when we leave campus with the royals. Naomi will have gotten us passage—I know we can depend on her for that. We'll hopefully be able to get some rest during the journey, because Taris and I are both exhausted.

We trudge back across campus to return our tools and use the workmen's showers near the shed. After, we change into new sets of stolen clothes, both knowing we'll likely have to wash again in another hour or so, but at least we're trying to be inconspicuous.

It's on our way back that Fate throws another complication at us. Because I suppose tonight hasn't been miserable enough.

At first, I think the figure we encounter on the path is merely some lightweight passed out on their way to bed. But then I see the splay of hair and even with her face covered, I recognize exactly who it is.

"Fate damn it," I hiss.

Taris makes a sound in either distress or irritation.

It's Lune, naturally. Foolish girl. She's not wearing the galaxy dress from the party, but is instead in simple, comfortable trousers and a tight-fitting tunic. Her butterfly knife sheath is strapped to the outside of her leg, and I notice she actually has two, right next to each other.

I'm half tempted to drag her back to the cabin, blindfold her, and demand answers. But there's no guarantee she'll tell me anything helpful.

Before I can say anything, Taris is already by her side, flipping her over to gently lay her on her back. There's still-wet blood all over her front, which I suppose explains her unconsciousness. Taris looks surprised at first, but since he doesn't say anything after checking her breathing and pulse, I assume she's fine. Or at least stable.

"Stop fussing with her," I hiss. "Let's finish what we started."

"We can't leave her," Taris sighs.

"Why not?"

"Because if she dies, Soleil, someone will find her, claim she's been murdered, and they'll shut down the entire campus to interrogate everyone. Tell me if I'm wrong, but I think we might have a problem if their find the bodies that you've had Korvaan hiding in the gardens, especially those that we've recently dug up and reburied."

"Point taken: what do we do?"

Taris runs a hand over his face, looking both exasperated and exhausted.

"Mmm. Take her to N'omi, get her patched up, and find someone to bring her back to her rooms," he decides. "And hope she doesn't think much of this tomorrow."

I groan, but I know he's right. Lune is too important a tool for me to worry about her dying now.

"Give her a look; see where she's injured, and we can try to stop the bleeding before we move her," I sigh.

It occurs to me that perhaps I should be the one to do such a thing, but Taris has already opened up her tunic and is clinically examining her bloody torso in search of an injury.

"I do not believe this is her blood," Taris whispers to me.

"What?"

"I can't find a major injury; I think this blood is someone else's."

But this is interesting. Lune might have injured or killed someone else tonight. Possibly the reason she met with her contact in the first place was to acquire her next target.

"Confession," I admit. "When I followed her earlier, I saw her with a man. Or heard her, really."

Taris raises an eyebrow. "The albino?"

"No, someone else," I say. "A Lijimi man. He sounded familiar, but…"

"Don't draw conclusions. I'll keep an eye out for any Lijimi. As well as our missing albino."

"Whatever his fluke is, it must be damned powerful for him to avoid us like this," I mutter.

"If she's not hurt, this changes things," Taris says, ignoring my last statement as he fixes Lune's tunic and covers her up. "I'll take her back to her room, so when she wakes up she'll think she managed to get herself there before falling unconscious. I'll meet you back at the cabin."

"No, I'll come with," I insist. "I'll check on Rian while we're there."

Taris doesn't seem pleased with my prolonged company, but he doesn't insist otherwise. He hoists Lune in his arms to carry her and I help rearrange the fabric of her tunic to make the blood less noticeable.

With the nobles moving on from the campus tomorrow, their building is all but abandoned, boxes and trunks packed up and sitting in the halls. I help Taris maneuver around them and bring Lune up to her room. The back staircase one might use to reach it discreetly is blocked off, but no one is in the hallways at this time of the morning.

I let Taris go on ahead to Lune's room and then split off to check on some of the nobles, in case one of them is out for a midnight stroll as well. But they're all safe and accounted for. Crispin is entertaining a restless sleep. I guess he gave up on looking for his sister, but is still worried. Asmer is tucked up comfortably in her own chambers, a travel bag and her clothes for tomorrow laid out at the foot of her bed. Magnus has a pair of bedmates, but they're all fast asleep. And from what I can hear from his room, Mercer has decided to stay up late and sleep off his nighttime entertainment on the journey tomorrow.

Rian, thankfully, is sprawled out in his bed, sleeping soundly with Mango curled up on his chest.

All is well.

I head down to meet Taris by the front entrance. I notice familiar faces of Rian's guard and am pleased to see that none of them have given in to drink or other substances despite tonight's festivities; they are alert and professional. My crown prince, I suspect, was in less danger tonight than my *khashak* and I.

Taris, of course, is downstairs, but he doesn't mock me for it. He looks quite troubled, and has good reason to be, but his expression leans more towards pensive than distraught. His father died tonight, but he is busy thinking about the albino, Lune's contact, and what Lune herself might have been doing out tonight.

We silently walk back to the cabin, this time determined not to let anything delay us. Morning approaches fast, and while the nobles aren't leaving at dawn, we're still running out of time.

We're about to leave the campus proper and cross to the cabin when a strange look flits across Taris' face and he pauses. Before I can ask, he leaps at me and grabs my arms, pulling me down. Something large and unnatural flaps loudly past us, nearly knocking Taris and me in the head as it gives out a screech. It disappears into the night as quickly as it appeared.

We both pant as Taris releases me and we go about righting ourselves. We stand and stare into the night, trying to see what that thing was and where it went, but there's no trace of it.

"What was that?"

"I'm not sure," Taris admits. "But if I didn't think you'd scoff at me, I'd say some kind of demon."

I hesitate before answering, and what I do say is clearly not what he expected.

"And I'd say 'demons don't exist', but at this point…"

"Ironically, the person to ask is probably Rian," Taris mutters.

"What?"

"Demons. If they're real or not. The Smiths, the Greys and the Wolffs were supposedly killers of demons and monsters in the old stories, were they not?"

"I'm starting to think there are many things it may be useful to ask Rian," I admit in a mutter.

"So, *ask.*"

"What?"

"Ask him," Taris presses, meeting my gaze sternly with his own. "This entire system—having you follow every piece of advice my father gave you like its law—it's ridiculous. How can you protect Rian to the best of your abilities if you don't even know who is after him and why?"

Taris has been so up and down emotionally tonight, it's almost annoying. One second, it's as if our partnership means something to him; the next, I'm the Dark's handmaiden, or something of the like.

"This is the best way to protect Rian," I say, though I'm only arguing because I'm irritated with him. My heart's not in it.

"You don't know that," Taris accuses. "Qhan protects the crown prince well, and they're friends. Close friends. And you can't say that Qhan wouldn't do an equally excellent job of keeping the crown prince safe, because you always kill the assassins before they can get close."

"Which is my job," I hiss.

"It's Qhan's job, too. And he's bigger than you. Stronger. A better killer."

My anger flares.

"This job isn't about killing."

"Exactly my point," he says, and I let him go on, because I thought he was going to argue with me, and he isn't. "You could be so much more useful if you were by Rian's side, Soleil."

He stands, waiting for a response, but I'm not going to give him one. Not now. Mostly because I'm not sure what I would say.

"Come on," I insist. "We've been gone too long. We'll discuss this later."

Taris grunts, but I can tell he's going to hound me about this. I'm starting to think he wants to do away with everything that made me Rian's *Khashtani* in the first place.

Korvaan has taken care of most of the mess in the cabin. It's uncomfortably warm inside, as he's burning whatever bloodstained wood he can while his sister kneels by the last of the bodies in the room.

"Took you long enough," Korvaan mutters when he notices us.

Naomi is with Nusk, who she and Korvaan have cleaned up some in a poor attempt to make him look at peace. She is sniffling, her fingers shaking as she struggles to paint the Signs of the Dead. I can tell every second she has to touch his body is torture for her. She can't finish.

"Don't bother," Taris says coldly, as Naomi's eyes flick up in shock. Taris continues to stare at his father. I don't know what to call the look on his face, but it resembles disgust. "Dead is dead."

"I'm sorry—I'll stop! I'm sorry!" Naomi stammers through her tears. I know I should say something, but I don't. I can't.

I can't stand to see Naomi this way. And to make matters worse, I'm the one who did this, hurt her this way. Even if he does not appear to be mourning, Taris is right: I'm the reason their father died. *This is my fault.*

"Here. Let me," I say.

I crouch next to N'omi, taking the pot from her hands to finish drawing the Signs. She lets me, but avoids looking at me. Korvaan leaves the fire to join us, and he won't look at me, either. He just watches my finger move as I finish the circle. I can tell his jaw is clenched, but he doesn't say anything. I almost wish they'd yell; that would be easier to endure.

"What's done is done," Taris says once I've sat back on my heels. "It will be best if we can move past this as soon as we can, together. For our own sake. And for the prince's sake."

Naomi sniffles again, her breath catching several times, but nods.

"Let us hope we can keep the crown prince alive until Comus Day," Korvaan mutters. "Without Soleil getting anyone else killed."

I'm shocked to hear such a thing from him. From Taris, definitely. But not from Korvaan, with whom I'd always thought I'd had a decent friendship. I suppose his closeness to his father surpasses any familial bonds we shared. The same bonds, I'm starting to worry, I've now destroyed.

I know I should stand up for myself, or chide him somehow. But what he says is so factual in nature, I can't muster the anger to hate him for it.

THE CHILDREN ALL CRY when they bid Rian farewell. Officially, they're meant to throw flowers for all the nobles' procession, but no one is fooled: they are here to see Rian off. All the young men and women, meanwhile, are going to cry over Asmer or Mercer's departures. The first Comus Day since New Isaaria's conception may be a historic event, but it does not feel like one, living it. There will be a celebration after its passing, but the days leading up to it are a chore for everyone, all those at the University included.

This is a great upheaval for them. Rian's classes must be covered by another teacher. No more public storytelling. No one to keep the ridiculous fantasy of Magicsmiths alive. The professors and high scholars will miss his banter, and Crispin's thoughtful introspection. There will be no looking forward to the returns of Crown Prince Mercer and his fantastic, worldly adventures. No gentle presence of the beautiful and innocent Lady Asmer.

Time will pass, and Comus Day will end. One day, these children will have children of their own, and will only have vague answers to their questions about the event. But no one is foolish enough to pretend that their personal life won't be affected by this. For once, politics are worth paying attention to. For once, what happens on the world stage on a specific day at a specific time will change everyone's lives—for better or worse.

Before leaving, Rian gives Ayla a set of bracelets that match his favorite earrings. He's discreet about it, but the secrets will have to stop soon: he'll be adopting her. He cannot hide from that.

Naomi did well to secure assignments for us. It was too difficult for her to get us all allocated to Rian, but Korvaan is traveling with him. Naomi and I have been dispensed to Lune, and Taris, to Crispin.

I have officially been promoted: instead of a night maid, I am a lady's maid. The entire infrastructure is ridiculous at times; I essentially have the exact same job, but I am now an attendant to Lune. I follow her around and see to her needs and indulge her when necessary. This would be a technical improvement over cleaning up after her if I cared, but I'm more pleased at the prospect of being closer to the Carsans.

Additionally, the uniforms are better.

I'll be quartered with Lune herself and her favorite maid, Romia. She's Native Isaarian, like me, but with lighter hair, and a prettier, milkier face. She's friendly enough, and does not ask why there are dark circles under my eyes and stiffness in my form. Likely she's assumed that I reveled late into the morning and is trying to be polite in her judgments.

She sticks close to Lune on the carriage ride to the train station, insisting on taking the lead when it comes to seeing to Lune's needs. I'm fine with letting her. The less work I have to do looking after Lune, the better.

Especially today: I'm exhausted. My neck is bruised and my voice a pained, hoarse whisper. I tell myself to make this a good thing: a reminder of my mistakes that will stay with me for at least a good two weeks.

I did not manage to sleep yet today. I'd been too worried about the journey to the capital, the albino, my horrid dreams, Nusk's death, the firebird conspiracy, the Carsans' potential treachery, and Rian's desire for a family. Once in the capital, I'll have more time to determine who we can trust, and who has a nefarious goal in mind. But until then, I have little to keep my mind busy other than obsessing over Nusk's death and the identity of those killers.

Lune is equally exhausted; she sleeps most of the way, in the most dramatic fashion possible, splayed all the way across the carriage seat. She only gets up to move when we transition to the train. Once aboard, Lune finds a spot to settle in, drags a blanket over herself before Romia can offer to help, and falls asleep once more. I have no way of knowing if she remembers Taris and me from last night, but her injuries do not appear to have affected her drastically. She moves stiffly, and her face is pale and drawn, but most folk likely assume this is from last evening's celebrations.

She barely even notices Romia, or me, or any of her other attendants.

At least I have something for my hands to do during the trip; somehow word spread amongst the lady's maids that I'm good with knots, so I've been given a tangled mess of Lune's necklaces to sort out. As if she'll ever wear any of these.

It gives me time to think while appearing busy. The look of concentration on my face will be attributed to my attempts with the necklaces, and I'll be free to act as distracted as I please.

My *khashak* and I barely managed to prepare in time for this morning, but here we are, scattered amongst the nobles, our belongings packed up with the rest of the servants'. We'll have rooms in the palace, keeping us even closer to Rian than before. Hopefully, this will give us the chance to keep a better eye on those I'm most suspicious of.

I haven't yet explained to Korvaan or Naomi what Taris and I intend, but there will be plenty of time, later. Even without all the answers, my two acting *khashak* have returned to following my directions. They're sullen, and they still refuse to look at me, but at least I can depend on them.

All I did manage to tell them is that they should watch the nobles carefully. That goes for their servants, guards, and entourages as well. Just because a noble is a friend to Rian does not mean everyone in their service is. And so, we have eyes on Crispin, Lune, Asmer, and Rian himself. That leaves Mercer and Magnus out, but I'm starting to think that, despite their blatant differences and relationships with Rian, they are the only trustworthy nobles around. Perhaps Asmer is naïve and innocent, but there are a few suspicious things about her. I have to keep reminding myself not to forget that.

That leaves Nissa Sondushki, Yụugo Ido, Detrus Lundan, and Vásan Pike. Four more heirs competing for Rian's crown, all of whom I haven't seen in years.

I ponder my memories of them as the train glides on. Romia joins Lune in dreamland after our lunch, but I stay awake. Thinking. Remembering. Trying to make sense of everything.

Hours pass, and I still feel as clueless as when we first left the station.

Eventually, the train slows to a stop to change tracks, marking the halfway point in our journey. Peering out the window, I can see farmers in the fields with their children and their wives, preparing to lay the last of the seeds of summer in the hopes of a bountiful harvest come autumn. It is a strange tableau, like a place lost in time.

The children careen about, some with kites trailing behind them. Possibly I can spot a few field fairies about, having left their nests in pursuit of pretty colored paper. I can't be sure if I imagine the sound of their laughter. The girls have kerchiefs on their heads, their hair flying out behind them, skirts tucked into apron ties. The boys' trousers are rolled to the knee, and their socks and shoes are missing. Most of the men are too far away to be more than specks, but those closer to the train are carrying mulch for the women to flatten with their spades and hoes. They whistle for their dogs, and wipe the backs of their hands over sweaty foreheads. The womenfolk wear their pretty patterned dresses to their ankles, though they've slipped their shoulders and arms free of their long billowing sleeves and tied them about their ribs to keep from dirtying them. Straw hats perch on their heads to keep off the sun. Some work behind the men, and others are calling the lot for a late lunch. There is definitely mirth as they call for the children, and the pack of younglings race back for food.

I bite at my lip as I watch their laborer's merriment. It takes me a moment to realize I'm feeling something akin to jealousy. I'm not sure why.

Perhaps my parents were farmers who could not keep me, and the memories are buried deep down in my head.

Too soon, the train moves again, leaving the people in the fields behind.

I force myself to settle back into my seat and turn away from the window with a frown no one will ever see, feeling somehow empty.

I need something to distract myself, but I've brought nothing with me. I've already untangled all of Lune's necklaces, and I'm so used to looking after Rian or exercising in my spare time that sitting in a train for hours is excruciating.

But then I realize: Rian. Of course.

I still have my earpiece, and I'm certain Rian is wearing his earrings. Unless he's asleep, he is having all sorts of interesting conversations with his cabin-mates. I can't recall if he's riding with Mercer or Asmer, but it hardly matters.

When I turn my earpiece on, the first thing I hear is a low rumbling noise that I quickly identify as Mango's purring. It's close, at first, as if he's nuzzling up against Rian's chest. But then he settles down into my crown prince's lap, and the sound fades so I'm able to hear.

"Tell me a dark story, with a good ending," I hear Asmer say sleepily.

Her voice crackles slightly over the distance, and my reception is hardly ideal. But if I lean my head on a hand, pretending to prop myself up, I can cover an ear and just barely make out their words. As a quick glance at Romia reveals that she is still asleep, I'm not worried about anyone else hearing.

"A dark one with a good ending?" Rian repeats. "Hmm. I'll have to think on that one."

"Are there not many stories like that?"

"Not many *good* ones, in my opinion. You tell me one first, while I think of something," Rian prompts.

Asmer sounds bashful. "I don't know any stories," she admits.

"Your parents didn't tell you any when you were little?" Rian teases. "Come on, Asmer, you must have something. It doesn't have to be 'a dark one with a good ending'," he adds. "Promise. I'm not that particular."

I try to hide a smile. Rian's always bringing out the best in other people, encouraging them to try things they'd never think to do themselves.

"Well, there's always Kajah and the Nine Powers," Asmer admits. "Raj and I used to beg our parents to tell us the story at night, but they'd only oblige us now and again. Father would be all the men, and Mother would do all the women's voices. And they'd switch on and off with the narration. Almost as if they practiced it."

"Sounds like quite the performance," Rian teases.

"I suppose so. I won't be able to tell it the same way," Asmer confesses. "I don't remember it that well. I could only give a summary of it, if anything."

"It's a Bhantan story, isn't it? I think I've heard the name before, but I'm not an expert on tales from the Ishtak Empire. What's it about, then?"

Asmer is halting and embarrassed as she sums up the tale. She's not good at storytelling. Granted, I get the gist by the end, but we've all been spoiled by Rian's mastery of the art.

"It's, um. Well, it's meant to teach a lesson, I think, about greed and *shanaan*," Asmer begins, mentioning the Bhantan concept of finding one's purpose in life. "Kajah is a girl born to a family after six sons. Having wanted seven sons, as is always important in older tales of magic, her parents were disappointed in her. She grew up bitterly, thinking herself inadequate and wishing there was a way for her to prove herself to everyone. The tale goes on, and she grows and, um…there are bits about some magical creatures and things."

"And then?" Rian says, engaged despite Asmer's awkwardness.

"And then when she's one of those golden ages—sixteen or something like that—Kajah is outside with the family's goats when the young Bhantan king rides by with his entourage, and he naturally falls in love with her instantly, and so on, and asks to marry her. Her family is thrilled, but Kajah is dubious and irritated, because she feels as if she hasn't done anything to deserve that.

"Of course, the king has a terrible, wicked nephew that wants to slowly poison him and take the throne, and if the king gets married to Kajah and they have children, he will no longer be the heir. When Kajah goes to meet the king, she is shrewd, and she realizes the nephew's wickedness. She devises that she can prove herself, marry the king, and save the kingdom all in one. After several months of living in the palace, she cleverly tricks the king and his nephew both into thinking they should send her on a set of trials to prove herself worthy of being queen, and so the nephew sets up some list of ridiculous things she has to do and sends her off on a journey.

"But Kajah decides to seek out the nine djinns of the desert and collect them, so that she can use the powers of each. She does so, and I can't remember all of the adventures and such, unfortunately…But by the time she's collected the ninth one, and returns to the kingdom, the king is dead and the nephew has taken over! He throws her in the dungeon and leaves her there. But Kajah still has the nine djinns, which she can use only once each. She begins to try and figure out how to use all of their powers, but by the time she's sorted everything out, she realizes that she loves the king, from when she lived in the palace with him. And the djinns tell her that she can bring him back to life, but she has to use up all their powers, and then can't use any more of their magic again.

"She agrees, and the king comes back, but the king is not the king anymore, his nephew is, so they escape and run away and find their own goat farm to live on. And they live, not always happily, but satisfied, and Kajah realizes she has had enough adventures, and is simply happy being who she is, without thinking she needs to prove herself to anyone."

There's a short, awkward silence.

"My parents tell it much better," Asmer says apologetically.

"No, no, I like it. I'll have to find a copy for myself, now, so thank you. Besides, now I've got one. Your 'Kajah and the Nine Powers' has given me a good idea," Rian admits.

"Is it another Magicsmith one?" Asmer says, but instead of teasing, the way Mercer might, she sounds eager. I think she's secretly just as interested in the mysteries of the Families Three as Rian is.

"It involves Magicsmiths," Rian admits. "Lots of the good stories do."

I roll my eyes at that, but I want to hear Rian talk more about Magicsmiths. Maybe it's because Magnus warned him not to talk about *Dadj'zcha* and the Families Three much. Maybe it's because Rian is an excellent storyteller. Or maybe it's because this is his entire life's work, and I want to hear about all the things he's been uncovering while I sat outside his window.

In any case, I'm glad for the tale. It takes up time, and I enjoy letting Rian's voice carry me away with everyone else.

"This is back around the time of Kryto Grey, before he became the leader of the Greys and…well, founded a certain art," Rian says, playfully avoiding the word. "At the time, there were seventeen other powerful-fluke-bearing members of the Grey family who appear in the story: eight women and nine men. I can rattle off the names, if you like, but I doubt—"

"Oh, please, do," Asmer chimes.

Rian is pleased she's said so. "Well, alongside Kryto, there were also Syra'ac, Rostyar, Drex, Carius, Celtan, Dax, Jukka, Roeinan, and Roenvan. As for the ladies: Evanna, Sorcha, Ilenna, Latona, Nasya, Nascha, Naja, and Aeli. It was a golden time for the Families Three, and the Greys were particularly powerful. They had all sorts of powerful abilities, as did the Smiths they worked alongside. The power of suggestion, healing, illusions, imitation of flukes—that sort of thing, for the Greys. And the likes of creationists and memory smiths, for the Smiths.

"This, of course, is just background knowledge," Rian explains. "The story itself doesn't give much in that way, and I had to infer certain things while piecing it all together. But I'm sure you've probably at least heard of the modern version of the tale—or the simplified version, as I call it. 'The Curse of the Dragon's Tooth'. Or, 'The Curse of Mwakil Rajak', in Lusch."

"Curse of the Dragon's Tooth? That's quite the interesting tale, Yakarami," I hear Magnus Oram say, startling me. "I think I've heard some bits of it before."

I had no idea he'd been sharing a cabin with them, he's been so quiet up until now. I half-wonder if he'd been sleeping, and woke when Rian started talking. That's the only reasonable explanation; he's usually much chattier.

"Oh, I'm sure," Rian agrees. "It's a much more popular version to tell than the one involving the Families Three. In fact, I've found a lot of our 'popular' stories are modified to leave the Families Three out. I always found that curious."

Magnus grunts. "Well. I'm sure if you think hard enough, you'll remember why that is," he mutters, but he doesn't stop Rian from going on.

"Now," Rian starts, slipping into his narrator's voice. "Back in these days, there was more magic alive in the land. Less folk were inclined to flukes in their blood than today, and the world was teeming with dragons and faeries, Fae, Fair-folk and mermaids, dryads and basilisks and centaurs. One couldn't step outside their house without checking where they trod for the littlest of dragons, sunning themselves on rocks, and one had to be wary when passing uncharted forests, for the call of the Fae may draw a person in, and trap them in a mindless world of fantasy."

I can feel Asmer's excitement. Even Magnus doesn't interrupt. Despite his prickliness, he can't help but let Rian enchant him, too.

"In these times, when the Families Three were well-known and whispered of, there was a place—a mountaintop in Lusch—where it was said the very first members of each of the Families received their gifted flukes. This place, now lost to time, was called Mwakil Rajak. The Dragon's Tooth. A place of truce and treaties, where the Families Three to gathered once every ten years to discuss what needed to be done in the world.

"Now, the Grey Family was led by a pair of brothers, Roeinan and Roenvan. Twins, in fact. Roeinan was wifeless and heirless, as his family had died not but five years prior, but Roenvan had a powerful and beautiful wife, Sorcha, and three sons: Kryto, Jukka, and Dax. Now, Kryto was not the eldest son, and should not have been the heir to the family, but he had a craftier mind than his elder brother, Jukka. While still a youth, he went to his father Roenvan and confessed he was tired of the old way of things—how the Families Three appeared always on the defensive, always killing themselves to protect humanity from unholy dark creatures. He wished to change that, and believed that, as head of the Grey family, he might succeed where others had failed.

"Roenvan was impressed, naturally, and proud of his son, but there was a problem: he and Roeinan were the patriarchs of the family, but they had a sister. Ilenna. She, too, was married, with children of her own. And Roeinan, the more dominant of the twins, had decided when he lost his own family that, when he died, the Grey family would be led by a matriarch, as they had not been for many, many years. He was determined that level-headed Ilenna and her children would inherit next, to prevent the sorts of follies that killed his own family from ever happening again.

"Even Roenvan's own wife, Sorcha, agreed with this judgement, relieved that her sons would never have to bear what she considered a great burden. So, what, then, was Roenvan to do? His son Kryto made excellent points, but these plans required risk. Sacrifice. Roenvan was certain Kryto was the answer—the one meant to lead the world into a better future—and yet, if he could not even convince his own wife of this, how could he convince the rest of the family?

"So, Roenvan went first to his elder twin, sure that the two of them together could make sense of this. They would find a solution, so that the world might benefit from it.

"He was to be greatly disappointed—"

I WAKE AT THE SOUND of a whistle blast, having accidentally drifted off. Last night's events have both exhausted me and set me on edge, and it takes me several seconds to calm down and remind myself neither Rian nor I, nor any of my *khashak* are in danger. The whistle is only routine. The train has stopped. We have reached our destination, and we will soon disembark to ride carriages up to the Pyrian Palace.

The royals and noblemen won't be moved until after their luggage, which is what I assume we're waiting on.

My earpiece is still on, and Rian is chattering. Still telling his story, only now, we're close to the ending. Perfect timing.

"—and so Roeinan perished before he could warn the Smiths or the Wolffs of what was to come; his, Ilenna's, and Sorcha's lifeblood staining the top of the Dragon's Tooth, never to be removed by snow or rain or shifting sediment. And with blood spilt on the mountain, they say an unbreakable curse was laid on the Grey family: no matter what its leaders tried to accomplish—for good or for ill—it would come at a painful cost. In his bitterness, Kryto Grey decided that if the Greys must sacrifice for the greater good, then why not have others sacrifice, too. After all, the Families Three had been the ones bearing the burden. It was time the rest of the world gave back.

"So, he offered his new art of *Dadj'zcha*, to teach witchcraft to the rest of the Greys, and enhance them once again with the powers they'd lost to their own greed. And the rest, as they say, is history."

There are the necessary moments of stunned silence while Asmer and Magnus awake from the spell of his tale.

"That's so sad," Asmer sighs, as Magnus mutters, "That's despicable."

"Well, it is what it is," Rian claims. "A good story with a dark ending."

Asmer huffs. "You got it backward," she chides.

"Even so. It's easy to label the Greys however we like, now, but it's hard to know what might have been embellished for the sake of creating proper villains. After all, in their own minds, they were the purported heroes, weren't they?"

"Purported being the key word, there," Magnus says. "But I agree with you, Yakarami. I might not like *Dadj'zcha*, and I find its practitioners untrustworthy, but as I warned you: those who believe in its power must think the Greys a family of gods."

"Yes, yes," Rian says, a little shortly. I can tell he doesn't like being reminded about that afternoon. "I'll take your advice to heart, crown prince. No more public stories about the Families Three and *Dadj'zcha* and such. Private ones, though, I think it's safe to amuse ourselves with."

There's a mischievous tone in his voice, at the end. I know exactly what smile he's smiling, right now, and it makes my mouth curve reflexively as well.

"Have you ever thought of penning your own story?" Asmer suggests. "I think you'd be very good at it. People would love to hear you tell some original tales. I think you could make a spectacle of it."

Rian laughs. "You think so? I must admit, the thought has crossed my mind…"

"On Magicsmiths and such?"

Magnus is mocking him, but Rian doesn't rise to the bait.

"Not exactly," my crown prince admits. "There's something else that I think would make a fascinating story, and I don't think one's ever been penned before. There's this Milashi tradition, you see. A certain bodyguarding practice that I find oh-so intriguing."

I swear, my heart stops.

Khashtani. Rian is talking about the *Khashtani*.

I can feel my heart. It's on the outside of my chest, now. Skipping beats. It's torturing me. If I didn't know better, I'd think he was making fun of me. I'm terrified by the idea that maybe he is, but…

There's a sudden sliding sound as the door to their compartment opens.

"Sir," Qhan says. "Your coach is ready for you, now. M'lady Asmer, Crown Prince," he addresses. "I'm sure yours will be brought around shortly. Please excuse Crown Prince Yakarami. It is best we not dawdle."

"Oh, go ahead, Khaleem," Magnus says. "Griffith will be around for me shortly. And I'll bring the Lady Asmer."

The door to our own compartment is wrenched open, and I quickly turn off my earpiece and drop my hands into my lap as Romia walks in. I hadn't even noticed, but she must have left while I was asleep. Lune slumbers on, but I'm so startled, I can feel my fingers tingle.

"Oh, I'm sorry," Romia apologizes sweetly. "I didn't mean to scare you. You and the lady were so tired. I thought it best to let you sleep."

I hum something in thanks, but try not to look at her while she kneels on the seat across from me to gently shake Lune awake. I take the next few seconds to subtly try and pull myself together, and make sure all my tools of the trade are handy. We're at the capital, now. An unpredictable metropolis.

"My lady," Romia says, her hand on Lune's shoulder.

Lune groans in an unladylike way.

"My lady, we have to leave, now," Romia says. "There's a coach to take us to the palace. And you've slept long enough. I need to fix your hair on the ride, and you must change into your dress. You're singing this afternoon, you remember."

"Would you like any help?" I offer.

"I can manage," Romia says, smiling at me.

She's strangely genuine, which I immediately distrust. I keep trying to see if she's mocking me, the way Taris would, but if so, she's being subtle about it.

She helps Lune out the door and down the train's hallway while I follow behind, watchful. Wary. Crispin happens to be approaching us from the other end of the train. He looks nervous.

He gives Lune an irritated look when he passes, but doesn't say anything. I just barely brush up against him and tag him with one of Taris' bugs. I have a whole pack of them in my coin purse.

I'm deciding Crispin is a more likely threat than Lune.

I could be wrong, but I think it's possible I've been following her around when I should have been following him.

Twelve

THERE ARE TWO PALACES for the king's household in Isaaria: the one in the capital, and the Summer Palace, in the northwest. I've only been to the Summer Palace a few times, but I recall it's a fanciful thing made of white and gold marble. The capital palace, often referred to as the Pyrian Palace for the nearby mountains and city, is not quite as pretty, but just as impressive.

It's a sprawling estate, with enough complexes to house representatives from the eight royal families and a larger central one for the king's household. Built of marble and tile, with swirling black iron gates and window decorations, its inner hallways are white stucco and the king's grounds alone include three different gardens, a decorative pool, and an underground one for swimming.

It also has one of the most magnificent meditation chambers in the country, made of domed glass and iron, at the top of a squat hexagonal tower. The roof can be retracted and opened up to the sky day or night, and the trees inside are some of Isaaria's proudest flora, their roots stretching all the way down to the ground below so a person is practically meditating in the treetops when they present themselves before the Almighty and his sun and moon.

It's called the Solunium Hub, and it's considered one of the most beautiful man-made places in all of Samioth. I might not have reason to do so myself, without a fluke, but I might try to experience the place.

My carriage with Lune and Romia is entering the grounds of the Palace in a long line of others. Rian, I think, is in the one behind us. I've left my earpiece off, for now. There would be too much interference, given the sounds of the carriages, the distance, and the many walls between us. The last thing I need is obvious feedback. For that same reason, I don't dare reach out to any of my *khashak*. We can spare a little less of each other's company, for now.

The palace grounds are surrounded by large brick walls, topped with twisted metal gating, and the front gates themselves are a matching black with curling designs. Once inside, the carriages roll up, up, up to the circular drive at the front of the palace, which is adorned with a multitude of impressive statues and fountains, plants and hedging. There's a courtyard in which everyone will gather before heading inside together, and I can see as we pull up that the University travelers are the last of those to arrive today. I disembark from our carriage first and wait while Romia fusses with Lune's appearance. It gives me time to see all there is to see.

Nissa, Yuugo, Detrus, and Vásan. Three crown princes, one crown princess. I have not been able to observe them over the years as I have the others, but I know they've kept in contact: with Magnus, with Mercer, with Crispin. Even Rian. They are not shadow-players waiting in the wings; none of them have excused themselves from the Comus Day proceedings, so each must believe they deserve the throne, or that pretending to want it will win them something significant.

I have limited time to make my assessments of them. But I do what I can.

Crown Princess Nissa Sondushki, the only female heir, is not a large woman, but there's no doubt she can hold her own. She sits perched on one of the pillar-stands at the foot of a statue: a bear with a woman carved inside it where the bulge of its stomach would otherwise be. It is as good a representation of Nissa as any, except in the old Kachin stories, the bear-woman eventually grew to desire a child, and I cannot see Princess Nissa feeling similarly.

She's dressed in impractical leathers that would do little to protect her sun-tanned skin in battle, but wrap around her lithe body in strips to show off its form. Her muted red hair is cut to her shoulders, and her ears are adorned with jewelry carved from bone. Beside her prowls a creature exotic to most Isaarians: a hyena, from the south. Nissa's fluke brought her charms over a familiar, and the hyena suits her well: not highly gregarious or social, but dangerous, and known to fight off creatures much larger than itself.

Everyone knows Nissa was raised in the far south of Isaaria, by the last of the migrant Hoitsokin and their wild ways. Her mother's people. She does not appear to have brought an entourage like the rest of the royals, but has come completely alone. Not even members of her father's court have come to support her.

I know not to underestimate her.

Crown Prince Yuugo Ido is the shortest and slightest of the male heirs, standing only about a hand taller than the petite Nissa. He's the youngest of the bunch, at twenty-three, and dresses in a neutral set of salmon pink Tourrannese heritage garb—*kundah*. He looks even smaller and younger in person than he ever did in pictures, and the last I saw him face-to-face; he was only seven. For some reason, he appears as if he has grown up least of all the heirs.

He is mixed Isaarian and Tourrannese, but favors the latter, and does not speak much. I know from reading a letter from him to Crispin a few years ago that he idolizes the Carsans heir, and has two younger brothers he hopes look up to him in turn. Otherwise, I know little about him. I'm fairly certain the only reason he hasn't excused himself from the Comus Day trials is because he does not want to be the first or only heir to do so. I can't imagine he has the confidence or tenacity to be king, and he must know that.

That leaves Crown Princes Detrus Lundan and Vásan Pike. Like Nissa, Detrus is red-haired, but their resemblance—and his resemblance to any of the other heirs, for that matter—stops there. Detrus is an impressively large man, with a wife too pretty for him. He has a great, bushy beard that he keeps meticulously groomed and arm muscles the size of small hams. His wife is a tall, blond woman with a somewhat large nose and a slim, boyish figure. One might assume she married him for his position, but from what I've heard, the two are madly in love with one another.

Detrus is the only married heir, which already changes my assessment of him. Even more importantly: his wife is with child. With a daughter already born and rumors of a son on the way, Detrus is the only one whose ascension would maintain a form of familial comfort; an overtly wholesome, pretty picture.

Aside from Rian, he's the most likeable crown prince. Even Mercer, though a joy to be around for most of his peers, is too rowdy, unpredictable and even scandalous to make a good king. His constant traveling does not help make him look particularly patriotic.

Yet, out of all of them, I am most wary of Vásan. He's the smartest of the lot; the shrewdest. He even looks it. Tall, slim, always gloved and poised to offer a clever opinion in cool, commanding tones. With medium-length, pale blond hair, a narrow face, and faded blue eyes, one might describe him as delicately featured, but such a thing may hint at a strong, powerful fluke: Vásan need not bulk muscle or curry favor with the courtiers and noblemen.

He can hold his own.

He has come with his younger brother, their widowed mother, and a handful of trusted supporters, but that's all. Nothing flamboyant, but he's not making an obvious statement, like Nissa is by coming alone.

Out of the corner of my eye, I catch sight of Asmer all but sobbing at a surprise reunion with her younger brother, Raj. I recall her claiming her parents and brother meant to remain in the south for Comus Day, which rings suspicious, but if this reunion is for show, then Asmer is a better actress than I thought.

Not far from me, I watch Crispin Carsans disembark from his own carriage. I eye him carefully, and briefly meet eyes with Taris. I didn't see him on the train, but he is now close behind Crispin as another one of his guards.

I've decided I've been underestimating the Carsans heir: despite his obvious discomfort on the train, Crispin is now his usual, pleasant self. He even tips the coachman generously, smiling. Then he moves forward, past where I'm still waiting for Romia and Lune. I follow him and Taris a few steps, hoping to keep an eye on them as they start to mingle.

"Crispiiiiiin!" a young voice calls, coming closer and louder before a slim, blond-haired boy of about eleven throws himself at Crispin, so hard that the two spin around a few times.

It's little Soren Carsans, the boy born to Grand Prince Alion Carsans and his wife Eliora long after they thought it impossible for them to have another child.

"You're out of your chair!" Crispin exclaims. "You're running!"

I'm selfishly glad that Soren's doing well; when his muscles fatigue or spasm, he can barely stand, and uses a wheeled chair. Not unlike Nusk's.

"Uh-huh!" Soren agrees cheerfully. "I can do it sometimes without any help, but mostly I use my walking sticks. I wanted to surprise you and Lune, though. I've been working hard at it. And I'm not supposed to know, but the doctors said I might be able to walk all on my own even more soon. Just slower than normal people, I guess."

I see Crispin stiffen. "You are 'normal people', Soren," he mutters.

Soren isn't listening.

"Where's Lune?" the boy demands.

Crispin manages a smile. "On her way. She stayed up too late last night."

Soren grins. If I weren't so desensitized to such things, I might note that it's a cheeky, adorable expression. But I'm wary of it, because while I've no doubt that Soren himself is an innocent child, I'm certain any one of his family members would do absolutely anything for him. That makes him dangerous.

I look back to the carriage to see what's keeping Lune. She's finally emerged, and is currently surrounded by a flock of women in habits and head coverings.

It's the nuns from the Rose Order, flocking around Lune excitedly and kissing her on the cheeks like they raised her themselves. I know Lune is exhausted, and the attention isn't helping, but she manages to smile and accept their greetings, exchanging pleasantries and promising to visit.

She either has reneged on casting aside her faith, or else is too much of a coward to mention it. Regardless: I know the Carsans family feels indebted to the Rose Order. The nuns have ensured Soren bathes monthly in their healing springs of Our Lady of Pyrian. A supposed apparition sight of the Queen of Heaven. Many travel to the mountain springs just a few miles outside the capital's limits, praying for miracles.

Soren's positive progress might be taken as one such miracle. I suppose.

"Lune!" Soren calls, and waves to her when she picks up her head.

Lune excuses herself graciously, then picks up the skirts of her elaborate costume and rushes over. Romia hurries behind, already cringing; she'll have to fix the lady's hair with its ornaments falling out and veil slipping. And, possibly, fix Lune's dress after the embrace she shares with her little brother.

I sigh and fall in with Romia.

"Did you miss me?" Soren's asking, his arms still wrapped around his sister's waist. His toes are barely touching the ground.

"Like a fish misses her river," Lune teases, and pokes his nose.

Soren laughs. "Fishes die without water—they can't just miss it!"

"Well. Then it's a good thing we're back together again, isn't it?" Lune says. "…I don't think I'm ready to die."

She has not noticed that she made Soren uncomfortable with that remark. Or if she did, she's quick to try and distract him from a thoughtless comment.

"You've gotten so strong," Lune compliments him. "Soon, you'll be carrying around Crispin and me like we're a pair of puppies!"

Soren scoffs. "No, I won't. That'd be a miracle."

"Miracles happen," she quips, though it sounds forced. "Where's Kaoli?" she asks after Soren's aide and bodyguard. "Are you giving her a break today, looking after yourself?"

Soren laughs again and finally releases Lune, making the chimes in her hair sound. He wavers before regaining his balance, but manages to stay standing.

"No. She's with Mallorie and Parker, and Mother and Father. Just over there," he answers, pointing back in the direction he came from.

Lune, Crispin and I all follow his finger.

Grand Prince Carsans and his princess are standing in wait for the arrival of their elder son and daughter. Both are imposing, stiff figures—the grand prince with curly, faded golden hair not unlike his sons', and princess with straight, white-blond hair scraped back into a ceremonial headpiece. Their bodyguards, Mallorie Courteau and Parker Aubrey, hover at their shoulders, with Soren's aide Kaoli Adder not far behind, carrying his canes in case he needs them.

I follow the Carsans party as Soren escorts his siblings back to their parents, and I am oddly reassured when Taris steps in close to me. I haven't seen Naomi yet, or Korvaan, but Rian is leaving his carriage, with Mango wrapped around his shoulders. I have eyes on him.

Alion and Eliora Carsans barely glance at me or Taris when their children reach them. I'd be insulted, but I'm glad I won't have to answer any personal questions about who I am and why I'm in the same position as Romia, whom they have known for years.

"Mother, Father," Crispin says. He bows to them, and accepts an embrace from each when he rises. "I hope you've been well."

"It's been some time, has it not?" Alion Carsans says.

"Soren has missed you so much, you know," Eliora adds. Her tone is somehow cold, chiding, and motherly all at once. "Despite your letters and such."

Soren doesn't confirm or deny this, but is still grinning, happy to have his family together again.

"Well, there will be no leaving, now," Crispin reassures them. "My days at the University are over. I'd like to be ready at all times for the king, whenever he might need something. Or queen."

"And Lune—don't hide behind your brother, there, let's see you," Alion says, motioning for his daughter.

Lune obliges him with an obtusely false smile. Even physically, she does not belong here, and she must know that. Her hair is several shades darker than her adoptive brothers', and her eyes are blue rather than honeyed brown. Her pale-as-the-moon skin does not tan under the summer sun like theirs, and her figure is shorter and slimmer than most in the Carsans clan. But I think the greatest irony is that she looks least like a member of her family not because of physical differences, but because of how formally her parents treat her.

I'm curious as to why the Grand Prince and Princess Carsans adopted Lune. They do not appear fond of her. Oh, they pretend, naturally but therein lies the problem: everyone knows it's a show.

Instead of an embrace, Lune only bows to them both. "Sir. Madam.

So glad to see Soren again, and to know he's been well. The nuns said he's improved greatly. How wonderful."

"Oh, dear, you've let your hair grow out again," Eliora tisks, holding Lune at arm's length while she looks her over. "It's dreadful while long."

She does not acknowledge Lune's praise of the youngest Carsans. She's only concerned about how long Lune's hair has gotten, and how it's started to frizz in humidity, despite the decorative braids and twists Romia so carefully put in.

"I'm sorry," Lune says, "I forgot to have it trimmed."

Eliora sighs. "Halved, I should think. Well, we've time, yet, to remedy it."

Lune frowns. "Time before…?"

"Have you been well otherwise, daughter?" Alion interrupts.

Their interaction is stilted, as if there is another conversation hiding beneath this frivolous one.

"Well, enough," Lune says, forcing her smile wider.

"Is that so? Crispin mentioned you've had several…fits, lately," Grand Prince Carsans says. I've no doubt he knows everything about Lune's actions these past few weeks.

"Oh. Yes, but I'm better now. Promise."

No one looks convinced of that. Even Soren is frowning, concerned.

I watch this family reunion with keen eyes and pricked ears, trying to read faces and deconstruct their words. I'm not as paranoid as Magnus Oram, but I don't trust the Carsans family. I know too little about them, on the whole. I've watched Lune and Crispin with Rian, naturally, but I don't know their wants and goals, nor their parents' desires.

Grand Prince Alion Carsans is a cool customer. Not as golden as his elder son or as dramatic as his daughter. I know what, legally and traditionally speaking, the Carsans family should be trying to achieve, which has constantly tempted me to excuse them from suspicion. But that does not mean it's the truth. It does not mean they are not angling to become more powerful. Prestigious.

Folk have said too many times, recently, that it is impossible for Crispin to become king, myself included. It's begun to worry me. I cannot help but wonder if the first Comus Day in history is Alion Carsans' opportunity to change that.

I'm not accusing Grand Prince Carsans of anything, yet. But I will not, and cannot, be a fool about this.

"Grand Prince Carsans!" someone calls, interrupting whatever Eliora is going to say to Lune next.

I don't bother to turn my head and look. I remember that voice; it's

Asmer's brother Raj al'Yibna. He's quite a bit older now than when Rian and I saw him last. His hair is longer, and worn in a short ponytail at the back of his head, with a decorative band about the top. As he approaches the Carsans, I realize he's also grown taller than me, and looks particularly impressive beside his tiny sister. Asmer does not follow him over, but is called off by some other noblewoman she hasn't seen in years.

This leaves me and Taris with Raj al'Yibna and the Carsans.

"And the entire family," Raj adds as he stops in front of us. He bows to the grand prince, and kisses the grand princess' hand. "Crispin, Lune… Soren," he adds for each of the Carsans' children. "How good to see you all again. It's been years, hasn't it? Soren, last I saw, you were only six years old; look at how big you've gotten!"

"And I can *walk!*" Soren announces proudly.

"So I see," Raj says, but then quickly moves on.

I think Asmer must have warned him about the sensitivity around Soren.

"I brought a gift for you," Raj claims. His accent is a mix of his father's northern Bhantan speech and southern Isaarian.

"What for?" Soren inquires.

"No reason, Soren," Raj laughs. "Only, Asmer and I have no little siblings to buy presents for. It's nice to have someone to dote on from time to time."

Soren narrows his eyes. "What kind of present?" he probes, all business, now.

Raj brings around the pack he's wearing. He begins to explain whilst digging around inside it, and the Carsans watch curiously. I can tell the grand prince and princess are pleased; it's highly traditional, in Isaaria, to bring a gift for the youngest of the family when visiting, particularly for diplomacy. Soren is happy only to receive a gift, but the rest of the Carsans, as well as myself and Taris, are more intrigued by what it is Raj has been sent to the capital to talk about.

It appears I was right to assume something significant must have changed since Asmer first said she'd attend Comus Day on her family's behalf.

I try to move closer, to bug Raj, but the angles aren't good. Someone would see. So, I hold myself back.

"I went down to visit our uncle, in Bhanta," Raj says.

"What's Bhanta?" Soren asks, and Crispin musses his hair.

"You need to study your geography more," he teases his brother. "It is a country in the Ishtak Empire, where Raj's and Asmer's grandfather is from."

"Exactly," Raj says. "And while I was there, I found something I thought Soren might be interested in."

He leans down closer to Soren's height and brings his hand around. He's holding a small, hexagonal board painted muted gold and green, with red dots spotted around the middle. Atop the board is a velvet bag that Soren digs into to pluck out metal figurines: sets of tigers, dogs, and goats.

"Everyone plays this in Bhanta," Raj explains, as Soren is captivated by the miniature figurines. "It's a strategy game. There are the goats, who must avoid the tigers, the tigers, who must capture all the goats, and the hounds, who must capture all the tigers while protecting the goats. Goats win if they all cross the board without capture by tigers or herding by the hounds."

Soren looks up with a wide grin. "And since there's three, Lune, Crispin and I can all play!"

His siblings withhold laughter, but I'm sure they will still oblige him on occasion. Even if Crispin is too busy, Kaoli could always sit in for him.

While Crispin and Lune both bend down to let their little brother show off his new gift, and Kaoli helps Soren hold everything, Raj takes the opportunity to lean closer to the grand prince. I turn on my earpiece discreetly, as I know I'm otherwise too far away to hear him.

"I need to speak with you urgently, sir. Privately," Raj al'Yibna whispers to Grand Prince Carsans.

I barely pick it up through the bug I put on Crispin, but even so: what an interesting thing to overhear.

I glance over and meet Taris' eyes; he'd heard that, too.

"What a gathering this is!" a voice suddenly announces over the crowd.

I hear the king before I see him, and so does everyone else; his voice is deep and rumbling. When I turn to look, I see his mane of thick, brownish-red ropy locks. He's tall enough that I can see the top of his head above everyone else, and the hints of his wife's black hair as well. The crowd quickly parts to let them through, but they've appeared without fanfare or even an announcement.

The Carsans are suddenly scrambling to look presentable, as is everyone else.

The king and queen are healthy, despite their age, and their rule has been a relatively good one for Isaaria. The Oram family has managed to keep the rest of hungry world at bay, and have handled external pressure with such grace and diplomacy that there are several foreign ambassadors attending Comus Day out of respect as well as to give their country a presence at an historic event, of course.

I have always found it odd that Magnus is their only child, but the

Orams have always been careful to keep their personal lives separate from matters of state, so there could be any number of private reasons for that.

Naturally, the royal pair make their way instantly to the Carsans, flustering them and amusing me and Taris.

"Alion!" the king greets, throwing an arm about the grand prince's shoulders. "It's so good to see all our children back safely in one place, wouldn't you agree?"

"I…I'm certain it is a great relief for all that Comus Day is finally here," Grand Prince Carsans says, clearly uncomfortable.

The king is already moving on. "And Crispin! Are you prepared to swear yourself to the new king?"

"I suppose that depends on who the new king is," Crispin says.

His tone makes the king laugh and the queen smile, because it's obviously meant to be said in jest, but his words unnerve me, and Lune looks twitchy.

"And me!" Soren announces, not to be forgotten. "I'll do whatever Crispin does. For Isaaria!"

"How patriotic of you," the queen whispers in her hoarse, strained voice. It is an effort for her to speak, but even she will do it for Soren.

The whole show is so disgustingly put on that I find myself impatient. I tune them all out, expecting Taris to still be listening, and glance around to see how everyone else is reacting to this show.

Magnus hovers, trying to avoid attention, interestingly enough. Griffith is directly behind him. Given the medal pinned to his chest, I suppose the king has given him some kind of award for keeping Magnus safe all these years. So, the king and queen slipped out quietly to greet their son before this spectacle with the Carsans.

I find Rian, who is standing with Mercer and feeding Mango some dried fruit while the dragon perches on his shoulders. The two are only half-paying attention to what's going on as they chat.

Detrus Lundan and Yuugo Ido are more interested in their own family reunions, and have made note of the king's presence without doing anything about it. However, I do catch Detrus looking directly at Vásan to give the other crown prince a nod. Vásan returns it, but is distracted by the Carsans. I cannot tell if he's looking at Crispin or Lune, but either way, I was right to suspect the Carsans were at the root of all this trouble.

Nissa has disappeared from her perch on the statue, I glimpse her vanishing inside the lofty palace doors, her beast prowling behind her. She is fed up with all the pomp, I suppose.

Taris nudges me in the arm, and I realize he's inched closer to do so. When I look at him, he widens his eyes and raises his eyebrows. I can practically hear him demanding I pay attention. I give him a scathing look back before returning my eyes and ears to those in front of me.

"I'd heard your daughter plans to grace us with the beauty of her voice during opening ceremonies," the king is saying to Alion. "I'm certain we all look forward to it. Last I heard you sing you were only a little thing, weren't you?" he adds to Lune.

One of the few people here who will likely ever speak directly to her, and he's the king himself. It's telling.

This means Magnus has decided not to share his suspicions with his parents. Or, he's kept from them his injury at Lune's hands. It's possible the king-incumbent is astutely planning to keep an eye on the Carsans, and has decided to start now, but I don't think he'd be able to treat Lune quite so pleasantly if he knew what she did to his son's neck.

"You're too kind, your majesty," Lune says with a genuine smile and a proper curtsey. "I believe you're right: it's been far too long since last I sang at the Pyrian Palace. I'm honored to have the chance to do so again. And for such a tremendous occasion."

"Well, if no one else opposes, and if you're prepared Lady Lune, I think it's high time we gathered for the opening ceremonies," the king says.

He's already taking his wife's arm to walk into the palace with her. Queen Clair can technically see with the use of her fluke, but it would be an exhausting practice to maintain. She's a quiet, almost demure queen, but is less frail than one might assume a blind and nearly-mute woman to be. I think she simply likes to observe things, and allow people to underestimate her.

She wears gloves, like the rest of the population, but they are thin, and sheer. I've heard that when she uses her fluke to sense her surroundings, there's almost a golden glow about her. There's part of me that wants to see if it's true.

Lune gives a small, perfect curtsy that somehow irritates her mother. "If you'll lead the way, your majesty," she says.

I stay close to Romia as the masses shuffle on. As we are near the king and the Carsans, we're at the front of the crowd streaming into the palace.

It's thankfully cool inside the hall, despite the mass of bodies moving into it, and it's as richly decorated as one might expect a palace to be. There are ornaments and chandeliers, paintings and carvings, all meant to remind Isaarians of what is most important: heaven, nature, the sun, and the moon. These are the things from which we draw our power, and we must always be grateful for them.

While the nobles are looking forward to entertainment, the palace staff will be hustling to get all their belongings into place while they're enjoying themselves. I'm grateful for my promotion, now; it will afford me more opportunities and keep me close to Rian.

There is a presentation arena built onto the palace grounds; I've never been entirely sure of what to call it, but Lune's sung there at least twice in the past. Sometimes, they put on plays or minstrel shows. Traveling performers are occasionally invited, and those with flashy flukes are always welcomed as part of the entertainment.

As Lune is meant to sing, and does not require our assistance, Romia and I are ushered off with the rest of the handmaids, off-duty guards, and the general public coming for the opening ceremony. Personally, I find it ridiculous we have an opening ceremony at all, what with this being a serious occasion and not some kind of sporting competition, but no one asked what I thought when they drew up the plans. And, as I know the Carsans are the ones who determined this week's scheduled events leading up to Comus Day, I'm extra wary of what lies ahead.

The ovular arena is at the far end of the palace's west wing, and can seat up to twenty thousand people. Half of those seats are intended for lesser nobles, their assistants and guests, but the other half is open to the public—whoever is lucky enough to win the lottery for tickets. I'm certain people would have sold one of their organs for an extra ticket to Comus Day, even merely for these opening ceremonies.

Scattered around the arena are nine boxes, eight of which are for the royal families and their guests. Today, most of those boxes sit empty, as the families find seats in or around the last, largest, and most impressive box, which is reserved for the current ruling family of Isaaria.

I sit with the maids, but choose a spot on an aisle. I spend the next few minutes making a point of searching out everyone in the crowd that I can while the other maids gossip. Lune is in one of the rooms beneath our seats, steeling her nerves. Crispin is seated with the rest of the princes, beside Rian, and Taris is standing naught but twenty paces behind them near an exit with the Carsans' other bodyguards. I turn on my earpiece discreetly while Romia is busy chatting.

Rian still has Mango curled around his shoulders, and the first thing I hear is the dragon's purring. That makes it difficult for me to hear Rian clearly, but it is better than silence.

He's talking with Mercer, who sits beside him looking both bored and uncomfortable. He nods vaguely response to Rian, but does not speak, which is odd for him. I think this event makes him nervous. He does not like reminders of his royal status.

I peer around the box, but I don't spot Talan Marques anywhere.

I beginning to wonder if the man's dead and Mercer simply never told anyone.

"I hear there's a special surprise for the public, on Comus Day itself," Rian says, which is what gets Mercer's attention.

"What, aside from a new king?"

"Or queen," Rian adds. "But yes. Did you not see all those boxes they were delivering, at the University?"

"...Mmm," Mercer says, but I can tell it's a topic he's interested in even as he feigns indifference.

Rian continues to talk, a steady stream of chatter that nearly puts me to sleep again. I likely would have dozed through Lune's performance if Romia did not accidentally nudge my arm and knock my chin off my hand. I hastily turn off my earpiece, as Rian would never talk through one of Lune's performances, and set my eyes on the arena below. Lune looks small and alone, from up high. She's a blue-clad speck whose hair, I note, is starting to come out of its adornments, and whose face, even at this distance, is white-pale.

Physically, she's disheveled. But the moment she opens her mouth, everyone forgets that.

Lune's song is a beautiful lament. It sounds tragic, though it is officially called a lullaby. There is sparse music to accompany her, giving us all the opportunity to hear how unique a voice she has: a deep, slightly nasal tone that soothes us all while remaining strong. This song is sung in Old Isaarian so that, while few of the words she sings are ones we still use today, we can all understand the lyrics.

She tells us to stay warm by the fire of her heart through winter, whilst waiting for spring. She tells us to dream pretty dreams, of looking upwards on a hillside, and seeing a pale blue sky full of white clouds. She says we must be gone away from each other, for now, but we will one day meet again.

I wonder why she chose this song, when there are cheerier traditional songs suitable for the occasion. I wonder who she sings it for.

Perhaps there is some hidden message, for a partner in treachery to hear and obey. After all, I realize, the last time Rian's life was seriously in danger was when Lune sang her concert on Fars'day.

I'm split between following that thought and reminding myself of the last time I heard Lune sing a lullaby. Or hum a lullaby, actually. One that I, for some reason, found familiar.

When she's finished, the arena is remains morose and silent. Thousands of royals, nobles, servants, guards, and even foreign emissaries all hold their breath as Lune's last notes ring in our ears.

No one applauds.

Several people, including Romia beside me, wipe away tears.

Even I feel strangely empty inside, but I think that has more to do with the fact that I haven't slept or eaten in a while. That's less worrisome than assuming Lune's melancholy is affecting me, too.

It's nearly a minute of silence before the king stands up in his royal box and speaks. His voice is a harsh contrast to Lune's singing, and I see several people flinch, or pull disappointed faces; they'd rather continue to hear her than the king, an additional side-effect her fluke has that I had not considered before. People want to listen to her.

She is the ultimate siren. Even as the king welcomes everyone to celebrate this tremendous occasion, few are absorbing his words. We care more about the woman standing in the arena below.

I force myself to listen to him, hoping to glean as much information as I can.

"...In just a few days' time, Isaaria will crown its new ruler," Oram is saying, careful not to specifically mention a king. "A new royal family will take charge of our country and, as the Carsans' prophecy proclaimed, will lead us into a better future than any of us could hope to imagine."

Here, he pauses before changing course a touch.

"These are dark times, as you all must know," the king admits. "Many of our neighbors have fallen and turned on each other, with war and violence. Our own Crown Prince Mercer Ralhan has seen the destruction such warmongering has provoked firsthand. Without prejudice towards one country or the other, he has attempted to help where he can."

I glance at Mercer again; he does not look pleased by this public recognition. In fact, he is purposefully keeping his gaze high, so that his eyes can't possibly meet those of anyone now staring at him.

"So Isaaria, too, must lend aid," the king says. "Our country has stayed out of conflict for years. We, alone, have remained a sanctuary of peace."

It leans too patriotic for my taste, but so it goes. This precedes the first Comus Day in history, after all; folks are nervous. I'm certain the king, or whoever wrote this speech for him, is trying to conjure whatever reserves of optimism Isaarians have left. Children are excited for this event, certainly, but their parents know better. They understand something must have gone wrong, for Isaaria to go so long without a new king.

"It is with this in mind that I thank all those spreading messages of charity and understanding," the king says. "We must do so with whatever talents the Almighty has blessed us with, fluke or no. I would especially like to thank Lady Lune, for the song she prepared for us all today, which, I am certain, will inspire anyone who heard it to—"

A loud burst of laughter elicits a sudden, shocked silence as it echoes through the arena. Only one person could have laughed loudly enough to drown out the king right now, and eyes slowly turn downwards again, to where Lune stands.

Even the king is too confused to remark upon her outburst.

I could be wrong, but I think Lune's mocking laughter stems from disbelief. She can't believe us stupid enough to think she was singing for our sakes.

"P-Pu-*Please* continue!" she says, though she's laughing so hard, I'm afraid she's going to pass out. "I'm s-s-so sorry! I can't take this s-s-seriously!"

I glance up at the royals and turn my earpiece on. Grand Princess Carsans is mortified. Her husband is white with anger and embarrassment.

A few seats below, Rian leans over to Crispin in concern.

"Is she quite well?" he whispers.

Crispin looks miserable. "Never."

Lune, still laughing, manages to cover her mouth, and flee off the side of the arena. The crowd begins to murmur, and the unrest builds louder with every passing second. The king does not know what to do, and is stunned Lune would interrupt him in such a way, especially after what seemed like a pleasant enough exchange outside the palace.

The queen has joined him to tug on his sleeve, and Grand Prince Carsans stands and straightens his suit with an angry jerk before going to speak on the family's behalf, to apologize for Lune's behavior, and beg the king to continue. I don't know how he plans to excuse this, but Lune's entire family will be furious with her save for Soren, who is merely distressed. I can just hear him through the earpiece as he talks with his brother: Soren wants to see what's wrong with Lune, but Crispin insists the boy stay and rest. He's exerted himself enough, for today.

Crispin then heads out himself, to chase after Lune for some answers.

"We'd best go see to her," Romia whispers to me.

She's already standing, nudging my legs and prompt me to lead the way. I am suspicious of such an opportunity to get close to a distressed Lune Carsans, but I cannot allow it to pass me by.

We leave the arena seating by a short, dark hallway, then find a stairwell down to where performers prepare for their shows. It's not hard to find Lune and Crispin, as the belly of the arena is mainly empty, and even though they are trying to keep their tones quiet, their voices echo.

"Come on, Lune: pull yourself together," Crispin is saying as we approach.

"I apologized," Lune snaps, crossing her arms. "I'm not going to repeat it."

Whatever was so funny to her before evidently isn't laughable now.

Crispin huffs. "It is not so simple. It does not disappear because you apologized, Lune, everyone saw. People will gossip on the radio, all of Isaaria will know! There were emissaries there! Ambassadors from other countries!"

"I couldn't give a Flick of Fate's Fingers," Lune says, and Crispin pales, as if he has never heard his little sister use such language and never expected to.

"Lune," he hisses. "Please. You are embarrassing our family. Yourself. Me. You must compose yourself. This is the most important thing to ever happen in our lives."

I cannot tell if they are referring to Comus Day or something else the Carsans might have planned. But he is being purposefully vague, now that Romia and I are present. Granted, he doesn't shoo us away, but that doesn't mean anything.

"Family," Lune sneers. "Funny, isn't it? Siblings calling themselves siblings when they have no loyalty to one another. Tell me, Crispin: am I really your sister? Or am I the replacement for the daughter your mother miscarried? It clearly did not fill the hole in her heart, did it? So, what's the point of me? What is Lune to the oh-so-proper Carsans family?"

Crispin stares at her, horrified and confused.

"What is wrong with you?" he demands.

"Ask what's right," Lune laughs. "It's a shorter list."

"My lady—" Romia tries, stepping forward.

She is interrupted by the sound of approaching footsteps. I'd dig out one of my weapons, but the way this person is walking is not threatening, and too purposeful, as if they like the sound their shoes make clacking on the hard floor.

I am not surprised to see Vásan Pike round the corner and approach us, but everyone else seems to be. Statistically, I assumed one of the heirs would come to check on Lune, but while Mercer or Rian were more likely, I know their steps well. Vásan walks more boldly than either of them. He stands tall, with perfect posture.

"Everything well down here?" he asks, raising a perfectly arched eyebrow.

He must not be worried about security much, because he has not brought any of his guards with him, or even a family member.

"Everything is fine," Crispin says tightly. "Go back to your seat."

"Yes," Lune sneers. "Go back. Enjoy the show."

The way she says that confirms to me that, at least to the Carsans, all of this is a charade. Manufactured.

Vásan does not leave. That eyebrow of his lifts even higher, in an admittedly impressive way.

"Everything is fine? Really?" he says, switching to Alarkian on the last word in a tone that emphasizes his doubt. "Given what happened a few minutes ago, I'd describe this as anything but fine."

"Suck an egg, Vásan; this is none of your business," Lune snaps.

"Anything that upsets my fiancée is my business," he says coolly.

Lune turns to stare at him, and then jerks her gaze back to her brother. It is telling that Crispin avoids her eyes. It takes Romia a moment, but then she gasps and covers her mouth.

"Oh, so none of them told you about that, yet?" Vásan says. "Your father decided to strike a deal with me, Lady Lune. We are to marry in three weeks, pending the approval of the new king. I wonder exactly when Alion was planning on telling you," he says. "Or Crispin: for shame. You have known for almost a year, now; you weren't going to tell your little sister she is engaged?"

Lune's stare is even more demanding. She looks about to cuss out either her brother or Vásan and cannot decide which one to start with.

"Is it true?" she finally asks, her low voice shaking slightly.

Crispin sighs. "We...I thought Father should tell you."

The silence Lune allows then is damaging. Even Vásan begins to frown after the first few seconds. He looks as if he thinks he should say something, but can't conjure words. Lune has not reacted the way he anticipated she would.

Finally, Lune turns to Vásan, her composure barely maintained.

Her face crinkles in a smile so forced, it looks hostile. "Would you excuse me and my brother, for a moment?" she asks tightly.

Vásan bows to her. "But of course, my lady. I apologize for the startling news, but I thought it improper to keep such a thing from you any longer."

"...Mmhmm."

Vásan sounds sincere, but he could also be a brilliant political actor. Either he truly did only say so because he hopes to spare Lune's feelings when their engagement is announced publicly, or because he wants to make the Carsans family splinter.

Lune grabs her brother's sleeve and stalks off, dragging him behind as she returns to the palace proper. Romia follows, holding her skirts up and beckoning to me. I am hoping the two Carsans siblings have it out with one another, and reveal some extra tidbits of information for me while they're at it.

She hasn't been in the Pyrian Palace for years, but Lune must have a good memory of it because she knows exactly where to go for privacy. She brushes past startled servants and guards alike before shoving her brother through a swinging door into what amounts to a large storage closet, complete with mops and buckets. It's awkward, cramming the four of us in the enclosure, but Lune doesn't seem to notice. Or care.

"What foolishness is this, Crispin?" she hisses. "What did Father do?"

Crispin sighs. I do not take pride in commiserating with Lune, but in this case, I can understand her rage. Her Father and Crispin have done something morally ambiguous, and even suspicious, by betrothing Lune behind her back.

"It was either him or Magnus, and—"

"Magnus? Magnus?!" Lune screeches.

"Yes! And you're welcome for pushing Father in the other direction!"

Lune blinks and then breaks into a cruel laugh. "Crispin, Crispin, Crispin. Don't give yourself so much credit: I told Magnus if he didn't stay away from me, I'd kill him. I'm sure he wrote to 'Grand Prince Carsans' immediately to pull out from the running."

She cannot be correct, as she has been engaged for longer than that, now, but she only intended to shock her brother. It has the intended effect. For a second, it looks like Crispin's about to grab his sister by the shoulders and shake her, which is so unlike my image of him that it's startling.

"I do not know if you have noticed, dear sister, but our family does not hold high standing, currently," Crispin snaps. "The Carsans family has but one job: maintain Comus Law. Ensure there is always a king. Yet: twenty-five years, *and no Fate-damned heir.* Marrying you to Vásan is a good move. Given what information Father's squeezed from the Currian Council, it will be either him or Magnus on the throne next."

"You think I want to be queen?" Lune scoffs.

"Lune. You know why this is important. What it could change…" Crispin starts, but sighs again and shakes his head. "I don't know why I bother."

"Because I don't try hard enough?" Lune sneers. "Because I'm not a good enough daughter for the Carsans family?"

"Because you're selfish. In fact, if you're going to be like this, don't come down to dinner tonight," he snaps at her. "There is too much at stake, Lune, you know that. We need Vásan to uphold his end of the deal."

"Fine," Lune snaps. "Maybe I'll spend the time designing a wedding dress. Assuming you and Father did not see to that already."

She picks up her skirts and pushes open the door so hard that it slams into the wall. Romia and I follow her, and neither of us bother to curtsey to Crispin. It's interesting, I think, that Crispin could be so cordial and unassuming for so many years, only to become a completely different person now that Comus Day looms over us all. I always thought he and Lune got along well, despite the differences in how their parents treat them.

I am beginning to wonder how much the monotony of the University hid. It truly was a refuge from the rest of the world. For everyone.

Lune's memory of the palace is terrifyingly good, and she finds her rooms with ease. All her luggage has been moved in, but not fully unpacked. The maids inside are scared out of their wits when Lune barges in, demanding they leave and ignoring their protests. She strips off her costume without preamble, down to her chemise, and that chases out everyone but me and Romia.

The maids are finishing their exodus when Rian of all people attempts to enter. He still has Mango wrapped around his shoulders and enters tentatively, but is determined to look in on Lune. The lady herself has disappeared into the wash-room, making even more of a mess as she goes.

Rian nods his head in the general direction of myself and Romia, but does not look at us long.

"Ah…Lune? Everything good?" my crown prince calls, and kicks one of Lune's layers of skirts out of the way before thinking twice, picking it up, and laying it down on the bed.

Romia hastens to pick up the rest of Lune's clothes, as if embarrassed she didn't think to do so earlier. In her defense, she's not accustomed to receiving the sort of shocking news Vásan gave us. I'm sure she doesn't know what to do with the information, or how to help. It makes her feel useless, unable to help her mistress. That is something I understand all too well.

"Oh, everything is wonderful," Lune snarls from the washroom. She is not bothered to have Rian here, or surprised that he came after her.

"Is there anything you would like to talk about?" Rian asks her, twisting the rings on his fingers nervously. He's clearly upset by her unusual behavior.

Lune slams something in the other room and then stalks out. She's pulled her hair loose of its fanciful braids, and it has frizzed and curled in the humidity. She is holding a brush, ignoring Romia's attempts to commandeer it. She does not want either of our help.

"Apparently, I'm engaged," she snaps, waving her hands dramatically so that I worry she will let go of that brush and hit Rian with it.

"Oh. I'm guessing you would not appreciate congratulations at this juncture?"

Lune snorts and rolls her eyes before flopping down in front of her vanity and yanking the brush through her hair.

"Do you mind if I ask—" Rian starts.

"Vásan," Lune says, and that startles him.

"Vásan?! Vásan Pike, the aloof, cold-blooded riddle? Why in the world would anyone think the two of you would pair well together?"

"Oh, don't ask," Lune sighs. "It's the usual political nonsense, that's all you need to know."

Rian is wringing his hands in a manner most unlike him. "Is that why you had that outburst? Downstairs?"

"That was…No, not exactly," she struggles to explain. "Don't worry about it. It has been expected. Bound to happen at some point…"

They are both silent, avoiding eye contact while she brushes her hair. I'm guessing she plans to spend the rest of the night unpacking her things alone. Or, perhaps, using that as a cover while she meets with one of her fellow conspirators.

"Lune, I cannot help but have noticed you acting strangely over the past few weeks," Rian says, concerned.

"I'm fine," Lune insists. "Things have merely been complicated of late."

"But you know that, if you ever need to talk to someone—"

"It's fine," she repeats. "Truly. I don't need to talk to anyone."

Rian nods, rubbing Mango's nose. He's frowning still, not fond of leaving Lune alone. He wants to know what's wrong, and is bothered that she won't tell anyone. Not even him.

"I need to return to the others, for the meeting," he finally says apologetically. "Do you want me to come back later tonight? Or Asmer? I can always send Asmer. Neither of us would mind."

"I'd rather be alone, tonight," Lune says. There's an awkward pause as she considers her words before adding, "Thank you. For trying to always think of me. It's not unappreciated."

Rian nods again, struggling to think of what to say, if anything.

"I'll leave you be, then," he finally decides, and bows to us all before slipping out. I catch sight of Qhan as the door opens and closes, which mollifies me a little, but I'd still rather be close by Rian's side myself.

Luckily for me, Fate apparently has something similar in mind. Poor Romia is trying to be helpful, trying to brush Lune's hair for her, asking if she'd like to have a bath drawn, or take some tea. Put some music on.

But as she said, the Lady Lune wants solitude. Complete solitude.

"You're dismissed for the night," Lune snaps. "All of you," she adds before Romia can open her mouth. "I don't want to see a single maid, attendant, noble, what have you—I don't want to see anyone."

"But, my lady…" Romia starts.

"Am I not being clear? Go. Leave me alone. If either of you say anything to anyone about what happened today, I will make you regret it," Lune warns.

"Yes, my lady," Romia says reluctantly.

She turns, gesturing for me to follow. But once we're back in the corridor, Romia turns to me with further instructions. She's either too loyal to obey Lune, or too stubborn to allow such a curt dismissal.

She sighs. "I will remain, in case the lady needs anything. You should go out and see if you can't enjoy the festivities in the city. Make sure you bring a pass with you, so the guards will let you back into the palace," she adds.

I nod to show I understand, and am about to leave when Romia speaks again.

"Are you a mute?" she asks with a curious frown.

"No, ma'am," I say. "…I simply don't talk much."

She considers this. "That's perhaps for the best. Please report back to work tomorrow morning, and don't say a word of this to anyone. If asked, say that Lady Lune, in her generosity, has given you the rest of the day off to enjoy yourself, understood?"

I nod again obediently, and let Romia send me on my way. The moment I'm far enough away from her, I turn on my earpiece, send a quick message to Taris, and run down the hall after Rian and Qhan.

Thirteen

I HAVE BUT MOMENTS to find a new uniform to change into. It helps that I have the entire layout of the grand Pyrian Palace memorized; impressive, perhaps, but also only thanks to Nusk, who insisted that my *khashak* and I know both the Pyrian and Summer Palaces inside and out. It's because of this that I know where to stash the clothing I'm discarding, to pick up later, and when to leave the palace proper to run across a small courtyard, where laundry is hung out to dry, to steal a new disguise.

Within minutes, I'm a new maid, my hair twisted up and hidden properly again, wearing a drabber uniform and a blanker, wide-eyed face.

Then I'm off, certain I know where to find Rian and Qhan. There is an official meeting room not far from here, for all eight of the royal families' representatives to gather for councils. Rian's must have left the opening celebrations early, to look in on Lune. He and Qhan will likely be taking a formal pathway there, but I know all the proper shortcuts.

Sure enough, as I cross from one hallway to the other, I see the royals on their way to the council chamber. The king leads the way, flocked by his bodyguards. The queen follows, her fingers splayed to help her see.

I skirt down a parallel passage to the same destination, then circle around their grand entrance to a servant's passage. There, near a table festooned with ice cold drinks, hand towels, and other refreshments, are several maids. Most of them are scurrying in and out of the council room, but one is standing near the table itching for a smoke, if the lighter she's flicking in one hand is any indication.

I wait until she's alone, and then approach her with my money pouch in hand.

"Twenty for you to swap with me. Please. I was promised I could work this shift, but then they moved me," I pant piteously.

The maid hesitates, but scoffs and starts to remove her head covering.

"You must be new. They're not that special, you know," she lectures, thinking I'm willing to pay so much simply to get close and serve the crown princes and princess.

"You'll be sick of them by the time Comus Day comes 'round," she adds, but sets her tray down on a nearby sideboard and prepares to head out.

I give her the gold. It's a larger amount than I should have offered, but as my *khashak* and I approach the most dangerous days of Rian's life, there is no better time to spend some extra coin.

When I join the other servants, none of them are surprised or bothered by the switch. We wait while the royals enter the chamber and take their places, and though I'm getting impatient, I steel myself. There's no reason for me to suspect anyone will try to hurt Rian, now. He's with Qhan. He is safe.

The head maid assigns tasks to the rest of us. I make certain that I am the one holding the tray of warm hand towels, because it will give me the opportunity to stay in the room with Rian. Those in charge of food and drink will come in and out, but I will be expected to stay, in case the nobles want to clean their hands from the stickiness of fruit and pastry and sweat from the sweltering summer heat.

I'm relieved when we finally enter the room and go about our tasks. I find Rian immediately as I take my place. A simple task, as he is the only representative of the Yakarami family. The only one still alive.

The other families are spread out along the large, oval table. The king, queen and Magnus are clustered at the head—the crown prince looking irritable and uncomfortable. Then, going about the table, there's Nissa and her hyena, the Idos, Lundans, Carsans (minus Lune and Soren), the Ralhans (Mercer has several cousins who have come to join him), Rian with Qhan, and the Pikes, represented by Vásan, his brother, and mother.

I have to note that Grand Princess Pike does not look pleased to be seated by Rian. There are empty seats between them, as Rian has come alone, but still. This is good information, especially knowing what I do about Vásan and Lune.

"…at which time, we will formally present our seven heirs and begin the trials," the king is saying. "Naturally, the Currian Council has requested that Grand Prince Carsans and I not reveal to any of the heirs what the trials will consist of—not even Princes Magnus or Crispin know," he adds pointedly. "But rest assured, they have been compiled in the manner we think best suited to choose the next ruler of Isaaria."

From my position, I can see Nissa give a slow, dramatic roll of her eyes. Of all the heirs present, she is the most irreverent; even Mercer is sitting up straight and proper, and dressed for the occasion. She's still in her leathers, with her legs folded under her and her arms crossed over her chest. If she desires to be queen, she's not acting like one.

"Might you reveal whether there will be a competition over fluke, your majesty?" Vásan inquires.

He is cold again, as if he has flicked a switch in his head and is not thinking at all about what happened a short while ago with Lune. Whoever he was then is gone now. It's impossible for me to tell which of his personas is him.

"We don't believe a direct showing trial is necessary," the king admits, only because he would need to alert them in advanced if there were. "With the heirs' permission, we would prefer to bring in a fluke reader, who in turn will be supervised by Crown Prince Rian's captain Qhan Khaleem."

He gestures to where Qhan is standing behind my crown prince, which visibly surprises several attendees, including Rian himself. Qhan only dips his head to the king in reverent supplication.

"Excuse me, your majesty?" Rian manages to say.

"I believe your captain's fluke is related to truth-telling—he'll be able to make certain the fluke reader does not lie to favor any one heir," the king says.

Around the table, all are nodding in agreement.

This further speaks to Rian's own trustworthiness: a fluke reader might lie or be paid off, but everyone expects a man like Qhan, who holds Rian's trust, would never lie for him.

"But I cannot pretend this body is gathered solely to discuss the trials of Comus Day," the king continues. "As I said in the opening ceremonies, these are dark times for the world and for our country, moving forward. Regardless of who becomes the next ruler of Isaaria, it will be important for the eight families to work together. To protect Isaaria, and its people."

He nods, and his son stands, pulling out several large scrolls. Griffith Reach steps forward to help Magnus unroll the scrolls across the table, one of which reveals a large map of New Isaaria. Spotted across it are different colored marks, concentrated in specific areas. The remaining maps are several other lands, colored with more frequent dots. I recognize Lijimata, Alarkia, Tourran, Milash, Kacha, and the Ishtak Empire among them.

This interests even Nissa, as she leans forward to read the maps.

"Over the past seven years, approximately, there has been a disturbing rise in so-called animal attacks across Isaaria," Magnus begins. "These attacks, according to the witnesses we managed to speak to, are bloody, violent, and appear to be caused by unknown creatures. At first, we thought such accounts were mistaken reports, or exaggerations. But in the third consecutive year of these attacks, my father asked me to monitor them as closely as I could. It was at this time that I joined Crispin and Lune Carsans, as well as Rian Yakarami, at the East High Courts University, to consult some of the most intelligent minds in Isaaria."

This explains Magnus' presence for the past five years. But I would never have thought he was working on this project. I never saw proof of it.

I think about that monster I saw in the road.

As Magnus continues to talk, I notice that Griffith is watching the Carsans family closely for their reactions. Clever. Magnus might not have told his father about his suspicions, yet, but he still wants to see if he can connect the Carsans family to these strange attacks he's now discussing.

"In my work, I discovered that these attacks are not happening in solely in Isaaria, but all over Samioth," Magnus continues. "In fact, they are happening least frequently in Isaaria, compared to others. Though he did not understand why at the time, I questioned Crown Prince Mercer Ralhan on what he might have seen in his travels. While he has not seen these creatures himself, he has tended to what he has described as peculiar injuries, particularly during his latest visit to Alarkia and Lijimata."

I glance at Mercer. He's surprised that Magnus is mentioning his travels at all.

"Is this true, Ralhan?" Vásan asks.

"Ah. Yes," Mercer says awkwardly.

"Could you describe these 'peculiar injuries' if necessary?" the king prompts.

"I suppose. I did not realize, at the time, that such things mattered. I would have kept better documentation, had I known," Mercer admits.

"I recorded our conversations. If need be, that will suffice," Magnus says, taking over once more.

He continues to talk, and I note Mercer's posture slump as he starts to fiddle with that necklace of his. I think he wishes he could have been more useful, and now hopes he can do more in the future. If not to prove himself, then to help the victims of these attacks.

"Though it is yet undetermined what these creatures are, after consulting with some of the eldest beings Isaaria hosts, I have come to the conclusion that these things are new monsters," Magnus says. "Not even the Fae could determine where they are coming from," he admits, which means he has met with Clanaugh at some point to see what he could learn.

"And no one has managed to capture or fell one of these so-called monsters?" Crown Prince Detrus asks.

"Not as of yet," Magnus admits. "I have had drawings rendered of what said creatures might look like, but reports of their appearance are often varied, and confused. Many of the witnesses were injured or scared out of their wits."

"I'd heard of several such attacks with the Hoitsokin," Nissa admits, speaking for the first time. There's a hint of surprise in her tone. "We thought they were stories. As you said. Tall tales. And you're certain this is a new threat? Not merely a known magical creature, perhaps entering Isaaria from elsewhere?"

"I've considered as much," Magnus says. "Early on, it seemed like the most reasonable explanation. But whatever these things are, there's no pattern to their movements. They sprout up here and there, but they aren't roaming. They aren't native to anywhere else in the world. They are something new. Perhaps."

"Or…perhaps not?" Detrus offers.

"There is one instance in which I've seen similar descriptions of said creatures before," Magnus says, and I realize where he's going with this just a few seconds before he says it. "It took me a while to force myself to believe it, but…"

He sighs.

"Much as I wish it were otherwise, there is someone in this room who might be able to explain things more adequately, and that person is Crown Prince Rian," Magnus says, gesturing as he says so. "The crown prince has been studying ancient myths and such for many years, now. The stories he has read, and the history he has unearthed, describes similar attacks during the time of the Families Three. Back when such creatures were referred to only as demons. Though I can't say if that is what these creatures are, I think the crown prince may be able to use his knowledge of the past to make sense out of all this. If anyone can."

Rian's hand has stilled on Mango's snout. Everyone is looking to him.

"Ah. Let's see, here. Then," he says, and clears his throat.

His eyes are darting around as he fidgets in his seat, and it's clear that he was not expecting this level of attention, nor is he fond of it. He straightens his spine and leans in to give the map a proper look. The room is silent as he does so, waiting. I notice a bead of sweat appear on his forehead; ah—so the man does sweat, after all.

"Red is for areas with the most frequency?" Rian asks, one of the only two questions he has for several minutes, and Magnus nods. "And folk are calling these demon attacks?"

"That has become the most popular theory, unfortunately," the king's son says. "Without proof to the contrary, citizens are turning only their meager knowledge of the old stories."

Rian thinks for a long time. I start to become nervous on his behalf, and I don't know why. Some part of me, I think, wants him to have all the answers. To be revered. A proper crown prince helping his country and people. But I also don't like this attention on him. This singling out. It makes me nervous.

"I do find it interesting that these attacks are occurring mainly in rural areas, along the borders of our territory," Rian finally says.

"Does that mean something?" the king prompts.

My prince shrugs. "It may. You see, folk are calling these things demons. Which, admittedly, sounds a bit ridiculous. But let's compare these attacks those of similar creatures that we are familiar with. Yes, Nightmares, Worgols, and Black-Eyes all attack in a similar manner, preying on folk in the night. But there would be some way to track them. Back to a point of origin, or a homestead. These monsters are different.

"Then, there's the fact that these attacks occur mainly at the borders of our country," Rian goes on, spreading out some of the other maps, "but appear to be both more scattered and heavily concentrated across other countries. I assume these reports are not perfectly accurate, but: I'm certain Crown Prince Magnus has done his best, and this is a decent amount of research to handle. An entirely new species of magical monster appearing all across the world about seven years ago, with no explanation, attacking more frequently in times of war? That sounds quite a lot like the 'demons' in the old stories."

"Which means what for Isaaria?" Detrus points out. "That these are demons? Questionable creatures from olden times come to life again?"

"Without being a certified expert," Rian says—which is funny, because he is, "I'd say it's entirely possible that, yes, these could be the demons referred to in the old stories, and yes, they could be a threat to our entire country, if not the world. If your maps and charts are all accurate, your majesty, and I'm assuming they are, these things appear to be drawn to chaos and panic, hence why Isaaria has been spared for the most part. That implies that fear of them is crucial to their existence. One could conclude, then, that so long as Isaaria stays balanced, uninvolved in war, and does not panic the public, we might be overlooked by…whatever this is."

The king raises an eyebrow, certain there's more that needs to be said. "But?"

"Well, it would be a massive assumption to make, your majesty, and one that could destroy us if I happen to be wrong," Rian allows. "Besides this, if we only took care of ourselves, we would be dooming the rest of the world. I am not saying we should intervene, only…"

He shrugs.

"It seems to be a complicated matter, your majesty," he says. "I'm not certain if I can accurately draw conclusions without more information."

"We only expect your best attempts, crown prince," the king says.

"I can have all of my gathered reports and findings brought to your rooms," Magnus offers, speaking to Rian but for his father's benefit. "With all that, do you think you could at least conclude whether these attacks are from demons?"

Rian scratches at his hair. "…Yes…Could do, possibly," he laughs nervously. "I know it sounds ludicrous, doesn't it, to be saying such things, but… I'll do my best to make accurate conclusions free of bias."

"I'm certain your expertise will be valuable," the king says gravely.

"Ah. Thank you. Your majesty," Rian says, swallowing uncomfortably.

Qhan motions one of the other servants on the edges of the room to bring the crown prince some water.

This explains why Magnus thinks it crucial to keep Rian safe: if he believes, as his father does, that our country may be under attack by monsters like the one that Taris and I saw, or the one in the road, Rian is the crown prince best suited to the task ahead.

I add this to my stock of information. By my count, Magnus has been working on this project for half a decade, now, and feels as if he can trust both Rian and Mercer. Meanwhile, he suspects the Carsans, who are receiving reports from the al'Yibna family about events in the south. As the Carsans have yet to reveal whatever Raj might report on, if he's reported yet, it implies that information carries great weight. Meanwhile, the Pikes are also connected to the Carsans, by Vásan and Lune's newly revealed engagement.

I understand, now, why Nusk always told me not to bother with politics.

I'm also starting to wonder if, by giving Rian a large research project on the week leading up to Comus Day, the king is inadvertently telling everyone that Rian is not being taken seriously as an heir. After all, the others will be spending this time preparing themselves for Comus Day. Rian has been given a project to manage and report on, regardless of who will be crowned next.

I'm struggling to decide how I feel about that.

Magnus' maps are cleared away, and given to Qhan. The meeting moves on to other, more trivial matters, none of them interesting to me. I vaguely listen as they go over the schedule for the coming days, discussing which events are mandatory for all the heirs, as opposed to what is optional or exclusive to a few. But I want to slip out and confer with Taris.

I'm overly vigilant about distributing all my hot towels, so I'll have a reason to leave the room. But instead of reloading my empty tray, I place it on the table outside the council chamber and head to a private corner while I wait for Rian to emerge from the meeting.

As I haven't seen Taris with Crispin or his parents, I'm guessing he has either been assigned to Soren, or he has been dismissed for the day. Either way, he should be able to respond to my inquiries.

I don't bother with much of a greeting when checking in. I don't know how much time I'll have before I have to follow Rian to his next appointment.

"Are you with Soren, or off?"

"Off, for now," Taris tells me.

"N'omi and Korvaan?"

"Naomi's working, Korvaan's sleeping so he can watch the prince tonight," he says. "From what we've seen, no one has tried to enter the palace who shouldn't be here. No one making much of a fuss. Other than Lune."

I snort. "We still need to find some time to rendezvous," I add.

"I have my own room. 71B," Taris admits, using the coding system Nusk gave us when he made us memorize the palace. "It's small, but private. We could use it as a base of operations. Rotate sleeping, when we need it. Leave messages for one another."

"How did you manage to get a private room at a time like this?"

"Crispin had master documents with him, on the train. He fell asleep, so when no one else was watching, I went through and edited it. I've lightened my schedule as best I can, too. Gives me more time to help with Rian."

"Will anyone notice that?"

"Unlikely. He was looking at so many lists, schedules, and venues for the coming days, I doubt he'll remember details. Again, it's small," Taris warns me. "But there will be a bed and a desk, and we can stick notes to the bottom of the latter, in case we can't reach one another."

"Good thinking," I admit.

From what I hear, the royals are now leaving their meeting.

"Find as many different uniforms as you can for us all, if you're able," I tell Taris. "Leave them in that room. Check back in with me later."

With that sorted, I circle back to one of the side corridors, waiting and watching. Rian and Mercer are the last to leave the room, letting everyone else go about their business around them as they stop outside the door. According to the schedule, I know there's to be a banquet tonight, but it is not a required event. In a few days' time, once all the foreign emissaries have arrived, there will be a mandatory dinner, but tonight, at least, is optional.

"Well, that was, ah, unexpected," Rian laughs, and scratches at the back of his neck with one hand.

Mango bats at Rian's fingers, thinking they're playing a game, and Rian swings the dragon around to let him crawl over his arms.

"You did well," Mercer reassures him. "Better than I did, anyway: I barely had anything to offer, and apparently those attacks were taking place right under my nose. But there you were, spouting off theories."

Rian sighs. "I think all I did was blather a great deal and perhaps confuse people. Really, I might have to start giving classes to educate everyone on their history before I even begin to talk about if these things are demons."

Mercer raises an eyebrow. "Do you not have an opinion, yet?"

"No, I do," Rian admits. "But it is more complicated than one might think. I'll try to explain later," he finally says. "Like I said. I might have to give classes."

"Who knew all your research on so-called 'dead history' would come in handy?" Mercer teases, nudging him.

"…Yes. Who would have thought…" Rian mutters.

He rubs at his eyes, suddenly looking exhausted. Today has gone in so many confusing directions, I'm sure Rian's head is spinning as much as mine.

"Will you be dressing for the evening's festivities, now, your majesty?" Qhan asks, noticing Rian's weariness. His question is partially a prompt, giving Rian the chance to return to his rooms, if he so chooses.

"I think I'll bathe first," Rian says with a lazy, feline stretch. "My muscles ache more now than ever before in my life."

Qhan dips his head. "As you wish, your majesty."

"In your rooms, or are you going to test out the public baths, with the underground spring?" Mercer poses, raising both eyebrows in invitation.

I can see Rian considering this while Mercer goes on.

"You could, now, since you're old enough. It really has been a long time since we've been to the palace, hasn't it?"

"Oh, why not," Rian decides. "I may as well try it now, or else I might never find another opportunity."

"Mind if I join you?" Mercer asks amiably, stretching his arms and back. "That trip in is a strain on a body."

Rian laughs. "Says the world traveler?"

"It's different, going at my own pace versus being jostled around in a train all day and then being expected to appear princely and proper until midnight."

"You don't have to attend the dinner," Rian reminds him. "It's optional. I won't stay for long, if I go at all. There are plenty of celebrations in the coming days for me to grace my presence with."

"But as you've said: I need to work on my image," Mercer says. "I doubt Lune will be there, though, huh?" he adds. "Poor kid. I wonder why Vásan."

From the way they continue to talk about it, I quickly determine that some announcement was made after I left. Rian would never have said anything to Mercer himself. Not after Lune told him in confidence.

Rian sighs. "She's definitely not happy about it. And not that I have anything against Vásan, but…"

"They do not make for a happy couple, do they?" Mercer drawls.

"I wouldn't think so," Rian says, and then tries to wrangle Mango again when the dragon leaps out of his arms to grab onto a nearby sideboard. "You are not going to let me have a bath in peace, are you?" he chides the hyperactive dragon.

"Here—let me take him outside," Mercer offers, reaching for the dragon. "I'll give him a good quarter hour to tire himself, bring him back to your rooms, ready myself, and then join you downstairs. You go on and get started without me."

Rian laughs, but allows Mango to scamper from his arms up to Mercer's shoulder. "If you say so, Merse. I appreciate it. My legs feel jellified, being folded up all day. A soak will do me good."

"Don't thank me yet—I'm using that time to get a little exercise of my own," his friend claims.

It's a joke, partially, but he likely will be running about after Mango. That fool of a dragon hasn't figured out he's a dragon yet, but he can run surprisingly fast on those stout legs.

"I'll send word ahead, your majesties. And make certain the baths are emptied for you" Qhan says, holding his scimitar hilt still with one hand as he bows to the princes.

Rian is about to insist that's not necessary, but then thinks better of it. He thanks Qhan, then bids farewell to Mercer, promising to see the other soon.

Rian takes the usual route to the underground baths. The baths are public to the royals and nobles, foreign ambassadors, and the like. They are separated by sex, and offer a number of health treatments if requested, but Rian likely only wants the simple pleasure of a hot soak. I decide to take an alternative route that will put me in position to watch the large cavern of pools without having to pass through a segregated dressing room. It would be difficult to hide the fact that I'm a woman in a royal bathhouse.

Nusk's diagrams of the palace were accurate, and now come in handy.

I find an empty, low-ceilinged servant's passageway and move with haste. The cooling system in the palace is old, so the passages are large enough for me to crawl through if I'm careful. It is a musty trip, and more cramped than the last time I was here, but it's the best way for me to follow Rian without being spotted.

When I was younger, I used to make Taris and Korvaan take shift whenever I thought I might have to follow Rian someplace with undressed men. The idea of seeing him or any other man unclothed made me squeamish, and my entire face would turn red. When I was a child, it was out of embarrassment. When I was older, for other reasons.

Now, I have fewer qualms. I've seen the human body countless times. I've seen people disemboweled, stabbed through the eye, garroted—sometimes I'm the one to do it. I have even seen Mercer and Magnus both with different women they like, in bed. I don't purposefully watch, but an occupation such as mine does not allow for bashful maidens.

The underground bathhouse has multiple rooms, but the main one is for soaking. By the time Rian sheds most of his clothes and emerges from the dressing rooms, I have found myself a position in the vents above, and though it's swelteringly hot, I have been in more uncomfortable situations.

Thanks to Qhan, the baths are completely empty, and quiet save for the faint sounds of moving water. Rian has a soft pair of white cotton trousers on beneath his robe, but nothing else, and his bare feet make a pleasant padding sound on the tiles as he walks to his pool of choice. He takes a moment to consider something, then descends the first of several steps into the pool, to wet his feet and wriggle his toes. The hem of his cloth trousers skims the surface of the water, but he does not mind.

"Ah, I already feel much better," he insists, tilting his head back to take a deep breath of the aromatherapeutic scents steaming in the air. "You know what—I've changed my mind. We'll have to tell Merse when he arrives. The three of us can spend a few hours here, and skip the dinner completely. We deserve it."

"As you wish, your majesty. I will send for a servant to bring your clothes from upstairs once you've finished," Qhan suggests.

Rian's smiling, pleased with the atmosphere. "Yes, I think that sounds—"

He's cut off by a banging. It's not cacophonous, but it's loud enough to echo in a place like this. Qhan and Rian both turn, startled: someone just entered the bathhouse dressing room.

"No one else is supposed to be here," Qhan says.

He's put his hand to his scimitar and is about to draw it when he's attacked.

It happens so fast; I know it's done with the use of a fluke. One second,

Qhan is standing there, hand on his sword. The next, he's been slammed against the far wall with such ferocity, the tiles on the wall crack, some of them even falling to the ground. At the same moment, something hits Rian in the chest and sends him flying backwards into the water. There's no blood that I can see, and he's moving, but he definitely has gotten the air knocked from his chest.

Qhan is struggling to his feet when he's picked up and slammed into the wall again. It's only after he's slumped to the floor that I can see his attacker at all: no one I recognize, but there is a glint of metal off his breast pocket. A pin. There are at least two more enemies that I can count. Qhan is alive, but has not risen. That leaves Rian alone, and vulnerable.

Fate dammit.

I kick out the opening in the vent and drop down into the pool in time to grab Rian by his shirtfront and haul him out of the way. Granted, I end up throwing him from one part of the pool into the other, but it's better than leaving him to that fellow with the speed fluke, who zips into the water so fast it splashes waves out onto the tiles.

Out comes my first knife, which I feign throwing, then wait for Rian's attacker to flee. The second I know his direction, I throw there instead. It's not a clean hit, but I do clip him in the side, and manage to down him. I cannot leave Rian for long, so I quickly retrieve my knife and finish the intruder. I know that I should want one of these attackers alive to try and question him. But not this one.

The water reddens. I return to Rian and drag him to his feet, determined to get out of the pools before this escalates further.

I notice Qhan was not knocked unconscious after all and has managed to keep the other two attackers away from us, so I could get to Rian. But he's definitely out of this fight, now: lying face-down on the tiles, still breathing, but otherwise completely motionless.

There's four now, that I can see. I stand on a strip of tiles between two pools, balanced on the balls of my feet. I keep in front of Rian, using my arms to push him behind me.

Get a count, Soleil, get a good, accurate count this time.

One, two, three, four, and the one down in the water.

I can hear myself breathing, panting. The floor is slippery.

All four of the attackers are hesitant, careful as they move to trap us.

"Well. You dropped in with perfect timing," my crown prince gasps behind me, sopping wet and still coughing from the water he swallowed.

"As one might expect, it did not take long for you to get yourself into trouble, your majesty," I scowl, but Rian, of course, smiles. I can hear it in his voice.

"And as one might expect, here you are to get me out of it again, my dear Soleil."

I am understandably startled to hear him say my name, and with such familiarity, but I force myself to push any suppositions from my mind. I need focus, now. His life may depend on it.

I see the female assassin slowly reach to her side to free a throwing knife.

"Stay back," I warn Rian, keeping my eyes on the assassins and brandishing my own knife in warning. "I have trained for this."

"Oh, yes, I know," Rian agrees. "So have I. But to be fair, you're better with knives than I am."

I watch the woman, certain she'll be the first to attack. I'm trying to determine if I should throw Rian to the ground or try to hit her dagger out of the air with my own when one of the men runs up from behind us. Rian notices and manages to dodge out of the way, allowing me to duck low, strike the fellow at his midline, then flip him over my shoulders and send him to the ground. I'd hoped he would crack his head on the tile, but he manages to catch himself.

The woman's knife flies, cutting open my forehead as I turn to avoid it. And then the woman herself is there. She slashes at me with another knife and I avoid her, pushing Rian back with my body as he regains his feet. I keep putting him off balance, especially on this slippery floor, but it's either that or risk his life.

I dodge the woman's swipes, timing it as well as I can, and return one of my own that forces her foot into a wet spot on the floor. She recovers herself in a side-lunged crouch, but that gives me time to advance. I let her catch my foot with both hands as I go to roundhouse her head, as it makes her drop her weapon. I bend my knee and throw myself straight into her, getting my elbow into her face and my knife toward her chest.

Then there's a hand in my hair, dragging me up and throwing me backwards. I recover just in time to take a hard hit across the face that leaves blood on my lip and a ringing in my ears. I know I'm about to be hit again, possibly in the throat or somewhere else vital.

But then Rian is there. He has stepped up to my side and caught the man's arm before the blow can land.

"It's not nice to hit a lady," he claims, and *sets the man's arm on fire.*

I don't know how Rian does it, but one second, he's caught the man's arm, and in the next fire crackles bright and hot with the smell of burning fabric and flesh. Screaming, the assassin runs for the pool, where I shoot him with a poison dart and let him fall into the water.

I glance at Rian, bewildered.

"What are you doing?"

"What do you think? Lending you a hand."

The woman's gotten to her feet again, which puts our count back up to three. Whatever armor she's wearing stopped my knife from going through, and she's pulled it out and thrown it away. She brings out a foreign weapon that looks like it has a curved, rotating blade attached to a handle, to be whipped around.

I note where my knife falls; I'll need to recover it, but at least I have another two strapped to my legs, and more darts.

I hastily rip the skirt of my uniform up the sides, and pull both knives. One longer, one shorter.

"Tell me now or regret it later: can you manage this?" I demand of Rian.

Damn me for doing this to my own principal, but given whatever he did with that fire, I'll save my questions for later and take whatever help he's offering now.

"If you take the lady, I'll keep the other two back," he promises.

I go for the woman, knives flashing. She thinks I'm targeting her torso, which is where I should aim if I were trying to be predictable. When she comes at me, swinging her own blade, I go for her weapon-hand instead. I miss, which means she now knows that weapon worries me, but I'll get another chance.

Behind me I feel the heat of fire, and sounds of commotion. I have to trust Rian to look after himself while I finish this. Usually, I wouldn't have any doubts in my own abilities, but my body still aches from yesterday's violence.

The woman swipes at me with that blade, letting it snick-snack from side to side. I'm sure it's managed to slice off at least a few strands of my hair, and cut up my clothes while I avoid it.

I back up. Get some distance between us. Time to change tactics.

She attacks again, but she's sloppy about it. She's guessed that I'm trying to disarm her, and she's smaller than I am; we both know that a hand-fight will end in my victory. I let her push me back, circling around the side of one of the pools so I can get a glimpse of Rian. He's faring well enough, but I still worry for him. Though I manage to creatively avoid the woman's blade, I know that if half my attention is on Rian, I'm bound to slip up.

She swings, and I duck and roll so that she smashes her blade against the wall behind me. It hopefully dulls her weapon while affording me time to get her where I want her.

The woman is quick to recover her weapon and whip around again, wary of me, but I've used my time for avoidance rather than attack. I give her two seconds to pant, letting her overthink it. Then I run at her. But instead of going after her arms, I drop to my knees, back bend, and slide on the watery tiles. And though it's practically cruel, I hamstring her.

She cries out as her legs buckle under her, her dark braided hair flying out. Determined to hold onto her weapon, she fails to catch herself and strikes her head on the ground. This time, she does not get up again.

I run towards Rian and the other two assassins, gain momentum, and jump to try and stab down into one of their necks. He avoids me, but given the burns on one side of his face, I know Rian's gotten to him at least once.

Another burst of fire pushes the remaining assassins back. But whatever sorcery Rian is capable of, it will exhaust him eventually. Assuming it works in the same manner as a fluke, Rian hasn't been outside all day, and we're now underground, on a manufactured floor, far from the sun or the moon.

I need to end this now.

If only.

"Oh, *little sun-child*," someone sings. A voice I recognize from just last night.

No.

I sheath my last knives, whirl, push Rian behind me again, and then throw myself onto him so we both drop to the ground to avoid the projectiles that have been shot at us. Though I know it must hurt him, I use Rian's body as a cushion and roll back over him, getting my hands on the tile to spring back to my feet.

Second knife: out.

I spin, build my momentum, and throw. The knife doesn't cut my target, but it knocks the gun out of his hand. The general whose pin I stole, whose men killed Nusk, is somehow alive. He's a fool for calling out to me instead of getting his shots off first, but as I found last night, he's the dramatic sort.

He's bigger than me, and stronger, and he knows my so-called weakness. But as long as I protect my neck and throat, I should be able to manage.

"I think you have something that belongs to me," the firebird general says with a nasty grin.

"I killed you," I snarl at him, narrowing my eyes. "We buried you."

He holds his arms out. "And yet."

I take a second to consider my options, then hit a button on my watch to alert Taris. But I don't have the luxury of assuming he'll reach us in time.

Behind me, Rian's forced himself to his feet again and shoots another burst of fire to cover us. He's prepared to help me take on the general, but I don't want him to. I need him to watch my back, but I can't let this monster get too close to him. He almost killed Taris last night; I refuse to even allow the possibility of him touching Rian.

"Can you take those two?" I ask the crown prince.

"Don't worry about me," Rian says, and then nods. "Go get him."

My longer knife isn't balanced for throwing, but I do so anyway, then follow it up with a barrage of poison darts. The general avoids all but the last one, which skims his arm. It rips his sleeve, but may not have opened a cut. At the very least, it gives me the opportunity to retrieve my short knife and get up close to him.

Block, block, swing, countered. So fast, I don't have time to think about my moves, just react. Bring up a leg, kick, down, side of knee. Swing arm, elbow strike. He grabs my arm with both hands before I can make contact, but that's fine. I adapt. That's the way to play this game: absorb and adapt. Every time a hit glances, or pushes me somewhere I don't want to go, I find a way out of it. Roll. Recover, get back on my feet. Stay light. Balanced. Keep him from using his advantages against me.

We're both too fast for each other. We get a few good hits in, each, but nothing powerful enough to take the other one out or cause serious damage. And while I've retrieved one of my knives, I haven't gotten a good opportunity to use it.

To try and combat his height, I go to knock him down on his knees, with the intention of getting my legs around his neck to put him in a modified choke-hold. My legs are stronger than my arms, after all.

He counters with a maneuver that sends me sprawling, and it takes a miracle on my part to keep from cracking my head on the ground like the woman before me. I snatch a wet robe off the floor—maybe Rian's, maybe not. As I get to my feet again, I spin it, twist it, use it as a whip. It won't cause serious damage, but it doesn't need to. It only needs to extend my reach.

I flick it out at him over and over, irritating him by smacking at his face and neck. Once I have an opening, I take my knife in hand and swing hard at his head.

He blocks my arm and chops the elbow, but while I drop the knife with one hand, I duck, spin, and catch it with the other. Hurl myself at him again. Keep my attacks quick and unpredictable. Not every attempt has my full force behind it; some are feints, some are genuine failed attempts. Just so long as he can't tell which is which.

Sweat drips into my eye. I ignore the sting and try to push the general back to the lip of one of the pools, so he might trip. I don't want to take this fight into the water, but he's too much taller than me out here. Too much taller than most people, in fact. I won't get a clean hit anywhere other than his torso this way, and I already know I can't take him out like that.

So, when I get the opportunity while his back is to one of the pools, I charge at him, drop into his abdomen, and slam the both of us into the water. I use my weight to keep him under as long as I can, but let him throw me off him. I don't want to try and stab him underwater.

I wait until he manages to stand and then throw the knife into his neck.

Or, I would have thrown it.

He's halfway into a lunge at me when I move to throw, a drastic change in position I didn't account for. It's by chance that I manage to grab a firm hold on my knife again to abort my throw while he returns the favor of my tackle and smashes into me, knocking me over. I already know what he's going to do. He knows I panic without air—he's going to try and drown me. I let him grab my head to hold me under, but keep myself from floundering. I can feel around for his face. And his neck.

He doesn't get the chance to block me this time, and I feel the blade sink in properly. Perhaps I'm not good at protecting my neck, but neither is he. I feel his grip on me loosen, and he falls into the water. If not lifeless, he soon will be.

That's for Nusk.

I stumble in the red water, sloshing to my feet. I'm dizzy, and my throat hurts from sucking in so much air after last night's debacle. But I've done it; I have killed this man twice, now. If I have to do it again, I'm cutting off his entire head.

My momentary triumph is cut short. Before I can stand, someone grabs the back of my head, fingers digging into my scalp, and forces me underwater. One of Rian's two opponents has slipped away from him. I don't have time to hold my breath beforehand, but at least I'm not reactive enough to immediately take in a breath once I'm submerged.

I'm trying to think of an escape when that hand is ripped off my scalp. It hurts, and he's taken a chunk of hair with him, but I'm freed. All I can think of, before I manage to stand and suck in a gulp of air, is that the water around me is suddenly freezing.

Once I've gotten air into me again, I see ice. Ice everywhere except for a little circle around me. Ice building up out of the water as it grows, capturing our remaining two enemies completely. I realize, all this time, Rian has wanted to get them in the water again. He's too weak, I think, to have done two elements at once, but somehow, he does have control of the elements. I don't understand it. It makes no sense, but there it is. Rian can control fire and water.

And he's turning this room into a skating rink.

I clamber out of the icy water and stare at him, panting. I'm sure confusion is spelled all across my face.

"You always seem to forget that I can do that," he says, and grins as his ice continues to fill the room.

There's blood trickling from a slight scratch on his forehead, but aside from that, bruises, and the soreness that'll be sure to hit hard tomorrow morning, he appears uninjured. I'm more concerned about Qhan, but know I must bring Rian to safety, first.

"Not that I can blame you, I suppose..." he starts.

"Why didn't you open with that?" I rasp.

"It's hard for me to move water and turn it to ice at the same time," he admits. "When I'm in the water, sure, that's fine. But when I'm not connected to an element with my own body, it's more challenging. Even the fire, I could not make from nothing," he says, and shows me a lighter he must have gotten from Qhan at some point.

So, the two of them are not completely unprepared after all.

I set my jaw and grab his arm. "Come on," I order, and pull Rian towards the bathhouse doors. Answers can wait until later, when I know that his life is no longer in immediate danger.

"Qhan—!" Rian starts, but I refuse to let him pull away.

"I'll send one of my *khashak*—" I rethink my words. "I'll have someone take care of him; I promise. But you have to come with me, now."

I yank on his arm again, and Rian obediently stumbles after me as I bring him towards a servant's passage. With one hand still clamped on the crown prince's wrist, I wriggle my other hand out of my watch, catch it, and press down on a button while I bring it up to my mouth.

"Taris," I snap into it, and he replies with his obligatory blip, letting me know he's listening. "Change of plans. I need you to wake up Korvaan. Bodies in the underground baths. Possibly one or two still alive. And Qhan is injured. I need you to carry him upstairs, to the sitting room connected to Rian's bedroom, and have Naomi get to work. After—you take the opportunity to get some sleep. Have Naomi watch Qhan, and Korvaan run perimeter. *I'm going to have a little chat with our crown prince."*

Fourteen

I DRAG RIAN TO his rooms using servant's passages, a knife clenched in my hand the entire time. He thankfully does not try to speak, and manages to keep pace with me, but I know he's thinking about the questions I'm sure to ask. It has finally occurred to me that the real truth, and the truths Nusk told me for what he thought were good reasons, are two different things.

I'm already assessing damage control. Qhan had the baths cleared out, and Korvaan will be there soon, with Taris, to recover Qhan, help him, and dispose of the bloody mess. They are smart enough to figure out a way to buy themselves time, if necessary. That, I'm not worried about.

But how Rian knows me, how he can fight, how he can control the elements... These things are worrisome, if only because they add several complicated angles to a situation already bloated with them.

We make it into Rian's rooms safely, but it's a petty victory. I fling Rian into his bedroom first, slam the door behind us, and lock it. I'm tempted to start building a barricade, but I'm not sure what good that would do. If someone happened to come through a window, it would hinder us.

Forcing myself to breathe, I take a look around the room, marking exits and entrances. Mango is curled up in his own bed, fast asleep. Mercer must now be in his own rooms further away in the palace, preparing to join Rian down in the baths. He cannot be allowed to see the carnage, there.

I whirl on the crown prince so fast it startles him.

"Call Mercer's rooms, now," I order, pointing to the telephone. "Tell him you're not feeling well, tell him the baths are closed. Tell him something, but make sure he stays away from that massacre."

"Yes, yes, calm down," Rian says, turning and heading for the telephone on his bedside table.

I huff, and try to do as he asked: calm my nerves. I need to take deep breaths and focus on one thing at a time. Ground myself in reality so hypotheticals don't spin me out of control.

While Rian handles Mercer, I cross the room to the floor-length mirror set between two large windows and look myself over. I will definitely have bruises. Another layer around my neck, as well as on my arms and possibly my back and shoulders. Then there's the split lip. Bloody scratches. An aching in my abdomen. A pulsing in my head.

I can endure, but my body aches. I'm tired. My spine feels weak and my muscles are already stiffening.

This next week is going to be a long and agonizing one.

I realize Rian has stopped talking, and am to him when I'm smacked in the chest by a pair of clothes. He has another set laid on the bed and is peeling off his sopping bathrobe.

"We should change," he says. "We'll get ourselves sick, otherwise."

I want to scowl, but he's right. With night fallen and the palace's cooling system working in earnest, it's chilly and we're both soaking wet, having come from a room of water and ice. So, I accept the new clothes, turn my back to him, and start to strip. There's nothing for me by way of suitable undergarment, but I tie Rian's offered undershirt up in a knot, put the second layer over the top, and slip into the trousers. I have to cuff the bottoms of what I realize are pajama pants, as Rian is significantly taller than me, but otherwise they are not a terrible fit.

The moment I'm redressed, though, it's time for some answers. I kick my wet clothes into a pile and stalk over to Rian, who is much more careful in laying his out on the wooden floor to dry.

"You," I say, stabbing a finger into his chest. "Explain. Now. I know we must have gone through several timelines already, or perhaps re-lived several days you've had us do over, but I—"

"You know," Rian says, "usually when one demands an explanation, they let the other party speak."

I try not to become indignant. Given my personality, this is difficult.

"I would, except…There's you! And you're…ridiculous! It's… Impossible! Nothing short of…A bad dream," I tell myself. I'm pacing, now. "Yes, that's it. This is another one of those horrible nightmares, and any second now, I'll wake up, and…and we'll start the day over again."

I turn to look at him, and stand there, waiting.

The crown prince looks unimpressed. "Almighty bless, Soleil, but this would be so much easier if you were better at sitting and listening."

"There! That!" I exclaim. "Start with that: how do you know my name?"

He gives me a tired look. "Well, which is it? Do you want me to start explaining, or are you convinced this is all still a dream and that there'd be no point in it?"

"I'm holding out for the latter," I admit, "but you'd best go on, in case of the former."

Rian looks at me for a long while and then sighs.

"Oh, you're exasperated with me?"

He surprises me by responding with: "How can I not be? You can't possibly understand," he rants, "how many times we've survived near-death experiences, you jumping in to save me and revealing yourself, me having to explain the whole damn thing multiple times over again, each time adding a new layer of this mess to remember—it's exhausting!"

I realize Rian's confirming that we've time traveled. Many times. At least during one of those cycles, we knew each other well enough for him to assume our closeness, now. But it feels impossible. Instead of answering questions, all it does is add more.

"Do you know how many times I've been this age? How many times we've started a life, only to go back?" he demands of me, bitter, angry, hateful, but not at me—at the world itself, it seems.

"I don't understand," I admit.

He gives a cold laugh. "Naturally. I could have said it for you—you never do. Not at this point. And when you do understand, you either send us back, or I die and you make us start over anyway! Do you know how many times I've died in your arms, and with my last breath begged you not to go back? To let me die and live your own life? I know you could go on, if you wanted to. It's I who can't live without you. I die for you. Always. Fate has made me this way. And then you make us do it again."

I stare at him. "But you have the power of time. You—"

"No, Soleil," he cuts me off, and sighs. He closes his eyes tightly, and when he opens them again, I see the pain there. "You do. The power of time is your birthright. It always has been. And every time you remember how to use it, our world erupts into chaos."

"No," I say. "No. That's not me. I don't have a fluke. Even if I did, the Carsans' prophecy—"

Rian groans and lets his head flop back and then forward again. "The Carsans prophecy, oh, yes. Excellent evidence."

"But you have a fluke," I insist. "You must."

Rian nods. "Yes."

"And it's over time, like the prophecy said—"

I understand I sound like a blubbering fool, but Nusk has repeated these facts to me so many times that I'm struggling to accept anything different.

"It's over the elements," Rian interrupts. "I can influence the elements, Soleil. You saw that downstairs for yourself. Which is rare and special, but it's nothing compared to the power you wield."

"But then, the Carsans' prophecy—" I try again.

"Would you stop it with that? You were lied to, understand? Most people have been. The Carsans' prophecy does not mean what people think. It has been... purposefully misinterpreted."

I cross my arms, defensively or for comfort, I'm not sure which. It is difficult to focus on one thing at a time, given what Rian has said. I don't know if I believe him, despite the evidence I've already been shown, because it's madness. It ruins everything I've known about my life and the world around me.

"If I leapt out this window, would you catch me?" I challenge him.

Rian laughs. "What sort of test would that be?"

"A good one. Turn back time, and you're a liar. Slow my descent, and you're telling the truth."

"Unless I have dual flukes," he reminds me.

"A rare and unlikely thing."

"Less rare, I should think, than controlling the turn of time."

There's an awkward beat.

"…I do," Rian says.

"You do what?"

"Have dual flukes."

"You're lying."

"If I was, would I tell you that in the first place? What purpose would it serve? I have dual flukes: one is over the elements; the other is some weak aura sensing. It's not important," he insists. "The important thing is that we know each other, Soleil, and we have for centuries. We have both lived so long, it's unthinkable. Only I remember, and you don't."

I keep my arms crossed. It's a defensive move, I decide.

For nearly two decades, I have looked after Rian as his secret bodyguard, ready to die to protect him. Now he's telling me he's known about me all along. That I have a fluke. That it's one of the most powerful flukes in the world. And, apparently, I've been using it.

"Tell me something to prove what you say is true," I demand.

"Like what?"

"Tell me something personal to prove you know me."

Rian thinks for a moment, and then steps closer to me. I barely resist the temptation to back away from him, mostly because I don't want him to know he makes me nervous.

"You've changed your hair color over and over again," he says. "Sometimes you wear cosmetics to change your face. Other times you cut your hair, wear wigs, swap uniforms, change the tone of your voice."

I snort. "That doesn't prove anyth—"

He suddenly leans closer. Close enough he can speak directly in my ear.

"But your eyes," he whispers. "You must remember—you promised me to never change your eyes."

I try to ignore how my heart is jumping in my chest. I feel a wave of heat wash from my face down to my gut.

"If you think that of all things would convince me, you're even more of a fool that I first thought," I whisper back to him.

Rian recoils at first, but then laughs. I suppose this is exactly what he expects from me, as he claims to know me so well.

"No matter what, you are still my Soleil," he notes.

He must know full-well how charming he can be. He must know that, as much as I call him a fool, I'm attracted to his confidence, and his brashness. The way he laughs at everything, including himself.

"Stop trying to be clever," I insist. "Fine, then: assuming I have the power over time, then what does the Carsans' prophecy mean? Because I'll tell you one thing: I am not a royal."

But Rian is undeterred.

"It's not about you or me, Soleil, it's about us. You become—"

"Your queen?!" I interrupt.

I sound horrified, but that's only because I've no idea what I'm feeling, nor do I know how to express it. It's foreign. And painful.

"I'm surprised it took you so long to realize it," Rian says. "You sound as if such a thing would be the worst Fate could have in store for you."

I scoff. "Not the worst, but not far from it."

"You don't have to be that gloomy about it."

"It's not my fault you're a narcissistic, daydreaming, foolhardy brat who couldn't cook his own rice if he had a steamer prepared for him."

Rian smirks. "Bold words for a bodyguard with her own servants. They've looked after you your whole life, haven't they? Can you cook rice on your own?"

I splutter because, I've realized, I can't.

"That's not the point. And my *khashak* aren't servants. They are a delegated position meant to serve an heir to the throne with a certain amount of duty and honor, and for that matter, it's their cultural system, not mine, and—"

"Aha!" he crows. "The lady concedes: neither of us can cook. You know how I knew that?"

"Because it's a fair guess?"

"Because I know you. You've never been able to cook. You've never had to."

I find I've tightened my jaw so much it hurts. "I'm certain I could ascertain the proper way to use a rice cooker if necessary—"

"So you agree! It's not necessary, and never has been!"

"Stop that," I growl.

"Stop what—making good points?"

"Stop. I don't know," I snap at him.

I back up until my legs hit the seat of a chair and let myself slump into it. If I thought my head hurt before, now it's pounding so hard I think it's vibrating the rest of my body.

The look Rian gives me makes me uncomfortable, because although it's not lewd, there is a bittersweet longing in his eyes, and when they flicker over me, it is as if he knows every inch of me, every corner of my mind. I know he wants to pull me into his arms and feel every particle of where our bodies touch.

I'm uncomfortable, I realize, because I want him to.

"By the Almighty, I love you," he sighs wistfully. "Every time I talk you into marrying me, I love you more and more."

"I would not bet on that happening this time," I say.

"You want to put money down on it?" he teases.

Teases me.

"You expect me to believe that all this time, and, in fact, every time, you've refused to take any other woman to bed because you're being loyal to me," I say.

It's not the question I should be posing right now, but to be fair to me, there are a lot of questions. The more personal Rian's claims are, the harder they are to believe.

The laugh Rian lets out is mocking, but I can't tell if it's directed towards me, or himself. "I know—how very conservative of me. How dare I desire anything more than a pleasing figure to amuse me."

"And why not?" I challenge him. "You must have been tempted. Especially if what you say is true—you could have taken up with someone else, only to have me wash back the timeline again, and it would be as if it never happened."

"This may come as a surprise to you," he says, his tone just biting enough, "but I believe enough in true love that waiting for you has been less of a challenge than you'd think. I'm not some beast that requires relieving.

I've waited because I love you, Soleil. No one else comes close. I could have chosen another woman, knowing you'd wind the clock back when we inevitably failed. But lost timelines or no, I would know. It would not mean nothing to me."

"So, you've pined after me for potentially hundreds of years instead."

He sighs. "Truly, Soleil? The fact that it sounds so irrational to you saddens me. I love you. I've always loved you. Every time we do this again, I only love you more. I won't claim I haven't noticed pretty women, because I am not a blind man. But beauty is temporary. The vows I made to you are forever."

He's such an overdramatic fool.

"I'm almost certain wedding vows are binding only until death," I accuse. "Besides, we would never work."

"Actually, I happen to think we make a good couple," Rian says confidently. "And I'm not the only one."

I groan.

"Look," I say. "You must understand: I have been raised as your *Khashtani*."

Rian nods, agreeing. "Yes."

"I was told you did not know I existed."

"Well, no. I know who you are, Soleil. The very first timeline, we were betrothed since we were children. I became king, we married. You've always been you, but you were a queen, once."

I tap my fingernails on the table next to me. "And Nusk knew all this."

"Yes."

"He raised me as your *Khashtani* on purpose."

"Yes."

"Why?"

Rian winces. Before he speaks, I know what he says will distress me.

"Because you told him to. Because, in that first timeline, I was assassinated. I died, Soleil. And you could not live with that. You never can. I'm sorry for it. Really, I am. All I do is die, but it still bothers me that I hurt you that much. So many times over again."

I stare at him.

I understand what he's telling me, but it feels impossible. Rian is claiming I was queen of Isaaria, that we married, that I was so in love with him I forced the entire world to rewind back to our childhoods, so I could try, many times over again, to save him. That I ordered Nusk to raise me as a nobody, so I could try and protect him myself.

It is strange, because while that feels and sounds like something I would do, I cannot picture myself as a queen. But there is some truth to what he's saying, because I hate thinking about even the possibility of Rian dying. I certainly cannot picture going a single day without him, let alone the rest of my life. So, knowing what I do about myself, it isn't exactly implausible that—should I have the power of time—I'd use it for his sake.

What bothers me most, I think, is the idea of loving him. I'm not sure what love is, and not because I think myself incapable of it. I simply do not understand it, emotionally speaking. I won't pretend like my teenage self didn't harbor secret fantasies of a ridiculous romance between myself and my principal. But I was young. Such things are expected.

Part of me wonders if, when I told myself it was time to grow out of those fantasies, I thought it meant I needed to grow out of love, too.

"Did we marry because the Carsans' prophecy said we should?" I must ask.

Rian shrugs. "We were betrothed because their prophecy said the 'great heir of Isaaria' was meant to be 'born out of fire and time itself, with a crown at his brow by his first breath'. Me, the elements—and you, time. We were meant to rule Isaaria. As well as our son after us."

For once he has the good sense to turn a bit red.

I stand and brush myself off unnecessarily as I take a deep breath.

"Fine," I decide. "If I have some unethically powerful fluke as you say, let's test it, shall we? I'll go back and make sure you never go to the baths in the first place, and that ought to—"

But before I can even start thinking of how I would go about doing that, Rian is there in front of me. He's grabbed my wrists to stop me from removing the bloody gloves I still wear.

"Soleil. You need to be careful. Your powers are strong, but unpredictable. Sometimes they surpass you. I don't know how it works, precisely, but I know that when you panic, you cannot hope to control them. So you say."

"It's impressive you think I'd be able to control them at all," I admit, yanking my wrists out of his grip. "Which is another thing! If I did not know I had a fluke, how could I be using it over and over again, hmm?"

Rian looks exhausted, and I feel a sting of guilt.

"I'm hardly an expert," he sighs. "You'll have to trust me. We are so close this time. We still have a chance to perhaps do what Fate originally intended for us."

"I want more proof," I say. "And, for another thing, if I'm the one with powers over time, how can you and Nusk remember things, but I can't, hmm?"

"Aha!" Rian crows, excited again. He's so loud, I almost instinctively leap on him to cover his mouth before I remember he's a crown prince. No one's going to care about how much noise he makes in his own rooms.

"That, I have an answer to, and perfect proof, and it's this!" he says, and dramatically shoves one of his hands in my face.

"This is your hand."

Rian rolls his eyes. "No, look at what's on my hand, you silly—"

He looks at his own hand and freezes. His face suddenly whitens.

"Oh, no. Oh, no, dear Almighty."

"What."

"I lost it. I lost it. How could I possibly lose it? I mean, yes, so, it was getting a bit loose, my fingers are getting skinnier. I think. Or the metal is stretching in the heat when my hands swell? But even so—"

I resist the urge to grab his head and make him look at me.

"Rian," I snap. "What are you on about?"

"My ring. The one I always wear—I'm sure you know it. I lost it. But I definitely had it on before the baths. I remember thinking I put it on the dresser, but I must not have—I think it's in Lune's room! Possibly she's assumed it's one of hers and put it in her jewelry box, but I must have it back, Soleil."

Given how much he was twisting that ring around his finger in Lune's room, wringing his hands in concern, I'm not surprised. The man is careless with his gestures; it might have fallen off at any time and he wouldn't have noticed.

"You want me to fetch it?" I offer dryly.

This man would never survive without me.

He grabs my shoulders. "Soleil. I need that ring."

I brush him off. "Yes, yes, I hear you. I'll get your damned ring back."

"It's very important."

"I'm not a halfwit. You need it, I'll get it. But stay put, would you?"

Rian shuts his mouth, thinks for a second, and nods.

Once outside Rian's rooms, I take my time to look around the hall and ensure he's locked the door behind me. I also teach him a secret code, so he'll know to only let me back in, and no one else. And advise him to scream, loudly, if anyone comes after him. Rian is not amused by this, but I wasn't trying to be humorous.

Cursing the entire scenario under my breath, I start down the already familiar path to Lune's rooms. I can hear a lively orchestra playing downstairs. The rest of the royals are enjoying the festivity, then. I'm tempted to take a detour to see who is in attendance, but I don't dare leave Rian for long.

There's no sign of Romia outside Lune's rooms. I suspect she's been sent off more firmly, or else finally gave in. Lune still has the door locked, but there are no lights shining from under the door, so possibly she has exhausted herself in her sullenness and gone to bed early.

It's around the time that I'm picking the lock that I remember I'm still wearing Rian's pajamas. At least I still have my own boots on, even if my socks are sodden.

I slip into Lune's rooms, glad that there's a short hall inside to house the entryway. The bedchamber is dark, except for the orange light of a flickering fire. My eyes adjust, and before me I can see Lune's vanity covered in facial creams and powders, lip paints and kohl. The vanity is but a few feet away, set against the center of the wall to my left. To my right is the bed, but she's not in it. Instead, the bedcovers have been dragged off it and pulled before the fireplace, including what looks like a fur coverlet.

I cannot see her at all until I inch across the floor, towards her vanity and the jewelry box upon it. At the end of the bed, her slim feet and ankles are poking out as she lays on the ground. Next to them are bigger feet, belonging to longer, larger legs, the coloring decidedly less fair, though the shadows cast by the fire make it difficult to tell the ethnicity for certain.

Lady Lune has taken a lover. And it is not her fiancé.

It is dark, but as he rubs his leg against hers, I can see that Lune's lover has a silver star-and-moon tattoo on his ankle; he is no one I know, then. I would have noticed someone permanently marking themselves like that, as a sign of their dedication to a woman named Lune.

I hear him kiss her, and she sighs.

I'm not concerned about them noticing me, so long as I'm quick and clever. I have slipped into more dangerous places, with more security, and come out unscathed and unseen. Lune and her lover are helping me, with their focus on each other. Even when they quiet again, I don't mind, because it means I can hear Lune when she moves.

She sits up, leaning on her left arm, her hair wild and tousled as it hangs loose around bare shoulders. She's wearing a fine silk nightgown, but the sleeves are thin, and it's open in the back down to her waist. The fire gleams off her naked skin, off those dotted scars crossing her back like a constellation. I wait, not daring to move lest glance my way. But she's distracted, lost in a pensive melancholy.

The fire crackles. Below us, I can faintly hear the orchestra. Lune sighs softly, and I pray she cannot hear my breathing as well as I can hear hers. I try to keep myself calm: I stare at the vanity. The wall. Her shoulder blades.

I stare at her left hand, and realize that the fire is also glinting off a pair of looped bands on her ring and middle fingers. She never wears them in public, but I'd bet Rian's life that the man she's lying beside has a matching set.

It's no wonder she's so angry about being matched up with Vásan.

Lune has secretly married a mystery suitor. His identity means nothing to me, but his existence begs an important question: if Lune is married, and seemingly in a relatively healthy relationship with her man given their current state, then why is she messing about with Rian?

My thoughts are interrupted by her lover himself. His voice is both soft and husky with desire, but I can think contextually enough to know he's said, "Lune."

She turns her head to him. I waste no time in continuing my slow trek to her jewelry box. He pulls her back to lay with him, and I can no longer see her head peeking up above the side of the bed. She's crying, though. I can hear it. I have to wonder, as I reach her vanity, what she could possibly have to cry over.

He kisses her, as if in attempted comfort, and she continues to sob, panting in pitiful little gasps.

I gently lift the lid of the box after wiping the putty grease from the arch of my boot onto its hinges, in case they squeak. Behind me, I can hear Lune's breath hitching. I can hear a sort of frustrated desperation from her lover when he says her name, trying to calm her, but I can't understand what that means, nor do I have any desire to.

"I'm sorry," she cries softly. "I'm sorry, I'm sorry…I'm so, so sorry…"

I don't know what she's done to anger her lover—what she could have done that needs apologizing for—and I don't care: Rian's ring isn't in her jewelry box.

I silently curse my bad fortune. There's almost no way for me to search the rest of the room without being noticed, so I tuck myself under the vanity, hoping that Lune and her lover fall asleep soon.

I'm forced to listen to Lune's crying, and her lover's attempts to settle her. She's blubbering, trying to sloppily apologize. I wonder if she's been drinking.

Her companion is much more eloquent, and somewhat revealing.

"Shhshhshh. Lune. Please. Don't talk. Don't cry."

"You. Y-You—" she stammers.

"I'm not upset."

"Liar."

"I'm not upset with you."

His voice is deep and murmuring with a southern Isaarian accent. He sounds like Taris, which alarms me at first before I allow reason to calm me: I've seen Taris' ankles enough times to know there is no tattoo on either of them. Besides, Taris has no love for Lune.

No, this is not Taris. But his vocal resemblance to Nusk's eldest son gives me a hint as to the origins of Lune's mystery lover. Possibly, it will give me some idea as to where some of Rian's enemies lie in wait, if Lune indeed is a spy and traitor both.

I keep my body pressed up firmly against Lune's furniture, hiding in the shadows, glad that the firelight is mostly blocked in this little dark corner.

"I need time alone," her lover finally says. His voice is a murmur, but there is something thick and choked about it that I can hear all the same.

"Yes, yes, of course," she insists, and sniffs, likely wiping away tears. "Will you come back to me?"

He answers her. Too quiet to hear, but I assume negatively.

"At least for a little," she begs him. "Half an hour. Please."

I do hear him when he answers that one: "You don't want half an hour."

Her silence tells us all he's right.

"Please. Why won't you stay?"

"Oh, sweet Lune. You know that we should not."

Then he pulls away from her, and stands. I can't decide which one of them is crueler to the other.

I get a good look at the back of him as he gathers his clothes, walks to her washroom, and closes the door. His hair is curlier than Taris' and his skin darker. He has no scars where I know Taris does, though the two are about the same size. I'll have to ask my *khashak* to keep an eye out for this man. I've no idea what he and Lune intend.

He turns on the water in her washroom.

I wait a minute, then slowly slide out from my hiding place. Lune's lover is upset about something—it will take him longer than most men's hasty wash to finish. I have five minutes, at least. Maybe up to half an hour, depending on what he's bent out of shape about.

The first thing I do is check on Lune. But luck is kinder to me than I would have thought: Lune lies half-curled on her side, tangled up with the sheets and the fur duvet, her nightgown scrunched up. Though her hair falls in her face, mussed from her lover's touch, I can still see her tear tracks on her cheeks. She's fallen asleep quickly. My sneaking won't rouse her.

Some small, sympathetic part of me wonders why she cried, but I tamp it down. From what I know of her, she's the sort of woman who cries when she's done something wrong. Her lover is angry with her, she cries, makes him feel guilty, and apologizes until he gives her what she wants.

I could kill her in her sleep, and easily handle her lover. But if I do, and there is someone controlling her movements, I will never know. Rian may be in danger from an unknown threat.

No, I will leave Lune alive, for now. Dangerous as her voice may be, it may be even worse to silence it.

I spend a good five useless, nerve-wracking minutes searching Lune's room for the ring. I'm about to decide Rian's wrong—that he lost it someplace else—when I realize I haven't checked the most obvious place yet. Dropping down, I lift the bedskirts and look underneath Lune's mattresses.

There's Rian's ring. Pushed under the bed. Typical. Lune probably hasn't even noticed it's here.

Ring in hand, I hurry from the room, concerned Lune's lover will emerge and catch me right up until the moment I'm outside Rian's door once more.

Before I rejoin the prince, I remember at the last second to check on Qhan. Naomi's still with him, but claims he suffered no serious head trauma, and barely needed two stitches. He should be fine in a day or two.

I'm grateful for this report, and glad that Naomi and Korvaan appear to have cleaned my mess up for me again, but I can't help but notice how Naomi doesn't look at me when she talks. I don't know if it's on purpose, but it bothers me. I hover for a moment, trying to think of what sort of apology I could possibly offer, then give up and leave the room. My *khashak* know I've revealed myself to Rian, but they don't yet know what he claims. They don't know about the power I supposedly have.

If they find out, I'm afraid they might hate me even more for how I choose to use it. Or not to use it.

Rian is pacing when I enter his room, and I can tell he's not pleased with how long I was away even before he opens his mouth.

"What took you?" he demands as I close the door and lock it. "I was worried."

"Sorry," I say, deciding not to elaborate.

I lean against the wall to rid myself of my socks and boots, which are still so wet that they've turned my feet white and wrinkled. Rian watches me, biting at his lip. It's strange, to see a side of him that he kept away from everyone all these years. I don't think I've ever seen him this nervous before.

Once barefoot, I present his recovered jewelry.

"Your ring," I say shortly.

Rian sighs. "Thank you."

He slides it onto his finger, examining it, making certain it's not damaged. I can't help but snort at him as I go to retrieve all my things and drop them in the same spot, near my boots.

"You're so dramatic. About everything."

"And why not? Life is rather dramatic, if you hadn't noticed," he claims. "I figure at least one of us crown princes should recognize that. All the others are all too caught up in their own heads, for the most part. Acting so serious all the time, as if we didn't all start out whining for our mothers."

"You say that, but they're all grown now. And they will eat you alive."

He might stay fit enough for appearances, but there's no doubt in my mind that Rian does not have the temperament of a warrior. His skills with a sword are too pretty to be practical. He may be of decent height, and appears well-proportioned, but his frame is smaller than Detrus's, Magnus's, or Crispin's.

"You are a book-burrower, not a fighter. Without me, you'd be dead by now."

"So says you," he allows. "But if you recall in stories, many-a-time have scholars drawn magic swords to slay beasts…serpents and demons alike."

I narrow my eyes at him and point at where his sword rests in a display on the far side of the room.

"If you're about to tell me, on top of your supposed dual flukes, that this is a weapon born of some ridiculous Magicsmith's tinkering, you can throw yourself out the window, this time."

It's as if the joking is over, and Rian stares at me. "You do remember—me throwing you out the window, you remember it!"

I scoff. "As if I could forget. You—"

But suddenly he flies to me, and wraps me in a tight embrace, picking me up off the ground in his excitement.

"I knew it was possible!" he cheers. "I knew it!"

"What?" I gasp out.

This harebrained man of mine is lucky I haven't killed him a dozen times over already, the way he keeps spiking my senses.

"You're remembering. Here, see—my ring, it's a charm that Asmer made for me—" he starts, putting me down but keeping an arm wrapped around me as he shows me the ring on his hand again.

"Asmer?"

"Well, I think it was Asmer. My memory of that time is hazy. I have no idea how I got it. I think I was possibly dying again," he chuckles. "Or maybe I was dying for the first time. I've died for you quite a lot."

"The exact opposite of what this relationship should be," I say. "And I think you're forgetting a very important fact, here."

"What's that?"

"Asmer can't have made this charm of yours. It's impossible. It's allowing you to keep memories of old lives that don't exist anymore. It's a magical object."

"So?"

"Rian," I sigh. "The only person who could do that, make something like that, is…" I struggle thinking up the proper words, "a Memory Smith.

And we don't know a Memory Smith, and, more importantly, Magicsmiths aren't real."

"But: what if they are?" Rian challenges playfully.

I am not in the mood.

"Give me proof and give me relevance to our current calamity, and I'll consider it," I say, which is at least a more open response than most give him.

He only laughs. "How much proof do you want from me, woman?"

"More," I claim. "Always more."

"Why?"

"Because I don't feel like I could love you. We've barely spoken to one another."

"So?" Rian challenges. "You know me better than anyone else. You've watched me all my life. And I know you better than anyone else in the world. I've grown up with you several times over, now. You're passionate. Fierce. You hate coffee and fleece. You like puzzle-solving games, but you've never any time for them. You love candied fruit, and you pout when Nusk doesn't let you have any. Because, yes, every time I've ever met you, even the first, Nusk raised you. I remember that much. And you love his children like siblings, all of them, even when Taris drives you mad."

It surprises me because it's true, and that's something no one should ever know by watching us, or simply looking at me. Rian would only know if I'd told him, and I can practically hear my voice moaning about Taris' temperament, flopping on Rian's bed—our bed. I can feel something familiar about it all, like a dream. A time when Rian and I might have been something more than what I believe we are now.

He has come closer to me, and this time, I find I don't have any urge to pull away. I don't think I ever did, but it's easier to deny oneself of desires that frighten them than to give in.

"You have a scar on the upper inside of your thigh," Rian murmurs to me. "You've always had it. You can't remember where you got it. But it's from falling off the palace wall when we were children. We would clamber over it to escape our entourages, driving my father mad. But Nusk would laugh. He'd say it was in your nature, and mine, too."

My hand almost flies to cover the scar on my leg, the one neither of us can see, but we both know. How could he know?

I force myself to calm down, then glare at Rian, considering the obvious.

"If we've really relived the same years over and over, shouldn't I not have this scar? Didn't that timeline never happen, if we've done it over again?"

Rian shrugs, surprising me by not fighting my claim. "I've no idea how your powers work, Soleil; I only think I know a few things about humankind.

Based on the fact that each human person has an individual soul, that means each of us only has one version of ourselves. Every time you use your power, then, you're manipulating time for everyone in the world. Each time you go back, you write over the past. There is no alternative universe where certain things do or do not happen, there's only our universe."

He seems so proud of this explanation that I almost don't have the heart to tell him it makes my head spin.

"But then—" I start, prepared to contract him in a million ways.

He interrupts. "Maybe some things are changeable, and some things are not. Perhaps you always have that scar, and earn it in different ways, but saving my life is flexible. Who knows?"

I can feel my forehead wrinkle. I don't know if they are memories that I've invented, or visions of past times buried deep inside my head, but I think I do remember growing up with Rian, a long time ago. I'm worried it's a fabrication, based on what I want. I'm worried I'm being selfish.

Yet, I have no reason to believe Rian would lie. The more he talks, the less likely I find it. He's being far too serious.

"You're possessive," he says deviously. "Particularly of me. 'Your' prince, you call me. Yours."

"And why shouldn't I?" I bristle. "I'm the one who has kept you alive all these years. I'm the one who sacrifices everything for you, my own life made trivial for your sake. Why shouldn't you be mine?"

"That's it!" Rian cheers. "Claim what's rightfully yours, Lady Soleil! Make me yours, if it pleases you."

"I'm not a lady," I tell him.

He doesn't stop grinning, the devil. "That's right. You were a no one, then a princess, then a queen. But never a lady. Nusk made sure you always knew that. Nusk would say—"

"Stop talking about him," I suddenly snap.

I don't mean to be so curt, but I am, and suddenly it's silent. Rian's potential words hang there, as I've now made him hesitant.

"Oh," Rian says. "Of course. I'm sorry. I should have known, at this point..."

I jerk my head at him. I don't know if I'm glaring, but he doesn't care.

"Some things change, Soleil. That never does. It is, I think, his time to die."

I can't open my mouth because I don't know what will come out. I clench my fists by my sides and look at the far wall, trying to regain control.

"As I said," Rian goes on quietly. "Some things are meant to happen at certain times, no matter what."

"It's not fair!" I cry, and I don't care how childish or immature it is as the tears start to fall. Angry tears, made hot by the embarrassment on my cheeks. I want to punch my fist through a wall.

I drop to a crouch instead, covering my face with my hands. I'm horribly embarrassed. I can feel myself shaking and I don't know why.

Rian is behind me. He wraps his arms around me, and the moment I feel him, I push my elbows into him to buck him off. I refuse to let anyone touch me. But while most other people would back away, knowing the damage I could do to them, he refuses to.

"Let me hold you, let me—let me," Rian says, his voice growing sterner until I give in.

Though it feels like a betrayal of my nature, of everything I've been made into, it's a relief to collapse into him. It's freeing to finally break this dam held back for twenty years, and know he won't think any less of me because of it. I don't care what anyone says about how I should be: if I should be impenetrable, rough, heartless, cold. I don't care at all how they would react to the death of the only father they ever knew. I need this.

Rian's body is comforting, the muscles of his arms and chest warm against my back. It feels so good to feel him breathe with me.

"Oh, Soleil," he whispers. "It's not weakness, to show your sorrow."

"It's my fault," I say, the words tumbling free of numb lips. "I never listened to him when I should have. I thought I knew how to keep everything as it should be. I thought nothing would change."

"It's not your fault," Rian insists.

He's stroking my hair. It's strangely comforting.

"I should have been able to stop it. It's my job to stop killers. I—"

"You're only one person, Soleil. You can't save everyone."

I never imagined failing. Never imagined that there would ever be a time where I would have to mourn and go on. I'd always assumed that, if any of us died, it would be me. I would sacrifice myself for Rian in some fate-altering way. He would never know what I'd done, but he would be alive.

"You don't how they look at me," I whisper. "They hate me, now."

"Mmm?"

"My *khashak*. He was their father, and I made the wrong decision, and he's dead. They're going to hate me forever. Naomi won't talk to me. Korvaan—"

"Will forgive you, in time," Rian soothes. "It is not in his nature to hate you for something that, deep down, he knows is not your fault."

"Of course," I say, and sniff. "Because you know everything and everyone."

Rian can't help but laugh at that. "Well, to be honest, I seem to remember little about your *khashak*. For some reason. Taris least of all, but he's always been a recluse, has he not?"

I consider this, then nod. I can't help but think about how Rian sees Taris as someone forever alone and I realize that I don't want that. A *Khashtani's* life is meant to be a lonely one of sacrifice, but I can't do that. I don't want to do that.

I want what Lune has with her mystery lover. If she can have it—that spoiled, delicate lady with her fancy dresses and petty complaints—then why can't I? Would it be so wrong to allow myself this one thing? I can still protect Rian, still stay close to him. The only difference would be that there was something more to our relationship. Something he claims is meant to be, anyway.

"What are you thinking?" he asks me, after I've stopped sniffling.

"I don't know who I am anymore. Can't you tell me?" I whisper.

Rian considers, then lets me go and comes around to kneel in front of me. He is still smiling. He always smiles. A small, adoring smile that I know he will only use for me. He takes both my hands.

"I rededicate in the same spirit that I once took you, for better, for worse, for richer, for poorer, in sickness and in health, to have and to hold, to love and to honor, until death. Soleil Marson, you are my wife," he claims. "There, how's that? Now you and I both know who you are, even if no one else does."

I stare at him, looking like some kind of swamp witch with my red eyes and damp hair. Yet, that means nothing to him. He can say such sweet words, and mean them, regardless.

I do know Rian's not perfect. I've watched him be imperfect for years, now. But he is still one of the best people I have ever seen, heard, watched, known. I don't care if he has faults, if he's an fool sometimes, if he trusts people too much. He makes me want to do things that I definitely shouldn't do. Cannot do.

Won't do. I won't do what I'm thinking about in my head, because I can't. I should not do this.

I'm not sure how it happens, physically speaking, but I find myself pushing Rian flat on his back and kissing him.

He chuckles against my lips. "Not quite so rough, Soleil, it's a kiss."

I huff and sit up. "Fine. Then you teach me how to do it."

Rian laughs again. "No one really knows how to do it, Soleil. It's a matter of preference."

"I don't like it yet, then," I admit. "I only want to kiss you, and I'm angry."

Rian pushes me off him and sits up. "You're angry that you want to kiss me?"

"I don't know. I'm angry about a lot of things—and I don't want to talk about it right now," I add when he opens his mouth.

"Noted: we won't talk about it," he agrees.

I go to kiss him again. Though I'll admit, I might have lunged a little.

"Hope's Head, woman—are you trying to eat me?"

"I'm trying to be in charge."

"Soleil: has it occurred to you that in this sort of relationship, neither one of us has to be in charge? Both of us can simply be? Together?"

I hesitate, but then decide to do something incredibly stupid, and give up my control. Rian's the one who leans in, who I let put an arm around my waist. Who I let tilt me back so I'm leaning against the foot of his bed.

His kiss is so slow, so light, so dizzying, that it almost makes me angry again. He kisses me like this for some time before I get my head around how it should be done. And then he grips me tighter, and I can feel the muscles in his arms. I make a sound I didn't know was waiting in my throat.

He wraps an arm back around my waist and kisses me slowly, gently. None of that frantic, silly scrambling I attempted. I can feel his fingers pushing into what little softness there is of my side before it gives way to muscle. It's strange, but whenever I imagined lovers caressing one another, I always thought of that pleasurable touch applying only to the obvious places. I would have never thought that simply having this man's arm about my waist, pressing against my side, would be enough to make me shiver.

Rian's right—he and I suit one another. My aggression brings out a darkly passionate side of him, yet his natural gentleness keeps us from completely devouring one another. This isn't lust: this is intimacy for its own sake. And we bring it out of it each other.

I'd always thought of this sort of closeness as a betrayal of the mind; that, the moment one decides to trust anyone with their body, they've made a fatal error, impossible to remedy. But it's different, here with Rian. He's been waiting all this time for me. I want more of him.

He's not Asmer's, not Lune's, not even Isaaria's. He's mine. And if this world is going to give him to me, I'll keep him.

WAKING UP IN Rian's bed is perhaps the worst thing I've done in my life, but also the best. I know I'm damned the moment my eyes snap open to his silk canopies above me, my own head sunk into the pillows at the top of the bed. He is tucked in close next to me, his arms constricting my waist, my breast as his pillow. He has purposefully bent his body so he can twine his legs with mine, the loose fabric of his soft trousers hiked up to his knees so I can feel the warmth of his skin against my own chilly limbs.

I glance down at him, and pull one of my arms from where I'd thrown them above my head to play with his hair. Sometimes, I've noticed, it dries oddly after a wash, and gives in to soft waves. Today will be one of those days, and I enjoy running my fingers through his silky, white locks.

I lean down to kiss the top of his head. "You are mine," I whisper to him, and feel us breathe together as my chest rises and falls, his hot breath warming my skin as he sighs in his sleep.

Sliding down further in his embrace, I treat myself to a different angle of him, almost face to face. Is this what love is like? Wanting to do nothing but gaze at him and memorize every feature? Or is that simply because I'm an obsessive, paranoid person, used to checking him for even a minor scrape?

If I please, I can tell myself I love Rian. When I look at him, that's what I think. But I'm not sure how to prove it. I know the clichés of what love looks like, but I'm not sure how to express it.

Yet he does bring out a different side of me. She burst out so quickly, it was all I could do not to let my *Khashtani* instincts smother her. I have to wonder if that's who I was in our first iterations, before I knew what horrors awaited me in later years and timelines. Or am I still her, simply presenting different sides of myself for Rian's sake: the angry killer when he needs a bodyguard, and the mischievous doting wife when we're both too exhausted to care any longer?

I at least know this: I cannot picture being anywhere but by this man's side, for the rest of my life.

Almighty forgive me, but I can't help myself. I begin to kiss Rian's jaw. He groans in his sleep, stirring, and mumbles.

"Mango…stop. Sle-eep…"

"I am not a Mango," I whisper in his ear.

By the time I've leaned back again, Rian's eyes have snapped open. It takes him a moment, but then he remembers and grins. He smiles so often one might think I would get sick of it, but I don't.

"Good morning, my queen," he greets.

"Don't get ahead of yourself," I warn him.

He pulls himself up me to kiss me, one hand behind my head, his other arm still wrapped around me, as if he never wishes to let go.

"You taste like stale chocolate," I accuse.

"I drank some late last night after you fell asleep…and then I fell asleep."

"Terrible for you, you know. Especially that late."

"You're jealous."

"Less jealous of what you'll have to do in the days ahead," I say.

"You're beautiful when smug," he claims, and kisses my wrinkled nose.

"Don't try to flatter me," I chide him.

He readjusts himself, now the smug one. "Ah, but you like it. You like it because even when you're angry, you want me to make you smile."

"You are damnably perfect," I tell him. "And you know it."

"I ought to. You've told me often enough. My spectacular, supercilious, sinfully stunning spouse."

"Not one of your better ones."

"I'll work on it," he claims, and leans down to kiss me.

I let him, for almost a full minute, before he breaks it off and we do nothing but breathe. Then he puts his head down to my shoulder to kiss there, instead. I'd never have thought to do that. And I might have enjoyed it, too, except there's a thought in the back of my head that's been bothering me since I decided to believe him last night. About everything.

"Rian?"

"Mmm."

"Did we ever have children?" I whisper, and he freezes. "I know…You said the Carsans' prophecy is about our firstborn, but did we ever…get to…"

Did we ever meet our child? Did I ever get to hold him, and name him, and tell him I loved him? I cannot picture myself as a mother, and yet I find myself craving the very thing I'd once thought the least of my desires. I want to know, I need to know, if I ever got the chance to have what so many other women take for granted, and sometimes even dread. What some see as a sign of restriction represents my ultimate freedom: to escape this world in which I do nothing but end life, and have the chance, with Rian, to create it instead.

I'd do anything for the children I've been promised and denied.

"I have never met our son," Rian says carefully.

There's a loud knock at the door that saves Rian from answering my next question. I throw him off of me, about to jump out of the bed, but he grabs my arm. I don't shake him off. Someone tries the door handle, but it's still locked from last night.

"Your majesty? Your majesty, are you awake?"

"Yes! Give me a few moments!" Rian calls back.

I move to flee again, but Rian's grip on my arm tightens.

"Rian. I have to. If they find me here—"

"So?" he challenges. "Are you not my wife? So someone finds you here?

You are the only woman I have ever taken to my bed, and they will know that. I want people to know that."

I glare at him. "If I am your woman, then you are my prince."

"Good. Tell me again, and maybe I'll give you another kiss."

I almost do it before I force myself to see sense. I throw myself down onto the pillows instead, groaning. I can't see Rian, but I can hear him moving further down the bed.

"This is an utter disaster," I say, and throw an arm over my eyes in disgrace.

How dare I. How could I. Where is my mind, and who scrambled it? There is no logical reason for me to abandon all my senses for the sake of sleeping with the man I've dedicated my life to protecting. No reason to put him at risk for some silly tumbling in the sheets.

And that's the worst part: it really was just messing about. The pajama shirt I borrowed from him is partially unbuttoned, but I might just have never done it up it properly in the first place. It's possible we might have done more, but he would not. He said I was too distraught. I fell asleep on him in exhaustion while he was playing with my hair, and perhaps that's for the best.

I slept in his bed, and slept so soundly, if an assassin had—

I feel his hand on my ankle, and then his lips on my calf, and bolt upright like a startled deer. Rian is smiling at me; that stupid, supercilious smile that tells me he knows that I like this.

"Oh, do stop it," I groan.

"Do you want me to?" he asks, his lips leaving my leg.

"No," I admit. "But you must. And I must."

I pull my leg away, swing over the side of the bed, and throw myself out of it. This big damned bed that has no business being this height. I scramble to find my clothes from yesterday, only to discover they're still damp. I snatch them up anyway. I need to forget last night. I need to pretend that there's something else I must do immediately, so I can get away from Rian and his smile and eyes and laugh and his dimples.

Except I can't. It's my job to stay as close to Rian as possible. I could call in one of my *khashak* to look after him, but then I would have to deal with an onslaught of questions. Given our positions, I'm sure at least one member of my *khashak* already knows I spent the night here, but it is worse, thinking of facing them and admitting to it myself.

"Would you allow me to have someone fetch you proper clothes?" Rian asks.

"We can't," I say. "Then people would know."

"Soleil, they're going to know anyway. You may as well let it happen now. Let me find you something to wear. Lune won't mind if you're not in uniform," he claims, and heads to his own armoire. "And you fit my night-clothes well enough—"

"You want me to wear your clothes?" I ask, horrified.

"Until I can fix up an alternative," he says. "Don't worry. No one will care."

He starts digging out whatever he thinks will suit me best.

I moan and flop back on the bed. A second later, Rian throws clothes at me, and after a few more lazy moments, I force myself to start dressing and retrieve my weaponry.

Rian heads to the washroom and I hear water start to run. The sound wakes up Mango. I suppose he wasn't bothered by our voices, but now the dragon is yawning and smacking his mouth, drowsy and hungry. I dress quickly, hoping to leave before Rian comes back out, but he returns while the water is still running to catch me. He knows me too well.

"Soleil," he says, and I hesitate before fleeing the room.

The way his tongue slips over my name makes me want to run to him. I feel betrayed by body and mind both—it is two against one, and I'm losing the fight.

"Soleil, some things were meant to be," he tells me. "We are meant to be. The world can't keep us apart, and you expect that you could?"

It is as if he's read my mind. Though if we've spent as much time together as he claims, why shouldn't he know every corner of me?

"How can you know we're not making a mistake?" I demand. "Simply because it is what we want, that's what makes it right?"

"No, Soleil. Because we bring out the best in each other. And don't deny it—you know it's true. Because I love you, Soleil."

"Stop saying my name," I mutter.

"Why? I like saying it."

"Because I like you saying it," I snap. "Would you marry me again?" I add in challenge.

"I always do."

I want to kiss his smile.

"I'll have you reassigned to me," Rian adds. "Lune won't miss you."

I cross my arms. "Don't you think you ought to ask me what I'd like?"

"Do you not want to be reassigned to me?"

"You know as well as I that it would make my job easier."

"And you'll never have to wear one of those drab uniforms again."

"Fine," I say, as if that's all it takes to convince me. "And get Taris, Korvaan, and N'omi if you can. That will simplify things magnificently."

“Then this will be the last morning you serve Lune. Come back soon for breakfast,” he insists.

“I will,” I promise. “We need to have a very, very long talk.”

Then I head to the doors, unlock them, and throw them open, taking Rian’s attendants on the other side by surprise. One of them almost falls over as I stride past them, and I’m sure they’re staring at me as I go. There will be rumors. But if Rian does not care, I suppose I don’t either. He was right: people were going to find out sometime or another.

We might have gotten away with it at the University, but in the palace, Rian is expected to be attended to properly. He has retainers that he never had before. He’ll have more guards assigned to him. More people around him. It would have been too much work, trying to keep our renewed relationship a secret. So, we won’t. And we’ll handle whatever complications arise from that decision.

I feel a smirk not unlike Rian’s creep onto my face as I stride triumphantly down the hall, the taste of him still fresh on my mouth. My prince is finally mine. And I am very pleased to have him.

Fifteen

I AM NOT MUCH inclined to trust, So, the first thing I do after leaving Rian's room is not to attend Lune. Instead, I go directly to where I know Taris should be sleeping, as I told him to last night. Because though Taris has told me over and over against to trust him, I don't. I'm not so stupid as not to put two and two together and realize that if the man with Lune last night sounded like Taris, there is a possibility, no matter how remote, that he is the one sleeping with her.

I pick the lock, throw the door open, and find Taris lying in the tiny room, his legs bent to fit into a bed too small for someone his height. He stirs at the light pouring in, but I don't give him any time to adjust.

"Have you been here all night?"

"What...in...Fate's...Fancy, Soleil?" he groans, cursing and shielding his eyes from the light. "What are you on about?"

"Stick out your foot," I demand.

Taris groans, but when I start digging under the blankets for his ankle, he obliges. Perhaps too roughly, I jerk up the leg of his sleepwear trousers and inspect his foot and ankle from just about every angle. But: no tattoo. Even when I insist on examining the other leg as well, there's nothing there. No layer of makeup, no fake bandage, no tattoo.

I feel foolish.

"Can I go back to sleep, now?" Taris mumbles. "You promised me until nine."

"Are you sleeping with Lune?" I demand abruptly.

He snorts and flops his head back down on his pillow. "I wish."

"Taris, I'm serious. Are you involved with her?"

"I'm serious, too: do you think I'd be in this tiny bed if I could be in hers?"

I grimace. "Don't be disgusting."

"I'm not. Her bed is huge and she's a midget. I could use that mattress."

"She's nearly my height."

"And you're short, too."

I'm not, and it annoys me that Taris says so. But at the same time, I'm relieved, because if he's teasing me, it means he doesn't hate me. I hope.

"Can I ask why you think I would be enjoying the nocturnal company of a highborn lady?" he yawns.

Though I'm already starting to feel embarrassed, I explain my experiences to Taris as well as my perhaps unwarranted suspicions.

"So might I assume anyone who shares my accent you might mistake for me, or will you do so only on occasion?" he says.

"Well, when you say it like that, it seems ridiculous," I admit.

"You're ridiculous," he grumbles, and pulls the blanket back around himself. "Give me my extra hour of sleep and I'll come find you and the prince."

"Is there much point in coveting that last hour?"

I hear him mutter some less than charitable things about me. This time, I can't blame him. Thankfully, he has not mentioned my clothes. So, he hasn't noticed, he doesn't care, or he isn't surprised. I'm not sure which is best.

I leave him and head to Lune's rooms instead, trying to ignore the guilt over my unnecessary accusation. There's quite a commotion inside Lune's rooms, which intrigues me, and for a moment I wonder if she and her lover were foolish enough to get caught. But when I enter, I see only Lune, sitting on the window seat and looking out the glass panes dismally. Her hair is knotted. She is still dressed in night clothes. Romia and several other maids are here, all worried and flustered.

"My lady, I thought you would wear your pink and gold gown—the one with the roses," poor Romia suggests, saying anything to try and engage Lune.

"That's fine," Lune sighs.

She sneezes twice, the movement jerking her entire body, and then shudders from her shoulders to her toes. She's too pale. Despite the heat, she shivers.

"And you ought to break your fast," Romia goes on.

"I'd rather not," Lune says.

It is unnerving to hear her speak so, as if she's in a trance.

"Please, eat something, my lady," Romia begs, but Lune's ignoring her.

"Nothing tastes good," she murmurs. "It always happens like this. I try to eat, but none of it tastes good. And then I give up…"

One of the maids near me gasps, and then covers her mouth and turns to start whispering to the girl near her. There's some gesturing, and a nervous, taut feeling suddenly descends on us all. I look to where the maid is pointing, and see a few drops of blood on the ground near Lune's feet. It's dripped all the way down her leg, off her ankle, and onto the wood.

It's only what happens to most women each month, but I'm embarrassed for Lune's sake that she hasn't noticed until now.

Lune glances down at the blood and does nothing for a moment. Then her mouth tightens and she throws herself to her feet to storm to her washroom, slamming the door behind her so that it shudders. There are several crashes as she breaks what I assume are the glass containers holding her soaps, and gives an ear-piercing scream. A second scream trails off weakly at the end, and turns into a sob as we hear her throw herself to the ground and cry.

Some of the maids flinch mutter to one another. Romia flies to the washroom and tries to enter, but Lune has locked the door.

I can hear rumors being born. Normally, I assume, Romia would whirl on the others and snap at them to quiet themselves. But when she turns to us, and the chaos she has on her hands, it takes her a long time to do anything at all.

She looks relieved when she recognizes me, as if we've become friends since yesterday. Romia approaches, does not say a word about what I'm wearing, and does not ask why. She takes me by the arm and pulls me toward the alcove by the door, leaving the other maids to talk.

"Should one of us fetch a doctor, maybe?" I suggest, just to get a conversation going. Whatever's wrong with Lune, a doctor can't fix it.

"No, no, don't," Romia insists. "But I need you to do something else."

"Find Grand Prince Carsans? Or the crown prince?" I suggest.

"No!" Romia says, horrified, then collects herself. "No, not that. But I need you to take today off. Again. Please. I'll give you a pass so you can go wherever you like, but I need you to help me keep rumors from spreading. Tell everyone, instead, that Lady Lune is not feeling well. She…has a chill. She doesn't want to see anyone until she's better."

"Do you know what's wrong with her?" I ask.

Romia sighs. "Please*?* Help me and don't ask questions."

I nod and take a brief moment to consider my options.

"Can I have a friend help? Naomi Qurvo? She—"

"Whatever you like," Romia says. "Help me contain this. Or Grand Prince Carsans will have both our heads."

I doubt that, but if this sends me back to Rian without complications, I'm more than happy to oblige. I'm tempted to ask Romia why she picked me, but I already know: she tested me, yesterday, and I passed. I didn't start rumors about Lune and Vásan's engagement, nor did I sell the story. The royals know, now, but it hasn't been publicly announced.

So, only a few minutes after I report for work in Lune's rooms, I am sent off again. It's as I exit Lune's rooms that I catch something out of the corner of my eye—someone ducking into the adjacent hallway, attempting to disappear up the tower staircase. Lune's lover. It takes me a moment, because I cannot believe finding him could be so easy. It's almost as if my finally being with Rian has ensured the strands Fate weaves are with my convenience in mind.

It's too fortuitous, but when Fate obliges me, I won't complain. Even if Lune's useless, I'm sure I can get answers from the man she's been using to warm her bed. It's possible he's part of this conspiracy as well.

I draw one of my knives and follow him. He's hurrying away as quickly as he can, but I'm faster. I decide that some answers are better than no answers, and when I catch him on the steps, I upset his balance and slam him against the wall. It's incredibly rude of me, and I understand that there's a small possibility that this man is completely innocent, but I prefer to start from the assumption that no one in this palace is harmless.

The poor fellow immediately holds his hands up in defense, and as if to show he is not reaching for a weapon. He wears a standard palace guard's uniform, but we both know it's stolen. He's pretending he belongs here as much as I am.

He's trying to say something, probably about how he has no money for me to steal, or that I have made a mistake.

"I saw you last night," I interrupt.

That quiets him.

"Why are you here? What are you here for?" I demand, and press the knife so close to his neck that it scratches his throat as he replies.

"For Lune! Only for Lune," he promises, sounding sincere. Then again, anyone can when they think their life is on the line.

"Why?"

"I…I love her," he confesses. "I swear it on my life, I'm here to help her. Things are so hard for her. I only want to be here for her."

"Then what is our Lady Lune up to, then, mmm?" I challenge him, tickling his throat again. "I know she's cleverer than she pretends. And she's a part of some plot or another: tell me the truth, now, and I'll see to it we spare her life."

"She isn't part of a plot!" he promises. "All she wants is the Lost Heir to take the throne! That's all!"

I feel a prickling at the base of my skull. My grip on the knife tightens.

"And has she said who that is?"

"I won't tell you," he says, setting himself up to potentially die for that secret. "I do not know who you are working for, but I won't let you harm the heir, if that's your intent."

Interesting. If this man and Lune are plotting against Rian, telling me nothing in this regard would be to their advantage. But this holds true as well if they're trying to keep him safe.

Beyond his word, there's no way to prove this man's intentions are pure.

Unless, of course, I take him to Qhan. If the bodyguard is awake, and in decent condition, he'll be able to see the truth in this man's words, if there's any to read in the first place.

I sheathe the knife and grab his arm.

"Come," I snap. "If you pass interrogation, I'll release you go. Otherwise…"

He pulls against me, but my grip tightens, and he does nothing more drastic to free himself despite the fact he's much larger than I am. So, he doesn't want to hurt me, then.

"I cannot go with you," he insists. "I cannot, do you understand? All of this is only a misunderstanding. I need you to let me go. I promise you, I haven't done anything wrong. I'm not conspiring against the crown. None of it matters to me!"

"If that's true, then you won't mind answering a few of my ques—"

"She lost the baby!" he interrupts.

I fall silent, trying to process what he's said. I release his arm, but he doesn't run. We stand there on the steps, each waiting for the other to say something.

"What?"

He's bitterly angry, now, and I can tell he's trying to use it to keep me from seeing the glistening in his eyes.

"Lune. She…We were going to have a baby. But..."

I continue to stare at him. Rude as that might be, I don't know how to handle things like this. It's strange, but I would never have guessed that Lune and her lover were meeting solely for personal reasons. Even now, part of me wants to believe that this is a smokescreen, a way of distracting me with a tragedy so I won't look deeper.

I don't know if I should believe him or not; the evidence I've found could support such a thing, but it does not explain everything.

"I thought that things would be different this time," he murmurs, and

I take a step back from him, suddenly uncomfortable. "She'd gotten so far along…"

"How many times?" I force myself to ask.

"This was the third."

I think about last night, about the times I've spied on Lune.

"Then why does she act as if this is more of a burden for you?" I challenge him. I'm lucky he doesn't realize I have been eavesdropping on them during some of their most intimate moments together.

He sighs. Whatever the truth is, he's doing a fine job of playing his part.

"Lune could only tell me about it remotely after it happened. We cannot see each other as often as we would like, but she wanted me to know. Lune is very giving," he claims. "She sees my pain and tries to push her own aside. Tries to pretend as if I am the only one suffering, and that she can manage it."

I'm skeptical. "If she really was expecting, why allow that to happen? Did you not mean to keep your relationship a secret?"

He's barely listening to me.

"They say death comes in fours," he says.

I know what he's implying; he does not want to lose her, but suspects Lune will be the next life to be taken from him. He wants to spend as much time as he can with her in the interim, yet being around her causes him pain.

I'm conflicted. I might not be the best person, but I'm not a monster. And now I have to ask myself: am I the sort of person who would drag a grieving man before Qhan and demand he relive his pain to satisfy my own curiosity? It's a sure way to know the truth, but what would Rian think of me, if he saw me do this? What would Korvaan and Naomi think?

I try to weigh potential outcomes. Yes, Qhan would be able to sense the truth or lack thereof in this man's words. But that's assuming he'd even talk. Given his outburst, I'm sure he knew I meant to bring him to Qhan, which means he's aware of more than I'd like, already. Yet if he really is only here to be with Lune…and he's a relative innocent…

"Leave," I hiss at him, making my decision. "If you love Lune, you will do as I say, and know that if I ever see your face here again, there will be consequences."

I go to stalk down the stairs, knowing I've technically done the right thing, but annoyed that it hasn't done me any immediate good.

But then he laughs at me.

"You think you can say whatever you want, hand out threats to strangers on a staircase, and I'll obey because you say so?"

Dear Almighty, give me the strength to restrain myself from violence.

"You'll leave the Pyrian Palace and keep out because you are not meant to be here," I snap at him. "And yes, I do expect you to do as I say. Leave. Or else Lune might have to pay for it."

His anger sparks. "You impudent, selfish—"

"Selfish?" I laugh.

I am tempted to keep goading him. If he attacks me, it will give me an excuse to fight back without worrying about the moral high ground of the situation.

"Maybe think next time, before you start with the insults," I go on. "You can only get away with generics for so long."

I see his fists clench but he doesn't move.

"Too genteel to hit a lady?" I taunt him.

"You're no lady, Soleil Marson."

The sound of my name in this man's mouth is enough; he does know me.

I reach for my knife again, and he reaches under his jacket. I wait before throwing, in case I need to dodge first. I don't want to lose one of my knives before I have to. But the fellow was not reaching for a weapon. In an instant, the entire stairwell is filled with smoke and I'm struggling to keep from coughing. Naturally, once I've recovered myself, he's gone. I'm not going to waste my time trying to chase him down.

What kind of overdramatic ass uses a smoke bomb in a stairwell?

I sheathe my knife and escape before anyone arrives to investigate. It's best to cut my losses at this point and rejoin Rian.

I sigh, mightily tempted to bang my head against the nearest wall.

A fluke-dreamer albino, a Lijimi, a disgraced Isaarian lady, and her southern lover all involved in a vague conspiracy for Almighty-knows what.

Sounds like the beginning of a bad joke.

And that doesn't even account for the rest of the Carsans. Or the firebird assassins. And whatever Nusk knew about them. So, once again, instead of finding answers, I've only dug up more questions.

I stalk back to Rian's rooms. I doubt he knows anything about Lune having a bedmate, but he definitely still knows more than I do about my own fluke.

I find Rian sitting at his desk with about eight different books around him, and Mango purring on his lap. My distracted crown prince doesn't notice me slip in, but the dragon does. He perks up to look at me with those huge, black eyes, which makes me oddly nervous. I have the vague remnants of memories or maybe merely counterfeit memories when it comes to me and Rian, but I don't remember anything about Mango, or if he liked me.

Dragons are emotional creatures, from the largest of them to the smallest. There aren't many breeds left in the world, and I don't know much about them on the whole. But I do know that they often like to bond themselves to things—people or animals or other dragons, even gold—and only the largest ones like being alone for long stretches of time. They can be greedy, selfish things, hoarding whatever they can get their claws on. But if Mango's proven anything to me, they can also be sweet, and loyal. Willing to do anything for those they've bonded to.

Because of this, I half-expect Mango to be defensive of Rian when it comes to sharing him with me. But when I approach, Mango leaps off of Rian's lap and starts twining between my legs, like it's been a long time since he's seen me and is excited that hiatus is over.

I crouch down to scratch his ears as Rian turns, sees me, and struggles to free himself of his desk. I think his intent was to stand up, sweep over, and give me a kiss, but he knocks his things about and I have to help him pick books, papers and pens up off the floor.

"You're back earlier than expected," he says with one of those perfect smiles.

"Lune's throwing a fit," I say. "I've been unofficially dismissed for today."

"Why do you smell like smoke?"

I sigh. "I ran into someone who may be in the conspiracy against you. I didn't get any answers out of him, before you ask."

Rian blinks at me. "Oh. Thank you for trying?"

"I have a week catch him again. What have you been working on?" I ask instead, hoping that Rian's gotten more done than I have.

He excitedly returns to his desk, shoving papers aside and putting the journal he's been using as a workbook on top.

"I have finished one of the family trees!" he crows. "Well, for the most part. But: you are looking at the first person to find the end of the Wolff family line."

I raise my eyebrows. That's not what I expected. On several fronts. Still, I won't deny I'm interested.

"The end of it?"

"Well, yes," Rian says. "You see, though I hadn't filled in every gap and blank, I had a little knowledge of the end of the line—supplemented by that wonderful book Mercer found for me in Alarkia—and all I had to do was piece a few more things together. Luckily! the Pyrian ancient library is rather expansive, and—"

"Rian," I interrupt. "I'm sorry, but most of what you're saying is running together for me. Could you say why this is so important to you? Or tell me something interesting you've found out," I suggest instead.

"Well, the Wolff line ended officially only about, fifteen years ago," he says. "I can't remember precisely. It's in my notes. Somewhere between fifteen and twenty. It all comes down to one man: Aldrich Wolff."

I frown. "So close to us?"

For some reason, even after Rian's discovery of significant evidence regarding the Families Three, I would have expected their lines to have died out hundreds of years ago, not a mere fifteen or twenty.

I don't think Rian heard me, because he's still gushing about Aldrich Wolff.

"You see, Aldrich Wolff is probably the single most impressive man to marry into the Wolff line in history. The Valeians had stories about him, so many stories, about the Alarkian man who found their island and stole the heart of their queen… But unfortunately, as he doesn't carry the blood, and he's the only one left, it's not as if there can be any more Wolffs…"

I check my watch while he talks; Taris' hour isn't quite up yet, which means there's no point in assembling my *khashak*. So, I seat myself in the lounge chair, a knife in hand for prudence's sake.

"He's a madman, but impressive. Not the sort of man I would ever want to cross," Rian is insisting, blathering like a schoolboy.

"He's really something then, is he?" I say, and that sets him off.

"He's a legend. I mean, not to most people, because it's so strange for them to think about how someone like that could still be alive."

"Someone like what?" I ask, and Rian opens his mouth, but stops himself.

"Oh, it's too long a story," he realizes. "And I've ordered breakfast, so—"

I interrupt him.

"There's time," I say, and smile. "Tell me all about Aldrich Wolff."

BREAKFAST, OR BRUNCH, rather, is Tourrannese in style per Rian's request, with delicate, lightly crisped fish filets, thin omelets filled with layers of seaweed chips and Isaaria's best cheeses, and plain rice with broth. It's a relatively simple breakfast mainly filled with protein, which I appreciate in a nutritional sense, but the flavors impress upon me how well the kitchens here adapt to the royals' whims.

I finish my meal quickly, scarfing down what I need most while Rian takes his time to consume everything else available. The lad doesn't like to let good food go to waste; I don't like wasting time.

It was good fun listening to him jabber about Aldrich Wolff for a time, but now we need to stay grounded in the relevant.

"We need somewhere to start," I say thoughtfully, sticking a pen between my teeth to give my mouth something to work on, so my teeth don't grind. After a moment's thought, I look to Rian. "I suppose we should start by you telling me absolutely everything that you remember from our first timeline. That seems most pertinent, wouldn't you say?"

But Rian freezes, and slowly looks up at me, grimacing. "You're going to be less than pleased…"

"What."

"So. The thing is," he says, "I don't remember much of the original timeline. I have pieces, but…it is as if someone has reached inside my head and scraped that iteration out. For the most part."

I stare at him, and Rian gives a nervous laugh.

"Unbelievable," I mutter.

Rian shrugs. "Sorry. I suppose we could go see Asmer and ask her about these charms of hers, but, ah, that's assuming she really is the one who made them. And that she kept one for herself."

But we can't work with potentials, only with what we know.

"What do you remember?" I sigh.

"First timeline?" Rian clarifies, considering. "Mmm. Well, I remember my parents. Growing up. I lived here at the palace, with them and my grandparents. The Carsans did, too, and so did Merse and his parents. A couple others, I think, but Mercer and I were the closest."

Some things don't change, then, and if Rian knows what's meant to be, he can at least ensure some continuity. I'm not sure what happens now because it is "meant to", and what happens because Rian ensures it does. Perhaps Fate's design is a combination of both.

"I've a few memories of showing my fluke when I was young, maybe four? And then my parents, of course, presented me to the Currian Council. We had to wait for the rest of the heirs to indicate their flukes, but otherwise it was an open and shut case. And I remember we first met when you were, mmm, perhaps six? I don't remember why your parents were at the palace in the first place, but—"

"My parents?" I yelp.

Rian blinks at me. "Well, yes, Soleil, you did come from somewhere. And before you ask, no, I don't think they were royals. Or, they weren't Isaarian nobles. I'd bet they came to present you, because you indicated your fluke, and they knew that meant Fate wanted us to marry."

He has the good sense to turn red when he says that, and clears his throat.

"Anyways, we became good friends, even before we knew what it meant to be betrothed. We were raised in the palace together."

"And my parents...left me?" I cannot help but ask.

"I suppose," Rian admits. "They left you at the palace so you could grow up as a princess, and learn all kinds of proper things as our future queen while I learned to be the future king. We grew up alongside the other crown princes, although they were grand princes, then, since we knew I was meant to be king. We were very good friends; you, and me, and Mercer and Asmer. But I don't remember Crispin and Lune being there much," he adds, and shrugs.

"What about my *khashak?"* I ask. "You've said you remember them?"

Rian shrugs. "Yes? I know Nusk has always, always had three children. I think he still raised them to look after the two of us, when you were a princess."

I can't help but snort.

Rian grins. "I know. But to be fair, it's not as if you were a proper princess. You and me, Mercer, and even Asmer—we got up to a fair bit of trouble. And I don't know if it's because we were told it was going to happen anyway, or because we were such good friends, but…we…fell in love."

"And were married," I add. "Then, I imagine, you got me in the family way."

Rian looks down and fiddles with his spoon. "…I never did get to meet our son," he admits, "but…I knew we were going to have one."

We're both silent for a few seconds.

"And then...I...died," Rian finally says. "Assassinated."

"And you have no idea how it happened?"

He gives me a look. "Ah, no, Soleil. I think I would have said something about it by now if I did, don't you?"

I stand and begin pacing.

"I suppose that's when I concocted my plan to go back in time and catch your killers before they got to you, and had Nusk help me. Only that clearly has not worked. Why has that not worked?"

Rian sighs. "Thing is—nothing ever happens exactly the same way twice. And it's a lot to remember. We've gotten close to stopping the killer, I think, but even that doesn't guarantee anything. Safe to assume it's some kind of hired assassin. And we have no idea who he's working for."

"Feels sloppy," I say. "And unlikely. How are we this bad at catching a killer?"

"Bad enough for us to understand seriously that whoever we're up against is definitely no joke," Rian admits. "Whoever they are, they're skilled, clever, and they likely have powerful flukes."

It is a keen observation. Either we are complete blundering idiots—which I'd like to think we're not—or our enemies are powerful.

A third option, naturally, is that we are idiots and we're facing down someone brilliant, but I'd like to give us some credit. Even if I'm pigheaded, Naomi or Taris could have put things together. Which leaves me to assume that in other timelines, we've never gotten far. We have never had this useful bump of time before Comus Day to try and investigate.

"So-leil," Rian complains, and I feel a pillow hit the back of my head. "Pay attention to me."

I turn on him. He really can't go more than a minute without attention. "What, are you a child?"

He grins.

"Let me think for a minute," I insist. "I'm trying to decide how we can best use the week we have to make things right. To make sure this is the last time I ever have to use my fluke."

"There's no point in you trying to protect me if you don't listen to me," Rian claims. "I may be a spoiled Crown Prince, but I know my own schedule. That is invaluable information for a bodyguard."

"Yes," I agree, "but I too know your habits and schedule."

Rian looks thoughtful. "Mmm, well. Given certain…special circumstances, it's possible those habits and that schedule may be modified. For my wife's sake."

I am not amused, and make certain my eyes tell him that. "Rian—this may come as a shock to you, but I'd rather have you alive and apart from me than next to me and dead."

"Or, we can use this week to do whatever we want, I give you my ring, and when we turn back time, we can use this one week over and over until we get it right. This time, with you able to remember everything."

"Rian, I'm serious,"

"No, you're Soleil," he says with a somewhat irritating smile.

I roll my eyes. "Ree-on…"

"What, you don't think we should get the chance to do whatever we want?" he says, using that same suggestive phrase.

"There is no time for something like that," I insist, though even I hear a lack of conviction in the words.

"And why not?" Rian retorts. "Soleil—I don't care about you roaming the halls, looking for would-be assassins, and acting as my *Khashtani*. I want you to be here. With me."

I can feel myself growing angry with him for his selective blindness. "That may be what you want emotionally, but it will likely result in your death—"

"So?" he challenges me, and throws up a hand. "You'll go back again. I try to stop you, try to talk you out of it, but you always do. If what I do never matters, I might as well do what I like with my wife, while I can."

I groan. "Rian. Let us focus on finding your assassin. And then we'll worry about our marriage."

"But you're meant to have our child in the coming year," Rian argues. "So, whether we like it or not, we're running out of time to make this the correct timeline. We either have our son, or we don't. But we do have to work a little for that, you know."

I sigh because he's right, but it's too early for me to be thinking the way that he is. I know that Rian and I marry. I know we're meant to have at least one child together. But it's difficult to fully comprehend.

"Rian, I understand," I say. "Really, I do. But there's no reason for us to try being together before I catch these killers. I need you alive."

"No, you don't. Not really. They never hurt you," he reminds me. "Not once. So, if I die one night in your arms, knowing you'll always wake up safely and will one day have our son, what better way is there for me to die?"

"Old age," I retort. "I value your life, *Crown Prince Rian.*"

"Soleil. I do wish you'd stop," he says, quieter. Serious, for once. "Everyone has lost someone. Does the world deserve to be caught in this coil of time because you cannot come to terms with losing me?"

I struggle with how to tell him that's not what's happening. I understand how he sees things—I understand how difficult it must be to have me make him tell me again the same things over and over. I'm confused as to why I don't have a ring of my own to help me remember each loop. I want to find a way to tell him that I can't let him die because I can't rule Isaaria without him. I can't raise Ayla and our son with a dead father when I have the power to prevent that.

"Can't you understand how that might make me feel? You've the fate of the world in your hands and time and time again, you sacrifice the greater good for me," Rian says.

"They are not warring sentiments," I say. "Our children are meant to do great things, Rian, that's the entire reason our enemies are trying to kill you. So long as I keep you safe, I keep the world safe."

"Maybe. Or maybe not. We don't the answers, do we? I'm tired, Soleil," he sighs. "I've lived through this too many times, and for too long. Why won't you spend whatever it is I have left and simply be with me?"

When I respond, I don't know if they're the right words. I can only say what's on my mind and hope that he understands me.

"Does the world deserve to end, then, because we can't shoulder our burdens? Everyone has a fight in their life, Rian. This is ours. And I will keep fighting as long as it takes to make things right. Why else would I have this power?"

Rian sighs. "I don't know. What use does this world have for me, so long as our son is born?"

I do not answer that because I do not wish to consider it even for a moment. But if Rian believes flukes are gifts from the Almighty as Theebins ought, why would I have my gift if not to save him? What torture is that?

"You've had the luxury of living many times over again," I remind him.

"And dying many times over again."

"With the knowledge that I will always, always go back for you. Because it's what needs to happen. We have forever, Rian. Would you really be so happy to see me again if some part of you wasn't prepared to continue doing this?"

"I'm not strong enough for this, Soleil," he insists. "If you're asking me? Really asking me? Then I want this to be the last time I have to remember. I cannot do this if it means knowing it is my destiny to die."

"…Then you'd better get to work helping me, so I can keep doing this for both of us," I insist.

"It's difficult to tell everything we have discovered," he confesses. "Think of all the things people write down to remember them: I've had to remember precise dates, precise times, names of people I don't know, things that look odd, things I thought were odd but weren't. I have to remember all those things for years and years and years of material. I have to remember what details change or not; what things we can change and what things we have no power over…"

He's growing more frustrated the longer he speaks. I can tell he is upset with himself, and realize, then, just how many times we have failed.

Rian is right. It's too much for him to remember. Most people could barely recall what they ate for breakfast a week ago, let alone what he's forced himself to memorize.

"Soleil," he whispers, horrified by his own words. "We have failed so many times, and we still don't know why."

"A lack of proper suspects is likely a contributor," I say, but my bluntness does little to lift his spirits. "Don't worry about what we might have to do again. Please, Rian. Trust me. I'll manage things."

He sighs again, but relents with a nod.

I start pacing again. Mango finds this confusing and starts to copy me, prancing back and forth,

"It is interesting that we've never once been able to uncover the traitors," I muse. "It makes me suspect there is a third party involved. But that doesn't make much sense, does it? I can't imagine a third-party having any motive…"

"Then you're assuming motive," Rian reminds me.

His voice is muffled, and I turn to see that he's found his way back to the bed to fall down face-first on the pillows. He could be taking this worse.

"I'm going to have to assume some things, Rian," I sigh. "I'm sorry, but you haven't given me much to work with."

"I can tell you whoever it is definitely has intimate knowledge of the palace, my life, our lives…"

"Then how do you know it's not Crispin? Or Mercer? Or Asmer or Lune?" I challenge him.

Rian props himself up on an elbow and sighs. Again.

"I don't," he rasps. "But Soleil: whether you like it or not, I refuse to punish people for things they haven't yet done. If we find the conspirators, yes, of course: imprison them before they can do anything to hurt me. But we can't assume someone's working against us and punish them for that. Even if we can't trust my friends, they're still my friends."

"So, who can you trust, then?"

"You," he admits. "And your *khashak*."

I roll my eyes. "And we're right back to where we started."

"Oh! And Qhan."

Oh, and Qhan. Brilliant.

"Fine," I relent. "Let's discuss my fluke instead. Now that I know I have one, I need to know how best to use it."

"Your fluke?" Rian repeats.

"Yes, anything you know about it," I clarify. "Because I need to know how to wind back the timeline if things go wrong."

"Well, first you ought to be in the sun for at least an hour every day," Rian admits, sitting up in bed. "You generally use your fluke…Instinctively? Winding back, at least. I know there are other things you can do, but you've relearned this many, many times over again. I think, at this point, you simply know what it is you must do."

"That's not confidence inspiring," I say. "I was hoping for instructions told piecemeal."

"What I can tell you is that you're very good at it," Rian offers. "And also that you tend to not think…before…you…use it."

"So, I act in panic."

"I think it's more a matter of when you panic, your fluke goes a little…"

He whistles and makes a compelling swirling shape with a finger.

"Otherwise," he goes on, "you're quite good at doing whatever it is you want to do so long as you're relaxed and focused."

"That explains the meditating Nusk wanted me to do, I suppose," I mutter. I wish he'd told me I had a fluke over time itself…Though, it's possible I might have abused that power on occasion. So maybe Nusk knew what he was doing.

"And before you ask," Rian adds, "no, you can't go forward. You can manipulate, wind back, and even stop time, but you've been heavily advised against going forward."

I frown. "The first time you said 'can't', second time you said I've been advised against it."

"What's your point?"

"My point is, which is it? Can I go forward in time or not?"

Rian sighs. "So-leil…"

"So, you don't know, then. What if I propel myself forward through time?" I pose. "I could move so fluidly around others. Do what I pleased. Though, one would think I'd have done so at this point, if I could—"

"Neither you or I know the entire depth of your powers, Soleil," Rian sighs.

"It's 'you nor I', Sir Linguistics," I say. "What kind of teacher are you if you can't even get that right?"

"First: I am a teacher who does not give a care about speaking correctly when he's off the clock. Second: I teach literature, not language. They are two different subjects."

I huff. "Oh, well then."

"And third of all," he adds. "You can't do that, Soleil. Well, I mean, you can, I suppose, but it's dangerous. You've done so before and almost gotten yourself killed. Do that and—"

"You'd be helpless!" I conclude, and Rian gives me a look.

"Well. Not helpless, dear. But we would not be able to go back again and fix things. I refuse to lose you. Well," he corrects. "I suppose we could always…"

He trails off and looks incredibly confused, and conflicted.

"What?" I say.

"That's strange," he says, putting a hand to his temples, as if he's suddenly contracted a painful headache. *"Ach.* I can't recall…"

"What?"

"I thought there was another way. Of resetting things. Without your fluke. But that would be impossible. Wouldn't it?"

"I can't say," I admit. "I'm still trying to get used to the idea of having a fluke."

I'm grinding my teeth, but this time I don't care. I have my suspicions that Rian knows more than he's saying—not that he's keeping things from me on purpose, but because he actually knows so much that it's hard for him to focus on what's most important.

"Now what are we going to do?" I mutter out loud.

"You call your *khashak* up to make whatever sort of plan you want, we check on Qhan, and we figure out what you want to do next," he offers.

"Yes," I decide. "Let us do that."

Except he hasn't moved, and I haven't moved.

"It's the watch," Rian reminds me. "You use that to call your *khashak*."

"I remember what the watch is for," I say. "Can you get off the bed, please?"

"What? Ah."

"Yes. Yes, please, stop lounging like that."

Rian's pretending not to smile as he hops off the bed. It was made before, but now it's untidied. If he has to call someone in to make it up again, they're going to think the worst.

"Come on. Put your shoes on," I tell him as I click on my watch. "We're going to visit Qhan, and then we're going to make a plan. Are you going to get all destitute and dramatic on me again?"

"Probably," he warns. "But even if you can't convince me that I should do things your way, I'll still do it."

"Fine," I say. "But don't expect me to ever give in to your doomsday gloom and agree to let you die."

"Could you at least promise to not rewind us eight-million times for my sake?"

"No. Follow me."

I practically grab him by the collar, keep a knife handy just in case, and pull him over to the room where Qhan is. Naomi's so startled that she has a gun half-drawn before she realizes it's me and Rian.

I suppose Romia made sure Naomi got the rest of the day off, then. And Naomi, good-hearted as she is, decided to come straight upstairs to see to Qhan.

Qhan is awake and eating, so I suppose he's on the mend. Naomi's got his head bandaged over top of some stitches, but the moment he sees Rian, his eyes widen and he immediately moves to stand and bow. So, no lasting damage.

"Your majesty—!" Qhan starts, but Rian's waving for him to sit back.

"Please. Finish your breakfast. We're all safe. That's what matters," he says.

Qhan doesn't look comfortable relaxing when he should be at work helping protect his crown prince, but he's also not about to disobey an order.

"How are you feeling?" Rian asks, perching on his bodyguard's bedside.

"Not as bad as I'm sure I looked yesterday, your majesty," Qhan promises him. "The important question is, are *you* feeling well? Those assassins got closer to you than they ever should have, and I apologize for that. In fact, if you'll allow me, I would like to resign from my post moving forward—"

"No!" Rian interrupts, horrified. "No, I will not allow it," he adds stoutly. "They shouldn't have been able to get into the Pyrian Palace in the first place. Lady Soleil here believes there's a chance we were...betrayed by someone."

Qhan frowns, looking both hesitant and concerned. "No one knew we were headed that way except for Crown Prince Mercer—"

He cuts himself off, thinks, and then sighs.

"Well, and the dozens of others you announced it to on our way there."

"And that's not counting spies," I add. "So, while Mercer is a suspect, so is everyone else."

Rian shoots me a look. "Mercer? Really?"

I shrug. "Sorry. We have to suspect everyone at this point."

Rian rolls his eyes. "Ah, yes, because my best friend from childhood, who has no desire to be king and wants to continue traveling the world, is the most likely person to try and kill me."

I shrug again.

"Face it—that's merely the most dramatic option, so you think it's the right option even if it makes no sense," Rian accuses.

He may be right, there. I've spent too much time listening to his stories and now I think I'm in one.

There's a peculiar knocking at the door before it opens—Korvaan's usual way of alerting us to his entry. He first meets eyes with his sister, who shakes her head at him and gives a small shrug. Then he looks at me, Qhan, and finally, Rian.

"I know," I say. "Come in, Korvaan. We're waiting for Taris, and then I'll explain."

"Yes, answers would be good, seeing as I've buried the same man twice now," Korvaan says as he finds a chair to perch in. "That man in the general's uniform? Does he have a Fate-damned twin*?* Is it a fluke? What the hell is that about?"

I sigh. I suppose that means we don't have any survivors to interrogate.

"Let's give Taris a minute, then we'll share information as best we can."

"Well, in the meantime," Rian says, and then crosses to shake hands with Korvaan and a startled N'omi. "Rian Yakarami. Nice to finally meet. I appreciate everything you've done to help keep me alive."

"Oh," Naomi says, not sure where to look when Rian shakes her head. She's turning pink at the attention.

"Uh," Korvaan manages, also shocked to be shaking a crown prince's hand so casually, especially since we've made Rian's business our business for the last two decades. It's surreal.

"You'll get used to the crown prince's peculiarities," Qhan reassures them, likely also confused, though I'm sure Naomi at least told him that I'm Rian's *Khashtani* and the Qurvos are my *khashak.*

"I'd also like to introduce my bodyguard and friend, Qhan Khaleem," Rian goes on, "as well as extend my sympathies. I'm sure these past few days have been difficult for you, so please, if there's anything I can do to help, let me know."

"We'll do that. Sir," Korvaan says, and Naomi nods and forces a smile.

It's then that Taris all but slams the door open and closed before locking it and glancing at all the windows to mark exits and entrances.

"Let's get this over with," he snaps.

His hair is damp, as if he's quickly washed. I'm guessing he accidentally slept than intended only to have my call over the watches wake him again.

"Someone's in poor spirits," Korvaan notes.

Taris' glares could kill if there were a fluke attached to them.

"Perhaps that's because someone decided it was a brilliant idea to wake me early to accuse me of bedding down Lune Carsans."

Everyone in the room stares at me.

"What the hell, Soleil," Rian says.

"That was unfair of me," I admit. "I apologize. It has since been confirmed you are not Lune's lover, hence why I currently smell like smoke, before anyone else asks, so, again. My apologies."

Taris grunts and crosses his arms over his chest. This is the only acceptance of my apology I am likely to receive.

"Ah, what's all this about Lune having a-a…" Rian starts, turning pink.

I sigh.

"Everyone: listen closely because I only wish to say all this once," I warn.

Then I explain about everything that I possibly can, and all the things I think I've discovered thus far. Rian and Taris chime in here and there with what they know, but all it does is round out the starting point for our mystery. There still aren't many questions that have been answered.

The only thing I leave out is what Lune's lover said this morning, about her miscarriages. The more I consider it, the more I'm starting to think they planned that as something to say if they were ever caught. It's tragic enough a revelation to keep most people from prying further. And it would also mean that Lune and her man were fooling around with one another for at least several years, if it were true. While I might not have caught that, one of my *khashak* would have.

Once I've finished, there's a good minute of complete silence before anyone speaks. I know it's a lot to take in, and Qhan, Naomi, and Korvaan have the most to reconcile. I'm especially concerned about how Naomi and Korvaan will react to the knowledge of my hidden fluke. No one is looking at me, but that might be because they're trying not to think about how Rian and I are meant to be married, and that I spent last night in his rooms.

"Question," Korvaan says, raising his hand like one of Rian's students. "And forgive me if I sound like a fool in saying so, but, ah, if the Carsans' prophecy is about your son, why in the world would you and Soleil become king and queen instead of, say, Magnus inheriting from his parents and then having your son replace him?"

"I can understand the confusion," Rian admits. "But the first time, when this was being decided, it was known that our son was meant to be 'born with a crown at his brow'. The Currian Council interpreted this to mean his parents, then, would already be king and queen."

"He does appear to have Fate's blessing," Taris drawls. "Given how things are meant to have turned out."

"Sir," Qhan says, frowning at Rian, "my fluke says this is all true, but I want to hear you say it yourself and then, I won't question your word again."

Rian sighs. "Well…Yes. Unfortunately. It's all true. I'm sure my parents would have been excellent to have now to help explain things, at least as far as my having a *Khashtani* is concerned, but unfortunately, ah: they're dead. So, you'll just have to trust that I haven't lost my mind, here. Though I'll admit, sometimes it feels like I have."

Qhan nods slowly. I know he'll be loyal to Rian no matter what, but it must be hard to get his head wrapped around this time traveling business.

"So, what's the plan?" Korvaan asks.

He's not looking at me, but he isn't snappish. I wonder if he and Naomi had a discussion about waiting until after Comus Day to kill me.

"We need to ensure Rian becomes king," I say. "And obviously, we need to apprehend whoever wants him dead, either as soon as possible, or right after Rian is crowned. To make sure that we can still save our future."

I give Rian a look to make sure he doesn't say anything about his alternative ideas. We can talk later in private, if we must, about how hard this has been on him. But I need Qhan and my *khashak* to move forward with confidence. It will make it difficult if they know Rian is struggling with the idea that this might not be the last time we have to go through the same lifetime to fix our mistakes.

I'll help him through it, our own way.

"This isn't just about us anymore," I press. "If Rian is meant to be king, for the sake of a prophecy that claims his heir is going to help heal the world, then we need to make sure that happens."

"I'm afraid I won't be much help to you in securing his majesty's crown," Qhan admits.

"Let Rian and me worry about the crown. The four of you need to make sure we don't compromise his safety," I add. "Someone doesn't want Rian on the throne. We'll worry about the 'why' when we can afford to—Nusk was right about that. We only need to uncover conspiracies and put a stop to them."

"You understand there's only *six* of us, yes?" Korvaan asks skeptically.

"We can do it because we must do it," I insist.

"It would help if you and his majesty made a public announcement," Qhan admits. "Something that will help you stay by his side."

"I'll formally announce something," Rian suggests. "That will give Soleil a chance to speak with everyone, and even ask questions out of 'ignorance'."

Qhan nods. "And I will interview all of his majesty's bodyguards to ensure their loyalty. No one will guard him who does not have his best interests at heart."

I thank him for this, glad he thought to do so.

"What is the schedule for the next few days?" Naomi presses on.

"Comus Day is eight days away, now," Taris says. "Tomorrow evening is the ball. The next morning, there's a brunch, but after that, there's no 'mandatory' events for the crown princes to attend."

"If that's the case, I want Rian wandering about as little as possible, unless there's good reason," I say. "When Comus Day itself arrives, we'll come forward and offer to prove Rian's legitimacy through other means."

Rian looks as if he's about to argue with me, but thinks better of it. "Well, I suppose some time locked up in my rooms will give me the opportunity to work on my project for Magnus and his father."

"You're going to worry about that now?" I criticize.

"Well, dearest, assuming everything works out, the king and queen of Isaaria ought to have an idea or two about how to save their country from potential demon attacks, so yes, I thought I'd get a head start on it," Rian volleys back.

He has a point.

"Our father must have known some of this," Naomi says, frowning.

That idea has clearly been weighing on her for some time. She looks to Taris for confirmation, but Rian is the one who speaks.

"Well, without having perfect recall: yes, he did. He's the one Soleil told to train her as a *Khashtani*. But whether he had his own agenda that deviated from whatever Soleil first told him, I suppose we cannot know."

"It would make things easier if we did," Korvaan mutters, and kicks at the tassels on the carpet.

"But we don't," Taris snaps. "We can't control what did or did not happen in the past. All we can do is move forward with the knowledge of what must still be done."

"We need to make contingencies," I say, hoping to move on from any discussions of Nusk. "I suppose I will do that. As for scheduling—I'll be with Rian every hour of the day, and Qhan will attend public functions with us. Taris and Korvaan, I want both of you at these events as well, but at a distance, and Naomi, you'll stand by. At any other time, you can organize things amongst yourselves, yes?"

"What about this investigation of ours?" Taris says.

"Yes, I need you to help with that. I'll…sort that out. Later. I suppose."

Taris raises an eyebrow in doubt. "Or you could sit down before you pass out and let me manage this."

"I'm not going to pass out," I insist.

"Soleil, you're even whiter than usual," Korvaan says, and for a moment, I feel a hint of his usual teasing.

"Sit down for a minute," Naomi says, moving out of the way so I can take the chair she'd been standing in front of.

Qhan passes her the glass of juice he didn't drink, and Naomi forces that into my hand.

"I am fine," I insist, but take a very long gulp and let Taris take charge.

Thank the Almighty for him. The man is more organized than the rest of us combined. For the next five hours, he forces each of us to explain exactly all we know, and manages to keep track of it all in his head. I can tell Qhan, especially, is impressed.

By late afternoon my *khashak* have organized security in the most efficient way, and Taris has decided that he, Rian, and I will investigate dependent on opportunity. As of right now, we can suspect nearly everyone in the palace. It will be a matter of narrowing that list in the next few days, and ensuring that, when Rian announces himself as the rightful heir on Comus Day, he will not be in danger while doing so.

In addition, we will move all our things from Taris' tiny closet to one of Rian's rooms. Since our crown prince prefers his bedroom, that leaves us with the guest room we're all in, now—which will likely be shared by anyone who needs some sleep—two washrooms, a small study, and a nook of a private dining room, for nights Rian doesn't want to fancy up for a banquet. Plenty of room for the six of us and one sunblood dragon.

We give ourselves a well-deserved rest. Rian insists on introducing Naomi and Korvaan to Mango, and Qhan accompanies them.

I'm about to go along with them, but I hesitate. This room has a balcony, and Taris has sequestered himself on it. Normally I'd leave him—it is not unusual for him to be alone. I'd respect that and give him space, but I still feel guilty after accusing him of being Lune's lover.

I join Taris out on the balcony. The sun is starting to set, though it will be a long while before Isaaria becomes properly dark. I suppose Rian will order dinner for us, we'll move our things in, go over tomorrow's plans, and lastly—to my partial chagrin—take care of the clothing issue. Now that we've all been moved to Rian's entourage, we cannot continue wearing what we have been.

This has been a surreal experience. I suppose everyone else feels similarly. Except while Naomi and Korvaan have been asking questions, trying to wrap their heads around it all, Taris hasn't. He acts as if he has the answers to everything when he doesn't, which makes me wonder what he's thinking.

"Is there something you wanted to tell me?" I ask him.

Taris glares at me. "At this point, I'd have said it if I could, yes?"

I return his look. "I'm not asking because I suspect you're keeping anything from me. But you're entitled to your own opinions. I want to know if you have any theories yet. You're smarter than I am," I add, and I mean it.

Taris considers this, and then bobs his shoulders, agreeing.

"I have suspicions," he admits. "But I don't want to influence your opinion until we have more evidence."

"But if we truly don't have any other options, you'll tell me, won't you?"

Taris makes a low sound. I think that's a yes.

"Did your father tell you any of this?" I have to ask.

"My father did not feel it necessary to share anything with me," Taris says.

"But you suspected him," I guess. "Given…"

"Given how much I hated him?"

"I didn't mean…"

"Don't try to backpedal, Soleil. So, what if I hated my father—I hate most people. I'm a misanthrope. I don't need you to try and fix me," he adds.

"I wasn't planning to," I say. "Sorry if you feel otherwise."

"Mm."

"We're all on edge, now. These past few days have been chaotic," I say.

Taris grunts. I swear, that man will do anything to avoid speaking.

"Thank you for helping," I make myself say.

I forget what else I was going to ask about, and simply stand on the balcony with him for a moment longer. I need to start standing out in the sun more, anyway, and even if my feet aren't touching the earth, this is a good start.

"I'm going to see if...That is, I'm going to join the others in Rian's bedroom. Are you coming?" I offer. "You don't have to."

"Then I won't."

It isn't the answer I wanted, even if I assumed it was the one I'd get.

"Fine," I sigh. "But at least come in when we order up dinner."

"Mmm."

Later, when we're all sitting to dinner on Rian's bedroom floor, Taris slips in to join us. We eat a simple supper today, Isaarian in style: assorted cheeses soft and hard, fresh bread to spread it on, olives, salted and roasted nuts, thinly sliced meats, and wine. Rian has already called Mercer to tell him he'd like some privacy this evening, as he "isn't feeling up to facing the other royals" and conveys he'll see everyone tomorrow for the ball.

We don't all eat at once, but have Korvaan, Qhan, and Taris rotate keeping our perimeter secure. Mango sniffs around at all of us so that we'll feed him bits of meat and bread, and I can tell that he has endeared himself to Naomi quickly. He finally settles on Rian's legs once he's full, but not after padding back and forth around Rian and Naomi both for some time.

It is strange, how simultaneously peaceful and claustrophobic our day and a half in Rian's rooms ended up being. After dinner, Rian called up a slew of seamstresses and tailors with highly specialized flukes to take measurements and determine what uniforms and formal wear my *khashak* and I should dress in. Given how much Rian's paying them, and the fact that they only have to keep quiet for about a day, I'm not worried about rumors. And they'll be busy with their work, in any case. Not much time left for gossip.

The entire process is exhausting, and I must say, if I have to endure many evenings like this one when I'm queen, I might limit the number of social events I attend simply so I don't need a new dress every time.

By the time they've all left, taking their measurements and fabrics and muslins with them, we're exhausted. But Taris confirms he'll happily take the night shift, since he slept well last night.

It is a relief to be alone with Rian again. While I am glad my *khashak* and Qhan are ready to support us, I don't have to worry about letting Rian see me tired, or overwhelmed, or confused. I must constantly stay strong and confident in front of my *khashak,* and I want to impress Qhan.

Rian knows me well enough to understand I can't be that person all the time.

Neither of us has said what we're going to do about sleeping arrangements, but I'm planning on claiming the sofa and letting Rian have the bed to himself. No point in tempting Fate, after all. As if to stake my claim, I throw myself down on said sofa and bend my legs so I'll fit comfortably.

Rian watches me for a few minutes from a chair, with the sort of hesitant silence that tells me there's something he wants to say but can't decide if now is the time to say it.

"What?" I demand after another full minute, sitting up after Mango decides he wants to try and knead my stomach into nest.

"There's the ball tomorrow, you know. And I would like to invite you to join me. Formally. As my…my fiancée."

I stare at him. I knew he was planning to make an announcement that would excuse our proximity, but I didn't think he'd decide upon a public engagement.

Rian starts to turn red.

"Only…because…You know. You see—"

"Yes."

It comes out aggressively, but at least it stops his blathering.

"Oh. Well. Good," he says, and smiles. "Because while you were all being measured for new clothes, I asked one of the seamstresses if she would not mind making something special, for you. For tomorrow. It won't be ready until mid-morning, but, ah…She left me a sketch."

He comes to sit next to me on the couch, unrolling filmy papers from a scroll. I had noticed Rian talking with one of the seamstresses while she sat at his desk, nodding and sketching, but I had been getting a muslin fitted to me, which meant standing exceptionally still in hopes of not getting stuck with a pin. So, I hadn't thought much of it at the time.

The dress on the paper is framed by scribbled notes that give me significant insight into its more interesting properties. It is a gray ballgown, but without too wide of a skirt, and after some reading, I realize what gives the dress volume at all in its lower half is the fact that between its long slits is a secondary skirt that hosts pockets, and can be easily tucked up to let me reach my knives. It can also be transformed quickly for ease of movement, with a sash that unwinds from the waist and tucks up the skirts.

The dress itself is beautiful, but what makes it so special to me is the fact that Rian has thought about what my complaints might be for a regular ball gown and modified it.

"It's perfect," I breathe, so pleased with the dress that I know Rian will be smug about this for weeks to come. I don't mind. He does know me well enough to boast, it seems. "It's so functional," I add.

Rian beams. "I thought you'd like it. And the fabric she's going to use washes well. So, if you get blood on it, somehow, you can still wear it again, if you like."

"I think I will like," I say.

And I lean over, turn his head with my hands, and give him a kiss.

"Thank you."

"If I buy you more 'functional' things, do I get more than a kiss?" Rian suggests mischievously.

I shove him off the couch, but say, "We shall see."

Because, at this point, I'm not sure what I want to have happen between us, and when. So dependent on what other so-called *functional* things Rian has in mind, perhaps I will give him more in the future.

It is not as if we don't all know that it's going to happen, at some point. It is, more than anything else in the world, inevitable.

Sixteen

RIAN AND I are meant to enter together this evening. He has ironically decided that he would like me to be a lady, and has given this evening's herald the instructions to announce, "Crown Prince Rian Yakarami and his fiancée, the Lady Soleil Marson", which means that after tonight, there is no more hiding. Everyone will know Rian's intentions towards me, making any rumors about the fact I've been in his rooms obsolete.

At about a quarter to eight, he decides we're fashionably late enough for an event that began at seven. We dress, me in my charcoal gown with the slits and gold bands, him in his suit of gray and royal red. My hair has, thankfully, decided to be reasonable today, and it falls with a soft curl to it. Rian's is no longer wavy, but stick-straight and adorned with those gold ornaments he likes. It's funny, in a way, but a quick glance of the two of us in a mirror tells me we look good together. I wouldn't have thought that, just a few days ago. I'd have insisted we were too different.

Naomi will be waiting tonight in Rian's rooms while Taris and Korvaan run perimeter. Qhan is well enough to accompany us, and I carry my knives on my legs. I am not expecting trouble, but it's good to be prepared.

When Rian and I enter the ballroom, at least half the room stares at us. I take the opportunity to stare back, and to observe all there is to see about the ballroom along with its occupants. There are two long tables, with white cloths and chairs tied with ribbons, sitting on the far side of the room, where guests can have food brought to them whenever they please. There are some dancers out on the floor, but most everyone stands about; talking, socializing, making quiet alliances and promises.

The eight royal families are in attendance, as well as emissaries from surrounding countries, other Isaarian nobles, and a variety of foreign guests. I did not manage to get my hands on a guest list, but through mere observation, I can tell that many private conversations can easily take place in the middle of this room, and no one will hear a thing over the music and general chatter.

When Rian and I reach the bottom of the steps, Vásan stands there. He is visibly irritated, holding his drink high with his other arm crossed over his chest. I know his brother and mother are around here somewhere, but he has elected to stand alone.

He barely flicks his eyes at us, though his mouth curls as he mutters his congratulations before stalking off. Lune is not in attendance tonight, which means Vásan had to enter alone when he should have been accompanied by his own fiancée. It must feel like a personal insult, having Rian and I make our own announcement tonight when it should have been him and Lune.

Besides Vásan, most folks react to me with curiosity rather than spite. I'll admit, I'm a touch nervous about this evening, but not because I care about all the staring and whispering. They can say whatever they want; I only want to make certain no one too suspicious comes close to Rian. Qhan is here to help, but still.

At least one person here tonight wants the heir of Isaaria dead. At least one person knows that their assassins in the bathhouse failed.

"Eat first, or socialize?" Rian asks me, his arm still linked with mine after our descent from the staircase.

"The latter," I say, disappointing him. "We need to host some conversations. See who we can trust and who we can't."

"Including Vásan, I suppose," he sighs, looking back over his shoulder after the aloof crown prince. "I say we should wait on him for a bit longer. Or else he might think we're mocking him."

"Agreed," I say. "Ideally, we should see to the ambassadors, first."

"I haven't met with the ambassadors often," Rian admits. "Last time I brushed paths with any of them, I think I was only about eighteen or so."

"Do you know all the countries represented tonight?" I ask.

Qhan is the one who answers, from behind us. "The Ishtak Empire, the Floating Islands, Rumshtama, Tourran, Kacha, and Lijimata, my lady, have all sent official ambassadors this evening."

I frown. "But not Milash or Alarkia?"

Those are two rather prominent countries to have snubbed us.

"I don't believe Alarkia's keen to send ambassadors to foreign courts after what happened seven years ago," Qhan admits. "The Lijimi are likely hunting for allies to support their war effort, but the Alarkians have no interest in auxiliary forces. Only money. And we've continued accepting their trades and buying their products. That's enough for them."

Rian sighs.

"I do miss the Alarkians," he laments. "Well, technically Ambassador Erikson and his daughter were the Alarkian ambassadors to Lijimata, but you know how these things function. Ambassadors end up everywhere at one point."

"They're the ones…?"

"Emmelina Voskoss had killed? That would be them."

"I'd forgotten you knew them," I confess, wracking my memory for the archive of such an event.

"Yes, well. It was a long time ago. They were both great fun to have around at parties, though. Tended to make things less…grim."

I don't like seeing him upset, but the Ambassador Erikson's death was seven years ago. Nothing to be done about it now.

I'm about to distract Rian by asking who he thinks we should start talking to when someone pushes their way through the crowd to reach us. I'm concerned until I see who it is, and can understand why he's sought us out.

"Rian Yakarami!" Mercer calls, shaking his head as he approaches. "You are unbelievable, do you know that? Unbelievable."

"Evening, Merse," Rian says. "Sorry about the secrecy, but ah, you know how it is. I was asked not to say anything to anyone until after the opening ceremonies."

A lie, but a kind one. Mercer is unhappy enough as it is to have a best friend keeping so many secrets from him. It would be too difficult to try to explain the real nature of our relationship, or the fact that Rian and I have already married at least a dozen times over again. Our so-called engagement is a formality, for the sake of everyone else. And propriety.

"I believe I specifically asked you about a fiancée, and you specifically denied it."

"Well, I don't know if that's exactly how it went…" Rian says, but Mercer's already moved on.

"First Lune and Vásan and now you! Any more secret engagements? Qhan—you seeing anyone?"

"Ah, no, your majesty," the bodyguard says, trying not to smile.

Mercer scoffs. "Well, thank the Almighty for that."

"Are you going to remember your manners or not?" Rian chides, and Mercer bows to me dramatically, sweeping his red and black coat back.

"My good lady," he says. "A pleasure to meet you. I'm sure Rian's told you at least a little about me, but I am Mercer Ralhan. Crown prince, but that's the least interesting thing about me."

"Soleil Marson," I respond, stretching an arm out to him. "Charmed."

"And where have you been hiding all this time?" he asks before kissing the back of my glove.

"With Rian, in his rooms," I say.

Mercer looks surprised. "Oh. You two have...christened the bed, then?"

I give him a coy smile. "A lady doesn't tell these things."

Mercer laughs. "I like her," he tells Rian.

"I'm glad you approve," I say. "Or we'd have to call off the wedding."

"Oh, a sense of humor on her," Mercer notes. "Any other surprises for me?"

"Only this," I quip, and use the string-pull on my skirts up to show off my knives. In general, it's a good idea not to let the populace know Rian Yakarami's fiancée wears knives under her skirt, but I can trust Mercer not to tell anyone.

"Impressive," Mercer whistles. "I hope your bark is worse than your bite."

"Naturally. Though you should be complimenting Rian. He is the one who picked out the lovely dress."

"Then you are a magnificent sculptor, my friend," Mercer compliments. "With the ability to make stone look soft."

Rian turns red.

"I look forward to seeing you both in white and gold on Comus Day," Mercer says theatrically. It may not sound like it, but it it's the highest compliment he could give me.

"Oh, I don't think we could get married on Comus Day," Rian insists. "For one thing, it wouldn't be appropriate. And for another, Ayla's not here! And we could not possibly have the wedding without her!"

Mercer opens his mouth, then closes it. He has the good sense to look chagrined. I've got it figured, but I guess Rian doesn't, because it takes him a second to even ask.

"What?"

"I may or may not have arranged to bring Ayla here. Tomorrow," Mercer cringes.

Rian stares at him.

"I thought it would be a nice surprise," Mercer goes on hopefully.

When Rian tries to recover his smile, I know he means to spare his best friend's feelings, though Ayla's visit will be anything but timely.

"Yes, that's…You are always so thoughtful, Merse!" Rian insists, and adds a laugh for good measure. "But it is a surprise. I was planning on waiting until after I announced my engagement to present Ayla to the court, but I suppose this will spare everyone the trouble of listening to me twice!"

"So, I suppose we could be married on Comus Day after all," I joke, poking Rian in the side.

Rian laughs, but it's uncomfortable and Mercer, Qhan and I can all tell.

"Don't mind him," I reassure Mercer. "It's only: Ayla has yet to meet me. I've been bothering him about it for ages, and here you've finally forced his hand! I suppose I should be thanking you."

That is enough to break the tension.

"You haven't even introduced your future wife to Ayla?" Mercer accuses.

"It...I had reasons!" Rian insists.

"He wanted to make sure I wasn't a madwoman first," I tease.

"Ah, well, I'm sure you'll both be fine. Just so long as you aren't one of those oddities who insists on not wearing their gloves," Mercer says, and rolls his eyes.

I'm suddenly reminded of that gloveless woman from Mallin's shop.

"What? Oh, no. Soleil wears her gloves all the time. Or...*Most* of the time," Rian says with a devilish grin.

We are a completely normal bride-and-groom to be. We are light-hearted and playful and fun.

"I hope you don't take umbrage with my mother, then, Ralhan," a new voice says. I recognize Magnus even before Rian and I turn to admit him into our circle. Griffith, as always, stands behind him as Qhan stands behind Rian, attentive but polite. The two bodyguards exchange nods.

I can see that Magnus' parents are not far behind, though they've been stopped by a man in a military uniform who wishes to pay his respects. I suppose this means I will be introduced to the king and queen soon.

"She occasionally goes without gloves. So that she may see," Magnus adds. His tone is perfectly polite, but he still manages to sneer that last part.

"As anyone will tell you, Magnus, I'm sure there's nothing the wonderful Queen Clair could do that anyone would take umbrage with," Mercer says, in such a way that even I almost believe he isn't mocking Magnus.

"Mm. And where are your parents, Ralhan? I suppose at least Yakarami's got an excuse, but you've decided to go it alone, haven't you? Even with this, Isaaria's first ever Comus Day?"

"They are with my sisters," Mercer claims with a shrug. "I told them I will never be king; I'm not even going to try. So, they stayed with Cora and Lucille. Cora is having her baby soon, anyway. My cousins' presence will suffice as representation for the Ralhan family."

"And Cora's the unmarried one, is she not?"

Rian interrupts to introduce me. It will be our routine, through the night, and will likely help save us from awkward conversations. It's a rarity, when the royal families are pleasant to one another. I suppose Rian brings it out in them, when he can.

"Ah, Magnus, you haven't met Soleil yet, have you? Soleil Marson. My fiancée," Rian says.

I plaster on a smile. "We're thinking next spring," I say, as if anticipating a question about our wedding date.

Magnus gives me a strange look, as if he recognizes me and can't remember where from. It takes him just long enough to decide what he wants to ask that his parents have arrived in time to witness it.

"You look familiar," Magnus says suspiciously.

I answer before either of his parents can chide him. Better to give him our own explanation, so he won't think to go snooping on his own.

"Forgive me for not introducing myself earlier, crown prince," I say. "Rian wanted to keep our relationship private, so I posed as a maid at the University. You and I may have passed each other on occasion."

"...I suppose so," Magnus admits.

"Oh, your majesties," Rian says, bowing to Magnus' parents and hastily moving the conversation along. "I suppose you have heard, then, and have come to meet the lovely lady herself? Soleil Marson! Soon to be Yakarami," he announces even as the king is answering.

Rian's probably the only person in the world who could get away with talking over the top of the king.

"Pleasure and honor to meet you, your majesties," I say with a curtsey.

"The pleasure is ours. Marson, hmm? Your father is western-Isaarian, then?" the king guesses. The "son" ending to my last name does seem to imply that.

"It's Marson-Qurvo, really," I decide. "I was adopted. My older brother Taris, actually, is one of Rian's guards. That's how we first met."

And so, our counterfeit history continues to unfold.

The king looks surprised, but politely interested. "Qurvo?"

"My adopted father was originally from Milash," I explain. "Khas Qurvo. He worked for the royal family there, for some time—that might be why you know the name. Taris is half-Isaarian, then."

Not that he'd be caught dead admitting it.

The king makes a sound of polite interest and the queen smiles. "Remind me to invite you somewhere for something at some point," the king proposes, as vaguely as he can to leave things entirely up to me. "I think a chat with you would be very interesting, Lady Marson."

"You'll have to wait in line, your majesty," Mercer jokes. "I've already got the happy couple booked."

"…Mercer," the king greets, and the queen's smile grows more genuine when she looks at him. "Hiding behind Crown Prince Rian again, I see," he adds.

It's more of a symbolic statement than a literal one.

The queen turns her face up and whispers something to her husband. The rest of us wait politely. I never did hear all the details on Queen Clair's accident about twenty-five years ago, but it nearly ruined her voice. And her blindness has been since birth. What's most interesting, though, is that she did not have a fluke at birth. She acquired one when she first lost her voice.

If she'd been born sighted and then lost it and gained a fluke, it would make more sense to me. Instead, her situation is one of the official miracles claimed by the grotto in the mountains, along with the fact that she recovered any of her voice at all. The details of what happened were kept very quiet. Officially, they announced it was a virus. But I don't think anyone believes that.

"…Marques…" the king suddenly says loudly, almost chidingly. "I know you're there. You can hide from just about anyone else, but not from my wife."

A man appears right behind Mercer, frightening me so much that my hand is halfway to drawing a knife before Rian catches it. It takes me a moment to realize that I would not have stopped myself, and that would have earned us a ridiculous line of intense questions.

Mercer grins and laughs. The tall, dark, broad, imposing bearded man behind him does not.

"Well spotted, your majesty," Mercer says with a playful bow to the queen. "Well done, indeed. You are the first person in ten years to pick out Marques when he doesn't want to be seen. Guess we'll have to start from scratch, now, eh?" he adds to Marques.

Marques does not look at all amused.

Rian is gripping my hand so hard it hurts.

Magnus is smirking on his gracious mother's behalf; he's proud of her.

Griffith and Qhan are irritated, and I am, too, because Mercer's bodyguard has a decent fluke for a bodyguard, but an incredible one for an assassin. And, given our occupations, Griffith, Qhan and I are used to knowing who is close to our principals at all times.

"Marques! I thought you'd died," Rian laughs, as if this is a game. "I suppose I should have known better. Someone's got to look after Merse on all his trips."

Marques leans into the obligatory bow, stiff as can be. "Your majesties," he says for everyone that applies to. Then he straightens and adds in his deep voice: "Khaleem. Reach…Lady Soleil."

A smile is a lady's defense. I remember hearing Lune tell Asmer that, once, back at the University. Despite everything else I don't like about her, Lune was right about that.

"It's no offense meant," Mercer's saying to all of us. "Marques prefers to stay unseen. And he's gotten good at it, after so many years of practice. It helps, you know, when I'm treating children abroad. They're usually petrified of him, but Marques won't leave me alone, so..."

He shrugs.

"And no offense taken," the king reassures. "Though I thank you for indulging our little fun. It's not often Clair gets to use her fluke for non-practical purposes."

"Then Marques and I are glad to be of service," Mercer says.

"Guess we'll have to work on an act for next time," Rian says to me, and gives my hand once last squeeze before letting go.

My nerves have settled. It's not Marques' fault, but I've become paranoid. I'm starting to wonder if it's only a matter of time before someone darts out of the crowd and tries to stab Rian in the gut.

I had not even considered someone having an invisibility fluke.

My watch vibrates against my wrist: it's Taris, telling me he saw that, and he and Korvaan will be on alert from now on. Not for anything involving Marques, but for other invisible threats. It would be just our luck for someone else with a similar fluke to be hanging about tonight.

There's a visible parting in the crowd to our left to admit Nissa Sondushki, who no one wants to be around tonight. The only crown princess of Isaaria is already an oddity, with her half-Hoitsokin heritage and tendency to wear revealing outfits—a habit she has not broken for the sake of this evening's dress code, I see, though she has bothered with something of a skirt, even if it's slit up past her hips on either side so that she is visibly not wearing anything underneath. Her hair, then, is worn loose and almost raggedly. She has bothered with jewelry, but it is all made out of gleaming, polished bones and beads. And she looks absolutely furious that her hyena was not allowed to attend the festivities.

She is creating even more of a stir than Rian and I are, or Vásan and Lune, which at least explains why I don't feel trapped under a spotlight. As hasty as my engagement to Rian is, it's not the most scandalous thing happening tonight.

"Crown princess—won't you join us?" the king calls pleasantly. "Come meet Prince Rian's fiancée."

I catch Nissa's grimace when she looks at Rian and me, but she masters her expression and comes to join us. Even she won't refuse the king, tenuous though his position is.

Unlike most, she doesn't bother dripping her tone in honey before she greets the king and queen. She's practical about it, but we all know she's acting out of obligation, not respect.

The king just barely manages to introduce me before someone else is already approaching him and the queen for a few minutes of their time. That leaves me and Rian with Mercer, Magnus, and Nissa. An interesting combination, to be sure.

Nissa observes me patently, and I maintain a cool expression while I let her. I don't care if she wants to compare the two of us, as long as she realizes I am not some pretty thing to hang on a prince's arm.

"Congratulations on finding yourself a bride," Nissa finally tells Rian.

"Ah. Thank. You?" Rian says.

"I'm sure she'll make a lovely Grand Princess," Nissa adds.

It is one thing to insinuate Rian is unlikely to be king, as others have. It's another to say so publicly, where anyone could overhear, and in front of two other crown princes themselves. If I was ever in doubt before, Nissa's now saying it loud and clear: she has every intention of making sure she's the one with the crown on her head come Comus Day. Even if she knows damn well she has no business being queen.

"And I'm sure you will as well," I say before anyone can stop me.

I hear Mercer mutter something about a catfight, though I'm sure only Marques, Qhan and I hear. I suppose I'm good for some entertainment after all.

Nissa turns her gaze on the other two princes and considers them.

"No," she finally says, pointing at Mercer, then Magnus. "Maybe. If you find someone as petty as you."

"Excuse me?" Magnus demands.

"He is never getting married," Nissa says, pointing again at Mercer. "The man doesn't want to be tied down. You, meanwhile, I suppose could. But again: she'd have to be petty."

Next to me, Rian is trying very hard not to laugh.

"Is this your way of nominating yourself, Nissa?" Mercer offers.

Magnus snorts. "I'd take Lune over you, and that's saying something."

Nissa considers responding with yet another insult, but I suppose she's impressed enough with the princes' quick retorts, because she doesn't bother.

"I suppose you're all enjoying the attention?" she sighs, waving a hand at everything around us.

"It's quite new to me," I deflect.

"I'm enjoying showing off Soleil," Rian confesses.

Mercer shrugs. "Not particularly."

"I definitely am," Magnus half-mutters.

He's looking off to the right, far above all our heads, to where Raj al'Yibna is trying to motion him over.

"Excuse me," he says without looking at any of us, then straightens his jacket and disappears into the crowd.

Griffith hesitates, bows to all of us, and then follows.

I don't dare look at Rian, but make a show of clearing my throat, so he takes note as well. I told him all I suspected, so he knows now that Grand Prince Carsans spoke to Raj al'Yibna in secret at some point, yesterday. And now Raj wants to speak to Magnus. Interesting.

It could be nothing. But I doubt it.

A glass of watered-down wine is being offered to me: Marques, who heard my coughing and, I suppose, misinterpreted. I thank him with another gracious smile.

"I thought you were dead," Nissa says as she raises an eyebrow at Marques.

"Not even remotely, your majesty," Marques says.

"Queen Clair exposed him," Mercer confesses. "And he'd best not disappear for the rest of the night, in case the king makes a show of his wife doing it again. Not that, you know, I'd mind, but…it does rather defeat the purpose of having an invisible bodyguard."

I half-expect Nissa to say something mildly rude again. Maybe about how Mercer isn't important enough to be worrying about assassins. Or how she's sure Marques has his work cut out for him given the rotating door in and out of Mercer's bedroom. But instead, she frowns, and narrows her eyes.

"It was when Lune Carsans was born, you know," she says.

"I'm sorry?" Mercer says.

"What?" I manage.

"The night the queen had her 'accident'. That was the night Lune was born," Nissa repeats. "She's a witch, with that voice of hers. She steals flukes."

"What?" I say again, confused. "I thought…Lune's not a Carsans by birth; they adopted her. I didn't think anyone knows who her parents were."

Nissa shrugs. "Her mother was a guest, here. Years and years ago. Everyone in the south knows it. The Hoitsokin helped bring the lady here, in secret. I was young, but my half-brother remembers. Lune's mother had her, saw what a monster she was, and left her here. That's why the Carsans are so wary of their own daughter. They adopted her, not out of the kindness of their hearts, but because they thought she'd be useful. In fact, the Hoitsokin were the first people to call her a siren, back when she first started singing in public. And do you know what sirens do to people?"

I don't say anything. Neither does Rian or Mercer.

Nissa gives me a disturbing smile. "They drown them."

I swear, her eyes flash when she says that. And I can't help but notice how incredibly pointed her incisors are. Like she's sharpened them.

Rian clears his throat. "What a lovely rumor, Nissa. Very mature, spreading that one around."

"Oh, it's not a rumor. Hopefully those of you who enjoy the Lady Carsans' company will figure that out before it's too late. Don't worry: I'll avenge you. I look forward to it…Have a good evening," she says as scornfully as possible, and then heads off into the crowd, which parts for her accordingly.

"Ugh. She gives me the creeps," Mercer admits with a shudder.

"Oh, don't be mean, Merse," Rian chides. "She's different; she can't help that. The Hoitsokin have a unique culture. A different way of thinking."

"So do the Kachin and the Milash, but they don't give me looks like they want to mount my head on a wall," Mercer says. "I mean, your Lady Soleil here is undoubtedly a capable woman, but even she can manage a few hours in a ballroom without giving out veiled death threats."

"You're too kind," I drawl, and he tips an invisible hat to me. "Did the, ah, Lady Carsans do something to make the crown princess angry?" I add, only half-pretending to be naïve about this.

Mercer rolls his eyes. "Oh, who knows. If she did, I doubt it was even Lune's fault. Though, speaking of, has anyone seen her lately? I wanted to talk to the poor girl. About…well, Rian, did you tell your fiancée about—"

"To your right, your majesties," Marques leans down to tell us.

It's unfortunate timing, since I was hoping to hear more of Mercer's opinion of what's happening with Lune. But when we look to where Marques has directed, I realize, with some relief, that we aren't about to be treated to another pointless exchange of insults between royals, because the impressive-looking man striding towards us is obviously Tourrannese. One of the ambassadors. An ambassador coming to speak with the two least likely heirs to become king.

Interesting. Though exhausting. I'd wanted to hold a conversation between myself, Rian, Mercer, and their bodyguards, after all. How hard can that be?

"Crown princes!" the Tourrannese ambassador announces as he sees us noticing him.

"Does this ever end?" I ask Rian through a plastered smile.

"Unfortunately, not, Lady Soleil," Qhan says sympathetically from behind us.

It's only when the ambassador draws near that I realize someone is following him. Someone smaller than him, and slighter. Not that this means much; the ambassador is incredibly tall for any man, regardless of race, and could pass for his own bodyguard. His beard is neat, black, and barely longer than a carefully groomed goatee. His garments are of modified and modernized Tourrannese cultural significance, and his jewelry, I'm sure, would tell me exactly how high he ranks in the Tourrannese royal family, were I knowledgeable on such matters.

It's then I remember that he is not just the ambassador for Tourran, but Kacha, also. A joint goodwill ambassador. Lord Aiko Renki, I recall, and more of Nusk's helpful teachings come back to me the longer I think on it.

"Lord Ambassador Aiko," Mercer greets. "How good to see you again. It's been a long time, hasn't it? Are you here to meet the lovely Lady Soleil, or have you sought myself and Crown Prince Rian out for other reasons?"

He's good with cutting through niceties without appearing rude. I must ask him later to help teach me the trick of it.

"I wanted to congratulate you both, as Comus Day approaches. You and all the crown princes," Aiko says, bowing to Rian and Mercer. "Though it is a pleasure to meet the Lady Soleil as well. I'm sure Isaaria is relieved to know the Yakarami family will not disappear from the eight."

He genuinely means that; it's not an insult. I appreciate that, though I still don't know enough about Aiko to understand what his angle is.

"I also wanted to take the opportunity to introduce my youngest son," Aiko goes on. "Shinya will be appointed as ambassador to Isaaria in a few years' time. Our representative, here. To foster goodwill between nations."

He gestures, and the figure hiding behind him is forced into the spotlight. The boy hesitates, and then hastens into a bow.

"Your majesties," he addresses the two crown princes as so many others have.

Aiko Shinya is a handsome young man, about seventeen or so. He is a little taller than medium height, with a slim though well-muscled build, and a fair complexion, likely from keeping out of the sun. Despite his mixed Tourrannese and Kachin heritage, his eyes are a startling cornflower blue. A genetic fluke: sometimes they happen naturally, but they are also more prevalent in highly magical families. Shinya's blue eyes aren't that surprising, considering who his mother is. And I, like many, have heard about his cousin Princess Mi-Sun's red hair.

He catches me noticing his eyes and flicks his gaze down for a moment to shield them under his long eyelashes, as if embarrassed. But his father has taught him well, and he handles the situation with careful diplomacy.

"A rare genetic expression brought on by magic," Aiko Shinya says, almost as if he's apologizing for not looking quite as we expected. "Blue eyes are unnatural in Tourran, but I assure you, I am my parents' son."

"Oh, I'm sure no one doubts that," Rian insists, smiling. I know he can tell as well that Aiko's son is nervous around us.

"Your Alarkian is very good," I note.

Most people in the world rely on Alarkian as their common tongue; it's the language of business and politics, and most Isaarian children learn it from birth along with our own mother tongue. But the Tourrannese take learning Alarkian to an entirely different extreme. It is a great compliment, then, for one's skills to be remarked upon.

"Thank you, Lady Soleil," the boy mumbles.

His father smacks his shoulder in irritation and Shinya repeats himself, louder and more clearly, before adding on:

"I am glad for the opportunity to practice it in such a place as the Pyrian Palace, and with such...important people."

This sounds like something he'd been told to script in advance, and he forgot the last bit. His improvisation in a second language is still impressive, but I can tell his father is unhappy. I think Shinya is meant to be a model of perfection; he has to be, to justify the fact that his birth made his mother grow sick and die.

At this point, Mercer and I know what's happened: Ambassador Aiko came here to make serious alliances with some of the royal families before Comus Day. And his son is, to be blunt, holding him back from such secret meetings.

He's here because Mercer and Rian are the least likely princes to be named king. He needs a Fate's-damned minder for his son.

I like him less, now, than I did at first.

Mercer, after another moment, hastens this awkward exchange along.

"Lord ambassador, if you would indulge me, might I trouble you for some of your time? You can leave the boy here; I'm sure he'll be excellent company for Crown Prince Rian and his lady," Mercer suggests, and I know he's doing this out of kindness. For poor Aiko Shinya's sake.

Perhaps he might be more inclined to enjoy himself if his father is not breathing down his neck. Not that Rian and I will get much out of his company, but still. If I have to drag the boy around for the rest of the evening, worse things have happened.

Mercer gives me a wink before escorting the lord ambassador off, probably intending to lose him in another five minutes or so. Marques follows, and poor Shinya watches the three leave, absolutely horrified to be discarded.

"Is this your first time in Isaaria?" Rian asks the boy politely. "I remember meeting your father, once, but I don't recall you accompanying him. And, well, I think I would have remembered."

"Oh, ah…No, I…I've been to Isaaria before…sir," Shinya says, struggling to discern if he should be looking at Rian or me. "When I was young. Six. But you weren't here. And then my father and I were…at Lijimata. For…some time."

He's reddening and looks at the ground again.

"Please don't tell me you're bashful on my account," Rian says. "I promise you, I am the least impressive of the heirs you might encounter tonight."

"Oh, not for us, sir," Shinya insists, looking up again. "In the east, you…are very highly regarded."

I almost snort at that, given what just happened, but Shinya's only seventeen. He might be speaking for the youth, not his father's generation.

"Really?" Rian says.

Shinya nods.

"Many people in Kacha named their male children after you. Because of things they've heard, and liked. One of my cousin's good friends is named 'Riyong', after you," he says.

That doesn't surprise me; teaching is very highly regarded in the east, and Rian seriously humbled himself to become a teacher of children. The Kachin, especially, would appreciate something like that.

Rian tries not to smile as widely as usual. "Is he? And which cousin is that?"

"Chimhwi. The younger one. You should meet him, and Bogun and Mi-Sun. I think they'd be most honored to meet a Crown Prince of Isaaria."

I don't know much about the royals in Kacha, except that they are the Aikos' cousins, the princess has startling red hair, and one of the princes is a bastard son with a Western mother, but I can't remember which. Chimhwi, I think.

Rian, meanwhile, can't help but laugh at Shinya's reverence. "Your cousins are all royals themselves, Shinya," he reminds the boy. "I doubt they're truly all that interested in meeting one of the eight potential heirs of Isaaria."

"But you're the Laughing Prince," Shinya points out. "The one who tells stories, and keeps a pet sunblood dragon, and researches Magicsmiths and all sorts of mystical things. Your Magicsmith thesis, it…could change the world if it's correct."

"The dragon is all thanks to Crown Prince Mercer," Rian admits. "But I do appreciate your enthusiasm, young man," he says. "I suppose I did not realize I was regarded so highly, in the East."

"…Perhaps not all over," Shinya confesses. "But…you are Tourrannese and Kachin. Like me."

Ah, so that was it. Poor boy.

"Well, and Isaarian," Rian says thoughtfully. "But yes, we definitely share a similar heritage, at least in that way. You know, since you'll be here for a while, anyway, you'll likely get the chance to meet Mango. It's a shame I couldn't bring him tonight..."

An anxious-looking servant is hovering nearby, trying to get Rian's attention without interrupting. Qhan finally has to point out the poor fellow.

"Sir, Crown Prince Magnus is asking for you," the messenger says.

Rian and I exchange looks. I nod.

We'll have to split up, for now. Yes, I'm paranoid, and yes, Marques scared me, but Rian will be with Qhan, with Taris and Korvaan watching. I trust them to look after the prince. Especially at a time like this, when we have an opportunity to learn what Raj al'Yibna's been whispering about.

"Then we shouldn't keep him, should we?" Rian says cheerfully. "Young Lord Aiko, you'll have to excuse me; I'm being summoned. But if you wouldn't mind keeping my future wife entertained, I would greatly appreciate it."

Shinya gives himself only a second to appear startled. "I would...it...Yes, I will do so for you, sir," he manages.

I think most times he plans out what he wants to say in his head beforehand, and sometimes he mixes different options for conveying it in Alarkian. But I meant what I said when I complimented him; Shinya must have studied his second language for a long time to be this fluent. I don't have to slow down my speech to accommodate him, and that's impressive all on its own.

"Don't be long," I tell Rian. Perfectly pleasant and casual, of course, but he knows the double meaning behind that.

"I'll come find you when Magnus is done with me," he says with a friendly, joking eye-roll.

He and Qhan part ways from Shinya and me. It takes me several awkward seconds to think of an acceptable topic of conversation for myself and Lord Aiko's son, during which time Shinya accidentally accepts three aperitifs and a drink he clearly has no idea what to do with.

"Well. I suppose I should offer you some kind of entertainment, shouldn't I?" I say as Shinya inches closer to a table to put down the cutlery he's juggling.

"I, ah. That's not necessary, Lady Soleil," he says awkwardly.

"Nonsense," I insist, curious to hear more of his thoughts. "Some chit-chat will pass the time. Ah, I know: tell me, who do you think will be the next ruler of this country?"

At first, Shinya tries to construct a polite way to avoid answering, but after a moment he gives in. He wants to give his opinion, and at least part of him is happy I've asked him. I doubt anyone else will.

I watch Shinya look around at all his options: Mercer, Rian, Nissa, Vásan, Magnus, Detrus, Yuugo.

"I don't know," he says carefully.

"Make an educated guess," I drawl.

Shinya frowns, and lets his eyes rove all around the room again.

"…Crown Prince Rian," he finally says, sounding almost a little surprised with himself, as if even he didn't think he'd come to that conclusion.

"That is not what your father thinks," I guess.

Shinya considers this. "Father's a good ambassador," he says carefully. "But he is not the best judge of character. Or, hmm…Not that. Exactly. Sometimes… he sees people, or does not see them, the way they could be. In potential."

He's struggling to explain in Alarkian, but I get the point.

"Well, we all have things we are good at, and things that seem to elude us even at the best of times," I say.

I'm thinking in particular of how I wish I was better at diplomacy than violence, but we can't have everything. Rian's apparently not good at solving mysteries, but I'm not going to hold that against him. Yet. When it's the eve of Comus Day, if we're still blundering about in the dark, then we'll talk.

"I suppose I'm good at black-ink painting and listening," Shinya's saying thoughtfully, "and Father's better at things with money, and talking."

"See? There you are," I say, trying not to sound absent, though I've allowed myself to become distracted.

Rian and Qhan are already returning, with Crispin and Soren Carsans close by Rian's side. Soren is in his chair tonight, pushed by Kaoli, but he is dressed to match his brother in garb befitting a young prince.

Interesting: Rian was sent to see Magnus, and he returns with Crispin and Soren. I suppose Rian will have to tell me what Magnus wanted at a later time, privately. Besides, we are meant to be mingling with as many people as we can, this evening. We were bound to get to the Carsans some time or another.

"Ah—Crispin and Soren, Soleil; Soleil, Crispin and Soren Carsans," Rian introduces casually when they reach us. "Oh, and Crispin: Lord Ambassador Aiko's son Shinya."

Crispin gives the boy a nod. "We've met."

"Oh? All the better," Rian claims.

Soren has been chattering his own personal introduction at me, and I have no idea what to do in response because I was listening to his brother and Rian.

"Soleil's certainly enjoying herself, are you not, Soleil?" Rian says, saving me.

I force another smile, though I'm afraid it's starting to become a grimace.

"Of course."

"Well, that's good," Soren says, as if it's his responsibility to check up on all the guests. He then peers at me with a frown, almost as if inspecting me for something.

"...Mother said you're getting married to hide the fact you're having a baby, but it doesn't look like you're having one to me," he finally says.

Qhan snorts. Shinya flushes, as if embarrassed to even think about such a thing happening between me and Rian. Rian himself looks aghast, but it's all I can do not to burst out laughing.

"Soren!" Crispin says, supposedly aghast, but he's not as careful as usual. He is not entirely convincing.

"There's no baby," I say. "Rian and I are getting married fast because we're tired of waiting. If having the wedding next spring is considered 'fast'. Though we do hope to have children. At some point."

"Oh," Soren says, sounding a little disappointed. "Well. I thought it would be nice not to be the youngest anymore."

"Crown Prince Detrus has children," I point out.

Rian is still trying to recover himself.

"That doesn't count," Soren sighs. "Because I don't know the Lundans all that well. But Crispin and Rian are friends. So, I'd see you a lot more."

I resist the urge to look at Crispin's and Rian's faces when he says that. A few days ago, they both would have considered themselves good friends. But I've told Rian to be suspicious of everybody. And I know Crispin's family is up to something.

An idea strikes me. Something that might work perfectly as a contingency plan, but I can't bring it up now. And there is still time, yet, to neutralize all threats before Comus Day. So, I store the thought away, for now, and try to re-engage in the present.

"It gets *boring* around here," Soren continues complaining. "There's *no one* my age."

"Well, Rian and I plan to adopt a girl just a few years younger than you," I tell him. "Maybe you can become friends."

"Really?" Soren says, brightening, and looks up at his brother. "Do you think that would be okay with Mother and Father? ...Crispin?" he adds, when it's clear his brother isn't paying attention.

"Sorry, Soren. Not right now...I'm starting to get nervous," Crispin admits to Rian. "Lune is still not down yet. She's supposed to be here."

"To announce their engagement?" Rian poses innocently.

"For several reasons," Crispin says.

"Would Vásan be angry with Lune, do you think?" I'm asking Soren as well, not about to dismiss him as quickly as Crispin does. "For not being here?"

Soren frowns. "I don't know. Probably not. He's nice to her."

"Well. When your sister does arrive, you'll have to find me and introduce us," I suggest. "You want a new friend in Ayla, but I need some friends for myself, too. I'm still very new to all this, you know."

Soren smiles, agreeing.

"And I'm sure the Lady Lune would like to meet you as well," I add, trying to pull Shinya back into the conversation some.

He slows his eating. "…I already know Lady Lune," he admits. "She was in Lijimata seven years ago. To…sing. For a celebration of theirs, shortly before the war started. I happened to be arriving with my father as she was leaving, and we were introduced."

I watch his eyes track someone across the room as he speaks to me. I follow to see who he's watching and have to stand to get a better look. It's not Lune, as I was hoping, but a well-dressed Lijimi man, followed by a boy with similar features. They wear long coats, open in the front, with bangled shoulder pads and buttons. Lijimi wear sashes not unlike Isaarian fashion, but theirs are worn around the waist, tied to one side, while ours are worn from shoulder to hip. The Lijimi ambassador, obviously. He looks as if he's actively avoiding us.

"Elias Voskoss," Rian says to me when he notices where I'm looking. "And the kid's his son, Hector."

"Those names mean nothing to me," I hiss back, irritated.

Luckily for both of us, Mercer has reappeared just over my shoulder with an appetizer, and notices my confusion. "Voskoss? He's a prince. Queen Emmelina's uncle. He had two sons, Javier and Hector. Javier was the older one. Got assassinated a few months ago. I think the three of them and Emmelina's half-sister Falisia are the only members of the royal family left."

"And why are they important to us?" I ask.

Mercer shrugs. "Emmelina recently appointed her uncle as ambassador of foreign affairs. The fact that he's here suggests the Lijimi are about to pander to whoever's named king—see if they can get us to help them in the war."

"And what do you think of him? Voskoss?" I ask him.

"Barely know him," Mercer claims. "I've met him…twice, I think?"

"That's very helpful, Merse," Rian drawls.

"And yet, still far better than anything you could offer," he points out.

"Elias Voskoss isn't the sort of man you trust unless you have to," Crispin informs the rest of us. "And that's not an opinion—he likes people to know that."

"Not a very good trait for an ambassador," Rian notes.

"Which tells us he wouldn't be Emmelina's first pick for ambassador if she had a choice," I say.

"He's very smart but pretends like he isn't," I hear Shinya murmur next to me, startling me a little.

I knew he was still here, of course, but he'd gotten so quiet.

"I was there, remember? I told you," he says when I turn to look at him. "I visited Lijimata with my father for years. Before the war."

"But that...You must have been only ten!"

He shrugs. "I said I was young, not stupid."

"Where in the world did you put Lord Ambassador Aiko?" Rian's asking Mercer.

There are too many of us in the group, now, and we're splitting into smaller conversations.

"I lost him to the Lundans—if one can call that losing," Mercer says. "No offense, kid," he adds to Shinya.

Shinya shrugs again.

I have a good feeling about the boy. There's something that tells me I can trust him, young though he is, and the way that Rian acts so casually around Shinya tells me he may have a vague memory of him being useful to us in times past. His father, I'm wary of. But Shinya has a good heart. I can tell.

"It's getting late, and Mother and Father told me not to let you stay up much past your bedtime," Crispin is telling his younger brother, holding his ground against Soren's pouting, "Aw…".

"Five more minutes?" the boy begs, shamelessly widening his eyes.

"Nice try. Go with Kaoli," Crispin says. "She'll get you into bed, and I'll make sure to see you first thing tomorrow morning."

"Did my father want me to join him?" Shinya is asking Mercer.

"Sorry, kid, he didn't mention it."

"You're welcome to stay with us, if you don't mind," Rian offers.

Shinya considers this, and nods. Soren bids his proper farewells to each of us, including Marques, before letting Kaoli take him out of the room. It's grown far later than I thought. Rian and I did decide to arrive a little tardy, after all. I wonder what the Carsans will do if Lune never shows tonight. I doubt Vásan will break off the engagement, but what will they all do if Lune simply refuses to cooperate?

And does it make me a bad person that I want to see that happen?

"Your father is an interesting man, Lord Shinya," Mercer says, trying to strike up a conversation with the young man. "He speaks plenty, but says little. It is an art."

"He is a very good ambassador," Shinya claims.

Implying that he thinks he is not. Interesting pathology, that boy.

"You'll get there, one day. And no one here is going to purposely sabotage you," Mercer promises. "We happen to quite like our connections with the east, don't we, Rian?"

"We do? I mean, yes, we *do,* naturally," he says with a nervous laugh for Shinya's benefit. "I just didn't think you'd care that much, Merse."

"To be perfectly honest," Mercer says, coming closer to all of us. "I'd like to do more traveling in the east next year, which would be easier if our countries were friendly with each other."

"I'll drink to that," I say, and snatch two glasses off a tray for Rian and myself. The last thing I need right now is Isaaria going to war on top of everything else.

"Oh, as a matter of fact: I gave your father something for you, kid. Just a small token from the Isaarian crown princes to Tourran. A sign of goodwill," Mercer says. He grins at Rian and winks. "See? Look how proper and princely I am."

"Yes, I'm very proud," Rian says dryly.

"I'm…not accustomed to receiving gifts," Shinya admits.

"You're not," Mercer claims. "You're receiving it on behalf of your country, from the Isaarian crown princes—as I am presenting it on the behalf of Isaaria. You see? …Besides, your father is the one I gave it to, directly. You're just the one I think it would suit best. You are going to be our ambassador, after all."

"Then thank you, Crown Prince Mercer," Shinya says, and bows. "I am sure I would be glad to act as a symbol of goodwill between our nations."

"Are you accustomed to being used as a symbol, Lord Aiko?" Crispin asks, an oddly insensitive question.

I force a nervous laugh. "I'm sorry—I must not be intelligent enough for this conversation. What is all this about symbols and ambassadors?"

"I only want to see if Lord Shinya intends to act as a proper ambassador between our countries, in the future, or if he'll do nothing but stand by and allow things to progress as they will," Crispin says.

"So why not just ask him outright?" I say before Shinya can open his mouth.

Crispin gives me a vague smile. Mercer, Shinya, Qhan, Marques and Rian are mainly an audience, now.

"Because politics are all about showmanship, Lady Soleil. It's something that comes with the territory. I hardly think of myself as particularly intelligent," he says with a laugh, "but I know many others in our circles do. I merely hope to help our ambassador-in-training prepare for Isaarian politics. We tend to be much less straightforward than those in Tourran."

"I am certain my father appreciates that, sir," Shinya says. "And I am glad to hear from all of you that you hope for nothing but healthy relations between your country and those I represent. It is a relieving acknowledgement."

He bows to all of us.

"Tonight has been very educational for a youth such as myself, I am sure."

I resist the temptation to cackle. There is nothing obvious to indicate that Shinya is speaking disrespectfully, but I can still tell he is not entirely as shy and demure as I first imagined.

"Educational for myself as well, I sup—" I start.

A loud commotion behind us interrupts me, and we all turn to see what's happening as partygoers scatter from around the drinks table, our bantering forgotten.

It's Lune, and she's a mess. She is less than decent in her nightclothes and dressing gown. Her hair isn't brushed, and she has not attempted to make up her face after crying. It looks as if she cut herself breaking that glass in her bathroom and has sloppily wrapped several of her fingers up, though the blood soaks through the cloth to smear across a bottle she's grabbed. Lune does not appear to notice this, and immediately starts to drink.

"Excuse me," Crispin says hastily, and is gone before Rian can ask what he might do to help.

Mercer sighs. "Oh, Lune..."

I glance around and quickly find Grand Prince and Princess Carsans. I'm too far away to see their expressions, but I'm sure they're less than pleased. All eyes are on Lune tonight, but for all the wrong reasons. Even if everyone had moved past Lune's outburst earlier, they're not going to forget this any time soon.

I'd like to look around for more reactions, but the next thing I know, Rian has grabbed my hand and is pulling me through the crowd closer to Lune. We lose Mercer at some point. Qhan sticks by us dutifully, and Shinya, I think, is still back near the dining table.

If he thought the conversation this evening was entertaining, he's in for a surprise. Crispin was right: Isaaria is very different than Tourran. Something like this would never happen, there.

Rian almost strides right up to Lune, but I twist free of his grip and grab his shirt to yank him back. I know he means well, but sometimes Rian means too well. He had already forgotten that there is a possibility Lune could hurt him. He tries to give me a questioning look, but Qhan agrees with my assessment and comes to assist. Rian is not to come close to Lune with her in this state.

"What's wrong?" Lune laughs, noticing the wide berth she's been given. "You've never seen a lady's legs before?"

"You ought to be ashamed of yourself," someone says.

Detrus' mother, I think.

Lune calls her a particularly rude word in old Isaarian that sends people into appalled titters.

"Lune, why don't you go back upstairs? You're not dressed properly for this sort of function," Crispin mutters as he reaches to try and coax the liquor away from her. "Lune? Come along. You need to—"

"Don't tell me what to do," Lune hisses, snatching the bottle back.

Crispin searches the crowd for his parents, but they are not going to be much help; they're likely finding the king and queen and apologizing profusely. But it's curious that one of the Carsans' bodyguards hadn't made an appearance to try and control Lune.

"Lune, put the knife down," Vásan says.

I look back and notice that Lune has been casually holding a knife in her hand while she drinks from her bottle with the other. Vásan, who was lurking near the back of the crowd a second ago, has now pushed his way to the front.

"Oh, you especially don't get to tell me what to do," Lune snaps at him.

Crispin gives the other crown prince a warning look, and Vásan wisely backs away. I can already see several bodyguards trying to evacuate their principals, given the circumstances, but Rian refuses to leave.

Lune puts her emptied bottle down clumsily, smashing several pieces of glassware in the process. Crispin takes the opportunity to grab for her, but she brushes him off with surprising strength and even takes a swipe at him with her knife.

"Don't interrupt me, I'm performing," she snarls with a disturbing amount of clarity. "Isn't that what you all wanted?"

She finds another open bottle, then, and starts drinking that as well.

She's still brandishing that knife of hers, but in a way that tells me she has spent a lot of time getting comfortable with the weapon. People continue to give her a wide berth as she moves, almost dancing around the room. Crispin keeps his distance, though I can tell he's just waiting for the opportunity to try and grab her again.

"Is this disruptive enough for you?" Lune hollers at the ceiling. This is all a mockery on her own behalf, but ours as well. "Have I done enough?!"

"Lune? Who are you talking to?"

"All of you!" She bellows so loud that it echoes. "All of you fools!"

Qhan and I make eye contact. I want him to get Rian out of here and take him back upstairs, but Rian still refuses to leave.

Lune has continued her drunken waltz, and is stumble-stepping her way towards a large open window.

"Look at all of you!" she crows, spinning in a circle. "Look at all you pretty, petty, lying pawns. Prancing around and preening at each other as if any of this means anything!"

"Lune, that's enough," Crispin says, trying to get closer to her.

She climbs up on the window ledge, giggling, and looks down at the ground far below. "This is all so-o-o pointless…"

"Lune, that's enough," Crispin says again, this time more forcefully.

When he steps forward again, she throws her bottle at his head with startling accuracy given her mental state. It clips his forehead, and he starts to bleed.

Lune turns around and steps backwards on the ledge. The crowd gives her exactly the reaction she wants. They are horrified, but also on the edge of their seats. I'm sure this does not feel real to them.

Lune laughs again. "None of you mean anything; none of this means anything!"

She almost tumbles out the window, and several people lunge as if they're considering trying to stop her, but Lune catches herself with one hand and uses the knife in the other to scare them off. My watch buzzes against my wrist.

"Cowards! Pawns! I will do it!" she says. It's almost a promise, as if she expects us to cheer her on as she leaps from the window. "And it won't mean a thing! And then I'll wake up and get to do everything all over again and again and again and again—!"

My watch buzzes again. And then, in my earpiece, I hear Taris. He sounds understandably panicked: a woman is about to jump to her death.

"Can I grab her? *Soleil, can I grab her?!"* he demands.

I'm taking too long to respond. Too long to consider if it's worth revealing Taris' position. She's going to fall.

"Soleil!" Taris snaps.

It's Mercer who seizes Lune and yanks her away from the ledge, seemingly from nowhere. There's a collective sigh of relief, and though whispering doesn't take long to start, I'm sure that at least most people here are glad they didn't see Lune jump to her death. No juicy rumor is worth that much.

I'm shocked back into action. I don't hear anything from Taris but his breathing, and that's enough. We're both relieved Lune didn't get the chance to jump. We both know Taris might not have had the chance to reach her.

I follow Rian as he and Qhan hurry to Mercer's side. Lune's struggling, but Mercer is much bigger and stronger than her. He has to work for it, but he can still restrain her. With Marques' help, and ignoring all onlookers, Mercer manages to get Lune prone, where it's easier to pin her. He digs under his dinner jacket to unzip a pouch full of capped needles and various medicines. I wonder if he suspected something might happen tonight, or if he always carries sedatives.

Lune sees the needle and panics. Even Rian is grimacing, distressed to see one of his friends this way, but he doesn't intervene.

Lune continues to resist, but she is clumsy and easily contained. Mercer steadily and professionally restrains Lune's arm and slides the needle under her skin. The sedative won't take effect straightaway, I know, but once Mercer pulls the needle out, Lune gives up, deflating. There's no getting it out of her, after all, and she begins to cry instead.

"I'm a bad person," she whimpers, her words almost incoherent. "A horrible, selfish person…" she continues, nearly choking on fresh tears.

Mercer slides his arms under her back and legs and stands to hoist her up. Asmer is quick to appear at his side, the first I've seen of her in a while. I'm sure she's struggling to know what to do. Before she can say much, Crispin appears to start pushing at Mercer, ushering him from the room to escape the stares.

"Let's get her out of here," he says. "For the sake of our family's reputation."

"…And her own sake," Mercer says.

I think part of him is still struggling to process that he just saved Lune's life.

"Asmer, stay here," Crispin says. "See if you can keep people from being too cruel about what they say."

Asmer presses her lips together, her brow furrowed with concern, but nods. I'm sure she wants to accompany her friend, but Lune's reputation is about to be destroyed, and she'll be little help in putting Lune to bed. At least, if she stays here, she might be able to assist in another way.

"I'll come up to check on her as soon as I can," Asmer promises, then dashes off to recruit her still-confused brother.

Behind us, Qhan is trying to pull at Rian's shoulder, prompting him in all ways physical and vocal to leave, but I disagree this time. Mercer and Crispin are exiting the room, led by a crowd-scattering Marques, and I'm watching them take my best chance at answers away with them. I need to have some idea of what's happening with Lune Carsans. Somehow, she's at the center of all this. I trust my gut too much on that to ignore it.

"Rian? What is Lune to us?" I ask him, pressing close by his side.

"I don't remember," he confesses. "But I know that to me, she has always been a friend. And I worry for her."

Seeing his concern, and the grave tone he's taken, I almost tell him about Lune's alleged baby.

"We should follow," I say. "To make certain she settles. As she's always been your friend," I add.

Rian is moving before he can finish his nod, numb to the murmurs and glances of the crowd.

I, meanwhile, take the opportunity to observe people's reactions as best I can. I'm hoping to see Vásan, but he seems to have vanished. His brother is still around, though. Bastien. He's watching us with interest, drinking his wine like he thinks it might be drugged and is curious to see what happens. The Carsans are, as I suspected, with the king and queen. Detrus is with his wife Irina and Nissa, of all people, who is smirking with an eyebrow raised as she watches Lune be carried out of the room.

Magnus is with Lord Ambassadors Aiko and Voskoss, and as I pass by, I manage to hear him:

"I apologize on the Crown Princes' behalf for the display. The lady has not been well."

I honestly cannot tell if he's politicking or attempting to do damage control, like Asmer. It's hard to tell, with Magnus.

I stick with Rian and Qhan as we follow a dozen or so paces behind Mercer. I can tell Qhan is wary about letting Rian go anywhere other than back up to his rooms, but Lune's chamber is at least much safer than the party we've just left. Besides, there's always Taris and Korvaan. Shocked as they still may be about the death they nearly witnessed, I know I can always count on them.

Once outside of Lune's rooms, it becomes apparent that the lady must have snuck out some other way besides the front door, because Marjorie Courteau is standing guard and looks completely appalled when she sees us approaching with Lune.

She bows to Crispin and Mercer, stammering an apology when Crispin tells her to open the door. Once inside, Mercer lays Lune limply on the bed, whilst Crispin frets and Rian stands helplessly a few paces away. He looks lost. Rian's motivations are pure, his intentions only to see Lune safely to bed, and he cannot fathom what might have happened to turn the exuberant young woman of a few weeks ago into this haggard ghost.

"Lady Soleil, are you certain it's wise to allow the crown prince to stay here?" Qhan murmurs to me, quiet enough that only I can hear.

"Lune's no threat, now," I whisper back, "but she may still reveal information we sorely need. We have to take the chance. We'll be taking a lot of chances, in the coming days. Consider it good practice."

I understand his confliction, because I feel it, too. But we've played safe for twenty years and have nothing to show for it. That time is over.

Crispin gently adjusts Lune's position, and allows Mercer to help cover her with a sheet, a wool blanket, and that fur duvet. Mercer tells Marjorie Courteau to leave and report to the Carsans. Marques and Qhan are here, to look after us. And, I suppose she should probably tell the Carsans that Lune was able to slip past her in the first place.

"Lu, let me brush your hair out for you?" Crispin asks.

Lune starts to cry again. Crispin watches his sister with obvious concern before making his decision. He finds her hairbrush, sits next to her on the bed, and combs through her tangled locks. He's right in assuming it will calm her, but that also may be the result of the drugs Mercer injected her with. She quiets, and settles into a deep sleep after only a few minutes, but Crispin continues to brush her hair, and Rian continues to hover.

"Do you know what happened?" he whispers to Crispin, who shrugs helplessly.

"I told you: she's been erratic," he says. "Lately, it's only gotten worse. I don't know what's causing it. I wanted her to see a doctor. But she absolutely refuses."

"I could look at her," Mercer suggests. "Do a thorough exam. Tomorrow. If you don't mind."

"I think it's a matter of her minding," Crispin sighs. "I don't know what to do: do I declare her unfit to make her own medical decisions and force her to stay in a hospital? Could I do that to her?"

Rian is quick to insist otherwise. I can tell he doesn't like the idea of sending Lune away to a hospital not of her own free will.

"If you declare her unfit, they won't even let her leave her bed without express permission," he goes on, panicked on her behalf. "If she tries to, they'd have every legal right to tie her down."

"Which maybe they ought to do," Crispin says.

There's an uncomfortable silence.

"Rian, she nearly jumped out a window," Crispin defends.

"I know, but…"

"I can keep her on sedatives for a while, if need be," Mercer starts slowly, as if he regrets even suggesting it. "So that we don't have to hover over her shoulder and invade her privacy, or send her to a hospital. I'll look after her. Whatever I can do to help."

Crispin sighs. "Thank you. I don't want to put you in this position, Mercer, but it may be for the best. Until Comus Day passes, at least."

Mercer nods. "I don't want to do it," he says, responding to the look Rian's giving him. "But it would at least be better than sending her away."

"I'm just glad Soren didn't see this," Crispin admits. "I don't know how I would explain it to him."

"He'll hear about it, anyway," Mercer warns.

"I know."

There's a beat of silence. I'm about to excuse myself and Rian—I don't think Lune will be spilling any secrets while unconscious—when there's a knock at the door. I put a hand to a knife under my skirt, just in case, and give Qhan a nod. He's barely opened the door when Vásan bursts in, pushing past him. Qhan reacts without thinking, grabbing the crown prince by the arm. Vásan stops, and gives Qhan a venomous look until he's released.

"I'm here about Lune," Vásan says coldly, looking directly at Crispin.

"If you want to call off the engagement, you should be talking to my father," Crispin sighs.

"No. I want to know what's wrong with her, and I want to know why your family's immediate reaction to her nearly killing herself is to try and protect your own reputations."

"Ah, Lune's health really should be her own business," Mercer says, standing and putting himself between Vásan and the rest of the room.

"She's my fiancée," Vásan insists, though his tone is too plain for me to tell if he is mocking or genuinely concerned. "I would like to know what it is that's sent her into such a state."

"She'll be fine," Mercer claims. "Women's issues. She became hysterical, so I gave her a sedative. Tomorrow, I'm sure, she'll be embarrassed about the whole ordeal. You can invite her to tea and chat with her about it, then. But I'm afraid I can't give you any more details, Pike. It's just not ethical."

Vásan frowns, giving Mercer an undeserved suspicious look. "I don't approve of you acting doctor to my future wife, Ralhan. Drugging her when you think it necessary."

"If you hadn't noticed, Vásan, it was the right thing to do, tonight," Crispin says. "Lune—"

"I'd like to take her to see some specialists," Vásan interrupts.

"Immediately. I find it irresponsible, to sedate her and leave her here. Pretending as if nothing's wrong, locking her away and hiding her like the 'problem' your family likes to claim she is, instead of taking her to doctors who could help her."

Rian is as shocked as I am by this amount of passion from Vásan; the crown prince's lip is almost curling with disgust as he speaks. I realize that it's possible Vásan has actual feelings for Lune, and he wants to see her treated well.

It occurs to me that I have no idea what Vásan's fluke is, only that it's powerful.

He could be some type of skin-walker. He could have been right under my nose. How painfully ironic would it be if Vásan was Lune's secret companion this entire time? They're both good enough actors to pull such a thing off. To pretend as if it's all for politics when they've been together all along.

"Pike, I am a doctor," Mercer says, stepping in again.

"You work mainly with children," Vásan scoffs. "And you've never been Lune's primary physician. You don't know her medical history."

"Wait," Crispin interrupts. "You…You want to still be stuck with Lune? Despite this evening? Why?"

"Because you said it like *that.*"

Mercer sighs. "Pike, a word? Perhaps I can explain the situation a little better," he says, gesturing for Vásan to lead the way out of Lune's bedroom. "Carsans—ice that forehead, would you?" he adds before pushing a still resistant Vásan out ahead of him.

"You should go as well," Crispin tells us. "I appreciate your concern for Lune, Rian—and Lady Soleil, I wish you could have met my sister under better circumstances. She's not well. Please, if you would…?"

He gestures for us to leave the room.

"Oh, of course," Rian insists. "Please tell Lune we're thinking of her, when she wakes. Remind her that I'm always free, if she needs someone to talk to."

Crispin nods, but doesn't confirm he'll pass on the message. I can tell that Rian would like to stay longer, but while it was my idea to come up here, it was done in hopes that Lune would spout off nonsense, not fall right to sleep. It's past time to go. Qhan hovers behind us as I lead the way, pulling Rian by the arm to get him into the hallway.

We head back towards his rooms, where I know Taris will be waiting to speak with me. I allowed myself to become distracted, and almost let Lune jump out a window. She is, or at least was, our best chance at answers, and she nearly died right in front of me because I couldn't bring myself to tell Taris to save her.

"Would you have guessed Vásan Pike wants to marry Lune for non-political reasons?" I demand from Rian as I hurry him along down the hall.

Rian thinks about this, biting on his lower lip. "Vásan's not the best person around. But I do know that he...likes Lune. So, I suppose it's... possible?"

"But if the Carsans want to hide Lune away as an embarrassment, why suggest marrying her to Vásan if they think he might be king?" I say.

Rian groans. "Soleil, I don't know. I've done a fairly good job of not looking like a threat, but unfortunately that means no one talks politics to me, much. I'm present, but not important."

"Mmm," I say.

"What do we do now?" he asks as we round a corner.

We're close to his rooms, now. Thankfully.

"You're not doing anything," I say. "This has been stressful enough for you, and far too contrived to be mere coincidence. I want you to get in your room, with Naomi and Korvaan, and stay there."

"I'm not sure if that's—"

"Please, Rian," I say. "I don't have the time or energy to worry about you constantly. There is too much at stake."

He nods, understanding, I hope.

I ask Taris and Qhan to join me in the spare room while Korvaan and Naomi stay with Rian. All is quiet, but I suspect that's only because everyone else is busy downstairs spreading rumors about Lune Carsans and her fiancé.

What a mess.

Qhan and Taris are waiting for me after I check the perimeter, and are doing nothing but standing around with their arms crossed not looking or speaking to one another.

"You two are the epitome of miserable," I inform them, closing the door.

"I apologize, Lady Soleil. I thought, given the circumstances—" Qhan starts.

"Ignore her, she's overly critical when she's upset," Taris says.

"At least no assassination attempts were made tonight," Qhan offers.

"They might have been planned, and Lune simply interrupted," I say. "But you're right: I don't think anyone meant Rian harm tonight. Which means that either we've subdued a major threat for now, or they otherwise simply couldn't get to him."

"Or didn't think they could get close to him," Taris corrects.

"Or Lune was meant to be the one to do it," I say, and though Taris gives me a dubious look, I haven't ruled that out as a possibility. "So long as Mercer's keeping her sedated, she isn't a threat for now. But whoever she's working for or with might be," I add.

Taris raises an eyebrow in full. "You really still think the Carsans are a threat?"

"Until we prove they aren't, everyone is."

"But Lune specifically?" he says.

"There's no proof she isn't."

Qhan nods, siding with me. He doesn't know me that well, but he's so loyal to Rian that as long as Rian trusts me, and Qhan can keep an eye on me himself, we can work together.

"Tomorrow morning at breakfast, we'll meet with Ayla and Mercer. I'll need to be with Rian for the most part," I admit. "So, Taris: I need you to have eyes and ears on Grand Prince and Princess Carsans. They might not slip up during breakfast, but just in case they do, I need you to be paying attention."

"If you insist," Taris says.

"Afterwards," I go on, "there should be High Mass around noon; most will attend, I'm sure, if only for the spectacle. Rian will go with Ayla, but I'm going to take the opportunity to see what I can find in a few people's rooms: Crispin, Vásan, and Magnus."

"Speaking of Magnus, and Raj al'Yibna, I have information I think you'll appreciate," Taris admits. "From when you and Rian split up."

"Oh?"

"Trouble, in the south. The king of Milash was murdered last week. His daughter is to be put on the throne, though she's only a child. And while the king's attacker was never apprehended, he was seen. And they know he was Hoitsokin."

"Hoitsokin?" I repeat, and frown, narrowing my eyes. "Nissa."

The Hoitsokin live in the south, where Asmer and Raj's father governs. They are a powerful assembly to cross on any day, though I'm not sure how Milash managed to provoke them.

"Why would the Hoitsokin want the king of Milash dead?" I ask, and Taris shrugs unhelpfully.

"All I know is that the Milash are trying to keep things quiet, for now. Most are not aware of the king's death, yet. But Adeem al'Yibna decided the Isaarian nobility would be wise to prepare for the worst. I suppose they thought it best to tell the Carsans first—they're the only permanent position around here while the rest vie for the throne. And the Carsans must have decided that most of the heirs deserved to know. Except Nissa."

"Hence why they're going around whispering in ears instead of calling a meeting," I say, nodding.

I consider that conversation Rian had with Crispin—the one I once thought was a dream and now, I assume, was not. Crispin does not appear to want war in Isaaria. Which means that whatever his family is after, they can at least be counted on to unite with the rest of the royal families against Milash. But I have a sneaking suspicion that Alion Carsans has decided now might be the perfect time to attempt a move on the throne. I don't know exactly how he plans to do that, and why he'd want to marry off his daughter to Vásan, but there it is.

...Unless Grand Prince Carsans thinks Vásan is the lost heir and approached him to cut a deal: Vásan would set aside his claim in exchange for Lune. And Vásan would play along because, well, he's not the true heir anyway, and he might have some long-harbored feelings for Lune.

"If the Milash want vengeance, they'll attack our southern border to get to the Hoitsokin," Qhan warns, breaking me out of my thoughts. "And given their refusal to acknowledge their king's death publicly, or send an ambassador to Isaaria to discuss what may have happened, it would seem as if they have no intention of trying for peace talks."

"Why didn't Rian tell me right away?" I sigh.

"He's overwhelmed. There's a lot happening in Isaaria, now," Taris reminds me. "Even if we manage to make Rian king, and keep him safe, he'll still have the safety of his people to consider."

"Very well," I sigh. "Looks as if I'll be investigating the Carsans, Magnus, Vásan, and Nissa Sondushki tomorrow. Though if all Raj is here for is to warn the capital of tensions in the south, that at least means it's unlikely the al'Yibnas are involved in a plot. Which is a relief."

"If you want my opinion, the al'Yibnas are not a likely threat to the crown prince," Qhan agrees. "They'd have nothing to gain from it."

"Noted," I say. "Now, we must narrow down the rest. In the meantime, keep Rian safe. Watch the ambassadors. I want to know if the Lijimi approach Rian at all and for what, and if Aiko really only wanted someone to watch his son for him, tonight, or if that was a misdirect."

"You were forthcoming with his son," Taris notes. "Did he know anything?"

"Shinya? If his father has plans, he's not a part of them," I say. "Or, at least, he has no knowledge of them. I wouldn't say we can involve the boy, but I get a good feeling from him."

I half-expect Taris to argue, insist I'm being foolish for putting any trust at all on a seventeen-year-old half-Kachin, half-Tourrannese ambassador's son. But all he does is nod. Whatever potential I see in Aiko Shinya, whether it be echoes of memories from lives past or not, Taris sees it, too. Given that he's meant to be ambassador to Isaaria, it's possible we made it far enough in some timeline, at some juncture, that he was appointed the position.

Playing a game of possibilities makes such wondering endless. I force myself to stop, and focus on the present. As Nusk would have wanted.

At least we all agree there are threats to be expunged, and the most likely culprits are the Carsans, the Pikes, and Nissa Sondushki. Even Soren Carsans might be aware of his family's intentions, slim though that possibility is. But we decide to leave Lune, at least for the time being. There is nothing we can do for her. And nothing she can do for us.

Seventeen

RIAN, BEING RIAN, decides to wake me up by throwing Mango onto the bed and letting him snuffle around my face. I grumble and try to swat the dragon away, but he thinks I mean to play with him and starts jumping about on my shoulder, trying to catch my fingers in his mouth. I stuff my arm back down under the blankets. I barely slept last night.

"So-leil," Rian says as he shakes my shoulder. "Up you get. We're expected by quarter to eight."

Mango is padding around by my knees, kneading the blankets with his tiny feet. I can see a clock ticking on Rian's bedside table, telling me it's half past six.

"Let us be fashionably late again," I mumble. "Or better yet, let's not go down at all. It's safer up here. And I'm tired."

"There's a breakfast. Food. *Quiche.*"

"Must we attend?" I mumble into the pillow.

"Mercer said Ayla is going to be there," Rian reminds me.

I drag myself out of bed, trying to think of what I need to prepare for the day. Rian's gone, disappeared into the washroom along with Mango, and I go about recovering my equipment. A knock comes at the door—five-two. That's Taris.

I have a knife in my hand when I open the door, but it really is only Taris. He gives me a once-over, taking in my crazed hair and bruised eyes.

"Sleep well?" he mocks me.

"Stuff it, Taris," I snap, and give him a warning glare.

"Qhan and I have taken a look at the breakfast hall downstairs," he says instead of retaliating. "Everything looks safe for the crown prince. We'll keep an eye on him, after you leave."

"I'll stay through breakfast," I decide. "Mass will be at least an hour. That will give me plenty of time."

"Have you thought up a decent excuse for why you're not attending?"

"I'm not yet converted. I'm considering my religious options. I'm not feeling well—must have been the eggs. I'd like to check up on poor Lune Carsans," I rattle off, and Taris nods, allowing it.

"Work on your delivery," he suggests. "You're not convincing when you sound so haughty about it."

"Obviously I'll be white as a sheet and moaning like I'm nauseated."

"Obviously. Let me in?"

"If I must," I sigh, and move out of the doorway.

Rian is showering, based off what I can hear. I decide I'm clean enough and don't want to risk giving my hair the chance to absorb any more moisture than it already has. Instead, I take a seat at the vanity and start to brush through my snarls. Taris leans up against the wall near the door and watches me struggle for a second.

"You're using the wrong brush," he says.

I snatch up the other brush on the table, and assume that's correct one because Taris doesn't say anything else. I have to admit, it does brush smoother than the other. That man notices more than I give him credit for.

"What are you here for, again?" I ask.

"No reason. Just wanted to make sure you were up. You're running late."

"I'd have been up by seven. I've run off of little to no sleep before."

"And yet you should have been asleep at a reasonable hour, given what time you went to bed."

"I couldn't sleep," I admit. "Too much to worry about. Too many people here who I'm positive are going to try and hurt Rian. Somehow."

"At least you can trust us. Even if we're the only ones you can."

"What's that supposed to mean?" I ask, brushing through a snarl.

"Nothing. What are your thoughts on Mercer? You want to use him?"

"I'm hoping we can, why? You see anything to suggest we shouldn't?"

"No. Mercer's about as predictable and reliable as you'd expect. Which is why I'd advise against whatever it is you're planning. I'll go along with it, if that's what you want, but Mercer's too loyal to Rian. He'd get himself killed, helping us. And Rian would not forgive you for that."

"If anything happens to Mercer, Rian would ask me to go back for him, and I would."

"And risk Rian getting hurt instead?"

I sigh as heavily as I can to let him know that he's not helping. "I'm doing the best I can, Taris. Leave me to that without poking holes in what little I've managed, would you?"

"I'm trying to be helpful."

"You'd be more helpful if you could act a lady's maid to me, but I don't think you're about to do that, now, are you?" I ask.

"I'll send Naomi in to help you," he says.

"Appreciate it."

"I do what I can."

It surprises me that he isn't mocking me. But I suppose Taris is tired of always being supercilious. Or else he's too tired to bother trying.

While waiting for Naomi, I manage to struggle through my hair, braid it into two plaits, and twist them into coils close against the back of my head. There are still loose strands curling around my ears and temples, but it'll have to do. If I can borrow some hair jewelry from Rian, perhaps no one will notice how plain and untidy a style it is.

Naomi is so quiet when she enters that I only notice her because I'm trained to, and because I can see her reflection in the mirror.

"Oh, excellent," I sigh. "Thank you, N'omi. I suspect Taris has already told you I need help pretending to be a lady? Not that any of you are surprised, I suppose, but at least I managed the hair."

"I'll fix it," Naomi says. She's a bit short, this morning. I assume she hasn't slept well, either. "I suspect you'll be in need of some clothes? The items the crown prince ordered for us were dropped off late last night."

"If you wouldn't mind. Pick something that won't be ruined if I spill," I say. "And please, don't worry about style, N'omi, let's keep this simple. I'm not trying to make a statement."

"I think maybe you should," N'omi sniffs.

"What?"

"Korvaan said the crown princess was making veiled threats last night. I think you should attend breakfast like a warrior queen. Put her in her place."

"Touching as it is that you're that concerned about my reputation, Naomi, I'm also going downstairs to meet the child who may or may not allow me to adopt her, so let's table the warrior queen idea for now and help me look a little more…"

"Motherly?"

"If possible."

"I think the best we can hope for is, 'less terrifying'."

I sigh, but nod in agreement. While it's useful to be considered terrifying now and again, it's never been something I've had to work at. I'm hoping Ayla doesn't see me and instantly think of the wicked stepmothers in fairy tales.

Naomi leaves the room briefly and returns with a dress that is likely simple, by royals' standards. She helps me into it, ensuring my weaponry is accessible but well-hidden. The gloves paired with it are unfortunately stiff, with the thick lace overlay decorating them, and that will make handling more delicate items difficult. But today's piece has no sleeves. That would not be acceptable if I was to attend mass with everyone else, but as I have no intention of going, I can make all the excuses I like.

Then it's on to making me look like a lady. A dress can only do so much, after all, and N'omi knows more about how to do up one's face. She helped me last night, and she'll help me now.

Rian must have brought all his things with him to shower, because he's shut the water off, now, and is humming animatedly to himself while he prepares. He's granted me the use of the vanity while he bothers with the washroom mirrors. He'll be ready with ample time, so hopefully I won't hold things up. Makeup and hair for a lady takes longer than whatever it is Rian's doing.

But Naomi is acting oddly this morning, taking up more time. She keeps making mistakes with my cosmetics, scowling to herself and tightening her jaw when she has to make corrections. She won't look directly at me or meet my eyes, and though she was just teasing me minutes ago, there was something stiff about it. Forced. She wants me to look like a proper queen, to best Nissa, but that doesn't mean she can't be annoyed with me about something else.

"I'm sensing you're upset with me," I say once we're nearly finished.

It's meant to be the start of a tease, but N'omi answers seriously. Almost worryingly so.

"Am I so obvious?"

"What did I do?" I sigh.

Naomi's brow furrows in rare anger. "Don't say it like that. As if my emotions are an annoyance to you. Just another thing you have to consider for the crown prince's sake."

I stop trying to smooth down the little frizzes of hair near my ears.

"Fine, then: Naomi, please tell me what's bothering you," I order, trying to be both calm and understanding. "I don't mean to demean whatever it is I've done."

"Whatever it is?" she repeats, awkward about her anger. She doesn't enjoy being frustrated with me, but she is, and she doesn't know how to reconcile that feeling with our relationship.

"Do you really not know? Has it not even occurred to you?"

"Has what occurred to me?" I ask, proving her point.

"Soleil, is this…Does any of this even matter?"

"What do you mean?"

Naomi hesitates, but goes on. "Korvaan and I talked about it, you know. And Taris and Qhan: Taris is going ahead with everything as if he isn't surprised at all, but that's Taris. And Qhan will do whatever, for Rian, but…"

She bites her lip.

"But what?"

"This is so much change, all at once. It feels so different. It goes against everything our father taught us."

I frown. "I thought you've taken this well, actually."

"Mostly because we were shocked, I think. Part of me keeps waiting to wake up back at the University, and Korvaan feels the same."

"I'm still not sure what this has to do with your being upset with me."

Naomi frowns. I think my ignorance in the matter is making her even more frustrated, but at least that means she'll stop dancing around the topic and get to her point.

"Soleil, you know that if this is all true, it means our father chose for us fake lives that mean almost nothing. What did Nusk and you and Rian change to make our lives different?"

I sigh. "I don't know, Naomi—I don't remember, either."

"But it's not the same for you!" she insists. She's not yelling, but this is as close as Naomi gets. "You make us go back. It's your power. Your fluke, and you…You make us go back!"

"Because I have to."

"All I'm saying is…maybe…You should think about how you're using your fluke. And why. Maybe you're doing the right thing, Soleil, but are you sure you're doing it for the right reasons?"

I frown. Didn't I have to explain all this to Rian? Convince him? Why does everyone seem to think I'm doing this for me? If I've gone back in time before to save Rian, it's only because I've had to. It's not for my sake, it's for the entire world's; why is it so hard for people to see that?

"You don't understand," Naomi says. "You don't understand at all."

"No, I suppose I don't," I admit, hoping that'll be the end of it.

I finish putting the last little sun ornament in my hair. Rian has decided that practically every piece of jewelry I now own should pay homage to the sun. Fitting, I suppose.

Naomi stands behind and watches me. I get the feeling I've somehow made things worse. And admittedly, if Naomi's angry with me for not considering her feelings, she's right to be. I didn't consider it. I assumed she and Korvaan were handling things as well as I wanted them to. But it's not my fault if she's bothered by our time travel. It's not my fault we have to do this.

"The minute after midnight post Comus Day, I'm leaving," she announces. "I don't know what Korvaan's doing. It's too surreal for him. But considering you might make us do all this over again anyway, I'm leaving with Valor Ondra and doing whatever the hell I want for as much time as I have."

"You're welcome to," I say. "I told you I'd release you from—"

"What I'm saying, Soleil, is that I'd leave regardless of whether you released us from your *khashak* or not," she interrupts me. "As far as I'm concerned, the reasons we became your *khashak* in the first place…It's all pointless, now, isn't it? With my father, we were useful, because he apparently remembered things. Without him? We're unnecessary surplus."

It occurs to me that Naomi might be somewhat jealous of how my attention has been diverted to Rian and Rian alone and how incredibly focused my life has become on his. Oh, he was always on the forefront of my mind before, but my *khashak* and I were all united in that. We had a closer bond, as a *khashak* and their *Khashtani.* It's different, now.

"Thank you, N'omi," I manage to call to her right before she leaves.

Her jaw is still clenched, but since I'm not arguing with her, it's difficult for her to stay mad. She nods once, shortly, and leaves. I think even she's unsure of why she's angry, or even who is at fault for what.

I don't know. I suppose I should feel guilty about it, but it's not entirely my fault. Technically, I'm a victim of Past Soleil's decisions, too.

Rian saves me from an existential crisis by exiting the washroom in a cloud of fragrant steam. I assume he's used his fluke to dry his hair, and he's got Mango balanced on his shoulders, gnawing at one of his gold bangles. He's smiling, and that always brightens my mood, no matter what.

"What's put you in such a foul temper?" Rian notices immediately. He comes around and kisses the top of my head. Mango takes the opportunity to try and jump after my hair ornaments, but between the two of us, we manage to grab him.

"It's nothing," I insist. "…Naomi and Korvaan might be mad at me. And I suppose they have a right to be. I'll talk with them later."

Rian raises an eyebrow. "Can I do anything?"

"No, I don't think so. Thank you, though."

"Well, the best way to forget about it is to give yourself something else to worry about," Rian claims.

"How can you be so cheerful about this?" I sigh.

"Because…breakfast. If we have to put ourselves in mortal danger on a regular basis, at least we're being fed. Not to mention, I'd heard there's going to be quiche," he adds.

I'm very tempted to roll my eyes at him for that.

Qhan joins us as we head down to the private dining hall. My *khashak,* I presume, are doing what they do best: keeping an eye on us while staying out of sight. Taris, likely, will be doing as I asked and watching those I suspect most.

We are neither first nor last to arrive, and few have taken their assigned seats yet. Breakfast has not begun, which leaves us to stand about the fringes of the room and socialize. I'm sure Rian would have liked to introduce me to Ayla straightaway, but Mercer went to pick her up from the train station early this morning and has not made it back yet. That's fine with me; Ayla is sweet, but she's a distraction. Hopefully I can get some work done before she makes an appearance.

It takes about three seconds after we enter the breakfast hall for Rian and me to be drawn into conversation. I only saw Asmer briefly, last night, but I suspect if Lune hadn't interrupted things, Rian would have made sure to introduce us. She excuses herself from her conversation with one of Crown Prince Yuugo's siblings and picks up her fluttering skirts to hurry towards us as fast as her little legs will allow without breaching the unspoken protocol of decorum.

"Rian! I was hoping you'd be here," she says when she reaches us.

"Were there rumors I wouldn't be?" Rian says.

"No, but after last night…I'm sorry, I forget myself," Asmer amends, and curtsies to me. "It's lovely to meet you, Lady Soleil. I've heard things about you and I apologize for not seeking you out sooner. You sound very interesting. And a good match for Rian."

I answer as I know I should: "Thank you. I'm glad we've finally met as well. Always a pleasure to get to know Rian's friends."

"I hope you don't find it too forward of me, approaching you like this. But I wanted to thank you both, for helping Lune," Asmer says. "I honestly expect it of you, Rian, but Miss Soleil—you barely know her. I don't think you've even met her, and you still went to check on her. That was very kind of you."

I hadn't considered how my interest in Lune last night might look to other people; after all, I've known Lune almost as long as I have Rian, but no one else knows that. I suppose that made me look as if I thought helping Lune was more important than making social and political connections last night. That's good for my reputation as Rian's fiancée, if anything.

"Any friend of Rian's, I hope, is a friend to me as well," I say.

"And you know me, Asmer," Rian says. "I can't forget about a friend in trouble. And I think we all know Lune's been in trouble for a while now."

Asmer sighs sadly. "Yes…She's been distant over the past few months. Well, you know, she's always a little distant. Even with me. But there are things she doesn't talk about. Things she's careful to deflect."

"We all have things we're secretive about," I say, as if lending her the benefit of the doubt.

"It's different with Lune, though," Asmer says. "I worry for her, Rian. I think she keeps too much locked up. It's starting to rot. And if I know the Carsans, they won't do what they must to help her. You know I love Crispin, Rian, I do, but…He will always do whatever his father wants. And Grand Prince Carsans has always prioritized politics over family."

"She'll be all right," Rian reassures. "It's a rough patch, that's all. Merse is looking after her now. He's going to take good care of her."

Asmer nods morosely. "I know. But we can't be there for her forever. You're getting married. Mercer can't stay in one place for long before he gets a wandering in his bones. And I…I suppose we've always known my time is limited."

"Don't say things like that, Asmer—"

"Please," she says. "I don't want to make this about me. I only want to ask you to please try to remember Lune in the future, if you can. She'll have Vásan, I suppose, but…He's not exactly the most emotionally available man, is he?"

"I've tried to get her to talk to me, Asmer, truly," Rian's trying to insist. "But she pushes—"

I move Rian out of the way just in time. All I've rescued him from is getting bumped into by the person entering the room behind us, but that's what we get for standing in the doorway.

Ambassador Elias Voskoss passes by us and, rather than apologize for the near collision, gives Rian such a disgusted look that I'm tempted to pull a knife.

"Did you say something to insult the Lijimi?" Asmer frowns as we watch Voskoss head around the table to join his son on the other side of the room.

"I don't think so," Rian admits. "In fact, I don't think I've even been formally introduced to the ambassador."

"Perhaps it's me he doesn't like," I offer, still watching Voskoss and his son.

Hector Voskoss is about twelve or thirteen. Maybe older and I can't tell, maybe younger and he has a mature face. He's quiet, but it's not like the quiet of Aiko Shinya. Shinya, I think, is a smart, observant young man who happens to be terrified of disappointing his father. But I could get him to speak with me.

Hector Voskoss, meanwhile, looks constantly afraid of everything around him. He flinches when people talk too loudly. His eyes dart around the room, trying to watch everything at once. And he rocks back and forth a little in his seat, as if trying to calm himself. It makes me think the poor boy has seen more than he should, including the deaths of his own aunt and uncle, and his older brother.

"Oh, and there's Merse," Rian says, gesturing to another one of the doors in this ridiculous room.

I have no idea who thought it would be a good idea to make a hexagonal room with six different entrances, but it enables folks to move in and out in a constant flow. It's hard to watch all the doors at once, and I'm sure Qhan is equally bothered. It's not practical, from a bodyguard's perspective. But since Mercer's just entered with Ayla, both of them dressed for breakfast at the palace, I know I'm expected to put away my *Khashtani* self and play my part.

"Please excuse us, Asmer," Rian says brightly, "but if you hadn't heard already, I've got an adoptee waiting to meet her mother."

Asmer smiles. I'm sure Mercer said something to her about it already. "Don't let me keep you," she says, and gives another demure and unnecessary curtsey. "Lady Soleil; I hope we get another chance to speak. And soon. I would like to become good friends."

"I'm certain we will," I say before allowing Rian to take my arm as we cross to the other side of the room.

Mercer is looking in all the wrong directions for us when Rian brings me up to him and Ayla. I have never seen Mercer look nervous before, and today is no exception, but he is fiddling with that Alarkian necklace of his, so I guess he has tells other than his facial expression. It makes sense: he wanted to bring Ayla here as a nice surprise for Rian, but he didn't know Ayla would be meeting me when he planned such a thing. He wants this to go well.

"Merse! Enjoy your ride in?" Rian asks as we approach.

"I've had worse," Mercer says with a smile and a shrug as he turns to us.

"I got to ride in two carriages! Fancy ones! And a train!" Ayla chirps as she throws herself at Rian for a hug. "And Crown Prince Mercer gave me this dress! Look!"

The dress is the nicest thing she's ever worn. It's knee-length, blush pink lace with short puffed sleeves and a flowered waistline. It's casual enough for breakfast, but is still beautiful, especially compared to Ayla's university frocks.

"Oh, you'll be getting many more fancy things in the coming days, Ayla," Rian laughs at her as she expresses how glad she is to see him. "I can promise you that."

"Crown Prince Mercer said I'd get a wardrobe of dresses," she informs him.

"Spending my money for me again, I see," Rian says wryly to his best friend.

"Kid—you can just call me Mercer. I told you that, and I meant it," Mercer tells Ayla rather than take Rian's bait. "Or even Uncle Mercer, if I'm being bold."

"Are you ever anything else?" I offer.

I see on his face that Mercer is glad to have me as an addition in Rian's life as well as his own. He appreciates my teasing commentary, which must make me seem more congenial than I am.

But now I've drawn attention to myself. Ayla is curious and looking up at Rian for an answer, as she can probably tell I'm someone of importance but isn't sure how. Rian puts his hands on her shoulders and leans down a little to her, as if presenting her to me.

"Ayla, may I introduce my fiancée. Soleil Marson," he says.

"You have big arms for a lady," Ayla notes, and continues before Rian can say anything about that indiscreet observation. "I bet that means you give really good hugs."

"Oh. She gives the best hugs," Rian decides, giving me a smile.

Fine, why not.

"It's lovely to meet you, Ayla," I offer, and crouch to her level. "Rian's told me so much about you."

Not really, but I've seen the two of you together before and I approve of this adoption wholeheartedly.

"Are you going to be my mother, then?" Ayla asks, innocently curious.

"Well, I suppose..." I start.

"Suppose she can be, if you approve," Rian says cheerfully, pulling me out of my stiff posture with an arm around my shoulders.

Ayla considers this. "I don't know why I wouldn't," she admits to Rian in a whisper. "Is she mean, like a wicked step-mother?"

"She's the greatest mother possibly in the cosmos," Rian claims.

"Then why do I have to approve?"

"Just say 'yes', Ayla."

"Then, I approve."

It's strange how relieved I am to hear that. I shouldn't worry. But it's nice to have Ayla's approval, even if she doesn't think she needs to give it. She didn't ask to be an orphan, and didn't ask for two new parents, either.

Especially since she's never met me before, and if she wants to be Rian's daughter, she's going to be stuck with me, too.

Ayla is quick to take to me, and is now asking me questions about how I met Rian and why we kept things a secret. I make my answers automatically, telling a few half-truths and occasionally letting full lies slip right off my tongue without hesitation. We'll have to explain everything to Ayla at some point, once this is all over, but now is not the time.

"How is Lune?" I hear Rian ask in a whisper while I've got Ayla's attention. We're comparing gloves right now. She's worried about getting her white lace dirty during breakfast.

"She was fine when I left to get Ayla," Mercer responds gravely. "Sleeping. I gave her a low dose, just to keep her calm and drowsy, but I don't want to keep her unconscious all the time, Rian. That doesn't seem right."

"No, no. I agree. Thank you, Merse. Asmer and I both want you to know we appreciate you helping with this. We don't want Lune sent away someplace."

"I like flowers on lace," Ayla is saying now, "but I think I like real flowers better. Did you know the Fae wear flowers and such in their clothes? I've seen pictures and things."

"Have you, now?" I say.

"Mmhmm. Rian says the Fae aren't that nice, though, even if they're pretty. It's easy to get tricked, because a lot of people think that pretty that means good, but I know better than that."

"Got a good head on your shoulders, then."

"I guess so. Thank you."

Rian's said what he wanted to Mercer, and bends back down to join Ayla and me, pressing his hands down near his knees. "Well, I'm glad my girls are getting along," he says. "Guess this means I'll be able to leave all the wedding planning up to the two of you."

Ayla gasps. "Really? I get to help?"

"You probably have better taste than either of us," I say, giving Rian a look.

"We'll have to leave it to Ayla and Qhan," Rian agrees. "The people who know what's good for us…I'd add Merse as well, but it's taken him years to figure out how to dress himself properly, and even now, he's just got that one piece of jewelry he's using over and over."

"At least it matches everything," I add. Which might have been a mistake, seeing as Mercer said that himself the first time he showed it to Rian, but the other crown prince doesn't seem to notice.

"Oh, perfect," he grumbles, suddenly frowning.

He'd been trying not to interrupt our wholesome moment while he crowd-watched, but the king and queen have entered. They're meant to be the last to arrive before breakfast starts, which means it's almost time for the show to begin.

"Something wrong?" Rian asks.

"The queen's brought her pora'bola," Mercer sighs. He's not that irritated, I don't think. He just likes to be dramatic.

"What's a pora-bo-la?" Ayla repeats, intrigued. She hasn't heard of that type of fairy before.

"Ah, take a look, see?" Rian says, pointing at the queen's right shoulder where the tiny, glowing gold fairy sits in all its bird-like glory. It even matches Clair's dress. "Pora'bola are mind-magic fairies, I guess you could say. They talk to each other by projecting their thoughts. But when they met humans, they liked our language so much that they'll read human thoughts and mimic them by speaking them out loud. They're usually mischievous little things, but if you have the time and patience, you can train them. Queen Clair has a bond with hers—she's raised it. She likes to bring it to private events to speak for her so she doesn't have to exhaust herself."

"Why doesn't everyone who can't talk have one, then?" Ayla points out.

"Maybe one day they will, but pora'bolas are expensive to keep and train. They have specific diets and needs. Not to mention, it's a toss-up as to whether they'll take to a person. I know for a fact they don't like folks with any kind of mind-related flukes. Probably because that magic challenges their own."

"Do I have to meet the king and queen just now?" Ayla asks with a worried expression.

Most children would probably be excited about such an opportunity, but Ayla's mature enough for her age to be worried. She doesn't want to dishonor new father by making a mistake.

"We can do it sometime after Mass," Rian promises her. "It will only take a few seconds. Promise."

"I don't want to be around the fairy thing," Ayla pleads, distressed by the idea. "I don't want it in my head!"

"Oh, don't worry," Mercer tries to reassure her, tickling her a little until she giggles. "We'll make it so quick, the fairy won't have time to hear anything. I, meanwhile, will have to play it safe," he sighs with an eye roll as he straightens back up. "I'm seated near the queen for breakfast."

"Oh? I suppose we'd better find our seats, then," Rian says. "Thanks for bringing Ayla, Merse," he adds. "Really. It was a thoughtful surprise."

"Just doing my job," Mercer says with a grin.

We part ways. Me with Rian, Qhan and Ayla, Mercer presumably alone, though I'm sure Marques is around here somewhere. Our spots at the table are unfortunately far from Mercer, whose company I would have appreciated, especially given my Comus Day back-up plan involving him. But at least that does mean we won't be near the queen's fairy. I'm with Ayla on this: I don't want that damned thing in my head.

Ayla is seated to Rian's left while I'm to be on his right, and Qhan will stand behind us, back against the wall. He's already eaten this morning, and it's his job to act bodyguard, but I still wish he was seated on my other side. I appreciate Qhan's company, and I'd like to know more about him than just what I've observed. But I'll have to make do with my other seat-mate for conversation, and given my investigation attempts, that's probably for the best.

I am seated next to Detrus Lundan for breakfast. I haven't officially met either of them, and I don't see them as particularly threatening. Perhaps that's a mistake, but whoever did the seating arrangements clearly thought we hadn't spent enough time together yet, because here we are.

Detrus takes his seat and gives me a welcoming nod. The interesting thing about Crown Prince Detrus Lundan is how unremarkable he is to me. He isn't ugly or handsome or endearingly adorable the way Rian is. He's a large man, but I almost don't notice it. In fact, I'm only ever reminded of how plain though large he is when he stands next to his pretty wife, but I don't see her here, now.

"Crown prince," I acknowledge once he's settled himself. "I'm sorry; I don't believe we're acquainted yet. I'm Soleil Marson. Rian's fiancée."

"Ah, of course. I heard you were introducing yourself last night—I'm sorry to have missed you," Detrus says. His voice is pleasant enough, but his tone is not quite as jolly as one might expect from the red-headed giant.

"Unfortunately, we ducked out early," I apologize. "My fiancé is close to Lady Lune, and, well…"

"Understandable," Detrus says. "It was an interesting night for everyone."

"Will your wife be joining us? I would love to meet her," I say to break the awkward pause that follows his statement.

"Irina isn't feeling well this morning," Detrus admits, and I see his mouth tilt towards a frown before he masters it. "I told her to stay upstairs and rest, and not to bother with all this. I've already made my apologies to the king and queen on her behalf."

"Too bad. I hope she feels better," I say. "Though I've heard such things are common for women expecting."

Detrus looks relieved when I say so. As though this is the explanation he's been waiting for. That's odd to me, because his wife already has one child. One would think Detrus would have some idea of what could happen when a woman becomes with child.

"I'm sure she will feel better tomorrow," he claims. "I can promise you'll meet her before you're married to Rian."

It's hard not to laugh at that. I've been telling people that Rian and I plan to marry next spring, but it's apparently gotten around that we're aiming for something a bit sooner.

"It'll be exciting for the public, at least," Detrus notes. "Having yourself and Rian engaged as well as Vásan and Lune, and a new king as well."

"Yes, well, the timing of it all could be better," I agree. "But Rian and I have kept our relationship quiet for a long time, now, and we didn't want to wait. Besides, we had no idea that Vásan and Lune were going to announce their engagement as well. Although I suppose that has not happened officially, yet, has it? At least, not as far as the public is concerned?"

"I believe the new plan is to wait until after Vásan is announced as king," Detrus says casually.

I give him a look of polite interest. "Is it all but decided, then?"

"It's what everyone knows but refuses to say: it's between him and Magnus, and I'm putting my money on Vásan."

"I thought the Currian Council would at least consider each of the heirs."

"Possibly, Miss Soleil, but ask yourself this: is your own fiancé doing much in preparation for Comus Day? Does he even care about who is king next? Because to everyone else, his nose is buried in books, Ralhan's is buried in the nearest bosom, Ido is too young, Crispin is irrelevant, and the princess is, well, not mentally stable."

"And what about yourself?" I respond in kind. "Are you planning to make your mark on the world as king of Isaaria?"

"I have a family, Miss Soleil," Detrus says, as if that's a proper excuse.

"Then I suppose we'll just have to be happy for Vásan and Lune," I claim.

There's that annoyed facial twitch I was looking for. Everyone has one. Now I've just seen Detrus'.

"Oh, I'm sorry—I thought you and Vásan were good friends?" I say. I remember that look and nod the two gave each other not long ago. You don't do that across a crowded courtyard to someone you're not fond of.

"I suppose we are, in the way that a man like Vásan keeps friends," Detrus says slowly.

I'm starting to think that Vásan's persona and who Vásan actually is are two different people, because given how concerned he's been about Lune, I wouldn't call him the cold-hearted bastard even I pegged him for at first.

It's at this time that breakfast is served, which is unfortunate given how quiet the room becomes with food present. Oh, conversation continues, but in hushed whispers. Anything I say to Detrus could easily be heard across the table.

Rian conducts a quiet conversation with Ayla while tucking into three different kinds of quiche, but there's not much to read into, there. Ayla is a child excited to be in a royal palace, and looking forward to being adopted by a crown prince. I have to play nice and naïve with Detrus, though. Keep things simple, even though I'm curious as to what his goals and motives are for Comus Day. Instead, we talk about mundane things. How I'm liking the palace. What I think of adopting Ayla. How Rian and I came to meet. All while paying due attention to our breakfasts.

Breakfast passes without any dramatics, but I'm not sure if that's a good sign or not. I learn very little from Detrus Lundan, other than the fact that he apparently has no desire to be king despite not bothering to withdraw from the running. Granted, Mercer hasn't done that either, but that's mainly because he sees no point in kicking up a fuss when everyone already knows he doesn't want to be king. Detrus is playing things close to the chest, in comparison. I wonder what he thinks he can gain from that.

Towards the end of breakfast, I begin to make my prearranged excuses about my decision not to attend Mass. Given Irina Lundan's current state and the rumors going around about me and Rian, I decide against feigning illness.

"It's not that I don't believe in anything at all," I'm informing Detrus as we leave our places. "It's only that I'm someplace in-between at the moment, if one can call it that. Some days, I simply don't feel as if Mass is the place I'm meant to be at the time."

"And Rian is supportive of this?" Detrus asks, still confused.

"If he isn't, he'd have told me as much," I claim. "Besides, I think he wants me to determine what I do believe in, if anything, and doesn't want to push or pull me in any direction by force. If I feel as if I'm meant to attend, I'll go, but this morning, I think I'd like some time to myself."

Though he still looks as if he doesn't understand my stance, Detrus is at least courteous enough not to make a fuss over it. And he'll do a good job of spreading the word about my absence as well. Though our conversations were brief, and Detrus hasn't struck me as much of a gossip, he strikes me as the sort of person who likes to be helpful. If anyone's wondering where I am, he'll tell them, just so they won't have to wonder any longer.

I stay close to Rian and Ayla as the breakfast hall empties. Rian has somehow procured a walking stick. I don't know how, and I don't know when. That man sometimes manages things that would worry me if he were anyone else.

"I'm going back up to the rooms for a bit," I tell Rian unnecessarily once we're a good way away from the breakfast hall doors. "Ayla: lovely to meet you, dear. I'll see you again shortly, yes?"

Ayla looks confused, but nods. Rian will have to explain to her. Or Qhan. I trust either to do a good job.

"Will you join us for a leisurely stroll through the gardens after Mass?" Rian asks, swinging the walking stick around.

"I'll meet you there," I say, and after a moment of hesitation, lean in and give him a peck on the cheek.

Rian lights up like he's eight years old and I've handed him a bag of gold in a candy shop. I decide it's a good idea to leave him with that before it occurs to him that it really was one very short kiss.

I take the hall back towards Rian's bedroom and raise my watch to my mouth.

"Taris," I check in with him.

"No one's said anything interesting," he reports. "The Lijimi are flattering Vásan, trying to make some preemptive deal, so I suppose they're assuming he's going to be king, too. I listened in on the bug you've got on Detrus, but he's given me nothing, yet, either. Mercer's skipping mass as well, though. He's going to check on Lune and stay with her. Asmer went with him."

"How noble."

"I suppose you could call it that."

"Keep listening."

"Surely."

Once I'm sure there isn't anyone around to see, I break into a run to save on time. If anyone asks, I'm sure I can come up with an excuse. Back in Rian's room, I decide against changing into something more suitable, in case I'm caught, but pick up a few more materials, including my lock-picking kit. I grab the sealed letters I wrote last night and tuck them away safely—my protection.

I've got several suites to break into, and not much time to search them. I'll start with Crispin, as his rooms are the closest to Rian's, relatively speaking. Then I'll check his parents, then Nissa, then Vásan. If I have time, I'll visit Magnus's room as well, but I'd like to think he's the least of my concerns.

I don't need my lock-picks for Crispin's rooms, but I do need my climbing hooks. He's left a guard outside—not uncommon, but annoying. I dart down a secondary hallway, find a window, and climb out and across.

It's a bit of a risky gamble that one of Crispin's windows will be unlocked, but it's a warm summer day, and I'm counting on him wanting fresh air. The palace has a cooling system, yes, but it isn't used when the royals are out of their rooms.

Crispin doesn't have a window unlocked, but I do find one with a loose handle. It's admittedly a strain, hanging on the wall with three limbs instead of four while I work to unscrew the handle and snake a wire inside to open the window. I manage it, but I've torn part of my dress even while having it tucked up to free my legs. Unfortunate.

The window deposits me in Crispin's washroom, where there isn't much to see. I search it thoroughly anyway, in case he's the clever sort who thinks of hiding bottles in the backs of toilet tanks, but there's nothing. The lackluster start to my search makes it so that, when I enter his bedroom, I'm not expecting to find much.

I am taken by complete surprise.

"Holy Hope," I mutter out loud before I can think better of it.

Turns out, most people will hide whatever they like in plain sight in their rooms. With a lock and a door and the general understanding is that such a place is a private sanctuary.

Crispin's room is absolutely covered with papers. Charts. Maps. They flutter in the breeze I've created, and I understand, now, why Crispin would keep his windows tightly shut. I have underestimated Crown Prince Carsans. What I wouldn't give for a photo camera.

I examine the papers over the walls, trying to commit what I can to memory. Trying to make sense of whatever it is Crispin is up to. There's so much of it, it's dizzying. I almost don't know where to start, until I recognize the handwriting on these pages as Lune's. These are her notes. This is her writing. With dates on some pages going back for several years. The reason I've never anything in Lune's rooms is because Crispin's been keeping it all for her.

Most of it, I can't make sense of. It's written in a foreign language—that same language Lune made up herself and often sings in. But sometimes I see names I recognize. All the crown princes, and the princess. Soren. Qhan. The king and queen. Some names I don't recognize, and others are clearly code names, though I'm not sure why Lune would be so inconsistent. Maybe she's struggling to remember everything. Possibly.

And then there's the maps. All different countries. Some of which, I note, look eerily familiar to the ones Magnus presented to Rian. But others look like Lune is trying to pin something down. Looking for something. Someplace, or someplaces, in the world. I note there are several places she's circled, though I can't tell why. One is in the uninhabitable mountains on the west coast of the land between Alarkia and Lijimata. Those mountains are dangerous, I've heard. No one crosses them but the brave or foolish.

Strange, then, that Lune would circle a part of them with a wide oval, and scribble something next to it like it's important.

The other maps marked in similar ways are Milash and Rumshtama. I don't know what she's looking for, or why, but there's apparently a shrewd researcher behind Lune's once bubbly façade.

The papers lead all the way into Crispin's sitting room as well, though his private dining room is empty of such things. Still, two full rooms of notes and charts. That's nothing I can afford to ignore.

A quick check of my watch tells me I need to move on, but not before something else stops me: a symbol with a whole page to itself that's been slapped onto a wall. The distinct though simplistic outline of a firebird, surrounded by a many-pointed sun.

It's time to move on, but I think I've seen enough to confirm my suspicions. I don't know how I'll tell Rian—he's still close friends with Lune and Crispin. He likes them. Cares for them. Trusts them. This will devastate him.

But it's clear to me now more than ever that we cannot trust them. If I had to guess, I'd say Lune and Crispin are working against the group belonging to that firebird pin, but not in our favor. The general knew who I was, and who Rian was. Lune and Crispin, I think, are trying to uncover the heir's identity for their own purposes.

I try and give them the benefit of the doubt—after all, Lune's lover did claim that she wanted the real Isaarian heir on the throne. But were those his exact words? I can't remember. And I can't trust him, anyways. Another possibility is that the Carsans have a tentative alliance with these firebird folk but haven't been told as much as they'd like, and are planning some kind of double-cross. Either way, I think they'd see Rian as a tool or a threat. The general and his folk know I'm the one with the powers over time, but I think the Carsans are still assuming it's one of the heirs. And maybe Alion Carsans wants that power for himself, and is using his children to get it.

It would make sense. Lune would find acceptance with her adoptive parents, if she succeeded. It would make the Carsans family very powerful. And if Lune began to suspect that Rian were the true heir—one of her very good friends, who she likely doesn't want to hurt—that would also explain her turmoil.

I make certain everything is where it belongs and then leave out the window again to head for Crispin's parents' chambers. Why hadn't I started doing this before? I'd searched Lune's room at the University, yes, but now I see I definitely should have been doing this much earlier.

There is more security to the Grand Prince and Princesses rooms than their son's, but it's nothing I can't manage. It's almost a relief to slip back into this role. I never realized how much I enjoy using my *Khashtani* skills.

The Carsans' room is incredibly neat, almost to the point of being unnatural. A person could divide the room down the middle into his and hers. The two of them must have a complicated marriage, given the gap between Crispin and Soren. But if they're up to anything seditious, they keep that material out of sight. Knowing Grand Prince Carsans, he likely keeps everything in his head. No paper trails.

I should be disappointed, but I'm still pleased by the results of my searching Crispin's room, so I move on to Nissa's expecting to get exactly the answers I want and need. Proof that Nissa has connections to the assassination of the king of Milash. A practical confessional written out for me.

It's at the last second that I realize I don't know where that hyena of hers is kept, and on the off-chance it's in her rooms, I don't want to make a bad first impression. So instead of picking the lock on her door, I find myself a window so I can have a good look around her bedroom. No hyena in sight, thankfully, but I'm careful in moving about Nissa's rooms regardless.

Of all the rooms I've seen, Nissa's is the barest. It's not simply neat, there's not much in it. Nothing personal aside from the clothes she brought with her, some toiletries, and a personal effect or two. She keeps some bone jewelry, but doesn't have a firebird pin.

If I had to conclude anything from the crown princess's rooms, it's that she doesn't plan on staying long. She appears to have packed last minute, as if the first Comus Day in history was a minor inconvenience. Yet, like Detrus, she hasn't recused herself. So, I'm forced to conclude that the both of them think that they can get something else out of these proceedings, beyond the throne neither of them wants.

I'd be tempted to search Detrus' rooms, too, but I know his wife is there, and she probably has their daughter with her. Even if I managed to get past Irina, there's no telling what will set infants off, and I don't even have the dark of night to help me. No: I'm good at what I do, but I won't tempt Fate.

With Nissa proven neither innocent nor guilty, I move on to Vásan Pike.

I decide not to go through the window and simply pick the lock on the bedroom door. Though nothing inside is as obviously suspicious as Crispin's rooms, I can tell there's something not quite right.

Vásan's rooms are as neat as Nissa's, but in his case it's due to meticulousness. He has plenty of belongings: fine clothes, jewelry, and an Alarkian flintlock pistol on display beside official-looking volumes on political theory and foreign history. A writing desk with inkwell, pen, and blank sheets of paper. Not a single note or personal touch aside from a photo-portrait of his family taken the year before his father's death.

I do find a decorative wooden box in his closet, housing a set of beautiful jewelry—earrings, necklace, and bracelets—with the obvious motif paying homage to the moon. An engagement gift for Lune, I'd assume. And then, when I look, I do notice that it looks as if Vásan is starting to organize and pack his belongings. So, wherever he plans on moving in with Lune, he's not taking her to this room on their wedding night. Interesting.

I can hear bells chiming in the distance. Mass is over. My time is up.

I make certain I've left no trace of my intrusion before leaving Vásan's rooms and relocking the door. I'm disappointed I don't have more time to search—I'm sure there's something for me to find in Vásan's rooms—but I'm hoping his association with the Carsans is enough to implicate him. As long as I get them, I've got him, too. That's one plot taken care of, at least…

"What in the world are you doing here?" I hear.

It hasn't been long since I was last snuck up on—that general managed it—but it's different, having it happen in the palace.

It's Bastien, the younger Pike. He shares most of Vásan's looks, but his hair is a few shades darker, and he's a tad shorter and more muscular. He's also not quite as sharply handsome, but that doesn't mean much for a prince. I'm sure women still swarm over him for the position alone.

"Oh, Prince Bastien," I say as I curtsey to him, glad that I straightened my clothes up before leaving Vásan's bedroom. "I'm so glad to have found you."

"Forgive me if I doubt that."

Given how cheerfully I saw him tucking into his breakfast this morning, his cold mimicry of his brother is not what I expected.

"I've something for your brother," I say, trying to still play the innocent card. "Would you mind acting courier for me? I planned to slip it under his door, but there's no gap."

Which is true. And also explains why he might have seen me crouching by the door as I relocked it from the outside. My tools are still hidden in my gloves, but I shift my weight and clasp my arms behind my back almost girlishly so I can tuck them someplace a little safer.

Bastien stares at me, his face impossible to read. "You're Soleil Marson."

"Ah, yes. Sorry I didn't introduce myself. It's been a busy few days."

"Yet, it seems you found time to meet my brother. Funny; he's never mentioned you."

What the hell is Bastien Pike? He's more two-faced than I would have imagined, given the show he's been putting on for the past few days. I suppose such a thing must run in the family.

"I'm sure Vásan—" I start, when I'm suddenly interrupted.

"What's this about me?"

Vásan himself rounds the corner, two of his bodyguards at either elbow as he approaches, fiddling with one of his gloves. He's looking much less withdrawn compared to this morning, but is still pale. Even paler than usual, to quote Korvaan. He looks almost sick.

"Lady Soleil," he says, looking down his nose at me as he brushes past his brother without even a hello. "To what do I owe the pleasure of your presence at my door?"

The way he says it assures me my presence is anything but a pleasure to him.

"I only came to give you this letter," I say. I take the letter I composed last night out from its spot next to with the other four I manufactured for a case such as this, and hand it over to him. "I wanted to thank you in person, but I felt as if it would be inappropriate, given our recent announcements."

"Thank me?" Vásan repeats, raising an eyebrow at me as he opens the letter.

"For doing what you thought was right on behalf of Lune Carsans," I say as he skims the contents. "I don't know her well, but she and Rian are good friends. I assume that means that we, too, may become close, if only by association?"

"Mmm."

He finishes reading the letter, refolds it precisely, and slides it back into the envelope. When he flicks it backwards, one of his bodyguards takes it from him and just like that, my letter is gone. Hopefully it's served its purpose, and hopefully Vásan keeps it. Seeing as I stuck one of Taris' little bugs into the wax when I sealed it. If Vásan puts it in a desk drawer to forget about, Taris might be able to pick something up. So far, I'm assuming, he hasn't heard anything of interest or urgency. He would have checked in, if he had.

"Spare a moment of your time, Lady Soleil?" Vásan asks, and beckons me to walk alongside him as he continues down the hallway.

"I was actually headed to join my fiancé, and Ayla. They're taking a walk in one of the gardens, I believe. I'd assume whichever one is closest to the church," I add with a little laugh.

"Then allow me to accompany you," he says.

Given the way his guards fill the hall with their breadth, I'm forced to keep pace with Vásan. We leave Bastien behind as if he was never there. Odd, for brothers to behave in such a way. But my only point of reference is Korvaan and Taris, so perhaps it is normal for noble siblings to be cold with one another.

At this point, I'm merely glad Vásan hasn't accused me of anything. Nor does he seem worried that I'd be the sort of person with lock-picking skills.

"Your letter. Interesting statement," he says after a minute of silence.

He walks with his hands behind his back. He is still gloved, but if he did wish to use his fluke, he could remove one of those gloves easily without my noticing.

"Interesting that I would want to make a formal introduction of myself and decided to use Lune as an excuse?" I say. "I wouldn't say that's so strange."

"Interesting seeing as you barely know her," Vásan notes.

I know I shouldn't rise to the bait, but I do. It slips out.

"Neither do you," I retort, and though Vásan takes care not to react, I'm sure that must sting a little.

With a few words, I've diverted whatever suspicions he might have had about that letter. It was a simple thing—truly more of an introduction of myself than a thank you on Lune's behalf. She's just the excuse I decided to use, in case I got the chance to dig for more information, which I now have.

"I know her well enough."

"For marriage?" I challenge. "She lived at the University for years, with Mercer, Crispin, Rian, Magnus and Asmer. I know she's close with them, but you haven't spoken to her much at all, have you?"

"I have watched a number of her performances," he says evasively. "And I have exchanged letters with her father frequently on the subject of marrying the lady for some time now."

We're headed down the stairs. I carefully hold my skirts to conceal the fact that I tore them getting into Crispin's room.

"If you don't mind me asking," I start, "why choose Lune at all? If you've lived at such a distance from one another?"

"I don't mind you asking," Vásan says calmly. "It's not so complicated as some might propose: I've considered the political and personal benefits of marriage and have decided that the Lady Lune is my best option. As she is a Carsans, no one will accuse me of marrying for power or to seek favor."

"Though they could always accuse you of choosing her because you thought it would help win you the throne and kingship," I point out.

"Oh, perhaps. But the Carsans have little power on the Currian Council, if any. Their opinions are, in a word, irrelevant."

Interesting. This is good to know, Vásan, thank you.

"So, it's a safe political move," I surmise, allowing myself to sound skeptical. Vásan does not strike me as the sort of man content to make the safe moves in life. Especially not if he's as interested in the throne as he seems to be.

"One might call it that," he agrees. "And, if I must admit it to satisfy you, I am attracted to Lady Carsans. So I am not concerned about producing heirs."

Instantly, I make the connection, at least in part. Assuming Lune and her lover are telling the truth: she can't have children. I have to wonder if Alion Carsans already knows this and has offered Lune to Vásan on purpose. After all, everyone knows Vásan is most likely going to be named heir. Vásan or Magnus. The two princes Alion considered marrying Lune off to.

It must be deliberate. Grand Prince Carsans saw an opportunity and decided not to waste it. Vásan is, apparently, highly attracted to Lune, and Magnus is at least mildly so. Either could be named heir by the Currian Council, only for no heir of their own to appear. A significant problem when one considers the prophecy and the truth I know of it.

Alion Carsans knows that the prophecy pertains to the current true-heir's son. He must know that. He's been keeping it from the public and from the royals on purpose, to reveal at a later time. So he can twist the truth however he likes. So he can finally get a Carsans on the throne. I haven't worked out all the details, but it's a theory. It's possible, especially if Lune Carsans is queen. A girl who can manipulate people by singing to them.

It's possible that Alion Carsans has known since Lune was a child that she is incapable of having children of her own. He is going to finagle an existing, true prophecy to crown his own son and win the Carsans a position of respect. They've been something of a joke for decades, now. Royalty in name only, with no prospects of ever becoming more. Grand prince after grand prince after grand prince. Never king.

I'm puzzling out the details I don't have when I realize Vásan has spoken and left an opening for me to respond. I have to guess, make an assumption, but as we're almost to the gardens, my time with him is almost up, anyways.

"I'm sorry for the interrogation," I say, making it seem like a jest. "I only know that Lune is important to Rian. He cares for her deeply. So, it is a relief to him, or would be a relief, to know your intentions toward her and why."

Vásan's satisfied enough with that, so I suppose the response fits whatever he asked me. I think he wanted to know if I found his answers satisfactory.

"If the concern is that I will abandon her due to recent events, rest assured, I have no such intentions," Vásan claims. "In fact, from what I've seen..."

He thinks better of what he was going to say to me and changes his mind.

"Well. You may tell your crown prince that he need not worry for Lune's sake. I'm certain Prince Ralhan is doing his best for her. And when she's my wife, I know that I will."

Yes, right up until the point you realize her father double-crossed you.

But I smile and nod, and then curtsey as I know I should. "I'll be sure to do that, your majesty. Thank you for the escort. Likely we'll be seeing much of each other in the coming days."

"I'm sure," Vásan agrees coolly.

I suppose in his mind, that's a proper farewell, because he turns with a dramatic flourish and walks between his guards to return upstairs. I wonder if he got from me what he expected to. He definitely didn't volunteer to walk me down here for no reason. And I know I got better than decent information out of him, if only through supposition.

I was right to suspect the Carsans were up to something. Now all I need is some viable proof and all this will be over with. Hopefully, once and for all.

Eighteen

INSTEAD OF WANDERING the gardens to look for Rian, I check in with Taris and let him direct me. As I stroll through the twists and turns of the flora, I can hear Rian chatting with Qhan while Ayla hums something to herself. So, they're alone, then. Qhan notices my approach and gives me a respectful nod, which alerts Rian. When he turns to see me, it's with such a broad smile that I'm tempted to roll my eyes at him. Ayla has him making a flower crown. She's already made five or six herself, but apparently that's not enough. She looks up and waves and calls hello to "Miss Soleil", but stays seated on her bench with her flowers.

"Have a good Mass?" I ask as I come to a stop before Rian and Qhan.

"Oh, I'd say so," Rian answers, and then perches on the side of the bench to help Ayla gather up her flowers. "Mind if we move this upstairs? I heard it's meant to rain today. Don't want you catching a cold."

"All right," Ayla agrees, scooping flowers and crowns into the skirt of her dress.

Now that I'm still, I can feel the electricity of the storm Rian's predicted. Our humid summer days are finally breaking into the wet season before we careen into the autumn. It occurs to me that, dependent on what happens in the coming days, we might never see this winter. What would otherwise be considered the normal progression of time, the inevitable ticking along year by year, is about to pause. Or stop entirely.

"Lady Soleil," Qhan says, coming to my side. "I would like you to know that the crown prince and I conducted an experiment of our own, this morning."

"Oh?"

"Yes, my lady. We decided that, though his majesty goes to Mass for religious reasons, we could not let the time pass without being productive."

"This productivity was subtle, I hope."

"Of course. Investigation disguised as conversation. With my fluke, we were able to determine who meant what they said when they claimed to have Isaaria's best interests at heart. I thought you should know that Crown Princes Magnus, Mercer, and Yuugo and the Lady Asmer are all the most loyal of Isaarians, and the Grand Prince and Princess Carsans were neither truthful nor lying, oddly. Crown Prince Detrus, however, was lying. And Crown Princess Nissa found a way around answering much at all so there was neither truth nor lie about it."

Detrus and the Carsans. Interesting. I would not have guessed that.

"What about Vásan or Crispin?"

"Unfortunately, I did not get the chance to listen to them, my lady," Qhan admits. Makes sense, if Vásan hurried out of Mass in time to catch me outside his rooms. "Though if one takes into account what happened last night, I would say that if they are both plotting against Isaaria's true king, they may be acting as separate entities."

"Well. Excellent work," I say. "Thank you."

"Anything I can do, Miss Soleil."

With Rian and Ayla finished gathering up her flower crowns—and one of them now perched on Rian's head, I note—we head back inside just as the first drops of rain start to fall. Ayla giggling and smiling as we run out of the rain feels out of place to me, and part of me is irritated with Mercer for bringing her here. Not that it's his fault; like everyone else, he's assumed there's no chance Rian would be the Lost Heir. This entire matter of Comus Day is an inconvenience to him, and he's assumed it would be the same for Rian.

There are gifts waiting outside Rian's rooms for Ayla, and I insist on having Qhan and Naomi go through them all before she touches them. I order Taris to meet up with me while Ayla begs for a story from Rian and my crown prince attempts to pacify Mango for abandoning him this morning. Korvaan, I assume, is still on duty, watching for threats. As he should be.

Taris looks tired when he joins me outside Rian's door, and I consider ordering him some coffee as we retire to the dining room. But that would just be one more cup to test for poison. One more thing to call someone for. So, I don't bother. If he needs something, Taris can take care of it himself.

"Before you ask, no one's said anything over the bugs. Qhan and Rian have discovered more today than I have," Taris warns me.

He sounds as if he's prepared for me to be angry with him, but I'm not. This is a lot of ground to cover, in a short period of time.

"Change of plans. I need you to find out what Vásan's fluke is," I tell him.

Taris raises an eyebrow. "Got a working theory, do you?"

"Possibly," I say. "At least, for one of the threats to Rian. But I need to know Vásan's fluke to confirm it. Otherwise, I can't prove anything. And while proof might not be necessary for us, the Currian Council won't listen to us unless we have some way of showing them the Carsans' threat is real."

"I'll do my best," Taris promises. "But from what I haven't been hearing on the bugs, it seems as if most folk arrived at the palace with their plans already laid. They're not particularly chatty."

"That is a problem," I sigh. "But leave it be for now. I want you to do only two things, from now on: keep Rian safe, and investigate the threat I believe the Carsans and Pikes are jointly posing."

"What about Detrus?"

"It might be nothing," I admit. "Let's not be too paranoid about this... They can't all be conspiring with one another. There's only one throne, after all."

"That means multiple disparate threats."

"Yes," I agree. "But some are more pressing than others, like the Carsans and the firebirds. I'd say that's the largest threat against Rian. I'll handle the firebird connection," I add before Taris can ask. "You look into the Pikes."

"Gladly."

I give him a look. "You have a problem with the Pikes?"

"Vásan is pretentious. It's starting to annoy me," he grumbles.

"As a misanthrope, doesn't everyone annoy you?"

"He's making a habit of it."

That's fair. I can understand why Taris might be irritated by the likes of Magnus and Vásan, who wield their power ostentatiously. Rian, despite his dramatics, is humble.

"What will you be up to, then?" Taris asks, and hides a yawn.

"You mean after a day with my now-adopted-daughter and fiancé?" I sigh. "Once Ayla's asleep, I'll get back to work. Depending on how he's doing, I might push Rian again. See if he can scour his memories for anything important. It will be hard for him, and I know it's not fair. But he's too great a resource for us to waste."

"No, I agree," Taris says. "Do what you have to. He's managed all this so far. If we can put an end to all this, he can endure a little longer. He's strong enough for that, even if he doesn't think he is."

I'm pleased to hear that from Taris. I know he cares for Rian and wants to protect him as much as I do, but part of me also thinks that, if circumstances were different, Taris might even want him for a friend.

"Get to it, then," I say. "And Taris—if you need to sleep do so. We have a week, still. There's time."

He nods. But while I do believe Taris usually makes reasonable choices for himself, he's let me see him yawn thrice, now, in just as many minutes. So perhaps I need to rethink that assumption.

I put on my Lady Soleil mask again for Ayla's sake, then join her and Rian. She wants to know all about his Magicsmith research, and Rian is more than happy to oblige. I fold myself onto the couch and let Mango treat my lap as his nest while I listen to Rian, once again, go into details of the Families Three and their origins. How they've been scrubbed from many of our most popular stories and replaced with less controversial, different characters.

When his voice gets tired, we order in hot drinks that I have Naomi test. Ayla opens some of the gifts that have been pronounced safe, most of which are politely generic. But Mercer has given her a book about different types of fairies around the world, after her interest in the pora'bola this morning. Asmer has sent an invitation on beautiful, decorated cardstock for Ayla to join her for a proper tea party one of these afternoons. Dependent on the next few days, I might let her attend so long as Naomi is willing to accompany her.

An invitation from Soren Carsans also arrives, but I won't tell Ayla about it until I've discussed it with Rian. I'm certain we could trust Asmer with Ayla, especially with one of my *khashak* present and at least another guard or two, but I don't want the Carsans anywhere near her.

I already know Rian and I might argue about that; despite the evidence I've found, I'm sure he'll still want to consider Lune and Crispin his friends after all these years. But he would never stake his daughter's life on the assumption that his friendship goes both ways, and the facts paint a damning picture.

We pull out a deck of cards to teach Ayla Eight Kings and Merchant's Bluff. She's impressively good at the latter, I'm pleased to find. Later in the afternoon, Ayla goes off to her new space in the study to take a nap, as she rose quite early this morning for the train ride in. After an hour passes, I go to wake her, but she looks so adorable that I let her sleep. Besides, I won't pass up a chance to speak with Rian without interruption.

"No Ayla?" he asks as sit down at his desk, looking for a pen and paper.

"She's exhausted," I excuse, finding a utensil and starting to record as much of my discoveries as I can.

"Hmm. That gives us time alone, doesn't it?" Rian says, kneeling beside me.

"It's hard to take you seriously with that flower crown on your head," I tell him. "And regardless, Rian: we need to ensure you're out of danger before you even think about dragging me back to bed, understand?"

Rian scoffs. "What do you mean back, we didn't do anything last time—"

"But we were still in bed, to-ge-ther," I remind him. "It counts."

I flick the pen at him to get ink splatters on his face and hair. I hope he'll be annoyed with me for that, so it might make him less interested in what we could get up to while alone, but he scrunches his nose up with a smile.

Rian waits another minute while I write and then starts kissing my arm, beginning down near the top of my hand and traveling upwards so that it is definitely keeping me from writing with a steady hand. He has his other hand on my leg.

"Could you stop trying to seduce me? I'm hunting for your killer."

"Have you ever heard the phrase, 'I'd happily die for' such and such…?"

I flick my eyes over to find him smiling stupidly. "You are not dying for 'me'."

Rian sighs and stands back up. "Fine," he complains. "But at some point, Soleil, you're going to recognize the fact that we need to do something about our so-called-savior son."

"And we will. On Comus Day. Apt, I should think."

He rolls his eyes at me, but grabs Mercer's book before throwing himself on the bed to read with Mango. We spend a good twenty minutes in silence while I scribble and he flips pages. But even after I've gotten down everything I can remember, including what I discovered about Vásan and the Carsans today, I still can't make complete sense of it all. Alion Carsans might want the crown for Crispin, but then why try to kill Rian? Even if he did know Rian was the heir, why not try to use him? Marry Lune off to him instead? In fact, given how Rian hasn't bothered to step forward and claim the kingship for himself, what threat does he pose to the other royals, really? Why would they assume him a threat? And what about those firebird people?

I stand up to pace. I'm used to a lot more physical exertion in a day, and this morning's investigation wasn't nearly enough to calm my jitters. What I lack is information. I suppose I could blame this on myself for never once questioning Nusk's methods, but that's hardly productive, and I'm more interested in finding answers than dwelling on might-have-beens.

Still, I'm so frustrated, I kick the side of the bed and dent the wood with the metal toe of my boot.

Rian leans over the side to look at the damage. "Bit early in our relationship to be breaking the bed, don't you think?"

"I am not in the mood for whatever joking innuendo that was meant to be," I warn him, but I have to turn away from him to hide my smile.

Damn and bless him for always being able to do that.

"The good news is that we can officially trust Mercer," I say. "If he had any ill intentions, the pora'bola would have picked it up during breakfast."

Rian snorts and rolls his eyes. "Yes. Because the man who wants the crown least of all, my best friend since birth, was a major suspect."

"You never know," I say defensively. "I'm trying to keep you safe."

"Which I appreciate, but not at the expense of logic."

He does have a point. I tend to wait for physical evidence before making my conclusions, and unfortunately that evidence more often than not takes the form of someone trying to kill Rian. I'm not much of a detective, and am not fond of assuming trust.

"Well, Mercer might not be conspiring with the other princes for the crown, but he could always be working with whoever wants you dead because of the prophecy nonsense," I contend. I don't mean it, though.

"Because the man who spends his time tending to casualties of war definitely wants more chaos."

I sigh. "I'm sorry, you're right. I've already told myself we can trust him. But I'm not inclined to trust, Rian."

"You trusted me with everything rather quick."

"That's different."

"If you say so."

He picks at the tassels on one of the pillows. "So, if it's the six of us, plus Mercer and Ayla, we might as well tell them everything, don't you think?"

"Possibly," I admit. "But only at the right time. Naomi and Korvaan are struggling with this, as it is. I wouldn't want to have something unfortunate happen when we tell Mercer. Especially given all the work he's put into trying to save lives."

Rian nods, understanding. After all, what would Mercer's hard work have been for if there's always the possibility of me scrubbing this timeline from existence? Thinking about it like that, I understand Naomi's issues with my new-found fluke even more.

"It makes you think about the inverse, some, though, doesn't it?" Rian points out thoughtfully.

"What inverse?"

"Well, Mercer has worked hard to save lives, and your power over time could be interpreted as making his work irrelevant. So, as for the opposite..."

"The opposite of what?"

He's dancing around the topic, but I won't let him. Rian finally sighs and takes off the flower crown to start picking at it. "Soleil, does it bother you? How many people you've killed?"

I try to dig deep and empathize with my victims.

"Not in the slightest."

"Really?"

"It's not as if I knifed them in the streets over a little coin. Every assassin or bodyguard knows what they're getting into."

"It truly doesn't bother you."

I shrug. "It annoys Taris, and it…"

Used to make Nusk lecture me on the cost of human life.

I barely flinch at killing, but his death nearly unraveled me. How hypocritical.

"I'm not the best of people," I tell him. "I killed my first man at nine. At this point, drawing the Marks of the Dead on everyone who's tried to murder you is almost a nuisance."

Rian hesitates. "You don't mean that."

"If you believe that, then you don't really know me."

"But I do. That's how I know you don't mean it. You only wish you did. Everything would be easier. In fact, if we didn't feel at all, we'd likely make better choices, given our positions and your abilities. But we do. I do. And I'm afraid that makes me both a terrible husband and king."

"Oh, stop that. And order up something to eat," I tell him. "I'm going to step outside for a minute to talk with Korvaan."

Even if I can't unravel the plots of the other royals, I might as well see to my disaster of a personal life.

Rian brightens, sitting up sharply and reaching for the telephone near his bed. "I'll get us something suited to the rainy weather, shall I?"

"Whatever you like, darling," I say. "And when the food arrives, have it tested before you bite, understand? And get enough so we can feed anyone who might be hungry."

"Yes, my lady."

I force myself to continue to the door instead of turning to see his smile. Since my *khashak* having been checking in with me on and off through the day, I know that Korvaan is currently standing in the hall, keeping an eye out. As his shift draws to an end for the day, he has to be tired, and possibly irritable, but I'd still rather face him than try Naomi again.

"All's quiet," Korvaan announces when he notices me. "Naomi and Qhan have finished with Ayla's gifts. No one sent her poisoned sweets. Nice to know folks will draw the line at killing a little girl, then, I suppose."

"Good to hear. If you don't mind, could I speak to you for a minute?" I ask.

Korvaan is puzzled, but nods. I lean against the wall next to him and cross my arms over my chest. I do that a lot, I've noticed.

"N'omi said the two of you were having doubts about all this," I say. "She also told me she's leaving. After Comus Day."

Korvaan doesn't say anything, forcing me to keep talking.

"I wanted to tell you: I understand this is confusing. And I know it's hard to even trust me, now. That's all fine. And if you want to leave, too, you can. But I want to apologize, first. I—"

"I don't blame you for Nusk," Korvaan interrupts. "I mean, I did, at first," he blathers on. And the words just pour out:

"I blamed you and Taris and the man who did it…I felt like there was so much you weren't telling us. But then I saw that body in the bathhouse. Again. And I guess it helps to know you got to kill him twice. For Nusk. So, I got to thinking, maybe there'll be a lot of things, now, that I don't understand. But I don't want to lose the rest of my family because of that. I don't understand this time-traveling fluke. Not any of it. But…if I'm not going to remember…I guess it doesn't matter, does it? So long as I make the right choices as often as I can, regardless. And I can't ask any more of you now than I did before I knew you had this fluke."

I'm so shocked by this speech that for a long time, we're silent. It's chilly in the hall, and I shiver, then sniff. Possibly I'm starting to catch a cold. I'll have to talk to Rian about a fall wardrobe, as ridiculous as that sounds.

I consider what I want to tell Korvaan back.

"Thank you," I say first. "I appreciate that. I do blame myself a little for Nusk," I admit. "But there's something else that is fully my responsibility that I do need to apologize for."

"...What?"

"That first cycle, when I first went back all the way to make us start over. When I told Nusk to raise me as Rian's *Khashtani*...I didn't give you a choice. I didn't ask what you wanted, or ask you to volunteer, I made the choice for you and expected you to go along. I suppose you did, because here we are, but maybe you didn't. Maybe I forced you. And that's wrong. So, I'm sorry. None of you could have known we'd have to go through this as many times as we have. You didn't ask for this."

Korvaan consider this. "You didn't, either—"

"I did, though," I argue. "Maybe not this version of me, but all of this was all the first Soleil's idea. And even if it doesn't seem like it, she's still… me. Which means I've been selfish. I'm sorry for the turmoil that might have caused you and your siblings. I hope that, at some point, you'll forgive me."

"Soleil, I meant it when I said you don't have to apologize," Korvaan insists. "I was mad, at you and Taris. For keeping secrets. But it's nice to think that maybe our father always dies at that time. Maybe he's meant to. And maybe, in other times, he's had a more peaceful death. Or maybe, we might be able to give him a peaceful one. At least once. Wouldn't that be nice?"

"Yes," I say after a moment. "Yes, I suppose it would be."

I don't have the heart to tell him that, if all goes well, I'm not planning to send us back again. Not if that's the only thing giving Korvaan peace. It's almost like, for a few minutes, I can stand in the hall with him and pretend that everything is as it once was.

THIS MORNING, I'M allowed to wake at seven the way I normally would. Rian is still asleep, his hair a particularly endearing mess today, and I'm tempted to pass the next hour playing with it. But I need to get up and get back to work. So, I rise, check in with Taris, and then prepare for the day ahead. The rain has let up, which means we might be going into the city today. Rian made a promise to Ayla we both must keep.

Just as I've gotten myself into one of those fancy garments again, there's a knock at the door. Rian stirs, but doesn't wake, so I answer it. I find a page standing outside, with Valor Ondra close to him. I've barely spoken a word to the guard Naomi's set her sights on, but I know she and Qhan both find the man trustworthy. If he thought this messenger harmless enough to even let him knock on the door, I'll hear whatever the poor fellow has to say.

"Can I help you?" I ask, setting my legs a little wider in the doorframe.

"The king has called a meeting of the royal families this afternoon, in light of some new information," the messenger says nervously. "He requests Crown Prince Yakarami's presence."

I nod and stifle a yawn. "I'll make sure he knows."

The messenger hesitates, still.

"What?"

"The king would also like you in attendance as the crown prince's intended, my lady," he says, as if he thinks I'd be annoyed. I wonder if my reputation is such that the rumors are saying I'm quick-tempered.

"I'll be there, too, then," I say, extending my hand for the official card.

"Thank. You," I add pointedly, and give the man another second in case there's anything else he wants to say before I close the door on him.

I tear open the card, but it doesn't reveal any more details about the meeting the king has called. Only the time and place and who needs to be in attendance. No ambassadors are invited, which I suppose isn't too odd, and I'm almost glad for it. I don't like the way that Lijimi ambassador acted towards Rian. And I'm not in the mood for more introductions, considering all those Rian and I haven't paid our respects to yet.

Throwing the card on the desk, I head to our dining room to see if breakfast has arrived. Naomi's there, standing in a corner and reading something, but she barely flicks her eyes at me when I enter. Her self-assigned charge for the day, sitting at the table with a particular book on fairies in front of her, is much more enthused to see me.

"Good morning," Ayla says with a smile.

"Morning. You're up early," I note.

She shrugs. "It's because of school. Is Rian up yet?"

"Not quite. Would you like to order up some breakfast while we wait?"

"Mr. Taris already went to get some breakfast for everyone," Ayla responds, and it's strange to hear her say Taris' name.

All we told her was that Taris, Korvaan and Naomi are my adopted siblings and that they help protect me and Rian. If we've adopted Ayla in every iteration of our lives, that means she'd know my *khashak* as her aunts and uncles. I hope for that, for her, one day.

It's hard to make myself stay, now that I know that Ayla's already been taken care of, and I'd like to disappear back to Rian's room for a while to organize myself for the day. But if Ayla's to be my daughter, I need to give her as much attention as I can. So, I make myself sit down at the table to ask after the different fairies in her book.

When Taris comes, bringing food that he claims to have already checked for nefarious ingredients, I start to eat without hesitating. I'm enjoying my time with Ayla too much to care about doubting my *khashak*. When Rian wanders in, fully dressed for the day with the king's invitation sticking out of his pocket, it almost feels like we're a family.

After a long morning and lunch in the city, we return to the palace laden with new belongings for both Ayla and myself. We're nearly on time for the meeting with the king; a few minutes early, perhaps, but close enough. Taris takes Ayla back up to Rian's rooms while the two of us report to the council room.

We have assigned seats for the meeting, and I'm placed next to Nissa, which irritates me because she's found a way to bring that damned hyena with her, and it's sitting curled at her feet. Whoever agreed to allow that thing in here was bribed.

The room slowly fills until almost all the seats are taken. Mercer wanders in before he can be properly late, and is sitting down just as the king and queen are announced. Detrus is here alone, so I suppose his wife still isn't feeling her best, as is Vásan, but that's no surprise. Crispin has both his parents present, but obviously no Soren. Raj al'Yibna is here, though, which is interesting. The only member of the lower nobility present is seated near the head of the table, next to Magnus, the latter of whom keeps looking around the table with a frown.

I run through the possibilities for all their flukes. Nissa's is obvious, and she seems to like it that way, but as for the rest, I cannot imagine. Hopefully, Taris will make progress on that within the next day or so. I can't afford to have him spend much more time on that side of the investigation. He's too valuable a resource.

"Thank you all, for obliging me," the king says, and I force myself to look at him as everyone else is. "I'm afraid this gathering has been called in light of an unfortunate development."

Given Raj's presence, it's not hard to guess what that development might be.

"I'm sure you have all been told about the tragic death of the king of Milash," the king says, and Nissa stiffens. Evidently, by avoiding a major announcement, Raj managed to ensure that he told his news to everyone but Nissa. Though everyone around the table still knows that she knows.

This is all just a game, these feints and maneuvers. Acting polite while fishing for answers. Not my playing field at all. At least, not this version of me.

"Without a perpetrator in custody, the government is looking for someone to blame," the king continues, electing to ignore Nissa's reaction. "Despite our best attempts to reach out to them, they are ignoring all overtures and have neglected to send an ambassador to our courts."

The king pauses. What he says next causes an uproar amongst the heirs.

"So, given disturbing current events in Alarkia, Lijimata and Milash, the Currian Council has decided to move up Comus Day," the king says.

The room erupts. Even Magnus wasn't aware of the change beforehand. And despite his playful nature, Mercer looks outraged or at the very least displeased by this turn of events. In fact, the only person who doesn't look bothered at all is Nissa. And that, considering her alleged role in all this, can't be good.

Almighty damn it. Mother of Heaven damn it. Prince of Earth damn it.

Fate damn it, Hope damn it, the Death damn it…The others whose titles I can't remember: damn, damn, *damn it.*

This is possibly the worst thing that could have happened. Here I've wasted an entire morning under the assumption that I'd have a week ahead of me to do as I pleased. Now, who knows how much time Taris and I have left?

"I understand this is in no way ideal," the king says, using that booming voice of his to speak over our protests. "But, as we may be facing war against one of our previously staunch allies, and as the Lijimi have obviously come here to ask favors of us in their own war, I decided we have no time to waste. We *must* have a king on the throne. And as soon as possible."

"Your majesty, when are we to hold Comus Day, then?" Mercer is quick to ask, standing and leaning over the table to get the king's attention.

"The day after tomorrow will be the new Comus Day," Oram answers calmly. He looks completely prepared to handle all our questions.

"Sir, how are we going to tell the public about this?" Detrus asks.

"An announcement will be made this afternoon," the king answers. "The past few days were spent making preparations around the country to compensate for this sudden change."

"Does this mean we'll be altering the schedule for Comus Day itself?"

"Everything will be the same, only sooner. There is inconvenience involved, of course, but while my days as Isaaria's king dwindle, I've decided this is what will be best for our country moving forward."

"Who else already knows?"

"Have the ambassadors been told?"

"Does this mean the Council has an idea of who they're going to choose?"

"You look displeased, Lady Soleil," Nissa says beside me, and I turn to find the most manufactured expression of concern I've ever seen. "To be honest, I'm not sure why anyone here cares. It's only the movement of a date, after all. Does something so trivial as that really worry you?"

"Certainly, it does. And it should," I reply, trying to still sound at least mildly pleasant. "It's unfortunate to hear that someone in the south might have wanted the king of Milash dead. Especially if it damages the relationships between our two countries."

Nissa's expression wavers. For a moment, there's an almost feral snarl playing at her lips before she faces forward again as if to ignore me. Good; if she didn't suspect we all knew about the assassin her people allegedly sent to Milash, now she does. I've tried to lessen my abrasive personality for the other nobles, but I think Naomi might have been right about how to handle Nissa. I need to show my teeth with that woman.

The king fights once again to be heard. "I understand this is unexpected for everyone. If any of you should like to excuse yourselves, now, to speak with those in your parties, please, feel free to leave. Everyone else, I'll answer your questions to the best of my abilities."

The next thing I know, Qhan is leaning down between me and Rian.

"Your majesties," he starts, "perhaps it would be best if we..."

He doesn't need to finish. I'm already pushing my chair out and grabbing Rian by the arm. Likely someone would have found this odd, if anyone was bothering to look at us. But for obvious reasons, we are the least interesting thing in the room just now.

"Is this really necessary?" Rian asks as I drag him out of the room.

"Yes," Qhan and I say at the same time.

Qhan knows which paths to take to keep us as far from others as possible on the way to Rian's rooms. Once we're on a staircase, far from listening ears, I immediately bring my watch up to contact Taris. I don't really suspect anything will happen right this moment, but we don't have the luxury of assuming that, anymore. I don't think the king moved these dates for any nefarious reasons, but it's possible someone else had an influence on him. Everyone save for Nissa was visibly upset about this switch.

Taris answers me immediately.

"Meeting. Everyone. As soon as possible," I tell him.

"Everyone?" Taris repeats.

"All of us, plus the best guards Qhan deems trustworthy. I assume he's told them something of what's going on already?"

"Excepting the truth of us, the prophecy, and the time traveling, yes."

"Good. Five minutes at most."

"I'll see it done."

"Thank you."

As much as I've found Taris an irritant in the past, he's turning out to be a gift from the Almighty, lately.

I'm apparently in the mood for slamming doors, because it's still rattling even after Qhan, Rian, and I are safely inside. Poor Ayla, who was sitting on the couch, all but jumps out of her skin, and only settles once Rian gives her a smile and apologizes for me. I don't have the time to do it myself—I'm making sure this door is locked so securely that no one could pick it without my noticing.

"Are we holding that meeting in here, then, Lady Soleil?" Qhan asks me.

"I think that might be best."

"What's going on?" Ayla asked, too confused to be scared yet.

"Only a change of plans," Rian says. "Your mother-to-be isn't fond of those…"

Things are somewhat chaotic over the next quarter hour. What I can say on behalf of Qhan and his men that they are impressively organized. It doesn't take long for them and my *khashak* to assemble in Rian's bedroom, staged all around so that we almost fill it. Some of them look understandably uncomfortable to be standing in their principal's bedroom with the woman they know he's been sleeping with. The context, I think, is a bit much for them.

Valor Ondra is among those present, and he and Naomi are making a point of not noticing each other.

"Well, we might as well get this over with," Korvaan sighs, the last of us to settle in. "What's all this about?"

I consider how to best go about this. Most people in the room are looking at me with confusion while their crown prince lounges on a couch. They're not sure why I'm the one giving instructions in the first place, let alone what dangers might be present for Rian. Ayla, sitting on the floor near Rian's feet, is frowning at me wearing a look that students usually give to let their teachers know they are concentrating intensely.

"Right, so, the long and short of it," I start, and give them what I find most necessary. "Most of you know me only as crown prince Rian's fiancée, but before that I was his *Khashtani*. The additions to his security, then, are not really new at all but are a part of my *khashak*. We've been looking after your prince for nearly two decades, now, though most of you were kept unawares on purpose. Apologies for the deceit, but it was a matter of professionalism."

Several of the guards are muttering among themselves, but they're being quiet about it, so I press on. No time to waste.

"Some of you may have suspected that Grand Prince and Princess Yakarami employed a *Khashtani* for their son, though I'm sure you did not suspect it was me when I first appeared. It is a Milash practice, but one the Yakaramis took particular interest in. As would anyone whose son was meant to be king."

They are doing more than just muttering, now, but a look from Qhan is enough to quiet them.

"It is the truth," he confirms. "And you all know I am able to tell. Our prince is the one Isaaria has been waiting for. The only reason he did not come forward before now was for the sake of his own safety. There have been many attempts on his life—many of them thwarted by Lady Soleil and her *khashak*. But there is no more time to hide, now. Isaaria needs its king. And it will be our job to protect him in the coming days."

"There are few people we can trust right now," I warn. "The only reason I'm telling any of you is because Qhan has found you reliable. And I trust him."

I pause. I don't expect these people to follow me without question, but they will do what Qhan tells them to. He's my conduit, the one person we can all trust to vouch for both sides.

"I have a plan," I assure them, "but it will require all of us. Plus, a key element I have yet to approach on the matter, but I need to know that all of you can do what I ask, first. No point in bothering the poor man, otherwise."

"Wait, key element? Who would that be?" Rian asks, frowning. And though I'd rather have told him about this plan in private, particularly the specifics of it, it appears there's no time for such luxuries. Whether Rian approves of this or not, he'll have to tell me in front of everyone

I take a deep breath. "If he agrees, I want to present Crown Prince Mercer as the true heir on Comus Day, in Rian's place. To draw out whoever wants to do Rian harm, and put a stop to these intrigues once and for all."

I watch Rian open his mouth, likely to argue that there's no possibility of stopping intrigue *forever,* but he shuts it again. In fact, as he does not offer any argument, I know he approves of my bringing Mercer into this. It's been hard for him to keep his identity a secret from his closest friend.

"If he agrees, my *khashak* will help protect Mercer while the rest of us keep a close watch on Rian. There are political and physical threats, both, against Rian and I am not entirely sure if these are all related to his inheritance. If we have Mercer make the claim, and use our own flukes to pass off *his* as something substantially related to the Carsans prophecy, only the people who know Rian is the real heir will try to do anything about it. And only those who want the crown for themselves badly enough to kill will reveal their positions. It would be too risky for them to allow Mercer to be crowned, otherwise."

Here, I pause again. If I thought it was difficult explaining things to my *khashak,* this is worse. And Qhan's men barely know the half of it. Many of them are looking from me to Qhan to Rian and some of them even to my *khashak,* who I'm sure they know vaguely by sight.

"Your majesty, do you agree with this? Is this what you would have us do?" one of them asks.

"I would," Rian insists.

"So it's true, then," Valor Ondra says. "You really are the Lost Heir?"

Even Ayla is looking at Rian with awe, wondering if it could possibly be true. For her, this is a storybook revelation. The man adopting her is meant to be king, which means she is most definitely about to become a princess.

"I'm not much one for dramatic titles," Rian admits. "But yes, if that's what you want to call me, I am."

"I've heard it as the truth myself," Qhan adds, and everyone in the room turns to look at him. "It is unexpected, but it does not surprise me. So, know, at least, that in helping to protect the crown prince, you are doing the most honorable work for Isaaria that you possibly could be."

The flattery is overdone, perhaps, but purposeful. These men were already loyal to Rian; Qhan has made sure of that. But now they're being asked to do even more than before. In fact, it's possible they might have to attack another of the crown princes for Rian's sake, which is tantamount to treason. But so long as Qhan and I reinforce in their heads that this is the moral, patriotic thing to do, they hopefully won't consider that.

"I'm sure you all have many questions," I admit. "If you'll adjourn to the next room over, I'll have Qhan do his best to answer them while I explain a little further to my own *khashak.*"

I look to Qhan and give him a nod, and he acknowledges me back. So long as his men have a general idea of what we'll have to do in the next few days, they'll know to obey my commands not just because I'm meant to marry Rian, but because their king's life depends on it.

"You made it up, then!" Ayla says, too excited to be angry that Rian lied to her. "You said you thought Crown Prince Pike would be king, but he's not! It's you!"

"Well, it wasn't entirely a lie," Rian claims. "If things proceeded as everyone assumes they will, I think Vásan would be crowned."

Ayla continues to babble at him, bombarding Rian with questions that he answers very carefully. The room grows briefly busier as Qhan moves his men over to the dining room, and during this time, Taris sidles up to me.

"There is a slight issue with your plan," Taris mutters to me.

"And what's that?"

"Mercer's been almost constantly looking after Lune."

"Like the good friend he is," I mutter. "What's your point?"

"He's almost never alone," Taris reminds me. "Crispin or Marjorie Corteau or Asmer or even all three of them are there with him. How are you going to make your proposal in front of them? Or otherwise lure him out of their presence without arousing suspicion?"

"I'll have Rian go," I say. "He'll visit under the guise of checking on Lune himself—they are good friends, so that's not odd. And while there, I'll have him strike up conversation about our wedding, asking Mercer to be his best man, something of that nature. And then he'll come to me."

"You'd use Rian to prompt Mercer into inviting you someplace," Taris says.

He sounds almost surprised by his own approval. As if he didn't expect such adept manipulation from me.

"I'll tell Rian to see if he can angle it towards a lunch," I go on. "I don't dare explain things in front of Mercer's bodyguards, in case they're not all reliable, but I'll slip him a note. Ask him to meet us later in the day, without his guards, to discuss things. Qhan and Korvaan can pick him up, if necessary."

Taris frowns. "Why add another layer of complications? Are you really that worried about his guards?"

"The likelihood of betrayal is slim," I admit. "But don't forget, Taris, people will do horrible things for money. All one of them has to do is get it into their heads that someone would pay a good deal for the identity of the Lost Heir. No—if we have to lure Mercer out and away from everyone, so be it. Better to be cautious and waste a little more time than to be hasty and dead."

Taris considers this, then shrugs. He cannot argue with that.

"Besides," I add, "this will work, Taris. You know Mercer as well as I do—do you think he wouldn't agree?"

Taris snorts. "No, he definitely will. In an instant. Though he'll claim to be annoyed at having such a secret kept from him. He'd do anything for Rian. And he's proven it before."

Not to mention, wealth does not appeal to Mercer, as evidenced by his gift of a priceless historical artifact to Rian. That Kachin hairpiece is proof enough of their friendship. And I'm sure, if he could, Mercer would have haggled away everything he had to get his hands on that Magic Mirror, too.

"Go scout, then come straight back," I order Taris. "Find out if it would be reasonable for me to send Rian to Lune's room, later."

Taris nods, and bows to me. Reflexively, I think.

"I'll see it done."

"And don't linger," I add. "I can't afford to have you getting into trouble."

Taris does not acknowledge that last part, but I know he heard me. He slips into the hall while everyone in the bedroom rearranges themselves. Eventually things quiet once more, leaving just me, Rian, Ayla, Naomi and Korvaan, but I can still hear muffled conversation from Qhan and his men in the next room. I hope I haven't made a mistake in telling them, but I need more hands to help protect Rian and Ayla.

"—like my aunt and uncle?" Ayla is asking excitedly.

She's still kneeling near the couch, but Rian and Korvaan have shuffled around, some. Rian's perched on the arm of the couch with his arms crossed, and Korvaan's laying on it, tossing a blue glass ball of Ayla's up and down in the air. The gold and paper snowflakes inside dance with each throw. It's one of Taris' pieces, highly popular with children.

Korvaan exchanges a look with Naomi. "Ah, I suppose so," he says.

"And you're assassins like Miss Soleil?"

"I'm a bodyguard, not an assassin," I correct as I rejoin them. "It's just that occasionally, protecting Rian means killing some people."

"Occasionally? I would say 'weekly'," Naomi says.

It's a thinly-veiled jab that I decide to let pass.

"If they didn't come after him, they wouldn't have to die. Which is still unfortunate, of course," I add for the little girl's benefit. "But sometimes I have to do what's necessary, regardless."

Ayla's got enough of a moral compass to understand, I hope.

"You'd think whoever keeps sending them would have picked up on that, at this point," Korvaan adds.

When he tosses that ball again, I snatch it out of the air, forcing him to sit up and pay attention.

"Why isn't Taris here?" he sighs.

"Because Taris is out scouting," I snap. "Now: listen. We have very limited time to decide the best course of action."

"Not my fault you two wasted time rolling around on your bed," Korvaan says.

"You can blame me for that one," Rian claims with a grin.

I flash him a warning look. *Not in front of Ayla.*

"First, we need a detailed schedule of the Comus Day plans," I say, moving on before Ayla can start asking uncomfortable questions. "I don't care who gets it, or how, but someone's going to need to steal it for me."

"I can!" Ayla volunteers, raising her hand like she's in class.

"Ah. Maybe next time, sweetheart," Rian says with a laugh.

"But I'd do a good job!" Ayla insists. "Because I'm small and quiet and no one would ever notice me."

"Mmm, you make good points," Rian says. "But I have another job for you, Ayla. You'd be much too busy to be sneaking around. Best leave that to one of your mother's *khashak.*"

"Another job?" Ayla repeats, already taken by that idea instead.

"Yes, but you'll have to wait to hear about it," Rian warns. "Let Soleil say everything else that has to be done, first."

Giving him time to think about it, I assume. Or give me time to think about it, knowing Rian.

"...Naomi, I want you to see what you can do about finding that schedule this evening," I say. "I'd rather have Taris do it, but he can't be in three places at once. If you can't get it tonight, tomorrow morning. But I'd like to know what the Currian Council expects to happen on Comus Day."

Naomi nods instead of arguing with me, which is a blessed relief. I have no idea what I would do if she started verbally attacking me in front of Ayla.

I used to believe I didn't care about what others think of me, but I know now for a fact that's blatantly untrue.

"What about me? What am I supposed to be doing?" Korvaan complains.

"Keeping bullets from killing my husband," I say, and give him a look to make sure he understands how serious I am. "You'll be working with Qhan, Korvaan. Keep Rian and Ayla safe."

"Bullets don't kill. *Speed* kills," he claims by way of response.

Naomi frowns. "I think the bullets may have something to do with it."

Korvaan's attempting a rebuttal when Taris slips quietly back in and gives me a nod. Quick one, he is.

I take a deep breath. "Rian, go visit Lune this afternoon. Mercer's still with her. And you know Merse; he'll want to talk with you. Use your charm, would you? Get him to want to meet me tomorrow. Complete privacy is impossible, I know—Marques would never allow that—but as secluded as we can make it."

"Will do," Rian nods.

"Meanwhile, Taris will be investigating the Pikes," I add. "I want to know what their flukes are. Ideally, I'd know everyone's fluke, but..."

I sigh.

"I can tell you mine!" Ayla says, hopping to her feet.

She truly wants to help. I don't know why she's already attached herself to me enough to want my approval, but she is an orphan. I suppose she's not used to having a mother figure. Only Rian.

I soften my tone and try to think matronly thoughts. Considering it's quite literally my destiny to become a mother, there's some irony involved when I take into account just how bad at it I am.

"I didn't know you even had a fluke, Ayla; you never said."

She shrugs. "At school they tell us over and over it's our right not to tell anyone if we don't want to, so long as we don't use it to do bad things. So, I didn't tell anyone because I didn't have to."

Rian considers this with an approving air about him. "More than fair enough, Ayla, though as your parents, I'd say we have something of a right to know."

"That's why I'm telling," she insists, as if such a thing should be obvious.

Rian and I exchange a look. He shrugs.

"What can you do then, Miss Ayla? Something flashy?" Korvaan says, teasing her like the good uncle he's adapting to be.

She shakes her head. "It's, um...Professor Bissier said I'm an editor."

Professor Bissier has the ability to read flukes. All the students can get a fluke reading as first years, if they haven't been brought by their parents already or otherwise made an indication.

"I can show you if you want," Ayla adds, when it's clear she isn't making herself understood. "I just need something made by a fluke."

"Here, allow me," Rian suggests, already pulling off a glove.

There's a glass nearby, sweating from the ice melted into it. With a flick of his wrist, Rian lifts the water out and freezes it so that it looks as if someone was trying to pour a drink in the middle of an especially cold winter. Rian's grinning at all of us, never one to waste a chance to show off. Though since he's somehow managed to secretly practice with his fluke all these years whenever we weren't watching him, I won't begrudge him that.

Ayla isn't at all surprised by this display, but I believe this is mainly because she's too young to have any idea of how exceptional it was. She walks over to the glass, removes her own gloves, and brushes her hands off on her skirt. She touches the ice, and it changes. She's sculpting it, I realize, into a completely different shape. Not just a splash of water, but a flower. Not a perfect rendering—she's just a child, after all—but Ayla's fluke is now obvious.

"She's a *fluke* editor," Naomi says, and Ayla turns back with a grin, glad that at least one of us has gotten it.

"Uh-huh! Apparently, we're not rare, but aren't commonplace. So, it's an in-between sort of fluke," Ayla says.

"I'm sorry, am I missing something?" Korvaan asks. "She's not an… ice… maker? Something of that sort?"

I suppose while Taris and I maintained an interest in flukes despite not having any ourselves, or believing I didn't have one in my case, Korvaan never bothered to read up on common flukes or their prominence in different parts of the world.

"Fluke editors are…Well, it's not a perfect name," Rian explains, "but simply put, Ayla here can take the results of someone else's fluke and… change it a little. And speaking of, little lady, that is some nice work," Rian adds, standing next to Ayla so he can ruffle her hair. "I'm especially proud. I might just have someone dig out a photo camera for a snapshot!"

And just like that, I have the perfect job for Ayla.

"Ayla, go wait for me in your little room for a second, would you?" I prompt her, interrupting her insistences to Rian that he didn't need to bring a camera. "I have that very special job for you. But it's a secret. No one else can know."

"I thought there was other stuff to talk about first?" Ayla says.

"Only a little more," I say. "But I want to tell you about your mission so you can get started right away. It's very important."

Calling it a mission does the trick. Ayla scurries off. She calls over her shoulder something I don't quite hear that makes Taris quirk an eyebrow, which I think is his version of a smile.

"What are you going to have her do?" Rian asks, intrigued.

"Why in the world would I tell you? It's a secret."

"Seriously, Soleil?"

"You'll find out in good time," I reassure them all. "But if I'm going to be Ayla's mother, I want a good relationship with her, and that starts with keeping secrets secret."

I catch Naomi's scoff, but since I don't feel like guessing why that's annoyed her, I pretend as if I didn't hear it.

There isn't that much more to say, since my *khashak* all have their temporary assignments. I try to make it quick, so as not to keep Ayla waiting, but do leave a few general orders to sustain them from now through Comus Day.

"Above all: keep a weather eye out," I warn. "If anyone, it is a *Khashtani's* duty to die for their principal. But none of you should feel compelled to die for me."

"Good. I don't plan on it," Naomi says coolly. "You can always go back in time, after all. The rest of us don't have the luxury."

"Well, I would!" Korvaan insists. "What, you think you can snatch up all the glory for yourself?" he accuses me. "Not a chance, Soleil. We're your *khashak*. That means we—"

"Do what I tell you to," I remind him, a warning in my tone.

"Taris doesn't," he complains.

"That's because Taris is a fool, and I'm not particularly worried about him giving his life for me."

Taris shrugs, nonplussed. We've reached a point, I think, where he knows that I'm teasing him.

"But if anything happens to you, Soleil, there's no point. The prince wouldn't last five minutes without you," Korvaan claims.

Rian, naturally, opposes this. "Oh-ho-ho, I beg to differ."

"Yakarami," Taris says gravely, "you cracked your head open when you were twelve after screaming, 'Quiche!' and reaching for a ceramic dish some halfwit left cooling on the top shelf."

"Halfwit," Rian agrees, "because they should have known better than to think that any height would keep me from reaching quiche."

Naomi looks to Taris. "You have a point—he needs bodyguards. Constantly. To save him from himself."

"Hey! I have dual flukes, you know!" Rian insists. "I don't need to have guards by my side every second of the day."

"Yes, you're very impressive, dear," I agree, "and, Qhan and Taris are going to stay by your side every second of the day until we can guarantee your safety."

"Do we have a secondary plan?" Korvaan asks. "In the face of, 'absolutely everything goes wrong'?"

"Yes: go see Mallin Cruz and get a-aall the good pipe weed while we ride this one out," Rian drawls.

I sigh. This meeting has gotten irredeemably far off track.

"Yes, this will be dangerous and precarious, and yes, we're all vulnerable for different reasons and need to look after one another as I said. Let us not talk in circles about it. You all have work to do. As do I."

"Really?" Rian says. "What are you doing, then?"

"After my little chat with Ayla? I'm going to practice," I claim. "If I've got a time-controlling fluke at the tip of my fingers, I want to know I can use it if necessary. Even if it's mostly instinctive," I add, interrupting Rian.

"That's not a bad idea," Rian admits. "If Qhan and Korvaan permit me, I might come find you later."

"It would be good for him to spend some time under the sky himself," Taris agrees before I can say something about the potential danger of it.

I know he's right. Rian' will be in perilous danger; the least we can do is make certain he has enough energy stored up to power his dual flukes. Or just the one fluke, I suppose. I don't think the aura-sensing one is going to be useful when it comes to defense. Rian himself doesn't seem understand what it is or what it can do, from what I can tell.

"Then I will see you later today for something of an evening stroll, dear," I drawl. I make my way out, grabbing Ayla's gloves from where she left them on the table. "Do us both a favor and bring a gun."

Nineteen

I SPEND A FEW minutes with Qhan first to get our stories straight before joining Ayla for some time. Once she's well on her way with her secret project, I leave to see what I can do about strengthening my fluke.

The grotto is the safest place to practice without worrying about someone seeing me—and, if I'm going to be dramatic, it's also considered the holiest place around the capital. Even if I don't belong to Rian's faith, I might still request intercession on his behalf. If the god he believes in does exist, maybe he'll take pity on us.

Though the grotto won't be entirely abandoned at this time, it's temporarily closed to the public given current events. The grounds are large enough that I know I will be able to find a small, quiet nook far from the religious site itself to use for my own purposes. I enjoy the long walk out, at least, which surprises but pleases me. Even after a few minutes under the setting sun, and I begin to feel calmer, more in control of my fate.

The grotto grounds host two prayer gardens. One of them is lit by candles at night: an underground cavern filled with statues and tributes to the grotto's story. Four different churches are scattered near the original chapel built above the most holy spot, where the healing waters spring. The story goes that an apparition of the Queen of Heaven appeared eight times to a pair of poor village children hundreds of years ago, when New Isaaria was still young. The children continued to return to the grotto to pray, as the queen asked them to, much to the dismay of many around. This was in the age where Isaarians often fled religious persecution, after all.

Sure enough, before the children could return for the ninth time, the entire village was slaughtered by intolerable folk from Isaaria's then-neighbors. The children were saved, though, along with four others who were at the grotto's site at the time. Their injuries were healed, and they were able to find help.

I don't know what happened afterward, but I'm sure the nuns who reside here happily fill in anyone who inquires for details. I do know that the children were supposed to be dead where they fell, but water sprang out of the ground and created a source of natural healing water that has yet to stop flowing.

It occurs to me that, once this is all over, I will live in the Pyrian Palace with Rian and Ayla, and we'll likely come to the grotto now and again. Rian and Ayla are both Theebin, so their religious principles make it a holy pilgrimage. In another year, I might know as much about the grotto as the nuns do.

It is an almost funny thought that sustains my good mood as I begin my work. I'm not certain how to practice with my fluke, but as Rian said my usage of it is usually reflexive, I decide to start practicing combat skills or something of the like and maybe, now that I know I have a fluke, I'll activate it.

I am not without some reservations. What if, while trying to practice, I accidentally throw us back a few days? I'd have to explain everything to everyone all over again.

I can see why Rian is tired of this. I don't think I could bear to go through that meeting a second time, let alone who-knows-how many times Rian's done it.

I try meditating, first. Not Nusk's way of meditating, but what I did out in the field with Korvaan. I focus on feeling the sun on my face and neck, and enjoying its warmth. I take my boots, socks, and gloves off as well and get as much contact with nature as I can. Oddly, it helps to buoy my spirits despite my nervousness.

Unfortunately, once the heat of the sun has vanished and I can't delay any longer, that good mood doesn't last.

I spend hours attempting to use my powers without much luck. I've brushed up on plenty of decent combat practice to the point where I'm worried I may be sore tomorrow, but I can't convince my brain I'm in real danger. I have to wonder if I'm doing something wrong, if some buried version of myself is refusing to let me waste my energy this way, or if whatever supernatural entity may or may not reside in the grotto has decided to block me for their own reasons.

Eventually, I'm forced to walk back to the palace, tired and beaten. During my stroll, I find myself at the foot of a pair of statues, not unlike those at the University. The Queen of Heaven should be an imposing figure, considering the height and the marble she's made of. Her son the prince, who is almost always standing as her match, definitely strikes that tone. But the queen is often rendered as a young girl with a head covering. Sometimes carrying a child.

One would think it impossible to look at such an innocent statue and be frustrated by it, but I am. I need something to take my anger out on.

"Nice of you to lend a girl a helping hand when needful," I sigh at the statue, looking up at it with my hands on my hips. "What, you only give miracles out to true believers? Because this is for Rian's sake."

For obvious reasons, the statue says nothing back.

"Must I grovel for assistance?" I say. "Obviously you've lent yours before. I'm not asking for anything big," I go on, truly venting, now. "Just something. Anything. Give me some kind of sign I'm doing the right thing."

I give it a minute. Still nothing.

"About what I expected," I snap. "Thanks for nothing."

I kick at the base of the statue, and instantly regret it. That's solid marble, and the toe of my boot is not quite as strong as I'd have liked to think. I'm jumping about, annoyed by the pain shooting through my foot, when I realize there is someone watching me. The only reason I don't pull a weapon is because I can tell who it is, and they aren't a threat.

I drop my foot down and try to recover what is left of my dignity before the young lord Aiko Shinya.

"Oh!...Lady…Soleil…I did not expect to find you here," he admits.

"You're not interrupting anything," I promise the poor boy. "Please—don't let me keep you from what you came here to do."

"I only wanted to see the grotto. I've heard much about it," Shinya says, still sounding apologetic.

"Then allow me to act as tour guide if you don't mind," I offer, deciding to try and see if I can make an ally of the Tourrannese. That way, my trip out-of-doors won't have been a complete failure. "Please. It will give me something to do to quiet my thoughts."

"You do seem as if you could use a distraction, Lady Soleil," Shinya admits.

My foot is throbs in a mocking reminder of my foolishness. I need to get it out of this boot and pray, I suppose, that I haven't broken a toe. If nothing else, at least I'll soak up extra energy. Still, it occurs to me as I'm removing my boots that my actions might seem odd without context.

"Do you mind?" I ask.

Shinya applies my words to the situation and realizes what I intend.

"Oh. Not at all, my lady."

"Usually I prefer the sun," I admit as I discard my boots and tie their laces together to carry. "But it has been some time. I suppose the moon will have to do."

Shinya nods. "I'm a rarity. Apparently. I don't have a preference."

Once I have my boots in hand, stockings stuffed inside, Shinya and I walk on. I'm still frustrated, but playing adult to Shinya's confused and shaken youth helps settle me. I want to act as a mentor to him, I find; it feels like practice, for raising Ayla. And I do genuinely like the boy.

"So, are you here for the impeccable scenery, or are you the religious type?" I ask him after a few moments.

Shinya is surprised for a second. "I...Apologize?"

"Apology accepted," I grant. "But the question stands if you don't mind sharing."

"Ah," Shinya says awkwardly. "Both, I suppose. And neither. I wanted to ask for guidance about something," he adds. "I've...asked the god of every other religion I can think of thus far, but no answer. I figured I should try the Theebin god as well. Just in case."

I nod, and start spewing sentimental advice before I can stop myself.

"A believer once told me that if you ask your god for something, He'll always answer, even if the answer is 'no'," I admit. "Sometimes we want things that aren't good for us, or want to be pushed in a path that would tangle Fate's threads. So while we might want it in that moment, it's sometimes good to be told 'no', just as children are."

Shinya considers this. "That is good advice," he says.

"My father told it to me," I say.

It's only the second time I've referred to Nusk that way, but now that I've said so, I'd go on to say he damned well deserves the title. More than whoever my biological father was, in any case.

I clear my throat.

"Right. What was the question you intended to ask? If it's not too private."

"It's not anything important. Only something personal," he mutters.

"Only?" I repeat. "Over half a person's motivations are personal."

"What about the other half?" Shinya asks curiously. He's opening up to me.

"Money."

The boy nods.

"My father says if your mind is occupied with something personal, you aren't doing your job as ambassador," he says. "All major concerns should be in respect to properly representing one's country, and keeping the peace."

"That's a hard thing to expect of anyone," I say carefully. "But possibly, your father's neglected to mention there is equal importance in maintaining healthy relationships between individuals. Countries are merely many millions of personal relationships all tied up together."

"I suppose," Shinya says. "But I can't imagine how personal relationships change a country, politically speaking."

"Well, consider your own question, whatever it is," I say. "And how it might relate to both."

"But it's…" he starts, and seems to realize he can't say more without giving himself away. "It's different."

Shinya surprises me, then, by deciding to tell me without proper cajoling.

"It's...I have…dreams. About a girl," he confesses. "I know what that sounds like, but it is peculiar, because though I've never met her before, I've dreamed of her since I was a child. More innocent things, back then, but now…"

He flushes.

"Decidedly less innocent things?" I say wryly.

Poor boy. But I can't help but tease him. The way his face reddens when he even thinks about his repressed desires is endearing. Having met his father, I'm sure Lord Aiko is not an easy man to speak to about such things. I think he would chastise Shinya for having any sort of personal distractions.

I am easier to speak to, because some part of Shinya thinks it's unlikely he will meet me again. I don't think he's considered the fact that if Rian becomes king as he's predicted, I will be queen. And he's meant to be an ambassador, here.

"I only want to know what it means," Shinya insists. "And who she is. I think I'm meant to help her. So you see? Not at all political."

"Hmm. Maybe it still is, merely not in the way you'd expect. Are you Theebin? A member of the Church of the Holy Three?" I ask. It occurs to me that Shinya asked me, but I never asked him.

Shinya shrugs. "It's the only church in the world that seems to believe that there's an afterlife for good people even if they didn't happen to be Theebin. They might have to work a little harder in the Otherworld, but they can still reach an afterlife. There are still rewards for people who follow a moral code."

"Is that so?" I say.

I think Shinya knows more about the philosophies of my fiancé's religion than I do. He seems like the sort to intensely research as much as he can about anything and everything.

Shinya nods. "Even off-shoots of the Theebin church, made up by people who didn't agree with all of it, claim that if you don't convert, you'll end up doomed for all eternity once you die. You could live a perfect, saintly life, but if you weren't baptized the way they wanted you to be…"

He shrugs again.

"I don't know if I believe in all of it," he admits. "But at this point, if I'm going to pretend I believe in anything, I might as well choose the one church that thinks there's a chance for me even if I believed in nothing."

I've forgotten exactly what I wanted this conversation to be in the first place. I recall hoping to fish for potential political allies, but Shinya's personal life sounds much more intriguing. Tonight, it seems, is to be frivolous for the both of us.

"What about you, Lady Soleil?" Shinya says. "Even if you're not Theebin, do you believe in anything else?"

I sigh, distracted. "I believe, at this point, I've killed too many people to hope for some kind of god to judge me when I finally die."

Shinya's staring at me, and I remember that he would have no reason to know I'm Rian's *Khashtani.* I've just confessed to multiple murders.

Fate dammit.

Shinya's stopped walking. I turn back to him, expecting to start damage control. Only, Shinya's not shocked. His expression is plain and carefully guarded.

"That's…" I start, and then grimace. There's nothing I can think of to say that would make any sense.

"My younger cousin, Prince Chimhwi—he has a very powerful fluke," Shinya finally starts. He speaks slowly, choosing his words with care. "And he can't always control it. It makes people scared of him. They avoid him, and many of his father's ministers submit appeals to force my cousin to cut his hands and heels, swear never to use his fluke, and take the White. That is, they want to lock him away where he'd never see the sun or the moon. So he could never possibly hurt anyone, even on accident. They have put him through violent exorcisms, claiming he is possessed by a demon, when I am certain this is not true."

"That…must be hard, for him," I say. "But why tell me?"

"Because when you said what you did just now, and realized you shouldn't have, the look on your face was the same one I have seen on my cousin's many times. You are afraid of how others react to you. You do not want to be seen as a terrible person, based off a few facts out of context.

"You need not worry about my spreading rumors, Lady Soleil," Shinya promises me. "If you've taken lives, I am certain you have done so in defense of yourself. Or of your crown prince."

I stare at him, surprised by his statements and forced to consider the potential truth in them. Shinya gestures for us to continue walking.

"Forgive my assumptions, Lady Soleil. To me, it is obvious you are protective of Crown Prince Rian, but it is not the usual way a woman is protective. I am sure you only mean to keep him safe."

I can't help but laugh after a second. "No need to ask for forgiveness, then. You're much smarter than your father gives you credit for, you know," I add, and I mean it. "But a little too open with me, given our lack of a relationship."

"I know how to tell the good people from the bad people," he claims. "I get…feelings, about them. I can tell, with you. You are a good person."

I raise an eyebrow. "Out of curiosity, are there any people here you don't get good feelings about?"

"Not particularly," he admits. "But I have spoken to you more than anyone else here. Besides my father."

Of course.

"Then I'm honored to be the one you've decided to speak with," I say.

"I am usually a dreadful conversationalist," Shinya admits, almost curiously. "I hate talking. There is so much thought that must be put into it. But with you, there is no effort. I am not afraid of insulting you. Somehow."

"Lord Aiko, even if you did insult me, you'd never know it," I promise.

He's not looking at me, but in front of his feet as we walk. There's a slight up-turning of his mouth, a subtle little movement, but it's the first time I've seen him smile.

We've come to an elaborate fountain. Its spurts of water are illuminated by lights planted around the ground. I can tell from his eyes that Shinya finds it visually stunning, so I stop walking, knowing he will mimic me.

"I'm sure you haven't offended anyone here at all," I add. "As you said yourself, you've barely spoken. You've done almost all you possibly could to adapt to our culture as well, including wearing gloves at almost all times."

Shinya looks down at his hands with dissatisfaction. "I am not fond of them," he says. "But you Isaarians do not seem to mind. You have all kinds of styles and colors and types."

"It's different, growing up with it as a cultural tradition," I say. "Do you primarily live in Tourran, then?"

Tourran is famous for its lenience about fluke-usage. And from what I've heard, Shinya's fluke is an impressive one. I'm sure his father found a way to make it politically useful. Based on what I can tell about Shinya, I'm sure some part of him enjoyed showing off as well. Not for the accolades and attention, but I think he gets genuine pleasure out of using his abilities. It's a relief for him.

"My father and I have a residence in Tourran that we frequently…" he struggles to find the right word. "Occupy?"

I nod.

"It is in Yobashi. Where I am from," he adds.

"It must be strange, living in different countries on and off again," I say. "I've never been outside Isaaria. I think I'd have a hard time adjusting, but you've done an excellent job."

Shinya blushes. "Thank you, Lady Soleil. I truly do not mind. For the most part. Only, I am used to using my...*fluke* much more often elsewhere, than here. It can be taxing, trying to keep...balanced."

I can tell this is another instance where his second language is not precise, but I still think I understand what he means.

"Well, if you do need to let off a little energy, I wouldn't mind seeing your fluke," I offer. "I know you're not allowed to use it in the palace, but we're not in the palace."

"I...That is very generous, Lady Soleil, but I do not think appropriate," Shinya says, taken aback.

I goad him on, for my own reasons.

"Oh, no one will know," I reassure him. "Besides, you've been letting me walk around without my gloves this entire time, anyway. You can always use that as insurance; I won't say a word."

He hesitates, but then his fine silk gloves fall abandoned on the ground. Whirling, he allows his hands to just barely skim the surface of the water of the fountain, and as he moves, he carries it with him. As if the water is wet paint on a canvas. He spins and sends it spiraling into the air, almost suspended, but connected to the fountain at the base. The more Shinya works, the more the floating water becomes like an abstract sculpture coiled in the air around us.

For a few moments, even I'm enchanted. Shinya's fluke is truly a gift. He's talented. Unique. He does not control the water, but seems to be... extending it, somehow. I've no doubt he can do the same for any other material.

I've never in my life heard of an ability such as his.

And then, suddenly, the water all freezes, and it takes Shinya a second to stop even after realizing he's now working with ice. Startled, Shinya turns just as I do to see Rian approaching us with a grin, applauding. Korvaan and Qhan are following him, and Mango is curled around his shoulders.

"Your majesty!" Shinya says, and quickly bends into a stiff bow.

He is attempting to compose an apology in Alarkian, in his head, but Rian makes certain he doesn't get a chance to finish.

"Ah, what perfect teamwork," he compliments.

He says so while sliding an arm around my waist as he admires the ice sculpture wrapped in the air around us. I would slip away, but I actually don't mind letting Shinya see, and I won't begrudge us a somewhat romantic moment as a couple. I note sweat on Rian's forehead and recall what he said to me, about freezing and manipulating water without contact. It is taxing. But he bothered, still.

Shinya is desperately trying to find his gloves. He is terrified, despite what I said, that he's made some disastrous error by taking them off, especially in order to display his fluke in front of me–an Isaarian prince's fiancée.

"I...I would *never* have...That is, please forgive me your majesty," the poor boy is attempting. "I wouldn't...It wasn't—"

"It was entirely necessary for a proper performance, and what a performance it was! You are quite talented," Rian compliments. "Your father should be proud of you."

Shinya is turning pink. He won't look at either of us. But Mango leaps off of Rian's shoulders and scampers onto Shinya's. The boy is startled at first, but Mango starts to sniff around at him, wide-eyed with curiosity. Then he licks Shinya's face and settles in.

"Would you look at that. He likes you," Rian says.

After another moment of letting Mango purr on his shoulder, Shinya reaches up to hesitantly pat the dragon's snout, smiling for the second time tonight. It's not a grand smile—it doesn't even show his teeth—but it's enough to completely transform his face. The boy is only seventeen.

"And I like you too, Lord Aiko," Rian adds thoughtfully. "I'm very glad to know that you're intended to represent your country here. In fact, if it pleases you, regardless of who is king, I'd like you to stay on. I know your father claims you're not yet ready to be ambassador, but I beg to differ."

"Thank you, your majesty," Shinya says. "Again, I apologize for—"

"Oh, don't bother with all that," Rian insists. "I know you wouldn't ever do Soleil any harm. I'm sure she forced you into it."

Shinya mumbles something in agreement, still clearly abashed. I almost feel guilt, but I know he wanted to show off just as much as I wanted to see his fluke. And now I know at least one person's fluke around here, which is almost a relief. It gives me some reassurance that I might be able to find out Vásan's in time, despite Taris' lack of success.

"Join us on our walk back to the palace, why don't you?" Rian offers. "I'm sure we'd appreciate the company, and since we're all going back anyw—"

A sneeze from the bushes interrupts him. Qhan and Korvaan jump to attention, but Rian waves them back. Korvaan looks to me, but I, too, suspect there's little danger afoot. I walk towards the bushes to take a look, wary, but not overly so. When I find our uninvited guest there, curled against a large urn, my instincts are proven correct.

It's Irina Lundan. Her dress is damp, her hair matted against her scalp as if she hasn't washed it in some time, and she's grey with cold. I almost did not recognize her, except she's still wearing the dress she had on the night Lune caused a fuss.

"Grand Princess Lundan?" I say.

She only sneezes again and curls up tighter. My companions have joined me, having deduced that what I've found is in no way a threat.

"Princess," Rian says, surprised. "What in the world are you doing out here?"

Irina doesn't answer him either, but her teeth are chattering.

"Is she all right?" Shinya asks.

"I think she's sick," Korvaan notes unnecessarily.

Qhan puts a hand to my elbow and draws closer to whisper something to me while the others are preoccupied trying to get answers out of Irina.

"I heard from Crown Prince Lundan's head of security that the princess has been missing since before the morning of the breakfast," Qhan says.

"Missing?" I repeat.

Detrus specifically said that Irina was feeling unwell and was staying upstairs. I'd assumed it was morning sickness.

"Detrus wanted it kept quiet," Qhan confirms.

I crouch next to Irina. She doesn't flinch away from me, too dazed to realize I'm a complete stranger. Wet, exhausted, and ill, she's forcing herself to stay out here. As if she thinks her life depends on it.

"Princess? Can you tell us what you're doing out here?" I ask her.

"I'm so worried about him," she whispers, wide-eyed. "He's acting strange, so strange…He's not my husband at all!"

"I'm sorry?" I say.

I know Irina's talking about Detrus. I suppose she's claiming she's out here to hide from him. But why? The first day we arrived, I noted the two of them standing together, acting still very much in love. And I think someone else would have noticed if something was wrong with Detrus.

"Princess? Have you been out here all this time?" I try again.

"He won't touch me. He won't look at me," she says, her mouth quivering. "He…He's not my husband."

She coughs, and I can hear phlegm stuck in her throat. She's shivering, but I cannot tell if it's from the cold, or fear.

"Where's your daughter?" I ask her.

Irina shakes her head. "Not here. I don't know. I don't know. She…I…"

I frown, confused and intrigued. "How can you not know? Princess?

Irina," I say, and put my hand to her shoulder. "Irina, where is your daughter?"

"Soleil, stop," Rian says, as if he doesn't understand how important getting this information could be. "She's unwell. We should get her back to the palace."

"I'll call for coaches," Korvaan suggests, already heading off to do so. "I don't think any of us should be walking back."

I shoot Rian a look.

"Do you think it's safe to take her back?...What she was saying, about Detrus..."

"I think we can't leave her out here like this, and that Detrus would never hurt her," Rian admits. "Being back in the capital in a time like this strains people. Changes them. That's all. Let's bring her to Mercer and let him check her over. Maybe settle her somewhere she can rest away from everything."

"Rian." I stand again. "What about their daughter? What if something has happened to her?"

"Why would anyone want to hurt Elodie Lundan? She's a child," Rian protests. "And the Isaarian people love Detrus. They got to watch him and Irina fall in love and get married—no one would ever harm their daughter. Detrus isn't even one of the likely princes to be crowned. I'm sure Irina's confused. She's sick. Elodie's probably with a nursemaid or someone of that station."

I know I should leave things be; whatever private issues the Lundans are having, it's none of our concern. And I don't have the time or energy to worry about Irina. So, I know I have to bring her back to the Pyrian Palace, and let someone else manage things for her. But the decision feels wrong.

"Then do me a favor," I mutter to Rian, while Shinya crouches down to try his hand at luring Irina out of the bushes.

"Anything," Rian says.

"Stay away from Detrus. For safety's sake."

Rian snorts. "Soleil, I'm not going near any of the other heirs. I can promise you that."

"Fine. Good. How did things go with Mercer?" I ask.

So long as Shinya is distracted, I might as well take the time to speak with Rian while we're out of the palace.

"Perfect. We couldn't meet alone—he was busy with Lune, so Crispin was there, and I'm sure there are eyes and ears everywhere—but I got him to think it would be a good idea to take you out to lunch tomorrow. Someplace private. I *also* have implied that you can more than take care of yourself. And me."

"Are you sure that's wise?"

Rian shrugs. "I don't think it'll be detrimental if folk know you can handle yourself, Soleil. I know you like to take people by surprise, but it might be better if they're intimidated by you."

I sigh.

"Rian, there are still so many unanswered questions—we're walking into this partially blind," I admit.

"Sometimes risks are necessary. Even if we relive this a hundred times more, we still won't know everything."

"Yes, but…"

I force myself to stop grinding my teeth.

"It has occurred to me that our enemies obviously know more than us in general, but what if they also have their own way of remembering what happens each loop, like how you have that ring?"

Korvaan's returning, calling something to us about a ten-minute wait for the coaches. I tell him to help Shinya with the princess and discreetly pull Rian even further away from them.

"And another thing," I mutter to him. "Rian, I think…I think it's possible that I'm stressing reality with all the use of my fluke."

"What's that supposed to mean?"

"This evening, Shinya told me he dreams vividly about a girl he's never met before. And he specifically mentioned he thinks he's *'meant to help her'.*"

"So?"

"So, I think people are starting to…not remember, exactly, but have emotional tugs. I think Shinya's remembering his future wife, because I've forced them to meet and fall in love so many times over again. And if he can remember that, who's to say others can't feel more concerning 'tugs'? What if there's no point in this ruse with Mercer in the first place, because—"

"So-*leil,"* Rian interrupts. "It will be fine. I cannot believe I'm the one telling you that. Look, we've long since discovered we've got at least several different camps of enemies working against us. We've definitely enemies outside and within the palace walls. But if Mercer comes forward as bait, we can flush out the enemies within who don't know who I am, and that will give us time to work on stopping the enemies outside who do know who I am. What I am."

Korvaan has picked Irina up out of the bushes and is returning to us, with Shinya trailing behind. We need to get out of the garden, I realize, and head towards a more open area for a coach to meet us. It will be impossible for me and Rian to talk, then, and he knows it.

"Everything's going to be fine, Soleil," Rian promises me. "We've failed so many times that by the universe's own rules, we eventually have to stumble into a way to make this work."

As our time to talk expires, I'm forced to nod in agreement. But perhaps it's for the best. I do have the tendency to mince my own plans when I have too long to think about them. I'm too prone to worry. I know there's a conspiracy about Rian, and I know there are people trying to kill him. Very dangerous people.

But my fear makes me jump at shadows. People have multiple motivations. Multiple goals. Really, aside from the Carsans and the Pikes, everyone else in the palace could be completely innocent when it comes to wishing harm on Rian.

Tomorrow, I'll recruit Mercer to our cause during our lunch. With his help, and the folks loyal to both him and Rian, we'll stand a chance of keeping the rightful heir to Isaaria safe.

This is the right thing to do.

RIAN SLEEPS IN again the next morning, but I can't make it past seven. I pluck an equally restless Mango up from his pattering at the end of the bed and see to sorting out breakfast. Afterwards, I remain in the dining room with Mango warming my lap, reading one of Rian's books to try and keep myself from overthinking. It is only half-working.

After returning last night from the grotto with a half-mad Irina Lundan and Lord Ambassador Aiko's son, there was definitely some talk about the palace. I'm sure Mercer will ask me about it today, and I have not decided what I will say, yet. If anything. It's not as if I should have to defend myself; Shinya is the one who stumbled upon me, and we found Irina completely by accident.

To be honest, I don't know how people could twist any worthwhile gossip out of it. The situation is merely one more irritation to weigh on my mind. If I could, I'd have my *khashak* look into the matter for me. To see what people are saying and to make sure Irina's doing well. But I can't spare any of them, now. And even if I asked Taris—who'd likely be best suited to the job—I don't think he'd do it.

The Pikes are, obviously, much more important.

Ayla helps distract me when she comes in to eat, excited to have half-finished her project. She claims she'll be spending at least part of the morning finishing up, since this afternoon she's accepting Asmer's invitation to tea.

Rian and I decided to let her go; we'd already declined the Carsans, after all, and have no desire to make anyone suspicious of what we know.

Besides, Naomi will go with. And Asmer's the least likely person here who'd think of doing Ayla harm.

The rest of our party slowly goes about their morning business, doing as I've ordered them while simultaneously trying to look after their own needs. Taris looks especially exhausted, and his curls are no longer as meticulously tamed as he'd like, but no one dares to tease him about it. I think he spent all night trying to get the information I've asked him for, with little success.

Rian spends most of his morning working on Magnus' project, but comes out to spend time with myself and Ayla. None of us have bothered to dress for the day, yet, but I suppose that's not uncommon for royals. And I have an excuse: I didn't want to dress only to have Rian or Naomi tell me I'd have to change again for lunch. This way, they can pick out whatever it is they think I should wear, and I won't receive a lecture.

When the time comes, I wear a dark blue skirt that hugs my sides down to my knees, with long slits up both sides, and black silk stockings beneath. Feminine high-heeled boots. A blouse with a thick lace neckline, and a posh, though serviceable, jacket, complete with a decorative sash that runs across my body from shoulder to hip. Black silk gloves. The skirt is easy to move in, without making it look like I expect trouble. This is simply a prince taking his best friend's lover to lunch, to get to know her better. It has nothing to do with Comus Day tomorrow and certainly nothing to do with our plans for it.

Naomi tries to help me pull my hair back nicely, a difficult feat for us both as it is particularly humid today. It's Taris, of all people, who nudges his sister aside to help me. I don't know for certain where he learned to do it, but I've suspected for a long while, now, that Taris had a wide array of lovers during our time at the University. He knows how to twist and braid my hair so that it looks attractive and smart. It's a strange talent for him, but then again, I suppose his glass-work is, too.

"She's getting jittery," Naomi notes to the room as Taris finishes and I stand. "Calm down, Soleil. Your suspicions are going to make everyone in the palace suspicious of you. Not everyone here has an agenda, you know."

"I have to assume they do, or else Rian could die," I snap, and instantly regret it. Naomi looks hurt.

"I'm not going to die, darling; we still haven't had our son yet," Rian says with a yawn from his sprawl on the couch.

"That jest has worn out its welcome, *darling,*" I respond through gritted teeth.

"She's in a mood," Korvaan notes to Qhan, who wisely decides to say nothing.

"Would it make you feel better if I told you I managed to get my hands on a copy of the Comus Day schedule?" Naomi offers.

"Oh, excellent. Give it," I say, holding out a hand, but she refuses.

"You can go over it after your lunch with Mercer. Use it as a carrot for yourself. A reward for a job-well-done maintaining a social life."

"Ah—starting a social life," Rian corrects, and I groan.

"I don't want to go to lunch with Mercer," I complain. "This is the worst idea I've had yet. I should be by your side at all times. Protecting you."

I know this was the right thing to do, but I'm suddenly extremely nervous. I hate leaving Rian, especially now.

Rian raises an eyebrow. "Out of curiosity, Soleil, how much trouble do you think I'll get into in my rooms with your *khashak* while you eat lunch with my best friend?"

I consider. "Likely none. But probability is a broken science. We should be careful."

"Soleil," he sighs, "you're being difficult. We asked him, he agreed. Now keep to your word. You're going to have to get used to it—people will expect you to when you are queen."

"What if I postpone," I suggest. "Beg off going out. Reschedule in…a week?"

"So-*leil*, now you're being ridiculous. We have a plan. It's a good plan. But we need Mercer, and this is the perfect opportunity to pull him in without looking suspicious. Go to lunch, hit it off, and when you think the time is right, slip him my proposal discreetly."

"What will we even talk about?" I ask. "I don't know how to talk about anything, except…well, you."

Even I have to admit: that's a little concerning. My life literally revolves around Rian. How pitiful.

Rian rolls his eyes. "Wonderful. This will be a fabulous opportunity for you to expand your horizons and figure out what you like in life besides me. Who knows: maybe you'll even, possibly, potentially, become friends. Again."

I accept defeat and check my watch with a scowl. Ten minutes until Mercer's meant to retrieve me.

"I'm leaving early," I decide, slipping an extra knife in my boot and pulling my stockings up properly.

"Mercer is to come pick you up—" Naomi starts.

"Yes," I say, "but there's no point in sitting here quietly panicking. I'll meet him halfway."

I'm already to the door, my hand on the knob.

"All of you; see to the jobs you have been assigned. Hopefully when I return, it will be with good news. Rian: stay out of trouble. Naomi: keep an eye on Ayla."

"Naturally, darling," Rian says cheerfully.

I'm mostly out the door when I hear Naomi call out, so I stop in the hall. She hurries after me to hand me a flask and cloth pouch that I can wear tucked under my sash.

"There's a hyssop concoction, for your throat," she lists, "and then mint and sage leaves, so you don't grind your teeth."

"My throat?" I say.

Naomi sighs in dramatic exasperation. "You might be queen one day, Soleil, but right now, you're just a woman with a dreadfully sore throat meeting with a crown prince."

"Am I still that dreadful?" I say, trying to listen to myself.

My neck aches from the times I have almost been choked, recently, but I didn't expect anyone else to notice. Or care.

"Your voice cracks every couple of sentences, and you are constantly clearing your throat. Mercer is bound to notice that. The hyssop should help. It is so you don't annoy him," she adds, but I know better.

Naomi's still looking after me.

"Thank you," I say.

I'm tempted to tell her about Ayla's secret project, but I don't want to push things. Naomi still has reason to be mad at me, and frustrated in general with our current predicament.

"Don't do anything stupid," she says.

I almost laugh, but nod instead before turning to leave.

Crown Prince Ralhan himself crosses my path about a five minutes' walk from Rian's rooms. He's startled at first, but recovers with ease. He's dressed finely, today, and I'm sure he's trying his best to impress.

"Lady Soleil! Looking lovely today," Mercer says, and comes close to kiss one of my gloves. "Oh, what am I saying? You've looked lovely every day."

I can't help but smile at his teasing. Already, I feel better.

"Flatterer."

"Only when I have to be," Mercer responds, and then holds out an arm. "Shall we? I've got the perfect place to lunch. I think you will be very pleased."

"When you put it that way, there's no time to waste," I say, and allow him to escort me down the halls as his guards fall in around us.

Instead of trying to guess our destination, I allow Mercer to entertain me with small talk. I sense he has many questions for me, but is saving them until after we've sat down to eat. And, likely, until we have more privacy. He and Rian are so close that I know they tell each other almost everything. The fact that Rian has supposedly kept me a secret from Mercer all this time means there's an entire side to him that Mercer thinks he hasn't seen.

We will be discussing Rian as much as myself, though I must not forget to keep my answers guarded and in alignment with what Rian and I have already said. We can't have contradicting stories floating about the next day. And, as I've already learned, rumors in the Pyrian Palace spread like wildfire.

"Ayla seems to be settling in well, here," Mercer notes.

"Ah, yes," I agree. Ayla is a safe topic to talk about. "She's definitely glad to be with me and Rian, not sitting in wait at the University."

Mercer brightens visibly. "Oh, good. Because, you see, that's exactly what I was thinking! No child wants to keep it a secret that she's going to be a princess. And Comus Day is historic. A once-in-a-lifetime experience…I figured Ayla would like to watch."

"You are right, it will be historic," I agree.

"Have you decided when to announce your engagement to the public?"

"Not quite. Soon," I say. "But I'd hate to upstage Comus Day. Rian and I will make things official within a few days. Our engagement, and our plans with Ayla."

"I look forward to it, then."

"Me as well."

I look forward to that day, because it means that Rian will be safe. All this chaos will be over with.

As we head down the hall, Vásan suddenly rounds a corner. He's walking quickly, and purposefully, as if he's late for a meeting. I half-expect him to say something to us as he draws near, but Vásan merely gives us a curious nod of acknowledgement before he continues on his way.

"He's looking a little grim," I note, probing to see if Mercer has an answer.

"He has some conference with the Grand Prince and Princess Carsans, I think. I can't be sure. No one tells me much of anything," Mercer says. "But that's fine by me—I'm glad to be left out of the politics."

I almost ask him for his opinion on Vásan and Lune, but catch myself. I'll save that for later. Right now, I'd like to get Mercer in a relatively secure location.

I'm surprised by our destination, though I probably shouldn't be. Mercer has arranged for us to take lunch at the Solunium Hub. Privately, I note, as it looks like the Hub is closed to anyone else.

The wide hallway leading to the Hub's arched entryway has no interior lighting, but that makes the approach more exciting. Beyond, I can see a series of round, white tables with matching chairs, and places set for diners. One could have their pick of the scenery, and I can distantly hear flowing water, hinting at fountains inside. Eating at the Hub must feel like dining in a Fae kingdom—or the closest humans can get to it safely. With its decorations and flora, numerous trees stretching over the cobblestone paths, and even birds chirping to one another, it is enchanting.

I've never been to the Solunium Hub, and I have heard it is acclaimed for its beauty and atmosphere. Having lunch inside it means much more to me than traversing the grotto did, blasphemous though that sentiment might be.

Mercer and I are stopped at the entrance by a man in uniform, who stands at a metal table before a wall of cabinets and baskets.

"Crown Prince Ralhan," the man says, offering Mercer a bow. "We are pleased you could make your appointment. Lunch will be served shortly."

"Wouldn't miss it," Mercer claims brightly.

"Very good. Please remove any weapons or electronic devices," the man says, and while Mercer starts to comply, I hesitate.

Naturally, he notices. And while Mercer is unaware of my *Khashtani* origins, it is not hard to guess why a noblewoman might be wary of relieving herself of all methods of self-defense. Especially since I haven't brought any bodyguards of my own; I am, to all appearances, completely dependent on Mercer's preparations. And he's realized that.

"I'll take you someplace else—" Mercer starts.

"It's fine," I say. "This is fine."

"Are you sure?" he asks, concerned for my comfort. "We can head out into the city. It's a beautiful day."

"Then we'll enjoy it from here," I respond. "Truly, this is lovely. I'm a little nervous, that's all."

I tell myself there is little reason for me to suspect a threat, here; firstly, Rian and I have established that assassins almost never target me, only him, and he has Qhan, Taris, Naomi, and Korvaan all watching him, in addition to his usual bodyguards. Besides, I may depend mainly on my knives, but I'm not exactly useless hand-to-hand. Additionally, the Solunium Hub is probably one of the few places in the palace that I can count on no one eavesdropping. No one would plant a bug there. No one would plant a spy. It's too open, and too obvious. Sacred is the wrong word, but it's the closest thing I can think of right now.

"Give me a minute," I say, and begin digging everything out. My knives, my darts, the poisons, my watch and earpiece. Everything except for the flask that Naomi gave me, and the pouch of leaves.

"Good Almighty, woman, are you expecting an invasion?" Mercer jokes.

"It pays to be prepared," I say.

He laughs, shaking his head, and helps deposit my belongings into a basket for safekeeping.

"You'll receive all your things back once you leave," I am reassured.

I follow Mercer inside the Hub, wary, but yet to see anything to warrant major suspicions.

Though I've told Mercer I don't mind being relieved of my weapons, I feel naked without them. There's a niggling voice in the back of my mind, routinely insisting that I've forgotten something.

"Mercer, do you trust your bodyguards?" I whisper to him.

He looks a little perplexed. "With my life. Obviously," he laughs.

"But do you trust them?"

"Completely and utterly," he says, reassuring now rather than teasing. "Marques especially. Even if I had an inkling otherwise, I at least have you here to protect me. Rian let slip that you're more than capable in combat. 'Incredible', even."

"Thank you," I mutter.

I don't care much for the compliment; I know I'm a decent bodyguard. That's why Rian's still alive. I'd rather have heard Mercer give me good reasons as to why he trusts his guards. Prove to me they can't be bought out. The fact that he's considered at all that I may need to use my skills means that there's some part of him that doesn't trust his bodyguards. It might be a very small part, and it might be a part Mercer isn't fully aware of, but it's still there.

I don't even notice myself slipping a fork into my coat pocket as we pass one of the standing tables.

I try to enjoy our surroundings, especially the sun streaming in through the glass roof. Mercer is nearly giddy with excitement. Possibly the last time he was here was as a boy, and I'm sure he's happy to be sharing the experience with me for my first time while reminding himself of the beautiful things humans can accomplish in tribute to the natural world. Even the tables and chairs have vines twined around them, some with flowers blooming.

Mercer and I are escorted to our table, and helped to take our seats. Mercer's guards try not to hover over us, and stand at least thirty paces away, all around. We're served iced water and tea, cheese and olives, and a carafe of wine before we're left alone by the staff.

"Do you approve of the location, then, Lady Soleil?" Mercer teases, and I realize that I've been staring up and around us for several minutes.

"Oh, the…yes," I admit, and take the wineglass he's filled for me. "I'm sure you knew I've never been here before. Only heard about it. I appreciate you sharing it with me, thank you."

Mercer shrugs. "All the royals like to dine here. The queen regularly takes tea every week with her attendants. I figured, as Rian's bride-to-be, you ought to share in the experience, wouldn't you say?"

I manage a smile. I'm not fond of the wine's flavor, I'm finding, but I keep drinking regardless. It's the only thing I can think to do when I don't know what to say. Mercer is natural at conversation, but I can only appear natural if I have a goal in mind. Small talk is beyond me.

My wineglass drains quickly. Mercer deftly pours me more to drink without appearing to think twice of it.

We continue to talk, almost meaninglessly, while we wait for the food. Mercer asks me personal questions about my interests, and I answer as best I can without lying outright. I do engage in physical activities regularly. I have taken training classes in combat. And I do enjoy Rian's stories and the way he is so easily excitable when he finds something new in his research.

I keep waiting for the right moment to complete my mission, but an opportunity does not present itself presently. It would be too awkward. Too abrupt of a change. Mercer would start asking too many questions if I slipped him the note now, and I finally decide, as I pick my way through two courses, that I'll wait until the end of lunch. I'll get a better opportunity, then. I hope.

"I suppose you and Rian will want to settle down quickly after the wedding, then," Mercer notes as he's tucking into his fish. "If your adopting Ayla is any indication."

"That's the plan," I say, but I'm uneasy, because I've never considered that not being the plan. I don't like how Mercer looks almost disappointed by it.

"I'd almost hoped you'd be the sort to refuse that type of thing," he claims. "So that, between the two of us, we might push Rian out the door. Get him to come see more of the world with me."

"Rian's not much one for traveling," I admit.

Mercer sighs. "Oh, don't I know it. He likes to stick in one place and do what he can, there. I'd imagine it's isolating, but if he likes it, he likes it. You know, if not for Comus Day, I'm sure he'd have wanted the three of you to spend the rest of your lives at that university."

I force a laugh. "Ah. Well. Maybe so."

"All I'm saying is, don't be surprised if that's the one place he continually wants to visit," Mercer warns. "Rian's a good man, but as I'm sure you know, sometimes his head's off someplace else. Putting together lost Magicsmith lines and the like."

"You tease, but still indulge him," I note. "Rian showed me that Kachin hairpiece you gave him. That was generous of you."

Mercer shrugs. "I knew he'd appreciate it. And I was curious, anyway, to find the piece in the west. If it belongs anywhere, it's back in Kacha, but given the current tensions between them and the Tourrannese, I hesitate to try and return anything of cultural importance. So, I thought Rian would be a good guardian for it."

I frown. "Tensions? What tensions?"

"I'm not surprised you hadn't heard," he admits. "They like to keep quiet about it. And it's a good move—sending out Lord Aiko and his son to represent both countries, pretending like they have a united front. But as we approach nearly one-hundred years of peace between the countries, I'm sure many in Kacha still remember what it was like for them, under Tourrannese rule. It can't be easy, trying to move on from that. And since the Lijimi and Alarkians have caved to their political and social tensions, also brought on by wars past…"

He trails off.

I sigh. It sounds as if, even after I get Rian safely on the throne, there will be no rest for us. The politics of the world will demand our attention.

"I hope you forgive me for saying so," I admit, trying not to grumble, "but it seems to me as if wars often happen for the most ridiculous reasons."

"Oh, most wars are complete nonsense," Mercer agrees. "And all the while, the innocents are the ones that pay the price. But I wouldn't be too quick to despair. You know I've been traveling in the west," he says in a way that tells me he's building up to something.

"I've heard as much," I say. "Lijimata and Alarkia, I thought."

"Among…a few other places," he says with a vague smile. "The sorts of places very few people ever see."

"Good for you," I say, and drain my wine again. I know I'm being rude, but I can't help myself. I hate being away from Rian.

"I encountered something…very curious, while there," he says, trying to entice me, I think.

"Oh?"

"One could call it a new way of thinking," Mercer admits, twirling his fork around his plate. I think he's enjoying the lunch more than I am. For some reason, nothing tastes right to me.

"Are you going to enlighten me, or do I have to ask?" I sigh.

"Oh, no, I'll tell you all about it. Fascinating stuff," he claims. "You see, we as individuals often go about our lives assuming that, to reach our highest, most lofty goals, we have to depend on others. A person might go around thinking, 'I wish there was peace in the world', or, 'I wish I never had to see children suffer', but it's always considered impossible. Especially for a single person to do anything about."

"I'm sorry, I'm getting a headache. What are you talking about?"

"I'm saying there are ways to reach those lofty goals of ours, so long as we turn to some more…unconventional methods. Push the boundaries a little."

"Mental boundaries? Moral ones?" I ask. I'm trying to decide if Mercer is about to lecture me on some new-age Western philosophy, because there are many, many topics of discussion that I would find much more interesting.

"All kinds of boundaries," Mercer claims. "Think about all the rules you believe to control the universe. And then picture someone revealing to you the lot of those boundaries are fictional."

"And who made them up, then?"

"Any number of people. Most religious entities. Sometimes governments. Sometimes philosophers who take it upon themselves to 'protect' humanity from itself. Speculation and guesswork becomes fact, and before you know it, no one's asking questions anymore."

"Uh-huh. Very interesting," I say, my head pounding. "And who told you all this? The same people who got you that Kachin hairpiece, maybe? Or, was there not some girl who made that book Rian loves so much? Magic-mirror girl?"

Mercer smiles. "Teresa."

"Oh, she has a name. That's lovely for her."

I don't know why I'm in such a terrible mood. Well, yes, I do. I feel terrible. But still, I should be able to maintain a pleasant façade for Mercer's sake.

"She's a lovely girl," Mercer agrees. "And she didn't make the book, exactly, but she did all the illustrations. Very talented. Illuminated manuscripts, they're called. But, yes. Her, ah, *fiancé's* family was the one I spent quite some time speaking with about stopping the destruction in Alarkia and Lijimata."

"Uh," I start, and promptly forget the rest of my sentence. "Hope you learned much, then," I say instead.

"Oh, I certainly did. The head of the family is brilliant. And his wife is an expert in poisons and medicines. Did you know a person can be exposed to certain plant-based tonics for months without effect until a secondary chemical is introduced? They're called *activative* substances. Fascinating stuff. And perhaps the most intriguing thing about them is that they're so rare, they're virtually incurable."

"Mmm. Glad no one…wants us all…dead in Alarkia…then," I manage to say.

It is suddenly very hard to string a sentence together.

Oh…no.

My entire life, I've been worried about someone trying to poison Rian.

I've never considered someone trying to poison me.

"Feeling well, Miss Soleil?" Mercer asks. He's still smiling at me, as if nothing is the matter at all.

"Why…would you…"

"You're resilient, Soleil," Mercer comments, leaning forward. "Really, *quite* resilient. Any other woman, and you'd be on the floor by now."

"The...are…What…"

My muscles are going slack. All my limbs are loose.

"Usually, I would never drug a woman," Mercer reassures. And I'm confused, because he still seems very much like Mercer. "Really, I wouldn't. For any reason. But you've got to understand, I'm not much of a fighter. And you're…"

He laughs.

"Well, you understand."

"Itsnotyou," I slur.

"No, Soleil, it's most definitely me," he says, laughing at my doubt. He then stands and turns to one of his men. "Subdue her…and put her with the other one."

But I'm not focused on his words. I'm busy looking at his hand, on the table, and forcing myself to keep looking, keep looking, Soleil. I can get past this. I haven't ingested enough of whatever he gave me for it to do much. I might not be perfectly immune to every poison, but this one isn't deadly, it seems.

Because I am resilient. Damn if I'm not resilient. And while my head still aches, the moment I realized I was drugged, it wasn't hard to start exaggerating the drug's effects. So long as I can keep my wits about me, and I think I can, I'll be able to get myself out of this mess. I don't need answers right now, I just need to get back to Rian as soon as possible. The details can wait.

I pull the fork out of my pocket and slam it down through Mercer's hand, and into the table beneath it.

He's so shocked for a second that he doesn't know what to do. And then he starts screaming, as a person ought to when a fork goes through his hand.

There's no time to lose. Marques appears to pull the fork out of

Mercer's hand, pressing the prince's hand up against his chest and yanking him backward. His goal is to protect his charge, and regardless of what Mercer intended for me, getting the crown prince away from danger is more important.

Now all I have to do is take care of Mercer's men.

The first thing I grab is a napkin. Not the most useful item, but I'll make do. And I don't have enough time to try worry about it—I've got men bearing down on me from both sides.

I kick my chair into the first one. Not fancy, I know, but hitting a person at their midline with a metal chair is at least enough to give me a few seconds. The other man is greeted with hit in his throat, and then I spin him around and wrap the napkin around his neck. Pull and tie it very tight so he's choking, then kick out the back of his knees so he's on the ground scrambling for air.

Keep moving, Soleil, keep moving.

I throw myself onto the nearest table. Grab the table's umbrella pole. Kick, swing, smack. It's easy to give a person a concussion from this angle. That's another one down.

Someone tries to grab my umbrella pole. I snatch up a nearby potted plant and smash it down onto their head. Smack the end of my pole into another's gut before whipping it around to smack a few more heads. To make sure they're not getting up again.

Another man goes for the pole again. I let him have it. Grab my salad fork and stab it in his neck. Pull it back out and slam it into the eye of another assailant so he's screaming.

And that's the last of them.

Mercer and Marques are gone, but I don't pursue. Whatever they do, they are going to try and wrap Mercer's hand first. That gives me time. Not much, but a little is all I need.

So, I run right out of the Solunium Hub, stopping to grab my knives on the way out, leaving the place a lot redder than when I came in.

Twenty

I RUN BACK DOWN THE HALL, tying the remnants of my decorative sash tightly around my arm to staunch the bleeding there. One of those bastards scratched and I didn't notice. In retrospect, a lot of things might have happened in that short minute of combat that I didn't notice. For one, I'm bleeding. I'm missing a boot. The other one's heel snapped off. I think someone shot me. Just a graze, but still. When I focus on my survival, I realize, I might be just as frightening as one of the villains we're facing.

But I am starting to feel significantly dizzy. Whatever it was Mercer drugged me with is not leaving my body without putting up a fight. I'm sure I look half-crazed, staggering down the hall in one broken boot, but I don't dare stop to try and rid myself of the defective footwear. I have to get back to Rian's rooms. I must warn everyone else.

I'm panicking as I run, sure I can hear Mercer sending someone after me. Certain I'm about to feel someone grab me. Stab me. Appear from nowhere, the way I know Marques can. I can feel myself shaking, and it takes me forever to open the door to Rian's room. When I finally get the lock unlatched, I practically fall inside and have to kick the door closed behind me.

I force myself to take a second to breathe, prepared to ignore a storm of questions. But there's a disturbing silence.

I flip myself over, a mistake I immediately regret, but even with my spotty vision, I can tell Rian's bedroom is empty. No one in sight. It's so quiet in his chambers, you could hear a pin drop two rooms over.

"Rian!" I call, forcing myself to my feet, my heart pounding.

There's no one in the spare room, or the dining room. But Ayla is waiting quietly in the sitting room, reading one of Rian's books. Mango is on her lap. She looks up, and when she sees it's me, she starts to smile. But then she notices my appearance. The blood staining not only my arm and sleeve, but my hands as well. Possibly there's some splattered on my face.

I must look like a monster. Or like one dragged me around for a bit.

Ayla's not scared. Plucky little orphan.

"I'll go get Prince Mercer!" she says, leaping down off her chair.

"No!" I interrupt.

Ayla is startled into freezing, thankfully, but she's confused. And rightfully so.

"No," I repeat, trying to steady my breathing and sound reasonable. In control.

Knives. I need all my knives. My darts. Everything.

I shake my head. There's too much to do. I can't concentrate.

"Where is everyone? Why are you here alone?" I demand.

"I was with Miss Naomi and Lady Asmer, and then Miss Naomi suddenly said something wasn't right and made me come back here and told me to stay put," Ayla says. "I don't know where anyone is. Or what's happening."

Right, then.

I turn and hurry back to Rian's bedroom. I can hear Ayla following me, but I can't think of what to say to her. I'm glad she's not asking questions, though I'm sure she wants to.

Without bothering to hide what I'm doing, I start digging in Rian's wardrobe, pulling out my spare weapons. My darts. My bow, even. Might as well bring whatever I can. I lament the loss of my watch, and I know I should have taken it before leaving the Hub, but there's nothing I can do about it now. I'm sure I wasn't thinking straight at the moment. Not with the blood pounding in my head.

"What's all that for?" Ayla finally asks once I've all my gear in place and am tying on a new pair of proper boots.

"Don't you worry about it," I tell her. "Everything's going to be fine. I promise."

"You're bleeding," she notes.

Mango leaps up on my shoulders, mewling in concern, and I'm so startled, I nearly throw him off. I force myself to gently take him by the back of his neck and deposit him into Ayla's arms. I don't want to leave her alone—I'm not sure what possessed Naomi to do so in the first place—but I don't think I have a choice. Ayla's safer her, than she would be if I brought her with me. And I don't have the time to find someone to look after her.

I bend down and take her by the shoulders. Look her right in the eye.

"Stay put. Ayla. Listen, are you listening? Stay here. Keep the doors locked. Don't let anyone inside. No one. Understand?"

I'm starting to scare her, I can tell, but that will help. That will make sure she listens to me.

"But what if it's you?"

"If it's me, I'll pick the lock, or come in through a window, but do not open the door. No matter who asks you to. Understand?"

"I un-un-understand," she stammers.

"Good. Look after Mango, yes? Read one of your books and don't look at a clock. Time will pass quicker that way."

Before Ayla can beg me not to go, I'm out the door again.

It's empty and quiet in the halls. Unnervingly so. In a place this big, with this many guests, the palace should be buzzing with activity. Maids, guards, cooks, cleaners, royals, attendants.

Now that I think about it, anything could have happened in the rest of the castle during the ninety minutes or so I spent in the Hub, and I wouldn't have heard a thing. Without my watch, Taris wouldn't be able to reach me. Stupid of me, to lose it. I could have pretended to put it in a basket and then hid it in my sleeve. I could have. I should have. I didn't.

I run through the halls, trying to ignore the pulsing in head with every step. I'm looking for someone, anyone, to question, but I don't bother breaking down doors or picking locks. And I know I won't be find Rian like that, anyway. If he's not in his rooms, for whatever reason, he must be in a public place.

Gardens? No. He wouldn't be so foolish. Baths? No, for much the same reason. In fact, to give Rian some credit—or at least give Qhan some credit—they wouldn't have left his rooms unless they had to. And Rian would never, never leave Ayla behind if, for some reason, they had to run.

Which means they must have been forced to leave. I didn't see any signs of a struggle, so Rian went willingly. He opened the door on his own and walked out. He would have put up a fight if someone came to get him, which means someone lured him out, or tricked him.

I try to think. Assuming Rian is someplace he does not wish to be, where would someone lure him to? Why bother luring him? If they wanted him dead and had that level of control over him, they could have killed him in his rooms, but they didn't. They haven't. They must want him in a public place. And the most public place that I can think of on the palace grounds is…

The arena.

I change course, running for the underground entrances. If someone wanted Rian in the arena, they'd want him down on the floor itself, not in the audience.

When I reach the arena halls, it's anyone's guess as to which entrance Rian might have used. I start running around the outside, checking every passage, looking for him. Imagine my relief when, after three tries, I finally spot his white hair on the fourth hallway.

"Rian!" My voice echoes down the hall.

I run towards him, confused by what I see. Rian is there, along with Taris and Qhan. But they are trying their hardest to hold Rian back. He looks like he's struggling. Fighting them.

"What is this?" I demand.

Taris and Qhan are both helpless to explain. They don't know how to go about it. And I suspect they think I'd barely listen to them, anyway. So, it becomes Rian's responsibility instead. And when he looks at me, there's a foreign fear in his eyes that worries me.

"Soleil, I can't stop," he insists.

"What are you talking about?" I demand.

No one's mentioned that my arm is bleeding. I think we all know we lost control of this situation a long time ago.

"He just started moving," Taris insists, still working hard to hold on to Rian. I know for a fact that Taris is naturally stronger than my crown prince.

"And you didn't find that strange?" I snap.

"All he did was change his clothes at first, my lady," Qhan insists, and for the first time, I notice that Rian is wearing the outfit reserved for Comus Day. The one he wore his last night at the University.

"But then he walked right out the door," Taris adds, grunting when one of Rian's arms tries to elbow him in the face.

"I am so sorry," Rian insists.

I watch him, my mind racing. Then I pull the flask out that Naomi gave me and dump its contents over his head.

Rian splutters for a second. Taris and Qhan look stunned. But then Rian's arms relax, and he stops fighting so much. They let him go, surprised, as I'm sure they tried everything they could to stop him, but didn't think of that.

"How did you—" Taris starts.

"Witchcraft is often disrupted by hyssop. And mint," I say, hastily stuffing the leaves under Rian's clothes, everywhere I can. "Naomi didn't know it, but she gave me the perfect defense."

"Against what?" Qhan asks.

I don't think he likes the use of the word, "witchcraft", or what that implies.

"Who the hell would have laid a spell on him?" Taris asks. "And how would they have done it? You need physical contact for that. Or at least hair, blood..."

"Your guess is as good as mine," I say. But I do have a guess. Two, actually. And neither of them spell good news. "Where's Naomi? And Korvaan?"

"Korvaan, we sent to get you," Rian says, trying to unsuccessfully wipe some of the dampness off his ruined suit. "Naomi, we've no idea."

"What about the rest of the guards?"

"Dead or in a state like the crown prince, here," Qhan admits.

"Mercer?" Taris asks, and I gesture to my arm and the blood over me.

"I have him to thank for this," I say.

Rian looks appalled. "No," he insists. "No, Mercer would never—"

"But he did. Why? At the moment, it doesn't matter. Right now, we need to regroup—" I start.

Shots are fired at us from down the tunnel.

Taris immediately grabs me, yanks me down, and puts himself between me and the gunfire. Qhan does the same for Rian. I can hear Taris yelling in my ear to move. We run the only direction we can afford to: into the arena ahead. He and Qhan return fire, but I don't see if their shots hit because I'm busy grabbing Rian's arm and sprinting into the arena with him. I intend to bring him across it, to another one of the tunnels, where we can exit and return to his room before retrieving Ayla and fleeing the palace. But it seems our adversaries have other plans.

The first thing I notice when we enter the arena is just that: it looks properly like an arena, now. Not just a stage for a pretty noblewoman to sing her heart out, oh no. There's sand and dirt beneath our feet. Royal banners hung. Garlands. Obstacles. This is a proper gladiatorial pit. As if the Currian Council wanted all the heirs to fight to the death.

Only, when the king spoke to all the heirs on that first day, he'd implied there would be no such contest. Which means that this display was planned and arranged by someone else entirely.

Sure enough, I can see Crispin Carsans in the stands with two men who look as if they've been working on the arena. His voice echoes, as he's just barely restrained from yelling at them. At first, I assume, because something isn't to his liking. Then I realize it's because nothing is to his liking.

"This isn't at all what's meant to be here," he's snapping, gesturing to some chart or diagram. "My father sent me here to ensure everything was in order for tomorrow. So, who gave you the instructions for this monstrosity?"

From what I can see, the workers have no idea what's gone wrong, either. They're stammering apologies and trying to defend themselves when one of them glances down and notices us. He stops talking, drawing Crispin's attention to us as well. I'm prepared to defend Rian, if necessary, but Crispin doesn't try anything. In fact, he looks incredibly confused.

"Rian? What are you doing here? And Lady Soleil, you're bleeding," he realizes.

I share a quick look with Rian. I don't know what, if anything, we can say. But then Qhan and Taris are running to join us. At least one person is still firing shots after them, but they haven't hit any of us yet. Crispin's brow furrows. He's about to demand a full explanation when, suddenly, the two men beside him look much less bashful about their mistakes.

They attack him, forcing him to his knees and restraining his arms.

"What do you think you're doing?" Crispin snaps, furious. "Unhand me this instant. Don't you know what my father will do to you if he learns of this?"

"Oh, I'm sure they do," someone else says, his voice loud enough to be heard echoing around us. "But it doesn't really matter, now."

We all look up.

It's Detrus, up in one of the boxes. The king's box. Vásan is next to him. And even from down here, I can see that Vásan is not looking his best. For one thing, his clothes are bloodied, and torn. Not his blood, I'd gather, except, perhaps, for a few drops on his collar and chest; someone's practically sliced his face open. They've ruined his looks, that's for sure. And from the scowl on his face, I can tell Crown Prince Pike is not pleased with that.

"What in Hope's Head?" Rian mutters next to me.

I'm about to take his arm and run, not caring about what the other crown princes have planned or why, when I realize there's nowhere to run to. There are men bearing the Lundan and Pike colors scattered all over the arena. Both up in the boxes and seats, and near the exits.

"Crown Prince Rian!" someone else calls, their voice thinner compared to Detrus. I see little Yuugo Ido is in on this conspiracy as well, then. Standing behind us, with his own loyal servants at the ready. "No one wants this to be a bloodbath. Just do what you're told and no one has to fire a shot."

"Shots have already been fired," Taris mutters, his eyes flicking to my arm. I already know that whatever Rian decides to do, Taris is going to fight. And he'll ignore any order to the contrary.

I'm with him. I will not take orders from these crown princes.

I flick out my knives, and several guns click.

"Wait! Peace! Let us have peace for a moment," Rian calls with a nervous laugh, holding his hands up. He has not surrendered, but he's making a show like he might. "I don't know what you think I've done to deserve this but, ah, I can promise you, I'm not…Well. It's not…Can we talk about this?" he finally poses desperately.

"Afraid not," Detrus says, and then his tone changes as he orders his men. "Take the lady alive, kill the guards. And at least try not to kill Yakarami. It would be a hassle to—"

"Wait!" a voice rings out, and for a moment, everything freezes.

It's as if Nusk is alive and well again, his charmed tongue smothering the wills of all who can hear him.

But a second later, I realize there is a tune to the words ringing through the arena.

Lune.

She's standing in one of the boxes reserved for minor nobles. Behind her, partially hidden by the curtains, I can see Asmer looking terrified and confused. Yet Lune has no illusions regarding our predicament.

"No one move!" Lune calls again, and though her voice is thin and strained—her fluke is weak, now—it is enough to at least give all of us pause.

"Prince Detrus… Vásan, what do you think you're doing?" she demands from them. "This is most unlike you. Either of you. Detrus, you don't want the crown. Vásan, you all but have it! You know you do! Why would Rian Yakarami be a threat to either of you? To any of you? Have you stopped to consider the consequences of what you're doing?"

Neither of them answer her. But from the way Vásan looks at her, I can tell: that is not the Vásan Pike that was in love with Lune Carsans. That's not the man who burst into her room demanding he know what happened to her.

I remember what Irina Lundan said about her husband.

I ought to have looked into that when I had the chance.

"Awake at last, then, princess," Vásan says. He does not sound like Vásan, and it is obvious, as if someone else is speaking through him. "However, now, did you manage that?"

"I'm very resilient," Lune claims. "Now let them go. Or you'll regret it."

"I don't think so," Detrus interrupts, and then points at Lune and Asmer. "Take them, too."

I feel Taris at my shoulder. He takes my arm.

"Time to go," he says, then raises his gun and fires up at the crown princes.

It doesn't matter that he won't hit them at this distance; Detrus and Vásan are forced to duck, for their own safety. The sound of Taris' pistol going off is loud and jarring, especially given the acoustics of our current location. Crispin takes the opportunity to attack the men trying to subdue him, and while they had the element of surprise on him before, he's much bigger. It only takes him a few seconds to free himself.

"Asmer, Lune, get out of here!" Crispin yells, and vaults over the railing, grabbing what he can as he makes his way down the arena. Hopefully to help us, possibly to act against us.

Lady Asmer has already stumbled backwards, taking off at a run for the back of their box. She's barely made it a few steps past the curtains when she runs into a soldier—not one of the ones loyal to either Crispin or Rian. He grabs her, and starts dragging her away when Lune raises her leg, pulls her butterfly knife from under her skirt, and stabs him. Asmer's screams fall into shocked silence. Lune pushes her away, likely telling her to run.

Then I watch as Lune opens that gaudy bracelet charm of hers, spits in it, then uses a finger to draw out the paste and trace Signs of the Dead on the soldier's forehead.

"Dammit," I mutter, and then shove Rian forward behind a prop barricade, just in time to protect him from any wayward bullets. I see Qhan and Taris take cover as well, not too far away.

I can't see what's happening above us, but focus on trying to keep Rian low to the ground. He manages to jerk his arm free of my grip and rips off his gloves. I guess there's no point in trying to keep his fluke a secret anymore, and Rian knows that, too. He commands the ground beneath us just as easily as he has fire and water before. He can't make mountains, but he can at least give us more cover. The crown princes' men haven't stopped shooting, but Rian's bought us time.

"We can't hold them off. We'll run out of rounds quickly, and at that point, they'll be able to take us," Qhan warns. "We need to get out of here."

"I'm working on it," I promise. "In the meantime, we need as much firepower as we can get our hands on."

"There!" Taris says, and points.

There's a rack with weaponry propped against it. Another part of the garish stage that's been set, here.

"Go!" I insist. "Give me the gun; I'll cover you."

Within seconds, Taris' weapon is in my hands as he sprints toward the weapons rack. We can't know for sure why such a thing has been staged here, but I can guess. And if the crown princes want Rian alive, I'm afraid it will only be so that they can kill him for sport. Despite our current predicament, the thought is enough to make me nauseated, especially because I thought I knew some of these people, or at least knew their natures.

I would not have expected this from Detrus or Yuugo. And the last person I'd suspect of wanting to kill Rian for his own enjoyment is Mercer.

I use Taris' gun to keep our enemies' fire trained on us, and away from him. I don't know what good I'm doing, considering the unfair advantage against us, based on my brief glimpses of him, Taris appears uninjured. Qhan acts similarly, focusing on those opponents behind us while maintaining cover with Rian's barricades. I keep Rian's head down, continually shoving him against the ground though I know he wants to help. I don't care. He could have the most powerful fluke in the world and I'd still keep him out of this fight.

I refuse to lose him today.

I break cover to snap off a few shots up above us, trying to get a look at our enemies. There are at least two dozen, currently, and while none of them dare try to fight up close, Rian's right: our luck won't last long. I don't see Detrus or Vásan anymore, and I'm sure Qhan doesn't have eyes on Yuugo.

That's worrisome. The last thing I want is crown princes with powerful flukes down here in the arena with us. I might be able to take one of them, but not all of them at once, not with Rian to worry about.

"Let me help," Rian's insisting, starting to rise now that I don't have an arm pinning his shoulders.

"Yakarami!" Taris shouts, and suddenly he's there, swinging Rian around and raising a metal shield just in time to prevent the enemy's fire from hitting him. Rian instantly uses his fluke to add to our barricades, which in turn protects the rest of us from the barrage. Still, I'm glad when he lets me and Qhan pull him back down next to us.

"Remind me to give you a raise," Rian pants.

"You're not paying me, your majesty," Taris says.

"No? I should start."

I return Taris's pistol, sure it will be of more use in his hands, and unsling my bow from my back. It's a slower weapon to wield, but can be just as deadly if my aim is true. Taris himself looks to have acquired a metal shield and several bladed options. Rian starts rifling through them and finds a sword that looks close enough to the kind he trained with. So long as Taris has an assortment, Qhan has his scimitar, and me my knives, I'm sure we'll dominate close-range combat.

Assuming a lack of fluke magic.

"Mind if I join? Sorry I'm late. But no one said there was going to be a gathering in the arena," a woman says, and I look over just in time to see Nissa Sondushki slide into our group. Her hyena isn't with her, but I'm sure the beast isn't far.

Qhan and I both have weapons trained on her, but Nissa doesn't return the favor. I'd stab her in the throat and be done with it—no point taking chances—but if she managed to run across the arena to join us, avoiding gunfire, she might be one of the only heirs left we can trust to help us.

"I'm not sure whose side I'm meant to be on, here," she admits, "but you four seem to be the only ones not currently trying to kill me, so I think I'll stick with you for now, if you don't mind."

"Swear your allegiance to his majesty, the next king of Isaaria," I demand. I can't trust her, I know that, but at least if she swears her loyalty to Rian in front of Qhan, I'll be able to see if she's lying.

She raises an eyebrow. "If it makes you happy, my lady, I'll swear it," she claims, kissing two fingers and placing them to her forehead. "On behalf of the Hoitsokin people, I swear allegiance to his majesty Rian Yakarami. Satisfied?"

I look to Qhan and he gives me a short nod. She's telling the truth.

"You watch our backs with Qhan," I say. "I need get us out of here. Once I've done so, the crown prince will use his fluke to protect us, but I don't want to risk exhausting him early. We're going to need him."

I say this as much for Qhan and Nissa's benefit as Rian's. He can't like how helpless he feels, now. But as the only one of us with a powerful combat fluke, Rian is our backup. Even if I could command my fluke at will, I'm not sure I'd want to risk it.

"Five against an army. Not exactly a fair fight," Nissa notes.

"Allow me to even the odds a little," someone says, and Crispin Carsans appears. His arm is cut open, and there's blood on his temple. His fancy suit is most definitely ruined, but he's clearly muscled his way out of whatever cage the other crown princes would have liked to keep him in.

"You stay back," I warn him. Crispin has the gall to look offended. "I wouldn't trust you if Rian's life depended on it."

"Which, ah, sweetheart, it sort of does," Rian reminds me, flinching every time a bullet strikes too close to our hiding spot.

"Let him help, Soleil," Taris snaps. "Whatever suspicions you had before, I think it is obvious circumstances have changed, wouldn't you agree?"

I'm conflicted—I do still harbor distrust towards the Carsans, but after what I've seen, I know Crispin is at least not siding with Mercer, Vásan and the rest. So, we'll need him, just as much as we now need Nissa.

"Fine," I snarl, though my voice is lost amidst a sudden and rapid burst of gunfire that oddly sounds as if it's not at all in our direction.

"Brilliant," Nissa says. "Six. That's so much better."

"Can't you count? It is clearly nine," someone else says as they slip in next to Taris, panting.

It's Lune. And Naomi and Korvaan. It's getting quite crowded in here.

"Lune!" Crispin snaps. He's cross to see her here. "I told you to run!"

"And I did!" she retorts, expertly reloading her pistol in a way that unnerves me given what I apparently don't know about her. "In this direction!"

Squeezed in next to her, my *khashak* are looking after one another. I barely hear them checking in, but catch enough to know that they came here to rejoin Taris, Rian and Qhan, only to run into Lune. Though I know I don't have the time to confer with them, a visual inspection reveals neither Naomi nor Korvaan have sustained injuries yet and they've both come prepared, with their weapons of choice.

"Everyone, quiet," I order. "Qhan, Taris: keep laying down cover fire. We're getting out of here."

"Got a plan, then?" Rian coughs, and I realize I've been pushing on him too hard in my attempts to both cover him with my body and keep him from trying to get up.

I gesture through a gap in our cover. I know not everyone will be able to see without moving around some, but they'll get the gist. "The arena's surrounded by those underground tunnels, the ones that lead down."

"To the preparation rooms below, yes," Crispin agrees. "Most of them do."

"Yes, but one leads only downstairs. There's no way back into the palace through there. At least, not a natural means."

"What's your point?" Nissa snaps.

"They won't be guarding it," I remind them. "There would be no point. All we have to do is run down, bust through a wall, and we're out."

"Because it's that easy to get through a wall," the crown princess accuses.

"My *khashak* carry small bombs. It should be enough."

"Not for an outer wall," Taris warns. "Palace walls are too thick. We'll have to bomb through an inner wall, into an adjoining room. Make it back to the palace proper. There are more exits there. Hidden ways out."

"Then that's the plan. Qhan—you stick close to me and Rian no matter what. Keep him safe. Naomi, Korvaan, Taris: ring around outside. Nissa, Crispin, Lune: second ring outside that. Stick together and move quickly. Rian—watch our heads, if you don't mind. Use your flukes only if you must. You'll want to call your hyena in," I add to Nissa.

Thankfully, she has no quippy retort for that.

"Taris, let me know when there's an opening," I say, though I'm still paying close enough attention to realize that the gunfire has gotten significantly sparser in the last ten seconds.

"Now or never," he replies.

I grab Rian's arm. "Let's go!"

There are a few awkward stumble-steps as I transition from crouching to standing, pulling Rian with me. But once I've got my feet under me, I sprint across the area, Rian's arm gripped tightly. Considering the wild circumstances that have suddenly thrown us together, the others are surprisingly good at following my orders. I suppose as Nissa pointed out, since we're the only ones not trying to kill each other, sticking with us seems like the best bet for her. Whatever got to the other heirs didn't manage to get to her.

The tunnel I have in mind is only about a hundred paces away when I realize this is far too easy. Yes, we're still under a barrage, but the accuracy of the average marksman plummets significantly when presented with moving targets at a distance, even if they're heading in a straight line. The suppressing fire we've managed, plus Rian's fluke, means we're doing well. It looks as if we're about to escape with ease. Part one of my plans complete and a rousing success.

That's when the dragon lands in front of me.

It's a brightback. The largest of the worldly dragons, and a firedrake as well. Or, at least, we now know it's the largest of the worldly dragons. As far as I'd previously been aware, its kind was extinct. I'm not sure which of the crown princes acquired such a creature, but if I had to hazard a guess, it would be Mercer. Now he's unleashed the creature on us: silver scales, gaping maw filled with teeth as thick as one of my arms, staggering wingspan, and a neck long enough to snap down at one of us with ease: one dragon facing nine of us and we are oh-so-obviously outclassed.

The brightback roars, the sound so jarring it vibrates my bones. Even if I didn't know this breed to be particularly vicious, I'd be terrified.

I mutter an oath. We scatter as it snaps down at us—we're forced to. The brightback is large enough that it could knock us all over like champagne flutes if we stand together. I'm sure our bones would shatter just as easily. Qhan, Taris and I happen to all dive in the same direction, trying to keep Rian covered.

I hear a number of names shouted, screamed. I whip my head around as I get back to my feet, trying to get a headcount. Nine still alive and not painted in red, as far as I can tell with a cursory glance.

"Get to the tunnel!" I yell. "Go!"

It doesn't matter if we go together anymore, so long as we can all manage to dodge around the brightback.

Nissa raises her fingers to her mouth, whistles to call her hyena, and runs for the exit without further prompting. She's small, alone, and first. We'll hold the brightback's attention while she makes her escape. Taris is still kneeling on the ground but has propped up that metal shield of his and is using it to reflect the sunlight, trying to keep the brightback blind to us. It roars, snapping around at what it hopes is the level of our heads. My hair's ruffled as its maw sweeps above us, but Taris has bought us a few seconds.

"Get him out!" I order Qhan, throwing Rian at him while I unsling my bow from my shoulder once more and scrape up a few of my arrows.

Qhan grabs the indignant crown prince and begins to ferry him safely to the tunnel, avoiding the brightback's tail while Taris and I keep it occupied. Korvaan, Naomi, and the Carsans have enemies of their own to worry about, as we are no longer the only people on the arena floor. The crown princes' men try to keep their distance from the dragon, but they'll still engage those furthest from the beast.

The brightback lights a fire in its belly and spews a fiery magma that burns a hole two inches deep in the ground before sitting there, smoldering. Though I'm nowhere close to the infernal puddle, I can still feel the heat on my skin, reminding me the fire doesn't need touch me to cause debilitating burns. In fact, if it touches me, I'm sure it'll burn to the bone. And through it.

I exchange a look with Taris: not good odds for us.

We split up. Taris grabs what weapons he can, and I nock an arrow to my bow as I run, ready to shoot. The moment the dragon opens its maw again, I let the arrow fly, hoping to hit something fleshy in its mouth or throat. My arrow hits, and lodges, but I suspect this feels like nothing but a splinter to the brightback. A little painful, and irritating, but I am more of a mosquito than a hornet. If it tries to kill me, it will be to end an annoyance, not because it's scared of the rest of the nest.

We can't kill a dragon. I know that. But we have to keep it away from everyone else long enough for them to find an opening, and escape.

Avoiding the brightback is more trouble than I first anticipated. Its sheer size alone is staggering without taking into account its ability to breathe fire. And then there's the fact that I'm making of point of drawing its attention my way. Taris and I try our best to move in opposite directions, both of us hitting the dragon on and off again to protect one another. Taris has run out of bullets, but he's still got a few spears from that weapons rack, and he has excellent aim.

He manages to pierce the dragon's hide just next to its eye, which absolutely enrages the beast. It roars, throwing its head back. It would have been the perfect opportunity for the rest of us to slip past, only the dragon doesn't merely toss its head. It begins flailing, stopping about and sweeping its tail back and forth over the ground in front of the tunnel entrance.

I might not be an expert on dragons, but I know enough from listening to Rian all day that this is not how a normal dragon would behave. I conclude brightbacks, in general, are either exceptionally spastic creatures, or this one in particular is damaged.

Our opportunity lost once again, I quickly put distance between myself and the dragon, backing up until I'm more in danger from the crown princes' men than the beast. Taris stays closer, continuing to antagonize it, but he doesn't get a good second shot at it. Nothing that will pierce its scales, anyway.

Behind the brightback, I notice Rian running back out of the tunnel, carrying something heavy in a large bucket. Qhan and Nissa are following him, with buckets of their own. Upon reaching the entrance, Rian drops the bucket on the ground and allows its contents to slosh out all over the ground.

Water. Rian's come running back to us with *water.*

"Taris!" I shout, and he turns his head.

Neither of us can read Rian's mind, but we might as well be able to. Taris turns and runs toward me, away from the dragon. Rian takes a step forward, arms at his sides, fingers splayed. I already know what it will look like when he moves. I know how he'll control the water. Turn it to ice. And I run because I know what Rian's going to do.

"Prince Carsans! Lune!" Taris shouts, and the latter turns her head in surprise to hear him say her name. He's waving for them to move, and when she notices Rian, Lune's eyes widen. She pushes Crispin toward the closest side of the arena.

"Korvaan, Naomi, get down, *now!"* I shout, and then manage to tackle Taris against our old barricade before a blistering heat passes nearby.

And then that heat curves, moving upwards. Following Rian as he uses his ice to slip and slide around the arena, drawing the dragon's attention like a fly buzzing around its head. The dragon does not rampage, but thinks it can burn Rian out of the sky with its flame. This is precisely what Rian wants.

He twists around the arena, drawing the flames after him, and lets the dragon burn us a passage back into the castle. One still so dangerously hot that, without Rian to lay down an ice trail, no one will be able to use it. We can escape that way.

Once he's finished, Rian turns to send ice directly down the brightback's throat, stifling its flames for now. He's ruddy-cheeked and grinning as he slides down his own ice and deposits himself right next to Taris and me, while we clamber to our feet.

"Are you mad?!" I shout at him.

"I was expecting more of a, 'thank you', but, ah, that'll do," Rian responds. "And, if I may add—"

"No time, let's go!" I shout.

I grab Rian's arm and don't bother to wait around to see who else is coming. We need to get out.

Taris hangs back, shouting names and drawing everyone's attention, trying to get them all to follow us across while the brightback chokes on melting ice, clawing and shaking its head. Qhan and Nissa run from the tunnel back across the arena, her hyena close by. Rian and I pick up the remnants of my *khashak* along the way, while the Carsans are the furthest out, and the last to move. It seems they took cover as far away from the dragon as they could, but like Nissa and Qhan, they need to cross the arena again.

Rian and I reach the opening to his newly formed passageway first, but Rian stops before laying down the ice. He turns, waiting to make sure everyone's across, expecting his little stunt has bought us all a chance to escape.

We don't get so lucky.

The Carsans are just over halfway across the arena when the brightback suddenly moves. It charges at them, its weight shaking the ground and sending us all staggering. Lune manages to dive forward, rolling before coming to a stop. She's dazed, and struggling to regain her feet. Her brother's further back, faring even worse. From her sprawl, Lune has a front row seat when the dragon reaches him.

"Crispin!" she screams.

Crispin Carsans gets to his feet just in time for the brightback's head to snake down and consume his upper half. When it raises its head again, the dragon pulls Crispin's body with it, chomping and gnawing at it, flicking bits up in the air to catch again in its mouth. For a few moments, I think the only thing we can all do is stare, Lune most especially. Some of what remains of her brother spatter over her.

Lune's mouth wavers for a few seconds, her lips trembling. Then she lets it fall open and screams.

Taris moves so fast, it's only when I see him running back for her that I realize he's not at my side anymore. Lune's still lying there, completely horrified, as even the remaining soldiers in the arena can do nothing but stare at what used to be Crown Prince Crispin. The dragon has about finished its meal when Taris reaches Lune. He picks her up and throws her over his shoulder, skidding on the ice Rian slides under him in a running stumble.

"We can't leave her; it'll tear her apart!" Taris explains before I can ask.

And while I once might have ordered him to drop her, I find I don't want to leave Lune to die, regardless of whether she's innocent or not. Rian's influence on me, I suppose.

No one speaks. Rian turns to spread ice across the path the dragon burned for us, and we all run together toward the insides of the palace, pretending we can't hear screams as the dragon starts targeting those remaining in the arena. Lune's making inarticulate sounds of distress. Naomi's coloring tells me it's likely she'll be sick all over the ground in the next minute or so.

Rian's using his fluke as best he can, but all the blood has drained from his face. I have to catch him twice as he stumbles while we run.

Chaos has replaced the palace's disturbing calm. Staff and nobility careen about, desperate to either escape or see what treasures they can make off with in the panic. No one pays our group a lick of attention as we fight the crowd to forge our own path. No one cares for royalty, anymore, only for themselves. It helps to have Qhan leading the way, using his bulk to push people aside and always keeping an arm stretched back to me and Rian.

I don't need to speak to Qhan for him to know exactly where to go. I suppose he has the palace memorized just as well as I do, and understands we need to escape someplace most of the crowd won't be headed. As it's now impossible to tell the difference between our friends and enemies, we do not bother to hide amongst the mob. Even if Rian's white-and-gold head didn't stand out like a Fate-damned beacon, there are too many people close to him for comfort.

Our best chances lie with the castle's less-popular passages. The servants' corridors, and tunnels meant for discretion. Just before we enter the nearest one—Nissa's hyena streaking ahead past Rian and I—Taris stops and looks to the side, towards a main staircase.

"Korvaan: carry her," Taris says, handing Lune over to him before his brother can protest.

"What? What are you doing—where are you going?!"

"There's something I have to do. Don't wait for me. I'll find you. Promise," he adds, looking at me. "Soleil. I promise you."

I hold his gaze for a moment, then nod. I trust him.

I pull Rian into a servant's passage before he can try and resist. To demand that Taris tell us what he's doing. I can feel my crown prince's reluctance to leave anyone behind, even someone he's not particularly close to like Taris.

Once the door closes behind us in the servant's passage, the din of the palace fades, and we're left to traverse the dimly lit corridors on our own. I keep an even pace, pulling Rian along with me. The two of us lead the way with Qhan in front, Nissa and a still-green Naomi in the middle, and Korvaan in the back. Lune has quieted, now.

After several minutes, we are forced to stop and wait while Naomi dry-heaves. She recovers quickly, but it gives Korvaan time to set down a subdued Lune. She doesn't say a word, and her eyes are unfocused. I know it cannot help, the fact that she's still covered in her brother's blood. I can see her arms shaking, though she's trying to remain stoic.

I might not like the woman, but I'm tempted to offer my sympathies. I wouldn't have wished Crispin's death on him, even if he did mean to help place an imposter on the throne.

Once Naomi has recovered, we continue on. We've made good progress when we come to an intersection offering several routes. There are two sets of stairs—one leading up and the other down, and three hallways splitting off from ours.

"Yakarami!" someone calls.

It is Crown Prince Magnus, with Griffith Reach not far behind, wielding a bloodied sword. Magnus likely has no idea what's happened, but he must now know how important keeping Rian alive is, because it looks as if he's about to lend us the aid we need.

The king's son and his bodyguard approach us from one of the halls and pause before Qhan and me, panting.

"Everyone's gone mad," Magnus snaps. "The other crown princes—they tried to kill me. If not for Griffith, I'd already be dead."

"Where are the king and queen?" Nissa snaps.

Magnus opens his mouth, but Griffith is the one who answers.

"I evacuated them, at the first sign of trouble. They are likely miles away, by now. I intend to have their son join them. If you wish to join us, that passage before you will take us there. It leads right to a discreet exit, close to the forest."

So, then, Magnus' parents are safe. I am sure no one will follow them. They are only still king and queen by a technicality, after all, and Rian, the true heir, is a much more desirable target.

"Then let's not dally," I order. "It's not safe, here. And I suspect the city is much the same."

"We can head into the forest," Nissa claims. "The Fae: if Yakarami really is the heir of Isaaria, he can invoke the right of the heir and they will be forced to help us. We just have to get close enough to their territory."

I am wary of trusting the Fae for any reason, but Nissa's plan is better than nothing. We can't afford to sit around trying to think of something else. Not if we all want to make it out of here alive.

"The forest, then," I agree.

I grab Rian's arm again.

"No!" Rian says, pulling against my grip. "Ayla! Where's Ayla? I'm not leaving without her—I refuse! And Asmer! Soren! They—!"

"Yakarami, there's no time!" Nissa snaps. "Do you want to die here?!"

"Sir, no one will hurt the Lady Asmer," Qhan reassures him. "She is worth far more alive and well."

"But the children," Rian insists.

No one here knows what to say, because he has a point. Asmer and Raj al'Yibna will be worth plenty in ransom to their father. But Ayla can be used only to threaten and coerce one person: Rian. Soren's fate, meanwhile, is dependent on what the traitors intend. They may kill him.

"I'll return and search for Ayla—" Qhan is starting to say.

"I'm sure that's what Taris…" Korvaan's posing.

"Oh, no need," comes a voice behind us. Cheerful. Mocking. Almost spiteful with how light his tone is.

On the staircase above us, heading around its curve as he slowly descends, is Mercer. His left hand is bandaged, and in his right, he's holding a sword. He looks rather confident with it, for someone who claimed he'd rather drug me than fight. Behind him, her biceps gripped by a guard, is Ayla. She's wearing a satchel and is clutching a flower crown in her hands so tightly her arms shake, and little crushed petals float to the floor.

I don't have to ask. I know what's in the satchel and why Ayla left Rian's rooms, trying to find me. Trying to help. I'm too worried for her to be angry she didn't listen to me. Here she is, held captive by one of Mercer's men. Mercer—the man she knows is her father's best friend. The man who brought her here in the first place.

This is my fault. I should have bothered to explain further to her. I should have realized she'd want to help me.

"Ayla!" Rian calls to her.

Qhan and Griffith both grab his arms before he can try and run to her. We bodyguards instinctively push the royals behind us, as well as Naomi. If anything were to happen to Korvaan and me, and without Taris, I want at least one of my *khashak* alive, for Rian.

Mercer's smile is eerily casual, and he swings that sword around in circles like it's a toy.

"I knew you'd try this way," he claims.

The most frightening thing about it is how much he still sounds like Mercer. Irina Lundan was babbling about how her husband was not himself. How she could tell it wasn't him. How different he was.

But this is Mercer. I might not understand why he's doing what he's doing—it might appear in all ways contrary to who I know him to be—and yet this is still undeniably Mercer making these decisions. The smile he's giving Rian is not at all vindictive, or mocking. No, it's genuine. As if they're still the best of friends, about to go out for celebratory drinks.

"It's almost as if we know each other so well, we know each other's minds!" Mercer adds with a laugh. "And I knew you'd want to see your daughter."

"Merse, please," Rian says shakily. "Whatever I've done, whatever you want, your grievance is with me. She's only a little girl."

Ayla's chest flutters in terrified pants. She bites her lip to stay quiet, but there are tears running down her face.

Mercer smirks. "Yes, she is," he agrees. "A little girl who—"

To hell with this.

I draw a throwing knife and hurl it straight at Mercer. Marques appears from nowhere to deflect it, his invisibility only maintainable if he doesn't interact with moving objects. Which, I figure as I run up the steps to meet him, means he can't turn invisible on me while I do my very best to cut off Mercer's head.

I must be careful, fighting Talan Marques. For one, the man is bigger than me, and I know he can match my skill. But at least the stairway is tight enough that he's forced to cater to my preferred weapon—my knives. So long as I can keep him from pulling a gun, no one else will dare try to shoot at us in this confined space.

We go at each other as our prince's gladiators. Marques is stronger, and better equipped for a fight. I'm faster, and I have fury on my side.

Behind Marques, and in front of me, I can see Mercer attempting a leisurely retreat. He's confident Marques can protect him, but he still does not want me anywhere near him. He steps to the side and grabs Ayla before ordering the other three men present to attack us instead.

That might have been a problem for me, but Griffith comes to my aid just as Marques and I find ourselves on a small, flat landing. It's easier to fight him here than trying to move up the steps, mainly because, while I'm shorter, at least I'm not standing below him. Griffith engages in a dance with Mercer's men, while Korvaan and Naomi, thank goodness, are trying to force Rian to escape. Nissa's helping them, sending her hyena ahead to make certain the way is safe.

Magnus, I think, is trying to help a still-despondent Lune.

I'm tiring from Marques, but am confident that Griffith will soon join me against him, and at that point, I'm sure we'll be able to end things here.

Imagine my surprise when Mercer steps forward and stabs Griffith straight through the chest.

Magnus sees this and abandons Lune in a fury, clearly intending to charge at Mercer. Marques throws me into the corner of the landing where I nearly crack my against the wall, and draws his gun. Before I can stand again, my ears are ringing painfully and a red spot has appeared on Magnus's forehead. His body collapses on the steps, blood slowly pooling.

On the steps behind a trembling Ayla, Vásan Pike appears. His face looks puzzlingly less mauled than I thought at a distance. Perhaps I imagined the worst of the damage.

Mercer struggles to pull his sword free of Griffith, and eventually has to use his foot to give the body a shove. I still have a long knife in hand, but I don't dare make a move when Marques levels the muzzle of his pistol at my temple. I glare at Mercer, who is trying to use a handkerchief to clean the blood off his sword.

"Vásan," he says, pleasantly surprised. He gestures at me. "Do me a favor."

Vásan slowly takes good look at Griffith and Magnus' bodies. At the curve of the stairwell. The landing, where I stand with Marques. Down below us, where Korvaan and Naomi, shocked by the deaths, have stopped trying to force Rian to leave; and where Lune still stands staring at Magnus' body not far from her feet. At Ayla, who has pressed herself up against the wall behind Mercer, looking from him to Vásan with terrified eyes.

And then he changes. And he's not Vásan anymore. Not at all.

It's Taris. *Taris.*

Who is not supposed to have a fluke.

Who has claimed for years, for our entire lives, that he does not.

He feigns going for Mercer, but only to draw Marques' attention. Once the gun is away from my temple, Taris grabs Ayla instead, and is flying down the staircase with her. I bring my knife up and slash Marques across the face before I follow them. I might be confident in my abilities, but I am no fool.

Even before we've reached the bottom of the stairs, the others have started to move. Nissa is long gone, following her hyena's trail. Naomi and Korvaan are running Rian now that Taris has brought Ayla. I grab Lune Carsans by the arm and pull her along. No one's close to following us, yet, but that won't last.

For once, I'm following rather than leading, and all I have to do is stare at Taris' back, trying not to think about his fluke.

Vásan was standing on the stairs. It looked like Vásan. And then it wasn't. Taris is a skin-walker. Taris has a Fate-damned fluke, and he hasn't said a word about it in over twenty years. Damn him. Damn Nusk. Why the *hell* would they keep this from me? What good could it have possibly done?

It's a relief when I see the dim, natural light of day ahead of us. As the last one out, I make sure to slam the door behind me. I don't have anything to barricade it with, so I pull out one of my remaining arrows and jab it into the lock, twisting until something snaps and breaks. That should buy us a few extra minutes, I hope.

The door let out into a small herb garden, as it's not far from the palace kitchens, and beyond that is nothing but the Isaarian forest.

There are no enemies waiting for us outside the exit of the servant's passage—few would consider an escape into the forests an escape, after all—but we do come across Raj al'Yibna, who looks like he chose the wrong time to take a walk, and has missed most of the coup.

"What's going on?" he asks in a panic, and looks to Rian, the man he knows is his sister's friend.

Raj's eyes flick over to Lune, then. At the blood still coating her.

"Are we taking him or killing him?" Nissa asks, reaching for her hunting knife.

"Raj, don't ask, just run," Rian says, and something in his tone tells Asmer's brother not to protest.

I don't know what Raj is thinking. I don't know how he can manage to join us, and run, knowing his sister's likely still trapped somewhere in the palace. But we can't save for Asmer, now. Nor Soren, nor anyone else. We few unlikely allies bunch together, the battle-worn survivors of a bloody massacre.

And we run out, into the growing dark.

Twenty-One

WE RUN UNTIL WE ARE well within the depths of the Isaarian forest. Magical dangers dwell within, but they pale in comparison to those within the Pyrian Palace. After perhaps an hour of flight, Qhan insists we stop and rest. Our pace is flagging, and we can't endure much longer without a rest. Once we've recovered a little, we'll continue on until we've reached the Fae's territory. That's the only place the other crown princes wouldn't dare follow us, knowing Rian can easily invoke the right of the Isaarian heir as the rightful king.

We take Qhan's suggestion, too tired to argue. We're dirty, torn, bloodied. Shocked. Confused. No one speaks. No one knows what to say.

After giving himself a few minutes, Qhan draws his scimitar and leaves to scout our surroundings. Nissa and her hyena join him. Rian holds Ayla in an attempt to comfort her, though I'm sure he has no idea what to tell her. Lune slumps to the dirt, staring at nothing. Raj al'Yibna is pale and quiet, struggling to understand how it is he came here to be with us while his defenseless sister remains trapped at the palace. About a minute after we stop running, he's sick up all over the ground. Who knows what he's imagining, given our blood-soaked party.

My *khashak* and I exchange breathless looks, struggling to trust one another now that Taris has revealed he lied to us all these years.

We're startled by a rustling in the trees. Someone is running in our direction. Korvaan and I throw ourselves back to our feet. Lune draws her knife, but looks too tired to fight. So, it is lucky for us that the person who bursts into our camp is a fellow escapee, and means us no harm.

We stare at him. He stares back.

It's Aiko Shinya, alive with only a gash on his cheek and a slice cutting open the back of his clothes that didn't manage to cut flesh. In his arms, he's carrying a shaking Soren Carsans.

For a few seconds, none of us react. Shinya is frozen. He hasn't made up his mind, yet, if he can trust us or if we're going to hurt him. Then Lune flips her knife closed again and sticks it in her sheath.

"Oh, thank the Almighty," she cries, and runs to take her brother from Shinya's arms.

Soren is almost too big for her to hold, and she won't be able to carry him far, but I think Shinya understands she needs this. From the way Soren clings to his sister, I suspect he needs it, too.

I don't know if Soren understands that the blood on Lune belongs to their brother, but I suspect he is aware of Crispin's death. He has his arms and legs wrapped as tightly as he can around his sister, and is crying with his head buried against her neck. Lune collapses to her knees.

I stare at Shinya. His eyes are large and fully black. Even standing still, his body trembles.

"I…Not everyone…dead," he manages in shocked, broken Alarkian.

"No, not everyone. How did you know to escape?" I ask. "And to get Soren?"

"…Crown Prince Vásan met Grand Prince and Princess Carsans and… Father," he says dully, dazed to have come upon other survivors. "Carsans had their boy. Vásan…killed them all. Their bodyguards. He tried to kill me…"

So, then, he grabbed Soren and ran. Shinya must be the reason Vásan was sporting that cut across his eye when I last saw him. This spoiled ambassador's son is tougher than he looks.

"How did you know to come here?" I ask, and Shinya can only shake his head.

"I don't know," he insists. "I don't…"

His legs give out from under him. I hurry to sit beside him, and make sure he doesn't hit his head. His breaths are coming short, and his hands are shaking. I'm surprised and impressed that he's made it this far without succumbing to exhaustion. Before I can ask anyone to help me, Taris is kneeling beside me, taking Shinya's wrists to feel his pulses.

"You're fine," Taris tells him. "Look at everything around you. See the forest. Hear it. Feel the grass under you. You aren't at the palace anymore. All that is gone. Forget it."

We both know Shinya will never forget what he saw in the Pyrian Palace for as long as he lives, but if he can take in his current surroundings and force his mind to recognize he's someplace safe, it will help. His body is convinced he's still in danger, and wants him to run. His mind is struggling to comprehend that he and Soren Carsans are now both orphaned by Vásan's hand.

"Breathe," Taris instructs him. "Breathe…In, out. Slowly, now."

He's placed his hands on the back of Shinya's head, and I know he's trying to help however he can. He doesn't have his needles, but there are other methods.

"It's all wrong," Shinya gasps, interspersed with Tourrannese laments of what I assume are the same sentiment. "Everything—wrong. The world's wrong."

"It will be all right," Taris promises him. "We'll fix it."

"What is happening?" Shinya asks. He sounds terrified. And so confused.

"Don't think about it now," Taris says. "Look around you. Look at the trees. Look at me. Think about your breath. Tell me where you are. Describe it. And keep breathing between every few words."

"I'm…in…Isaaria," Shinya manages, trying to get his ragged breathing under control. "In the…forest. There are trees. And…flowers. There's a rock in…my shoe…I'm with…Crown Prince Rian and his…wife."

No one corrects him.

"Good. That's good," Taris says, and slowly releases Shinya. "I'll be back with you in a minute. Do you have your tonic with you?"

Shinya stares at him.

"Your medicine," Taris repeats. "I know you have to take some, Lord Aiko, it's not exactly a secret. Balancing your fluke overwhelms you and I suspect you used it to escape from Vásan. Do you have any with you?"

I try to shoot him a look, but Taris' full attention is on Shinya.

"Yes. I…I always have to…to carry some," Shinya manages, struggling to think of the proper Alarkian at a time like this.

"Take a dose," Taris orders him. "And keep breathing like I said."

Shinya takes time to process this before giving a slow nod. And another. He closes his eyes, takes a deep breath in through his nose, and shakily lets it out. This will not be an easy recovery for him. For any of us. But Taris must feel he's at least out of physical danger, because he stands to rejoin his siblings; I wait a moment before falling into step beside him. Taris knows as well as I that we all need to talk, even if this is a dreaded conversation.

"How did you know? About Aiko Shinya's medicine?" I ask him coldly. I'm curious about what else Taris might be keeping from the rest of us.

"I overhear things, Soleil; it's my job," Taris says shortly.

It's strange, hearing him lie to me. It makes me wonder how many times he's managed to do so before simply because I did not know what it sounded like. But now I have a reference. Now I know how easily Taris can dull his voice and sound tired, or bored, while lying oh-so-casually, making me feel ashamed of myself for doubting him. The absolute bastard.

Korvaan and Naomi hover not far from where Lune sits on the ground with her little brother. Korvaan's arms are crossed over his chest, and Naomi is trying to shift her weight comfortably so she can continue to stand like the rest of us, though it's obvious her legs need a rest.

Lune does not look up at them, or at Taris and me when we approach. She strokes Soren's hair as he rests his head in her lap, and then she begins to hum. I recognize the tune immediately as the one she sang in the carriage. Even now, the familiar song sends a zing of nostalgia through me, but I'm too tired to let it stir me to action. The feeling passes, and I'm left standing with the three people I consider my siblings, who I had only recently, and perhaps erroneously, decided I could trust with my life, with my whole self.

I'm angry at myself for every time I suppressed my own doubts about Taris.

He. Is. A. Liar.

Taris allows a few seconds of uncomfortable silence to pass before he sighs.

"Well. Go on," he prompts tiredly. "Let's get this over with."

"You have a fluke?" Korvaan blurts. I can't tell if he's more shocked or angry.

"Why didn't you ever tell us?" Naomi asks. She's more hurt. It's a betrayal.

"Yes," I agree, glaring at Taris. "Why didn't you tell us?"

He looks around our little group and sighs again. I can tell that he's too worn to rise so easily to our emotional bait. He possibly even has a good excuse for his deception. But I've already made up my mind to be angry with him. I want him to feel all my frustration.

"You're not going to like this, but it was for you, Soleil. It's been easier to look after you this way," Taris explains. "You never notice I am there, when I change my appearance to look like someone else."

I splutter, "Me? Look after me?!"

"Yes, you stupid woman!" Taris roars back. "Do you realize how much of a danger-prone fool you are?"

"I am Crown Prince Rian's *Khashtani!*"

"Not if you're dead, you won't be!"

His volume is enough to give us pause, mainly because we can't afford make this much noise. It forces us all to take a few seconds to breathe, as Taris told Shinya to do. Korvaan and Naomi exchange looks.

"That is my job," I hiss at Taris. "My privilege. To die for him."

"And it's never occurred to you he might take issue with that?"

And that's when it all becomes very clear.

"Ree-an!" I snap, and leave my *khashak* to stalk towards my fiancé.

Rian looks up from where he sits with Ayla. He glances from me to my *khashak,* noting Taris' expression, and puts things together easily.

"Oh. So, you've found out about that, then."

"You've been ordering my *khashak* to protect me?" I demand, furious.

"Just the one, actually," he says, nodding at Taris.

"You can't do that," I say.

"Technically, I'm to be king; I can do whatever I want."

I clench my fists. "Don't play that card," I warn him. *"Don't."*

But Rian doesn't back down. Even while sitting before me, he's not at all intimidated by my anger.

"Why? Because you, the all-knowing Soleil Marson, is the only one allowed to worry about the people you love?"

I bristle, because he has a valid argument, but I'm too angry to agree. Too angry to see anyone else's point of view beside my own. If I were a better person, with a calmer head and more maternal gentleness, perhaps I would temper my voice for Ayla's sake. She's been through an ordeal, and here we are, fighting without even bothering to hide it.

"How long? How long have you been in contact with Taris; how long have you been asking him to look after me?"

"Does it really matter, now?" Rian sighs.

I feel Taris come up beside me and deliberately move away. I know I'm being completely unfair, but it doesn't matter to me. I don't care if Lune, Raj, Soren, Ayla, and Shinya are all here to watch this. All I care about is letting my anger hide how frightened I am.

"Yes," I insist to Rian. "Yes, it matters. It matters to me! It matters to Korvaan and Naomi!" I add, flinging an arm back at them. "You lied to us! You both lied to us! Why?!"

"Because this is the way it often is. The way it always has to be," Taris says.

It's the tone of his voice, the grimly wearied way he says it. I've only heard that kind of emotional exhaustion once before, and it was when Rian tried to convince me not to turn back time again.

I turn and stand in front of Taris. It takes me a few seconds to force myself, but then I grab for one of his arms. He doesn't resist in the slightest. I pull at his hands, inspecting them for jewelry, then look to his ears for rings besides the one we used for our communications, and then—

I pull up the metal chain around his neck, and from the depths of his neckline, I free the only piece of truly beautiful jewelry that I've ever seen Taris wear. And it matches Rian's ring.

"Do you understand?" Taris says while I stand in silent shock. "Can you… begin to comprehend?"

Rian stands and dusts himself off.

"I'm sorry, Soleil," he says. Genuinely. "I wouldn't lie to you if I didn't have to. But during our third cycle, when I knew what you planned to do, over and over again…I had to do something. To make sure you were protected. Safe."

"This…This is why Nusk couldn't make you Rian's *Khashtani,"* I say to Taris, not daring to answer Rian directly yet. I can hear how choked I sound, and I hate that. I hate that I'm touched by it.

I'm the emotional thing Taris refused to let go of, to become Rian's *Khashtani* as his father wanted. I'm significant. I'm significant to him. And here, I always thought he hated me.

"My king ordered me to protect his wife in his absence," Taris says simply. "I've done so."

"It is not a *khashak's* job to die for their *Khashtani*," I choke.

"I have never been one of your *khashak*," Taris says.

I look to Rian, blinking furiously. I'm trying to maintain my fury, but I'm tired.

"Why could you not tell me?" I demand of him.

"See, darling, you seem insulted, as if we all sat down one day and I decided, 'Ah, I know what's a brilliant idea: lying to my wife! Everyone, be not to tell Soleil the following things…!' But, it was more like, 'Well, last time we told Soleil this, things…didn't go well. I'm going to skip that bit this time around and pray that as a result, fewer people die'. Make sense, now?"

"Vaguely, but I'm still angry," I insist.

"Well, it would be handy if we had, say, some sort of map that told us what simple actions resulted in which horrifying results, but the fact of the matter is, as I'd like it to be otherwise, human beings are absolutely terrible at foreseeing the consequences of our actions."

"Did you know the other crown princes would do this?"

"No, Soleil, of course not!" he says. He sounds dismayed I'd think so. "For the most part, I've told you the truth. The only thing I've ever kept from you…is that I asked Taris to protect you."

I believe him. Though I can't say the same for Taris, the only secret Rian's kept from me, is that he wanted to keep me safe. He wanted to make sure that though he couldn't be there for me, someone always would be.

I slowly turn back to Korvaan and Naomi. This has made me less angry at Taris, for lying about his fluke, but I know it will not hold the same resonance for them. First, they hear from me that I'm really our principal's future queen, with a powerful fluke I can barely use, and now they learn their brother has hidden his own fluke from them all their lives.

Naomi had to grow up learning to manage her fluke alone. Learning all the things fluke-users must do that others need not bother with. All this time, Korvaan thought he and his brother shared a common trait—some of the few people magic didn't take to in a world saturated with it.

They don't say anything, now, because they don't know what to think.

It's somewhat of a relief to hear footsteps approaching: Nissa and Qhan, reentering our temporary camp right behind Lune and Soren. Given our scouts' haste, the rest of us all know they do not bear good news.

"We must run," Qhan says, pulling Lune to her feet and helping her gather up Soren so she can carry him. "They've sent a hunting party after us."

"Hunting?" I repeat, narrowing my eyes. "Surely you don't—"

"Yes, hunting, Lady Soleil. With bullets, and arrows," Nissa snaps.

"On horseback?" Taris thinks to ask.

"At least some of them," Qhan responds.

"We won't be able to outrun that, even with the trees to help," Naomi says.

"We won't have to. Trust me, I know these woods," Rian says. "We're close to part of the lands Clanaugh has claimed for the Fae."

Shinya and Raj have forced themselves to join us, though the latter is visibly uncomfortable with our company.

"But will that be enough?" Nissa challenges. "We don't want to fight on the run. They'll be able to pick us off easily. It won't end well."

"I'll stay back. I can stall them," Lune promises. "If I'm captured, you can always come back for me. Eventually. But you must find a way to bring Rian back to the capital, and get the chance to explain things to all of Isaaria! So long as you do that, you may all be safe! The country might be saved!"

I glance at Rian. I know he wants to insist she needn't do that. That no one needs to stay—to be left behind. But Nissa is Hoitsokin. A practiced huntress. If she suspects we cannot outrun our pursuers, someone needs to prevent that. Someone has to stay behind, to buy the rest of us time.

"It shouldn't be her," Taris starts, and Lune jerks her head to look at him, but Taris isn't paying attention. "What could she do, sing them into submission? No. I'll stay."

Lune bristles. "I can handle myself," she claims, and then looks to Rian to say something rather telling. "If you'll think for a second, I'm sure you'll remember. And you know I'm your best chance."

"...Her fluke," Rian says, a realization or memory or both coming to him at the same time. "You're not a siren. You're a chameleon."

He looks to Lune almost in awe. I know he's going to let her stay behind for us, and I'm glad it's her and not Taris. But I also know that this is hard for Rian. None of us will say it out loud, especially since Soren's now starting to panic at the idea of being left with us, but Lune is not coming back.

"Promise me, you will not simply run and hide," Lune demands. "If I'm going to stay behind, I need you to promise. You will go back into the city and explain things. Explain everything. Isaaria cannot go to war, do you understand?"

"It won't," Rians says haltingly.

"You have everything you need," Lune tells him. "If Septimus—"

We can hear horses approaching, the call of the hunt. We're out of time.

Nissa curses under her breath, whistles to her hyena, and runs off into the forest. She's not waiting around for the rest of us. Raj barely hesitates before following her, and I nod to Korvaan and Naomi to do the same. Naomi grabs Ayla's hand and runs. Korvaan waves to Shinya, ushering the ambassador's son ahead of him.

Taris grimaces, but bends to pick up a protesting Soren. The boy beats at Taris's shoulders, crying for his sister and demanding to be put down. But someone has to carry him; we all know he won't be able to run.

"Rian—give me your hand!" Lune snaps, offering her own to him.

Rian doesn›t hesitate. He takes her hand.

"Fire," she demands. "Think of fire. Give me fire!"

Rian's startled, but manages to shake his head. "I…can't," he insists. "Not so close to the Fae's territory—they'd kill us."

"Then ice. Water. Give me that," Lune begs. "There's a body of water near us, I know it. I'll draw from there. I'll use that to stall them."

I can see Rian's about to suggest earth instead, but thinks better of it. If we can't use fire, for fear of angering the Fae, I'm sure they wouldn't appreciate Lune uprooting the trees in their territory, either.

Lune closes her eyes for a second, takes a deep breath, and lets it out. There is, strangely, a light about her. It's not enough light to see by in the darkening wood, but even so. She releases Rian's hand and avoids looking at any of us, then turns to run back the way we've come. That's when Soren finally manages to sob her name. He is reaching out for her over Taris' shoulder, begging her not to go. Lune allows herself another few seconds to clasp her little brother's hand and push his bangs off his forehead.

"Soren, Soren, please don't. Don't cry," she urges breathlessly. Desperately. We all know her next words for lies. "They will not kill me. They won't, I promise. I'll come back. I'll come find you, I promise."

She kisses his hand, then peels his fingers off of hers and runs. Soren screams her name after her, to the point where I'm sure Taris' ears must be ringing, but Lune doesn't look back.

"Your majesty," Qhan insists, grabbing Rian's arm.

Though Rian is reluctant, he, Qhan, Taris and I run. We head deeper into the forest, and leave Lune to buy us time. We can't move as quickly as the others, but I refuse to abandon Soren and Taris, though Qhan is trying his best to force Rian to.

Soren is sobbing so hard that his face is red and his nose running. He no longer has the breath to scream for his sister, but has limply collapsed against the shoulder of Taris' uniform, wetting the fabric with his tears.

I can't help but glance back at Lune now and again as we flee. I want to know what Soren can see, and, honestly, I'm interested in the workings of her fluke.

I've since discovered the secret to it: Lune's fluke is to copy others. So long as she makes physical contact, she can take on their power. Possibly, given how she asked Rian, she needs their permission, but I cannot say that for sure. Otherwise, there seems to be only one catch, something that makes her borrowed abilities less than a perfect copy. In Rian's case, she can only use one of his elements at a time. When controlling people with her voice, she must be singing.

Rian has given her the command over water, and Lune has used it to find its nearest source. She's snaked a living stream of water to herself, intending to use it however she sees fit. Her command is impressive, and her control admirable. Lune isn't the sort of person I would expect to credit with this level of discipline, especially with a borrowed fluke.

I will admit: her power is immense. I find myself surprised by the idea that I ever considered her a threat, as it is clear to me now that she could have easily taken us all apart had she so desired. Instead, she's willing to die to give Rian the chance to be king. I admire her for that.

After another few paces, Lune has disappeared from sight. We can still hear the fading sounds. We can tell when the hunters reach her: there are shouts, and the calls of panicked horses. Lune does not scream.

I can't make myself look at Soren. I don't want to know what he's thinking.

I can still see the others strung out ahead of us, including Nissa. She might have been quick to run from danger, but she has proven twice now that she's not willing to abandon us. Besides, I am sure she knows she must stay close to Rian, if she wants the protection of the Fae.

I can't say for certain when we reach the Fae's territory, or how I know we're there, but I know. There is a change to the atmosphere, to the forest itself. The colors of the trees and foliage somehow look and feel different.

Earthy, floral scents grow more potent. The chirping and rustling of wildlife feels much closer, and much more aloof to our presence.

Rian has brought us to the Fae. I'm certain at least a handful of them are even watching us, now. Curious. Amused.

"Clanaugh!" Rian bellows, barely able to pull enough air to call out while running. "I invoke the right of the Isaarian heir!"

We do not dare stop moving; while Lune's actions were heroic, she will not last long fighting on her own.

"Clanaugh!" Rian repeats, starting to sound frustrated. Annoyed. "I know you hear me! This is Rian Yakarami and I invoke the right of the Isaarian hei—"

There's a crackling sound and a flash of blinding light. For a second, I'm sure I've been somehow struck by lightning. When my sight rushes back, we are not in the forest anymore.

Or, we are in the forest, but it's as if we've run into a completely different portion of it. It is lighter, here, even though I know full dark should be almost upon us. Our group is no longer spread thin as we run, but lumped together now in the center of an impressive clearing. Around us, the trees, roots, and even more delicate plants have twisted and contorted into furniture, archways, stairs up into the treetops, and all manner of impressive decorations. This is the Fae's Pyrian Palace. This is the sanctuary Rian has been granted.

"I heard you the first time, boy," a deep voice drawls. "There was no need to be so dramatic."

I find it impossible to describe the Fae's voice, and can say only that it thrums and crackles. Groans like the stretching of an old tree about to be felled.

I don't know what my expectations were, but Clanaugh both meets and surpasses them. He and the other Fae around us are, as Rian once described, simultaneously the most beautiful and hideous things I've ever seen. It is as if they spent several lifetimes trying to perfect the human form and never stopped revising. There is considerable variety among them, but Clanaugh and the female Fae beside him are both copper-skinned, dark-haired, and green-eyed. Those eyes, naturally, are terrifyingly large and knowing.

Clanaugh smiles at us to bare gleaming white teeth, each one wickedly sharp. He wears a twisted crown, made from some type of Fae magic, and clearly adorns himself only with the most impressive of wares suited to his station. The female Fae next to him is similarly ornamented, and I'm sure her identity is that of Clanaugh's infamous sister, Kaetscha.

According to Rian, she is no better than her more roguish brother; only more gentle and caring with the human pets she steals.

I have no idea how they make their clothing, or from what it's made, but they are all dressed in the most spectacular of garments. Pieces that look as if they should not exist. Skirts that look like waterfalls when they move. Tunics that ripple like a lizard's skin. Jewels and flowers and ornaments I have no names for, but somehow know that they do not exist outside this forest.

Yet, like the Fae themselves, there is something tainted about it all. I can admire the aspects of beauty, yes, but the humanness in me warns to stay away. I have no desire to wear those sorts of clothes, or to gaze at a Fae for hours on end the way I have wanted to with Rian. Humans have flaws that make us individuals. That make us all feel more at ease with one another. Standing before a being that truly thinks it's perfect is unnerving.

"And so, I, Clanaugh, grant you the right of the Isaarian heir," the king of the Fae goes on, giving Rian a dramatic, mocking bow. "I wondered when you would bother making that announcement."

Clanaugh is, at the very least, claiming to have known Rian's identity all along. And what he says next supports that claim, somewhat, though his arrogance does not help his credibility.

"Oh, and the irritatingly powerful Soleil Marson. Lovely," Clanaugh sighs. "Nothing like having the turn of time at your command, is there? Not that I would know."

I glance at Rian, tempted to ask several pertinent questions, but keep quiet.

"We need sanctuary, at least for tonight," Rian says. It is a command, not a request. "And you must swear to uphold the right of the heir: you and yours may not, under any circumstances, attempt to enslave any of my party to you."

"Yes, yes," Clanaugh agrees irritably.

He acts as if such a thing is a given, but I can see his sister staring at Shinya with gleaming eyes. She is not bothering to hide how much she wants him.

"You may relax," Clanaugh continues. "Make yourselves at home. I swear to you, no item you hold nor substance you consume within this clearing will do you harm. In any form."

"That remains to be seen," Rian says. "But I am sure we are appreciative of your willingness to cooperate."

Given how Kaetscha is still staring at Shinya, I am rather dubious. I can tell she desires him for whatever collection she has hidden away. Shinya has a powerful fluke, powerful enough that it can hurt him if he's not careful. The Fae can smell that. They hunger for it.

My concerns are interrupted by a baby's cry. I look to our left in time to see a Fae hand a human child to one of its fellows. The child is not quite an infant, as I supposed, but she can't be any more than a year old. I recognize the motifs on her dressing gown. The lilies. The wild horses.

"That is Irina Lundan's child," I say.

Silence stretches taut for several seconds. I watch Nissa reach behind her back for the hunting knife sheathed at her waist. Taris has yet to put down Soren Carsans, though he must be exhausted.

"Poor thing was wandering about in the woods," Kaetscha croons, sounding too much like a predator for my peace of mind. "Following a glymph. We found her."

"The child's too young to trade her name," Rian warns the Fae. "You can't keep her. She'd have to give herself or be given, and she can't, and we won't."

"Perhaps there will be some reward for looking after the daughter of an Isaarian princess. Particularly such a negligent princess, to have let her own child wander off into our forest," Clanaugh suggests, smiling as he tilts his head at Rian.

"Perhaps there is," Rian says noncommittally. "But for now, I'd prefer if one of us took charge of the Little Lundan, if you don't mind."

Clanaugh waits a long beat, his expression preternaturally unreadable.

"Of course," he finally grants. "We would never deliberately separate a babe from its own kind."

I nod to Naomi, prompting her to collect Elodie Lundan. She is wary as she approaches the Fae, and brushes against it as she collects the child, but her nerve holds firm.

Clanaugh announces something else in the Fae's own language that causes most of those around us to hiss in disappointment. They begin to disperse at once, slinking off into their trees. Their king has ordered them to give us some privacy, though if left to their own devices, I have no doubt the Fae would be happy to do nothing but stand and stare at us. Time has a different meaning, for them. They could do nothing but watch us for an entire day and not find that time wasted.

"You will not be disturbed by my subjects, while you are here," Clanaugh promises, and though Rian's expression remains skeptical, he doesn't accuse the Fae of anything outright.

Clanaugh disappears into the trees as well. His sister pouts, but stalks off after him, practically strutting on her much-too-long legs.

It's only after they've both gone that Rian sighs in relief and lets the weight of his exhaustion curl his shoulders forward.

"I'm impressed, Yakarami," Nissa admits. "They seem to respect you."

"They respect the right of the Isaarian heir, as set down many hundreds of years ago," Rian corrects her. "Clanaugh finds me amusing and childish."

"Regardless, I am less concerned about our safety here than I once was…Get some rest. Everyone," Nissa instructs. "Even if you cannot sleep, lay down and close your eyes for a few minutes. It will help."

"We don't have the tim—" I start.

"We do, though," she snaps. "None of us know what to do next, and you won't think on it any better while exhausted. The body shuts down after such trying events, trust me. I know."

I want to argue with her, because Nissa is confrontational and it is in my nature to meet that directly, but I know she is right. Even now, I can feel my body begging me to at least sit for a few minutes. The arm wound I sustained during my escape from the Solunium Hub has decided to remind me of its presence in a continual throb.

"…Taris, let us have you put Soren down," I finally sigh. "Over there, perhaps," I say, and gesture to a patch of curled and twisted tree roots that look strangely comfortable. There will be plenty for support for Soren and plenty for him to use as handholds should he want to pull himself to his feet.

The rest of us settle in as best we can. Rian kisses Ayla on the forehead and sends her after Soren, instructing her to look after him, then pulls Qhan aside to talk. Not far from them, Nissa is lounging in one of those Fae chairs, sharpening her hunting knives. Raj throws himself into the chair across from her, and lowers his head into his hands.

Shinya goes off a little way by himself to settle in a twist of roots of his own. He looks too tired to think, and I'm sure he will be asleep within seconds, propped up against that tree. Naomi's handed Elodie off to a bewildered Korvaan so she can see to anyone with injuries, stitching them back up. She must be able to tell how drowsy Shinya is, because she goes to him first. It doesn't take long for us to discover that, whatever we want, the Fae's magic procures instantly. All we have to do is look around.

My head's too fuzzy to think, but I know that if I try to sleep, I'll feel both restless and useless. Eventually, I force myself into a spot between Shinya and where Taris is caring for Soren and Ayla. Even if all I can do is sit and stare off blankly for a few minutes, at least I'll be sitting.

I could have spent ten or fifteen minutes like that before I'm snapped out of my daze. Naomi's beside me, ordering me to show her the cut on my arm. We have to cut away my sleeve, and I wince as Naomi pulls threads from the red-stained sash I used to staunch the blood, but at least most of my arm movement is unhindered.

Naomi is silent as she goes about her stitching. I do my best not to move, and grind my teeth to cope. I only jolt once, and it's because Rian's given a surprised, happy cry. Naomi and I both look to see that Ayla has taken off her satchel to open it up. From inside it springs a sunblood dragon, who bounds over to Rian and scampers up his leg.

I'm smiling vaguely at Mango, but Naomi's staring at the other items Ayla's unpacking from her satchel. She's hunting for something near the bottom of the bag, something she thinks will help Soren maybe, and on the ground next to her, perfectly folded, is the beautiful coat Naomi made for me, the matching gloves resting on top.

"I…I thought you ruined that," Naomi stammers.

"I did," I say. "I had Ayla fix it."

Naomi continues to stare for another few seconds, then mumbles something about excusing herself and hurries off. Naomi knows Ayla's secret project, now. She can make of that whatever she pleases. I am too tired to explain myself.

I sit for another few minutes, then force myself back up to my feet and join Rian and Qhan. It's not pleasant, seeing Rian sigh when I approach.

"Soleil, please. I can't think right now," he insists.

"I'll give you your hour of rest," I promise. "Only consider this: the longer we wait to act, the more time the other crown princes have to spread their lies to the public. And it will be hard for us to recover from that."

Rian nods, glumly. "I'm sorry, Soleil," he says. That makes me feel terrible for opening my mouth in the first place.

"Never mind," I backpedal. "Try not to think about that, if you can."

"Too late," Qhan says.

Rian absently pats Mango's nose. "There's just too much to worry about. I don't know where to start."

"A shame to see you distressed," Clanaugh's voice sounds from the trees behind us.

Qhan and I whirl on him. Qhan's even put a hand to his scimitar.

"Are you sure there's nothing I could help you with?" Clanaugh adds, trying to play a game with Rian. "Let me keep your Magicsmith, and I will give you back your kingdom," he offers.

"No deal," Rian says, "we already have one, between you and the kings of Isaaria. I'm invoking it. No new deal needs to be made."

"We don't have a Magicsmith," I add. "Sorry to disappoint."

Clanaugh just smiles at me.

"Do you know that?" he challenges gleefully.

"Do you?" I retort.

"I know everything."

"He doesn't," Rian says. "He only likes to act as if he does."

"I know more than your kind can comprehend, at least," Clanaugh amends. "Which, when it comes to speaking with humans, justifies my saying, 'everything'. I know 'everything' you might want to know."

"Should I be insulted by that?" I ask.

"Only if you want to be," the Fae says. "You humans are a young species, with much to learn, still. You've no business carrying magic in your bones. All you know to do with your so-called 'flukes' is kill one another. A tragedy. And things like you are the worst," Clanaugh tells me. "Grubby little humans with magic-hungry bodies, soaking up all the power and not even daring to use it."

"I feel not one drop of guilt," I claim, and I can tell this irritates Clanaugh.

He meant to make me feel uncomfortable.

"Besides, apparently I can only use my fluke if I genuinely think I'm about to die. Or if Rian dies," I say.

I'm surprised by Clanaugh's reply. "Oh, that's because you've forgotten how to use it," he says dismissively. "You've been made to forget, except for in very specific cases. Some human thought that was for the best."

"Nusk," I realize, shocked.

But Clanaugh chuckles. "Wrong again," he mocks. I'm still trying to figure out what my first blunder was when he continues. "I can undo it, of course, but there's no telling how long it will be until you're fully capable of channeling your magic once more."

"Am I going to owe you anything?" I ask, and Clanaugh laughs more fully.

"Only if you have something you want to give."

"She doesn't," Rian interrupts.

Clanaugh smiles, pretending serenity, then raises a hand and snaps his long, thin fingers while saying something in his own language. I wait for several seconds.

"I don't feel any different," I admit.

Clanaugh continues to smile, and shrugs. That motion looks too human for him, and the effect is likely not what he intended.

"I assure you, it is done," he says. "It will take its time. But his work always does."

I know Clanaugh's baiting me, but I can't resist.

"Whose?"

His smile is so disgustingly wide, I want to punch him. It occurs to me that he smiles even more than the Laughing Prince, and that's annoying.

"Fine," I say. "Thank you for whatever it is you did."

"You are most welcome," Clanaugh says.

"And while I'm asking for favors, I want to wash this blood off me."

"I'm sure you'll find yourself a pool just there," Clanaugh claims, waving a negligent arm toward a tree not far from Shinya.

Sure enough, there's water springing from the wood, spurting into a series of small pools created from divots and curves of the tree's impressive roots.

I don't care for what I should or shouldn't be doing in my present company; I strip off my bloodied jacket and blouse, crouching to wash the blood off myself and soak my clothes as best I can, though I already know they are ruined. I don't care who sees me in my underclothes, at this point, and I don't think anyone here would care, either.

Most of my upper body and skirt are still wet when I go to retrieve the black coat Ayla left out on the ground. As I am shrugging it on, I notice Kaetscha has found herself back on the outskirts of our clearing. She's leaning over a sleeping Shinya with her head tilted to one side, staring at him with a haunting look of desire that no human could ever replicate. Clanaugh has disappeared from Rian's side to join his sister, and is watching her with almost humanlike disinterest compared to her strange Fae-emotions.

"Don't push your luck, Kaetscha; I would hate to anger the king," Clanaugh says.

"Oh, I so want to give him a gift…" Kaetscha pouts as she twirls a lock of Shinya's hair. "He's such a pretty thing. I'd hate to see him slit open, all his insides spilling out where they don't belong…"

She turns to her brother, her eyes glinting with terrifying silver tears. "Let me give him the golden leaf tea. Please…He's so pretty…Almost as pretty as a Fae child. I want him to stay with me forever."

Clanaugh snorts. "It hardly matters, Kaetscha. He won't get far enough this time around for it to be useful. But if he ever visits us again…"

I give him a warning look and take a few steps closer. Clanaugh puts a hand to his sister's arm, keeping her from touching Shinya again. Another second and they are gone, but I'm sure they're hanging back to watch us. Clanaugh promised his subjects would not bother us, but he made no such assurances on behalf of himself or his sister.

Making a mental note to check on Shinya every few minutes, I head over to Soren and Ayla to see how they are faring. Taris has left the children for now, electing to join the others gathered near Nissa and Raj's table. They're talking quietly, but they won't be sharing information, yet. Not without me.

Ayla, bless her heart, is stroking Soren's golden hair, trying to comfort him. He's still crying, his chest heaving with great wracking sobs. In less than a day, the poor boy has lost his entire family. He has seen horrific things. In fact, he is only here with us now because a young man he barely knew saw a child in danger and plucked him up before running for his life. He was saved by chance, and he knows it. It is probably, partially, what is tormenting him.

I might have had my suspicions about the heads of the Carsans family, but watching Soren cry for them and his siblings is painful. I feel an urge to comfort him and Ayla both.

I crouch before Ayla, noting the blood on her dress and the bruise starting to form at the base of her neck. I try to ignore it, but can't; I'm going to kill Mercer Ralhan. I don't care what his excuses are. For bruising Ayla, I will kill him.

"Are you alright?" I ask her, and Ayla gives me a stout nod.

I'm sure she's distressed after what happened, but her eyes are clear of tears. Having someone to take care of has helped her forget to be scared.

Soren sits up at the sound of my voice, and pushes away help from either Ayla or me as he rearranges himself as best he can. I'm sure his legs have seized up, his muscles tightly contracted, and it must be difficult for him to move them that way. But he would rather do it on his own than let me touch him.

"You let Lune go back," he accuses me. He's trying to sound grown up, but his voice shakes and cracks. "You let Lune leave. I-I-If she dies, it's your fault."

I sigh. "Soren…She did what she thought right. She only wanted to protect you. Protect all of us. That's what Crispin was doing, too. They're good, brave people. Soren, they've sacrificed themselves for Isaaria," I explain to him gently. Even if I don't believe every word coming out of my mouth, I know it's what I have to say. "They made a choice for—"

"I don't care," Soren interrupts. "I don't care about Isaaria or doing the right thing or any of that! I don't care about any of you!"

He bursts into tears once again and buries his head in his arms.

I can't help but grimace to hear him cry.

Why must I have such a weakness for children? Why couldn't I have just stayed away and let Soren sob his eyes out with Ayla, instead of giving in to my Fate-damned need to make things better?

"Soren…" I try again, quietly. I'm hesitant to touch him. "I'm so, so sorry."

I am glad when Ayla leans over to wrap her arms around Soren. She hangs onto him for some time, carefully balancing her own weight so she won't push him over. Soren's sobbing doesn't last long, but that's mainly because he's running out of tears. He must have a headache, at this point, and exhaustion will soon set in.

"Try to get some sleep," I tell them both. "You'll feel better afterwards, I promise. It might not seem like it now, but…This will get better."

"I want my parents. I want Kaoli," Soren whispers, rubbing at his eyes and nose with a sleeve.

"I know you do," I sigh.

"I'm so useless," Soren claims, and absolute conviction in his voice when he says so both startles and saddens me.

"Don't say th—"

"If I could run properly, they'd all still be alive," he interrupts.

I'm forced to fall silent. Because while I want to do nothing more than insist otherwise, I wasn't there. I don't know. Whether Soren's statement is accurate or not is irrelevant if it's how he saw things.

"That's not true," I say. "Soren, I understand you don't know me well, but trust me: you can't think that."

"They wanted to protect me. Crown Prince Vásan didn't even try to hurt me first, but everyone—*everyone* still went to protect me," Soren says. "Instead of themselves. Because I'm me. Because I was in my chair. Because they knew I…I c-c-couldn't run away. Mallorie, and Parker, and Kaoli, and Romia, a-a-and my -pa-par-r-rents, a-a-and now *Lune*—"

"Just don't think about it. Soren, don't think about it. Please."

"But it's my fau—"

"It is not your fault," I tell him. Perhaps a little too sharply, but I mean it. "It's not. If you can only think of one thing to try and get yourself to sleep, tell yourself that. Over and over. It's not your fault."

This time, I don't hesitate. I pull Soren forward and let him cry on my shoulder. I hold him because I know he needs someone to, and Lune is gone. She might have promised Soren she'd come back—others, here, might promise him she'll come back—but I know she won't.

A little hitch of breath interrupts my thoughts, and I look up to see that Ayla's about to cry as well.

"Ayla? What's wrong?"

"I'm so sorry," she says. "I'm sorry I left the room! I'm sorry I didn't listen!"

I open my other arm to her, and Ayla throws herself into me. She, Soren, and I are all awkwardly clumped together, and I have to rearrange myself a bit to hold on to them, but they're both so small. It's not difficult. Instinctively, I start to shush Ayla. Trying to calm her down.

"It's all right. I'm not angry," I promise her.

Frustrated, yes. But mostly with myself. She is only eight, and I expected her to do as I said simply because I told her to do it, with no explanation.

"It's not your fault, either," I tell her. "None of this. You only wanted to help. You are alright," I tell them both. "You're safe. It's not your fault."

I hold both children close and let them cry themselves out, knowing I won't let go until well after they do.

There's a mewling to my right, and I look down to find Mango looking up at me with his head tilted. He isn't used to human tears, but like the good little dragon he is, he wants to help.

Ayla lets go of me first, and then sits back against a nestling of tree roots wiping her eyes. The moment the thought comes into my head, a pile of thick blankets appears naught but a few feet away from me. Damned Fae. Yet, this is exactly what I need. When Soren finally releases his grip, too, I reach over and take the blankets to make a nest for him and Ayla.

"Here. The two of you do me a favor and protect Mango," I tell the children. "See if you can get him to go to sleep. Lie down and cuddle with him, maybe. He's a very snuggly dragon."

And hopefully, in doing so, the two of them will fall asleep. Nothing else I say is going to make them feel comfortable enough to try, but Mango might be able to distract them. Thank goodness for him.

I hover near Soren and Ayla a little longer, to see if they'll settle in some. Mango is happily curled on the ground between them, purring, his eyes closed and wings twitching slightly in happiness. Soren absently strokes the dragon's nose, which Mango enjoys, and Ayla's got a hand between his wings.

After a few minutes, both children at least have their eyes closed, even though Soren's hand is still moving, and I count that as a victory for today. Neither of them is crying or bleeding, now, and they have Mango to look after them.

Sighing, I sit back against a tree. I tell myself that I'll rest only for a few minutes, but I don't know how long I'm asleep before Qhan shakes me awake. Soren and Ayla are fast asleep with Mango between them, and someone has tucked Elodie Lundan in to a blanket-nest of her own. I don't know what we'll do about feeding these children when they wake, but hopefully Clanaugh is to be trusted on that front. Otherwise, we won't be staying here for long.

I join the others as we gather to plan. We've all laid grudges and frustrations aside, at this point. Even when I look at Taris, I find I am no longer angry at him. I don't have the energy for it.

"First: answers," I order, and look first to Raj al'Yibna, startling the poor lad. "Your sister brought Lune to us in the arena. To help us. How."

Raj swallows. He seemed so confident and cheerful, that first day at the palace. He's frazzled and young, now.

"Asmer…She was having tea with little lady Ayla," he starts nervously. "But she came back early. Said that Ayla and her attendant, ah—her," he clarifies, pointing at Naomi, "left. Because something wasn't right. Asmer sent me to look for Crown Prince Rian and then said she was going to get Lune. I went outside to check the gardens, because I thought he might be there, but…I don't know how Asmer woke Lune up. She must have. Crown Prince Mercer was keeping her sedated. Wasn't he?"

I've no doubt Mercer was doing all he could to keep Lune unconscious. But given her knowledge of the Signs of the Dead, and that hideous bracelet she wears everywhere, I know there is more to Lune than what she pretends. Possibly she is highly resilient, especially if someone was helping to wean her off of Mercer's medications. Possibly, Asmer ensured she was never given as much as Mercer intended.

It's a good enough explanation, for now. And I know I won't get more out of Raj; he wasn't there when Asmer collected Lune. He wouldn't know.

I look to Naomi, my eyes demanding *her* portion of the story.

"I happened to look out the window and saw a maid running through the courtyard, screaming. Lune's maid," she confessed. "…She was covered in blood. Someone chased her down and killed her."

"Romia," I say. "She was with the Carsans. When Vásan killed them."

"I knew something was wrong," Naomi agrees. "So, I brought Ayla back to the rooms. No one else was there—no one. So I told her to stay put and went looking. Lune found me first. And Korvaan. He said he went to fetch you. And to find something to break whatever spell the crown prince was under."

"You inadvertently gave me something," I admit, relying on my tone to imply my thanks. If I stop to parcel out gratitude to everyone I owe for the past few hours, things would become painfully monotonous. "But it still doesn't answer how someone managed to use *Dadj'zcha* on Rian in the first place."

"Are you sure that's what it was?" Qhan questions.

"It almost has to be," I say. "How else could someone have made him leave the room, seemingly of his own free will? And let's face it, Qhan: you and Taris are much stronger than Rian. So something else was walking him to that arena. For whatever reason…"

I trail off, trying to think. Controlling someone with Dadj'zcha requires a very high level of training. Someone who'd only been practicing a few months could never have managed something so complex, especially if they were seeing to other arrangements. That eliminates Mercer, Vásan, Yuugo, and Detrus.

Mercer did make some implications about that family he visited, but…

"You only need someone's hair to potentially control them, for a skilled practitioner," Taris mutters. "Though one would need blood and hair, both, to puppet completely against their will. Make them empty husks."

I suppose Rian's hair would not be difficult to get ahold of, particularly for Mercer. But then, there is the issue of Mercer himself, again.

"None of this makes any sense," I insist. I'm grinding my teeth again. By the end of this, I'll be lucky if I have anything left to eat with. "Why would Mercer want you dead?" I ask Rian.

Rian sighs. "He wouldn't."

"Unless he wants the crown for himself," Raj mutters.

"He doesn't," Rian insists, sounding irritated. "He has never desired it. And it wouldn't make sense for him to do it this way, anyhow."

"Or, he's much cleverer than you ever gave him credit for, and he's been playing the long game this entire time," Nissa poses.

"No, listen: that's not it," Rian insists, "I know Mercer. That's not him. And for all the crown princes to turn against us? That doesn't seem right. They can't all be king. They must know that."

"The only reason they would want to kill you that publicly, after making it known that you're the rightful heir, is…if they wanted to start a war," I realize, thinking back to what Lune said.

Now that I think about it, half of the attempts on Rian's life have been public attacks. Out in the open, or else so utterly lacking in discretion that it couldn't possibly be ruled an accident.

"Rian—what would any of the princes have to gain from a war in Isaaria?"

He shrugs miserably. "Nothing. Nothing at all. Our country would tear itself apart. There wouldn't be anything left to rule."

"Then something happened to him," I insist. "Mercer. When he was out west. He started talking about it, when he took me out to lunch."

And tried to kill me, I think grimly. But even that's not quite true, is it? He tried to incapacitate me, but not kill me. That is an important distinction.

"Then what about the others?" Rian demands. "Vásan, Yuugo, Detrus. *Marques*. What about *them?*"

I sigh. "I don't know. *Dadj'zcha*?"

"Possibly," Taris mutters.

"Why would anyone in the world want me dead?" Rian asks. He sounds tired and irritated and, surprisingly enough, angry. "I haven't done anything. I'm not even king yet!"

"To stop our son from ever existing, I presume," I muse.

"Well, yes, I suppose, but our son is meant to bring peace and prosperity. Who wouldn't want that?!"

"I don't know," I groan again. "None of this makes any sense."

I glance over at Taris, narrowing my eyes. "You wouldn't happen to know anything more, would you?"

He snorts, but looks away from me.

"Trust me—if I did, I would have said something by now."

There are several seconds of silence.

"You are lying," I realize.

Because now I know exactly what that sounds like.

Everyone looks at Taris. Those of us who know him better—know him well enough to understand what his lie means—are staring. Nissa raises an eyebrow, properly intrigued by these proceedings, and Raj is simply confused and tired. Qhan looks ready to pull a weapon on Taris, if he must, but I know Taris is no traitor. I just can't conceive of a reason for him to lie to me.

I reach into my pocket and pull out the pin that I've been carrying around every single day since the night I ripped it off the jacket of the firebird general.

"Do you know what this means?" I demand. "The firebird over the sun—do you know who they are?"

He hesitates for just a beat too long before attempting a chuckle. "Soleil, you're...You must be confused."

"Yes," I snap. "I am. I thought we were a team. Working together. The two of us, trying to sort this out. Ever since Fars'day."

Taris' eyes flick around our circle. This is the first time, I think, that I've ever seen him nervous.

"Soleil, you know I'd tell you things if I could," he tries again.

"So, you do have answers," I interrupt.

"Soleil, I can't—"

"Try."

"...The people who carry this symbol, they're...they are...in... th-th-the we-we-wesssst." He starts out speaking quickly, but as he goes on it becomes clear that he's straining himself to continue. "Th-th-they're c-c-c-call-ll-lled t-t-th..."

His hand flashes out to grip the back of Nissa's chair, and she angles away from him, watching with a mix of confusion and interest.

"They're a not just an assembly, they're a-a-a-a..." Taris tries, but gets stuck again. I watch his knuckles whiten on the back of the chair. It looks almost as if it's physically painful to try and speak.

"Lune!" he chokes out, though he's almost doubled over, now. "Lune, the missing Lijimi prince—they knew! Know! Working... together! Against...*them.*"

I frown, but think I am beginning to understand a little.

"Lune and Castel Voskoss knew each other," I verify. "Lune knew about the… *these* people," I add, waving the pin about.

Taris closes his eyes and nods.

"She was trying to find where they were hiding?" I say, trying to think back to the charts and papers I found in Crispin Carsans' rooms.

Taris doesn't give me any response.

"Did Nusk know that Lune Carsans knew this?"

Taris makes himself nod again, but it looks painful.

"Did Nusk know what you're trying to tell me?"

Another nod.

"…Do you know who the albino man is?" I suddenly think to ask.

I don't know where the thought comes from. It's been such a long time since I considered that man as part of this equation. I haven't seen any trace of him, not in weeks and weeks.

Taris is all but choking, but he forces himself to give a nearly imperceptible nod. His nose has started to bleed, and his eyes are shut tight. He is kneeling on the ground, now.

I crouch in front of him, ignoring everyone else, and lift his head. I can feel his entire body shaking.

"Taris, look at me," I demand.

It takes him a long time, but he opens his eyes.

"Your father had his own plans," I say. "I understand that, now. He did not want Rian and me to rule because he believed it would put us in even more danger, didn't he? He thought if he could get us past Comus Day and have another placed on the throne, the people trying to kill Rian might stop. And he wouldn't have to see me miserable as a *Khashtani*. But you disagreed with him, am I right?"

I don't need Taris to respond to know the answer to that one.

"Nusk remembered things, too," I say. "But he loved us. In his own way. He remembered watching us grow up—he raised us dozens of times over again. And he chose to keep us safe instead of letting Fate's loom weave the way it was meant to go. That's why he said you acted too much on emotion. That's why he told me he acted too much on emotion…Your father put orders in your head, didn't he? You remember things I don't. That Rian doesn't. So did Nusk. And he ordered you not to say a word."

Taris' nose is still bleeding, and his eyes are starting to glaze, but he still manages to nod again. I can feel Korvaan and Naomi's horror, but neither of them do anything to intervene.

"The man I took the pin from," I say. "I have killed him before. In other timelines. He did know you. And you knew him."

"…Amerson," Taris says. He is struggling to answer further, but I don't need confirmation. I know I'm right.

"Does Lune know what you know?" I ask.

Taris coughs before managing to choke out: "How am I to know what Lune knows?"

I press my tongue against the sharpest of my teeth to keep me from grinding them together. I'm just about to ask Taris something else when Rian grabs my shoulder.

"Soleil, that's enough. He'd tell us more if he could. Leave him be."

"He could give us all the answers we seek, now."

"Yet, Nusk's power remains strong even in death, it seems," Rian says. "Let it be. Perhaps it will fade in time."

I say nothing. As if to prove Rian correct, I watch Taris struggle for another minute to try and say what he wants to, but he cannot. I have to wonder how many times Nusk used his fluke on his son, reinforcing the same rules, over and over, to the point that it causes Taris this much agony to try and break through.

I love Nusk. I always will, and I will always appreciate the love I now realize he had for me and Rian. But I don't know if I can forgive him for doing this to his own blood. His own son. I don't know how he could excuse doing what he did out of love for me, while using his fluke to put Taris in such a position.

Even those with the best intentions can use love to justify the most horrific things. I realize, now, that does not exclude the man I call my father.

Taris collapses on his side, gasping for air. He looks frustrated with himself, and upset. Hurt. It's a wide variety of emotions all of a sudden, and I don't like it. Despite our differences, I've been able to depend on Taris. I hate seeing him like this. I hate knowing he wants to tell us all he knows, and cannot, because Nusk decided that if I knew what Taris knows, I would endanger myself.

This, naturally, only makes me more determined to find out.

Naomi kneels beside Taris and helps him sit, whispering to him in concern. Taris nods, brushing her off. I stand and cross my arms, trying to decide if I believe in the concept of goodness anymore.

"Well," Nissa says, breaking in again. "As exciting as all this is, I don't think you're getting very far interrogating your…brother? Is it?"

I mutter something less than polite.

"Sounds as if you've got several groups trying to kill the so-called rightful king, here," she continues. "Some, possibly with the intent of starting a war?"

"Many of the attempts on Rian's life by these…*pin* people were public events," I admit. "And possibly they had several plans in motion. I think they wanted to kill him with many people watching. And in a way that could be blamed on another of the crown princes. So that…they could get Isaaria involved in a war with itself. Or Alarkia, even," I add, remembering the Fars'day assassins. "Though why anyone would want that is beyond me."

"So, some of these assassins belong to the Order of the Pin," Nissa claims, giving a ridiculous but useful name to whoever ensnared Mercer and the other crown princes. "The subtler ones you're implying, then, were probably done by Vásan's mother or foreign entities not related to the Pin. And—I'll admit—it's possible the Hoitsokin sent assassins after all the other heirs on my behalf."

Qhan gives her a disgusted look.

"I did not say I approved," Nissa defends herself. "But they wanted me to be queen, and they knew I wasn't the rightful heir. The math is simple enough."

"Vásan's mother?" Rian says, surprised by that one.

Nissa rolls her eyes. "Let us not all pretend as if we didn't know the Pikes have been angling to get Vásan on the throne for decades now. His father was a fair man, who went about it in a fair manner. But his mother would rather have done away with us all. Myself included. Anything that would make things easier for her two precious sons."

"That is despicable, and yet, almost…touching?" Korvaan offers.

"I'm starting to think the Pikes are a very peculiar family," Raj mutters. I wonder what else he has heard about them to have come to that conclusion.

"Now that I think about it, some of those 'subtle' killers were probably from Alarkia or Lijimata even without intervention," Rian muses, disappointed in the realization, but too smart not to make it. "I played my cards too well; they thought me the least useful prince to Isaaria, but a prince all the same. They could kill me, blame the other side, and ensure Isaaria joined the war on their behalf."

"That explains the Lijimi ambassador's reaction to you," I say.

I am thinking, now, about a war being purposefully started in the west, too. I'm trying to put it all together, make sense of all the pieces. But it still feels like we are missing something significant. A driving purpose. Perhaps we have the who, given this mysterious firebird-pin Order, and part of the how, but not all of the why. Not in the slightest.

"He was probably annoyed none of his attempts worked," Taris agrees, coughing and clearing his throat as he rejoins the conversation. I cannot make myself look at him, and he won't look at me, but I appreciate his insight. "If the Lijimi could have you killed off and then blame Alarkia, it would have made their campaigning for assistance easier."

"Which still leads me back to the Pin. Whoever these people are, they must have gotten to Mercer at some point when he was abroad," I say.

Rian frowns. "But Mercer was in Lijimata and Alarkia. And they were already trying to kill me subtly and blame the other side. So, who are these firebird people?"

"I'm not sure." Even as I admit to it, a thought comes to me, building off the one I had before.

I look around at everyone.

"Who here knows their history? Who can best explain to me why the Lijimi and Alarkians went to war?"

"Probably me," comes a quiet voice.

Aiko Shinya. I had thought he was still asleep. Ayla is awake, too; our voices must have woken her. She is sitting with her knees pulled up to her chest and a blanket around her shoulders, watching and listening.

"I was there," Shinya adds. "…In Lijimata. I was ten. But I remember."

He stares ahead at nothing and takes a few seconds to steel himself.

"They killed his daughter first."

"The ambassador's daughter?" Rian clarifies.

Shinya nods dully. "Louisa. They blamed her for killing the king and queen. Emmelina's parents. They did not have any proof, but still, they blamed her. Because a Lijimi royal said she must have done it. They would not let her talk," he says haltingly. His chest is shuddering as he tries to control his breathing.

It's painful, and I hate making him describe it all, but these are details we need.

"They said she was hiding a fluke—or, casting, that is what the Lijimi call them. That she could control people, with her voice. So, they would not...un-gag...her."

I frown. The similarities to the accusations against Louisa Erikson and how Lune used her fluke are not lost on me.

"Do you think it is possible she did kill the king and queen? You were there. And you saw how Vásan acted, killing the Carsans. Do you think Louisa Erikson could have been influenced the same way?"

Shinya shakes his head. "No," he says hoarsely. "But someone else in the court might have been. Someone might have framed her. It was a strange time. Even while I was young, it seemed…odd. How they all jumped to conclusions so quickly. How they were so quick to execute her within minutes. And they killed her father, too. With even less proof of his involvement."

Given the disturbing experience that must have been, I know it is possible Shinya is not remembering things clearly. But I have heard enough.

"The simplest explanation, then," I say, and when I finish, the relieved look on Taris' face tells me I'm at least on the right track. "Someone wants all of these countries at war with one another, to destroy us from within. Maybe some sort of doomsday cult. And they're willing to do anything to accomplish that goal."

"But they must know they can't prosper off of countries devouring one another," Naomi points out. "Eventually, there won't be anything left. Nothing to conquer. If not money or power, why bother?"

"Anarchy for the sake of anarchy?" Korvaan suggests weakly.

"Yes, but if a person wants anarchy across the world, doesn't it rather defeat the purpose to create an organization with the intent of doing so?" Rian says.

"That's a matter of opinion, though, isn't it, your majesty?" Clanaugh's gleeful voice comes from behind me. I jump nearly a foot in the air.

"Fate's! *Fingers!*" I curse, and glare at the Fae. "If you do that to me again…"

Clanaugh is giving me an innocent look. His height, built, and general demeanor as a Fae make it a hard sell.

"I am only here for my own edification," he promises, holding up a hand mirror in a somehow elegantly dramatic pose. "I was taking a gander at the chaos you all have caused when I noticed something I do not have a name for."

I stare. I've been doing a lot of that lately. "Is that a *magic mirror,* by chance?"

"What else could it be?" Clanaugh asks condescendingly. "I use it from time to time to see what you humans are up to."

"Brief aside, but did, ah, the Fae happen to create Magic Mirrors?" Rian asks, thinking he's sly.

If a Fae could snort, that is exactly what Clanaugh does. "Don't be ridiculous, little king. Everyone knows that was the Magicsmiths."

"I knew it," Rian mutters under his breath.

"Here, give it to me," I say, holding a hand out for Clanaugh's magic mirror.

One of his fingers brushes mine as he hands it over, and a shiver runs through my entire body. I pretend as if I do not notice, but the way Clanaugh smiles makes me sure we each felt our magic clash with the other's.

"I have no idea what I'm looking at," I admit after staring at the scene in the magic mirror.

Shinya and Rian move closer on either side of me while everyone else attempts to crowd around for a look.

"Those are screens," Raj says.

His view is upside down, but still, he recognizes them.

"Screens?" I repeat, confused. I have seen bathing screens before, but the large black shiny things being set up in the middle of Pyrian City look nothing like those. They're plain and admittedly ugly, but look like new technology, to me.

"Yes, and then those things, there, are cameras. Audio-visual cameras," Raj adds. "Video. I've read something about them. They are becoming very popular, for those who can afford them."

"Vid-e-o," I repeat. Sounds like a non-word.

"I've seen them before," Shinya confirms. "They are Alarkian. It is like a photo camera, only it captures seconds and seconds of what is happening. Not a snapshot in time, but recording time itself."

"And they can show these seconds back on screens like that?" I prompt, a sick feeling settling in my stomach.

Shinya nods. "They are not standard, yet, but for big events, one could easily broadcast what is happening. Using flukes and signals from the radio towers. So that common people can watch bits of Comus Day themselves instead of having to hear about it later."

I realize why the crown princes wanted to take Rian alive, but weren't too worried about failing to do so.

"They want to kill you in front of the entire country," I gasp. "They want to show Isaaria the crown princes turning on each other, and that is the most dramatic way. Those big boxes that arrived at the University: the Comus Day surprise. They're going to let everyone see the events of Comus Day right in front of their eyes. It's meant to be for celebration, but it's going to end in a bloodbath. Panic. Instant chaos…

"Mercer must have only just found out about them," I go on. "Even you didn't know, Rian, so he must have changed plans when the king moved Comus Day forward. The other attempts: the bathhouse, on Fars'day… He wanted to have you killed and then make it look like he did it, like in the baths, but couldn't stomach doing it himself. Or he wanted it done in front of a large crowd like on Fars'day and make it look like *Dadj'zcha* was involved."

I remember the bodies Taris and I dug up. Those cuts, and the missing hair.

"I doubt Mercer knows a lick of *Dadj'zcha* himself, but he's working with people who do," I go on. "If you had died on campus, they would have searched everyone's rooms. Including Mercer's, even if he wasn't there. I bet they would have found some kind of proof that it was him who had you killed, and then…An Isaarian war."

"But I'm right here," Rian says, starting to panic. "What are they going to do now, tomorrow? They can't kill me if I'm not there!"

"Does it matter?" Taris snaps. "They can always kill each other. I think it's clear to everyone at this point that the crown princes, excluding Mercer, are not acting under their own free will."

"We still don't know about Mercer," Rian protests. "He'd never. He wouldn't."

He's shaking his head, refusing to believe it. But I spent over an hour with Mercer in the Hub. I've watched him grow up with Rian for over two decades. Everything he said at lunch: that was Mercer. There was nothing to indicate he was not himself, and if Irina Lundan's shaky testimony is anything to go by, if he was being controlled by someone else, I should have noticed something. Irina knew Detrus wasn't himself. That someone else was using him.

"This doesn't make any sense to me," I sigh, and sit, rubbing my eyes.

I still have a headache from that drugged wine, but I've grown so used to it that I only remember once I give myself a second of silence. I am tempted to ask the Fae if they have anything to help with that, but I don't want Clanaugh to think he can trick Rian into a debt.

"Maybe it does not have to make sense," Rian offers, joining me. "So long as we can make it through this alive."

"…I do have an idea," I admit.

"You do?" Rian repeats, and everyone save for Clanaugh looks surprised to hear this. As if they thought I was doing nothing in my head this entire time.

"I have enough of a plan, and if we begin in the next few hours, I think we will have enough time to pull it off. But some of you aren't going to like it…And Lord Aiko," I add, addressing him, "your assistance would not go unrewarded, if you would not mind lending it."

Shinya tightens his mouth and gives a stout nod. "I have no wish to see anyone else die as a catalyst for war. I will do whatever you think necessary to prevent that."

"Crown Princess, Lord al'Yibna," I say to Nissa and Raj, "you can do as you please, but I will not refuse your help."

Nissa snorts. "As if I'd miss the chance to get back at the bastards who tried to kill me. If your theory is correct about this cult tearing countries apart, I have no doubt they framed my people for killing the Milash king as well. I will help. But not for you, for me. For the Hoitsokin."

Good enough.

"All I want is to free my sister," Raj says.

"We will find her," I promise.

I know Mercer, at least, would never hurt her, and he would keep the other crown princes from doing anything to her. The only reason he has tried to do Rian harm is because Rian's meant to be king, and because, I'm starting to think, Mercer knows about the prophecy and our son. It is not practical to have a supposed savior on the way when one is working with anarchists.

I look past Shinya and meet Ayla's eyes. She is still sitting on the ground with her blanket wrapped around her shoulders. She stands and approaches when I beckon her.

"Ayla. I need you to use your fluke to do something for me," I begin, trying to be as gentle as I can without undercutting the seriousness of my request. She deserves to be spoken to as an equal, at this point.

"Can you try?" I ask her directly.

Ayla glances to Rian beside me, and he gives he a reassuring nod.

"I can…I can do my best," she offers, nervous, but determined.

"That is all I can ask for," I claim, and then look up and around at the rest of them, all standing around. Waiting for me to tell them what to do. Waiting to hear what I have to say that might fix this once and for all.

"That's all I can ask from any of you."

Twenty-Two

WHILE THE REST of us plan to return to either the palace or Pyrian City, Raj is staying behind with the children. I don't trust the Fae, particularly not their wily leader, but Raj is smart enough not to cut any deals. I pray.

Before we depart, I make everyone with and without a fluke stand barefoot in the morning sun. It is difficult to meditate given what I have planned for today, but I don't find it as impossible as I once did. And I know I will need the energy. If Clanaugh told me the truth, I should have full access to my fluke, now.

I will likely be putting it to good use.

Eventually, we split paths and depart. We have some time, yet, to implement my plan, but not much. The Comus Day proceedings are not meant to start until noon, but while the Fae deposit us back where they found us, it takes time for me and my companion to return to the outskirts of the palace grounds. Almost everyone else is heading into Pyrian City, their own missions in mind, and the last of us has already found his own way inside the palace, to do some reconnaissance for me.

I have decided to re-enter the palace by the least-guarded place, which is to say, the front entrance. Because it's a large door, locked tightly, with gates, it is easy to set a patrol to pass by it every now and again, but otherwise the guards are circling the palace in search of craftier intruders.

Stealing into the courtyard and avoiding the patrols is easy enough. Finding a spot to lay low until I can make sense of the guard's cycles and find the perfect time to pick the lock: time consuming, but not difficult. My legs ache as I crouch in the dirt on the balls of my feet, but my weaponry is not heavy. And the sun heating my back is a welcome visitor.

"We're going straight in, then?" Rian's voice comes from just behind my ear.

I flinch and nearly elbow him in the head. I turn to give him a warning glare, and find that the serious look on his face is not one I'm used to seeing. It would be worrisome, if not for our plan.

"We're going to find the traitor princes," I say, and wait until the way is clear before continuing. "And, it seems, that means going right in. Come on!" I hiss, and then dart forward, confident he is not far behind me.

I don't have my full lock-picking kit with me, but Clanaugh was gleeful at the opportunity to lend us further aid. He did, in fact, offer me something more magical in nature, but I declined, wary of tricks. Given the mild disappointment I sensed from Clanaugh, I suspect that was the correct choice.

It takes me a full minute to pick the lock, out of the minute and a half we have. I can feel Rian sweating behind me, nervous, but I stay calm and collected.

Once inside, we lock the doors behind us and bar them. It is uncomfortably quiet in the palace, and it still smells strongly of copper. There are no bodies to be seen, and no dramatic smearing of blood across the floor, but still. I have to wonder how many people have died, since yesterday. How many people were killed simply for their loyalties to the Carsans, the Orams, or to Rian.

The best I can do is avenge them. At least, that is what I tell myself. It is easier than thinking about how, if Rian died yesterday, I'd have gone back again already. And all these victims would get the chance to live their lives over again, perhaps with a completely different outcome.

"I am sure the others would be bolstered by the fact we're already inside. Qhan seemed dubious you could pick the lock on the front door," Rian comments.

"I have nimble fingers. Besides; no radio contact," I remind him tightly.

"You know how I feel about that."

"Yes, but there is no helping it. Who knows if they had an ability to intercept our radio frequencies? Now, follow me. We have a schedule to keep."

First order of business: find Asmer and give her the opportunity to escape. We promised Raj, and given the chaos I am about to unleash, I don't want her to be forgotten about.

There is no dungeon in the Pyrian Palace. Long ago, back when it was built, the king decided it was too dangerous to keep one's family and enemies in the same building, separated only by some bars and locks. So, in the absence of the traditional gloomy lock-up, I figure Mercer would have thrown Asmer in her room and locked the door. She could be perfectly comfortable, and he could all but forget about her. After all, Asmer's room is several floors high, and I don't think anyone would expect her to try climbing out the window.

I pull out a smaller set of lock-picking tools once we reach Asmer's room and begin working on the door while Rian stands guard. It doesn't take long before the lock pops and I stand to swing the door open. Inside, Asmer stops mid-pace to stare, then runs toward us in relief when I enter the room with Rian. I raise a finger to my mouth, and she nods.

"Thank Kilaj you're alive," Asmer whispers. "I thought…I didn't know what to think," she says, slipping the statue of her raven-headed goddess into her pocket.

"A handful of us made it out," I say. "Including your brother. He is hiding in the forest, with Alya and Soren Carsans."

"What about your *khashak?"* Asmer whispers.

I blink at her. "What—?"

"Yes, I know who you are," she says quickly. "The first time, you ordered me to stand by and look after Rian for you. As a friend."

"How much do you remember?" I demand.

Asmer raises her wrist and yanks her sleeve down to bare a thin, metal band of a bracelet. "Not much. But enough. Enough to always be loyal to you, my lady."

"Why give yourself one of those charms if you weren't going to make a good one?" I ask her. "…The memory charms. Rian said he thought he got his from you. That's your fluke, isn't it?"

Her brow furrows. "I...These are not mine."

"What?"

"I didn't make them," Asmer insists, shaking her head. "I do not know where they came from. All I remember is you giving one to me. So many cycles ago. And yes, I gave Rian's to him for you, and explained its use, but that's all."

"Soleil..." comes Rian's voice from behind me.

I shush him. "Tell me what you can, now. As much as you can. We haven't much time."

But Asmer makes a negative sound.

"I don't know anything more than what Rian would have. Even less. I don't understand how these things work," she adds, jangling her bracelet again. "Only that those of us who have the charms can remember some things from lives that could have been, and are no longer. But there's so much missing...I..."

"Never mind," I interrupt her. "Don't strain yourself. Do they have Lune somewhere close by?"

Her eyes suddenly widen, and her lower lip trembles.

"L-Lune...i-i-is..." Asmer stammers, and then bursts into tears.

I hear and feel Rian's form stiffen behind me. The sound of his breathing changes; he is furious.

"What about Irina?" I ask instead, forcing Asmer to calm herself in order to answer me.

She swallows back tears and nods. Her voice shakes when she speaks, but she is trying her best.

"Irina is here. All they did was put her in her room. I don't think they even locked the door. She is...When I saw her, she was acting strangely. Kept insisting that Detrus wasn't her husband. I think she cannot accept the facts. As they are."

Or Irina is completely correct, and most of the crown princes are not acting under their own free will, but *Dadj'zcha* puppeteers.

"Is anyone guarding Irina?" I ask.

"I don't believe so," Asmer says. "She is not in the best shape."

"But she is not bedridden, yes? Could she leave?"

"I suppose, if someone helped her."

"Then take Irina and flee," I instruct. "Be quick, quiet, and careful. Take her to the woods and call upon the Fae using Rian's name—I know it's dangerous, but trust me. Clanaugh will keep you and Irina safe. If she refuses to go, tell her that her daughter is out there."

Asmer's eyes widen. "Is that true?"

"Raj has her. She wandered off from Irina when she first fled the palace. Now, you won't be able to take Irina out through the front, or any conventional exit. You'll be spotted. Find a room on the first floor, wait until there's an opening in the guard's rotation, then open the window and run. Easy as that. Understand?"

Asmer's nodding fervently, rubbing to clear her still-moist eyes. "I-Is this going to be the last time?" she asks me, looking up at me in a way that makes me wish I could tell her yes.

"Let us hope so. But if not, continue to do as you always have. You are a loyal friend," I say, then turn to Rian. "Come. We've a meeting we can't be late for. Asmer: good luck. Keep your wits about you."

Then we're off, again. If Asmer is careful, she should be able to slip away without any trouble. As soon as I make it known that Rian Yakarami and I are back in the palace, I doubt anyone will bother trying to capture Asmer and Irina even if they are spotted.

I take Rian and find a servant's passage, all the way across the palace, to meet Aiko Shinya outside of Mercer's rooms. If my hunch is correct, someone clinically minded like Mercer keeps track of everywhere he has traveled, everyone he has treated medically, and everyone whose fluke he knows.

It's the last of these that is most important to me.

Shinya is waiting for us when we arrive. Quick, that boy.

"What did you find for me?" I ask, crouching next to where he's hidden himself in an alcove. "And how much time do we have?"

"At least ten minutes," Shinya whispers back. "I slipped in with some workmen—they are setting up the cameras, in the arena. No sign of that brightback. They must have locked it back up somewhere."

"You didn't happen to find a receipt of purchase amongst Mercer's things, did you?" I hear Rian whisper.

Shinya shakes his head. "I do not think it is his. Something as rare as a brightback is not sold full-grown. He would have to barter at a high-end egg auction. And they would not have those in the west. They think it is immoral to auction endangered species. Besides, I think it belongs to a woman."

A shiver runs down my spine. "Tall as Rian? Older than me? Doesn't wear gloves?"

"She was not wearing gloves," Shinya admits. "But she looked only a few years my senior. And she was not exceptionally tall. Around your height, maybe. She had dark hair, and looked as if she was from a foreign country I do not know. She wore one of those pins," he adds, remembering.

I exchange a look with Rian. Amerson, too, looked foreign in that manner.

"Leave it for now, Soleil," he warns me. "One thing at a time."

"Any luck with the other crown princes?" I ask instead.

Shinya nods. "You were right. Crown Prince Mercer did have a list. I think he was trying to determine how to kill each of them in a fight, if things do not go the way he intends. Or, perhaps, if things do go as he intends…"

"Unfortunately, I need that, too," I say.

He obliges me. "I did not understand all of the writing, even though it was in Alarkian. But Crown Prince Lundan's fluke is accuracy. And, apparently, he prefers throwing-axes. Crown Prince Ido's is inhuman strength and resilience to injury. I am not sure how those go together, exactly, but I think perhaps his fluke is simply 'resilience', and that can be applied to many things in many ways so long as he trains himself."

I raise an eyebrow. Detrus' fluke is a bit more subtle than I'd have thought, though he apparently uses it aggressively, and Yuugo's is much more physical.

I admit, "I would not have guessed those. Please tell me Vásan's was written down, too?"

"Crown Prince Pike's fluke is with the mind," Shinya says. "He can make reality seem...different."

"How so?" Rian asks. His voice almost makes me jump again.

"He can make one thing seem like another, in your head. A hangman's noose could be a necklace. A piece of meat on your plate suddenly becomes a mouse and scurries off. That sort of illusion."

"That seems to fit," I mutter. It is not charitable, but I don't have a reason to be. "Good work, Shinya. Go meet Lady Asmer downstairs. Help her."

But as much as he might seem like a good, obedient boy, Shinya has some youthful rebelliousness about him.

"I am staying," he insists. "You had wagered at least one of the heirs would not have a fluke, but they all have one. If it is only the two of you going to fight them, that is four princes with flukes and one invisible bodyguard. You know I could help."

"Out of the question," I deny him. "You're seventeen, Shinya. I don't want you anywhere near these people. Vásan already tried to kill you once."

"My apologies, Lady Soleil, but you are not queen yet. And you cannot make me leave."

Before I can speak, I hear Rian sigh beside me.

"Let him come, Soleil. The boy's right; we could use his help."

Two against one. I'm not winning this.

"Fine," I say. "But stay close to me, understand? And do as I say. Your fluke is powerful, but you are still a child. A liability."

"Yes, your majesty," Shinya promises. "...The crown princes are back at the arena," he adds. "I can show you where they are exactly, if you like."

"We know the way."

I walk with my bow in my hands, my quiver stocked with phoenix-feathered arrows thanks to the Fae. My knives are perfectly sharp. Rian is beside me with a sword, also gifted from Clanaugh, though I know he'll never use it again after today. Shinya bears no weapon but his fluke, and though that worries me, I would rather he utilize his own skills—with a power he's familiar with—than a weapon he does not know how to use.

I have never used the main entrance to the arena, but it is a spacious gallery built to make the royals forget they are about to enter a stadium filled more with commoners than peers. A relic of a time when the division between classes was significantly more severe than today.

But Mercer is the dramatic sort. He always has been.

It is ironic, then, that of those waiting for us, Mercer is the only one missing. No doubt he is still in the arena proper. I suppose he couldn't stomach what the others were doing. Hypocrite.

What husks remain of Vásan, Detrus, and Yuugo wait for us in a large, circular room with a stone floor and tapestries celebrating Isaaria's eight royal families. They are looking at the mess on the ground in utter disappointment, as if none of them can think of what to do with it now that it can no longer deny them answers. What is left of Lune is lying on her back, legs in a figure four, arms flopped loosely out by her sides. Her skin is white, and her hair looks darker than usual.

Even without the blood coating her, it is obvious that she is dead.

Rian's breath stutters when he sees her. I'm sure Shinya is horrified, though he tries to maintain his stoicism.

The crown princes all look up at us at the exact same time. As if they want us to know, at this point, that they are possessed.

"You ready for this?" I ask.

"Yes," I hear Rian say behind me. His voice is deep, and low.

He is going to help me kill these princes knowing that it is not their fault, what they've done. But we know better than to try and leave them alive. Vásan has a brother to take his place. Yuugo has two. Detrus has a daughter, and another child on the way. They all have someone within their families to take their places—we won't be ending an entire family line today.

I know Rian will be going after Vásan. I decide I will face Detrus—long-range for long-range—leaving Shinya with Yuugo. Physically, at least, I don't have to worry about Shinya much. I've no doubt his fluke is stronger than the crown prince's. Their contest is only a matter of how long he can use it before it exhausts him.

I don't give Detrus the time to pull an axe. In one smooth motion, I nock an arrow and let it fly directly at his head. He manages to roll out of the way, but I have already gained the upper hand; it is harder to throw an axe from the ground than from standing. So long as I can keep Detrus from throwing, he cannot use his fluke against me.

Unfortunately, Detrus seems to have the same idea about me and my arrows because instead of going for a weapon, he charges me. I don't have enough time for a full-draw, and barely have an arrow in hand when he crashes into me. It will be better for him to take this fight to the ground, with his size advantage. My bow is knocked from my hand, along with the breath from my lungs when my back hits the ground, but I've still got an arrow in my fist.

I jab it at his throat. Detrus manages to catch my wrist, but this frees up my other arm and I drive the heel of my hand into his face. I don't manage to break the nose, but that's still a tender spot to be hit. I free my legs and manage to prop my feet against the ground so I can throw Detrus over my head. We get to our feet about the same time, but he's closer to my weapon than I am and knows it. Detrus brings a foot down on my bow, snapping it in half.

So much for that, then. I abandon my quiver and draw a knife instead.

I open aggressively, hoping to draw blood however I can. With his longer reach, Detrus is able to throw a good punch so long as he times it well. I am the superior fighter technically, but I am already tiring. After the past week of nonstop strain and combat, my long-term endurance is starting to wane.

In my hand, my knife suddenly moves against my skin. It's scaly. Slithering. I nearly drop the snake I think I'm holding in surprise, but manage to tighten my grip at the last second. Absolute panic crashes over me when the creature hisses, and I'm sure, for a moment, that I have made a mistake. I'll have gotten this far only to die from snake venom.

But when I glance up again to check on Detrus' movements, I can see my knife out of the corner of my eye. Vásan's trying to manipulate me, even while he's occupied with his own opponent. Clever.

My hesitation gives Detrus enough time to pull his axe, though, which is exactly what I didn't want. When he throws it, all I can think to do is raise my arms towards my head to try and protect it. I would rather lose an arm today than the rest of my faculties.

But the axe doesn't hit me. Because Shinya has stepped in, dragging his hand against a wall and throwing it out. The wall slides, extending like the water did the night he and Rian sculpted it. It thins, naturally, as the material runs out, but is enough to act as a shield for me.

I do not allow myself to be shocked. I merely step out from behind the shield and hurl a throwing knife right through Detrus' eye.

His body staggers, then thuds to the floor. A quick glance to my left reveals that before coming to help me, Shinya made a handy prison for Crown Prince Yuugo by sliding out the wall again to make a stone cage. On the inside, I can already hear Yuugo trying to break out, but it will take him some time. If I leave Shinya here as I plan to, he can always reinforce the prison as he sees fit.

Rian is the last to finish off his opponent, but only because he is taking the time to stab Vásan through twice.

I take a minute to catch my breath and check the grand, gilded clock hanging above the doorway. Ten in the morning. Two hours remain. Or so Mercer thinks.

I look to Rian as he stands to wipe the blood off his sword, but he does not meet my eyes. I know I should say something about the rage radiating off of him, but I don't. Regardless, I'm sure our ploy will work. Mercer is too confident at this point for it not to.

"Stay here," I order Shinya, and though he hesitates, he nods.

I pass by the three bodies on the floor, forcing myself not to look at them. Not to think about the consequences of this. I head through the main tunnel to the arena, knives drawn, knowing I'm not alone. The tunnel splits off, offering staircases to the royals' boxes, but I continue to the floor of the arena itself. That is where Mercer will be.

As I enter the very grounds I fought to escape from yesterday, I notice the blood left from the dragon's carnage. Sand has been thrown atop the more gruesome spots, to soak up any pools, but it still leaves a stain. I can see the exact spot where Crispin died. Mercer is standing not far from it, in the center of the arena under the fullness of the sun. He is wearing that red suit of his; the one meant for Comus Day, just as Rian was meant to dress in black and silver. Ever the showman, our Crown Prince Ralhan. His necklace glints in the morning sun. I found it endearing, before, his constant wearing of it. Now I'm annoyed. It's not a damned firebird pin, but it may as well be.

"I thought I heard something of a commotion," he calls as Rian and I approach.

We are not alone in the arena. In the stands are the workers that Shinya must have slipped in with, testing those imported cameras. They are large, clunky black things that I'm sure must be drawing the heat in a most unfortunate way. Naomi's black coat does the same for me, but I take my power from the sun. It is most welcome on my shoulders.

"I'll admit, the last thing I expected was for you to come back," Mercer laughs as Rian and I come to a halt perhaps two dozen paces away. "Not after you let poor Lune die, so you could escape in the forest. You want a fight, then? Something to make you feel as if all this has been worthwhile?"

"That depends," I say. "Are you going to be fair about it?"

"Marques will come out when he's good and ready," Mercer replies.

"I've got Marques," I hear Rian reassure me. "...Get him."

"Bait? I don't have another throwing knife," I remind him, already regretting leaving mine in Detrus' eye.

"I've a better idea," Rian says.

Before I can stop him, he hefts his sword and charges directly at Mercer. Foolish man. It works, though: Marques appears from thin air to block Rian's blade with his own. Mercer heads to the left as if he intends to sneak off and away, entirely. Of course, he finds me there, blocking his way. I swipe at him and he dances back, quickly putting distance between us.

"Don't make me kill you," I warn him. "I will, if I have to, for Rian's sake, but I don't want to."

"Confident, aren't we?" he says.

"You don't have a weapon."

"Look around us," he reminds me, gesturing to the restocked weapons racks, though we're nowhere near one. "I'll manage."

"How's the hand? Certain you don't you want your dragon?"

Mercer merely smiles. "Interesting idea, Soleil, but I didn't authorize its use in the first place. It's a little too…impersonal, don't you think?"

I charge him again before he can finish his sentence. I need to bait him into using his fluke, preferably in a non-lethal way, so I can decide how to best him. But as Mercer is much more agile than Detrus, this proves difficult.

I do manage to get close, though: a well-aimed swipe that rips through the front of his lovely suit. As he dances away from me with a scowl, Mercer drags his hand across one of the prop barricades. For a moment, I assume he has a similar fluke to Shinya's. But then the barricade disappears completely. I slide to a halt, confused and surprised, and barely manage to throw myself out of the way in time as the barricade crashes back to the ground from above. By the time I've gotten to my feet, I have to dodge out of the way of a spear Mercer has thrown my way.

We are still nowhere near the weapons rack. He is a relocator. He can take an object and put it anywhere he likes, whether that be in his own hand or up in the air above me.

"So, you don't have to touch things, then," I muse. "To relocate them."

Mercer shrugs and smiles, another spear already appearing in his hand. "I have to be close to them, though. The larger they are, the closer I must be. But you are not so heavy, Soleil. Not compared to one of these barricades."

I'm suspicious of how easily he gave up that information. Mercer isn't the sort to make such a foolish mistake to an enemy, unless—

Of course. I'm fighting Mercer with long knives. And if I get any closer to him than I am now, he can move me with his mind. He could stick me high into the air and watch me fall to my death.

Fate's Fingers, I should have brought a gun.

"Give up, Soleil," Mercer sighs, twirling the spear around in his hand. "Rian's death: well, I am sorry it must happen. Genuinely. But what were you thinking? Bringing him back here?...Marques will kill him. This is over. You can't win."

"Why, because you're recording all this?" I say, and Mercer looks confused. "I know about the plan, *Merse.* Record yourself killing Rian, so everyone in Isaaria gets to watch? What was going to happen after that? Were you going to release the rest of the crown princes' minds? Let them all declare war on you and on each other, throwing blame? Or were you going to keep them under your control, and make them go to war using the public death of Rian Yakarami as an excuse? Because I think you'll find that impossible, now."

"If it all seems messy to you, it's because that's often the way things are when one's prime directive is to create chaos," Mercer claims, still trying to pretend he's in control.

I'm circling around him, slowly getting closer, like a predator would before pouncing. Mercer notices this, and relocates me. Thankfully, he doesn't put me high up in the air. He just pushes me back a few paces, in warning.

"Nice try, Soleil," he says with a smile. "Do you want to surrender, now, or do you want to do this all day? At least let me be a gentleman. You and Marques can go inside. I won't make you watch me kill poor Rian."

"Rian?" I repeat. "Rian is not here."

Mercer's smile falters. "Yes…He is."

"Sloppy of you, Mercer: falling for the same trick twice."

Mercer stares behind me. Because, naturally, it is not Rian that I brought with me back to the Pyrian Palace, right into the arms of his enemies. I would never dare. But as long as I brought a facsimile of Rian, he and I—the two most tempting targets—could act as a distraction, so that the real Rian would have time to make sure Isaaria knew the truth. So that our country did not fracture, splitting to back whichever of the eight royal families they favored.

All I needed to do was have Taris copy Rian's skin. Taris is taller, but I knew no one would notice. With Ayla's ability to edit the flukes—things like a false skin and stolen identity—Taris sounds like Rian, too.

It was a stretch of Ayla's magical capabilities to say the least, and sent her directly to sleep afterward, but it worked well enough to fool Mercer.

"Rian is in Pyrian City," I continue. "On the radio, right now, giving an emergency broadcast as far and wide as he can. I imagine it will be hard for you to get Isaaria to tear itself apart through civil war when its rightful king has just revealed himself to rally the country together. As soon as the Orams have the opportunity, I've no doubt they will answer in kind. We will keep you from destroying Isaaria."

Mercer is furious. I can feel it. But he grits his teeth and tries not to let me see.

"Marques!" he calls, and gestures to Taris. "Don't bother playing. Kill him."

Despite myself, in my worry for Taris, I turn. I barely get my wits about me again to avoid the spear Mercer has thrown. It's a good thing I decide to go to the ground instead of dodging, too, because Mercer can relocate that damned thing midair. This means he can throw it at me straight on, then move it so it comes at me from the side, or behind, or above.

Damn, but that's a useful fluke. Though I can throw these long knives if I must, it is a gamble. Even if I have the perfect spin, the perfect torque. Even if I could get a bead on Mercer, he could always relocate my knife before it gets anywhere near him. Or he can relocate me up into the air, and it won't matter what happens in the world, because I'll be dead. No more resets.

But if I can turn back time minutely in a matter of seconds, no: milliseconds…And turn it back only for myself, the way that Rian warned me to never try, lest my powers prove too much for me…

I know it is a risk. I have no practice using my fluke, only the distant memories of lives that never really happened.

But maybe that knowledge, regardless of whether it's real or imagined, is enough.

I run at Mercer. I run at him, and at the last second, just before he relocates me so high up in the air that I'm in the clouds, I throw my knife.

FREE FALL, AS it turns out, is not as thrilling as I'd imagined. I have had a flying dream once or twice in my life, but I can now say there is nothing romantic about the notion of flight when one doesn't have wings to depend on.

I'm falling, tumbling, and spinning. I can see the arena getting closer and closer at such a rapid speed that I know I have less than a few seconds at most before I'm nothing more than a smear on the ground. I don't have time to look into myself and concentrate. Reflect. All I can do is draw upon the confidence in the power I have been told over and over again that I have. I might be exhausted by recent events, but there's still a small reserve left. Just a little more...

I reach in, pull on that. Time is just a construct. It's all in my head. Today, I can't imagine ten days from now. Ten days from now, today is a vague memory. Today, I don't know if I'll get through this. In years, when I'm falling asleep to the sound of Rian telling stories to our son and Ayla on a cold winter afternoon, this day will be a distant heartache. Details that fade further and further with every hour that passes.

It's all in my mind. As time itself tumbles forward, I imagine it doing the opposite.

That hand on the clock begins ticking backwards.

The grains in the hourglass fall up.

Fate's loom unweaves, strand by strand, only for me.

Only for the time as I think of it.

I spread my arms out and away from my sides, and I start to slow. Not just because I have spread myself out, but also because time is ticking back until I'm no longer falling, but hovering. And then I'm moving upwards. Backwards in time. Back, back, back, until I'm higher up in the air, and then, suddenly, I am on the ground, again.

The version of myself that Mercer threw up into the air both exists and doesn't at the same time.

My world is blurred around me, and shaking. Colors bleed into each other like someone threw water over an artist's unfinished work. It is only when things start to go gray that I remember to release the hold I have on my own strand of Fate's loom and slam my reality back into the one everyone else knows.

I am in the arena, standing on the ground, exactly in the spot I was before Mercer sent me up in the air. I'm bent forward, gasping and panting, my head pounding so hard that I can barely hear.

But it worked.

I've remastered my powers dozens of times over again, over the span of hundreds of years. It seems that mastery has paid off, because here I am, both feet on the ground, decidedly not a splatter of gore. There is Mercer, collapsed on his back in front of me, my knife driven right into the base of his neck, under his throat.

He could only relocate one thing at a time, after all.

He should have chosen the knife.

My headache starts to fade beneath my triumph. I stagger towards Mercer to lean over him. Letting him see I'm alive, and he has failed. I don't think he has the energy to look surprised as his life slowly drains away. He might not even be able to think enough to remember he'd put me high up in the air at all.

His body and mind are panicking. He is dying, and all his deception's been for nothing.

"That was very clever of you, Sun-girl," he says, choking on his own blood. "You've always been so-o smart. Just not smart enough."

I don't care what that means. I only know I must glean answers him before he dies. Mercer might no longer be a threat, but there's always the question of who recruited him to their cause in the first place. Those firebird folk. That albino that has been haunting me ever since Fars'day. What Taris knows. What Lune knew.

I kneel next to Mercer.

"Where are the rest of your allies?" I demand from him. "I know there's at least one other, here. The woman who owns the dragon. Where is she? And the brightback?"

Mercer just coughs. I grab him by the front of his shirt.

"Why did you do this?" I hiss.

Mercer smiles so blood leaks out over his lips.

"Who told you to do this?"

"His…name...is Kryto Grey," Mercer says, and then laughs.

It is all I can do not to hit him, and settle for snarling in disgust. There is no point in trying to beat an answer out of him; he might well name characters from stories Rian has told until he bleeds out. I have no time for that, as I am sure he's well aware.

I drop him back to the ground and stand, turning to see if Taris needs my help only to find him limping toward me. He is back to looking and sounding like himself, too tired to bother using his fluke to keep up a useless illusion. He is covered in blood, but Marques is the one lying dead.

"It's done," I say as Taris joins me.

My brother collapses to the ground at the news. He takes off his borrowed overcoat from Rian, the sleeves noticeably too short, and begins to tear its fine fabric to bind up his bleeding leg. His chest is bleeding as well, but not as badly, and his injuries are not so egregious that he won't survive.

"Still alive, is he?" Taris rasps, jerking his head at Mercer.

"Not for much longer," I admit. "…Can you stand?"

"Likely," Taris grunts.

"Because we should join the others as soon as we can," I continue. "I'm sure Rian's worri—"

Mercer suddenly gives another blood-gurgling laugh. Still alive, then, yes, and still so needy for attention. I turn to stand over him again, prepared to let the last thing he hears in this world be an insult I have been saving a long time for him, when he speaks first.

"Don't fret, Soleil. I'll say hello to Rian for you. *I think I'll be seeing him first*," Mercer claims vindictively. And then he dies with an eerie smile on his face.

Taris and I take about a moment each to consider what that could possibly mean. While Mercer might be lying—might just be trying to get in one last deception before his death—it's a chance we can't afford to take. Taris and I both know that full well. We haven't come this far for failure.

"Go!" Taris orders urgently. "Go, go, now!"

I am already running. I sprint past where we've left Shinya, and though he is startled, he instantly picks himself up and runs after me. I told him to stick close to me, and that's what he is doing. I might appreciate that if I wasn't suddenly so terrified.

I need to reach Rian. I'm running as fast as I possibly can, but it still doesn't feel fast enough. With Shinya on my heels, I sprint back the way we came, then take a shortcut towards the front of the palace. It's only at the last second that I remember we barricaded the front door, and I change course. I raise an arm up to hopefully protect my face some, add a burst of speed, and then jump up and throw myself through one of the palace's front-facing windows.

I feel a shard of glass cut open the side of my face, but Naomi's coat protects my body from the rest. I tumble to the ground on the other side of the window, startling two passing guards so badly that they don't try to stop me as I roll to my feet again and continue running. Shinya manages to climb more carefully through the window after me and follows.

It'll be a drain on my remaining energy, running to the city, but I don't have the time to wait for a coach or try to hijack one. And I'm fast, now. Incredibly fast. It is possible I am accidentally slowing time with my fluke as I dash through reality at normal speed, which explains why everything is so dizzying, but I don't care what I should or should not be doing. I need to reach Rian.

I know the way. I know how to reach the building that houses the most successful radio station in all of Isaaria, where Rian has likely just concluded his interview or speech or whatever it is he ended up broadcasting to his entire country. It hardly matters to me—it was his job to orchestrate that portion of the plan. All I was supposed to do was stop Mercer. Which I did.

I pray.

I know I'm not moving fast enough. I'm barging past and through the crowds, throwing myself over obstacles when they aren't moved out of the way in time. I'm bloody and dirty. A hooligan barging past these well-dressed city-folk whose shouts die off as they stare after me, trying to process exactly what has dashed past them.

And then their annoyed shouts repeat as Shinya follows me, calling sincere apologies after himself in Isaarian.

I'd find that endearing, and hilarious, in any other circumstances.

Towards the end of my flight, I'm foolish enough to panic and think it's possible I've gotten myself lost. I should be near the building, now, after all. It should be here. But my feet know better than I do, and deftly deliver me to my destination.

There is a well-dressed man walking out of the building's gold-and-glass doors with a stack of papers. I barely avoid knocking into him as I run past, letting him inadvertently hold the door for me. A woman in an ankle-length skirt, suit, and heels was following him, probably heading for an early lunch break, and I do have to throw myself out of the way to avoid knocking her over. The bottom of my boot skids on the floor, practically leaving a mark.

In front of me, an elevator dings, opening to reveal several businessmen who pause their cheery conversation to stare at the bloody madwoman tearing past them to reach the stairs, and the well-dressed eastern nobleman hurrying behind her, apologizing to everyone on her behalf.

I read the lists of offices on landing of each floor as I pass. Though I have never been inside this building before, it is just what a person should expect given its grand exterior and reputation. The radio station offices are on the top floor—naturally, but at least this means that once I'm at the top, I'm there. Destination reached.

I barge through the large, fancy doors into the suite and past a flustered secretary who calls after me that I cannot enter.

I head for the door with the red light over the top, with only a vague idea of what I'm doing, and throw open the door. It is almost a shock to see familiar faces inside. There is recording equipment, as well as telephones and mufflers, to keep sound from echoing in the tiny room.

Korvaan is perched on the corner of the desk with the recording equipment, chatting with the man who must have acted as Rian's host. Nissa is lounging in a chair while her hyena gnaws on a chicken bone left over from someone's lunch. Naomi is leaning against the wall, stifling a yawn. Qhan is standing outside a door on the far side. But no Rian.

"Soleil! You're… I honestly don't think any of us were expecting you this soon. Rian wanted a second alone, he is in the manager's offi—" Naomi starts, but I'm already running through the door she's pointing at, past where Qhan stands guard outside it.

I'm moving so fast off my own momentum that I have to grab the doorframe to swing myself inside, or else I would have run right into the far wall of the office. Breathless, I take in the room to find Rian standing by the desk. His back is to the windows that lead out onto a balcony, granting anyone who wishes it a view of the city beyond.

Rian looks up and gives me the most brilliant smile I've ever seen from him. He raps his knuckles against the desk and Mango crawls down his shoulders onto the desktop.

"Oh, good, you're alive then—" Rian starts.

I run straight for him and throw my body into his just as a bullet cracks through the windowpane, aimed directly for his head. Rian and I slam onto the ground, the bullet skimming past to clip the left side of his head before lodging in the far wall. I'm sure Rian's back must ache, but I at least thought to put a hand to the back of his head to cradle it.

Granted, my hand's aching, now, but at least Rian's skull is safe.

I'm panting, barely able to comprehend the fact that I arrived in time to save Rian. Mercer was not lying, and thank the Almighty I had not assumed he was.

I close my eyes, moan, and let myself drop my head onto Rian's chest.

I have stopped the assassination that has killed Rian dozens of times over again on this day. It's over. No more turning back time. No more rehashed realities. No more talk of whether I've done the right thing or not—it doesn't matter, and I don't care. I'm alive. Rian's alive. That's enough.

It's Shinya's voice that makes me pick up my head, remembering things aren't quite over yet.

"Lady Soleil!" he calls, about to enter the room with Qhan on his heels.

"Stay back! Stay away from the windows!" I call.

Shinya must have gotten a glimpse of the broken glass, because he disappears back into the studio again.

I can hear the others already creating a fuss. Shinya has reassuring them he saw Rian and me both alive. Rian's host is saying he is going to call for the city peacekeepers. Nissa is offering to hunt the would-be assassin herself.

They can manage all that. I don't care. I can feel Rian's chest under me as he breathes. He's alive.

"Just in time as always, Soleil, aren't you?" he says, smiling up at me.

"Shut up," I say. I feel like sobbing, I am so relieved. "Don't ever do anything like this to me again," I order him.

"Naturally, dear, I don't plan on it," Rian promises me, and then reaches up to touch where the bullet skimmed by his temple, pulling his fingers away bloody.

"I could have been a second too late," I warn him.

"But you weren't," he reminds me. "And I should have known you wouldn't be."

I guess my lying on him is too good of an opportunity to pass up, because Rian reaches up and puts his hand to the back of my head so he can pull me in and kiss me. But when Rian leans in for a second one, I put one a hand over his mouth to intercept him.

"Stop. We've still an assassin on the rooftops," I warn him.

"Eh. I'm fine with that as long as we can stay like this a little longer," Rian claims, smiling against my fingertips.

But I roll off him and smack his hands from wandering.

"Follow me," I tell him, and make my way to the side of the room.

Rian, still grinning, does so. Once we're out of sight of the window, we stand to sidle around the side of the wall. I make it to the door. Rian is following behind me when he staggers. At first, I have the luxury of thinking he's merely being clumsy. He just barely escaped death once again, after all; he has an excuse to be dazed by the experience.

But then he staggers again, and falls into the wall.

"I'm sorry," he says, and gives me one of those charming smiles of his. "I don't feel so well."

He folds to the ground.

"No!"

I can't help but scream it.

I hurry to Rian's side, desperately trying to find what's wrong with him. At my cry, Qhan and Shinya both run into the room. Korvaan comes to the doorway, sees me and Rian, then leans back out to yell at someone to call for a doctor before he joins us.

Shinya kneels next to me and moves my hands away as I pat at Rian's clothes, trying to find a second wound. Qhan is asking me where the prince is hurt, but I don't know and Rian can't say. It does look as if his only injury is where the bullet barely scraped him. I am hopeful, for a second, that all is still well. Perhaps the impact of hitting the floor was still enough to daze Rian, and my hand did not do enough to soften things. Maybe. Maybe that's all it is.

But deep in my gut, I know better.

"Soleil, I think there's something on this bullet," Korvaan says as he examines the evidence lodged in the wall.

"...Activative substances," I mutter under my breath, remembering my talk with Mercer in the Solunium Hub.

"What?" Qhan demands.

"Poison," I say. "It's a rare poison, on the bullet."

"It can't have acted that fast," Qhan says.

"...It could. It could if its only purpose was to activate a poison that's been in Rian's blood for weeks."

And instantly, I know where the first poison is. How Rian could have gotten it on himself: the Kachin hairpin. It must be. He has been poisoned, all this time, ever since Mercer got back to the University. It simply never took effect because it had to have the right trigger.

It was a backup. A way to assassinate Rian, in case we managed something clever like this.

I jerk my head up and look to the window, following the trail of the bullet up to a nearby roof. I can see someone there, moving. Packing up their equipment, I gather.

At this point, I can do nothing to save Rian. Nothing.

But there's something else I can do. And I'm good at it.

"You'll want to catch him," Korvaan says gravely, and meets my eyes briefly.

I'm already off.

I run for the window, using my body to slam it open, then climb up onto the railing of the balcony and swing myself up onto the roof of the building. I'm too low down, from here, to try and jump to that higher roof, but I can use my surroundings like a good *Khashtani* should. Telephone poles. Wires. Adjacent buildings. Balconies. Window ledges.

I'm getting up there. I will catch the bastard that did this, and when I do, I am going to wring every answer I please from him, slowly. And then, when I turn back time, I am saving Rian once and for all, with the full knowledge of this shadow organization trying so hard to kill him.

The assassin's running across his rooftop as I reach it, and I give chase. Strangely enough, my previous exhaustion now means nothing to me. I am driven by something that I never thought could give me so much ambition, so much motivation, but it does. For Rian.

Revenge.

Mercer had a painful enough death. This man's demise will be even slower.

The assassin is not a large man, perhaps only my size, but he is fast despite the rifle slung over his shoulder. We run, both weaving to avoid the air filtration systems spinning on the roof to keep the buildings cool during the end to this sweltering summer. We leap across rooftops, barely thinking twice before we hurl ourselves from one place to another.

I catch up to him, flick one of my knives back out, and slash. He manages to avoid my every move. Pulls out a blade of his own and swipes back at me.

After a few passes at each other, I fail to lean back in time and he barely catches the same side of my face that the glass sliced open. Fresh blood drips down to land on my collarbone. Distracting.

The assassin leaps off the edge of our roof to a series of conjoined apartment buildings and scrambles to regain his balance after landing on the angled tiles. I don't hesitate before making the same leap, but land too close to the edge, and panic spikes in my brain for a moment before I adjust my body accordingly. I ache as I get to my feet and begin running after the assassin again, but now he has even more of a lead. If I make one more mistake, I will lose him. He will be gone and Rian will be dead. It'll all be completely for nothing.

But then a sunblood dragon glides down and lands right on top of the man's head. Startled, the killer's foot slips. He slides, tumbling down the roof tiles to fall onto a balcony, where I'm sure he's broken at least three bones.

Good boy, Mango. You've figured out you're a real dragon after all.

I slide down the tiles of the roof and drop down to the balcony below before stalking to the assassin, crouching beside him as he coughs and moans. Mango circles his head smugly. I suppose all he needed was a little motivation, too. I let Mango clamber up one of my arms and coil around my shoulders before I reach over and pull off the hood that's been obscuring the assassin's features.

It takes me a second to find my voice. I don't know what I was expecting, but it certainly wasn't this: olive skin, angular face, wavy dark hair, slim figure. No one I recognize. And yet.

"You're...!"

A boy. Younger than Shinya. Fifteen, I'd guess, and an excellent shot, especially for his age.

It makes me hesitate, but the silver firebird pin glinting on his breast helps me find my anger again.

I am forced to remind myself that though he may look like a mere child, there is evidence to suggest our enemies are aware of my timelines past. Perhaps with similar charms to the ones Taris, Asmer, and Rian have. This boy could have the mind of someone twice, thrice, four times his age.

I grab him by the front of his jacket and shake him.

"You're over," I hiss at him. "Every one of you. You are finished."

He just gives me a weak, shaky smile.

"It does not matter. The Dark will rise," he rasps. "And we will kill it."

Something starts to foam, in his mouth. I don't hesitate before jabbing a finger into his mouth, digging around until I pull out a capsule. Poison. This fifteen-year-old boy would rather commit suicide than reside in the camp of his enemies. Given his age, and the relative youth of the firebird general, I have to wonder who has been giving them orders.

The body has stopped shaking uncontrollably, but one of the boy's feet keeps twitching. I set down the body and examine it again, trying to see if I recognize who this is, but I don't.. Whoever this is, he means nothing to me.

I tear the pin off his jacket.

I've two, now. Maybe I'll start a collection.

I'm not sure how I make it back to the radio building, back to that room, back to Rian. I think I manage to answer a few questions about the assassin in one-word bursts, but I can't be sure. It's more important, to me, to kneel next to Rian and take his hand.

Everyone else backs away. Qhan, I think, has left to retrieve the body of the assassin.

Rian is still cognizant. He knows it's me here, at least, and though he's trembling, he tries to grip my hand back. His face is gray. He keeps trying to mutter something, but he's stuttering, and none of his words make any sense.

I don't say anything back to him, just hold his hand and kneel there. Waiting. Korvaan, Naomi, and Shinya all stand around, silent. I do not know where Nissa is, and I don't care. I don't care if Asmer managed to escape to the forest with Irina. I don't care if Clanaugh is right this second trying to trick Raj into making a deal with him.

Absolutely none of it matters. Because we're going to have to do it all over again, anyway.

I notice Korvaan's expression change, as he reaches for his pistol. I draw a knife and whirl, only to see someone familiar at the door. Someone unexpected.

The albino.

He is as young and mysterious and strange as I remember. He is standing there in the doorway, grimly, watching us. He doesn't move when we brandish our weapons at him. He looks tired.

Behind him is a young girl with wavy hair that hangs in her face. She clings to his arm and hides behind him. She's looking at Rian with large, horrified eyes.

Shinya is staring at her as if he's seen a ghost. His face is completely white.

"So, here we are again," the albino sighs. He looks disappointed, but not surprised.

"Is…Is he dying?" the girl whispers.

I am struggling to decide what to say. It's Shinya who manages to speak first. Though he's clearly as confused as I am. If not more so.

"She…It's you," he manages, completely incredulous by this girl's presence. "It's you…Teresa," he says, gasping the name. The girl looks over, startled.

"I'm sorry?" she says. "Do I know you? I don't think I do…"

But still, she tilts her head to the side as she looks at him.

He crosses the room in a few short steps. Shinya almost touches her with a shaking hand, but then pulls it back, as if he thinks she is mere illusion.

"You are...You're her. But...but you are so young..."

The girl frowns. "I'm fourteen."

Shinya doesn't hear her. The blood has drained out of his face. "I marry you," he whispers. "I think…you are my wife."

She looks even more perplexed. "But you can't be. Because I'm—"

"Teresa," the albino man snaps. "I told you to say nothing."

"Resa," Shinya says. He and the girl are both ignoring the other man, now. "Resa. You are Resa. My Resa."

The albino sighs and rolls his eyes.

"You cannot remember her, you've never seen her before in your life," he snaps, and then pushes against Shinya's head so the boy staggers and nearly topples.

"I don't…I don't feel good," Teresa says, her legs buckling under her.

Her companion deftly supports her, lowering her to the ground so she can sit.

"That's not surprising, unfortunately," he mutters. "You're not meant to be meeting him, now. And he's not supposed to remember."

"What did you do to him?" I demand.

I don't leave Rian, and Korvaan doesn't shoot, because there's something about this albino that keeps us from doing so. Shinya slumps against the wall, then slowly lets himself slide down to sit on the floor. He looks dazed.

"Stay put, dear. This will all be over soon," the albino says absently to his companion instead of answering me.

He comes and kneels across from me, and for the first time, Rian gets the chance to see who it is. Confusion flits across his face, but then his eyes bulge and he grips my hand so tightly that it hurts.

"Y-Y-You! Y-Y-You!" he stammers out. "Soleil. Soleil. D-D-Don't go back. Don't. Don't. Don't—"

"Shh…" the albino man says sympathetically, and leans forward to put his fingers to Rian's forehead.

Rian groans and lets his eyes flutter closed. But he seems more peaceful, so I don't raise a fuss.

The albino man looks up to me.

"Don't listen to him; he's speaking nonsense. He often does, near death. He can't help it. He's tired, and I don't blame him. We all are."

"What?" I say, my voice so hoarse the sound barely leaves my throat.

"Go back," the albino man snaps. "You must. You've ruined this loop."

I stare at him, trying to memorize his features. "Who are you?" I whisper. "Are you…some kind of a god?"

His lip twitches and he gives a self-deprecating chuckle.

"…Some kind. Maybe."

I don't have the energy or mental capacity to care about what that means.

"I'll go back a few minutes," I say. "A few minutes, and then that'll be enough. I can get here in time. I can save him—"

The albino man interrupts me in exasperation. "The other crown princes will still be under the influence of your enemy. They will still be known across Isaaria as traitors. The eight families will still go to war. There will be war in Isaaria and, what—you'll be happy with that ending? With a completely destroyed world, so long as you have each other?"

I flounder. "Then…then I'll go back and…and stop Mercer from going to the west," I decide. "That's…that's, what, six months? Six months. That will be enough time—"

"And the west will still tear itself apart, and eventually those horrors will find their way here regardless of what you try to do to stop them."

"Then…seven years! Eight years!" I snap at him. "I'll go back until…"

"Until what?" the albino challenges me, sighing. "Look, you've worked hard. But you were always going to fail. It's as simple as that."

I've begun to cry, and I'm not even that ashamed of it. "I don't understand."

"The only true future is one in which Rian becomes king and you queen, would you agree with that?" he asks.

"Yes," I whisper.

"And are you willing to live two, seven, twelve times over to find that future?"

I look at Rian, then up at Korvaan and Naomi, who are watching all this just as stunned as I am. Korvaan has lowered his gun. Naomi is huddled by his side. The albino man's words have made me think of her. Made me remember the promise I made that I am about to break. I understand, now, why it was so easy for me to force everyone else to live many times over again, for Rian's sake. I did it then, and I'll do it again, now. I don't care how angry it makes them, either.

Because I'll do anything to have Rian back again.

I look away from Korvaan and Naomi. I don't want to see their faces.

"Yes."

He looks down at Rian's hand and slips Rian's ring off.

"You're done, though," he says. "I don't think you can take another full round. And I'm starting to think that maybe you shouldn't."

He turns and looks at Korvaan.

"You'll do," he says. After a second of gripping it tightly in his hand, closing his eyes and concentrating, he tosses Rian's ring to Korvaan. "I've updated it. Which means the rest of the charms should be updated as well. Taris's, Nusk's, Lune's, and Asmer's."

"I'm sorry?" Korvaan says.

"Put the ring on," the albino man says. "When Soleil rewinds everything, you'll still have the ring. I've charmed it that way. You'll remember what I want you to remember, for the reasons I want you to. You'll know what I want you to do, and, aside from Taris, at least, you'll do what I ask. Which means I'll only have one wild card to deal with, because you and

Nusk are going to keep Taris from corrupting Soleil and making her do foolish things. Understand?"

Korvaan clearly does not understand, but if what the albino man is saying is true, if he puts that ring on, he soon will.

Rian's breathing stutters.

"Right, then," the albino says. "Out of time. Let's go back, Soleil."

"But what do I do?" I cry.

"You act his *Khashtani*. Keep him alive. Only this time, I'll have Nusk let you know your principal. He'll grow up, and marry Asmer, and become king, and you'll keep him safe. You have to be willing to try everything—try to keep him alive as long as you possibly can—so that we'll have enough time to fix the source."

I frown. "The…source? I don't…How—"

"It's best not to think about it," the albino man sighs. "It's beyond you in many ways."

Sudden anger flares in me.

"Don't assume my intelligence," I hiss at him.

"Don't assume you're the one meant to fix everything, Soleil Marson," the albino man snaps back. "I have worked for centuries for this. And I will work for centuries more, to straighten Fate's tangled web. That is my destiny."

"What are you saying?"

"I'm saying that there is a reason I never wanted you to remember everything. You always interfere. Sometimes that's good, most times it's not. I need Rian alive for as long as possible, because he is meant to live, and every time he dies, you go back and make me a child again.

"I am the one meant to fix the timeline, Soleil," he continues. "All of this—the proper and natural destiny of our entire world, as Fate intended—rests on me. Not you. You're just the stubborn woman with the gift over time. Which is why I need you."

"Why can't you explain everything to me," I complain. "Tell me what to do?"

"Oh. Things do not go well when I explain everything," the albino man claims. "Not well at all."

"Do you really think me so impulsive?"

"Usually you are," the albino says. "And…Ugh, it will be faster if I do it like this."

Before I can flinch away, he presses two of his fingers against my forehead. I feel something go through me like an electric jolt. And though I am not fully aware of what I know, I know things. I know how to go back in time. It's as easy for me as snapping my fingers. I know things that I'll forget, again, once we go back.

By the time I've recovered, the albino's turned to talk to Korvaan again.

"You'll have all these memories, but the body of a child," he warns. "It will be confusing, but you'll manage. You won't remember me, of course, but you'll remember the idea of me. See if you can make it so that Lune is not given to Carsans family," he adds as an afterthought. "That might help keep her a live a little longer. I hope."

"I don't know how to do that," Korvaan admits.

Next to him, Naomi's crying quietly, but she's not trying to stop any of this. So, she must understand it's going to happen whether she wants it to or not.

"Tell Nusk. He'll know what to do."

I grab the albino man's arm so he'll turn back to me again, and look at me with those pale, pale eyes of his.

"Promise me it will be different this time," I demand from him. "Promise me this all means something. This will be worth something."

"It will be. I swear it. I know what to do to ensure some eventualities. Some, not all. But it's close. Closer. I'm almost there. One more time, I think. Just one more jump back. One more, after this time, and then…Then I'll have it."

It's not the answer I want. But it will have to be enough.

I release him, and move closer to Rian, leaning over him. I let myself watch him breathe for another second until his chest flutters and he coughs. I lean down and let myself kiss Rian's forehead, once. The albino man is right: we're out of time.

"I swear, I will find a way to save you," I promise Rian. "Even if it means you cannot be mine."

I let go of his hand, and close my eyes. I call on the power that's been my birthright for centuries. The ability I've mastered so completely that Fate himself must worry over my influence.

And we jump back.

Twenty-Three

I AM TWENTY-SEVEN YEARS OLD, *and a half,* as the king likes to remind me. He and I practically share half-birthdays each at polar solstices, and as he is a romantic, this pleases him greatly. He is lucky his fiancée is not the jealous sort, or else she might begrudge how oddly intimate the king is with one of his bodyguards.

In fact, Asmer goes out of her way to often thank me for my service. Kind as everyone knows she is, I privately admit this makes me uncomfortable. Even worse, sometimes she looks at me with such a sad smile, it is as if she's seen my death and already misses me.

Unfortunately, I suspect I will be forced to endure similar looks often in the future. Rude as it may be, I have always been able to evade Asmer, when I please, and have variable excuses ready on my lips. But after today, she and the king will be married. She will be unavoidable.

I'm standing in the king's bedroom, which would be inappropriate if not for the fact that I've known him for years and have always needed to be close to him, for his safety. Besides, I've a companion in Taris Qurvo—one of my mentor's children, who often trained alongside me in our youth and has now become a bodyguard himself. He usually does not say much to me, but I believe we are friends, after a fashion. We were both raised by his father, at least, and that has formed a necessary bond.

The king is standing before a full-length mirror, looking himself over and scowling on occasion, pulling different faces. His miniature sunblood dragon, Mango, twirls between his feet, playing with the swish of his cape. Someone has been brave enough to snap a fanciful collar around the little beast, and though the dragon found it irritating at first, he has since grown used to it.

"I wish we could skip over today. I hate this. I swear, I've never been so nervous before in my life," Rian complains.

"You? Nervous?" I tease him. "I'd think such a thing impossible."

"And yet, I have this dreadful uneasy feeling," he says, shifting his weight and fiddling with the ornaments clasping the ceremonial gold cape to his shoulders.

The rest of his suit is entirely white, as Asmer's dress will be. It is a custom from Rian's religion he and Asmer have both agreed to, as well as the Theebin-style wedding. The reception is catered entirely to Asmer's liking, after all.

"Try to enjoy yourself," I say. "You will hopefully only marry once, your majesty; make the most of it."

He ruffles at his own hair, mussing it. His attendants will be annoyed with him if they see that.

"It is a political match," Rian complains.

"You like Asmer," I remind him.

"Not as…Not in…"

He's starting to turn bright red with embarrassment and frustration. I cannot help but laugh.

The door opens to admit Qhan Khaleem, my most impressive peer aside from Taris. Likely he's here to report that the chapel and venue have been secured, and there are guards standing at the ready every step of the way.

"Your majesty," he announces with a bow. "They are ready for you, if you'd grace us all with your presence."

Qhan is the only person I know who can say that and both mean it seriously and in jest.

"Thank you, Qhan." Rian stops his fidgeting, turning from the mirror. "Give me another minute to let myself panic, and I will be with you presently."

Qhan nods and steps back outside to relay the message in a more diplomatic manner. On his way out the door, he has to maneuver around someone else bouncing in.

It is Ayla, Rian's adopted daughter who he met two years ago after going to visit Isaaria's East High Court's University. She's smiling ear-to-ear, beautiful as an angel carving in her cream and blush-pink dress. I'll admit, I have a significant soft-spot for the child, and one might say I spoil her, when I can. She's a sweet girl, with an endearing though unrealistic view of her father, and though she's shy around Asmer still, Ayla is strangely drawn to me.

She gasps when she gets a good look at her father.

"You look like you're from one of your stories!" Ayla exclaims.

That, at least, makes Rian chuckle a little. "Thank you, Ayla. I suppose I do clean up nicely after the professionals have their way, don't I?"

"Well. You're always handsome," Ayla corrects herself. "But now you look even better than normal. Which is good, since you're getting married today."

"Really, Ayla, I'm glad you approve," Rian admits. "You do know I'd never have agreed to the wedding if you didn't like Asmer, don't you? Politics or no, I would have found a way around it."

"I like Lady Asmer," Ayla says. "She's nice. And she always has presents for me."

There's an unspoken disapproval, still, there, and though Rian is curious, he doesn't press. He knows better than to try, and Ayla will feign innocence if he does, anyway. She's a clever child.

There is another knock at the door, and in walks Ayla's attending lady, who she routinely tries to escape from.

Naomi Qurvo is beautiful. Her hair has grown quite long since her marriage three years ago; she and her Isaarian husband, Valor, have had no children, but that is not surprising, as the two rarely spend many nights together. They are both kept busy with work, and are often in two different cities, connected only by telephone and letter.

I suspect her brother Korvaan's own head is likely to be covered in a light fuzz, soon; he's been making moon eyes at Kaoli Adder, who attends the Carsans' younger son, Soren. Apparently, he likes her aggressiveness, and she finds his dopey adoration endearing.

"Oh, there you are. Why am I not surprised? My apologies, Majesty. I'd tell you it won't happen again, but I think we both know it will…Come along, now, Ayla," Naomi says, herding the girl out of the room again. "You've got to take your place."

"But I'll be standing there and waiting," Ayla complains.

"Yes," Naomi agrees, "though you'd do well to remember that you'll be with Soren Carsans. I'm certain the two of you can think of something to entertain yourselves with for twenty minutes."

"Soren!" Ayla squeals, and runs out the door calling goodbyes and well-wishes.

Naomi bows to the king and then straightens to follow.

"Captain," she acknowledges as she passes me.

"Miss Qurvo," I respond.

She gives me a nod, then follows Ayla out the door without another word. Not that I anticipated much conversation. The two of us are not close, but since Naomi's father raised me and Taris together and trained us, she is at least used to me. We are cordial acquaintances more than we could ever be friends, and that is probably for the best.

Her brother Korvaan, though, tries a bit harder. I'm not sure why.

"Your majesty, we should be leaving," I tell the king. "We're running out of time before people start to gossip. Wondering why you're late to your own wedding."

"Well, since it's my wedding, I can't really be late, can I?" the king challenges, but sighs and nods. "I know, I know. You're right. And I'm going."

He fiddles once more with his cape, and then takes purposeful strides out the door. I haven't given his attendants the chance to fix his hair, now, but I'll admit I prefer it messier, like this. And though I understand that what I like does not matter in the slightest—especially when it comes to the king—sometimes I cannot help but indulge myself in these little ways.

Taris and I follow the king out the door, and Qhan falls into step beside me. We collect the rest of the king's guard and make our way to the chapel. Constant reports of confirmation run in my ear: the way for the king is secure, safe. I have nothing to worry about, and yet my stomach twists in knots. It almost, strangely, feels as if this is my wedding. What a hilarious concept.

We reach the chapel and stand in the entryway, lined up properly. The king's guard adjust their positions, so as not to ruin the aesthetic of it all. We have these fancy new Alarkian cameras meant to record the event, and the wedding is going to be broadcasted to the entire country in short clips. Maybe to some other countries, as well, though I doubt the west cares much, what with their war going on.

In front of Rian, in a line with their significant others or designated family member, are the grand princes and princess of Isaaria: Magnus Oram and some noblewoman lucky enough to currently hold his attention, Yuugo Ido and his "just a friend", Vásan Pike and his wife Yvette—a woman everyone knows he does not love, Crispin Carsans and his brother Soren—whose chair Ayla will be pushing into the chapel, honored as she is to do so. Nissa Sondushki is here with her half-brothers, and when she notices Rian, she turns back and gives a toothy grin and a wink. She has to look past Detrus Lundan and his wife Irina to do so, which makes Irina turn to give me a smile.

Irina Lundan is a grand princess, and a mother of two, though the first is currently in the care of a nursemaid and the second is still in her womb. I would not call her a friend, but she is courteous to me, and sweet in temperament, though a wry joke can occasionally escape her lips.

Still, Nissa should have had to look past another row of royals. But there is no best man standing before Rian, and though everyone knows why, no one says a thing. Just as no one mentions the scar that runs across part of my face, a souvenir from the wound that only just healed four months ago. The person who would stand as Rian's best man, now, is the same man who gave that scar to me. The same man that, I found, was not so good a friend after all.

But Rian mourns the memories, and likely always will. He and Grand Prince Mercer Ralhan were close ever since childhood. It pains him, now, to know his best friend is dead. Executed for treason, last year.

He could not even give the order. Grand Prince Carsans had to, on his behalf.

The event pains me as well, mainly because I feel somewhat responsible. I was the one, after all, who gave Mercer leave to travel the world to help others in need with his medical expertise. I have no doubt that it was during his travels that he was convinced to turn against Rian. It is a lucky thing I received a tip regarding his treachery and handled a secret investigation that revealed his intentions.

I don't know if Rian will ever fully recover from that betrayal. After all, if Mercer could be swayed to turn against him, who couldn't be?

I'm sure, at this point, that Taris, Qhan and I are the only people Rian truly trusts in the world. Not even Asmer, Naomi or Korvaan are granted that same confidence. And though I'll never say so to anyone, that can't be a good sign for his impending marriage.

Reports muttering in my earpiece distract me. I note the voice of Taris behind me, responding, confirming it is time to begin the procession in. They bring Asmer out to join Rian at the last minute, so they will walk in together, as is tradition. She is stunningly beautiful, in her gown of white. It is Bhantan in style, and suits her completely. Her hair is covered with a veil and a large crown of flowers that will be replaced with a real crown by the end of the ceremony. Her brother Raj and parents are already inside the chapel, eager to see her married to the king. It is an exciting time for their entire family, and for the country.

Their king is finally marrying. The royal family is complete. And Asmer is a sweet, kind, beautiful queen.

The doors are opened as the music begins. Once Rian and Asmer enter, much to the delight of all, Taris and I wait a few seconds, then walk into the back and close the doors behind us. We hold to those posts throughout the entire two hours of High Mass and ceremony, making certain everything runs smoothly while most others present are here only to watch the spectacle.

When the guests are applauding at the end of the ceremony and the newlyweds leave down the aisle together, Taris peels away from the wall and exits just in front of them while I stay behind. I will wait until every last guest has been transferred from here to the reception hall, and then will check in with our security before I return to escort the king and his new wife to their suite for the night.

It is when the last of the guests are just trickling out the doors that I notice someone is staying behind, hovering until he can get the chance to speak with me. Lord Ambassador Aiko's son Shinya is meant to remain in Isaaria after the wedding, when he will be named as the Tourrannese-Kachin ambassador to Isaaria. He is representing both countries for the wedding, as his father could not attend.

I make eye contact with him and beckon him over. Whatever he wants, I'd rather he tell me now while the last few guests are leaving, so it won't force me to rearrange my schedule.

"Captain Marson," he says, bowing to me. I've told him several times that he need not do that, but it's a habit he's yet to break. "I apologize for disturbing you. I have some unfortunate news. Which I also apologize for bringing to you, now."

"Whatever it is, Lord Shinya, know that I would not want you to keep it from me simply because of the wedding," I say. "Unfortunate news is unfortunate news, no matter when it arrives."

Shinya nods, as if he believes I've given him invaluable advice. A real proverb for the ages.

"In that case, I will not delay with niceties: I'm afraid I must leave Isaaria and return to Tourran at once. There are tensions in the east which threaten us with war. Whatever diplomatic services I might have offered to Isaaria are needed back in my homeland."

"I see," I say carefully.

As we have not yet announced Shinya's position as our delegate to the east, this will spare us social embarrassment, but the politics involved make this change of plans a trickier feat. Not that it is something I need to worry about—politics mean almost nothing to me, given my position—but I know it will worry the king. And that displeases me. The king likes Aiko Shinya. He'll be sad to see the boy go, and even more upset by the news of disturbances in the east.

"Would it not be helpful for Tourran to have you here in Isaaria, in case we might offer our own aid in these troubled times?" I point out.

"Unfortunately, Captain, it is not the Tourrannese way to ask outsiders to solve our problems for us," Shinya says, sounding truly apologetic.

I suspect he has different thoughts on the matter, but he won't disobey his father or political betters. If he's being called home, he'll make his excuses and return. A responsible young man, at only seventeen.

"In that case, I wish the very best for you, and do not begrudge your leaving," I tell him. "But I have to ask, Lord Aiko: I'm not sure what political good you thought it would do, giving your farewells to the king's bodyguard. I may wish you well, but I have no say in politics."

"The answer is simpler than most would imagine. I could have told someone else—one of the grand princes, perhaps—but the king trusts you, which means I can trust you to be discreet," Shinya says. "My father told me to let as few people as possible know. I figured I should have you tell the king."

I nod. His explanation makes sense, especially from an easterner's point of view. They strive to always save face, preserve their honor, and maintain good standing. Shinya was concerned one of the grand princes would not keep this a clandestine secret, or might be insulted by his departure. By telling me alone, he avoids those possibilities entirely.

"Ah. Then I understand. Thank you, for what service you managed to offer during your time here," I say. "I am sure the king appreciates it."

"Again, I apologize for bringing you this news at a time like this," our young would-be ambassador says earnestly. "But I thought it would be best for me to slip out before anyone announces I was meant to remain here, as ambassador. So that the king might not have to make excuses for me."

"I wouldn't worry; I'm sure the king will understand," I say. "Don't let it disturb you. And try to rest, on your travels. You look weary."

He nods, rubbing at his eyes. I'm not the first person today to tell him this.

"Stress?" I pose, understanding.

"...Bad dreams," he mutters.

He clears his throat, straightens, and gives me another unnecessary bow.

"Thank you for the audience, Captain. And for understanding."

"Won't you at least stay for the reception?"

But he shakes his head. "I have a train to take to the coast. A ship is waiting there for me, and I would not want to force an inconvenience on them."

"Then please have a safe journey, Lord Aiko. I hope we might see each other again, one day, but if not: the best to you," I say.

I bow to him—as it should be—with a hand on my sword to keep it out of my way. Then I straighten, turn, and leave to join the reception, my mood admittedly dampened by his news. I like Aiko Shinya, and I found his presence in the Pyrian Palace a pleasant one.

I think it would have done all our countries good, having him as ambassador here. And perhaps he will return one day to fill that position. We shall simply have to wait and see.

Inside the grand ballroom, no one is missing myself or Lord Aiko Shinya. His absence will be noted by a handful, perhaps, but given tonight's festivities, even those few will forget quickly.

I check in with all my underlings, and then Taris and Qhan. Nothing is amiss tonight. No last-minute objectors to the wedding. No attempts to enter the grounds by those disappointed they didn't receive an invite. We even manage to corral every representative of the media, and keep them from poking around the palace in places they don't belong.

By the time the fireworks go off at midnight, the day the king was so worried about has passed by smoothly. He now walks between a circle made of myself, Taris, Qhan, and a number of his guards. His arm is looped with his new wife's, who still cannot manage to look up at him without turning red.

We climb the steps to the wedding suite as the king prattles away about how adorable he thought Ayla and Soren were together. How he enjoyed every bit of the wedding, especially the food at the reception, and how he found it highly entertaining when Nissa's hyena managed to enter the reception to find her when Yvette Pike had expressly asked that the beast stay away.

When we reach the suite, I find I am disappointed. Yes, it means my job for the evening is, for the most part, complete. I can take a brief respite before I'm expected on my rounds again. But I'll miss the king's chatter. I'm around him so much that I'm not used to silence. Though I suppose, now that he has a wife to see to, there will be many times I cannot be by his side.

Before they leave us for the evening, the queen hesitates and frees her arm from her new husband's. The king waits at the door for her as she approaches me. The second person to surprise me this way, tonight.

"Is there anything I can do for you, your majesty?" I ask her.

"Oh, no. I only wanted to thank you, Captain. For everything," she tells me.

She then stands on her tiptoes to give me a surprising, brief embrace and a kiss on the cheek. When she draws back again, I see tears in her eyes.

"I accept the gratitude, your majesty, though I'm not entirely sure what I've done to deserve it," I admit. "Please—it is my job to do what I do. In fact, if anyone ever asks, you may tell them I say I enjoy it."

Queen Asmer gives a watery smile and laughs, but it sounds sad to me. I wonder what she's thinking about. What she knows that I, for some reason, do not.

"Yes, well…" she starts, and then quickly lowers her voice to a whisper. "To be honest, I never pictured myself marrying Rian. I always thought he would prefer…someone like you."

She looks at me earnestly, like she expects me to agree with her.

"As entertaining a thought as that is, your majesty, I am the king's *Khashtani* and on occasion, if he is not too irritated with me to admit it, his friend. But nothing more than that, I assure you. Now, I must bid you goodnight, my queen. It has been a long day for you and your new husband both. I'm sure you would appreciate some time together with only the quiet to disrupt you."

I can tell the queen would like to say more, but I am uncomfortable with the direction she was attempting to take our conversation. And though she sighs, and fiddles with that simple band of a bracelet she always wears, the queen thanks me again before bidding me goodnight. The king holds the door to their room open for her, but he, too, lingers to speak with me briefly.

How popular I am, this evening.

"You're not going to tell me what that was about, are you?" he complains.

"I'm afraid not, your majesty," I say. "The queen's secrets are safe with me."

He snorts, but grins at me. "And here I thought you were *my Khashtani.*"

"Oh dear, your majesty. You're not jealous, are you?"

The king scoffs dramatically. I think he might have had a little too much wine, tonight.

"Jealous? Me? Ne-ever," he says, and then looks to Taris. "You didn't happen to hear any of that, did you?"

"Even if I did, your majesty, I think we both know I would claim otherwise," Taris responds.

He does not indulge the king quite as much as I do.

"Oh, very well, then," the king sighs. "I suppose I should see to my wife, shouldn't I?" he adds, sounding as if he regrets that fact to the point that I'm insulted on the queen's behalf.

"Yes, you really should," I say. "And mind your manners, your majesty. The queen is a lovely woman. You should feel lucky to have her to wife."

"You won't go far, though, will you?" the king asks me.

I nearly laugh at him, and catch myself just in time.

"I won't be far," I promise, though I'm tempted to roll my eyes at him for this. Only my principal would be worried about the location of his bodyguards on his own wedding night.

"Well. Good," the king says, nodding to himself. "…Goodnight, Captain. Taris. Qhan."

The king disappears into his room, and as soon as the door is shut, Qhan and I lock it in two places, with the keys each of us wear around our necks. The king and queen also have copies, so that they may leave the suite, if need be, of course, but otherwise, no one should enter through that door.

The double-paned windows have locks, as well, and guards patrolling below. I made sure of it.

"Good night, then," I say to Taris and Qhan both. "Long day. I'll see you both tomorrow morning."

"Captain," Qhan says, tilting his head to me in acknowledgement. Taris does the same, wordlessly.

Qhan will continue to stand guard through the night, rotating with Taris around sunrise, and then come to meet with me as he does every morning for the seven o'clock report. I'll then check in with Taris, make certain whatever breakfast the king and queen order isn't poisoned (though I doubt either of them will be up before noon), and so on and so on.

I wasn't lying to the queen when I told her I enjoy my job, but it is tiresome, and somewhat monotonous. Monotony is good, yes: it means no one is trying to kill the king. But it's the little things that help me through it. Like Ayla's adoration of me and her friendship with Soren Carsans. Irina Lundan's kindness and Korvaan's awkward attempts to befriend me. Nissa Sondushki's insistence on being contrary to everything she's meant to be as a grand princess. The king's endearing smiles, and the way he complains about his daily schedule even when he has a meeting with someone he likes.

I'm thinking of such things as I descend a short, quiet set of stairs to my room, which is situated closely to the king's usual suite. He will move back there with the queen within a few weeks, likely, but having a honeymoon suite is traditional. And expected. And—

Damn. I just realized I forgot to tell the king about Aiko Shinya's departure.

Tomorrow, then. Or, in a few days. After he and his new wife have gotten the chance to grow more accustomed to one another.

I am in the middle of stifling a yawn when I hear a strange sound that makes me stop and take a look around. I'm headed down a hall adorned with windows that grant me an excellent view of the fireworks outside. Given the distant cheers of the many citizens gathered to watch the show, and the pops of fireworks as they spray color across the sky, I'm convincing myself I imagined the sound when I sense a presence behind me.

I whirl just in time to see metal flash. A blade. I'm in the middle of drawing my own weapon when my would-be attacker is, strangely, impaled from behind. When the figure crumples, I see Taris there, holding the sword that saved my life, completely unfazed by what he's done. He must have followed me this way, I realize, instead of returning to his own room. But why he'd think to do so, I can't imagine, and I can't find my tongue to ask—

"Taris!" a woman's voice calls.

As Taris frees his weapon from the body, I turn once more to see a woman running towards us from the direction I'd originally been heading.

I don't recognize her in the slightest, but she is a curious sight. Her mess of hair is falling out of its pins. She is dressed in what looks like custom-made clothing that should help her blend in and potentially even disappear completely in dark corners. There is blood splashed on her. Not her own, I realize, given the bloody weapon she holds in her hand.

"About time," I hear Taris mutter.

"I'm sorry," the woman gasps, wiping blood from her forehead as she stops beside us. "I had to move the bodies. I did not want anyone to find them. I'll bury them properly later, but we have more pressing matters."

"Still. You are better than this," Taris tells her. His tone is sharp, but there's something else in it. Almost as if he's poking fun at her?

"Qurvo, what's the meaning of this?" I demand.

He ignores me completely. The nerve.

"We'd best move quickly," he says. "If we hurry, we can get the queen out of the city within the hour. Move her someplace more secure—"

"Someone is after Queen Asmer?" I say, surprised.

Both of them turn to look at me and snap in a startling unison, "No, *you.*"

While I'm still registering this, they have started speaking to one another again. The strange woman has grabbed my arm and is pulling me along down the hall, continuing the way I was going in the first place.

From the perspective of someone used to acting bodyguard to another, if I were this woman, I'd be concerned about the length of this hallway. It is a bad place to be trapped.

"I don't know how they found out, this time," she's chattering, talking over my attempts to question them. "Sep said he wasn't going to tell them anything, no matter what. They must have divined it some other way. I don't know how much they know, but they know who she is. And how many times we've done this."

"That is unfortunate. Are they trying for the Uniting of the Three route instead, this time?"

"No. It's too late for that, I think. Besides, they already killed Jax, and Erikson, and Aldrich has disappeared with his daughter. They know they will never find him if he doesn't want to be found. So, they will be here for Yakarami soon enough. But they must know there's no point in doing that if they don't have control of the reset. Otherwise, all the work will have been for nothing."

"That's…even more unfortunate," Taris mutters.

I glare over at him. "Qurvo, you'd best have a damned good explanation for this," I warn him crossly. "And I expect it shortly—"

"Oh, shut up," Taris says, flicking his eyes up at the ceiling.

I'm so stunned he'd dare say that, I am speechless.

"I'm going to need you to—" he's starting.

He's interrupted, as it turns out my attacker did not come alone. With their swords already drawn, the two beside me are quick to raise blades and fight. They are fast, and skillful, and I must say that despite my irritation with him, and my confusion over this woman's presence, Taris fights well with her. Almost as if they were trained to do so. A pair of partners.

I go to draw my own weapon, but the woman is there to grab my wrist.

"Don't get involved!" she snaps at me, and then spins and flicks her sword across the face of an opponent, sending blood into his eyes before she disarms him and stabs him through.

"Slow tonight, aren't you, dearest?" Taris notes as he wields his own sword deftly. "Feeling a little under the weather?"

"I prefer my knives," she snaps at him.

"So, use your knives," Taris says.

They are bickering like an old married couple.

The woman mutters a mild curse at him under her breath, then sticks her sword in the body of the man she just felled and draws the daggers from the sheathes strapped at her hips instead.

She and Taris continue to fight, pushing and pulling me out of the way whenever I try to assist them, or whenever I am standing in a spot that they apparently do not like. I am impressed, but confused, and even more perplexed by the number of adversaries that have, apparently, been sent here after me.

"Come on!" the woman says once the two of them have finished.

She grabs my arm again, pulling me along as we weave through the bodies on the ground. I count six as we pass. We finally make it to the end of this dreaded hall, Taris close behind us, and reach the second staircase at the end. The woman hurries down the spiraling steps, one of her hands gripping a dagger, the other holding tight to me. As if I'm an errant child.

"How in the hell did these people get past our security?" I snap, incredulous and angry.

"They must be getting desperate," the woman says, but she's talking to Taris, not me. "They must have decided to put the Anomaly to use. He can only use it once like this, after all. I guess he decided Soleil was worth it."

"I'm flattered," I can't help but say sarcastically.

We reach the bottom of the staircase and take a sharp left. Whoever this woman is, she seems to know her way around the palace. She knows all the right paths to take to keep us as far away from traffic. I don't know if this is because she doesn't want to be seen or if she doesn't want to risk collateral damage, but I am further impressed with her either way.

We are now in the least-occupied part of the palace, where the Ralhans would stay, were they in residence. After Mercer's betrayal and execution, the rest of his family has stayed far from the Pyrian Palace in penance. They were even excused from the wedding, to make certain they were never close to the king.

Mercer might have been the only traitor amongst them, as proven by extensive questioning, but the shame he brought on their family remains. There will not be another Ralhan in the palace until Mercer's nephew, Adrian, enters politics.

The woman barges into a suite of rooms, empty and quiet, and pulls me inside after her. We're out of the hallways, now, moving through adjoining rooms instead. I think she wants to find servants' passages meant especially for the Ralhans, so they can sneak me out of the palace discreetly.

"Could one of you at least explain to me why I can't fight?" I complain. "I think you know I'm quite talented that way, Taris."

"Can't let you think you might die. Just in case," the woman pants. "It's better if we protect you. You'll feel safer that way."

"And why can't I think—"

I'm suddenly, unceremoniously, thrown to the floor. For a moment, I'm sure it's the woman who's done this to me. Only, when I look, I see she's on the ground next to me, rubbing her temple where she smacked it on the tiles.

When I flip myself over, I see Taris engaged in combat with a man I have not seen in months, a man I honestly suspected I'd never see again: Marques. Mercer's former bodyguard. We never did apprehend him. I suppose this at least explains how these intruders know the layout of the palace so well.

Taris is continually moving to keep Marques from getting anywhere near me, though he's hindered significantly by the knife sticking out of his side. His body is partially hunched over and he's keeping a hand pressed around the knife, to try and hold back the blood or keep it from moving, or both. I don't know who Marques was aiming for with that—me, or the woman escorting me around—but with his fluke, he must have been standing here in wait, or following us invisibly, waiting for his chance to attack.

The woman springs to her feet, both her daggers out once more as she joins the fight. Marques is talented, and a formidable opponent, but I'd say my mystery woman and Taris combined easily outmatch him. Especially with rage to fuel the former.

She attacks Marques with moves that I myself have used before, aiming for the backs of the knees, using her legs with high kicks most opponents don't expect when there are knives in play. She supports Taris, and eventually takes over for him, as, by the time Marques is dead on the ground with her knives in him, Taris has collapsed as well.

I crawl to Taris' side as the woman drops to her knees next to him, already trying to pull his hands away from the knife in his side so she can look at the injury. She starts ripping up the still-clean parts of her clothes for bandages.

"Don't bother," Taris says. "That's not going to heal. Not unless you develop a new fluke in the next two minutes."

"Would you shut up," she snaps. "Stop moving. Let me wrap this. And then we'll go. I'll take you to a doctor, and then—"

"Sweetheart, I think we both know I am not going anywhere," Taris interrupts, placing a hand over hers.

"Stop it," she says, and goes back to trying to cover Taris' wound. "It's not that bad. It's not that bad, right?" she says, looking to me for confirmation.

Without a word, I move both their hands aside to get a good look at it.

The knife is a dirk. A long one. Chances are, it punctured something important, and given the odd gleam to it, it's possibly poisoned. Taris is right: he's only going to last another minute or so, and it is pointless to pretend otherwise. But I'm so shocked by this sudden turn of events, by this chaos that has suddenly invaded my life, that I can't find the words to say what I intend.

But Taris can read on my face what I can't say.

"That's what I thought," he says.

He doesn't sound surprised, or upset. He's not angry, or disappointed, or desperate. The woman seems to be cycling through all those emotions, but he is stoic about this. As if he thought it inevitable.

Taris lets his head fall back and sighs. "Well. I tried," he says. "No one can say I didn't try."

"Stop it," the woman mutters again. When I glance at her, I see tears in her eyes. "Stop it. You cannot do this to me."

"And why not? You've done it to me about a dozen times, dear. My turn, now," he says. As if he's still trying to tease her during all this.

But there is something else in his tone. A hint of fear. He is putting on a brave face for her sake, I realize, but he doesn't want to die.

"At the very least..." he continues, his breathing starting to hitch, his voice getting weaker. More strained. "...There are worse ways to die."

He flicks his eyes at me.

"After all. There's no nobler act than to give your life for a friend," Taris says.

His voice is not choked. He says it plainly and clearly. And then the coughing starts, and he spits up blood. I can't tell if the expression on his face is a bittersweet smile or simply a grimace, and while he struggles to breathe, his skin going blueish, I panic. I can feel his heart rate increasing, and I can't stop it.

I don't know how to describe the sound he makes when his heart stops, but it horrifies me. I never thought Taris liked me much. I certainly never thought I'd sit with a stranger while he died in our arms, protecting me.

I don't know how to feel. I'm confused. And conflicted.

I am certain there are many things I should understand, right now, but I don't, and the result is a strange numbness. All I can think is: how am I going to tell Korvaan and Naomi? They are the only family he has, since Nusk died a few months back. How am I going to tell them that they have lost a father and a brother all in one summer?

The young woman starts to cry. She covers her mouth with a shaking hand, her entire body trembling. All I can do is stare at her for several seconds before it occurs to me that I have no idea why she's crying. I don't know what Taris means to her. Or what she meant to him.

"...We need to alert the rest of the king's guard," I force myself to say, trying to think of what protocol should be in a situation like this. "We need to make certain the king and queen are safe."

"What? No. You fool," she cries. "We told you! They're not here for Rian—they're here for you. I am your *Khashtani!*"

"What?" I manage.

I cannot decide if I'm more shocked by the idea that someone appointed me a *Khashtani,* or that she called the king by his first name so informally.

"I have always been your *Khashtani!* Always!" she cries again, and the way she says it confuses me even further. "Every time!"

Every time? Every time of what?

"Where is the rest of your *khashak*? If you are a traditional *Khashtani,* you should have one, shouldn't you?" I ask her, but she's shaking her head as she wipes away her tears.

"Only him. Only Taris..."

I stop my fumbling for words and stare at her. I consider the pet names Taris has been calling her, and I realize, then, that he had not meant that merely in jest. Though I'm not sure how they could have gone unnoticed for so long, I suppose the two of them were lovers. Perhaps even more than that.

While I am still concerned for the king's safety, I don't try to hurry my apparent *Khashtani* along. The way she looks at Taris is the way I imagine a person should their spouse. Their better half. She has set her face in frustration in a pointless attempt to stop further tears.

She finally picks up his cold hand and presses it to her lips, closes her eyes, and says something against his fingers—words I do not understand. There are a few more tears, sliding down her cheeks to land on his skin.

"Who are you?" I ask her. "Please. I give you permission to tell me."

But she refuses to say. "It has never mattered to you before. It won't matter to you, now…I am never anyone for long, anyway."

Letting that statement hang in the air, she spends several more seconds looking at Taris. But then her spine straightens. I can practically see her ears prick, and the hairs stand up on her arms. In a moment, she is crouched on her feet, her knives drawn again, and she has pulled me to my feet, too. Keeping me well behind her as she backs up.

We are no longer alone with Taris' body. There is a man in the doorway we used to enter this room. Standing there, watching us coolly. I cannot tell how old he is, but I know he's from the west. He has the look about him. He is dressed in what appears to be some kind of modified uniform, though I don't recognize his clothes as a part of any military group I am aware of. My only clue is a silver pin his wears at his breast, but the simplistic outline of a firebird over some kind of sun means nothing to me.

I can't say the same for my *Khashtani.*

"I should have known there was another one of you hanging back," she spits. "They wouldn't have sent Marques with these men. Not an outsider… Which one are you, then? You are not one of his sons."

"You may call me Korsiko," the man says simply, calmly, and flicks his eyes over both of us. "…We have met before, but I suppose you wouldn't remember. I do usually pale in comparison to my master's sons. They are rather the dramatic sort, and I've no fluke to compete with."

"Ah. So where are the three demons?" my *Khashtani* snaps. "Too scared to face us again?"

Us? Again?

"My lord decided it was a poor choice to send his sons so young. I am a better option. And I will serve well," Korsiko says coolly.

She smirks. "Amerson get himself killed one time too many?"

She is fishing for information. I don't know what her plan is, or if she thinks she can manage this man on her own, but she is looking for answers.

And she is giving me enough information to, perhaps, start asking the right questions.

"The reason why is irrelevant," Korsiko claims. "Just know that I did not come here with the intention of fighting. In fact, if you'd have allowed us to take her without interfering, perhaps he would not have had to die," he says, nodding toward Taris.

"But I would," my *Khashtani* says.

"It is unfortunate, but true. You are a Magicsmith," he says, nodding to her. "Like the Lady Soleil here. A shame she is the greater of you; if it were otherwise, you could have lived."

"You can't have her," my *Khashtani* hisses.

"All Magicsmiths belong to my lord," Korsiko claims. "To do with as he sees fit. And this one has immeasurable uses."

"No," my *Khashtani* says.

And, now that she's gotten a fair bit of distance between me and the man who says he's come to take me, she charges at him. Korsiko raises the arm he's kept hidden by his side to fire off a crossbow bolt at her. He manages to clip her arm. She grimaces, but does not let the injury stop her.

Then she's on him, like a feral creature. I swear, every time her knives flash, she cuts him. Korsiko fights back, naturally, but the two are fast. They are so engaged with one another that I don't dare try to interrupt, because I have no idea which of them I would be helping if I did. Whoever thought to give me a *Khashtani* chose well. She is dangerous. A naturally violent creature hidden away in the form of a statistically slim woman whose appearance as a fighter would be nothing to speak of if I weren't currently watching her.

My *Khashtani* prefers her knives. Korsiko, apparently, is the sort who'd either shoot his opponent between the eyes or slowly beat them to death with spiked knuckle cuffs. Every time he hits her, he cuts her, but she is resilient.

Their fight lasts half a minute at the most before she manages to stab one of her knives through his neck, then slams the other one down through his skull unnecessarily as he goes down. The relative silence, afterwards, is so deafening that the woman's breathing sounds monstrously loud.

Her fists are clenched, and her shoulders heaving. She is watching Korsiko's body, as if she suspects he lied about not having a fluke and might somehow, suddenly, rise from the grave.

I can see there are goosebumps raised on the skin of her arms, visible from where she tore off her sleeves to try and bind Taris' fatal wound.

She's quite pale, even for someone with fair skin. At first, I think it's from exhaustion: mental and physical. But then she crumples to the ground.

I instinctively rush to her side, to see if I somehow missed a part of their fight. If Korsiko managed to give her a deeper wound than expected. But while every drop of blood seems to come from a superficial injury, my *Khashtani* is shaking. Her skin is turning gray.

After a glance around the room, I find the crossbow bolt that skimmed my *Khashtani's* arm and examine it. Touch a finger to the tip, taste it, then spit. Poisoned, then, like the knife that killed Taris. Whoever these people are, they don't like taking chances…Which means they must know enough about us to understand they can't afford to take chances.

My mind is buzzing with questions, my stomach churning from the overwhelming smell of blood in the room, but I don't have time to think, and I don't have enough information to conjure answers on my own. The woman is clawing at my arm, struggling to get my attention. Whatever is killing her is different than what triggered Taris' death, but it is still fast-acting.

Though I have no idea who she is, I owe her my life. If I can witness her last moments instead of instantly running to report this incident, I will honor her that way. It is the least I can do.

So, I sit on the floor and pull her in my arms. Her body is shaking intensely, so that her arms flail and her legs kick out. I reach around her and cradle her, pinning her arms to her sides to hold her while she trembles. The way she is stammering, I'm certain she is trying to tell me something, but she cannot and it aggravates her. Blood trickles from her nose, and she starts crying. She gives a frustrated moan, then gives up and simply lets her body weaken.

From her sounds of panicked distress, I can tell she's in great pain, and she is afraid. Like Taris, she doesn't want to die. She is an admirable fighter, and a strong young woman, but she is scared. She has every right to be. The tears on her face are not of weakness.

"So-*leil!*" she cries, and for some reason that cuts me to the core.

I don't know why, but I shush her, and I rock her. I don't know if this comforts her any, but she sounds less distressed, even if it's only because she's growing weaker.

Another second passes. Another. Her body stops jerking about, but her eyes are still flickering, looking all about the room before finally settling on me. It's horrifying, watching the light drain out of her eyes, but I cannot look away. She deserves my seeing this through to the end.

"Soleil. Promise. Never forget me," she finally pleads in a weak whisper. I can see the horror in her eyes, the desperation, the fear. And then it fades away with her last shuddering breath, and there is nothing in her eyes at all.

She dies in my arms, this strange woman who has saved my life, and I am too much of a coward to admit to her in her last moments that I still have no idea who she is.

Twenty-Four

WE PERFORMED FUNERAL RITES for Taris and the mystery woman both, and buried them; Taris near his father's grave, where he belonged, and the woman in an available lot. It is hard to say whether I did as she asked. To remember her properly, I would have to know who she was. I had no idea, and neither did anyone else. She was just another *Khashtani,* dead young and early for their principal. No one had a name, nor any idea where she'd come from, or why she'd been appointed *Khashtani* for the king's bodyguard.

We did attempt an investigation, but found little. The only additional secret I uncovered was a tattoo I didn't know Taris had on his ankle, of a moon and stars.

Mysteries without answers. It troubled the king, especially, when he was brought to see the bodies. I saw he thought he should recognize the woman, but could not. I know the confusion he must have felt, because I felt the same.

The king spent a good, long time looking at the body and asking me the same questions repeatedly. I acknowledged to him that she claimed to have been my *Khashtani,* but that didn't help much. If I did have a *Khashtani,* then the king had been completely unaware of her existence. Though, oddly enough, when the burial rites were to take place for the woman and Taris, the king did not want the Signs of the Dead drawn in the traditional fashion, nor in gold to signify their sacrifice for royalty.

"No. Silver," he interrupted, stopping the priests about to use gold.

They paused and said nothing, but looked to me to help.

"Your majesty?" I asked him, and the king stared at the bodies for a long time, biting at his lip, his expression tortured by a memory he couldn't quite recall.

"I don't know," he admitted. "But…I think they need to be silver."

It was his tone of voice that convinced me not to press the matter. He had no explanation, or at least no explanation that he thought we would find satisfactory. He had the urge to honor these two highly with saintly silver, and since he was king, he technically did not need a reason, even if the priests were curious for one.

"Oblige his majesty," I ordered them. "Paint the marks in silver."

There was still hesitation over the matter, but it was done as the king asked.

The funerals were small and rather plain affairs. Naomi and Korvaan Qurvo were both upset by their brother's death, but there were few tears shed, which seemed to imply they suspected this was always his fate. Their brother worked as a bodyguard for a king, and often put himself in the way of danger for said king's sake.

As cold as it seemed, Taris' death was, is, and perhaps always will be seen as an eventuality.

TIME PASSED. YEARS. I still have no idea what truly happened that day, but whatever the man called Korsiko had come for, those who sent him do not try again. Granted, there are threats against the king from time to time, but Qhan and I manage them with relative ease. Some are worse than others. But we never catch anyone willing to tell the truth. And since no one ever gets too close to the king, most of these attempts seem unrelated to me.

The king does his duty to Isaaria well. The people like him. He makes fair decisions and keeps the government from meddling where it shouldn't. He doesn't have much of a personal life, but always makes time for Ayla. The two are very close, especially considering her position as the king and queen's only heir. Since Crispin Carsans' accidental death, there have been many rumors about what may or may not happen if there is no future Carsans to pick Isaaria's next heir. No one expects Soren to sire children.

Queen Asmer dies in her thirty-fourth year, leaving no child of her own behind, but a single adopted daughter and a morose, widower of a king.

He does not remarry.

The years march on. I am in my forty-sixth year, near forty-seventh. The king, his forty-eighth. We have watched the world slowly crumble into chaos around us, but not Isaaria. Isaaria stands strong, for now. We have managed to keep out of the affairs of other countries, for better or worse, though I'm afraid that won't last for much longer. In fact, the concern came to be so strong that Qhan and I decided to take certain precautions, and the king brought the military to order.

Most of the castle's inhabitants have already been moved to the Summer Palace—it is safer there, as its position better suits it for defense against invaders, and has more space to keep refugees safe. The king insists on staying in Pyrian until the end, to make sure no one is left behind and nothing has been overlooked. While this is a noble goal, it causes me great anxiety.

He still has Ayla, his guard, and me, Korvaan, Naomi and Qhan. A few other members of the staff, in certain areas, to help keep the palace clean and the king fed and safe. There are still maids and several cooks, attendants, and the ever-elusive Grand Princess Nissa, who stops in with her hyena now and again to reassure me that the pathway straight to the Summer Palace is still secure, whenever the king is ready to leave.

I don't know how to tell her that I'm less worried about the journey out in the open, and more worried about assassins and spies hiding in the wings of the palace we have closed off.

I spend most of my days wandering around behind the king, conferring with Qhan and consuming disgusting amounts of caffeine to stay awake.

But for a long time, nothing happens to remind me about the night Taris died. Until one day, as I'm about to retire for the evening, Korvaan appears to tell me that we have foreign visitors.

I am annoyed to be kept from sleep, but my curiosity gets the better of me. I make my way to the throne room where, aside from the usual guards posted about, there are four people waiting for me. While I refuse to allow his majesty to meet with anyone before I know their business, two of these newcomers are children, making me more intrigued than wary.

The children are both boys, both young, perhaps a year apart. The elder has especially memorable hair: a bluish black so poignant a color I know it is from magic. The younger one's hair is a lighter brownish-blonde, like his mother's. He is perhaps four years old. Too old to be carried, but he is obliged anyway. He drowsily rests his cheek on his mother's shoulder, while she leans her weight back to counteract his.

That is, I'm almost positive the woman holding the younger boy is their mother. She looks tired. There's a gauntness to her face, and a delicate pallor to her skin that makes her appear ill: a delicate, perhaps weak, woman. Her eyes have a glazed look about them, as if she cannot see well, and a lack of spectacles tells me she is either vain, or she has lost the lenses. Given her tattered clothing, made of once-fine fabric and patterns, I assume the latter is more likely.

But perhaps the most intriguing thing about her are the scars on her face: tiny, round, muted pink, just a few shades darker than her skin. I've never seen them before, only the open reddish sores, but those are scars from magic-sickness. Those are the result of an infection with tainted magic—and recovery. She clearly barely survived, but she did survive.

The last of our guests turns when he hears me on the steps. For a moment, his appearance startles me. Because of Rian's past explorations with hair dye, this man's white hair was not shocking to me when I first saw it, and yet, when I take in his entire image, I realize he is an albino. His skin is chalky, and his eyes are hauntingly clear, framed by long white lashes. Unlike the woman, he at first seems more prepared for a presentation before royalty. But as I let my eyes take in further details, I note that his clothes are just as abused as hers, only he has cleaned and pressed them out of habit, or perhaps pride.

His suit is clearly a uniform, but it is unfamiliar to me. This fellow stands and moves like a military man, but I have the military uniforms of every country memorized from their navies to their armies, and this man's clothing is alien.

There's a silver pin on his left lapel, but from this distance, I can't quite make out the decoration on it.

"My lady Soleil," he says, and bows to me.

I take exception to this. People don't bow to me the way he did, aside from in polite greeting. They salute and tilt their heads respectfully, but this man has practically allowed his nose to scrape the ground on my behalf. As if I am royalty to him. And people never call me a lady, or address me by my first name. It is nothing but Captain Marson. Always.

The woman bows as well, and gestures for her elder son to do the same.

"I hope you don't mind," the albino man continues. "But I requested the lights be dimmed. I am sensitive to bright things."

"Who are you?" I demand, watching them carefully.

I don't like the woman, and it takes me several seconds to determine why: she resembles the mystery *Khashtani* that saved my life, years ago. The woman that Taris died with. They are hardly twins, and it is possible my memory is hazy after all these years, but they could be family.

"My name is Septimus," the albino man says. "This is Teresa, my sister. And her children. We have come from the west."

The pause he allows then is significant, and I say nothing. The west is war-torn, all by destroyed. We've avoided the damage so far, but I've discussed it with the king and his councilors, and we know that those who destroyed the west might come for us next.

There are rumors, of monsters and magical objects, and rare flukes. I have heard so many things, I'm not sure what's true.

"Is that supposed to mean something to me?" I say.

The albino man, Septimus, opens his mouth.

"We are your cousins," Teresa interrupts.

I bristle. "Is that so."

"We are Magicsmiths," she claims without elaborating on that pertinent familial claim. "Which means that you are, too."

"Magicsmiths," I repeat dubiously.

She bobs her head. "It is the truth. Before I wed, my name was Teresa Smith. My brother is Septimus Smith. My father, Janos Smith, was your mother Olivia's younger brother."

"I never knew my mother," I say coldly. "The name 'Olivia' means nothing to me, nor does the surname 'Smith'. Now, unless you have something more worth my time, I am not interested in playing this game with you," I say, and turn, already dismissive as I start to call for a guard to see them out.

"You are in love with the king!" Teresa blurts, and I whirl back on them so fast that my head buzzes.

"What did you say?" I snap.

For a moment, there is silence. Septimus closes his eyes and curses under his breath. Teresa makes herself swallow, frightened of me, but determined.

"You're in love with the king and you always have been," she says.

"And what makes you say that. What makes you think that?" I demand.

"Because we know you, Soleil," Teresa says. "You just don't remember."

This isn't much of an answer, but I'm still shocked by someone announcing the very thing I've been trying my best to hide for decades. It is upsetting.

"You have a fluke," Teresa continues, as if she's rattling off a script, "it's over time itself, you can turn back and recreate our lives over and over again, rewriting the old ones. Changing things. This version of yourself—when you act as captain of the guard and *Khashtani* to the king, you only exist like this because Septimus made you do it. He needed you to do it, to give us enough time on his side, so that Rian wouldn't die. It's the only variable. The only way he doesn't die is if the two of you aren't together. But it's wrong. Because you're meant to be the queen of Isaaria, and you're meant to have a son who will finally bring peace to our world. The first-born son of Soleil and Rian Yakarami."

"How dare you," I start, but she's still talking.

"We come from the west having escaped those who want to keep that future from happening. Who think they have their own way of fixing the world. It's insanity, their plan, but makes a twisted sort of sense, when you know it. They're the ones responsible. For the collapse of most of our world's civilizations. How have you not noticed the great influx of monsters wrongly called demons in your country?" she challenges me desperately. "In the world. The horrors, the hopelessness, the destruction. Can you really watch all this and think nothing of it?"

"You're getting to your point, I trust?"

"We share an enemy," she claims. "And that enemy…is responsible. For all of this. If you want to save the ones you love, you have to trust us," she pleads, looking at me with those glassy eyes of hers. "Please."

I look at her for a few seconds, then sigh and turn to Septimus Smith instead.

"Could you please explain what your sister is blathering about? Why do I need to trust you? What's all this about having multiple lives and lost memories and common enemies?"

"It would be easier for me to show you than to tell you," he admits.

"Explain."

"I am a Memorysmith," Septimus claims. "I've been doing my damnedest to balance keeping you all sane while you traverse time itself, insisting on remembering all sorts of horrific ordeals. And sometimes, I erase those memories anyway, when I think it necessary."

I remain skeptical.

"Those with flukes of memory—" I start, but this brazen man interrupts.

"It's different. Being a Smith," he claims. "A Magicsmith. Those with flukes of memory can at most touch a little upon what I can do, but for me, the mindscape is open. Easily manipulated. I can create memories—real ones, false ones. Bring back old ones. Read new ones. They can be of any length, from any time, and any place. And I can remember your intricate web of timelines, Lady Soleil," he adds. "The only person who can. Without assistance, that is, but as I supplied said assistance, my point still stands."

"Mmm," I say thoughtfully, and look to Teresa again. "What about you, then? What's your ridiculous, imaginary fluke?"

"I…I'm a Creationist," she says, flicking her eyes nervously at her brother. "I can…make things. If I have an idea in my head…I can… make…it."

"Anything," I repeat. "Like so-called demons? Monsters?"

I'm an odd feeling in my stomach. Because there have been monster attacks across Isaaria. Things people are calling demons, though the king is skeptical about their origins as such given the nature of Theebin demons.

But despite everything, at least some of what the Smiths are saying is starting to make sense.

I don't like that.

Teresa's eyes flicker to her brother, and I know I've guessed correctly. Or, at least, I've touched upon the truth of the matter enough that she can't hide it.

"And your sons—they are Magicsmiths, too?" I challenge.

I don't imagine Teresa holding her younger son tighter. Septimus puts his hand on the elder one's shoulder, as if to pull him back at any second. To protect him, from me.

"Please, leave them out of this," Teresa begs, her voice barely a whisper. "I promise, they are only children. They are no threat to you."

"But you are."

"I…I am a threat to everyone," she confesses morosely.

"It's not her fault," Septimus insists, aggressive all of a sudden. "We didn't ask for these gifts any more than you did. Let me show you," he suggests. "Let me give you back at least some of your memory. So that you will understand."

I raise an eyebrow at him. "Can you not simply do as you please with your fluke, then, Sir Magicsmith?"

"I could," Septimus admits. "But I prefer consent. It helps keep me in my place," he adds, and I notice he's turned slightly pink.

"I'm not giving you permission to do anything to me," I warn him.

Septimus sighs very heavily. "Then I'm sorry for this."

And before I can do anything to stop him, he snaps his fingers.

At first, nothing happens.

Then the Smiths are gone. And I see. I *see* things, like a great, big, tapestry, unfolded before me, stories woven together.

We were in the Pyrian Palace. I was a child of perhaps eight. I stood at the front of a crowd, with Nusk holding my hand with one of his. His other hand grips that of a girl I thought I'd forgotten about a long time ago. A girl I should not have remembered, but upon seeing her, I do. She would grow up to be the woman I knew as my *Khashtani*. She would, at least once, die for me.

Lune.

A little Korvaan stood to my right, and a young Taris stood to Lune's left, mussing her hair with a hand while keeping Naomi on his shoulders with the other, so she might have a good view.

Each of us were dressed in fine clothes I would never have imagined wearing as a child. A soft pink and white dress with a series of layered, flared skirts, with a golden brooch pinned to the front in Rian's family crest. A pale green sash worn from my shoulder down to a bow at my opposite hip.

My sandals looked gold. Gold.

A giddy Rian stood on the dais before us, with his father and Grand Prince Alion Carsans before them. Crispin was standing off to the side with his mother and the people of their court. Rian's grin was wide and perfect (despite several missing small-teeth). When he surveyed the crowd and caught my eye, he gave me a brief, excited wave. Child-me gave him an enthusiastic wave back and a gap-toothed smile of my own.

The crowd cheered. Rian had been named the future King of Isaaria. He bowed to us all, promising his service in our favor for as long as he lived.

He was a boy-king, only half-prepared for what lay ahead of him.

The child version of me was not surprised, but I am unprepared as I watch myself being taken up to the dais and brought before Rian. I held out both my arms to him and he took my hands. And then I watch as, while only children, Rian and I are betrothed to one another. As all of Isaaria is told in this first timeline, so very, very long ago, that Rian and I are meant to marry and that our son will help restore balance to the world. I watched the crowd cheer again, erupting, excited, cheering for me and Rian.

And then I see, later that day, myself in rooms fit for a princess. For someone of Ayla's station. I was being helped out of my elaborate finery by a child version of Asmer, who is still prim and proper and lady-like. Still the Little Flower of Isaaria. She was, once and only once in a lifetime, my best friend.

Lune was there as well, but I wasn't paying her much attention. She annoyed me, somewhat. I wanted a sister more like Asmer, and Lune was too loud and emotional and dramatic for my taste. But she never noticed this, and practically adored me. Worshipped me, in a way, because I was her older sister and she loved me.

She was especially excited about my engagement to Rian, though I was still so young that it meant little to me. I didn't care about being a princess, only that I got to marry Rian. And though I didn't know anything about marriage, I knew that Rian was my best friend aside from Asmer, and marrying him meant that we would stay together forever.

Lune was the one who wanted to be a princess, in fact. But she was so excited that I got to be one—her sister—that she wasn't jealous. Or, at least, I never realized if she was jealous.

A woman was admitted to the room, and Asmer instantly bowed to her and left, as if to give us privacy. I don't know how I recognize her, as I have not seen her for centuries, but I do. I know her just as much as I know everything else I am being shown.

Mother. My mother. She stood there with a smile, speaking only to me despite how Lune was clearly the one excited to see her.

"I don't have time to stay," she claimed. "Only a few minutes. But I wanted to let you know, before I leave, Soleil: I am so proud of you. And I love you."

"If you love me, why are you leaving?" I challenged my mother coolly.

She sighed. As if we'd had this conversation many times. "Soleil, I don't expect you to understand. But you are happy here, aren't you? You'll get the chance to grow up alongside Rian, and Asmer. They are good friends of yours."

My poor mother stood there, trying to explain to me, and my only response was to turn away from her and fiddle with my hair in the vanity mirror.

A man opened the door, standing within its threshold, without entering. My father, I think. Or the man who helped give me life, at least. Nusk was always truly my father.

"Olivia," he said. "It is time."

Lune suddenly gripped onto our mother tightly, wrapping her arms around Olivia's legs and starting to cry. As if that would do anything.

"I don't want you to go," Lune sobbed. "Stay here! Stay with us!"

I am ashamed to note that my past self was embarrassed and annoyed by Lune's outburst. Lune was a six-year-old child, whose mother and father were leaving her. Not to be the future queen of a country. Oh, no. My little sister had a much less desirable fate in store.

"Oh, darling, I wish it could be so," our mother said, stroking Lune's hair. "But there are many things that still must be done, to ensure that this world survives. And though I may wish one of those things was staying with my girls, I'm afraid it cannot be."

"Make it be anyway!" Lune wailed. "Where are you going? Why do you have to leave?"

"I'm going west, darling. To look after your cousins," our mother said. "And while I'm away, you must protect your sister, understand? You will continue your training with Nusk and become a *Khashtani* for her."

Lune continued to sob. "I don't want to!"

"But you love your sister, don't you?" our mother asked, and Lune nodded vigorously. "And you want nothing bad to happen to her?"

Lune nodded again, to the point that I was sure she must have acquired a headache from it.

"Then you must become her *Khashtani.* It will be hard for you, Lune. But I know you can do it. Keep your sister safe no matter the cost, as Taris will keep the young king safe."

Our mother untangled herself from Lune long enough to pick up a box she'd entered with, and placed on my tea table. She crouched next to Lune and lifted the lid off the box, revealing a full set of simple but beautiful jewelry. The jewelry was sized for adults, not children, and would be too big for Lune or me, I noted, but Lune did not observe such a thing.

"Here. This should help. These are gifts," Olivia said, letting Lune look over them all. "For you and your sister, from your Uncle Janos, and your little cousin. Septimus. They are Magicsmiths, like you and me and Soleil. They cannot come and meet you, not ever. They live with another family. But your uncle wanted you to know about them. So, he sent you over some presents."

"What are they?" Lune sniffed, wiping her eyes dry.

"They're special charms. So that if Soleil uses her fluke to start over, you'll remember things that no longer exist. Just in case."

Lune picked through the jewelry, poking through the different matching pieces, before deciding on one of the bracelets. She put it on, and tilted her head to the side to admire it, though I could tell this gift was not going to deter her from wailing and pouting and making an absolute spectacle of herself after our mother walked out that door.

That day, with my betrothal to Rian, and the gifts received from our cousins in the west, was the last time I ever saw my mother. In any timeline. And I barely bothered to give her a goodbye.

My mother Olivia meant very little to my life, then. I forgot about her easily as I grew accustomed to life at the palace. Growing up alongside Rian. Mercer. Asmer. Nusk's children. And my own sister, Lune Marson. My *Khashtani.*

I did not get along well with Lune, mainly because I did not know her. Though Nusk took it upon himself to raise us both, he kept us apart. Lune, he trained as my *Khashtani,* as he trained Taris to be Rian's, and I was given lessons of a different sort. Lessons on how to, one day, make a good, strong queen for Isaaria. How to speak for my people. How to lead.

As the years passed, Rian, Mercer and Asmer became my closest and best friends. Rian was the link between us all, including Taris, with whom he became so close that the two became more like brothers than principal and *Khashtani.* And wherever Taris went, Lune would inevitably come trailing behind.

It went that way for our entire lives. At first, Taris didn't care. Then he found it annoying. Then flattering. And then...

I quietly kept an eye on that developing relationship, pretending to find it tiresome and annoying, though it intrigued me to see how much Taris and

Lune cared for one another. I helped keep their relationship a secret until after Nusk passed away, just before my wedding to Rian.

At that point, Rian and I made the decision to retire Lune and Taris as our *Khashtani* ahead of schedule, and allow them simpler positions as bodyguards so that they might have their own lives. Taris stayed on to handle our security. Lune hung about as well, but more likely because she wanted to stay near Taris, not because she enjoyed her job.

My spies whispered to me about the two of them kissing in the dark. I was sure Rian's told him much the same. Lune did not own much jewelry, but what few pieces she did have, besides the gifts from our cousins, were all made of blown glass. Every last piece.

Our two *Khashtani* broke their most crucial law by falling in love; they were going to become sloppy and useless anyway. We might as well have let them go before they started making mistakes.

I married Rian, and despite budding problems in the west, Isaaria rejoiced at it. They'd waited nearly twenty years to see it happen, after all, and they knew a prophecy had foretold the coming of our son and a time of peace. Asmer cried and embraced me after the ceremony, sobbing so hard it was difficult to hear her say she was glad she lived long enough to see me married. Mercer presented Rian and me with a little sunblood dragon as a wedding gift, which Rian named Mango and trained to follow him everywhere.

We adopted an orphan named Ayla from the East Courts Academy, where Rian often visited.

We stayed up late, put on parties, and spent hours and hours talking with Mercer and Asmer about the most ridiculous topics.

So, no one was particularly concerned about the turmoil in the rest of the world when we had that promise to look forward to.

Especially when, after just a few months, I found myself expecting.

Another few months, and it was confirmed: a boy. Our long-awaited son.

Rian was so happy about it, it was absurd. He liked to mention at least ten times a day to his council, his retainers, his aides and the grand princes, all about his wife and son.

And though I rolled my eyes, and poked fun at his excitement, deep down, I was excited, too. Every week that passed was a week closer to meeting my son. And whenever he became rowdy, kicking, Lune liked to put a hand on the spot with this silly, absent smile on her face. She'd written a lullaby for him that she often hummed, citing a study Mercer dug up about how children in the womb can hear outside. I'd claim I didn't believe it, but I still let Lune sing.

We were all so looking forward to meeting my son that waiting each day to pass started to become unbearable to me.

There is no way to fully describe the anticipation to someone who is not called to be a mother, but meeting my son was one of the things I'd wanted since the moment it was foretold he was meant to exist. No, I did not always understand what would go into having a child. I didn't know the details, the complications. I couldn't. But I'd been named queen and mother of Isaaria when I was a child, myself. I chose to take up the responsibility the Carsans put on my tiny shoulders, certain I could do it all, and bear it all, with Rian. My best friend. With the promise of a child that I'd always wanted.

Then reality set back in. Taris came to me, one day, with information he'd gathered about those in the west who might wish my son harm. About attacks in our own country, reportedly by creatures folk could only describe as demons.

"Your son is in danger," Taris warned me when I refused to believe it, out of fear. "Our country is in turmoil. We stand on the brink of war—enemies without and enemies within. Spies and traitors everywhere who want every member of the royal family dead."

"Is it not your duty to handle such things?" I snapped at him. "If my son is in danger, it is your job to protect him. You can swap skins like a snake. If you cannot uncover such traitors, who can?"

"You," Taris retorted, so fast it stunned me. "You know what you could do, your majesty. Use your fluke. Go back in time and fix things before it comes to this. Make this land a land of peace, at least so that your children have the chance to start their lives in a world full of opportunity, not hatred."

This surprised me. I had been trained to use my fluke, and I was skillful, but I mainly practiced only with the equivalent of parlor tricks. I had been taught not to abuse my gift, after all; that it was meant, truly, only for emergencies. But part of me had assumed that such an emergency would never happen. To hear Taris say otherwise was terrifying.

"You would pass your responsibilities off to me?" I demanded.

"No, your majesty," Taris said, so softly that my anger wilted. "You know that if you use your fluke to begin it all again, my future will suffer more. My wedding to Lune is tomorrow. If you go back now, I will lose that. It might never happen. But Lune and I discussed it, and we've decided that we are willing to risk it. For the future of our country. And our nephew. For the world."

He had me call Rian in, and together he and Lune presented a plan in which we would use the gifts our Magicsmith cousins had sent us so long ago. They would allow us to remember the events of our lives while I rewound time itself, and gave us a chance to stop the torments of today. And the more Taris and Lune spoke, the more their plan made sense.

I hated it, because it meant I would have to wait years longer to meet my son. But if it would give my child the chance to be born into a world not already crumbling at his feet, if it set him up for the best chance at life possible, if it meant I wouldn't have to worry about someone coming to kill him while he lay in his cradle…Then I would do it.

Rian agreed, but had a better understanding of what Taris and Lune were willing to sacrifice for us.

"If we do this, you may lose Lune," Rian warned gently. "And you've only just gotten her."

"As I told your wife," Taris said. "We're willing to risk that."

"Then please. Let us give you your wedding day, at least," Rian suggested with one of his signature grins. "Something you can look back to fondly, when things are hard."

Taris bowed his head gratefully. "Thank you, your majesty. Lune and I will not forget that."

"Nor will we forget your offered sacrifice," Rian said. "We will discuss this again tomorrow, and see what can be done. But you must have at least one night with your bride. There is no telling what the future might bring."

So, with our tentative plan in place, we made the foolish mistake of thinking we had even one more day to spare. A day for a celebration, before we were forced to work for our happy ending.

Events such as a wedding, naturally, were bloated with potential security breaches. Annoyances. Interruptions that turned out to be nothing more than curious citizens sneaking about where they shouldn't be. But of all the days for someone to succeed in killing the king of Isaaria; of all the days for someone to even get close, of course it had to be Taris and Lune's wedding day. The one day Rian gave them that he shouldn't have.

I watch my own reaction, the first time I see Rian die in front of me. When he was shot from a nearby rooftop, and everyone around us flew into a panic to save him, even though I knew he was dead the moment he hit the ground. I, too, naturally, panicked. But while others' reactions were to scream and sob, and try to revive Rian by any means possible, mine was to *break time.*

I ran it back. Rewound it by several seconds so I could push Rian out of the way. But if I did that, then Korvaan, standing behind him, was shot. So, I rewound again, a bit further, and made sure Rian was not in view of a sniper, from that angle. And a shot was never taken…not then. Instead, he was killed when we went to congratulate Taris and Lune.

So, I went back again and told the guards. Then went back again and moved the wedding abruptly. Then canceled it. Then had it in secret earlier, and felt a meager relief only to later reach the same date and watch Rian die anyway, in some other manner. Sometimes Korvaan would die on the same day, dependent on what I did to try and stop my husband's death and how, but one thing stayed absolutely the same: Rian died. I lived it over and over, until I often woke up crying, but Rian always died.

And because that version of me did not know who the traitors were—did not know that the oh-so-loyal Grand Prince Mercer, with the fluke to relocate objects anywhere he pleased, had been corrupted during his time in the west; because I could not know that Mercer was the sharpshooter to kill my husband, his own best friend, and then join the concerned crowd of those trying to save him as he bled out—I did not know where to look.

I did not know how to save him.

The last time I tried, I'd rewound six months. Half a year of living everything over again, feeling dizzy and overwhelmed and constantly exhausted. Suffering from sleepless nights. Caught between the anxiety of my husband's and unborn child's lives both in mortal danger. Causing Rian misery as well, as he watched me slowly fall apart. I'd tried everything. Everything. Until I wasn't sure if my new ideas were old ones, or if I'd only played them out in my imagination.

And all this time, Asmer, and Taris and Lune—with whom we trusted portions of the jewelry we'd been given—did their best to help me come up with solutions. We tried all sorts of things. Everything we could think of. But it was too much. It was exhausting.

Until I finally decided the only way to save Rian was to fix the world, to start over completely. I knew I couldn't remember having a life with him. If I did, I'd never be able to endure it. I'd never be able to put the rest of the world first. I'd be too busy anxiously obsessing over the clock slowly ticking closer to the time I knew he'd be killed.

It was a cycle in which I lost Rian, Korvaan, and Naomi, all, that finally broke me. When I met with Asmer, Lune and Taris after experiencing all that death, I told them what we'd be doing. How far back I planned to set us. And how I wanted to be raised away from Rian, by Nusk.

How I didn't want to remember anything.

Asmer stared at me, horrified. "Your majesty—!"

"Don't argue with me," I said. "Let Taris remember. Let Lune remember. Let Rian remember everything but them. Make sure you, too, will remember. Make sure you all have charms. And I will send us all back again to a time where we might do things right."

She swallowed hard, a tear sliding down her face. "Your majesty, I… How can we do that? How will that help, I don't unders—"

"It is not your duty to understand, only to obey," I ordered. "Instead of coming forward when the Carsans reveal their prophecy, we will keep silent, and conceal Rian until such a time as when we might unmask whatever traitors lie within our walls. I will not be raised in the palace, nor will Taris, Naomi, or Korvaan. I will become Rian's *Khashtani,* and they will be my *khashak.* Nusk will train me to be a bodyguard. A Living Shield. A killer. A protector. Until a time when Rian is safe, and then he will tell me the truth. And we can be together again. That is the only way that I can save both him and our child…And ensure our son has a father."

"You cannot possibly know how things will change," Asmer warned me. "Your majesty, if you go back, now, and do this…You may make things even worse than they are now!"

"Then I will go back again!" I cried. "I will go back as many times as needed, but I refuse to live this life! With a dead husband? With a son who will die? Korvaan dead? Naomi dead? She was like a sister to me," I hissed. "I will not live that life; I refuse."

"You still have a sister," Asmer whispered, looking down.

I stared at her, then swung my head to where Taris and Lune were standing nearby. Taris continued to stare at me, hard, and gave me a nod. Lune hastily bowed before me.

"You know I will do as you ask, your majesty," she said.

"Then you cannot let me know about myself and Rian," I instructed them. "If you do, I'll begin to make decisions with my heart instead of my head. It'll put him in more jeopardy. Likewise, I forbid any of you from telling me of my fluke. Forbid it. You'll be the ones to prompt me to turn back time if necessary. But I don't trust myself to make that call any longer."

"How can we do that if you forbid us from telling you?" Taris posed.

"Put my life at risk. Stab me. Push me out a window. Anything. I'll turn back time instinctively, to protect myself."

Lune put a hand on Taris' shoulder. "That means you must make her walk the earth now and again, in bare feet. To make sure she'll be able to use her fluke if necessary. She prefers the sun," she adds. "It makes her fluke stronger."

"Tell Nusk to give Lune to the Carsans," Asmer told Taris. "I swear to you, the Carsans and I—we will look after her for you."

Taris tightened his jaw. "Thank you."

I remember watching him and Lune say their goodbyes. I remember, at the time, thinking they were quite dramatic about it.

I was selfish. And self-centered. Re-watching it, now, it hurts. Because I remember Lune. I watch this knowing she will die for me. Many times. So will Taris. And yet, every single cycle, they continue to assume their roles. Trying their best to protect Rian and me. To give us just one more chance.

"I love you," Lune told Taris. "But there is no greater thing than giving one's life for a friend," Lune reminded him, and kissed his lips gently. "We decided, Taris. We must do this. For Soleil and Rian's son.

"Never forget me," I heard Lune whisper in his ear. She kissed him one last time, then made him let her go.

I saw Taris crying silently for her, for how he was losing her. Giving her up for me and Rian. Watching the future they might have had together slip away from them both, perhaps forever.

Watching now, I hate my old self for seeing this sacrifice as something I deserved. Something that Lune and Taris owed us, after Rian and I released them from their *Khashtani* bonds.

They never asked to be *Khashtani.* They never asked to be released. Those were choices made for them. Choices that ran their lives, and forced them apart, and made it so that Taris now has had to watch his wife die in a million different ways in a million different timelines, trying to protect me from my own brazenness.

No wonder he hated me.

I gave him hope he could marry Lune and have a happy life, then snatched it away and let her die for me, instead. I have expected her to die for me. My own sister. She has never once complained. She keeps enduring it, trying to keep me and Rian safe. But I can put all the pieces together now, and all her eccentrics, her erratic nature, her mood: they all make sense. In fact, her sorrow and Taris' is made worse by the fact that Lune is not only unable to bear children, but the way I made them take up these roles, I've taken away any opportunity for them to adopt.

I see the times I did discover Taris and Lune's real identities, usually after one of her bloody miscarriages. My wild, angry shouting matches with him. My inability to understand why they would still care so damn much about wanting to have a child—why they would jeopardize everything, just for the opportunity to try one more time despite the vague promise he and Lune made, of living only to keep my portion of the family safe.

I see how Taris' anger and frustration has expounded and grown each time he's forced to endure another loop of agony. Each time he was forced to act a puppet on my orders, passed down to him through the controlling tongue of his father. Forced to keep certain secrets from me as Nusk's own agenda morphed over time, to be denied the few, simple things he ever wanted in life. Conflicted by clashing emotions running over themselves again and again. I watch the man who Rian and I both thought of as our brother slowly lose his mind, being forced to endure, to remember, every single timeline. Every time his father died. Every time N'omi or Korvaan died. Every child Lune lost. Every time we've failed to save Rian's life.

Nothing about Taris is a mystery to me anymore.

I'm impressed that he's managed to find the strength to go on, and give me any sort of assistance these past few timelines.

I am impressed and profoundly saddened, by Taris' and Lune's lost story.

And I am filled with furious loathing at myself.

How could I. How dare I.

Who was I?

Back in the throne room, where I am only vaguely aware I still exist, I fall to my knees, knowing the hard stone floor will bruise them.

Oh, Lune.

Oh, poor, sweet, Lune; how could I do this to you?

The information is too much to handle—too much to possibly remember, but I will forever be haunted by every repeated image of my little sister sobbing, *"It's not* fair*!"*, and crying so hard it exhausted her.

I will forever be haunted by the fact that though I pity her and hate myself in memory, I was able to once stand there and watch her suffer and feel nothing.

I have fully reset our lives a total of thirty-seven times, either to my childhood or back even further, to Lune's birth. Thirty-seven times, not counting minor instances in which I've used my powers to rewind a year or less. I have made Lune endure at least thirty-seven deaths.

By the time I'm fully back in the throne room, where the four Smiths wait for me to return, my head is buzzing. I remember too much. Too many timelines. Too many cycles in which we've tried different things, and Rian still dies. And yet, I know, somehow, that Septimus did not give me everything. Did not show me everything.

There are things missing. He's missing, for the most part, despite their claims of knowing me. I have no memories of him, except for those in one timeline, before our current one, in which he frequently haunted me. Manipulated me. But I know that I've met him and Teresa before, many times. So, I know there are things he's hiding from me.

I still cannot trust him.

"What did you show me?" I demand as I force myself to climb to my feet again, voice hoarse and knees aching. "What was that?"

"Your history," Septimus says. "And I know you know that."

I'm panting. My chest feels tight, and I think I'm shaking. I have never felt this way before.

"I don't…It still…"

"You're confused. You have many questions," Septimus guesses calmly. "That's expected. You never knew everything, and I didn't show you everything, though you're smart enough to figure it out on your own if you bothered to pay more attention to your king's research. Or really, to be fair, I haven't allowed you to remember everything that I bothered to tell you in the first place."

"Why?" I snap, glaring up at him.

Septimus shrugs. "Several reasons. One is that you, like most people, experience emotion. If I give all that back to you, it might break you. Not that I'm blaming you, of course," he adds. "People forget so easily what it's really like: to kill, to watch your loved ones die in front of you—"

"Stop it," I hiss.

"Another," he goes on, ignoring me, "is that I'm not a very good person, Soleil. Not at all. And, to be honest, I don't want to be held accountable by you for things I've done in the past that I now regret."

For a few seconds, I manage to hate him more than I've ever hated anyone before in my life. Teresa can see that gleam in my eyes, and it frightens her, but Septimus looks directly at me and does not flinch. I don't scare him, even at my most terrifying. And that unnerves me.

"You…You've used us. Me. Taris. Lune."

"Yes."

"My sister," I spit at him. "You used my *little sister.*"

Septimus shrugs. "So did you."

What happens when I try to lunge at him is probably for the best. My legs tremble, and I nearly fall to my knees again. I am forced to catch myself, trying to maintain what remains of my dignity before the people I now know to be my cousins.

"What...What have you done to me?" I demand.

I know what Septimus has done, of course, but I don't understand how my own memories returning to me could make me so weak. I am not accustomed to feeling weak. Or helpless. The last time I felt that way, in fact, was the latest time I watched Lune and Taris die.

Septimus sighs. "I'm sorry," he says. "It must be overwhelming. But I have given you back as many memories as I think you can manage right now."

"Give me everything," I order.

I am trying to sound venomous, and sharp, but I am exhausted.

Septimus shakes his head. "I'm afraid I can't do that. Even if I thought it was a good idea, it would break you. And besides that, it is not a good idea. Not with an impulsive person like you."

"Yet you would purposefully withhold information from an 'impulsive person like me'," I threaten.

"You're impulsive, Soleil, but you would never hurt me," Septimus says. Every word that comes out of his mouth makes me angrier. "You wouldn't hurt me, and you certainly would never hurt my sister. Or her sons. I know you wouldn't. Because I know you."

"No, you don't," I hiss at him.

I muster all my strength to stand straight. I whirl and stalk back the way I first entered this room, behind the thrones. Each step feels heavy and awkward, and I know what I'm about to do is wrong, but I don't care. I'm angry. I'm confused. I'm horrified by who I am, and it hurts.

"Kor-vaaaan!" I bellow.

He appears within seconds at my elbow, and walks with me as I try to get myself as far away from Septimus and Teresa Smith as possible.

"Yes, Captain?"

"The guests in the other room: put them somewhere. Anywhere. I don't care. But lock them in. And don't let them leave…Except for the man," I amend. "I want him to know what it feels to be the helpless one, for once."

"…Captain?" Korvaan repeats uneasily.

And I remember, then, that Korvaan has one of Septimus' charms. He remembers, at least as much as Septimus wants him to remember. He simply does not know what I remember, yet.

"Lock him in the wine cellar and leave him there," I hiss.

I all but flee from Korvaan then, certain that he will do as I ask even if he doesn't want to. I'm thankful he doesn't try to follow me, and that no one stops me as hurry through halls, trying to find someplace where I can escape from everything.

My memories continue to crash in on me, not as vividly as in the throne room, but just as painfully.

I remember arguing with Nusk, over and over, about having him use his fluke to prevent certain things from coming to pass. Telling him not to get in my way, when I rewashed the timeline. His frustration, nearly equal to his son's, as he watched the woman he thought of as a daughter do what I thought necessary and what he thought foolish.

Nusk wanted a good life for me. Rian wanted a good life for me—away from him, if necessary. Septimus, I now know, wanted to keep us all sane enough to live the same dreadful events over and over, so he might have a chance at keeping the world safe. I suppose it never occurred to me that the three of them would act on their own authority. That Septimus would delete, remove, or alter our memories for the sake of pushing a certain narrative forward. That Rian would ask Nusk to do his best to give me good life, and to ask Taris, who he did not remember loving as his brother, to protect me. That Nusk would, in turn, try to balance out his wishes for the world and for me, and order Taris not to tell me anything, lest he push our timeline in the wrong direction. Lest too much be revealed to me, and I accidentally ruin Septimus' careful planning.

I can oddly understand how all of their thoughts and feelings have influenced their decisions, and yet, as I can now see things objectively, I find it difficult to say if any one of their tactics is strictly good or bad.

I want to rail at Nusk for such idiocy—I want to feel nothing but anger for how he manipulated all of us, keeping us suspended, if only temporarily, in a sort of strange haven at the University. But it feels selfish to be angry, when I know he only wanted what was best for me.

So, I want to be angry with Rian instead, and his selfishness. His foolish reasoning, and his complicated decisions. But now that I know what it's like to be forced to look at all these iterations of our history, and consider having to be the one to make such decisions not only for my spouse but for the entire world, I can understand his struggle.

I could not have known it then, but when I decided who would remember, and who would not, I was damning those with memories to long, painful, and confusing lives. When asking them to choose between the ones they loved and the fate of the world, how long did I really think I could force them to make the noble sacrifice before it broke them?

The choices I made, dozens of lifetimes ago, were wrong ones. But I cannot look at the choices of those I care about and judge them so easily. Intellectually, I can. But emotionally, I am impressed with them. I have no such stamina; if I lived through what Taris has, I don't know who I would be today.

I find, in the end, that in a desperate attempt to escape from the choices life wants me to make, I head to the roof of the palace. There are few places a person can reach the roof, and as it is mainly a dangerous maze, few would dare to. But there is one spot, near the Solunium Hub, that offers a beautiful view. And while the view is not what I'm after, there will, perhaps, be peace.

The king is already there, looking out at the night, and I know Septimus must have given both of us our memories back. Mango is there, too. The little sunblood dragon is asleep, no longer young and spry. He is blissfully ignorant of the mental turmoil the king and I are now enduring.

No, not "the king". Rian.

I am quiet when I join him, but Rian still turns at my approach.

I see the sorrow in his eyes just as clearly as I feel it in my heart. He has long since stopped dyeing his hair, but these long years have earned him hints of silver and white stripes amidst the black. We are growing old together, I realize. But we've wasted so many years. So much time, not knowing. Letting others sacrifice for us, while we blunder along in meaningless lives.

We only hesitate for a moment before we find ourselves in an embrace.

"You saw," I say.

"Yes."

"That really happened. That is our past."

"Yes," Rian says again.

For a long while, that's all either of us can say.

"He was like a brother to me," Rian manages to say, and swallows. "I always wanted a brother, so Taris became mine. As Lune was…was my little sister."

He has to close his eyes tight, as a few tears escape. I feel his chest shudder. His breathing starts to become erratic.

"I didn't…know…He…All that time…For me. They did it for me."

They did it for us. Taris did it out of love for the man he considered a brother, and Lune did it for her own blood sister, who never once showed her the love she deserved.

"Should we go back?" I ask him, frowning. "And try to save them?"

I watch Rian consider, and watch the pain in his face distort his features.

"I'm not sure I can say, now," he says. "Do I go back, sacrificing this version of reality? Do I give up knowing you are safe to save the lives of two of my friends, whom I did not remember until this moment, or do I find another way to honor their sacrifice? Is it within our rights to go back at all? Do we dare attempt to control Fate, Soleil?"

I say nothing, because I don't know the answer to that. Or, I suppose I do. I know the arguments I have made to Rian, over and over again, every time he falls into this despair, but I can't bring myself to repeat them. If I've never been able to convince him that going back again is the right thing to do, then saying it once more won't change anything.

"I'm asking, Soleil, because I don't know. I don't know if we should go back to save Lune and Taris, because I don' t know if we can. But I felt her soul cry, when she died," he confessed. "First Taris', and then hers…Soleil: I nearly fell down a staircase…I've never felt that before, when someone dies. I do not know what that means."

I am tempted to ask him why he was traversing a staircase when he was supposed to be with Asmer on their wedding night, but it's a passing thought, and I don't care for the answer. All I can think about is how much I want to go back. How much I need to go back. Not for myself, this time, and not just for Rian. But because I owe Lune that much, at least, to try and save her.

"My sister lived a thousand hells for me, and I barely cared for her," I tremble. I understand Rian's conundrum, but Lune…Lune suffered so much for me, and I did nothing for her.

As a *Khashtani,* I thought I would grow completely immune to the pain of death. When you see it occur in such rapid succession, with so many different people, it's hard to see them for what they really are, at times. But Nusk did his best to teach me, to value human life. I try to pretend as if I don't, but his lessons sunk too deep: there is meaning in ending a life. There is pain.

I feel something wet on my face, and though I understand I have been crying, I can't fully comprehend it.

Why is Fate so cruel a creature that he would steal my little sister's time early, and take her in a way so that I would never really know her?

"Taris and Lune, and you and I—no matter who remembers and who doesn't, no matter how many times we go back, they—we…We always end up together. We find each other," I say. "It is meant to be."

"Our fate," Rian murmurs.

"And if they are meant to be, if we are meant to be…Rian," I whisper. "…Our child, our children—"

"It is too late, now," he interrupts, and turns away from me.

I say nothing, but we both think it. If I am too old to have children, it must mean we go back. At least once more. However many times it takes for us to reach the proper outcome. Because each human person has a unique soul—Rian and I both believe that. So, if we now live in a world where our children cannot exist, then it is our destiny, it is our fate, to go back at least once more, knowing everything. So that things can be as they are meant to be.

"Let us at least take some time, to think it over first," he finally says quietly.

"Time is certainly something we have," I agree.

Rian looks out away from me, into the sky. For several very long seconds, neither of us say anything. Then he moves closer to the edge of the roof and sits, the sky open before him so that it must seem to take up all of the world. I wait barely a moment before I decide to join him. I sit close by, my legs crossed under me, my weight propped on my hands. I don't say anything, but Rian knows. I've said it so many times to him, I don't need to say it again now.

"The sky is beautiful tonight," he says, and rests his hand on mine.

"Yes, it is."

So, we sit there together in the silence, until the sun comes up behind the broken clouds and the stars fade from the sky.

Cast of Characters

(alphabetical by first name)

ABSOLUM ORAM, current king of Isaaria, father of Crown Prince Magnus

ADEEM AL'YIBNA, father of Lady Asmer al'Yibna

AIDEN SMITH, second son of Teresa Smith

ALION CARSANS, Grand Prince; Crispin, Lune, and Soren's father

ALOYSIUS PIKE, Grand Prince, father of Vásan and Bastien, deceased

AMERSON, the "firebird general", of whom little is known as of yet

ASMER AL'YIBNA, court lady, daughter of Lord Adeem al'Yibna

AYLA YAKARAMI, one of Rian's favorite students and adopted daughter

BASTIEN PIKE, younger brother of Grand Prince Vásan Pike

BOGUN PARK, crown prince of Kacha, cousin of Aiko Shinya

CASTEL VOSKOSS, prince of Lijimata, missing for over seven years

CHIMHWI PARK, young prince of Kacha, cousin of Aiko Shinya

CLAIR ORAM, current queen of Isaaria, mother of Magnus, wife of Absolum

CLANAUGH, king of the Fae

CRISPIN CARSANS, Grand Prince, son of Alion Carsans

DAMEN SMITH, elder son of Teresa Smith

DETRUS LUNDAN, Crown Prince of Isaaria

EMMELINA VOSKOSS, Queen of Lijimata, elder sister of Castel

ELIAS VOSKOSS, Emmelina's uncle, Javier and Hector's father, ambassador

ELIORA CARSANS, Grand Princess; Crispin, Lune, and Soren's mother

ELODIE LUNDAN, daughter of Detrus and Irina

FALISIA VOKSOSS, Emmelina and Castel Voskoss's elder half-sister

GRIFFITH REACH, Magnus Oram's head bodyguard

HECTOR VOSKOSS, Emmelina's cousin, Elias's son, Jave's younger brother

IRINA LUNDAN, Detrus's wife, pregnant with their second child

JAVIER VOSKOSS, cousin of Emmelina, Elias's elder son, Hector's brother

KAOLI ADDER, aide and guard to Soren Carsans

KAETSCHA, Clanaugh's sister

KORSIKO, assassin who has some knowledge of the Magicsmiths

KORVAAN QURVO, second son of Nusk, middle Qurvo child

LOUISA ERIKSON, daughter of the Alarkian ambassador, executed

LUC ERIKSON, the former Alarkian ambassador, executed by Emmelina

LUNE CARSANS, adopted by the Carsans, Soren and Crispin's sister

MAGNUS ORAM, Crown Prince of Isaaria

MALLIN CRUZ, underhanded but discreet apothecary

MALLORIE COURTEAU, one of the Carsans' bodyguards

MANGO, Rian Yakarami's miniature sunblood dragon,

MERCER RALHAN, Crown Prince, Rian's best friend

MI-SUN KIM, queen of Kacha from ancient times, gifted a magic hairpin

MI-SUN PARK, princess of Kacha, cousin of Aiko Shinya

NAOMI QURVO, only daughter of Nusk, youngest of the Qurvos

NISSA SONDUSHKI, Crown Princess of Isaaria

NUSK QURVO, former Khashtani, Soleil's trainer and father-figure

PARKER AUBREY, one of the Carsans' bodyguards

QHAN KHALEEM, Rian's favorite and most reliable bodyguards

RAJ AL'YIBNA, younger brother of Asmer and son of Adeem al'Yibna

RENKI AIKO, Tourrannese-Kachin ambassador and lord

RIAN YAKARAMI, Crown Prince and the Lost Heir of Isaaria

RIYONG JIN, friend of Prince Park Chimhwi

ROMIA NOUIRE, a loyal maid of Lune Carsans

SAKIA YAKARAMI, grandmother of Rian Yakarami, former princess

SEPTIMUS SMITH, elder brother of Teresa, uncle of Damen and Aiden

SHINYA AIKO, Tourrannese-Kachin ambassador-to-be, son of Aiko Renki

SOREN CARSANS, much younger brother of Crispin and Lune Carsans

SOLEIL MARSON, *Khashtani* to Crown Prince Rian

TALAN MARQUES, Mercer Ralhan's bodyguard

TARIS QURVO, eldest son of Nusk, half-sibling of Korvaan and Naomi

TERESA SMITH, sister of Septimus, mother of Damen and Aiden

VÁSAN PIKE, Crown Prince of Isaaria

VALOR ONDRA, one of Rian's guards, Naomi's gentleman caller

YUUGO IDO, Crown Prince of Isaaria

YVETTE PIKE, Vásan's young wife, whom he does not love

Acknowledgements

First off, the greatest thanks go to Emily, for being my long-suffering beta reader, enduring my stupid typos and incomplete sentences, and listening to me blather on and on about my works. Similar thanks to Simon, Joey, and Kristina. This series of mine may not be your favorite, but your support and love of the Nyrïan Chronicles has helped me to keep writing even when it feels pointless. Thanks for showing me, before anyone else, that people will love my writing (enough to beg and threaten for the next installments, even!) And thank you to Ben, for enduring our eleven-mile long runs on Saturday mornings when we'd chatter about our endeavors, and to Meggie, for all the comforting hugs.

Next, same sentiments for Grace. Don't worry: the Dread World saga has not been abandoned! I will return to the story of Nate, Ebony, Ivory and (of course) Spencer Crue. In fact, most of the series is already written, merely sitting in wait. An additional thank-you to you, as well, for helping me with your graphic design expertise. I have no such talents, as I'm sure you know!

Thank you, Mom and Dad, of course, for raising me in such a way that I've been able to utilize my imagination to create dozens of different universes and a plethora of characters I love. You taught me that stories have meaning, and I hope my stories will be a part of a renewed movement of fiction that does just that. Thank you especially, Mom, for cheering me on and telling me I could do anything even when I thought I couldn't.

Special thanks to Aunt Lori, Uncle Larry, Abby, Jake, Annie and (again) Joey for letting me spend two years in your home while I used almost every waking minute outside of work and running to write. Thanks for all the love and support and hospitality. In the same way, a thanks goes out to Aunt Sandy for your artistic eye and fabulous dinner dates, and Uncle Pat, for taking me skydiving and introducing me to a new, beloved hobby that gave me insight into how to write Soleil's "fall". A thank you as well goes out to my grandparents, for their love and support, as well as their guidance my faith.

A thank you as well to all the artists—cover and promotional art both—who shared their talents with me and helped create something that fit my vision and that, I hope, others will appreciate as well.

Finally, a thank you to the students of Yeongyang Girl's Middle and High School, especially the class of 2019-2020 and Hong Ji-Yeon. Thank you for letting me spend an incredible year as your English teacher and for inspiring me to keep writing for the next generation. I wish you all the best. Fighting!